Try A Little Tenderness
&
Stay As Sweet As You Are

Try A Little Tenderness
&
Stay As Sweet As You Are

Joan Jonker

LONDON   NEW YORK   SYDNEY   TORONTO

This omnibus edition published 1999
by BCA
By arrangement with Headline Book Publishing,
a division of Hodder Headline PLC

CN 4271

Try A Little Tenderness © 1998 Joan Jonker
Stay As Sweet As You Are © 1999 Joan Jonker

The right of Joan Jonker to be identified as the Author of
the Work has been asserted by her in accordance with
the Copyright, Designs and Patents Act 1988.

Printed and bound in Great Britain by
Mackays of Chatham PLC, Chatham, Kent

Contents

Try A Little Tenderness

To my Down's Syndrome son, Philip, who is the nicest person I know.

He knows not greed or envy, speaks ill of no one and walks
away from raised voices. He enjoys life and appreciates everything.
With his ever-ready smile he is a joy to know and I
love the bones of him. If there were more people like Philip,
wouldn't the world be a better place?

A friendly greeting from Joan

Come with me back in time to the mid-1930s and meet the
Nightingale family. Stan and Mary and their two daughters,
Laura and Jenny. Both girls are beautiful to look at, but as
different in nature as chalk and cheese. And meet their friends
and neighbours, the Hanleys and the Moynihans. Bring these
characters together and you have a recipe for fun and laughter
all the way. There may be the odd tear of sadness, because
that's life. But mostly the tears rolling down your cheeks will
be tears of laughter. I hope you enjoy meeting my new friends.

Chapter One

'I want me skipping-rope back, Laura, yer've had it for ages and it's not fair because it was my birthday present.'

'Oh, stop yer moaning.' Laura Nightingale threw her sister Jenny a dirty look. 'Me mam said yer had to give me a go.'

'Yeah, but she didn't mean yer could keep it all to yerself.' Jenny stamped her foot in indignation at the injustice of it. At twelve years of age, she was eighteen months younger than her sister and always came off worse when it came to sharing. 'When you got a book for yer birthday, yer wouldn't even read me a story from it, never mind let me read it.'

'That's 'cos I didn't want yer to get dirty marks on it.' Laura was skipping with her arms crossed and jumping on one foot. It wasn't often she got the chance to skip with a proper skipping-rope. Usually it was a piece of clothes-line, but this one had real wooden handles painted in a bright red. 'I'll swap yer me book for yer rope.'

'No! The book's all torn now, I don't want it.' Jenny could see her sister had no intention of relinquishing the rope until she got fed up with it. 'I'm going to tell me mam if yer don't give it to me *now*.'

Laura smirked and kept on skipping. 'Go and tell her, I don't care.'

Near to tears, Jenny ran into the house. She found her mother in the kitchen putting some clothes through the mangle. 'Mam, our Laura won't give me back me skipping-rope. I haven't even had a turn, and it's my birthday present.'

Mary Nightingale sighed as she rubbed her wet hands down the front of her pinny. Mother and daughter were as alike as two peas in a pod. Both were slim, with pale golden hair, a fair complexion and vivid blue eyes. They had the same nature, too. Kind, easygoing and with a sense of humour that brought a ready smile to their faces.

'She's a selfish article, our Laura. She thinks the world revolves around her and what she wants.' Mary made her way to the front door. 'It's about time she learned there are other people beside herself.'

When Laura saw her mother, she laughed. 'Went crying to her mammy, did she? She's like a flippin' baby.'

'Give her the rope, Laura, it's her birthday present.'

1

'I'll give it to her in a minute, when I've had a go skipping backwards.' There was a brazen look on Laura's face. 'Just a couple more minutes.'

'Yer heard what I said.' Mary was trying to contain her rising temper. 'Give it to her now or I'll give yer a clip around the ears.'

Still the girl went on skipping as though daring her mother to carry out her threat. 'I said in a minute.'

Mary stepped forward and caught the rope in mid-flight. 'Do as ye're told and hand it over.'

'I won't, not until I'm ready.' When she felt her mother tugging at the rope, Laura gripped it tight and refused to let go. And all the while she had a smirk on her face. With her dark hair, greeny-hazel eyes and swarthy complexion, there was no resemblance between her and the woman with whom she was having a tug of war. And the war wasn't about the rope, it was about her getting her own way, showing who was the boss.

Mary could no longer stand the insolence and delivered a stinging smack to the side of her daughter's face. 'You asked for that, you impudent, selfish madam. Don't yer ever dare answer me back like that again.' She pulled the rope which was now hanging loose and passed it to Jenny. 'Here yer are, sunshine, and don't let her take it off yer again.'

Laura looked stunned as she held a hand to her cheek. 'You just wait until me dad gets in, he'll have something to say about this. Yer'll be sorry.'

'I warned yer dad twelve years ago that he was spoiling yer and making a rod for his own back. The trouble is, he's made one for my back as well. And everybody else that has to put up with yer selfishness and insolence.' With that Mary turned her back and went into the house. She knew there'd be a row when Stan came in, he wouldn't take her side, never did. But there was only so much a mother could take from a child who was out of hand, and she'd taken enough. They had two daughters and they should be treated equally. But they weren't, not by their father. Laura could do no wrong in his eyes, he thought the sun shone out of her backside. She lied herself out of trouble, always laying the blame at her sister's door. If there was a fight, it was always Jenny who started it. If anything went missing, it was Jenny who'd taken it. And Stan fell for it every time, believing her without question.

Mary put her hip to the side of the mangle and pushed it back into the corner of the tiny kitchen of the two-up-two-down house that had been her home since the day she married, fifteen years ago. She loved her husband, and they'd been happy, until favouritism had reared its ugly head and blighted that happiness. She'd tried to reason with Stan when Laura started getting out of hand, but he wouldn't listen. He couldn't see further than the end of his nose where she was concerned. Poor Jenny didn't get a look in. Although she was the youngest, she was the one who was sent to the corner shop for his five Woodbines when Laura didn't feel like going. She was the one sent down the yard for a shovelful of coal because Laura didn't like the cold. Yet she never complained. She did everything she was asked, because from the time she could toddle she realised her sister was more special to her father than she was. But in the last year she'd begun to rebel against the unfairness and was fighting back.

Mary lifted the lid off the pan of stew and sniffed up in appreciation. 'That should put a lining on their tummies.' She spoke aloud to the empty room. 'I'll set the table and then call the girls in.'

She was laying the knives and forks out when her husband came in, his face red with anger. 'Have you just slapped our Laura for nothing?'

'No, I have not slapped our Laura for nothing.' Mary sighed as she shook her head. 'I slapped her for giving me cheek and for not doing as she was told.'

'Yer made a holy show of her in front of the whole street, that's what yer did. And all over a bleedin' skipping-rope.'

Her anger high, Mary's answer was sharp. 'I think yer should get yer facts straight, Stan Nightingale. And yer won't get them straight off that wayward daughter of ours. Huh! In front of the whole street, was it? I didn't see anyone around, but if there was then they'd have heard her giving her mother cheek, the hard-faced little faggot. And the bleedin' skipping-rope ye're talking about was Jenny's birthday present! She wasn't even allowed to get her hands on it because of your darling Laura. Or had yer forgotten it was Jenny's birthday? Mind you, it wouldn't surprise me. There are times when I think yer've forgotten yer've even got another daughter, all the notice yer take of her.'

'Well, I don't want yer hittin' her no more.' Stan hung his peaked cap on the nail behind the kitchen door. 'If there's any telling-off to do, I'll do it.'

He was about to walk away when Mary grabbed his arm and spun him around. 'You tell our Laura off! That's a good one, that is. I've never known yer raise yer voice to her, nor yer hand, more's the pity. A few smacks when she was younger would have put her on the straight and narrow, taught her right from wrong. But it's too late now, she's set in her ways, lying, cheating and bloody selfish. Yer'll live to rue the day, Stan Nightingale, mark my words. She'll bring trouble to this door, and it'll all be your fault.'

Stan, whose dark colouring Laura had inherited, flushed. 'Yer've always had it in for the girl, yer've never had any time for her. But in future, leave me to deal with her.'

3

Once again he made to walk away and Mary pulled him back. 'Let's get this straight, once and for all. She's my daughter as well as yours, and while she's in this house she does as she's told. If she misbehaves and deserves a crack, I'll give her one. If she's good, we'll get on fine and this house will be a happier place. The choice is hers. But I'll tell yer this, Stan, and yer can take it from me that I mean every word of it. I'm fed up to the back teeth of her getting pampered and our Jenny left out in the cold. I won't tolerate it any longer. Either Laura pulls her socks up and behaves in a reasonable manner, or I'll wash me hands of her and she can run riot for all I care. She'd be your responsibility then. And that is only right, because you made her what she is.' She pushed his arm. 'Go and call the girls in for their dinner. Oh, and unless the words stick in yer throat, wish Jenny a Happy Birthday.

They sat down to their meal in silence. But Laura's eyes were going from her mother to her father. She wasn't satisfied that she'd received the sympathy she thought she deserved. 'Is me face red, Dad, where me mam slapped me?'

Stan's eyes were on his plate when Mary answered. 'I can't see any red. But I'll slap yer again if it's a red face yer want.'

'Did yer hear that, Dad? She said she'd slap me again.'

'Get on with yer dinner,' he grunted, 'before it gets cold.'

Mary pursed her lips. She shouldn't say any more to aggravate the situation, it would make her as childish as her daughter. But in the end she couldn't hold it back. Her and Stan had never argued before, not until Laura started to come between them with her shenanigans. 'Don't call me "she" either. They say that "she" is the cat's mother. So if I'm a "she", what does that make you?'

Jenny was feeling miserable, her heart in her boots. She couldn't bear it when there was an atmosphere in the house, and this time she was to blame. She should have let her sister keep the blinking rope – look at the trouble it had caused. She could tell her mam was upset, and she didn't deserve to be. So Jenny tried to make amends. 'Did yer see me skipping-rope. Dad? It's a smasher, all me mates will be green with envy.'

Laura wasn't having that. She was her dad's favourite, not Jenny. 'Seeing as all your mates are green anyway, no one will notice the difference. They're all as thick as two short planks, every one of them.'

Stan raised his head, his knife and fork standing one in each hand like sentinels. 'That's enough of that, there's no need to be sarky. Get on with yer dinner and have less to say.'

Laura's eyes flew open in surprise. Her dad never spoke to her like that. But she knew who had put him up to it – her mother. But she better hadn't say anything now, not while her dad was there. She'd get her own back though, she vowed as she speared a carrot. If her mother thought she was going to be a goody-goody, like their Jenny, then she had another think coming.

As the meal continued in silence, Laura was wrapped up in thoughts of the future. Only another six months and she'd be leaving school and getting herself a job. She was so selfish, all she dreamed of was having her own money and being able to buy the clothes she liked instead of having to wear the drab things her mother bought for her. Never once had it entered her empty head that her mother had to scrimp and scrape every week to buy those clothes. No, all Laura was concerned about was herself. Not for her the pride of handing over her wages every week in the knowledge that they would make life easier for all the family. She'd already made up her mind that she was entitled to keep more for herself in pocket-money than she handed over. After all, she would be the one going to work so why should she hand it over? In her narrow mind there was only one person in her life that she really loved – Laura Nightingale.

Mary was hanging the washing on the line on the Monday morning when a smile crossed her face. Amy Hanley, her neighbour and best friend, was singing at the top of her voice in the next yard. Over the wall came the strains of a song that had been popular a few years ago. Mind you, it had been sung then by Kate Smith, and Amy was certainly not in the same league as the well-known singer. It wasn't that she was tone deaf, she just sounded like someone who had been thrown out of the pub at closing time after her throat had been oiled by half-a-dozen bottles of stout.

> 'When the moon comes over the mountains,
> I'm alone with my memories of you.
> We kissed and said goodbye,
> You cried and so did I,
> Now do you wonder why I'm lonely?'

Mary took a peg from her mouth, and giggling, she shouted, 'Yer missed a verse out there, Amy. What happened to the "rose-covered valley we knew"?'

'Oh, ye're there, are yer? Well, I'm not in the mood for rose-covered valleys today, girl, I want to be alone with me bleedin' memories.'

'What memories are they, Amy? Must be miserable from the sound of yer.'

'I'm always miserable on wash-day, girl. If the sun was shining and I had nowt to do, and me purse had a few bob in it, me memories would be happy ones. Like remembering when my feller used to put his hands around me waist and tell me I was the most beautiful girl in the world, bar none. He hasn't said that for years, girl. Mind you, I haven't had a bleedin' waist for years, either.'

Although there was a brick wall separating them, Mary could see her friend as clearly as if she was standing next to her. She was only five foot, was Amy, and as round as she was tall. Right now her mousy-coloured hair would be covered by a mobcap which would be down to her eyebrows because the elastic had withered, the pocket of her pinny would be bulging with clothes pegs, her stockings would be wrinkled around her ankles and her face would be creased in a smile.

'Another memory keeps coming back to me, girl, but I have a bit of trouble with it 'cos it's faded with age. It was when we were first married, before the kids came along, and my feller was that eager he used to carry me upstairs to the bedroom.' Amy's laugh was so loud they must have been able to hear it in the next street. 'Now it takes him all his time to carry himself up. And the most I get out of him in bed is, "Don't let me oversleep, d'yer hear?".'

'Well, the men are tired after a hard day's work, Amy, yer've got to make allowances for them. The first flush of youth isn't there any more.'

'What the bleedin' hell do they think we do all day? Sit on our ruddy backsides? I'd willingly swap places with my feller and go out to work while he minded the three kids. He wouldn't know what had hit him, having to polish and scrub, wash, iron, get the shopping in, see to the dinners, do the darning . . . I'd give him a week and he'd be pleading for mercy.'

'Some good could come of it, Amy,' Mary chuckled. 'If he was at home all day he could put his feet up for a couple of hours, then he'd have the energy to carry yer up the stairs to bed again.'

'He'd need more than energy to carry me up the stairs now, girl – he'd need a bleedin' hoist. And by the end of all that palaver he'd have lost the urge.' Amy finished pegging the washing on the line and stood back to gaze with satisfaction at the clothes blowing in the wind. They'd be dry in no time and she could start ironing before the two kids came in from school and got under her feet. 'Ay, girl, yer don't happen to have any custard creams in, do yer?'

'I might have a couple, I think. Why? Are yer having visitors?'

'I'm not, girl – you are! I'm inviting meself in for a cup of tea and a chinwag. There's nothing better to chase the blues away than a good old gossip.' Her chubby face did contortions. 'Yer don't need to get yer best china out for me, girl, I'm not a snob.'

'Don't be funny, Amy Hanley, yer know I haven't got no china cups.'

'That's why I said yer didn't need to get them out, girl, I knew yer didn't have none. I didn't want yer rummaging in yer cupboards for something yer haven't got. And don't be coming over all embarrassed when yer give me a cup with a chip in, 'cos like I said, I'm not a snob.'

'Ye're a bloody scream, you are, Amy! Yer invite yerself over without a by-your-leave, then have the nerve to criticise me crockery before yer come. And ye're expecting custard creams into the bargain.'

'Only one, girl, I don't expect no more. And yer'll get yer money's worth, 'cos I can tell by yer voice that yer need cheering up.' Amy raised her voice to a shout. 'You put the kettle on, girl, while I stick the guard in front of the fire.'

'You're well-off having a fire this time of the morning, aren't yer? Has your feller had a win on the gee-gees?'

Back came a whispered, 'Fooling the neighbours, girl, that's all. I bet a pound to a pinch of snuff that nosy Annie Baxter has had her ear to the wall, listening to every word we've said. She'll be round to Lily Farmer's as fast as her skinny legs will carry her. And by the time she's put her own interpretation on our conversation, it'll end up something like this. "Ay, what d'yer think, Lily? Monday morning, and that Amy Hanley's got a fire up the chimney. And yer'll never guess where she got the money from for a bag of coal. What's that yer said, Lily? Oh, yer'll have three guesses . . . okay. No, she didn't get it on tick off the coalman. No, she didn't find a two-bob piece. No, yer silly cow, the bag hadn't fallen off the bleedin' coal-cart. That's yer three guesses, Lily, and I knew yer wouldn't get it in a month of Sundays. Just wait till I tell yer, yer won't believe it. She got it off her feller for letting him carry her upstairs so he could have his wicked way with her. How about that, eh? Dirty pair of buggers".'

On the other side of the yard wall, Mary was in stitches. Amy might not be able to sing like Kate Smith, but her impersonation of the street gossip was perfect. 'That was very good, Amy, yer sounded just like her.'

'If I had false teeth, girl, I could do it better. Yer know how her teeth are always clicking when she talks – well, I can't do that. Still, it's not worth having all me teeth out just to sound as miserable as she does. I'm all for getting things right, but that would be carrying it a bit too far.'

'It's to be hoped she's not listening to yer now, Amy.'

'I couldn't give a sod, girl, and that's the truth. If she wants to listen in to private conversations, then she doesn't deserve to hear anything good about herself.'

'Ye're right there, sunshine. Anyway, I'm going in or the day will be gone before we know it. I'll have a cuppa on the table in ten minutes. Oh, and I won't forget yer custard cream. It won't be a

7

whole one because I could only afford half-a-pound of broken biscuits, but I'll see if I can stick two together for yer, seeing as ye're me best mate.'

'This is more like it, girl!' Amy faced her friend across the table. 'I've always wanted to be a lady of leisure. If someone could trace me family tree, I'm sure they'd find me ancestors were very wealthy. They could even have been of the nobility, 'cos I've always had the feeling that I was cut out for better things.' Her body shook with laughter. 'Don't worry, girl, I won't be expecting yer to curtsy to me. A slight nod of yer head will do.'

'D'yer think one of yer ancestors lost the family wealth through gambling and loose women?' Mary's face was deadpan. 'That could account for yer being reduced to sitting in the living room of a two-up two-down house, eating broken biscuits. It could also account for yer obsession with what goes on in the bedroom.'

Amy laced her chubby fingers and nodded her head. 'Someone's got a lot to answer for, haven't they, girl? Dragging me down from riches to rags.'

'Money doesn't always bring happiness, sunshine.'

'No, I know that, but at least yer can be miserable in comfort. I wouldn't mind the kids running riot if I was stretched out on one of those chaise longue things, with a glass of whisky in one hand and a big box of Cadbury's in the other.'

'We don't do too bad, Amy, we're better off than some in the street. At least Stan and Ben are working, even if they do get a lousy wage. We've always managed to scrape along somehow. And things can only get better with the kids growing up.' Mary topped the cups up and put the cosy back on the teapot. 'Yer've got your John working already, bringing in a few bob, and Eddy will be leaving school in eighteen months, same time as our Jenny. Then yer'll only have Edna at home, and yer won't know yerself. Yer'll be living the life of Riley.'

Amy grinned. 'I wish I knew this Riley feller, he could give me a few tips. I don't know what he's got that nobody else has, but I'd like a bit of it.' Her brows drew together. 'What are yer looking at, girl?'

'Unless I'm seeing things it's starting to rain. Hang on, I'll make sure.' Mary opened the kitchen door and groaned. 'It's only spitting at the moment, but there's a dirty big black cloud overhead so we could be in for a downpour.'

Amy's legs were too short to reach the floor, so she had to shuffle her bottom to the edge of the chair before she could push herself up. 'Damn, blast and bugger it! I was hoping to have the washing dried and ironed before teatime. There's nothing I hate more than wet clothes drippin' on me bleedin' head while I'm seeing to the dinner. The kitchen gets full of condensation and the steam's so thick yer've

8

got to fight yer way through it.' She adopted the stance of a boxer, her shoulders hunched and her clenched fists stabbing the air while her feet danced in time with them. For a small woman carrying a lot of weight she could certainly move. 'Like this, girl, that's how I fight me way through the steam.'

'Yer've got a screw loose, Amy Hanley.' Mary grinned at the woman who never failed to cheer her up. There might be black clouds in the sky, but when her mate smiled, and her pretty face creased, she brought sunshine into the house. 'Yer'll need to be able to fight if Annie Baxter heard yer talking about her. She'll have yer guts for garters.'

'Huh! She's small fry, that one. I wouldn't need to fight *her* – one good puff and she'd be out for the count.'

'What if she's got her mate with her? Lily Farmer's not half big, she'd make two of you.'

'Ay, well, I've got to admit that Lily's a different kettle of fish. But I've got one thing in my favour, I can run faster than her. I might have a screw loose, girl, but I know me limitations and Lily Farmer is definitely outside of them.' Amy pushed the chair under the table and her face took on a thoughtful expression. 'It's funny yer should mention a loose screw, girl, 'cos I think ye're right. Every time I turn me neck sharply, I can feel this thing rattling around in me head. Could that be the loose screw yer were talking about?'

'Amy, I don't want to rush yer, sunshine, but the rain is teeming down. I'm bringing my washing in now before it's wringing sopping wet. If the weather clears I can put it out again when I come back from the shops.'

'I'll come to the shops with yer, girl, keep yer company. What time are yer going?'

'In about twenty minutes.'

'Just enough time for me to spend a penny, give me face a cat's lick and a promise, pull me stockings up and comb me hair. I don't need to cake me face with powder or lipstick, not with my natural beauty.'

'Ta-ra, sunshine, on yer way! I'll see yer later.' Mary left her friend and dashed out into the heavy rain. She sighed as she unpegged the clothes that were a damn sight more wet than when she'd put them out in the first place. Her eyes went to the heavens. 'Please God, take pity on us poor women, we don't do no one no harm.' She could feel the dampness as the rain soaked her dress, but she managed a smile. 'Only with words, God, and we don't really mean half we say. Besides, words don't harm no one.'

Mary turned into the butcher's shop with Amy in her wake. 'Good morning, Wilf, lovely weather for ducks, isn't it?'

9

'I'm happy for the ducks, Mary, but it's bloody awful weather for business.' The butcher feigned horror when his eyes lit on Amy. 'Oh dear, yer've brought the menace with yer. D'yer not think I've got enough problems without blighting me life with Amy Hanley?'

Amy slowly lowered her basket to the floor before placing her hands on her ample hips. 'Any more lip out of you, Wilf Burnett, and I'll take me custom elsewhere. I don't have to stand here and be insulted by the likes of you, yer know. All I've got to do is walk to the butcher's in the next block and let him insult me. He's better at it than you; some of his insults really get yer here.' With a dramatic gesture she placed a hand where she thought her heart was. 'Cut to the quick I've been, several times. In fact, and Mary here can bear me out, I was once that upset I had an attack of the vapours and someone had to hold a bottle of smelling salts to me nose, to bring me round.'

Wilf was shaking with laughter. He was a middle-aged man with thinning sandy hair and twinkling blue eyes. 'Yer mean sal volatile, Amy?'

Amy dropped her pose. 'What's salvotily when it's out?'

'Smelling salts.'

'That's what I said, yer silly bugger! D'yer know what? Yer've talked that much I've forgotten what I've come in for. It's no wonder yer've got no bleedin' customers, yer've probably talked them to bloody death.' She turned to Mary and gave her a broad wink. 'That funeral that's just passed us, I bet the poor sod used to shop here.'

'Well, I'm going to make amends for insulting yer, Amy, by giving yer a little bit of advice,' Wilf said. 'Next time yer do yer drama queen act, try putting yer hand where yer heart is. Yer were miles out.'

'I'll return the favour and give you a bit of advice, Wilf Burnett. You just keep yer eyes off my . . . off my . . . off my thingummybobs. My Ben wouldn't take kindly to yer weighing me up and down the way yer are. It's not your fault, 'cos men are drawn to me like a moth to a flame, but yer've got to be strong and keep yerself under control. I know yer mean well, and to put yer mind at ease, I do know where me heart is. It's well-covered, like, but it's in there somewhere.'

Mary banged on the counter, and when Wilf turned her way, she waggled her fingers. 'Yer do know I'm still here, don't yer? I hate to split you two up, but I would like serving.'

'Ah, she's jealous.' Amy shook her head and pouted her lips. 'I get this with her all the time, Wilf. If a man looks at me with longing in his eyes, she goes into a deep sulk. I feel sorry for her, 'cos she's me bestest mate. But I can't help being desirable, can I? It's not as though I'm a vampire, God forbid.'

When Mary and Wilf doubled up with laughter, Amy looked

10

surprised. 'Is it a private joke, or can anyone join in?'

Wilf reached for a clean piece of meat cloth and dabbed his eyes before answering. 'Amy, a vampire sucks blood. The word you should have used was vamp, which means a flirt.'

'Go 'way! Well, yer live and learn. I came in here for three-quarters of shin beef and get a lesson in geography and English. Not that I needed the geography lesson 'cos I know where me own bleedin' heart is, but a vampire sucks blood, eh?' Amy curled her fist and rested her chin on it. 'We haven't got none of them living in our street, have we, girl?'

'How about the woman in number seven, sunshine? It looks like bright red lipstick from a distance, but yer never know.'

'I'll weigh the shin beef while you two crucify the poor woman in number seven.' Wilf was reaching into the shop window for a tray of meat when Mary stayed his hand.

'Oh no, you don't! First in, first served, that's how it should be. I'd like a round neck of lamb, please, the leanest yer've got. And will yer chop it into four for us?'

Two more customers came into the shop then, and the friends were soon served and on their way to the greengrocer's. When Mary shopped on her own, she was around the shops in no time. After giving her order in and passing a few pleasant remarks, she was on her way. But shopping with Amy was a different experience altogether.

'Don't be trying to palm me off with a rotten cabbage, Billy Nelson, 'cos I haven't just come over, yer know.'

'What are yer on about, Amy?' Billy scratched his head. He was short and stocky, with a mop of black curly hair and a cheeky grin. 'I'll have yer know that that cabbage was in a field yesterday; it's as fresh as you are.'

'Pull the other one, Billy, it's got bells on. And when the bells start ringing everybody will think it's Sunday and get themselves ready for Mass.'

'Five o'clock this morning I was at the market getting me fruit and veg, Amy. Even the bleedin' birds were still asleep. I'm telling yer, that cabbage is as fresh as yer'll get.'

Mary thought it time to intervene, otherwise they'd be here all day. 'What's wrong with the ruddy cabbage? It looks all right to me.'

'I dunno, girl, I can't put me finger on it but I just don't like the look of it. It might be the shape of the bleedin' thing, or the colour.'

Billy slapped an open palm on his forehead. 'Ah, yer wanted a pink one, did yer, Amy? Or did yer fancy one in pale blue?'

Amy squared her shoulders and pretended to take the huff. 'Ay, Billy Nelson, you get sarky with me and I'll clock yer one. Buying a cabbage is just like buying a hat, yer either like it or yer don't like it.

11

And I'm telling yer now, I don't like that bleedin' cabbage.'

Holding the offending cabbage in the crook of his arm, Billy bent down and took another one out of the wooden box. 'How about this one, yer moaning so-and-so? Is it the right colour and shape for yer? Or would yer like one with a slim waist and a big bust?'

'Nah, we can't have two big busts in the house, we wouldn't be able to pass each other in our small kitchen. That one will do me fine, I've taken a liking to it.' Amy picked a well-worn purse from her basket, asking, 'Did yer say it was a penny, Billy?'

Billy looked forward to Amy's visit, you could always get a laugh out of her. And she didn't get upset if the laugh was at her own expense. Not like some moaning Minnies who came in the shop. 'There's a bloody big sign on the box, Amy, and it says the cabbages are tuppence.'

'Daylight robbery, that's what it is,' Amy said, passing a threepenny bit over. 'Ye're like that Ben Turpin feller who used to waylay people on the highway and rob them.'

Billy threw the coin in the big pocket of his apron and fished out a penny. 'Here's yer change, Amy. And it was Dick Turpin, not Ben.'

'What was Dick Turpin?'

'The highwayman.'

'Oh, it was Dick, was it? Was he Ben's brother?'

'No, Amy, Ben Turpin is a film star.'

'Well, I never!' Amy turned wide eyes on Mary. 'D'yer know what, girl? I've had more education in the last half hour than I had in me nine years at school.'

'I'm afraid yer've had yer last lesson for today, sunshine, 'cos it's time to get home and put the dinner on.' Mary took tight hold of her friend's arm and pulled her through the shop doorway, calling, 'Ta-ra, Billy, we'll leave yer in peace now.'

'Ta-ra, girls, see yer tomorrow.'

Amy was grinning as she moved the basket to her other arm so she could walk on the inside and link her friend. 'I enjoyed, that, girl. We had a good laugh, didn't we? And in case yer haven't noticed, the rain's gone off.'

'It went off twenty minutes ago, sunshine, but you were too busy talking to notice. I'm going to get me stew on, then put me clothes out again. With a bit of luck we'll get them dry this afternoon.'

Amy looked at Mary out of the corner of her eye. 'I heard yer telling your Laura off on Friday night, girl. Had she been giving yer cheek?'

'That's nothing unusual, is it, Amy? She's gone really hard-faced and is always giving me cheek. She went too far on Friday, though, and I slapped her face.'

'She is cheeky, I'll grant yer that. Not only to you, either.' Amy wanted to say more, but bit on her tongue. She could tell Mary a lot about that eldest daughter of hers, so could many of the neighbours in the street. But everybody kept quiet because, apart from Laura, the Nightingales were well-liked and respected. 'CNever mind, she'll change when she starts work. It'll be a case of having to, 'cos if she gets a job in a factory none of the women will take any lip from her.'

'I hope ye're right, Amy, because I do worry about her.'

'Of course I'm right.' Amy squeezed her arm. 'Vampires are always right, aren't they?'

Chapter Two

Mary sat one side of the hearth sewing a seam that had come undone in Jenny's gymslip, while Stan sat facing her, reading the evening paper. It was the best time of the day for Mary, when the girls were in bed and she and her husband could discuss the events of the day, or sit in companionable silence. At the moment the only sounds in the room were the rustle of newspaper when Stan turned a page, the ticking of the clock and an occasional spurt from one of the coals.

With a sigh of contentment, Mary sewed the last stitch and snapped the cotton between her teeth. 'That's one job done, thank goodness. With a bit of luck Jenny will get a few more months' wear out of it.' She rubbed her eyes with the heel of her hands. 'I'll leave your socks until tomorrow, it's hopeless trying to sew in this light.'

Stan looked over the top of the paper. 'I think the gas is going, love, it's taking me all me time to read. Yer'd best put a penny in the meter before it goes altogether and we're left in the dark.'

'I can remember the time when yer'd have been glad to sit in the dark.' Mary grinned. 'Stealing kisses when me mam and dad had gone to bed.'

Stan lowered the paper to his lap. 'That brings back a few memories. I used to dread the sound of yer mam knocking on the floor with her shoe.' He chuckled. 'If she didn't hear me leave right away, she used to bang so hard I expected the ceiling to cave in on us. I got the distinct impression she didn't trust me.'

'All mothers are like that with their daughters. I used to call her for everything, saying she was treating me like a child. Now I've got daughters of me own, I understand why she was so protective. I'll always regret not telling her that she'd been a good mother and I loved her dearly. The trouble is, yer think yer've got plenty of time to say all these things; yer don't expect yer mam to die at fifty-two.'

'Yer mam didn't need telling, pet, she knew yer loved her.'

'She probably thought me dad loved her, as well. Yer would after being married for nearly thirty years, wouldn't yer? I thought he doted on her, they always seemed so happy.' Mary gave a deep sigh. 'But he couldn't have loved her that much, could he? Not to have married again six months after she died. And to a girl only half his age. A man of fifty-five, trying to act as young as the girl he'd wed. I'll

15

never forget the first night he brought her here and she was all over him. She seemed to be flaunting him, as though to say "Look what I've got". I didn't know where to put meself, and me older than her. He didn't take long to forget me mam, and I don't think I'll ever forgive him for that.'

'Yeah, I've got to say it was the biggest surprise I've ever had in me life. If she'd been older I might have understood him marrying for companionship, but she's a fly turn, just out for a good time. I've seen them a few times down Walton Road, and a stranger seeing them would take them for father and daughter until they saw the antics out of them. Stupid bugger, that's all I can say.'

'I often wonder what me mam's old neighbours make of it. Especially the woman next door, Monica Platt. Her and me mam were real good mates. All the years they lived next door to each other never a cross word passed between them. And me dad used to be friendly with her husband, Phil – they used to go to the pub together a couple of times a week. I bet they're not so friendly now he's married a slip of a girl. They probably think he's lost the run of his senses, and they wouldn't be far wrong.'

The gas-light started to flicker and Mary jumped to her feet. 'I'd better feed the meter while I can still see it, save me fumbling around in the dark.'

'Here yer are, I've got a penny in me pocket.'

'No, I've got me week's supply on the kitchen shelf.' Mary reached up to where she kept the pennies, and as her hand covered the one at the top of the pile, a frown crossed her face. She lifted them all down and her frown deepened when she counted them. She'd put six there when she'd got back from the shops, she was certain of that, and now there were only four. When one had gone missing last week she'd put it down to a mistake on her part and thought no more of it. But she hadn't made a mistake today, that was definite.

Mary bent down and pressed a penny into the meter slot, then she turned the knob and waited for the coin to drop. Someone had taken two pennies and it wasn't something you could just brush aside. But if she mentioned it to Stan now, it would only cause trouble and spoil the closeness there'd been between them. He hadn't taken them, that was a cert, so that left the two girls. She'd have a word with them in the morning – try to sort it out without involving her husband. And she pushed aside the thought that there was no need to have a word with both of them because, God forgive her, she knew which one would be the thief.

Stan folded the paper up when Mary came back into the room. 'How about a cup of tea and then an early night in bed, love?' There was that special look in his hazel eyes which never failed to set Mary's

16

pulses racing. 'It's yer own fault for reminding me of the days when we were courting.'

'You cheeky beggar!' Mary didn't need to put a smile on her face, it came of its own free will. She'd sort out the problem of the missing pennies tomorrow, and make sure it didn't happen again. But tonight belonged to her and Stan. 'I've a good mind to tell yer I've got a headache, that would dampen yer passion.' She huffed. 'Reminding indeed! That's an insult, that is. I'm going to have to ask Amy for some tips, see where I'm going wrong. She said every time Ben looks at her his eyes fill with desire for her voluptuous body.'

'She's a corker, she is.' Stan laughed. 'She's got a voluptuous body all right, yer could lose yerself in it.'

'I'll put the kettle on while you dream of Amy's body. When I see her tomorrow I'll tell her what yer said and she'll be over the moon.'

'Ooh, don't tell her, love, I'd never hear the end of it. She'd be waiting for me coming home from work and she'd make a holy show of me in the street.'

'Be a coward and come in the back way, then.' Mary was chuckling as she walked through to the kitchen. 'By dinnertime tomorrow, Wilf the butcher, Billy the greengrocer and Greg from the Maypole will all know that yer fancy her.' She popped her head around the door. 'Of course, if yer treat me right I promise not to tell her.'

'That's blackmail, that is.'

'Yeah, I know. Isn't it lovely? I've got yer in me clutches now, so behave yerself.' She gave him a broad wink. 'No, on second thoughts, I don't want yer to behave yerself.'

'I've no intention of behaving meself, love, not tonight.'

'That's all right, then. I'll see if I've got a Beechams Powder in the house, just in case I feel a headache coming on.'

Mary carried a plate of toast through the next morning and placed it on the table. The two girls were sitting next to each other and Mary stood opposite, her knuckles white as she leaned her weight on the table. Since Stan had left for work she'd been rehearsing in her mind how she would broach the subject. But there was no nice way of doing it, so she gazed from one to the other, and said, 'There's two pennies missing from me gas money. Who knows anything about it?'

Laura's reply came quickly. 'Don't look at me, I don't know nothing about it.'

Jenny looked puzzled. 'What d'yer mean, Mam, two pennies have gone missing?'

'Just what I said, sunshine. I put six pennies on the shelf when I came back from the shops, but when I went to get one for the meter last night, there were only four there. And they couldn't have walked away by themselves.'

Laura bit off a piece of toast and talked through a mouthful of the crispy golden bread. 'Me dad must have taken them for his fare. Ask him when he comes home.'

'And shall I ask him if he took the one that went missing last week? No, yer can leave yer dad out of this, he didn't take them. So I want to know what you two know about it?'

Jenny's head was bent over her plate and her voice was low. 'I didn't take them, Mam. That would be stealing.'

'Ooh, listen to Miss Goody Two-shoes,' Laura mocked. 'Never does nothing wrong.'

'Less of that, Laura.' Mary's voice was sharp. 'Your sister's said she didn't take them, so what have you got to say for yerself?'

'I didn't take yer rotten pennies.' Laura chewed on the last bit of toast, a bold look in her green eyes. 'They must have dropped off the shelf and fallen behind the cupboard.' She licked her fingers before pushing her chair back. 'Or yer could have been mistaken and only put four there in the first place. Anyway, it's time we were on our way to school if we don't want to get the cane for being late.'

'Sit down,' Mary said, her face set. 'Neither of yer leaves this house until we find out what happened to those pennies. I'm not so well off I can afford to lose them, but that's not the real issue. If there's a thief in this house I want to know who it is.'

Laura laughed. 'Don't be stupid! Yer can't keep us off school, me dad would go hairless if yer did that.'

Mary leaned forward so her face was on a level with her daughter's. 'Don't you ever dare call me stupid or I'll give yer the hiding of yer life. If I say yer not going to school, then that's the end of the matter. And don't threaten me with telling your father, because yer won't need to, I'll do it meself.'

'Mam, we will get into trouble if we don't go to school,' Jenny said. 'We'll get six strokes of the cane and be behind with our lessons.'

'No, yer won't get the cane because I'll give yer a note to take in. But neither of yer leave here until the matter is settled. If a thief gets away with it once, they'll steal again, and I'll not entertain it in this house.'

Jenny was near to tears. She enjoyed school and was an eager pupil. If she missed a day she'd be behind her friends. 'That's not fair, Mam, 'cos I haven't done nothing wrong. I haven't got the pennies and keeping me off won't help yer find them.'

'Oh, shut yer face,' Laura said, giving her sister a sharp dig in the ribs. 'Ye're a proper whinger, you are.'

'I'd rather be a whinger than a thief.' Jenny had put up with a lot over the years, taken the blame too often for her sister's misdeeds. She'd tolerated it for a quiet life, but having to miss school was the last straw. 'I think me mam's two pennies are in yer shoe. I saw yer messing around when I was getting dressed but thought nothing of it.'

Before Mary realised what was happening, Laura had grabbed locks of her sister's long golden hair in both hands and was pulling hard, a vicious look on her face. 'You rotten liar! I haven't got nothing in me shoes.'

Jenny was wincing with pain as she pleaded, 'Let go, ye're hurting me.'

Mary rounded the table and took hold of a handful of Laura's dark hair. 'Let go, or I'll give yer a dose of yer own medicine.' The threat didn't work, but a sharp tug did. 'Now stop this fighting right away, d'yer hear me? Sit up straight in yer chairs and behave yerselves.'

Mary sighed as she gazed down at her daughters. Was she going too far? Making a mountain out of a molehill? No, she told herself, she couldn't just let it go. It was one penny last week, two pennies today, what would she do when it came to sixpences – let that go as well?

'Laura, have you got the money?'

'No, I haven't! She's a liar, trying to get me into trouble.'

Jenny's face was white. 'I might be wrong, Mam.'

'Right, well you go off to school now, sunshine, and Laura will follow in five minutes. I'm not having the two of yer fighting in the street. If yer run all the way, yer'll make it in time.'

Jenny grabbed her coat off the hook behind the door and was out of the house like greased lightning. She knew her sister would have it in for her, but if Laura hit her she wouldn't just stand there like she usually did, she'd fight back this time.

Mary waited until she heard the front door close, then sighed. 'I'll ask yer again, Laura. Have yer got the money in yer shoe?'

'No, I haven't, so there!' Laura tossed her hair. 'I told yer that once, so why ask?'

'In that case, yer won't mind taking yer shoes off for me.'

'Oh yes, I would mind! I'm going to tell me dad on yer, he'll have something to say.'

'If I were you I wouldn't mention it to yer dad, he'd be so disappointed in yer. If yer've got the money, hand it over and we'll say no more about it. I won't tell yer dad or Jenny, or anyone. Unless it happens again, and then I will shout my mouth off.'

Laura glared. All this for two lousy pennies. But she could tell by the set of her mother's jaw that she meant every word she said. 'Oh, all right.' She bent down and took a shoe off then emptied it over the table. The two coins rolled towards Mary, who stopped them with her hand. 'I wouldn't have to pinch if yer gave us enough pocket-money.'

Mary felt no anger, only sadness. 'We give you as much pocket-money as we can afford. I have to rob Peter to pay Paul every week, but you wouldn't understand that. Well, yer might understand, but yer wouldn't care. All yer think about, Laura, is yerself. I've always known yer were selfish, but I never dreamt yer would stoop to stealing from yer own mother. I won't tell yer dad about this because it would kill him. So I'll give yer one more chance. But a word of warning . . . nobody likes a liar or a thief and yer could end up without a friend in the world.'

Laura bent to put her shoe back on. 'Yer won't tell anyone, will yer?'

Mary sighed and shook her head. 'No, not this time. But do it again, sunshine, and I'll be the one who goes running to yer dad.' She waited until her daughter straightened up and held out her arms. 'Come and give us a kiss and say ye're sorry, and promise me faithfully yer'll never do it again. Yer see, Laura, if anyone found out, they'd never trust yer again, and yer don't want that, do yer?'

When Laura walked into her mother's arms, sobbing that she definitely wouldn't do it again, the tears she shed were not of shame or remorse. They were tears of relief that her father wasn't going to find out, and regret that she'd been caught. And there was a certain amount of self-pity as she told herself she was stupid to have taken the two pennies. If only she'd been satisfied with one, like last week, her mother probably wouldn't have noticed.

'Come on, now, sunshine, wipe yer eyes and get going. If yer run like the wind yer might just make it before the bell goes and the gates are closed.'

Mary's heart was heavy as she watched her daughter running down the street. She'd keep her promise and not mention the matter to a living soul. But as she closed the front door, she let out a deep sigh. She wanted to believe Laura when she promised not to do it again, but try as she might, Mary couldn't help feeling that the tears and promises were an act put on to get her out of trouble. And she doubted that her daughter meant a word of what she'd said.

Gasping for breath, Laura slipped through the school gate just as it was being closed by Mr Johnston, one of the teachers from the boys' school. The two schools were housed in the same building, but the two sexes never mixed. Even the playground was divided by high iron railings.

'Leave the house earlier in future, or you'll be locked out.' Mr Johnston's voice was stern, his eyes angry. 'All the children are in assembly now, so wait in the corridor until prayers are over, then report to Miss Harrison's office.'

Laura gaped. You only reported to the headmistress's office if you were going to get the cane. 'I couldn't help being a bit late, Mr Johnston, it wasn't my fault. Me mam's not feeling well and sent me on a message to the corner shop.' The lies dripped off her tongue. 'And I ran all the way, honest. I ran that fast I've got a pain in me chest.'

'You have missed assembly and Miss Harrison will want to know why.' The giant key to the school gate was tapped on the palm of the teacher's open hand. 'I suggest you make your excuses to her and she will judge whether you deserve to be punished or not.'

He walked ahead of Laura through the double doors, and without a backward glance he turned sharp left towards the ever-locked door which separated the two schools. The girl was so angry she felt like pulling tongues behind his back, but thought better of it. She was in enough trouble without asking for more. With a bit of luck the headmistress might believe her story about being sent to the shops, especially if she offered to bring a note in tomorrow from home.

The corridors were empty and quiet with everyone in assembly, and as Laura stood outside Miss Harrison's office the silence played on her nerves. The headmistress was very strict and feared by all the children. A smile on her face was a rare sight indeed. It wasn't going to be easy to pull the wool over her eyes, but she could only try. Getting six strokes of the cane off a woman who looked as though she thoroughly enjoyed inflicting pain, was no laughing matter.

Laura didn't lay any of the blame for her predicament at her own door. If their Jenny hadn't snitched on her she wouldn't be standing here now, shivering with apprehension. Her mother would never have dreamt of looking in her shoe for the missing pennies if her sister hadn't put the idea into her head. Well, she'd be sorry she hadn't kept her mouth shut by the time Laura had finished with her. She'd get her in the playground when they had their mid-morning break and Miss Goody Two-shoes would regret clatting on her.

The double doors of the assembly hall burst open and a stream of girls rushed out, chattering as they headed for their classrooms. Some of them sneered behind their hands when they saw Laura, who was unpopular with most of the girls because she was always bullying the younger children and causing trouble. Two of her mates stopped, curious to know what she'd done to warrant a visit to the dreaded office, but she hissed that she'd tell them later. Her eyes were peeled for sight of her sister, and when Jenny passed, Laura bared her teeth in a snarl. 'I'll get you for this, just see if I don't.'

Jenny shrugged her shoulders and walked on. Another time she might have been frightened by her sister's threat, but not now. She wasn't sorry for what she'd done, and she'd do it again if need be. Laura had played some dirty tricks in her life but stealing from her

21

own mother was a terrible thing to do. Especially when their mam had a struggle every week to make ends meet.

Laura stood to attention when the headmistress strode towards her, her figure squat and her walk manly. One look at the severe expression on the plain face told the girl she could expect no sympathy from that quarter. 'Good morning, Miss Harrison.'

Ignoring the greeting, the headmistress turned the handle on the office door and pushed it open. Her face only an inch away from the terrified girl, she barked, 'Enter.'

Laura nearly jumped out of her skin. And as she entered the office, tears welled up in her eyes and she allowed them to flow freely down her cheeks.

'Stop that snivelling, girl!' Miss Harrison sat down at the far side of the desk and with the end of her pencil, began a rhythmic tapping on the wooden top. 'Mr Johnston tells me you were late for school.'

Laura made no attempt to stem the flow of tears. She needed all the help she could get right now. 'I got in before the gate closed, Miss Harrison. And it wasn't my fault. I was ready for school in time but me mam's not well and she sent me on a message for her. She was going to write me a note, explaining, but I would have been worse late.'

'Worse late, Nightingale!' The dark grey eyebrows nearly touched the matching grey hairline. 'Your grammar is atrocious! Have you learned nothing in your nine years of schooling?'

'I'm sorry, Miss.'

'Being sorry won't get you a job when you leave school, my girl. Now stop that blabbering and listen to me. You will bring a note from your mother in the morning, and if I'm convinced that you haven't written it yourself, you'll be excused punishment for being late. But you will be punished for your treatment of the English language. You will stay in the classroom during playtime this morning and this afternoon, and you will write out fifty sentences, each sentence containing one of these words.' Miss Harrison reached for a pad lying on the side of her desk and began to write quickly. Then she tore the page off and held it out. 'Read them to me and tell me if you understand their meaning.'

Laura stared down at the paper and read the words aloud. 'Late, later, latest, lately and lateness.' She looked up and kept her face a picture of innocence, even though she was seething inside. Fifty sentences meant twenty-five this morning and the same in the afternoon. She'd never do that many in fifteen minutes. And she wasn't good at English, she'd make all sorts of mistakes with no one to copy off. But their Jenny could do it, she was always top of the class in English. 'If I don't get them all done, Miss, can I take them home and finish them there?'

'If you put your mind to it, Nightingale, instead of staring out of the window, you should have no trouble writing short sentences in a matter of seconds. How about, "I was late today"? Or have you forgotten the reason you are standing in my office? Now, away to your classroom and I'll expect you to report back here at half-past three with the finished work, all neat and tidy and without any spelling errors.' She waved a dismissive hand. 'Now, go.'

Laura forced herself to turn slowly and leave the room, closing the door quietly behind her. Once in the corridor, though, she gave vent to her anger. Her fists clenched, she swore vengeance on her sister. It was through Jenny she was going to miss playtime and be a laughing stock in the classroom. She knew most of the girls disliked her and would get great pleasure out of seeing her humiliated. Well, they'd be in for a bigger treat tomorrow because there was no way she could do fifty sentences, let alone without a spelling error. And that would earn her the wrath of Miss Harrison and six strokes of the cane.

But luck was on Laura's side when she got to her classroom and found herself sitting next to one of the cleverest girls in the class. She never had a kind word for the girl usually, always skitting her for being a brainbox. The task the headmistress had set would be no problem to this girl, a fact Laura's crafty mind was quick to work out. So as she lifted the lid of her desk she gave her a bright smile. 'Hello, Helen.'

Helen's brown eyes were suspicious. 'What have you been up to?'

Laura made sure the teacher's back was towards them before she answered. 'Nothing. I was late getting in and I've got to bring a note tomorrow from me mam to say why.' She closed the lid of the desk and slid the piece of paper across. 'Could you write fifty short sentences using one of those words in each?'

Helen fingered the paper. 'Of course I could, easy.'

'I bet yer couldn't do it in half-an-hour.'

The girl's smile was smug. 'I could, but then I'm not a dunce like you.'

Laura bit on her tongue. 'Go on, show us then. I bet yer any money yer can't do it.'

The teacher, Miss Baldwin, had been chalking on the blackboard and she now turned to face the class. 'These are your sums for today. Copy them into your book and I want them completed and on my desk before the bell goes.'

Helen dutifully opened her exercise book and began to copy the sums in her neat writing. There were never any dirty fingermarks on her pages, nor any altered figures. She turned her head when Laura poked her on the arm. 'Don't be stupid, I can't do them now.'

'Yer'll be finished with the sums before anyone else, so yer could

23

do a few sentences. Just to prove to me that yer can do it.'

Casting doubt on her ability was something Helen wouldn't tolerate. She finished her sums before Laura was halfway through hers, then, keeping a watchful eye on the teacher, she tore a page from the middle of her exercise book. After checking the words on the piece of paper Laura had put in front of her, she began to write. And when the bell went to announce the morning break, she slid the sheet of paper across to Laura with a supercilious grin on her face. 'There you are, twenty-five sentences. You could never do that, ye're too thick.'

Laura smiled as she gazed down at the neatly written sentences. Once she had copied them into her exercise book, she was halfway there. And now Helen had given her an idea of what to write, all she had to do for the next twenty-five was to alter each sentence a little. Her troubles were over, and for that she'd let Helen get away with saying she was thick. Although, when you came to think about it, it was Helen who was thick for walking into her trap. 'That's great, that is. Yer are clever, Helen.'

The girls lined up to put their books on the teacher's desk, then hurried out, eager to be away from the eagle eye of Miss Baldwin. Laura stayed at her desk waiting for the classroom to empty, and when one of her friends stopped to ask if she was coming, she explained that she'd been given lines to do by the headmistress and warned her not to let on to any of the other girls. Helen need never know she'd been duped because the lesson after playtime was history, and that was taken by Miss Hawkins in a different classroom. And the chances of sitting next to Helen again were remote, Laura would make sure of that.

History and geography were Laura's worst subjects. They didn't interest her and she could see no sense in them. After all, what good did it do you to know that the Battle of Hastings was fought in 1066? How many times in her life was she going to be asked that? No, when she left school in a couple of months she'd be too busy going out with boys, to the pictures or dancing, to give a thought to the likes of Henry VIII and all his blinking wives.

When Mary answered the knock on the door her eyes flew open in surprise. 'Dad! I never expected to see you! Aren't yer at work today?'

Joe Steadman took his cap off and ran his fingers nervously back and forth along the stiffened peak. 'Yeah, I'm working near here and thought I'd nip along and see yer in me dinner hour.'

Mary opened the door wider and waved a hand. 'Come on in, don't be standing on me step or the neighbours will think ye're the club-man and I owe yer money.' She closed the door behind him and bustled through to the kitchen. 'I'll put the kettle on and make yer a sandwich. It won't be much, mind, 'cos I haven't got much in.'

'There's no need, lass, I've got me carry-out with me. But a cup of tea would go down a real treat.' Joe took a small parcel from his pocket before sitting down. He gazed around the room, noting everything was neat and tidy, and spotlessly clean. He closed his eyes as a feeling of sadness descended on him. It must be nearly a year since he'd been in this house. His marrying Celia so soon after his wife died had caused a rift between him and his daughter which he bitterly regretted. She was his own flesh and blood, and he missed her so much, and Stan and the two girls. He wouldn't have stayed away so long, but he knew the sight of him and his young wife upset and embarrassed Mary and he thought it was for the best. But his longing to see her had grown stronger over the months and today he could no longer resist that longing. He hadn't been sure of the reception he'd get, but at least she hadn't closed the door in his face.

In the kitchen Mary lit the gas-ring under the kettle then leaned against the sink to sort her thoughts out. She'd called her father all the names under the sun since her mam died, but when she saw him standing on her step, looking like a little boy who was hoping the person opening the door would be glad to see him, her heart went out to him. He was her dad and she still loved him. Although she'd never admitted it, for the last year there'd been a void in her life without him. She would never change her view that what he did was wrong, but she still had fond memories of the man who used to tickle her tummy to make her laugh, gave her piggy-backs and took her to the swings in the park. She remembered how full of fun he always was and how happy their home had been.

The kettle gave out a piercing whistle and she turned the gas off before reaching for a cloth to wrap around the hot handle. 'Won't be long now, Dad. I'll just let it brew for a few minutes because I know yer like yer tea strong enough to stand a spoon up in.'

'Don't worry, lass, I'll drink it as it comes.'

He was sitting in Stan's chair when Mary carried two steaming cups through, and she tutted. 'Why don't yer sit at the table and I'll give yer a plate to put yer sandwiches on? Anyone would think we were poverty-stricken if they saw yer eating from the paper.' She pulled a chair out and sat down. 'Come on, sit at the table in a proper manner.'

'I haven't got long, lass, we only get an hour for dinner.' He lowered his eyes to the plate. 'I just wanted to see yer and make sure yer were all right. It's been over a year now, and I have missed yer.'

'Yeah, it's been too long, Dad.' Mary frowned as she watched him transfer the sandwiches from the paper to the plate. 'In the name of

God, Dad, what d'yer call them? They don't look very appetising, and there's not enough there to feed a bird.'

Joe Steadman flushed and averted his eyes. 'I made them meself and I'm not very good at it.' He lifted his head and attempted a smile. 'I've never been house-trained, yer see.'

'Yer don't need to be house-trained when yer've got a wife to look after yer.' Mary studied his face and it suddenly struck her that he was a lot thinner than he'd ever been. And there were a lot more lines on his face, adding years to his appearance. 'Doesn't she get out of bed to see to yer breakfast and carry-out?'

'It's not worth her getting up for that, I can manage meself.'

'Yer've lost a lot of weight, Dad. It seems to me she doesn't feed yer proper.'

'She does her best, but she's only young and yer can't expect miracles.'

'Miracles! A pan of scouse isn't a miracle, Dad! Even our Laura and Jenny could make a really good stew if it came to the push. They help me at the weekend making the dinner and they're not bad little cooks for their age. And they're only schoolkids, Dad – a lot younger than the one you married. If they can do it, why can't she?'

'She wasn't used to housework and she's still learning.' Joe couldn't hold back the sigh that escaped. 'She'll be all right, given time.'

One part of Mary's mind was telling her to mind her own business, another was reminding her that Joe was her father – and he had certainly gone down the nick since she last saw him. She couldn't just ignore it. 'So, while she's learning, playing mothers and fathers, like, you're going to starve to death? Buck yer ideas up, Dad, and be firm with her. Otherwise she'll act the fool for the rest of her life. She's a grown woman, for crying out loud, not a ruddy chit of a girl. She wanted to get married and be a housewife, so for heaven's sake make her get on with it.'

Twelve months ago, Joe would have risen to his new wife's defence, but not now, he was too weary. 'I've tried, lass, but talking to her is like water off a duck's back. She's still a child, never quite grown up. And I'm beginning to think she never will.'

'She never will, unless yer put yer foot down with her!' Mary sighed with frustration. 'My God, she knew a soft touch when she saw one.' She knew she was walking on eggshells, but she couldn't keep the words back. 'Does she keep yer house like me mam used to?'

'She does her best.' Joe pushed the plate away and leaned his elbows on the table. 'I'll have to be more firm with her, that's all.'

At that moment, Mary knew in her heart that her father rued the day when he'd married the young Celia. She'd chased after him, flattered him and made him feel young again. Their honeymoon had been a whirl of pubs, pictures and dances, and had lasted three months. After that, Celia didn't bother putting up a pretence and allowed her real self to surface. Her real self being lazy, brazen and man-mad.

'Well, that's your business, Dad. I won't say any more except don't be daft with her. It's no good our falling out the first time we meet in twelve months.' Mary laced her fingers and rested her chin on them. 'Yer said yer were working near here, where exactly is that?'

Joe was a plumber and had been with the same firm since he left school. 'We're working on a school in Bedford Road, laying some new pipes and putting in a couple of wash-basins. It's not a big job, we'll be finished this week.'

Mary glanced at the clock. 'It's a good ten-minute walk, Dad, yer'd better watch the time.'

'Yeah, I'll just have another half a cup of tea, then I'll be off.'

As she poured the tea, Mary asked, 'Why don't yer come tomorrow dinnertime and I'll have something ready for yer? It won't be a banquet, but even egg on toast would be better than those ruddy sandwiches yer've just had.' She smiled across the table. 'Anyway, I'd like to see yer again.'

Joe's face showed his pleasure. 'As long as yer don't mind. I don't want to put yer out, be any bother.'

'No bother at all. Just wait until I tell Stan and the girls yer've been, they'll be dead jealous they didn't get to see yer.'

'I'll call in one night and see them.' Joe saw his daughter's eyes cloud over and was quick to put her mind at rest. 'Celia goes out with a mate sometimes. I'll come on one of the nights she's going out.'

When Mary was seeing him out, Joe bent to kiss her cheek. 'I was worried about coming, but I'm glad I did. We've broken the ice, now, haven't we, lass?'

'Yes, Dad, we've broken the ice and it'll stay broken.' She felt quite emotional as she gave him a big hug. 'I'll see yer tomorrow. Ta-ra.'

'You're late.' Mary turned the tap off when Laura came through to the kitchen. 'Our Jenny got home ages ago.'

'I had to go to Miss Harrison's office after classes and she kept me waiting in the corridor for about ten minutes. I got into trouble for being late and she gave me lines to do during playtime. And on top of that she wants you to give me a note to take in tomorrow. I told her I had to go on a message for yer. It was dead unfair, though, 'cos I got through the gate before Mr Johnston had closed it. He could have let me off but he's too miserable. I'll be glad when I leave school, I hate it.'

Knowing her daughter's writing was terrible and she couldn't spell for toffee, Mary was apprehensive when she asked, 'And these lines yer had to do, did Miss Harrison check them before yer left?'

Laura tossed her head and looked really superior. 'She checked them all right, with a blinking fine-tooth comb. I felt like asking her if she wanted a magnifying glass. But she couldn't find any mistakes and I felt like pulling faces at her.'

'Yer did well, sunshine, not to make any mistakes. But if she wants a note off me, explaining why yer were late, why did she give yer lines to do?'

'Because she likes to throw her weight around, that's why.' Laura decided her best policy would be to make herself scarce before awkward questions started to be asked. 'I'm going out to see Cynthia, but I'll only be in the street if yer want me.' She was smiling as she walked away with a jaunty air, feeling very proud of herself as she remembered the look of suspicion on the headmistress's face as she tried to find fault with her work. But she couldn't because it was faultless. And that was all down to good old 'brainbox' Helen. She was as dull as ditchwater, but she had come in useful today. Without her, Laura would have been in real trouble and her hands would now be stinging from six strokes of the cane.

Laura saw her friend, Cynthia, coming towards her and waved. In a couple of months she'd never have to worry about the cane again; she'd be a working girl who could buy her own clothes, go to the pictures if she wanted, stay out late and go with boys.

Chapter Three

Mary sat at the table with her Christmas club cards spread out before her. She'd been adding up how much she'd paid into each and there was a smile of pleasure on her face because she was better off than she thought she was. There was enough in the greengrocer's to pay for the potatoes, the vegetables and fruit, and what she had in the butcher's should cover her for a small turkey and a chicken. She had been hoping to buy a Christmas tree this year, but it wouldn't run to it. Next year, though, with a few bob coming in from Laura they'd definitely have a tree, and all the trimmings.

She saw a shadow pass the back window and the next minute Amy's face was pressed against the glass pane, her nose squashed flat like a prize-fighter's. Mary lowered her head pretending she hadn't seen, and feigned interest in the cards while chuckling to herself. But two seconds later she regretted her action when Amy's knock on the window was so hard it seemed that not only was the glass pane in danger of coming in, but the whole window frame with it. She sprang to her feet, telling herself it served her right for trying to play a prank on her neighbour.

'Good God, Amy, yer almost put the flamin' window in!' Mary held the back door open and her friend hurried past, rubbing her arms briskly to warm them up. 'Apart from making me nearly jump out of me skin.'

'It's too cold to hang about outside, girl, it's bleedin' freezing. If I was a monkey I'd have had me you know whats frozen off by now.'

'Get over by the fire, then, and let me close this door to keep the draught out.'

'Blimey, girl, do yer call this a fire? I'd get more heat if yer breathed on me.'

'Ye're lucky I've got a fire at all, yer moaning so-and-so. I'm trying to save coal so we can have a bit extra for over the Christmas holidays. Anyway, if you've got a fire roaring up the chimney, why didn't yer stay in yer own house?'

' 'Cos it's like the frozen wastes of Siberia in there, girl, that's why. Yer see, I haven't got no fire at all, that's why I came in here to get a warm and scrounge a cup of tea.'

Mary's blue eyes were laughing as she pointed a finger. 'Yer might not have any fire, Mrs Woman, but yer've got plenty of cheek to make up for it. The nerve of yer, telling me ye're saving yer coal and tea, then having the brass neck to moan at me because me fire's low! I suppose yer'd like me to put a shovelful of coal on the fire before I make yer a cup of tea, would yer? And while ye're at it, why not go the whole hog and ask me for a round of toast to go with it?'

'That's neighbourly of yer, girl, I must say.' Amy folded her chubby arms across her tummy so her friend couldn't see it shaking with laughter. Adopting an innocent expression and adding a plaintive catch to her voice, she asked, 'I don't suppose yer've got an egg yer could put on the toast, have yer? Now that would be what I call real neighbourly.'

'Sod off, Amy Hanley! I'm beginning to think I can't afford you for a friend, yer friendship is costing me too much money.'

'Bloody hell, girl, yer get yer money's worth out of me. For a lousy cup of tea and round of toast, yer'll get all the gossip of the neighbourhood. I've a good mind to take me business elsewhere, where I'm appreciated.'

'Like yer neighbour on the other side, I suppose, the nosy Annie Baxter?'

'That's a thought, girl. I'd definitely get a poached egg on me toast if I went to her with the juicy gossip I've got in my possession.' Amy's lips were pursed as she nodded her head. 'Hot off the presses, it is. Hasn't had time to get around the street yet.'

Mary pulled out a chair. 'Yer've got me curious, now, sunshine, so sit yerself down and tell us what this hot news is.'

'Uh, uh! Ye're not soft, are yer, girl? Not a word passes me lips until me tea and toast is on the table in front of me. I want to see what I'm getting for me information. And if I think yer've been skinny with the margarine, I'll only tell yer half the story. I'll leave the best bit out.'

'Ye're a hard woman to do business with, Amy Hanley, and I'm a ruddy fool for falling for it.' Mary clicked her tongue on the roof of her mouth and rolled her eyes towards the ceiling. 'I'll make a pot of tea, and do yer a round of toast, but this gossip better be good. Something like Elsie Blackburn's husband catching her in bed with the milkman. Now that wouldn't be news, but it would be gossip.'

Amy's brows drew together. 'What d'yer mean? I know everything what goes on in this street and I've never heard that about Elsie Blackburn. How come you know about it and I don't?'

'How come I know what, sunshine?'

'About Elsie Blackburn.'

'What about Elsie Blackburn?'

'So help me, I'll strangle yer in a minute, Mary Nightingale. Yer know damn well what I'm talking about – her husband catching her in bed with the milkman.'

30

Mary let her mouth gape in feigned horror. 'He didn't, did he? Ooh, he wouldn't like that, would he? Did he give her and the milkman a good hiding?'

Amy's face was set for a few seconds, then her infectious laughter filled the room. 'Yer had me going for a while, there, girl. I thought to meself, aye aye, she must be pinching me job off me 'cos her gossip's better than mine. Me own common sense should have told me yer were having me on. I mean, the state of Elsie! A feller would have to be blind to go with Elsie, and the milkman's not blind. He's flat-footed, got a squint in one eye and yer can count the hairs on his head, but blind he ain't.'

'May God forgive us, Amy Hanley, for talking about them like that. Elsie's a nice woman, wouldn't say boo to a goose, and the milkman, Harry, is a decent bloke and a happily married man. Neither of them are bad-looking, either! Anyone would think we were Jean Harlow lookalikes, to hear us talk.'

'It's only in fun, girl, we're not doing no one any harm. I know I don't look like Jean Harlow because I haven't got blonde hair.' Amy pinched on her bottom lip, her eyes narrowed in thought. 'No, I'd say I'm more yer Joan Bennett type – slim, sultry and dark-haired.'

Mary grinned. 'I'll go and put the kettle on and leave yer to yer wishful thinking. Yer've got such a vivid imagination, sunshine, can't yer imagine Joan Bennett sitting at the table in her big Hollywood mansion, saying, "I'm a dead ringer for that Amy Hanley what lives in Liverpool. I'm lucky she doesn't live in Hollywood, or she'd be pinching me job off me".'

Amy waited until her friend had filled the kettle and lit the gas-ring before calling through to the kitchen. 'Many a true word is spoken in jest, girl, remember that. One of these days I will catch the eye of one of them talent scouts, then I'll be on me way up in the world. The new sex siren, that's what they'll call me. But I won't let it go to me head, girl, I'll always remember me friends. Yer'll always be welcome in my mansion, and there'll always be a cup of tea and a round of toast for yer.'

Mary popped her head around the door. 'D'yer mean I've got to wait until ye're a film star before I get a cup of tea off yer?'

Amy's face took on what she thought was a haughty expression. 'Sarcasm does not become you, Mary Nightingale. And have you forgotten that cup of tea you had in my house last Pancake Tuesday?'

'I most certainly have not! It was such a red-letter day, I made a note of it.' Mary gave a low cry. 'Ooh, I've forgotten yer flippin' toast – it'll be burnt to a cinder.'

'Put plenty of marge on it, girl, and I won't notice.' Amy picked up one of the cards lying on the table. 'Counting yer club money, were yer, girl?'

'Yeah.' Mary put a plate down in front of her neighbour and hurried back for the two cups of tea. 'I've done better than I thought and I'm dead pleased with meself.'

'That's what I came in for, to talk about Christmas, but yer put me off me stroke talking about Elsie Blackburn. A right bit of useless information, that was.'

'You cheeky beggar! Yer came in here to do a deal, that's what. A cup of tea and a round of toast in exchange for the latest gossip. I've kept my part of the bargain, so start talking, sunshine, and make it good.'

Amy folded the round of toast and took a big bite. She grinned as she chewed, her short legs swinging backwards under the chair. 'I did that so yer couldn't take it back off me if yer thought what I've got to tell yer wasn't worth it.'

'It's such a long time ago, Amy, I've lost interest, anyway.'

'I know how yer feel, girl, 'cos I've lost interest meself. I thought it was funny when I first heard it, but now it's as stale as this piece of bread.' When Mary's mouth opened to protest, Amy raised her hand. 'Only kidding, girl, don't get yer knickers in a twist. I'll tell yer quick, then we can talk about me plans for Christmas.' She finished the last of the toast and licked her fingers. 'Sammy Cooper staggered home last night, dead drunk. And Aggie did no more than hit him over the head with a rolling pin. I believe he's gone to work this morning with a lump on his head as big as an egg.' Amy's tummy rumbled with laughter. 'The part that tickled me was, he couldn't remember anything and asked Aggie if he'd fallen out of bed. She told him she didn't know because she was sound asleep, but if he had fallen he must have picked himself up again because she certainly didn't.'

'Ah, she shouldn't have done that, the poor man hardly ever goes out. She's twice the size of him, too, she could have killed him.'

'Don't worry, she won't do it again. Frightened the life out of herself, she did. And to make it up to him, she's giving him his favourite meal – liver and onions. The silly cow doesn't realise he'll twig something's up. He'll be sitting at the table wondering how he came by this ruddy big lump, and she'll put a plate of liver and onions in front of him. That's never been known on a Tuesday night before, so he's bound to put two and two together. And if he does we can expect to see Aggie with a black eye tomorrow.' Amy rested her elbows on the table. 'Now that's out of the way, let's get down to business. How about us having a party on Christmas night? We could go halfy-halfy with the food and it wouldn't cost that much. We've never had a real knees-up, jars out party, on account of the kids. But they're old enough now, so let's have a bit of fun and enjoy ourselves.'

'I won't have any money to spare, Amy, I've only got what's in me clubs.'

'That's all yer'd need, girl! We could do some turkey sandwiches, make a jelly and blancmange and bake some fairy cakes. Yer don't need a lot of food to enjoy yerself, just some good company.'

Mary's face lit up. 'Yeah, ye're right, sunshine, let's go for it. We'll share what we've got and I'll give yer a hand with the table and everything.'

Amy curled a fist and rested her chin on it. 'How d'yer mean, girl, yer'll give me a hand? I thought we were having the party here?'

Mary gasped. 'Amy Hanley, even by your standards, that's barefaced cheek, that is. It was your idea to have a party, I wouldn't have thought of it.'

'Ah well, yer see, girl, the idea was my contribution to the party. Your contribution is to have the jollification in your house. Now yer can't say that's not fair, can yer? Without me, there wouldn't have been no party.'

'I'm speechless! Why can't we have it in *your* house? They're exactly the same size, it's not as though I've got more room.'

'No, yer haven't got more room, girl, I'll grant yer that. What yer have got, though, is more nous. Ye're very good at arranging things, doing them proper, like.'

'Don't you be buttering me up, Amy Hanley, I know when I'm being taken for a sucker. How soft you are! Let's have a knees-up, jars out party, yer said. Let's have some fun and enjoy ourselves. And soft girl here fell for it! I must want me bumps feeling for listening to yer.'

Her face as innocent as a baby's, Amy asked, 'So it's all settled, is it, girl? Christmas night at the Nightingales'? Ay, hasn't that got a nice ring to it? Christmas night at the Nightingales'. It sounds proper posh. Just wait until I tell my Ben he's been invited to a party, he'll be over the moon. I'll have to make sure I get his suit out of the pawnshop so he'll look the part.'

'Just hang on a minute, sunshine! I don't remember agreeing to it.'

'Of course yer agreed to it, girl. Yer just weren't listening to yerself when yer said it. And I'll say here and now, with me hand on me heart, that I think it's real magam ... er, manig ... er, real good of yer.'

'What yer were trying to say, sunshine, is that it's magnanimous of me.'

'There yer are, yer see, you think ye're that as well! And that's another reason why yer make a better hostess than me – yer know all the big words.'

'For the life of me, sunshine, I can't see what big words have got to do with a party.'

'Well, it's like this, yer see, girl. They say God made everybody

33

good at something. To you He gave the gift of words, to me He gave the gift of craftiness. And they'll both come in useful at our party. When you're handing the plates of sandwiches around, all yer've got to do is throw in a few of those big words and they'll be that flabbergasted they won't notice the sandwiches are brawn, and not turkey.'

Mary couldn't hold out any longer and she shook with laughter. What could you do with someone who had an answer for everything? With tears running down her cheeks, she answered herself. You could have a party for her, that's what.

The knock on the front door had Mary pushing her chair back as she wiped her eyes. 'Who on earth can this be?'

'Unfortunately, girl, God didn't give me the gift of seeing through walls, so I'm afraid the only way yer'll find out is to open the bleedin' door.'

When Mary saw who her visitor was, her smile widened. 'Hello, Molly, get yerself inside out of the cold.'

'It's yerself, then, Mary? Sure, haven't I been knocking so long I was beginning to think there was no one at home.' It was ten years since Molly Moynihan left the shores of Ireland but the lovely lilting accent was as strong as ever. She was a tall woman, well built, with a shock of light gingery hair, pale blue eyes and a face that was never far from a smile. As she stepped into the hall she peered down at Mary, concern in her blue eyes. 'Have yer been crying, me darlin'?'

'I'm having an attack of hysterics, Molly, which means I don't know whether to laugh or cry.' Mary winked at the woman who had lived in the house opposite for ten years and was a good friend. 'And as yer might know, it's me mate what's brought about this state of affairs. She's in there now, but take my advice and don't mention the word Christmas if yer know what's good for yer.'

Amy's voice came through to them. 'Ay, I heard that! Don't you be blackening my name, Mary Nightingale, or I'll have yer up for slander.'

Molly was laughing as Mary pushed her into the living room. 'Oh, it's yerself, Amy Hanley. And what mischief has the good Lord allowed yer to be up to now?'

Amy spread out her hands, a real hard-done by look on her face. 'I can't believe anyone can be as ungrateful as this one. I did her a big favour by sharing me great knowledge and experience with her, and do I get any thanks in return? Do I heckerslike! A load of abuse, that's what I get. I tell yer what, Molly, it puts yer off helping people. They take yer kindness and throw it back in yer face.'

'Me heart bleeds for yer, so it does.' Molly pulled out a chair and sat facing Amy. 'And it's surprised I am that yer best friend doesn't appreciate yer kindness. What was it yer were offering that she threw back in yer face?'

'Don't ask, Molly, or yer'll live to regret it.' Mary got in quickly before her friend. 'I'll tell yer how crafty this one is. She's sitting there looking all angelic, as though butter wouldn't melt in her mouth, but behind that mask she's dead devious. I'll tell yer the story, word for word, and yer can judge for yerself. It started off with her coming in to scrounge a cup of tea and get a warm by my fire because she's too mean to have one of her own . . .'

Molly and Amy leaned their elbows on the table and waited to be entertained. They knew how good Mary was at imitating her neighbour, she had the voice and facial expressions off to perfection. And they weren't disappointed. Their giggles turned to chuckles, and then loud guffaws as Mary took them from the round of toast to Elsie Blackburn and the milkman, Sammy Cooper with the lump on his head and the meal of liver and onions his wife was going to set before him as a peace offering. But when it came to the Christmas party, and how Amy had skilfully worked it around so that Mary, thinking she was being invited as a guest to the Hanleys', was inveigled into becoming the hostess, the Irishwoman was banging the table as she rocked back and forth with laughter. 'Holy Mother of God, Amy Hanley, is there no end to yer trickery?'

Amy was sitting back with her arms folded, looking extremely pleased with herself. She found Mary's version of events very funny, and thought she herself came out of it very well. 'I didn't trick her, Molly Moynihan, she walked straight into it. She'd fall for the cat, she's that gullital.'

Mary spluttered. 'Yer mean I'm gullible, yer daft nit, not gullital.'

'There yer are, Molly, she admits I'm right. Now yer can't argue with that, yer heard it with yer own ears.' Amy tilted her head and narrowed her eyes. 'By the way, Molly, just out of curiosity, like, is your room any bigger than this?'

'Oh, I'm wise to yer, Amy Hanley, so I am. Yer'll not be catching me out so easy, indeed yer'll not.'

Amy sighed as she gazed at Mary. 'I'm sorry, girl, but yer can't say I didn't do me level best for yer. It looks as though you're stuck with having the party, like it or not.' She turned to Molly. 'Seeing as ye're too miserable to have the party at your house, how would yer like to come to our party? And Seamus, of course, and your Mick.'

Mary dropped her head in her hands and groaned. More often than not Amy's jokes turned into reality. 'What about Annie Baxter and her husband, Amy? And, of course, yer could ask Lily Farmer and her feller.'

'Nah, I can't stand them two, they get on me bleedin' nerves. And after what yer've told me about the antics of Elsie Blackburn and the milkman, I wouldn't associate meself with the likes of them. If yer invite any of them, girl, then even though it would grieve me, I'd have to turn down yer kind invitation.'

Molly chuckled. 'Oh, it's invitation only, is it?'

'I haven't even said I'll have a party yet!' Mary shook a fist in Amy's face. 'All this started because yer were too mean to light a flaming fire! I should have told yer to sling yer hook and I'd have been spared all this.'

'Then yer'd better make it plain, me darlin',' Molly patted her arm, 'before yer friend here invites the whole street.'

'I wouldn't invite the whole street, I'm not that daft.' Amy bit on her bottom lip to try and stop a smile appearing. 'Half the street, perhaps.'

'What would yer do with her?' Mary spread her hands and shrugged her shoulders. 'Okay, I give in. The Hanleys and the Moynihans are invited to a friendly get-together on Christmas night. But yer'll have to help out with the food, otherwise I won't be able to afford it.'

Amy beamed at Molly. 'There yer are! I bet when yer knocked on the door yer didn't expect to get an invite to a party, did yer?' She eyed the Irishwoman with curiosity. 'By the way, what *did* yer knock for?'

'Amy!' Mary blushed with embarrassment. 'Yer'll get me hung one of these days, yer cheeky article. What's it got to do with you why Molly knocked?'

'Yer don't have any secrets from me, do yer, girl?'

'I should be that lucky! You wouldn't let me have any secrets.'

'In that case, Molly may as well tell me what she's come for, save me shouting over the wall to yer later.'

'Well, now, I'd hate yer to have to stand on a bucket to see over the wall, that I would. Sure, I'd never forgive meself if yer fell off and broke a leg.' Molly was glad she had come, the last half-hour had brightened up her day. She had no family here to visit, they were all back in Ireland, so she was grateful that she'd been able to make friends with her neighbours. Life would have been very lonely without them. Particularly these two, who were guaranteed to put a smile on the most miserable of faces. 'A secret is something yer don't want anyone else to know about, but I don't think an ounce of Golden Virginia comes into that category, do you? Seamus asked me to get it for him, but I don't need to go to the shops for anything so I came to see if Mary would get it if she's going out. It's lazy I'm getting in me old age, and that's the truth of it.'

'Yes, I'll get it for yer. I've got to run to the shops, so it's no bother. That's if I can ever get rid of me mate, here.'

Amy shuffled her bottom to the edge of her chair. 'Ye're getting rid of me right now, but not for long. I'm going home to get me coat,

36

then I'm coming to the shops with yer.' She linked her arm through Molly's. 'I'll take yer out with me so yer can't talk about me. Never mind about paying her for the baccy now, yer can see her later.'

Laura rushed in from school that night, her face flushed with excitement. 'Mam, we're all being allowed time off tomorrow to go to the Labour Exchange. Teacher said they give us a card and tell us where to go for a job. If there's any jobs going, we can go for an interview the day after.' She took a deep breath and let her heartbeat slow down. 'Wouldn't it be the gear if I got a job to start after Christmas?'

'It certainly would!' Mary took her hands out of the soapy water and shook them before leaning against the sink. She was pleased for her daughter and privately hoping that getting a job would be the makings of her. 'You'll have to look clean and smart tomorrow, then. I'll press yer gymslip tonight and you can give yer shoes a good polish. Appearances are very important, sunshine, as are first impressions. If yer look scruffy then yer don't stand much chance.'

'We're not going for interviews tomorrow, Mam, only to the Labour Exchange.'

'Yes, I know that, sunshine, but they're the ones who separate the wheat from the chaff. They know what the employers are looking for, and they'll give out cards for interviews accordingly.' Mary wasn't worried about her daughter's appearance, she knew she could stand up against anybody. She was a pretty girl, with a nice slim figure, rich dark hair, finely arched eyebrows, full lips and wide eyes that were constantly changing from hazel to green. Dressed properly she stood as good a chance as any of the other girls. It was her attitude that worried Mary. She was far too self-assured for her age and too fond of answering back. 'Just be pleasant and polite, Laura, and yer'll do fine.'

Laura's hair swung across her face as she shook her head, her green eyes flashing. 'I'm not a kid, yer know, Mam. I do know how to behave meself.'

'It's important yer remember that tomorrow, sunshine, if yer want to get a job.'

Laura tossed her head again as she flounced out of the room. 'I'm going to Cynthia's.'

Mary sighed as she turned and plunged her hands into the water where she'd been washing some socks and knickers. Her daughter wouldn't take criticism, she flew off the handle for the least thing. She was in for a rude awakening when she started work, for no boss would tolerate her high-handed attitude.

Mary rinsed the clothes through and wrung the wet out of them before folding them and placing them on the draining board. It was too late to hang them out now, she'd do it first thing in the morning, weather permitting. She lowered the gas-rings under the pans on the stove, then popped her head around the door to glance at the clock on the mantelpiece. It was a quarter of an hour before Stan was due in, she might as well put her feet up for a few minutes. It was then her eye caught the glint of gold paper on the sideboard and her hand went to her mouth. 'Oh Lord, I forgot to take the baccy over to Molly. I'd better go now before I start putting the dinner out.'

Molly saw her neighbour crossing the cobbled street and when she opened the door she had the exact money in her hand. 'It's an angel, yer are, me darlin'. When yer want the favour returning, all yer have to do is shout out.'

Mary passed the tobacco over and took the money. 'It was no bother, Molly, I had to go out anyway. Besides, shopping with Amy is as good entertainment as yer'll get anywhere. Every shop we go in, she causes mayhem. Honestly, she never ceases to amaze me, the things she comes out with. I'm pretty quick on the uptake, and I think I've got a sense of humour, but she leaves me standing.'

'Sure, she's on her own when it comes to humour, and that's a fact. And she's a heart as big as a week, I'll say that for her.' Molly leaned against the door jamb and folded her arms. 'But don't be talked into having a party on Christmas night, me darlin', 'cos that's taking a joke a bit too far.'

'Oh, I'm not that soft, Molly, believe me. I'll admit I wouldn't have thought of it only for Amy sowing the seed, but I'm quite taken with the idea now. It won't be a lavish affair, and yer'll all have to muck in with the food, but it would be nice for the three families to get together for a few hours, don't yer think?'

'It would be grand, me darlin', and I mean that sincerely. But, sure, I'd be happy to invite yer over here, save you the bother.'

Mary shook her head. 'No, it's all arranged now, Molly.' She grinned. 'Another of Amy's bright ideas was that I should send invitations out and do the job properly. Actually, her exact words were, "Show them yer were brought up, girl, and not dragged up." But I'll settle for asking yer by word of mouth. Seven o'clock, Christmas night, at the Nightingales'.'

Molly straightened up, a wide smile on her face. 'Will yer look at these two fine-looking men coming down the street. The two finest specimens of manhood ye're likely to see in the whole of Liverpool.'

Mary followed her neighbour's eyes and saw Seamus Moynihan, with his son Mick, walking down the street. And as Molly had said, they were fine-looking men. Seamus was taller and broader than his sixteen-year-old son, but both were as handsome as they come. They would stand out in any crowd, with their raven black hair, deep blue eyes, strong white teeth and dimpled cheeks.

'Good evening to yer, Mary.' Seamus swept off his cap with a flourish. 'Sure I hope the Good Lord is looking after yer, keeping yer fit and well.'

'Hello, Seamus, and you, Mick. I'm fine, thank you. On top of the world, as yer might say in Ireland.'

'Yer can thank Mary for getting yer baccy for yer, Seamus Moynihan. I wasn't in the mood for shopping, so Mary was kind enough to oblige. If it hadn't been for her yer'd have been puffing on an empty pipe all night, and with the divil's own temper in yer.'

When Mick laughed, Mary thought what a handsome lad he was. He'd be breaking many a girl's heart in years to come. 'Take no notice, Mrs Nightingale, me dad isn't allowed to have a temper.' He'd been six years old when his parents brought him to England and, although there was still a trace of his Irish accent, it was now mixed with the Liverpool twang. 'There's only one boss in our house, and although I won't tell yer who it is, I will tell yer that it's not me or me dad.'

Molly shook an admonishing finger, but there was love and laughter in her eyes. 'It's not too old for a spanking, yer are, Mick Moynihan, and don't yer be forgetting that.'

'Not too old, Mam, but I think yer'd have a job putting me across yer knees. Yer see, yer'd need yer two hands to stop me from slipping off.'

Mary saw Stan's familiar figure turn the corner of the street and she laid a hand on Molly's arm. 'Ay out, here's my feller. I'll see yer tomorrow, sunshine. Ta-ra Seamus, ta-ra Mick.' She couldn't resist patting the boy's cheek. 'If I was twenty years younger, sunshine, I'd be running after yer.'

'If yer were twenty years younger, Mrs Nightingale,' he called after her, 'yer wouldn't have to run fast, I'd be letting yer catch me.'

'I'm going to be stuck for money,' Mary told her friend as they sat facing each other across the table. 'I'm all right for food, but it's the presents. The two girls want clothes, and Stan could do with a new shirt and pullover. The few bob I'll have isn't going to run to it.'

'Do what I'm doing,' Amy said, her hands curled around the cup. 'Get a cheque off yer club woman. I'm just as broke as you are, so it's a case of having to.' Her chubby face creased in a smile. 'I'll be cursing the poor woman every week when she's due, hoping she falls and breaks a leg before she gets to our house.' She saw Mary shaking her head and chuckled. 'Yer know I don't really hope she breaks a leg, I'm not that wicked. Just a sprained ankle would do, that would be enough to keep her off work.'

'Amy Hanley, I don't know how you sleep at night. God will pay yer back one day, you just mark my words.'

'Nah, He wouldn't do that. Yer see, girl, God's got a good sense of humour, which is more than can be said for you.'

'I've got a sense of humour, sunshine, but it isn't warped, like yours is. Anyway, I think I'll take yer advice and ask the club woman for a two-pound cheque. That would save me scrimping and scraping. And with our Laura passing that interview for a job at Ogdens, I'll be able to afford to pay an extra bob a week.'

'I bet she was over the moon, was she?'

'Like a dog with two tails. Honestly, she never stopped talking. Anyone would think she was the only one ever to get a job. And what she's going to do with her pocket-money is no one's business. Talk about breaking eggs with a big stick, isn't in it.'

'I know someone who used to work there, and she said the money wasn't bad and they were a good firm to work for. She was on packing the cigarettes, and she said they got so many for nothing each week. So your Stan could come up lucky.' Amy put the cup down on the saucer and wiped the back of her hand across her mouth. 'It's to be hoped your Laura doesn't start smoking, though, girl. I can't stand to see a woman with a fag hanging out of the side of her mouth. Always reminds me of a gangster's moll.'

'Yeah, I think they look as common as muck.'

'My grandma used to smoke a clay pipe, mind. I was only little, but I can remember her as plain as day. She used to shuffle to the corner pub every night, with a jug hidden under her shawl for a pint of stout. And she'd sit in her rocking chair, as happy as Larry, puffing at this clay pipe and drinking her stout. Deaf as a doorpost she was, couldn't hear a word yer said to her. Yer could tell her someone had died, and she'd laugh her bleedin' head off. Didn't do her no harm either, 'cos she lived until she was ninety.'

'There yer are, yer see, a warped sense of humour runs in your family.' Mary stood up and reached for the cups. 'Let's get down to the shops before they close for dinner. I want to get all the ironing done this afternoon, that'll be one thing off me mind.'

'I'm ready, girl, I brought me coat with me. I don't want much shopping, so I can put me things in your basket.'

Mary came back from putting the cups in the kitchen. 'Yer may have a warped sense of humour, sunshine, and yer may be wicked, but no one could ever say yer were daft. Use my basket indeed, and let me do the carrying.'

'For crying out loud, girl, I only want a couple of things from the Maypole. It's not as if I'd asked yer to get me a hundredweight of bleedin' coal.'

'Shut yer face, Amy Hanley, and let's get cracking. And do us a favour, try and behave yerself.'

Their first stop was the Maypole. A young girl assistant came over, smiling. 'What can I get for yer?'

'Nothing against you, girl, but I want to see the manager,' Amy

40

said, pulling herself to her full height and thrusting her bosom forward. 'I have a complaint to make.'

Mary grabbed her arm. 'Amy, for heaven's sake, don't be making a scene.'

'Me! Make a scene! Now as if I would.'

The manager, Greg, came in answer to the young assistant's call. 'Good morning, ladies, can I help yer?'

Amy's face was so serious, no one would guess the laughter that was going on inside of her. 'I've got a bone to pick with you. Well, I don't know whether bone's the right word to use. Do bluebottles have bones?'

Greg looked to Mary for guidance, but as she was as wise as he was, she could only shrug her shoulders. 'Why do you ask, Mrs Hanley?'

' 'Cos the half of margarine I got off yer yesterday had a ruddy big bluebottle in the middle of it. Fair made me sick, it did.'

Mary stepped back so she was standing behind her friend, and she shook her head at the bewildered manager. 'She's pulling yer leg,' she mouthed.

'I'm sorry about that, Mrs Hanley.' Greg kept his face straight. 'But you can rest assured I did not charge yer for the bluebottle.'

'I never said yer did, did I? No, I'm a fair-minded woman, and I only want what's due to me. What I'm asking for is me money back for the margarine the bleedin' bluebottle ate.' The shoulders were stiffened and the jaw set. 'I can't afford to be feeding no ruddy bluebottles, and yer should have seen the ruddy big hole in the margarine, yer wouldn't believe it.'

'Yer should have brought it back, Mrs Hanley.'

'Brought what back – the hole? Oh, I couldn't do that! Yer see, I used the hole for me husband's carry-out.'

All the staff and customers were listening by this time. Amy was noted in the neighbourhood for pulling people's legs, and if there was free entertainment going, they wanted some.

'Well, you should have brought the bluebottle back. At least that would have been some proof that what ye're saying is true.'

'Ah, I couldn't bring that back.' Amy's eyes went around her audience. 'Yer'll all cry yer eyes out when yer hear this, it's that sad. Yer see, poor Bluey died from over-eating. Near broke me heart it did, to see him on his back, his little legs waving about until the end finally came. I put him in a matchbox, but I haven't buried him yet because yer can't have a burial without flowers. So to give him a decent send-off, I'm here to collect for a wreath for him – and I know yer'll all be generous. Especially you, Greg, because it's your fault he's dead. If you hadn't been careless enough to let him fly on my margarine, the poor bugger would be still alive. He'd be sitting in

41

your window right now, flying from the brawn to the bacon, really enjoying himself with his sister. She's sitting on yer boiled ham right now, using it as a lavvy, and wondering where he is.'

The Maypole was usually a very quiet shop, except when Amy Hanley was in it.

Chapter Four

'Ay, isn't this the gear, girl?' Amy's round face beamed. 'All the food and presents in, and nowt to do but sit back and enjoy ourselves.'

'You're looking on the bright side, aren't yer?' Mary had finished wrapping the dress she'd bought Laura for Christmas and was tying the parcel with green string. 'What about preparing all the spuds and veg, cooking the turkey, making the stuffing and gravy? There's stacks of jobs to do yet, and I'm going to start on them as soon as yer've gone, save standing in the kitchen all night.' She patted the stack of presents and smiled with pleasure. 'That's them seen to. I just hope they like them.'

'Of course they will! And as I was saying to meself as I was wrapping mine, it's too bleedin' bad if they don't like them. Yer can only do so much with the money yer've got, and we've both done that, girl. I mean, me and God are the best of friends, but even He draws the line at performing miracles for me.'

'He performed one for me last night,' Mary said. 'I nearly died when Seamus knocked at the door to say he was getting their Christmas tree today off some bloke he knows who works at the market, and that he'd cadge one off him for us. It's years since we had a tree, but I've still got some decorations upstairs I can use. Apart from brightening the place up, it'll be nice to come down in the morning to see the presents hanging from it.'

'Don't try and hang that pullover of Stan's on it, it's so heavy it'll pull the bleedin' tree over, then yer'll have a right mess.'

'Credit me with some sense, sunshine, I ain't exactly brainless. Anything too heavy, I'll put underneath it.' Mary picked the parcels up and put them on the sideboard. 'They can stay there until the tree comes. Molly is expecting her men home about three o'clock and she said she'll send Mick over as soon as they arrive. That gives me time to prepare tomorrow's dinner and get this place dusted. The girls are really excited, they can't wait to help me decorate it.'

'How is your Laura these days? Still playing yer up, is she?'

'I'm hoping that when she starts work she'll have some of the insolence knocked out of her. She's far too forward for her age.'

Amy lowered her eyes. She'd seen Laura in the entry last night, kissing a boy from the top of the street. And it was the girl who was doing the kissing. It wasn't the first time she'd caught her at it either, and each time it was with a different boy. Other women had witnessed it too, and many tongues had wagged. One woman had seen Laura take her son's hand and lead him into a side entry that ran through to the next street. She'd done no more than chase after them, boxed her son's ears in front of the girl and told him if it happened again she'd get his father to take his belt to him. According to the woman, Laura hadn't run away or shown fear at being caught. Even the threat of her mother being told didn't make her turn a hair. She'd just stood by and brazened it out.

Amy sighed silently. Laura Nightingale was more than forward, but how did you tell her mother that when she was your best friend? And not only your best friend, but a thoroughly nice person who deserved better from her eldest daughter. 'I agree with yer, girl, she is a hard-clock if ever there was one. In her case a few smacks when she was younger wouldn't have gone amiss, instead of being spoiled rotten.'

'Stan's to blame for that, he can't see any wrong in her. Mind you, I've seen him taking more notice lately and I think the penny has finally dropped. Let's hope it's not too late, or she'll never have any decent friends.'

'She hasn't got any now, girl! That Cynthia is a real hard-faced article, as tough as old rope. She treats her mother like a piece of dirt, but like your Laura, she's as nice as pie to her father. They're two of a kind and it would be a good thing if they were split up.'

'I know, I've never liked that girl. Laura wanted to ask her to the party but I put my foot down over that.'

Amy laid her arms flat on the table. 'I've been meaning to ask yer, girl, have yer invited yer dad and his wife?'

Mary shook her head. 'I've had sleepless nights over that. He's me dad, I love him and we're getting on fine together now. But seeing him with her would spoil the whole thing for me. Just put yerself in my shoes, Amy, and see how you'd like it. She's younger than me, hasn't got an ounce of sense in her head and I know she doesn't look after him properly. To invite her here and be nice to her would be hypocritical. I can't, and won't do it.'

'I'm not blaming yer, girl, I'd probably feel the same in your place. But it's such a shame 'cos I've always liked your dad. And it's sad that he won't see his grandchildren over Christmas. Sad for them, as well.'

'He will see them, sunshine, he's coming in the morning with presents for them. And I've got socks and hankies for them to give him.'

Amy looked puzzled. 'How can he come in the morning? There's no trams or buses running on Christmas Day.'

44

'He said he'll walk. I was honest with him, told him about the party and the way I feel. He said he understood but he wasn't going to miss seeing us tomorrow, so he's decided to use shanks's pony. He'll do it in half an hour, he said.'

Amy sniffed up. 'It's sad, that is. I'll be crying in a minute.'

'If yer do, it'll be in yer own house. I want yer to be a good girl and go home, so I can start on the spuds.'

Amy's bottom shuffled to the edge of the chair. 'Bleedin' marvellous, isn't it, when yer best friend tells yer to bugger off. I mean, even though yer said it nicely, it still means the same, doesn't it? So I'll do as yer ask and take me body elsewhere. But before I go, what about tomorrow? Are we all sorted out?'

'Yeah. Molly's making a jelly and a dish of trifle, you're making two dozen fairy cakes and I'm doing the sandwiches. If yer'll bring them in about six, I can get the table set for seven o'clock.'

Amy swayed towards the door. 'D'yer want any help making the sandwiches?'

'No, I've got the girls to help me.' Mary put her arms around her friend and hugged her tight. 'A Merry Christmas, sunshine.'

Amy hugged her back. 'And you too, girl. And you too.'

Mary sat back and watched the girls decorating the tree. 'It looks nice, doesn't it, love? I'm really grateful to Seamus.'

Stan returned her smile. 'Yeah, it looks great. It's a good one, too, nice thick branches. Did yer say he got it for nothing?'

'That's what he told me. Off some feller he knows at the market.' Mary was pleased to see her two daughters laughing as they hung the strips of red and green bunting on the tree. It was a rare sight to see Laura being friendly and close to her sister. 'You can spread the big presents out underneath now, and hang the small ones on the branches.'

The girls elbowed each other out of the way to be first at the sideboard. As usual, Jenny gave way to her sister and let her take the big presents. 'This is for you, Dad,' Laura said, balancing the parcel on her hand. 'It's not half heavy.'

'D'yer think it could be two bricks?' Stan laughed. 'They'd be handy to put in the oven to warm, and I could take them to bed with me to put me feet on.'

'This one's for me.' Laura fingered the parcel before looking at her mother. 'I hope it's not one of those frumpy, old-fashioned dresses yer usually buy me.'

In a split second, Stan saw the pleasure leave his wife's face and Jenny's happy smile turn to sadness. 'Don't you dare talk to yer mam like that.' His voice was sharp. 'Now say ye're sorry, go on.'

'I didn't mean nothing, Dad, it was only a joke.'

'I didn't think it was funny, Laura, so do as ye're told and apologise.'

'I'm sorry.' The words were said with ill-grace as Laura shrugged her shoulders and turned back to the tree. 'It was only a flippin' joke.'

When Mary saw Stan's face redden and his hands grip the arms of the chair, she touched his lightly. 'Leave it be, love, we don't want any rows, tonight of all nights.'

'If you say so, love.' He took her hand and held it in his. 'But she is getting too big for her boots and I should have listened to yer years ago.'

Mary was up very early the next morning and her first task was to spoon the stuffing into the turkey before putting it in the oven on a low light to cook slowly. Then she set about cleaning the grate and lighting a fire. Soon the coals were burning brightly and she put a kettle on the hob ready to make a pot of tea. There was no sound from upstairs so she sat in Stan's armchair enjoying the peace of the house. The tree looked lovely, and with the presents spread out beneath its branches it gave the room a real festive air. She'd done a lot of moaning in the last week with the extra work and worrying about whether she was going to be able to eke her money out. But right now she felt it had been well worth it. A spark from a coal hissed as it spurted out, bringing Mary to her feet to stamp it out before it had time to singe the hearthrug. Not that another scorch-mark would be noticed, the poor mat had put up with a lot of wear over the years. It had been made from bits of old clothes, and she remembered how her mother had sat with her many a night pegging the strips of cloth through the canvas.

Mary shook herself to chase away the sadness. This was a day for happiness and she didn't want the family to come down and see her looking miserable. She hugged herself as she gazed into the dancing flames. There was a lot to look forward to, with her dad coming this morning and then the party tonight. She had never had a party before, but she was going to take Amy's advice and not worry. So what if her friend's fairy cakes did turn out as hard as rocks, or Molly's jelly hadn't set properly? The world wouldn't come to an end, they would still enjoy themselves.

She was so wrapped up in her thoughts, Mary didn't hear the stairs creaking and jumped when her two daughters burst into the room, chorusing, 'Merry Christmas, Mam.'

'Oh, I must have been miles away, I didn't hear a sound.' Mary hugged and kissed each of them. 'Merry Christmas, sunshine, and I hope yer both like what Father Christmas brought for yer.'

Laura's face was eager. 'Can we open our presents now?'

46

'Not until yer dad's up, I don't want him to miss any of the fun. Give him a shout while I see to a pot of tea.'

When Stan came down he was carrying a parcel which he put with the others under the tree. He grinned at his wife. 'That's for you, love. I hid it under the bed last night.'

Mary clapped her hands together. 'Ooh, what is it?'

'Yer'll find out soon enough, just be patient. And if yer don't like it yer can tell yer mate off, because she got it for me.'

'Oh dear, in that case it'll be a joke. When I open it, it'll probably blow up in me face.'

Stan's head dropped back and he gave a hearty chuckle. 'Fancy thinking that about yer best mate! I admit I had doubts meself about asking her to get yer something, but I think she's done yer proud.'

'Dad, can I open my presents now?' Laura asked. 'I can't wait.'

'Just hold yer horses, sunshine.' Mary pushed Stan gently down on to the couch, then handed him a cup of tea. 'Me and yer dad will sit and watch. I think the youngest should go first, so let Jenny open hers.'

Jenny opened the small parcel first, and much to Laura's annoyance, insisted upon trying the woollen gloves on. Then she laid them to one side and ripped open the large parcel. Her shriek of delight as she held the dress up brought a glow to Mary's heart. The dress was deep blue with a round collar, long sleeves and belted waist. It was in a heavy cotton, suitable for wear in any weather. The style was plain, but it was the simplicity that made it attractive. 'Oh, it's lovely.' Jenny held the dress close to her chest as she bent and kissed her parents. 'Thank you, Mam and Dad. Can I wear it today?'

'Of course yer can,' Mary said. 'Yer can get all dolled up for yer grandad coming. He won't know yer, think he's come to the wrong house.'

'I'm opening mine now.' Laura's face was set with impatience. But when the small parcel revealed her first pair of grown-up long rayon stockings, she jumped for joy. 'Just what I wanted. I'm over the moon, Mam, they're brilliant! I was frightened I'd have to go to work in me school socks.'

'I hope yer like yer other present as much.' Mary had her doubts. She'd spent a long time choosing a dress for her eldest daughter, trying to find a style that was neither too young, nor too old. And it was with apprehension she watched her daughter undo the parcel. But when she saw Laura's face, she knew her fears were groundless.

The girl was lost for words when she held up the cherry-red dress. She gazed with open mouth at the sweetheart neck, the long sleeves and the full flared skirt. 'It's beautiful! It's the most beautiful dress I've ever seen. I bet Cynthia doesn't get anything as nice as this.' She twirled round, holding the dress to her. 'I'm going to put it on right now.'

47

'Excuse me, young lady,' Stan said. 'Have you lost yer manners? Don't yer ever thank anyone when they give yer a present?'

'I'm sorry, Mam, I'm just that excited.' The tone of her voice and the offhand peck on her mother's cheek made it clear Laura's heart wasn't in it. She was doing what she was told to do, but her mind was elsewhere. 'I'm going upstairs! I can't wait to see what me dress looks like on.'

Jenny stepped into her sister's path, barring her exit. 'Aren't yer going to wait and see what me mam and dad got for Christmas?'

Laura looked surprised by the question. 'No, I want to go and try me dress on. Anyway, I know what me dad's got so there's no point.'

Laura tried to sidestep her sister but Jenny anticipated the movement and stood her ground. She knew how her mother had struggled to buy those clothes and she thought the least her sister could do was show some gratitude and not be so selfish. 'Me mam knew what we were getting because she was the one who had to find the money for them. But it didn't stop her from being interested enough to want to see our faces when we opened the presents. You're not the only one in the house, yer know, Laura.'

'Oh, you get on my wick, you do.' Laura tried to push her sister aside. 'Get out of me way and mind yer own business.'

Stan was rising from his chair to intervene when Mary gripped his arm and motioned for him to stay out of it. 'Let her go, Jenny, there's a good girl. Yer can't make anyone be interested if they don't want to be.'

Laura sneered into her sister's face before flouncing out of the room, leaving Jenny shaking her head. She always had a vision of families being close on Christmas morning, laughing and joking as they shared the pleasure of presents given and received. But looking back, Laura had always been the first to rip open her presents. They'd been mostly toys when they were younger, and her sister would sit at the table with them and not even throw a glance to see what the others had got. 'She's dead mean, Mam.'

'I know, sunshine, but that's her problem, and her loss. Now, you can go in the kitchen if yer like, and try your dress on.'

Jenny shook her head as she sat down. 'No, I want to see what you and me dad have got. I don't want to miss anything.'

'Then you can give them out, love.' Stan was realising he had a lot of ground to make up with his youngest daughter. He'd spoilt Laura by always putting her first, and he could see now that he hadn't done her any favours. If he hadn't given in to her every whim, she might have grown up to be as good and caring as Jenny. 'Yer mam can go first, then we can have a laugh if Amy has set a booby trap.'

'I'll kill her if she has,' Mary said, taking the parcel. 'This is one day of the year when I can do without me mate's practical jokes.'

She was tearing at the paper as she spoke. 'She's probably wrapped a dead mouse in an old towel, or something.'

'In that case, I want me money back,' Stan said, watching his wife's face closely. 'She's not diddling me.'

The only sound from Mary was a gasp, as she stared down at the neatly folded, deep blue fleecy dressing gown. Then came a long drawn-out sigh. 'Oh Stan, it's lovely. But how could yer afford it? I hope yer haven't gone into debt.'

'That's the last thing I'd do, love. Yer know how I feel about borrowing money. Once yer get into debt yer never get out of it. No, I was determined that this year I'd get yer a decent present. It's always you buying for others, never getting much back for yerself.' Stan took her hand and smiled into her face. 'So, since September, I've only been buying ten Woodbines a day, instead of me usual twenty. And the odd times I do go to the pub, I've only been having a half, instead of a pint. I've put the money away each week religiously, and it soon mounted up. I feel dead chuffed with meself – even gave meself a pat on the back.'

'Oh Stan, it's beautiful and I do love yer.' There were tears in Mary's eyes. 'But yer shouldn't have skinted yerself, I know how much yer enjoy yer ciggies.'

'It hasn't done me no harm, love, and I won't be going back to me twenty fags a day. Instead, we'll go to the pictures more than once every blue moon. The girls are old enough to be left on their own now, and it's about time you and me got out a bit more.'

Jenny was watching them with her head tilted and a smile on her face. Seeing her parents like this brought a warm glow to her heart. 'Mam, will yer show us yer dressing gown now, please? I can only see the colour of it from here.'

'I'll do better than that, sunshine, I'll model it for yer.' Mary felt happier than she had for a long time. Fancy her Stan going without his cigarettes so he could buy her a present. He had to be the best husband in the world. She stood up and passed the gown to Jenny. 'You undo the buttons, sunshine, while I give yer dad a big kiss.' She sat on Stan's knee and put her arms around his neck. Her first kiss was soft and gentle. 'That's because I love yer.' Then she kissed him with passion. 'And that's for being so nice I couldn't help but love yer.'

Jenny coughed gently. 'When you two soppy beggars have finished, can I see me mam in her new dressing gown?'

Mary sprang to her feet, laughing. 'Yeah, all good things must come to an end. If we don't put a move on, me dad will be here before we've had any breakfast.'

With her arms spread, Mary was doing a twirl when Laura came in. 'Ooh I say, the state of you and the price of fish.' She eyed the dressing gown with envy. 'I'll be borrowing that for when I have to get up early to go to work.'

'Like hell you will.' Mary held her daughter's eyes. 'This is the first thing I've had in the last twelve years that hasn't been bought second-hand from a stall in the market, or on a Sturla's cheque. So you will keep your hands off it. Understood?'

Laura pulled a face and shrugged her shoulders. 'Okay, keep yer flippin' hair on. Anyway, isn't anyone going to say they like me dress?' Not realising her appearance and attitude had put a damper on a happy scene, she appealed to her father first, expecting to be heaped with praise. 'It suits me, doesn't it, Dad?'

'Yeah, it's a nice dress.'

'It does suit yer,' Jenny said, feeling guilty for the bad thoughts she was having about her sister. 'It's a lovely colour.'

'It looks a treat on yer, sunshine,' Mary said, determined that nothing or no one was going to spoil this day. 'Turn around and let's see it properly.' The dress fitted Laura to perfection and the colour complemented her dark complexion and black hair. She was a pretty girl, there were no two ways about it. And as she grew older and her figure filled out, she had the makings of a very attractive woman. Her eyes were her outstanding feature, but somehow her smile never reached them. 'Yes, I don't think yer could have got anything to suit yer better.'

'Excuse me,' Stan said, 'but didn't Father Christmas bring me any toys?'

'Ah, you poor thing!' Jenny picked up his presents and placed them on his knee. 'We saved the best till the last.'

Laura was bored stiff having to sit and pretend to be excited about a flipping shirt and pullover, it was all so childish. But she knew she'd blotted her copybook and went out of her way to join in the enjoyment. But while she was laughing, her mind was on the party tonight. How she'd swank in front of John, the boy from next door, and Mick from across the street. They wouldn't half get their eyes open when they saw her in her new dress.

Stan opened the door to his father-in-law and quickly stepped aside to let him pass. 'Come in, Joe, yer must be freezing walking all that way.'

'I'm all right. I set meself a fair pace and soon got warm.' Joe took a glove off and extended his hand. 'Compliments of the season, Stan.'

'Same to you.' Stan opened the living-room door. 'Here he is, the man himself.'

Mary dashed forward to be first to her father. She took his face in her hands and rained kisses on him. 'A Merry Christmas, Dad, and may you be granted everything yer wish for.'

50

'And the same to you, sweetheart.'

There was a trace of sadness in Joe's eyes and Mary knew he was remembering the other Christmases when her mam was alive. There'd been so much love and warmth then, he was bound to miss it. 'Take yer coat off and get by the fire.'

But the two girls claimed him first. Hanging on to his arms, they stood on tiptoe to kiss him. 'It's lovely to see yer, Grandad,' Jenny said, her face aglow. 'We're never in when yer come to see me mam.'

'I won't stay away so long again, lass, I promise.' There was affection in his eyes as he patted her arm. How proud he and Ada had been when these two grandchildren came along, and how they'd doted on them. 'I'll call in on a Saturday afternoon on me way home from work.'

Laura moved away from him and spread her arms wide. 'How d'yer like me new dress, Grandad, isn't it lovely?'

'Not as lovely as the girl wearing it. And I see that Jenny is also looking very glamorous in her new finery. I'm lucky to be blessed with two of the most beautiful granddaughters yer'd see in a month of Sundays.'

Laura was eyeing the parcel tucked under his arm but for once was wise enough not to ask what he'd brought for them. Instead, she enquired, 'Where's Celia? Why hasn't she come with yer?'

'She's at home seeing to the Christmas dinner.' Joe had prepared himself for this question. 'But she sends her best wishes.'

'Ah,' Laura pouted, 'I wanted her to see me new dress. Can yer bring her tomorrow?'

'I'm sorry, queen, but we've arranged to go somewhere tomorrow.'

'That's enough now,' Stan waved the two girls away. 'Let the poor man come up for air, will yer? Take yer coat off, Joe, and sit down by the fire. Mary's making yer a cup of tea, she'll not be long.'

Joe put the parcel on the chair while he took his coat off. 'The tree looks grand, and there's a delicious smell coming from the kitchen.'

When he was seated, Jenny squatted on the floor at the side of his chair. 'Me and Laura decorated the tree, Grandad. And it's the turkey yer can smell. Me mam was up very early to get it in the oven, and she had the fire lit and everything before we got up.'

'Yer've got a good mother, sweetheart, I hope yer appreciate her.'

'Oh I do, Grandad, she's the best mother in the whole world.' Jenny drew her legs up to her chin and wrapped her arms around them. Her pretty face was animated as she asked, 'Tell us what you got off Father Christmas.'

'I haven't opened me presents yet. I thought I'd leave them until I got back and open them before I have me turkey dinner.' Joe was lying through his teeth. His wife had gone out with one of her mates last night and hadn't come home until the early hours. He'd pretended to

51

be asleep because he was too weary for any more arguments. God knows, he'd tried everything he could to make her see that as a married woman she had a responsibility to her husband and home. But it was a waste of time; she'd never change because she didn't want to. There was no Christmas tree in their house, and no smell of turkey coming from the kitchen – because his wife was still in bed when he left and would probably still be there when he got home.

'Here yer are, Dad, get this down yer, it'll warm the cockles of yer heart.' There was a wide smile on Mary's face when she passed him the cup of tea, but deep down there was an anger building up. She'd been listening to the conversation as she stood in the kitchen waiting for the kettle to boil, and knew with a certainty she couldn't explain, that her father was telling lies. There were no presents, she'd bet any money on that, and there probably wouldn't even be a Christmas dinner. 'The girls have got yer a couple of presents, Dad, but they're not very exciting, I'm afraid.'

Joe balanced his cup on the arm of the chair before reaching for the parcel at his side. 'These are not very exciting either, lass, but it's the thought that counts.'

Mary opened the brown paper parcel to find four smaller ones inside. They were badly wrapped and Mary told herself there was no woman's touch here, her dad had wrapped them himself. This fuelled her anger further. How dare this woman marry her father and then treat him so badly? He was a good man, he deserved better than this. Of course he should never have married the girl, he should have had the sense to see the pitfalls that lay ahead, Mary would never change her mind about that. But neither would she stand by and see the father she loved neglected and humiliated. Her mam would want her to look out for him, see he was well cared for.

Mary and the two girls were given underskirts and they were delighted. Mary's was blue, Laura's pink and Jenny's in a pale lemon. They were in rayon, and each had an inset of white lace in the front. Stan was given a packet of twenty Capstan Full Strength and he lost no time in lighting up. These were a luxury to a man who could only afford Woodbines, and there was a look of contentment on his face as he sat back, crossed his legs and drew on the cigarette before making smoke rings in the air.

When Joe had opened his presents and expressed pleasure in the socks and hankies the girls gave to him, Laura and Jenny went upstairs, eager to put on their new underskirts. 'They're over the moon, Dad, yer couldn't have bought anything to please them more.' Mary walked to the sideboard, and with her back to her father, she asked casually, 'Our dinner's nearly ready. Why don't yer stop and have a bite with us? The long walk back would give yer an appetite for another one when yer get home.'

'Yeah, why don't yer do that, Joe?' Stan asked, knowing how his wife's mind was working. 'Ye're more than welcome, yer know that.'

'I know that, Stan, and I'm beholden to both of yer.' There was nothing Joe would have liked more than to stay in this warm, cosy room, surrounded by those he loved and who loved him in return. But he was too proud a man to give even a hint of the bleakness of his life. 'Still, I think it's only fair I go home. I'll rest me legs for half an hour, then make tracks.'

Mary came to perch on the arm of his chair. 'Tell yer what, Dad, I'll save some turkey and have a nice dinner ready for yer the day after tomorrow, when ye're back at work.' She put an arm across his shoulders and kissed his temple. 'You and me will have a Christmas dinner all on our own, eh?'

Chapter Five

Jenny stood in the middle of the kitchen, her blue eyes wide and her hands clasped together under her chin. 'All this food, Mam, I've never seen so much in all me life. It looks so tempting me mouth is watering.'

'I didn't expect so much,' Mary said. 'Amy and Molly have excelled themselves.' The draining board was filled with plates of sandwiches and cakes, and the stove had been covered by a piece of wood to make space for the jelly creams, trifles, and biscuits. And under the sink stood the crate of stout that Seamus had brought over, the bottle of port that had been Ben's contribution, and bottles of lemonade that Mary had bought. 'It does look nice, doesn't it? Even yer Auntie Amy's fairy cakes have turned out all right. And, God love her, nobody is more surprised than she is.'

Jenny put her arms around her mother's waist and hugged her tight. 'It's been a lovely day, hasn't it, Mam?'

'It has, sunshine, it really has. If every day was like today, yer wouldn't hear me complaining. All we need is for the party to go down well and I'll go to bed tonight and sleep the sleep of the just.'

Stan came to stand at the kitchen door, and seeing his wife and Jenny holding each other close, he thought his youngest daughter was growing more like Mary every day. Both had a peaches and cream complexion, an abundance of golden hair, wide blue eyes, tip-tilted noses and mouths that were made for turning upwards into a smile. Jenny was almost as tall as her mother, too, there were only a few inches in it. Funny how he'd never noticed all this before. His daughter was twelve and a half years old and it was as if he was really seeing her for the first time.

Mary caught his eye. 'Are you spying on us, Stan Nightingale? Making sure we're not helping ourselves to the goodies?'

'No, I just heard yer saying that yer hope the party goes down well. I don't know what ye're worrying about, not when Amy and Molly will be here. Amy could entertain us all night on her own, never mind with Molly to help her. If we're not careful, between the two of them they could bring the house down.'

'Aye, well, we'll soon know, they'll be here in half an hour. And our Laura hasn't come back from Cynthia's yet, the little faggot. She always does a bunk when she knows there's work to be done.'

'I'll go down for her, Mam, while you get yerself ready.' Jenny walked through to the living room, saying over her shoulder, 'I'll drag her back if I have to.'

Amy and Ben arrived first, with their son, John. With them they brought the two extra dining chairs needed to seat everyone. 'Are yer all right, girl?' Amy asked, a big grin on her face. 'Have yer got everything under control?'

Mary laughed as she took her coat and handed it to Jenny to take upstairs. 'I did have, sunshine, but you'll soon alter that, won't yer?' She waited until her neighbour had settled on one of the wooden chairs before asking, 'Are you sure your Eddy and Edna are all right to be left on their own? I feel lousy leaving them out.'

'Oh, stop yer worrying, girl, they'll be fine. If anything untoward happens, all they've got to do is knock on the bleedin' wall. It's not as though I'm spending Christmas night on the other side of the world.'

'There's a knock, love,' Stan said. 'I'll answer it, it'll be the Moynihans.'

The room became alive then as hands were shaken and compliments of the season were exchanged. And while Molly was chatting to Amy, Seamus took Stan's elbow and ushered him out to the kitchen. He took a half bottle of whisky from his pocket and pushed it into Stan's hand. 'It's a Christmas box from me boss, God bless him, so you and Ben, and meself, can toast the dear man for having a heart of gold.'

Stan chuckled. 'I'm not used to the hard stuff, Seamus. One glass and I'd be as drunk as a lord.'

'Begorrah, is that right, now? Then I'll be after helping yer, so I will. Add a little drop of water to it, just until yer get the taste, then yer'll be fine. It's a sacrilege, I have to tell yer, to add water to a fine whisky, but I don't think yer'll be making a habit of it.'

Mary came into the kitchen and eyed the men with suspicion. 'Oh aye, what are you two being so secretive about?'

'A glass of whisky isn't a secret, Mary, me darlin', it's the nectar of the gods.'

'I'll have less of yer blarney, Seamus Moynihan. And I'll thank yer not to be teaching me husband any bad habits.'

'Well, it's sorry I am about that, Mary. Yer leave me with no alternative but to drink the whole bottle meself.'

'And have yer giving this house a bad name by rolling out of here blind drunk, singing at the top of yer voice? Not on your life, Seamus Moynihan, yer can just share that bottle with my husband and Ben Hanley.'

Stan wrapped his arms around her. 'Ye're as pretty as a picture, Mary Nightingale, and I love the bones of yer.'

Seamus clapped his hands together. 'Will yer just listen to the man, and not a drop has passed his lips yet.'

'Ay, you lot!' Amy's loud voice boomed. 'Get yerselves in here pronto, and let's get the bleedin' show on the road.'

Mary popped her head into the living room. 'Don't yer want to eat first?'

Amy's legs were six inches short of reaching the floor and she was swinging them back and forth. 'No, I don't want nothing to eat. I want a glass of sherry in this hand, and a glass of stout in this one. After that I'll give yer a song. Then I'll have another sherry and bottle of stout, and I'll give yer two songs and throw a dance in for free.'

Ben groaned loudly. 'For heaven's sake, take pity on me and don't let me wife get to the third sherry and stout. That's when she's just had enough to want to do the dance of the seven veils.'

'Ooh, ay, yeah!' Amy turned to her husband and thumped him so hard on the arm he nearly fell off the chair. 'That's me speciality, that is, when I do me Salome act. Yer'll think there's something wrong with yer eyes when yer see me belly dance.' She gazed at Mary with wide innocent eyes. 'Yer don't happen to have seven veils, do yer, girl?' Then she grimaced and shook her head. 'Of course yer haven't, what a silly question. How about seven scarves?'

Her son, John, was standing with Mick Moynihan and they both had wide grins on their faces. 'Being optimistic, aren't yer, Mam? Wouldn't seven tablecloths be more like it?'

She smiled sweetly. 'Another crack like that, son, and we won't be talking tablecloths we'll be talking sheets. The kind they have in hospitals.'

John held his tummy while he doubled up with laughter. 'One of these days I'll get the better of you, Mam.'

Mick tapped him on the shoulder. 'I wouldn't hold yer breath, John, 'cos yer've not got a snowball's chance of ever getting the better of yer mam.' His white teeth gleamed and his dimples deepened. 'Unless yer catch her when she's asleep.'

Amy preened as she gazed at Molly. 'That's a very clever son yer have, Mrs Moynihan. I don't suppose yer'd think of doing a swap, would yer? I'm in a generous mood now I've got me sherry and me stout, so I'll strike a bargain with yer. My three kids for your one. Now yer wouldn't get a better bargain than that even at Paddy's Market.'

Seamus had been helping Stan serve the drinks, now he stopped in front of Amy and bent until his face was on a level with hers. 'Yer'll not have much luck there, me darlin'. Sure isn't Mick the apple of his mother's eye? There's only one thing I can think of that she'd swap him for, and that's the key to the kingdom of heaven.' He looked up at the ceiling, closed his eyes and roared with laughter. 'And with the key there'd have to be a ticket for a seat at the side of the Good Lord Himself.'

'I could get yer the key, that's no problem, 'cos I know a feller what makes keys.' Amy's pursed lips gave her face an earnest look. 'But I couldn't get a ticket 'cos I don't know no one what knows Saint Peter. He's the one what guards the Pearly Gates, and I've heard he's red hot on not letting anyone through unless they've got a ticket.' She gave a deep sigh. 'Oh well, it looks as though I'm stuck with the three kids.'

'Never mind, love,' Ben said. 'Look on the bright side, it could be worse. We could have had six kids.'

'Where d'yer get the "we" from, Ben Hanley? You didn't have no kids – I had that bleedin' pleasure.' Amy handed her glasses to Jenny to hold before turning to Molly. With her arms folded and her bosom hitched almost to her chin, she said, 'Did yer hear that, Molly? Men are not soft, are they? While we're in bed, riddled with pain, they go down to the pub to wet the baby's head! Did yer ever hear the likes of it? Propping the bar up, they are, their chests sticking out a mile because they've proved what a clever man they are! Huh! I bet a bleedin' tanner that if it was the men who had the babies, we wouldn't have got any further than our John. And I'll also bet that we wouldn't be here tonight, because although our John's fourteen, Ben would still be in bed recuperating.'

'Sure, men are funny creatures, so they are,' Molly grinned. 'Hasn't Seamus Moynihan been wetting the baby's head every night since Mick was born – sixteen years ago.'

Ben tapped his wife on the shoulder. 'Ye're wasting valuable drinking time, love, so come on, get it down yer.'

True to form, Amy was the first to sing. Her rendition of 'Daisy–Daisy' had them not knowing whether to laugh or sing. She always mimed to her songs, her facial expressions and her hands making exaggerated moves to suit the words. It was difficult for those watching to join in the singing while laughing their heads off. And at the end of the song she got a rousing cheer which she accepted by bowing graciously.

Then Seamus and Molly sang a duet, 'When Irish Eyes Are Smiling', and they surprised everyone with their clear, strong voices. They also showed the strength of their love for each other by holding hands and facing each other as they sang, their devotion clear for everyone to see. They refused pleas for an encore, saying they'd sing later when they had a few more drinks down them.

The Moynihans' double act put poor Ben in the dog-house. 'Ay, you, light of my life,' Amy said, 'why don't you sing with me and hold my hand? Got no bleedin' romance in yer, that's why. Jeanette MacDonald's got Nelson Eddy, Molly's got Seamus, but if I want a partner I'll have to buy a singing canary.'

Jenny was sitting on the floor by her mam and dad. This was her first grown-up party and she was having the time of her life. She knew Auntie Amy was always telling jokes and making people laugh, but she'd never seen her in such good form. And the Moynihans were just as funny; there'd never been a dull moment since they'd arrived.

Laura meanwhile was standing near to John and Mick. She was disappointed because not one person had told her she looked nice in her new dress. But then, apart from the two lads, all the others were old fogeys and wouldn't know what was nice and what wasn't.

'I think we'll have a break for eats now,' Mary said, her heart light now the party was going so well. 'Come on, Laura and Jenny, give me a hand to pass the plates around.'

Laura pulled a face at the two lads. 'I hope no one spills anything on me new dress.' She half turned, then asked, 'D'yer like me new dress?'

John shrugged his shoulders. What did he know about girls' dresses? 'Yeah, it's nice.'

'Lovely colour,' Mick said with a smile. 'It suits yer.'

It amazed Mary how quickly the piled-high plates were emptied. 'I thought we had enough food to feed an army,' she told her husband, 'but it's nearly all gone.'

Stan grinned. 'Drink always makes yer peckish.' He put his arms around her waist and held her close. 'I told yer not to worry, didn't I? Everyone's having a whale of a time.'

Her eyes went to the door. 'Let me go, yer daft nit, before someone comes out.'

'It isn't a crime to cuddle yer wife, love.'

'Still, and all, behave yerself and see to the drinks.'

There was a lot of chattering going on when Amy happened to see her son going into the kitchen with his empty plate. Then she saw Laura follow him out. She was off her chair like a shot. 'Excuse me, folks, but I'll have to get meself a glass of water because me throat's so dry I could spit feathers.'

When Amy reached the kitchen door she saw Laura standing in front of her son, who was blushing to the roots of his hair. And she heard the girl say, 'Me grandad said I look beautiful in me new dress, John. Do you think I look beautiful?'

Amy bustled in. Her face was smiling, but her eyes weren't. 'Is yer grandad's eyesight failing, girl? Poor old bugger.' She watched Laura toss her head and flounce out of the kitchen, then turned to her son

59

who was looking relieved. 'Do yerself a favour, John, and keep well away from her. She's one hard-faced little madam.'

'It's her house, Mam. I could hardly tell her to scram.'

Amy smiled at the son who had inherited her sense of fun. 'Come and sit on me knee, yer'll be safe there.'

John returned the smile of the mother he adored. She never complained, was always bright and cheerful. 'Did yer bring me dummy with yer?'

It was one o'clock in the morning when Mary and Stan stood at the door seeing their friends out. They'd all had a wonderful time and were loud in their praises. Mary was worried about the noise they were making but Stan whispered, 'Don't worry, it's the first party we've ever had. And Christmas comes but once a year.'

'Ay, girl,' Amy said, her voice loud and slurred, 'what about New Year's night? Are we being invited again?'

'Sod off, Amy Hanley, and go home. You can have the next party.'

'Charming, that is,' Amy chuckled as Ben led her away. 'And, God help me, she's supposed to be me best mate.'

Seamus shouted from across the street: 'New Year's night in the Moynihans'. How does that suit yer?'

Mary grinned as she was closing the door and heard Amy call back, 'I always knew yer were a man after me own heart, Seamus. Invitation accepted with thanks.'

Mary stood at the bottom of the stairs and shouted, 'If yer don't put a move on, Laura, yer'll be late for yer first day at work.'

'For heaven's sake, keep yer hair on.' Laura appeared on the landing. 'I've got plenty of time yet.'

'You're supposed to start work the same time as yer dad, and he's nearly ready to leave.' Mary sighed. If she had to go through this every morning to get her daughter out of bed, she'd be a bundle of nerves after the first week. 'You haven't even had yer breakfast yet.'

Laura came down the stairs slowly, as though she had all the time in the world. 'It won't take me long to have a swill and eat me breakfast. I don't know what ye're getting yourself all het up for.'

'Neither do I, sunshine.' Mary walked through to the living room. 'In future I'll call yer once and yer can please yerself. If ye're late for work and lose yer job, then it'll be yer own fault.'

Stan was putting his coat on, but his daughter didn't even glance his way. She saw the plate of toast ready for her and the pot of tea in front of her cup and saucer. 'Pour me tea out while I get washed.'

Mary looked at her husband, sighed and shrugged her shoulders. 'She's going to be a real bundle of joy every morning.'

Stan walked to the kitchen door. 'Your mother is not yer servant – pour yer own tea out.'

Laura had her hands in a bowl of water, her face sulky. 'I'm going to work now, same as you, so why can't she pour me tea out? She waits on you.'

'A servant or waitress waits on people, and your mother is neither of those. Yer should have got up when yer were first called, same as I do, instead of leaving it until the last minute. If yer think yer can carry on like this every morning, then yer've got another think coming. In future yer either come down when called, or do without breakfast.' Stan picked up the tin with his carry-out in before kissing his wife's cheek. 'If she gives yer any lip, let me know and I'll deal with her tonight.'

'Me voice is hoarse with calling her, Stan, so she's on her own now. She can just get on with it. I'm going upstairs to wake our Jenny.'

There was no need to wake Jenny, she'd been wide awake since the shouting started. The two sisters shared a bed and she'd given Laura a few digs in the ribs to try and get her to move but all she got for her efforts were a few digs back from a very angry sister. She sat up in bed with a smile on her face. 'I'm getting up now, Mam. I was just waiting until the coast was clear. There was enough racket going on to wake the dead.'

They heard the slam of the front door and Mary hurried through to the front bedroom. She lifted the net curtains to see Laura running up the street eating a piece. What a good start to her working life! You would expect her to be excited and eager about her first day at work, not running hell for leather up the street with a piece of toast in her hand a very strong possibility of being late. Mary recalled the first day she started work, and the memory brought a smile to her face. She'd been so frightened of being late she'd arrived at the gates of the factory half an hour early!

Mary let the curtains fall back into place and made her way downstairs. She'd make a fresh pot of tea and sit at the table for ten minutes while Jenny had her breakfast. That should calm her nerves before she started on the housework. But she hoped this morning's shenanigans weren't a sign of things to come. She couldn't cope with it.

Mary was cleaning her teeth at the kitchen sink when something hit one of the panes of glass in the window and frightened the life out of her. She cupped one of her hands under the tap, filled it with water and rinsed her mouth out. Reaching for the towel hanging on a nail on the door, she told herself one of the slates must have fallen off the roof and she'd have to see the landlord to have it fixed. Otherwise, if they had a downpour, the rain could come into one of the bedrooms. She put the towel back on the nail, and as she lifted the door latch she muttered, 'This is turning into a right miserable day.'

'Is that you, girl?' Amy's voice came floating over the wall. 'I've been shouting me bleedin' head off for ages. I was beginning to think yer'd gone and died on me.'

Mary screwed up her eyes as she stepped down into the yard. 'Yer wouldn't by any chance have been daft enough to throw something at the window, would yer?'

There was silence for a few seconds, then Amy shouted, 'I cannot tell a lie, girl, 'cos God always pays me back when I tell a lie. So, yes, I did throw something at yer window . . . a feather.'

'A feather!' Mary put a hand over her mouth and willed herself not to laugh. After all, it could have ended up with her having to fork out for a pane of glass. 'From the sound it made, I can only assume you were attached to the feather?'

'Nah, I'm not that daft, girl, 'cos I'd have hurt meself. It was a brick.'

'A brick! Well, now I've heard it all. And who, pray, was going to pay for a new window if yer'd broken it?'

'It wasn't a whole brick, yer soft article, only a little piece of one. And I gave it a good talking to before I threw it. I said if it broke me mate's window I'd come around there and crush it under me feet.'

'Amy Hanley, the older yer get, the worse yer get.'

'Well, I was worried about yer, girl! I shouted and shouted, but yer didn't answer. If I never move from this spot, I really thought yer'd fell off yer perch. D'yer know what I said to meself? I said, "I bet that inconsiderate cow has gone and died on me. It's just the sort of thing she would do when I want to borrow a cup of sugar. The only one she ever thinks about is herself." That's what I said, girl, cross my heart.'

'Well, I'm sorry to disappoint yer, sunshine, but I am still alive and kicking. I might not be the happiest person in the world, but I am still breathing.'

'What's the matter, girl, why aren't yer happy?'

'Oh, I dunno. Monday morning blues, I suppose.'

'Are we going to the shops?'

'Yes, I've only got to comb me hair then I'm ready.' Mary undid the ties of her wraparound pinny. 'I've got to get something in for the dinner, there's no turkey or chicken left.'

'Same here, girl. Me cupboard's as bare as Old Mother Hubbard's. I'll give yer a knock in five minutes.'

'Just a light tap will do, Amy, don't put the door in.' As she stepped into the kitchen, Mary could hear her friend chuckling and suddenly her gloom lifted. Half an hour in Amy's company and she'd be as right as rain. Ready for anything.

Arm-in-arm they entered the butcher's shop to be met by Wilf's smiling face. 'Thank God for that,' he said, 'I've only had two customers so far this morning.'

'What d'yer expect after Christmas?' Amy was eyeing the rabbits hanging on a hook from the ceiling. 'Most folk will be eating the leftovers for a few days. It's only greedy buggers like me and me mate here what have been eaten out of house and home.'

'I'll have three-quarters of stewing beef, Wilf,' Mary said. 'It's easier to make a pan of stew than anything else.'

'Ay, girl.' Amy gave her a dig before pointing upwards. 'How about getting one of those rabbits between us? It's a while since we had rabbit.'

'But they're not skinned yet.'

'That won't take me long.' Wilf took a long pole and lifted down two rabbits which were tied together. 'Yer can hang on until I do it, or yer can get the rest of yer shopping done.'

'We'll get our shopping done.' Mary linked her friend's arm. 'When yer've skinned it, Wilf, will yer cut it in half down the middle, so there's no arguing over one getting more than the other? Otherwise me mate will have the tape measure out when we get home. We'll be back in twenty minutes, unless Amy starts gabbing to someone.'

'Just hold yer horses, girl.' Amy gazed down at the two rabbits lying on the counter. Then she pointed to one. 'I don't want that one.'

Mary tugged on her arm. 'For crying out loud, Amy, they're both the same!'

'They're not, girl, just look at them. That one's cock-eyed.'

Wilf pushed his straw hat to the back of his head. 'Amy, when yer come back it'll be decapitated. Yer won't see the eyes because it won't have no head.'

'Ah, yer won't hurt it, will yer?'

'Amy, the bleedin' rabbit is as dead as a dodo.'

'I know, Wilf, and I won't say keep yer hair on 'cos yer haven't got that much to keep on. But yer see, me saying it was cross-eyed was just an excuse. The truth is, it reminds me of my feller.'

Mary gasped. 'Amy Hanley, how can yer say such a thing?'

Amy turned wide eyes on her friend. 'Yer haven't seen my feller in bed, fast asleep, have yer, girl?'

'I should hope not!'

'Well, yer don't need to now, 'cos I'm telling yer, that's what he looks like . . . except the rabbit's better-looking.'

Mary slipped her arm from her friend's and put two hands on her ample waist. 'Out, Amy Hanley.' She pushed the reluctant woman towards the door, calling over her shoulder, 'Twenty minutes, Wilf. And if I'm on me own, yer'll know I've pushed this one under a tram.'

'That won't do yer no good, Mary, she'd only buckle the wheels.'

Laura was in a very happy frame of mind when she came in from work. She never stopped talking as they were eating their meal, her eyes shining and her arms waving. 'It's the gear, Dad, and the women are smashing. Dead friendly, they are.'

Stan was happy to see the change in his daughter. This was how she should be. How he wanted her to be. 'What exactly do yer do, love?'

'The cigarettes are in packets when they come to our bench, and we have to put them in cardboard boxes. There's a supervisor keeping an eye on us all the time to make sure we pack them properly. Her name's Miss Birch and she's got the eyes of an eagle, but she's nice. And as long as we get on with our work we can talk as much as we like.'

'Don't tell yer Auntie Amy that,' Mary laughed, 'or she'll be applying for a job. She'd be in her apple-cart getting paid for talking.'

'She wouldn't be able to work there, 'cos ye're on the go all the time and she's too fat.' Laura was looking down at her plate and missed her mother's expression change. 'Besides, she isn't me real auntie.'

'I'm sure Mrs Hanley is delighted she's not yer real auntie.' Mary wasn't going to sit and listen to her best friend being run down by her own daughter. 'And as for being too fat, she'd run circles round you, any day of the week.'

Laura smirked. 'Aye, in her sleep.'

'That's quite enough now, Laura. Yer'd be advised to keep a civil tongue in yer head.' Why does she have to go and spoil things, Stan asked himself as his heart plummeted. 'Amy Hanley is one of our best friends and yer'd travel a long way to find a nicer woman.'

'Yeah, she's all right, I suppose.' Laura pushed her plate away and swivelled sideways on her chair. 'I'm going up to Cynthia's to see how she got on in her job.'

'Stay right where you are,' Stan ordered. 'It's bad manners to leave the table until everyone has finished eating, and yer mam hasn't finished. And before yer buzz off out, yer can help with the washing up.'

'Ah, ay, Dad! I've been on me feet all day. Let our Jenny help to wash up.'

'Oh, I suppose yer think yer mam's been lounging on the couch all day reading, do yer? I wonder who made the beds, cleaned up,

64

did the washing, and after that went to the shops and came home and made the dinner? D'yer think a fairy with a magic wand did all that?'

'I'll do the dishes, Dad,' Jenny said, hoping to calm things down. 'It won't take me long and I don't mind, honest.'

'Let her go up to her mates, if that's what she wants.' Mary nodded her head in Laura's direction as she collected the dirty plates. 'The mood she's in, she wouldn't wash them properly, anyway. Me and Jenny will see to them.'

Laura didn't wait to hear what her father had to say, she was off the chair and out of the door like a flash of lightning. 'Yer should have made her stay, love. Yer told me off for spoiling her and now you're giving in to her.'

'I'm not spoiling her, Stan, just fed up with her. If she can't see for herself how selfish she is, then there's no use making her do anything against her will because it would be done grudgingly.' Mary smiled at Jenny. 'Come on, sunshine, you and me will have them done in no time.'

'I don't need you to help me, Mam, I'll do them on me own. You sit down and tell me dad about Auntie Amy and the rabbits.' Jenny took the plates from her mother. 'Go on, give him a good laugh.'

Stan was laughing already. 'What's she been up to now?'

'Don't you ever repeat to Ben what I'm going to tell yer.' Mary sat down, rested her elbows on the table and laced her fingers. And while she told the tale, she giggled at the memory of Amy's face, while Stan roared his head off.

'She's a caution, she is,' he said, wiping his eyes. 'Ben wouldn't be upset over that, he'd be the first to see the joke.'

'That's not all she got up to today. She had Billy Nelson pulling his hair out.'

Jenny came running in, water dripping from her hands. 'Yer didn't tell me about that, Mam, so the dishes can wait for a few minutes. Go on, tell us.'

'Well, I'd been served and Amy asked for five pound of potatoes. She stood there and watched Billy weighing them out, and never said a dickie-bird. Then, when he was emptying them into a piece of newspaper she pointed, and said, "Yer can take those little ones out, I don't want them. Me knife's a bleedin' big thing, like what the butcher has, how d'yer expect me to peel those fiddling little things with it? Anyway, by the time they're peeled there'll be nothing left of them. Me hand will be cut to ribbons, blood running down me pinny and making a pool on the kitchen floor, and the only thing in me hand will be fresh air, the bleedin' potato will have vanished".'

Mary's shoulders were shaking. 'I can see Billy's face now. He didn't know whether to laugh or throw the potatoes at her. But he kept his cool, and asked, in a very quiet voice, "Amy, why didn't yer ask for big ones?" And yer know how she squares her shoulders when she gets in a huff – well, she did that, then looking like a little angel, she said, "I've kept this secret for years, Billy, but now I'm going to open me heart to yer. I know yer fancy me, 'cos I can see it in yer eyes every time yer look at me. And I want yer to know that I feel the same way about you. Nothing can come of it, lad, because we're both married, so yer'll have to control yer emotions. But that doesn't mean we can't love each other from afar, does it?" '

Stan reached into his pocket for a hankie to wipe his eyes. 'She's a corker, all right. What happened next?'

'There was no sign of a smile on Billy's face when he asked, "What's all that got to do with potatoes? Or am I missing something?" And with a hand on her heart, me mate says, "It bought me an extra five minutes in yer company. I'll dream of yer tonight in bed and go over every precious word yer've spoken. I'll even dream of yer picking those fiddling little potatoes out and replacing them with decent-sized ones. And, my secret love, I'd be grateful if yer'd put a bleedin' move on 'cos I haven't got all day to stand here listening to you yapping. They say women can talk, but by God, they've got nothing on you".'

Mary stretched out an arm. 'Lend me that hankie, love.' She shook her head as she conjured up the scene in her mind. 'Billy's face was a picture, I can tell yer. He said, "I haven't spoken a dozen flippin' words! It's you what's done all the yapping." And me mate just grinned at him. "That's why I love yer," she said. "I've always fancied the strong and silent type. Yer remind me of Gary Cooper, except yer haven't got no horse".'

'How does Auntie Amy think of all these things?' Jenny asked. 'She's not just funny sometimes, she's funny all the time.'

'Ah, but Billy had an answer for her. He said, "What d'yer mean I haven't got no horse? How d'yer think I got these bow legs? I certainly didn't get them sitting on a twenty-two tram. No, I got them riding the range on me faithful steed, Silver".'

'Did Amy appreciate the joke?' Stan asked. 'I bet she laughed her head off.'

'Oh, she did more than that, did Amy Hanley. Yer know what she's like for having the last word. She gave me a dig in the ribs, and said, "We've seen his horse, girl. It's the one what pulls our coalman's cart. It's a dirty beggar, Billy Nelson, yer should train him proper. Every time he stops outside our door he decides he wants to go to the lavvy. I wouldn't mind so much if we had rose bushes to put it on, but the ruddy horse can see we haven't. Why doesn't he wait until he's outside a house with a garden?" '

'These shopkeepers don't take her serious, do they?' Stan asked.

'I mean, they must know every time she opens her mouth she's having them on.'

'Of course they know she's having them on! They look forward to her coming because they know they'll get a laugh. And they're as quick off the mark as she is. As we were leaving the shop, Billy shouted after her, "Why don't yer put a sign up outside yer house, Amy, saying USE OF TOILET 1d? Yer could make yerself a few coppers, 'cos lots of people get caught short when they're out, not only horses". With that me mate marches back into the shop, shakes a fist at Billy, and says, "Not bleedin' likely! Me first customer would be that nosy cow from next door, Annie Baxter. She's been trying to get into my house for the last ten years. Then she'd tell her mate, Lily Farmer, and before long there'd be a queue a mile long outside me house. Nah, that's a stupid idea, Billy Nelson. In fact, it's fair put me off yer. My feller's got more brains than you have. He'd be smart enough to up the price to tuppence if they wanted paper thrown in".'

Jenny was smiling as she went back to finish off the dishes. She could hear her parents laughing and felt a warm glow spread through her body. Now she was getting older she was allowed to stay up later and she was seeing more of her dad. They were getting to know each other and were closer than they'd ever been. She knew Laura had always been his favourite, but perhaps that was only natural as she was the firstborn and that made her special.

They were sitting around the fire when Laura came in, and as soon as Mary saw her daughter's face as she sat on the arm of Stan's chair, she knew she was after something. And it wasn't long before she was proved right.

'Dad, can I go up to Cynthia's on New Year's Eve? She can't go to the Moynihans' so there won't be much fun for her with just her mam and dad.' Laura neglected to say that her friend had invited two lads she'd met in work. 'Go on, say I can.'

Stan looked at Mary and raised his brows. 'What d'yer think, love?'

'I don't mind, as long as we know where she is.'

'I'll only be in Cynthia's, honest! She is me mate, and we can keep each other company.' Laura twisted a lock of her dark hair around her finger then let it spring back into place. 'Me and Cynthia have been talking about next week, when we get our first week's wages. How much will I have to give me mam out of me wage-packet, Dad?'

Mary opened her mouth, then decided not to voice an opinion until she'd heard what her husband had to say.

'Yer've got it the wrong way round, Laura,' Stan said. 'You hand yer mam yer wage-packet and she gives you pocket-money back.'

Laura's eyes flashed. 'That's not fair! They're my wages, I have to work for them.'

'I pass my packet over to yer mam, and you'll do the same. She's the one who has to run the house and that's the way it should be.' Stan's voice was stern. 'So let's have no argument over it.'

'I don't see why I should hand me packet over, not when I've worked for the money,' Laura said, her face sullen as she put an arm around her father's neck. 'Cynthia's not handing hers over, Dad. She'll be getting seven and six a week, same as me, and she's giving her mam four shillings out of it.'

'That's very big of her, I must say!' Mary laced her fingers together and pressed tight to remind herself to keep her temper under control. 'But I wonder how much say her mother had in it? From what I've heard, the poor woman doesn't have a say in anything, she's treated like a skivvy.'

'Forget Cynthia, and her mother. What goes on in this house has nothing to do with them.' Stan moved Laura's arm away from his neck. She was trying to worm her way into his good books but he wasn't being soft-soaped, not this time. 'Me and yer mam will decide how much pocket-money yer get, not you, or yer mate Cynthia.'

Jenny stood up and stretched her arms. She didn't want to hear any more arguments, nor see her mother get upset. 'I'm going to bed, Mam, I'm dead tired.'

'I'll come with yer, sunshine, I'm tired meself.' Mary stood at the door and gave Stan a look that said he could sort this out. Then, as she climbed the stairs behind Jenny, she could feel tears stinging her eyes. She'd always done the best she could for her girls, gone without things herself so they always went to school looking neat and tidy. She hadn't minded wearing second-hand clothes from the market, as long as her daughters were all right. And it hurt her to think that now life could be a little easier with Laura's money coming in, every penny she got would be begrudged to her.

Standing on the tiny landing, Jenny put her arms around her mother. 'Good night and God bless, Mam. And don't worry about our Laura, she doesn't always mean what she says. She acts tough, but she's not, really.'

Mary managed a smile. 'I hope not, sunshine, because sometimes she sounds as tough as an old pair of leather boots.' She kissed her daughter's cheek. 'Good night and God bless, sunshine. We've got the party to look forward to – that should cheer us up.'

Seamus Moynihan was very well organised. Five minutes after the Nightingales and Hanleys arrived, they were sitting with glasses in their hands, and within half an hour the party was in full swing. They all joined in as Seamus and Molly sang 'Danny Boy', then came the 'Bonnie, Bonnie Banks O'Loch Lomond', followed with gusto by 'She's A Lassie From Lancashire'.

Then a halt was called to refill the glasses. And while the men were busy pouring, Mary crossed the room to where Amy was sitting, her legs dangling six inches from the floor. 'I've been watching you, sunshine, and I'm getting worried.'

'Why's that, girl? There's no need to worry about me, I'm having the time of me life.'

'I know yer too well, Amy Hanley, and I think ye're up to something.'

'Me? Up to something? I'm sitting here minding me own business, girl, and I've got nothing to get up to.'

'Ye're too quiet for my liking. It's never been known for you to refuse to sing, so unless ye're sickening for something, I smell dirty work at the crossroads.'

'Nah, I'm not sickening for anything, girl, I'll give a turn when I've had a few more bottles of stout. Yer'll soon see there's nowt wrong with me.'

Two bottles of stout later, Amy said she'd give them a turn. 'But I'm going to do it proper, like they do at the Metropole. Seamus can introduce me and I'll make my grand entrance from the kitchen.' With her hips swaying, she tapped a finger on Seamus's chin as she passed him, fluttered her eyelashes and in her best Mae West voice, drawled, 'I'll give a shout when I'm ready, big boy, and make it good.'

Seamus thought it was hilarious, and when Amy called, he threw an arm out towards the kitchen door. 'Put your hands together for Kirkdale's own, the one and only – *Amy Hanley*!'

The applause was loud as the door opened slowly. Then, apart from gasps, everything went quiet as a chubby bare leg, with a fancy blue satin garter above the knee, began to kick in and out. Ben closed his eyes and groaned. 'What's that flippin' wife of mine up to now?'

'I knew it!' Mary said. 'I knew she had something up her sleeve.'

Then a chubby hand appeared and moved seductively up and down the door. There wasn't a sound in the room, apart from Ben's, 'So help me, I'll kill her.'

'I hope ye're all ready for this.' Amy's voice preceded her entrance, which knocked everyone for six. She'd cut an old dress up, hacking the sleeves out, making a high neck into a low round one, and cut the hem-line to mid-thigh. And around the bottom she'd sewn a blue silk fringe which danced as she began to Charleston. And every ounce of her fat danced with the fringe. She didn't know the words to the song, so as she kicked her heels backwards and swung her arms, she kept repeating, 'Do the Charleston . . . doh-doh-dee-oh-doh.'

Within a split second, the tune changed and so did Amy's movements. With her arms outstretched she began to shake her shoulders and hips, and to whistles and cheers, she made her way across the room to stand in front of Ben, who looked as though he'd been struck by lightning. 'If I Could Shimmy Like My Sister Kate' she warbled . . . and as she sang, Amy put her all into the dance that had been the craze when she was younger. And as everyone was to say later, they'd never seen a better shimmy.

Ben looked up into eyes that were dancing with devilment, and he grinned. 'Yer could always shimmy better than yer sister Kate.'

The dancing stopped and Amy put her hands on her hips. 'I haven't got no bleedin' sister called Kate.'

'I know yer haven't, love, that's why yer've got to be better than her. Stands to sense, that, doesn't it?'

Amy cut such a comical figure in a dress that showed her figure in all its glory, that everyone was in stitches. Mary and Molly cried tears of laughter into each other's shoulders, Mick and John were doubled up, and Jenny's pretty face was alive. She'd been embarrassed at first at Auntie Amy showing off so much of her body, but oh dear, she was really so funny you couldn't help but laugh.

Seamus bent down to whisper in Stan's ear, and grinning like two schoolboys, they stole up behind Amy. Before she realised what was happening, they'd each put a hand under her armpits, then their other hand went behind her knees and they scooped her up. They lifted her as high as they could, with Seamus saying, 'Here she is, folks, the lovely and very talented, Amy Hanley.'

'Sod off, Seamus Moynihan, yer silly bugger,' Amy called from her great height. 'Yer nearly knocked me bleedin' head off on the gas-light.'

John looked at his mother, and laughing so much he could hardly get his words out, he said, 'Ay, Mam, I don't think the flappers used to wear blue fleecy-lined bloomers.'

'More fool them, son.' Amy looked down to see she wasn't showing anything she shouldn't, otherwise she wouldn't half get it off Ben when they got home. 'Now we know why they were always shimmying and shaking – it was to keep themselves warm. Fancy using all that energy when all they needed was a pair of fleecy-lined bloomers.'

'Ye're right there, Mrs Hanley.' Mick's dimples deepened. 'A pair of those would have kept them warm up to their chins.'

Amy patted the two men on the head. 'Yer can let me down now, boys, and I'll make meself presentable. And as it's eleven o'clock I think it's time the guests were offered something to eat. We can start the party again when the clock strikes midnight.'

It was a quarter past eleven when a knock came on the door and Mick put his plate down on the sideboard. 'I'll go, Mam.'

The chattering stopped when Laura walked into the room. She didn't look as sure of herself as usual, and her laugh was nervous. 'I

70

thought I'd see how yer were getting on. Is that all right, Mrs Moynihan?'

'Of course it is, child. Get the girl a plate, Mick, and she can help herself to whatever she wants to eat.'

'What got into you?' Stan asked. 'I thought yer wanted to be with yer friend.'

'Cynthia's mam wasn't feeling well and went to bed early.' That was true, but the real reason for Laura's early departure was that the two boys hadn't turned up and she had no intention of sitting listening to her mate's dad prattling on about his work. Not when she knew there was a party going on just up the street. And that there'd be two boys there. 'It wasn't worth staying because we couldn't have celebrated the New Year, not with her in bed and us frightened to make a noise.'

There'd been very few words exchanged between Mary and her daughter since the night Stan had put his foot down and said Laura must turn up five shillings towards the housekeeping and pay her own tramfares to work out of the remaining half-a-crown. The girl seemed to put the blame on her mother and had sulked ever since. But she looked so ill at ease with all eyes on her, Mary's motherly instinct came to the fore. 'Get yourself something to eat, sunshine, then come and sit on the floor next to Jenny.'

Seamus Moynihan hadn't stinted on the drinks, and his wife certainly hadn't stinted on the food. Molly had refused help from her neighbours, saying that she had more money coming into the house, and fewer mouths to feed. So it was a heavily laden table that Laura stood in front of. 'Ooh, I don't know where to start, there's so much,' she told Mick, who was being very gentlemanly and holding the plate for her to fill.

'Pick what takes yer fancy, then yer can always come back for more.'

His attention put Laura in a very happy frame of mind, and when she squatted on the floor beside her sister there was a genuine smile on her face. 'What's been going on, kid? Have I missed anything?'

While Jenny was telling her sister that she had missed a real treat, Mick was back standing next to John who was pulling his leg. 'Got yer eye on Laura, have yer, Mick? Be careful there, mate, she'd eat yer for breakfast.'

'I was only doing what me mam told me to do, looking after the guests.' Mick glanced over to where the two sisters sat. 'I'm waiting for Jenny to grow up.'

'Yer'll have a long wait, mate, she's not thirteen yet.'

'I'm only sixteen meself, so I've plenty of time. I know a lot of water will flow under the bridge before she's old enough, and I also know I might meet someone else before then, or that she might not fancy me anyway. But I've been drawn to her since I first saw her. She was only about three, but I remember thinking the colour of her hair reminded me of a wheatfield back home in Ireland.'

'Blimey, you've got it bad, haven't yer?' John's face gave nothing away as he leaned towards Mick and said softly, 'Yer can get in the queue, mate. I'm before you.'

Mick chuckled. 'We'll continue this conversation in three years' time, when we'll probably both be courting strong and Jenny will be going out with a feller in the next street.'

'Yer could be right,' John said, nodding his head. 'But if not, remember all's fair in love and war.'

So it was, that when the tugs on the Mersey sounded their hooters at the stroke of midnight to herald the arrival of 1934, and all the grown-ups were hugging and kissing each other, Mick and John, armed with a piece of mistletoe, made their way to the sisters. Jenny, not thirteen for another four months, blushed to the roots of her hair and twisted her neck so the kisses landed on her cheek. While Laura puckered her lips, eager and willing.

Chapter Six

'Just look at the time, Stan – ten minutes to eleven and that little faggot still isn't in.' Mary paced the floor, her mood half anger, half worry. 'She knows she's to be in by half ten, and that we'll be waiting up for her.'

'You go to bed, love, I'll wait for her.' Stan rapped his fingers on the arm of his chair. 'And she'll get a piece of my mind.'

'D'yer really think that will make any difference to Laura? She won't take a ha'porth of notice of yer. She treats this place like a hotel, just comes and goes as she pleases, and to hell with anyone else.' Mary glanced at the clock. 'Eleven o'clock. Doesn't it enter her head that we might be worried about her? She's not sixteen yet, and if something awful were to happen to her, we're the ones that would get the blame for letting her stay out till this time of night.'

When the knock came on the door, Mary flew into the tiny hall. 'Where the hell d'yer think you've been, you little madam?' She closed the door and followed her daughter into the room. 'Yer do realise we've been waiting up for yer?'

Stan was standing, his feet astride, his hands locked in front of him. 'Where've yer been until this time of night?'

'If yer let me have me own key, yer wouldn't have to wait up for me.'

'Don't you ever use that tone of voice to me, Laura, I'm warning yer. Push me too far and yer'll find out ye're not too old to get a good hiding. And as for having yer own key, yer can forget that 'cos yer can't be trusted.' Stan unlocked his hands and pointed a finger. 'Now, tell us where yer've been, and I want the truth.'

Laura tossed her head. 'If yer must know, I've been to me grandad's.'

Mary gasped. 'Never! Me dad wouldn't let yer stay until this time, he'd know we'd be worried about yer.'

'Well, that's where I've been.' Out of the three people in the room, Laura was the coolest. She looked bored stiff, as though she just couldn't understand what all the fuss was about. 'Me grandad went to bed early and I stayed talking to Celia. That's all we've been doing, talking. And I can't see any harm in that.'

'She should have more sense than to keep a girl of your age out until this time, knowing that yer'd be walking home alone, in the dark. And *you* should have had more sense, as well. Yer've got eyes in yer head, yer could see the time, and yer knew yer were told to be in by half ten. In future, yer do as ye're told, understand?'

'Dad, I was only keeping Celia company. She said she gets lonely because me grandad goes to bed early every night and she was glad to have someone young to talk to for a change.'

Mary was blazing. How dare that woman talk about her father like that! She was the one who talked him into marriage. If she'd wanted someone younger to talk to, she should have married someone younger. 'She is a married woman and has no right to talk about her husband to a fifteen-year-old girl, who just happens to be his granddaughter, and who is supposed to think the world of him.'

'I'm nearly sixteen, not a baby.'

'Then don't act like one,' Stan said. 'I'm not finished with yer, Laura, not by a long chalk. But we'll leave it for now because it's late and I'm tired. Get to bed now, but be careful yer don't wake Jenny, she's got to get up early for work, too.'

'Yer don't call what she does work, do yer? Sitting on her bottom all day in an office is not my idea of hard work.' Relations between the two sisters had worsened since Jenny left school two months ago, and with excellent references from the headmistress had got herself a job as a clerk in the office of a small toolmaking firm. Laura was so envious she gave her sister a hard time. 'A right stuck-up little snob, she is.'

'It's taking me all me time to keep me hands off yer, Laura.' Mary ground the words out through clenched teeth. 'If yer know what's good for yer, yer'll get up those stairs and out of my sight.'

After Laura flounced out of the room, Mary and Stan looked at each other with sadness and frustration in their eyes. 'I don't know what we're going to do with her,' Mary sighed. 'If she keeps on like this she'll send me to an early grave.'

'It's my fault for not listening to yer.' Stan ran fingers through his thick mop of dark hair. 'They say there's none so blind as they who will not see.' He walked to his wife and took her in his arms, pressing her head against his shoulder. 'Nothing we say has any effect on her, it's in one ear and out the other. We may as well talk to the wall.'

'We'd be better off talking to the wall – at least it wouldn't answer us back.'

Stan held her away from him and kissed her forehead. 'We're both too tired to talk about it now. Let's leave it until tomorrow when we can think straight.' He put an arm across her shoulders and led her to the door. 'I'm absolutely whacked, me brain won't think straight.'

They were cuddled up in bed when Mary said, 'I do love her, yer know, Stan. And I worry about her, wondering what's going to happen to her.'

74

'I know, love, I feel the same way. But she might surprise us all in a year or two, yer never know. Perhaps she'll meet a nice bloke who'll tame her down.'

'I hope so.' Mary kissed his cheek. 'Good night and God bless.' Then she turned on her side and began to pray for her wayward daughter.

'Don't say anything to her,' Mary said next morning as she put her husband's breakfast in front of him. 'I don't want to start the day being upset. Wait until we've had our meal tonight and we'll just sit down and have a quiet word with her.'

'Whatever you say, love.' Stan cut the top off his boiled egg and grinned at her. 'Nice and runny, just the way I like it.'

They both looked up in surprise when Laura came through the door, bright and breezy. It was the first time since she started work that she'd got up without being called half-a-dozen times. 'You're up early,' Mary smiled, determined there would be no angry words exchanged over breakfast, otherwise she'd have a splitting headache all day. 'Pour yerself a cup of tea out while I put yer egg on to boil.' As she was walking to the kitchen, she muttered aloud, 'I may as well put our Jenny's on at the same time.'

'She's on her way down now,' Laura called through. 'Yer know what Miss Prim and Proper's like for being early. She doesn't start work until half eight, but she needs the time to titivate herself up.'

Stan dipped a finger of toast into his egg and kept his head down. That was another thing he wanted to talk to Laura about, the way she treated her sister. Young Jenny had done well for herself, but she'd worked for what she'd got and deserved it. And there'd been no argument over pocket-money, like there had been with Laura. She handed her wage-packet over to Mary and took what she was given with a smile.

'Good morning!' Jenny's bright smile seemed out of place in the room, but she appeared not to notice. 'It looks as though it's going to be a nice day, the sun's trying to shine.'

Mary came to the door and glanced at the clock on the mantel-piece. 'The eggs will only be two minutes, so pour yerself a cup of tea, sunshine. I hope ye're right about the weather because me and Amy are going into town for a couple of hours.'

'Are yer going to buy something nice, Mam?' Jenny put the cosy back on the teapot. 'Yer could do with a new dress.'

'I could do with a lot of things but they'll have to wait. We desperately need pillowcases, the ones we've got are on their last legs.'

'Ooh, would yer let me embroider one, Mam?' Jenny's face was eager. 'I can do it, I learned it at school. Just some flowers and leaves in the corner to make it look nice.'

'Of course yer can, sunshine, but yer need coloured silk thread for that and there's none in the house.'

'You could get some in town, I'll pay for it. I'd only need green and pink to be going on with, until I get me hand in. We only learned a few stitches in school, but when I've had some practise I can try more intricate patterns.'

'More intricate patterns? Oh, how exciting!' Laura's voice was mocking. 'All on a flippin' pillowslip that no one will ever see. Yer'll be making yer own clothes, next.'

Jenny turned and looked her sister straight in the eyes. 'Seeing as ye're so interested, and for your information, I have every intention of learning how to make me own clothes. One of the women in the office makes all hers and yer'd never know they were homemade. She can make a dress for a couple of shillings, and that includes the cotton.'

Mary came through with an eggcup in each hand just as Stan was pushing his chair back. 'Ye're off, are yer, love?'

'Yeah, it's a nice morning so I won't bother with the tram, I'll go on shanks's pony.' Stan reached for his donkey jacket. 'If yer see a dress yer like, love, you get it for yerself. It's about time yer started thinking of yerself, instead of everybody else.'

'I can't afford it, Stan, there's things we badly need for the house.'

'To hell with the house. It'll be here when we're dead and gone,' Stan said gruffly as he picked up his carry-out. 'I'll give yer a bob towards it.'

'And me, too!' Jenny's offer came quickly. 'I don't spend all me pocket-money so I can help towards a new dress for yer.'

'If yer've got money to spare, pass it over here,' Laura said, spooning the yolk of the egg on to a piece of toast. 'I can always find a use for it.'

Mary clamped her lips together as she followed her husband to the door. Why couldn't Laura see for herself how selfish she was? Never once, since she started work, had she bought a sweet for anyone. Mary didn't mind for herself, but she felt for her husband. He'd always been generous with his firstborn, spoiled her rotten, yet she couldn't even buy him five Woodbines. Jenny did. Every Saturday she came home with a packet of ciggies for her dad and a slab of chocolate for her. Laura knew this, but it didn't put her to shame. Every halfpenny she could get her hands on was spent on herself.

Mary stood on the top step and looked down at her husband. 'I'll see yer tonight, love. You take care now.'

'And you get that dress, d'yer hear? I'll be annoyed if I come home and yer tell me yer've got pillowslips but no dress.'

'Ah well, we can't have you getting annoyed, can we?' Mary ran a finger down his cheek. 'If me purse runs to it, I'll mug meself – okay?'

She waited until he reached the end of the street, like she always did, and returned his wave. Then she went back into the living room to find Laura standing in front of the mirror liberally applying bright red lipstick. 'You'd better put a move on if yer don't want to be late. And why yer have to put so much make-up on, I'll never know. Yer look much nicer without it.'

'Ye're old-fashioned, Mam – all the girls wear make-up.'

Mary sighed. She wanted to say that all the girls didn't put it on with a trowel, but what was the use? The only person Laura listened to was herself. 'You get yerself ready, Jenny, while I put the kettle on for a fresh pot of tea. I'm going to park me backside for ten minutes before I start on the beds.'

While she was in the kitchen, Mary heard the front door slam and knew Laura had, as usual, gone off without a word of goodbye. Then she heard Jenny's footsteps running lightly up the stairs. How was it possible for two people like her and Stan, who loved each other dearly, to bring two daughters into the world who were so different in every way? She just couldn't fathom it out, there was no sense nor make in it. If Laura had been badly treated as a child then there could be an excuse for her being so hard. But she hadn't. There'd always been plenty of love and they'd given her everything it was in their power to give her.

Mary carried the fresh pot of tea through just as Jenny came downstairs. 'Sit down, sunshine, and relax for ten minutes.'

Jenny pulled out a chair facing her mother and as she sat down she slid half-a-crown across the table. 'The silk shouldn't come to more than sixpence, Mam, so the other two bob can go towards yer dress.'

'I'm not taking any money off yer. That half-a-crown is yer whole week's pocket-money. Yer haven't exactly got a wardrobe full of clothes yerself, sunshine, so splash out and mug yerself to whatever yer want.'

'I've still got some money left upstairs, Mam, 'cos I don't spend very much. Anyway, I want you to to have it, so take it to please me. As me dad said, it's about time yer started looking after yerself for a change. So take it, as a little gift from me for being the best mam in the world. And because I love the bones of yer.'

Mary swallowed hard. 'Keep that up, sunshine, and there'll be more tears in me cup than there is tea! But to keep you and yer dad happy, I'll buy meself a dress. And I'll have it on when yer come home from work, so yer can see where yer money's gone.' She studied her daughter's face. 'Aren't there any young girls where yer work, someone yer could go to the pictures with?'

Jenny shook her head. 'There's only three of us in the office, and the other two are at least three times my age. They're very nice, and

I get on well with them, but they're too old to make friends with.'

'Yer could do with a friend, sunshine, 'cos a young girl shouldn't be sitting in every night with two oldies like me and yer dad. What about Janet, yer friend from school?'

'I haven't seen her since we started work. I could go around to her house, though, she only lives two streets away.' Jenny glanced at the clock before getting to her feet. 'I'll go round tonight, Mam, and see how she's getting on.'

'Ask her to go to the pictures with yer one night, it'll do you good to get out with someone yer own age. Everybody needs a friend, sunshine.' Mary deliberated as she watched her daughter pick up her bag, then decided quickly. 'Laura was very late getting in last night and although me and yer dad both told her off, we want to sit her down and give her a real good talking to. So if you could go out for an hour after we've had our tea, it would give us the chance. She might pay more attention if you're not here. Yer know how quick she is to flare up and you listening wouldn't help.'

'Yeah, okay, Mam.' Jenny rested her handbag on the table. 'I heard her coming in. I stayed awake because if I'd gone to sleep she'd only have woke me up getting into bed. Where had she been until that time?'

'She went to yer grandad's.'

Jenny's eyebrows lifted in surprise. 'What made her go there? She's never done that before. I'm surprised Grandad didn't chase her home earlier.'

'Aye, well, we didn't go into it last night because it was so late. But we'll have a good talk to her tonight and get to the bottom of it.' Mary put her palms flat on the table and pushed herself up. 'You'd better go, sunshine, or yer'll have to run for it. I'll see yer out.'

Jenny never left the house without giving her mother a kiss and a hug. 'Don't forget the dress, will yer? And get a blue one, 'cos yer don't half look nice in blue.'

'I'll get one, even if it's only to keep you and yer dad happy.'

'Here's the tram, girl, you get on first so I can take me time.' Amy waited until Mary was on the platform, then, with a look of determination on her face, she wrapped her two hands around the steel post and pulled herself up. 'Why the hell they have to make the bleedin' steps so high, I'll never know.' She prodded the driver on his arm. 'Did yer hear that, Mr Tram Driver?'

'Did I hear what, missus?'

'Whoever made those bleedin' steps so high, they must have a wicked streak in them. How is someone with short legs supposed to manage?'

'How should I know? Have you got short legs, missus? If ye're not sure, I could measure them for yer and put in a complaint on your behalf.' The tram driver was delighted by the diversion. It got really boring standing there all day like a lemon, with yer eyes peeled for some stupid bugger who might walk out in front of you. 'I could say that your legs are too short for the tram steps or, if yer'd rather, I could say the tram steps are too high for your short legs. I can put a good letter together when I put me mind to it, even if I do say so meself.'

'Yer cheeky bugger! Did yer hear that, Mary?'

There came the clattering of feet as the conductor descended from the top deck. 'What's the hold-up, Jim? I've rung the ruddy bell six times.'

'Well, it's like this, Tom.' The driver was chuckling. 'This lady wants me to measure her legs for her, so she can put a complaint in. She reckons they're too short, yer see?' He rubbed his chin. 'Or did she say our steps are too high? I'm not sure now.'

The conductor looked at Amy and tutted, 'Oh, it's you, is it? I might have known. Whenever you get on me tram, I may as well throw the timetable away. We'll have people moaning at every flippin' stop now because we're late.'

'So, yer know the lady, do yer, Tom?'

'Know her! She's the bane of me life!' But Tom was smiling. 'If I'd have been downstairs I'd have made yer go past the stop and let the next tram pick her up. Let some other poor bugger put up with her shenanigans.' His grin turned into a full-blown laugh. 'D'yer know why she's got short legs? It's because her mother used to pat her on the head a lot when she was little, and it stunted her growth.'

'Huh! Ye're a fine one to talk, you are. Yer remind me of a flippin' bean stalk, ye're that tall and skinny. While my mother was patting me on the head, yours must have been putting yer through the mangle.'

With the chortling of the men ringing in her ears, Mary put her arm through Amy's and pulled with all her might until she had her in the aisle. Pointing to a seat, she said, 'Sit down, sunshine, for heaven's sake, and let the men get on with their work.'

Amy's friendly grin covered the passengers who were enjoying themselves so much they wouldn't have cared if the tram never took off. 'Do yerself a favour, girl, and you sit by the window. If I get in first there'll be no room on the seat for yer backside, even though the one yer've got is that small it's not worth writing home about.'

'I dunno,' Mary said as she slipped along the seat. 'Coming out with you is becoming a test of endurance. We've only been out of the house five minutes and me nerves are shattered. I hope ye're not going to carry on like that in TJs, I couldn't stand it.' She turned to see her friend gripping the bar that ran across the back of the seat in front with both hands to keep herself from falling off, while half of her backside was suspended in mid-air. And as she clung on like grim death, her face was set and her tongue was sticking out of the side of her mouth. Mary felt a rush of tenderness towards the woman who could bring smiles to a tramfull of people, all because she had short legs. 'Just look at the state of yer,' she said. 'Why don't yer go and sit over there and have a whole seat to yerself?'

'No, I'll stick with you, girl.' Amy just managed to throw herself sideways as the tram lurched around a corner and threatened to unseat her. 'That's the worst of having a backside the size of a rhinoceros – they don't make seats big enough to accommodate it. Mind you, it wouldn't be worth their while when yer come to think of it because they probably don't get many rhinoceroses round here.' The eyes she turned on Mary were full of laughter. 'Except for that Madge Phillips – have yer seen the backside on her? Blimey, she puts me in the meg specks.'

Tom and Jim were talking on the platform when the tram came to a halt in London Road, and they watched with amusement as Amy prepared herself for the step down. 'Close yer eyes, love, and jump for it,' Jim laughed. 'That's the best way.'

'Sod off, the pair of yer.' Amy reached down to where Mary was standing on the pavement with her hand extended ready to help. And when she was safely on the ground, she gave one of her cheeky grins. 'If me prayers are answered, some big bloke is going to give one of yer a black eye for not running on time and making him late for work. Yer'd be laughing the other side of yer faces, then.'

'Amy, will yer knock it off and let's get to the shops? And if yer start acting the goat in TJs I'll pretend ye're not with me.'

'I'll be as good as gold, girl, you wait and see. I'll be that quiet yer won't even know I'm beside yer.'

Jenny was the first home from work and the first to be greeted by her mother wearing her new dress. 'Oh, Mam! Yer look lovely!' Her eyes were bright with pleasure and her heart filled with pride. The pale blue cotton dress was set off by a deep frill around the neck and short sleeves, and it fitted to perfection. 'It really suits yer, and yer look young enough to be me sister. Ooh, wait till me dad sees it, he'll be made up.'

'Yeah, I'm pleased with it meself. It was a bargain, reduced in the sale from seven and eleven to five and eleven.' Holding the skirt out, Mary did a twirl. 'Not bad, eh?'

'It's beautiful. I wouldn't mind one meself. If I nip down on Saturday straight from work, d'yer think they'll have any left?'

'I couldn't tell yer, sunshine. I did think about yer, and if I'd had

80

the money I'd have bought one for yer. But by the time I'd bought two pillowcases and this, I was skint.'

'I know what I can do! I can go in me dinner hour tomorrow! It's only ten minutes on the tram to London Road, and I can eat me sandwiches on the way.' Jenny clapped her hands. 'That's a good idea, isn't it? They won't be sold out by then, will they?'

'You can but try, sunshine, you can but try.'

Laura arrived home then and she eyed her mother up and down. 'Mmm! Not bad!'

Jenny put a hand on her hip and glared at her sister. 'Not bad! It's a beautiful dress and me mam looks lovely in it. I'm going to TJs tomorrow in me dinner hour, to get one for meself. And if I look as nice in mine, I'll be more than happy.'

'How much was it, Mam?' Laura asked.

'Reduced in the sale to five and eleven.'

'I wouldn't mind one meself, in a different style and colour.' Laura put her handbag on the sideboard and pulled out a chair. 'Yer can get me one when yer go down, our kid.'

Jenny glanced at her mother before holding her hand out. 'I'll take the money off yer now, if yer don't mind.'

'I haven't got it now, I'll pay yer on Saturday when I get me wages.'

Jenny saw her mother walk through to the kitchen and knew it was because she didn't want to get involved, didn't want to take sides. Anyway, this row was between her and her sister, and it had been brewing for a long time. 'Some hope you've got! Where d'yer think I'm getting the money from?'

'Yer never go anywhere to spend yer money, and yer said this morning that yer had some saved up. Don't be so flaming miserable, yer'll get it back on Saturday.'

Jenny narrowed her eyes, and although she knew what the answer would be, she asked, 'Give me half of it now, then, and I'll get yer one.'

'I can't give yer half, I haven't got it! I've told yer, I'll give it yer when I get me wages, so stop harping on it, for crying out loud.'

'I'd have to be pretty stupid if I couldn't work out that yer don't get enough pocket-money to pay me back. Don't take me for a sucker, Laura. I choose to save me money, that's my business, nothing to do with you. You choose to spend yours, that's your business and nothing to do with me. So let's leave it that way, eh?'

'You tight-fisted little cow!' Laura's eyes were blazing. She wasn't used to her kid sister refusing her, or answering her back. 'It's no wonder yer never go anywhere. No one would want a misery guts like you for a friend.'

Mary stood in the kitchen, her hands gripping the edge of the sink. She was vexed over Laura calling her sister a little cow, and was in two minds whether to interfere. But Jenny seemed to be holding her own, so perhaps it was better to keep out of it. So she listened, ready to move quickly if things got out of hand.

'I might be a tight-fisted little cow, but I'm the one with the money to buy meself a dress. You've spent all your money, now ye're scrounging off me because yer can't bear to see anyone having something that you can't have.' The main reason Jenny was standing up to Laura had nothing to do with money. She was angry at the thought that her mam very seldom bought anything new for herself, and now the pleasure was being taken out of it by her selfish sister. 'I don't like coming down to your level, Laura, it goes against the grain. But you have asked for it and it's the only language you understand. You are a greedy, selfish little cow who only thinks of herself.'

When Mary heard Laura's cry of anger, followed by the sound of her chair scraping back, she rushed into the room, at the same time as Stan came through from the hall. 'What on earth is all the shouting about?'

Jenny turned. 'It's nothing, Dad, just me and Laura acting soft.'

'No, it's not, yer little liar.' Laura was so angry she didn't realise she was being offered a truce. 'D'yer know what she called me, Dad? She said I was a greedy, selfish little cow.'

Stan looked taken aback. He couldn't imagine Jenny uttering such words. 'Yer didn't, did yer?'

Jenny's eyes never wavered. 'Yes, I did, Dad.'

'What for?'

'Ask Laura.'

'It was for nothing, Dad!' Laura saw her mother watching and listening. She must have heard every word so she couldn't lie herself out of it. 'All I asked was for her to lend me the money to buy a dress like me mam's, that's all. And she took off on me.'

Stan's expression softened when he looked at his wife. 'Yer look very pretty, love.'

'I'm sorry I bothered now, all the fuss it's caused.'

Stan looked from one daughter to the other. 'Yer mam only gets a new dress every blue moon, and you two have to start an argument over it! Jenny, I'm really disappointed in yer, I never thought I'd ever hear yer call anyone a cow, let alone yer own sister. What made yer say such a thing?'

'I'd rather Laura told her herself. Let's see if she can tell the truth.'

Mary banged her fist on the table. 'Enough is enough! While all this is going on, the dinner is in the oven getting ruined. To cut a long story short, the word "cow" came from Laura first, and Jenny retaliated. It's as simple as that. So can we have this table cleared, otherwise the dinner will only be fit for the back of the fire.'

'I'm going round to Janet's, Mam, but I won't be out late.' Jenny kissed her mother's cheek. 'Yer look lovely. I bet me dad will fall for yer all over again.'

There had been tension throughout the meal, but looking at Jenny's open face, Stan knew it had not been caused by his youngest daughter. 'Ye're right there, love, she looks good enough to eat.'

When she heard the front door bang behind her sister, Laura got to her feet, her pretty face marred by a sulky expression. 'I'm going to Cynthia's.'

'Stay where yer are, Laura. Me and yer mam want to talk to you.'

Laura remained standing. 'What about? Can't it wait until I come back?'

'No, it can't! Now sit down.'

Defiant to the last, Laura jerked her head in disgust as she pulled the chair out and sat down heavily. 'Blimey, it'll be time to come home before I get out.'

'Any lip out of you, Laura, and it's up the stairs yer'll be going, not out of the door.' Stan glanced at Mary. 'Do you want to start, love, or shall I?'

'You can do it, but first I'd like Laura to tell yer the truth about the row yer heard when yer came in. Ever since she was a baby Jenny has taken the blame for Laura's wrongdoing, and I think it's time to put the record straight.'

Laura, reluctantly and with a scowl, related what had happened. But because in her selfish mind she couldn't see why her sister wouldn't get the dress for her, her tone was full of self-pity. She ended by saying, 'There was no need for it, Dad. It wouldn't have hurt her to get me one while she's getting one for herself, and I'd have paid her back on Saturday.'

'Where would yer have got the money from?'

'Well,' Laura blustered, 'I could have given her half on Saturday and the rest next week.'

'You get an extra shilling a week pocket-money since yer got yer raise, so yer have more in yer pocket than Jenny does. Don't ever ask her again, d'yer hear? And while we're on the subject, yer whole attitude to her is just not on. God knows, she does her best to make friends with yer, but all she gets back is a load of abuse and sarcasm. Sisters are supposed to be close, and love each other. What's gone wrong in your case, I don't know. But from now on yer treat her with respect and civility, or yer'll have me to answer to.' Stan leaned his arms on the table and laced his fingers. 'Now to last night. Yer'll come in at the time ye're told to, not when it suits yer. I'm not telling you yer can't go to yer grandad's, but whether he goes to bed early or not, ye're to leave in time to get home for half ten. You are not to stay talking to Celia, she's too old for yer. Now, have yer got that straight?'

'I heard yer, Dad, I haven't got doll's ears.' Laura wasn't liking this one little bit. She was nearly sixteen, for heaven's sake, old enough to know what she was doing. 'I don't know what yer've got against Celia, she's nice At least she doesn't treat me like a child.'

'I'm not going to argue the toss with yer, Laura, so just get it into that big head of yours that I mean every word I say. You'll be more pleasant in the house, nicer to yer sister, and yer'll be in by half-ten every night. It's not much to ask, and it would make life easier for everyone. But keep on as yer are, with an attitude that stinks, then I'll come down hard on yer and yer won't know what's hit yer.'

'Yeah, okay.' Laura would have agreed to anything to get out of the house. She and Cynthia were meeting two boys and she was ten minutes late. 'Is it all right if I go now?'

'Have you listened to a word I've said?'

'Of course I have, Dad.' Laura left her seat, picked up her handbag from the sideboard and made for the door. 'I'll be in by half ten, I promise.'

Stan and Mary watched her flying past the front window, her black hair bouncing on her shoulders. They looked at each other and sighed. 'I may as well have been talking to meself. I don't think it penetrated the first layer, did it, love?'

Mary shook her head. 'No, it didn't, sunshine, but at least yer've made a start. Yer'll have to keep it up, though, otherwise she'll go off the rails altogether. And I'll do my bit, too.'

Stan felt cheered when he saw a smile light up his wife's face. 'I don't know what's brought the smile on, but it suits yer, and it suits the dress.'

'I was thinking of our Jenny. Yer should have seen the way she stood up to Laura. She gave back word for word, and even though I was as mad as hell, I felt like clapping.' Mary cupped her husband's face. 'Yer know, love, it wouldn't surprise me if it's our Jenny who brings Laura to her senses. It may take a while, but I think she started tonight.'

Chapter Seven

'I've a good mind to go up and see that Celia meself.' Mary spoke to the empty room as she walked around the bed tucking the ends of the overhanging blanket under the mattress. 'She has no right to discuss what goes on between her and me dad with our Laura. Fancy talking to a fifteen-year-old like that, and our Laura feeling sorry for her, too! She's old enough in the head as it is, without the bold Celia telling her things that should be private between her and me dad.'

Mary gave the eiderdown a good shake before throwing it over the bed. 'I'd like to tell her to her face exactly what I think about her, the brazen hussy.' She rubbed her temples to ease the headache that had started during the night as she'd tossed and turned, unable to sleep with the worry on her mind. Any idea of friendship between her daughter and the older woman had to be nipped in the bud before it took hold. It was no good telling Laura because she wouldn't take any notice of them. Oh, she'd agree with them, promise them anything they wanted to hear, but she would do as she pleased on the sly. They had no idea where she got to every night because she didn't tell them. And Mary didn't want to involve her father, he must have enough problems with his wayward wife without her adding to them.

She gave a deep sigh. She'd never been back to her old home since her dad had married the girl younger than his own daughter, because she couldn't bear to see her taking the place of her beloved mother. But she would know no peace until she'd voiced her fears. And the only way to do that was to face the woman who was the cause of her headache and upset tummy.

Still talking aloud, Mary made her way downstairs. 'I'll go now and be back in time to go to the shops with Amy.'

Her neighbour's brows shot up when she opened the door. 'In the name of God, girl, has yer clock gone wonky or something? It's not ten o'clock yet.'

'I'm going on a message, but I'll be home to go to the shops with yer.'

A frown crossed Amy's chubby face. 'What d'yer mean, ye're going on a message? Yer never go on a message without me.'

'It's not that sort of message, sunshine, it's personal.' Mary tutted, wondering how she ever, for one moment, thought she'd get away without her mate worming the truth out of her. 'Oh, all right, I'll have to tell yer I suppose, or yer'll plague the flaming life out of me. I'm going to me dad's to have a word with Celia.' Briefly, she told of the reason for her going. 'But yer keep that to yerself, d'yer hear? I'll never speak to yer again if it gets out.'

Amy's answer was prompt. 'I'm coming with yer.'

'You are not! This is something I've got to do by meself.'

'I'm coming with yer in case she thumps yer one.' Amy nodded her head and her chins quivered in agreement. 'You won't be able to thump her back because yer'll be flat out on the floor, so I can do it for yer.'

'I'm quite capable of looking after meself, sunshine, and I'd rather go on me own. But I do appreciate the offer.'

'That's what mates are for, isn't it? To help each other out in times of trouble.'

'I don't know how long I'll be gone because I can't walk past me mam's old neighbour, Mrs Platt, without giving her a knock. So I might be a couple of hours. But don't worry – no matter how long I am, I won't be getting meself into trouble.' Mary turned to walk away. 'I'll try to get back before the shops close for dinner.'

'Don't worry, girl, I'll wait for yer.'

After turning to wave, Mary increased her pace. She wasn't looking forward to this one little bit, so the sooner it was over, the better.

Mary stood outside her childhood home and felt like crying. Her mam used to have the place looking like a little palace, with windows shining, lace curtains as white as snow, front doorstep scrubbed every morning and the red-raddled window sill polished until you could see your face in it. If it hadn't been for the number on the door, Mary would have thought she was at the wrong house. Behind the dirty net curtains the draw curtains were still closed. The windows were filthy, as was the step and window sill. It was as if nothing had been touched since her mam had died. The house was a disgrace, the scruffiest in the street. And as she knocked on the door, Mary thought how ashamed her dad must be, having to come home to this every day. He was a proud man and this must be so humiliating for him.

As she lifted the knocker for the third time, the next door opened and Monica Platt's head appeared. 'Yer'll not get an answer there before twelve.' Then when recognition dawned a wide smile lit up her face and she almost jumped from the top step to embrace the daughter of the woman who'd been her neighbour and best mate for years. 'Mary, sweetheart, it's good to see yer. Me and Phil often talk about yer, and wonder how you and Stan are, and the girls.'

'I came to have a word with Celia, but she must have gone out.'

Monica Platt's smile disappeared. 'Come inside, sweetheart, and I'll make us a cuppa.' With her arm across Mary's shoulders, she led her up the step and into the hall. 'I'm glad yer've come, there's things need saying.'

While Monica put the kettle on, Mary gazed around the room that had been like a second home to her when she was young. Nothing had changed, the same brown chenille cloth covered the table, the same clock ticked away on the mantelpiece, the aspidistra still stood on a small table under the window and the statue of the Whistling Boy had pride of place on the sideboard. The room was homely, comfortable and spotlessly clean. Like her mam had been, Monica Platt was very houseproud.

'There yer are, sweetheart, drink it while it's hot.' Monica set a dainty cup and saucer in front of Mary before sitting down on the opposite side of the table. 'It does me heart good to see yer, and that's the truth.'

Mary sipped on the hot tea, hoping it would chase away the hard lump that had formed in her throat and quell the tears that were threatening to spill. But she was so devastated by what she'd seen of her old home she had no control over her emotions. 'I'm sorry, Auntie Monica, but I'm going to cry.'

'You go ahead, sweetheart. I've cried buckets meself over the last year or so.'

Mary put the cup back on the saucer and the sobs came. 'Me mam must be looking down with sadness at the little house she was so proud of. And she must be disappointed in me for not doing something about it. But I was so hurt and angry when me dad married again so soon after her death, I fell out with him.' Mary sniffed up as she wiped the back of her hand across her eyes. 'I didn't see him for well over a year, but we've made it up now and he calls in every Saturday afternoon and sometimes a night through the week. But he comes alone because I won't have her in my house. I think she only married him so he could keep her and she wouldn't have to work. I can't stand the woman.'

'Did yer come with a message for her? I don't even pass her the time of day if I can help it, but I don't mind passing a message on if it'll save yer hanging around.'

Mary shook her head. 'Our Laura came to see her grandad a few nights ago, and apparently he went to bed early leaving Laura with Celia. Things were said about me dad that I didn't like, so I came to have it out with her. I came early, hoping to catch her before she went to the shops, but she must go to work, does she?'

'Work! Work, did yer say? She couldn't even spell it, never mind

87

do it.' There was disgust on Monica's face. 'She's in bed, sweetheart. She'll have heard yer knocking, but she never surfaces until twelve o'clock. She's the laziest bitch I've ever known. Never does a hand's turn in the house, it's like a tip. If yer think the outside looks bad, yer should see inside, it's like a muck-midden.'

Mary narrowed her eyes. 'Yer mean she's in bed now?'

'Yes, sweetheart, she's in bed now. Twelve o'clock she gets up, not a minute before. And she seldom goes to the shops, except the one on the corner for her ciggies. Yer never see her in the butcher's buying meat, nor have I ever seen her carrying potatoes or veg.'

'Doesn't she ever have a dinner ready for me dad when he comes home from work?'

'I don't want yer to think I'm nosy, sweetheart, but I'd have to be blind, deaf and dumb not to know what's going on next door. There's never any smells coming from the kitchen, never any sign of activity, until your dad comes home. Any cooking done in there is done by him. All she's fit for is making her face up, painting her nails, reading magazines and flirting with every man in the street. Anything in trousers and she's fluttering her eyelashes. Any of the neighbours will tell yer that what I'm saying is true, there's not one has a good word for her.'

Monica leaned her elbows on the table and laced her fingers. 'I don't know whether I should be telling you all this, but me and Phil think a lot of Joe, and we worry about him. He never moans or criticises her, but I've watched him walking up the street on his way home from work, and he looks so unhappy and weary, my heart goes out to him.'

Mary's face was set, her anger boiling over. 'And yer say she's in bed now?'

'Yes, sweetheart, she's in bed now and hasn't got a care in the world.'

Mary pushed her chair back and stood up. 'Right, we'll soon put a stop to that. I'll give her something to care about.' She put her arms around the older woman and gave her a hug. 'Yer did right to tell me, Auntie Monica, so don't worry.'

'She probably won't open the door for yer, 'cos as I said, yer never see sight nor light of her until dinnertime. But if she does, watch out for her, sweetheart, she's got a vile temper. I don't know how Joe puts up with the way she shouts at him – my Phil wouldn't.'

'She'll open the door all right, otherwise I'll put a window in. I'm so angry now I would willingly strangle her with me bare hands. I'm not going to stand by and see a fly turn like her make a fool of my dad.'

'If yer get into trouble, sweetheart, just knock on the wall and I'll come running.'

'The way I feel now, Auntie Monica, if anyone does any running, it'll be the queer one who me dad was soft enough to marry.' Mary was shaking her head as she stepped into the street. 'And by God, he's paying dearly for it now.'

Monica stood on the pavement and watched as Mary banged on the knocker next door. The bangs became louder, but still there was no response from inside. The woman from next door but one came out to see what all the noise was about, but at a sign from Monica she held her tongue and just stood silently watching and wondering what Joe Steadman's daughter was up to. If her face was anything to go by, it boded ill for the lazy so-and-so inside. Perhaps she was going to get her comeuppance, and it wouldn't be before time.

Mary lifted the letter box and bent to put her mouth as near to the opening as she could get. Then, at the top of her voice, she yelled, 'Get out of that bed right now, and open this door! Did yer hear what I said, or shall I start breaking a few windows?' She stood back, looked up at the bedroom and saw the curtains twitch. 'I haven't got all day, so make it snappy.'

Three women from the houses opposite had come to their doors when they heard the shouting and were now standing in a small group with their arms folded. There was a look of pleasant expectancy on their faces that the chit of a girl who'd dragged Joe Steadman down to the gutter, was going to be confronted by his very angry-looking daughter. 'I hope she belts her one,' said Maggie Smith. 'She certainly deserves it.'

'Yer never spoke a truer word, Maggie,' Nellie Mitchell said, hitching up her ample bosom. 'Many's the time I've felt like clocking her one.'

'Aye, poor Ada, God rest her soul.' Lizzie Thompson made the sign of the cross. 'She must be turning in her grave at what's happened to her husband and her little house.'

The door to Joe's house opened slowly and Celia's head appeared. 'What the bleedin' hell are yer making all that racket for? What d'yer want?'

'I came to talk to you. I'm coming in.'

'Like hell yer are!' The door was opened wider and Celia stood on the step, a cigarette dangling from lips that bore traces of yesterday's lipstick. Her hair was tousled and the scrap of nightdress she was wearing looked as though it had never been washed. 'Yer don't live here, this is not your house, so get lost.'

'Just try and keep me out.' Mary acted so quickly the girl was unprepared for what happened. With one hand on the door, and the other on Celia's chest, Mary pushed with all her might. The door crashed back against the hall wall and Celia was sent reeling backwards. 'This is my father's house and I'll enter it whenever I want to.'

To the dismay of the onlookers, who were in the mood for cheering, Mary stepped into the hall and closed the door behind her. Dusting her hands together as though they'd been in contact with something unpleasant, she walked into the living room to find Celia standing by the table, waiting for her, with eyes blazing.

'You can't come barging in here as though yer own the bleedin' place. Just wait until I tell Joe, he'll have plenty to say about it, don't you worry.' Celia took a long drag on the cigarette before throwing it in the direction of the fireplace. 'Now yer can just sod off, I don't want yer in here.'

Mary's eyes followed the flying cigarette and she gasped at what she saw. The grate still held the remains of last night's fire and the hearth was overflowing with ashes, cigarette stubs, sweet papers and an apple core. Then Mary took stock of the room. As Monica Platt had said, it was like a muck-midden. The furniture was thick with dust, curtains and cushion covers were filthy, there were clothes flung everywhere and the floor was strewn with shoes and papers. But it was the overpowering smell of dirt and neglect that had Mary clenching her fists. There was nothing here to remind her of her childhood and her mother. 'You dirty bitch! You dirty, lazy bitch! Lounging in bed all morning, too flaming idle to keep the place clean. Yer should be ashamed of yerself.'

'Don't you come here lecturing me, this is my house and I'll please meself what I do in it.' The brazen look was on Celia's face again as she reached for the cigarette packet on the table. She never took her eyes off Mary as she deliberately took her time selecting a cigarette and then lighting it. Just as deliberately, she drew deeply on it before blowing the smoke into Mary's face. 'Now, get yer skates on and vamoose, before I throw yer out on yer arse.'

'I'll go when I'm good and ready, and not before. And I wouldn't advise yer to lay one finger on me if yer know what's good for yer.' Mary resisted the temptation to take her by the shoulders and give her a good shake. 'Tell me, is this what my father comes home to every night? A lazy good-for-nothing wife and a filthy house?'

'So what if he does? I don't hear him complaining.'

'I'll complain for him then, shall I? And as yer don't seem to know what being a wife's all about, I'll explain that to yer. I'll do it slowly, so yer can't say yer don't understand. When a woman marries a man, she pledges her love and vows to care for him. That means giving him love, warmth and a clean comfortable home. And as you were so keen to marry me dad yer practically threw yerself at him, I believed yer did love him. So I'd like to know why the dirt is meeting him at the door when he comes home from work, why there's no dinner ready for him, and why his wife has turned into a lazy slut? Or would I be right in thinking yer never loved him, yer just wanted a meal ticket? And the real truth is, yer've always been a lazy slut?'

'I'll break yer bleedin' neck, talking to me like that. Who the hell d'yer think yer are?' Celia lunged forward to grab at Mary's hair, but the move was anticipated and Mary pushed her arm away.

'Don't try that again or I'll brain yer.' Mary sighed. She hadn't come with the intention of fighting with her father's wife, just to talk to her. But seeing the way her mam's home had been left to go to rack and ruin, she couldn't help herself. And now she'd probably made things worse for her father. 'I won't tell me dad I've been today because he'd be so ashamed that I'd seen the way he lives. If you want to tell him, that's your business.'

'Oh, I'll be telling him all right, everything yer said. And he'll be straight up to yours to tell yer what he thinks about yer.' There was spite in Celia's eyes. 'There'll be no more Saturday visits from him, that's a dead cert.'

'Please yerself, but when ye're crying down his ear, put a blindfold on him so he can't see that every word I've spoken is the truth. And don't forget about me calling yer a lazy slut, I wouldn't want yer to miss that out.' Mary hoped she was right in thinking Celia wouldn't dare even mention she'd been in case the whole thing backfired on her. 'Anyway, all this is not why I'm here. I came to tell yer not to talk to Laura about intimate details of your life. And yer must never run me dad down to her. The girl isn't sixteen yet, and I'll not have yer putting an old head on young shoulders.'

'I didn't tell her nothing but the truth. He's like an old man, going to bed every night about nine or ten and leaving me on me own. What sort of life is that for me?'

'Perhaps he goes to bed so he won't have to sit in this squalor. Try cleaning the place up and make it comfortable for him, then he won't be going to bed early.'

'Your dad is an old man. He goes to bed because he's tired. But what about me? I'm still young.' Celia's top lip curled. 'And there's no fun in me going to bed with him because all he does is sleep. He's not capable of doing anything else these days.'

As quick as a flash, Mary let swing with her arm, delivering a resounding smack across Celia's cheek. 'How dare you! How dare you talk about my father like that. Your mouth and your thoughts are dirtier than this room, and that's saying something. Cheap, nasty, and as common as muck, that's you. Ye're not fit to wipe my father's shoes. And I can promise you that if I ever hear yer've talked dirty to my daughter, I'll be down here to wash yer mouth out with carbolic soap. Then I'll drag yer out of this house and down the street by yer hair. And don't think I can't, or won't, because when anything threatens my family I'll protect them with me life.'

Mary turned and was halfway down the hall when she felt a blow in the small of her back that knocked the wind out of her. She bent double, and was gasping for breath when she heard soft laughter behind her, and although the movement spread pain right through her body, she straightened up, determined not to give the other woman the satisfaction of seeing she'd been hurt.

Celia was leaning against the wall, an evil smile on her face as she rubbed her knuckles. 'Nobody hits me and gets away with it. And that's only a taste of what yer'll get if yer ever come to this bleedin' house again, with yer preaching and high-falutin', holier-than-thou attitude. To hear yer talk, anyone would think yer were a cut above the rest, but all yer are is a stuck-up bitch. Now get going, and I can say goodbye to bad rubbish.'

Mustering all her courage, Mary walked back and faced her. 'Ye're wrong there. When I go, I'll be leaving the rubbish behind.' She lowered her gaze to Celia's feet, then slowly let her eyes travel the length of the woman until she reached her face. 'You should feel quite at home here with all the muck and rubbish – it's where yer belong. The house could be made clean with the help of some elbow grease, but no one could change you; ye're wicked right through to the core of yer.'

There came a knocking at the door, then Monica's voice. 'Are yer coming, Mary, I've made a pot of tea.'

'Yeah, I'm coming now, I've finished me business in here.' Mary waited for a few seconds to see if Celia had anything more to say, but the woman remained silent, a sneer her only sign of retaliation. So Mary opened the front door and stepped into the street to face the concern in Monica's eyes.

'I've been worried to death about yer, sweetheart, yer've been that long.'

'I'm all right, honest. I said what I wanted to say and got it all off me chest. Actually, I said more than I intended because of the state of the house. She wasn't very happy about it and gave me a load of lip, but it's off me chest now and I feel better for it.'

'Are yer coming in for a cuppa?'

'No, I'll have to get home because me mate's waiting for me. But why don't you come up to ours one day? We could have a good natter and I'd enjoy that.'

'I'll do that, sweetheart. I've got yer address so I'll write and tell yer what day I'm coming. Give my love to Stan and the girls,' Monica hugged her tight, 'and I'll see yer soon.'

Celia stood with her ear pressed against the door and heard every word. And when the talking stopped, she made her way back to the living room, saying softly, 'So yer feel better now, do yer? Protect yer family with yer life, will yer? Well, there's one member of yer family who doesn't think the sun shines out of yer backside. She's the weak link, is Laura, and it's through her I'll get me own back on yer, Mary Nightingale. Yer'll rue the bleedin' day yer ever came here throwing yer weight around because I'm going to make yer pay for it.'

Amy was standing on the doorstep when Mary came up the street. 'My God, girl, I was beginning to think she'd killed yer.'

'Not quite, sunshine, not quite.' Mary had only taken the tram for two stops because every time it swayed she felt like crying out with the pain. So thinking it best to keep her body in motion, she'd walked the rest of the way. She was glad she had now because the pain had eased off a lot. 'Get yer coat and I'll tell yer all about it on the way to the shops.'

'Okay, girl, just give me one minute.' Amy bustled down the hall and was back within seconds, struggling into the sleeves of her coat. 'Let me make sure I've got everything. Me keys, me purse and me basket, all present and accounted for.' She pulled the door behind her and linked her arm through Mary's. 'Right, I'm all ears now, girl. How did yer get on with yer stepmother?'

'Don't call her that, Amy, she's no relation of mine. If she's anyone's stepmother, it's the devil.' As they walked, Mary recounted everything that had happened. And they'd just reached the Maypole when she came to the part where she'd slapped Celia's face.

'Hang on a minute.' Amy pulled her to a halt. 'I can't take all this in so quickly. Yer mean yer really slapped her face?'

'I couldn't help meself, not the way she was talking about me dad. Anyway, she got her own back with a vengeance.' Mary continued her tale right up to where she parted from Monica Platt. 'So, there yer have it. The whole sorry story.'

For once Amy was at a loss for words. Mary was so good at describing things, Amy felt she'd actually been there. In her mind's eye she could see the dirty state of the house and the two women squaring up to each other. 'The hard-faced, brazen bitch! I asked yer to let me go with yer, but yer wouldn't have it. I'd have knocked bleedin' spots off her. In fact, I've a good mind to go up there now and give her a good hiding.' Amy was blazing. She knew what the girl was the first time she'd set eyes on her. She had brazen hussy written all over her. Joe Steadman must have been out of his mind to have got himself involved with the likes of her. 'And yer said some of the neighbours were out?'

'Yeah, me mam's old mates. Women I used to run messages for and played with their children. I didn't get a chance to talk to them, apart from Monica Platt, but I had a feeling they were cheering me on.'

'And to think I missed all this,' Amy said, shaking her head. 'Did yer really threaten to put a window in?'

'Yeah, sunshine, I did. But I can't say I'm pleased with meself, shouting in the street like a common fish-wife.'

'I wonder what yer dad will make of it?'

'I'm not going to say a dickie bird to anyone, Amy, and I'm relying on you to keep it to yerself. I'm not even going to tell Stan.'

'Yer can't keep it a secret, girl, 'cos the queer one is bound to tell yer dad.'

'I doubt it, Amy, I really doubt it. She's not that soft, she knows me dad wouldn't take her part, not now. Yer see, although he's never said anything, I think he wishes he could wake up one morning and find he's been having a nightmare, and there's no such person as Celia. There's no wedded bliss in that house, I can tell yer. There couldn't be, there's no room for it with all the dirt.'

Amy blew out a long, deep sigh. 'Come on, girl, let's get the shopping in. I'll mug us to two cream buns, to have with a cup of tea when we get home. And then yer can go all over it again in slow motion, so I haven't missed anything.'

Mary pushed open the door of the Maypole, but before stepping inside, she turned her head. 'What I've told yer was for your ears only, remember that. Not even a word in Ben's ear when ye're in bed.'

'Ay, girl, when I'm in bed I'm too busy being otherwise engaged to talk. That's for when yer've read all the *Echo* and there's nowt on the wireless worth listening to.'

When Amy saw a smile light up Mary's face, her heart lifted. After a cup of tea and a cream bun, her friend's worries would have all but disappeared. Please God.

Chapter Eight

Janet Porter's smile was wide when she opened the front door. 'Jenny! Oh, am I glad to see you! I've been going to come round to yours a few times, but I was worried that yer might have gone a bit stuck up, now ye're working in an office.'

'Don't be daft, it's just a job, same as any other.' Jenny was pleased with the smile of welcome from the girl who had been her friend all through school. 'D'yer feel like coming for a walk, so we can have a good gab and catch up with our news?'

Janet held the door wide. 'I'm helping me mam wash the dishes, so yer can come in and wait for us, I won't be long. She'll be glad to see yer, she's always asking about yer.'

Jenny followed her friend into the living room where her father and brother were seated at the table. 'Hello, Mr Porter. Hi-ya, Bill.'

'Hello, stranger, long time no see.' Vincent Porter flicked the butt of his cigarette into the fireplace and hooked his thumbs into his braces. 'How's the job going, lass?'

'It's fine, I love it.'

The sounds from the kitchen stopped and Janet's mother came through, drying her hands on her pinny. 'Well, well, a stranger in the camp. It's good to see yer, queen, I thought yer'd fallen out with us.'

Jenny smiled. 'Now as if I would. Me and Janet have never fallen out, have we, Jan?'

'No, not once.' Janet pointed to a chair. 'Sit down, Jenny, while I help me mam finish the dishes, then we can go out.'

Martha Porter shook her head. 'Yer don't have to help, queen, I've nearly finished. But don't be rushing off out, I want to hear about Jenny's job.'

Jenny sat down facing Janet's sixteen-year-old brother, Bill, who had so far not opened his mouth. He couldn't think of anything to say to the girl whose leg he used to pull something terrible. But she wasn't a schoolgirl any more, she was a young lady, and a very attractive one at that.

'I'm only a filing clerk, really,' Jenny told them, the grin never leaving her face and her eyes shining. 'But the manager is letting me practise on one of the typewriters and I'm hoping I make the grade as a typist.' Her familiar infectious giggle brought smiles to the other four faces. 'It'll be years before I get me speed up to match the other women, though. Their fingers just fly over the keys so fast they make yer dizzy. So far I'm only using the one finger on each hand, although I was daring this morning and tried with two.'

'Yer'll get there, queen, don't worry,' Martha said with conviction. 'Yer know what they say about Rome not being built in a day.'

'If they'd only been using two fingers, Mrs Porter, it would never have got built.' Jenny could feel Bill's eyes on her. 'What's the matter with you, Bill Porter? Ye're staring at me as though I've got horns sticking out of me head.'

'I'm trying to make out who yer are.' Like his parents and sister, Bill had rich chestnut-coloured hair, eyes that were constantly changing from brown to hazel, a square chin and a broad nose. 'They keep calling yer Jenny, but the only Jenny I know is one who cadged a bull's-eye off me last time I saw her, and she was wearing a gymslip.'

Her eyes dancing, Jenny leaned closer. 'What's the matter, Bill, d'yer want yer bull's-eye back?'

Janet was getting impatient. 'Ay, come on, Jenny, let's go for a walk.'

'I'll come with yer,' Bill said, bringing a smile to his mother's face. 'A bit of fresh air will do me good.'

'Yer will not!' Janet was indignant. 'Me and Jenny want to talk, and it wouldn't interest you 'cos it's girls' talk.'

'Oh, let him go with yer,' Martha said, thinking to do her son a favour. 'Get him out of our way for an hour.'

'Ah, ay, Mam! I'm not having me brother traipsing around with us! Me and Jenny want to catch up on our news and we won't be able to talk with him there.'

'Just hang on a minute.' Bill sat upright in his chair. 'What about when I used to have to traipse around with *you*? I couldn't go to the Saturday matinée without yer crying to come with me. I couldn't even have a game of footie with me mates without dragging you along. I used to get me leg pulled soft over you. And yer were a proper little pest, always whinging.'

Janet was having a quick change of heart. If he mentioned that she used to wet her knickers she'd die of humiliation. 'What d'yer think, Jenny?'

'I don't mind, honestly. Although I think he'd be bored stiff.'

'No chance of that.' Bill was looking decidedly pleased with himself. 'I've always wondered what girls find to talk about. And yer should be pleased to have a handsome escort, who can see yer both safely home.'

Martha and Vincent exchanged knowing looks. Their son must have taken a shine to young Jenny, that was the only reason they could think of. Wild horses wouldn't have dragged him out of the door to go for a walk with his sister. 'Make sure Jenny's home by ten,' Martha said, 'in case her mother worries where she is.'

When Bill got to his feet, Jenny gaped. 'Good grief, you haven't half got big since the last time I saw yer.'

While Bill grew two inches in stature, his mother did the bragging. 'Five feet ten inches, he is, and still growing. And he takes a size ten shoe.'

'If he keeps on at that rate, Mrs Porter,' Jenny said as she slipped her handbag over her arm, 'yer'll have to be looking for another house.'

After seeing the youngsters out, Martha came back chuckling. 'D'yer know what, love? I think the penny's just dropped with our Bill. He's finally noticed the difference between boys and girls.'

Much to Bill's dismay, the two girls linked arms with Jenny walking on the inside. Wanting to make a good impression, the boy had no option but to act the gentleman and walk on the outside, putting him next to his sister.

Jenny was in a very happy frame of mind. It was lovely to be with her old schoolfriend again. 'How's your job, Janet, d'yer like it?'

'Very hot and very tiring.' Janet was working in the pressing room of a laundry. 'The women are nice, and we have a good laugh, but in the hot weather it's killing. What with the heat from the pressers and the steam, the sweat just pours off yer. I never thought I'd hear meself say this, but I'll be glad when the winter comes.'

'It's a job, our kid, that's the main thing,' Bill said. 'If yer think it's hot in your place, yer should try working with me, in the tannery. But when I get me wage-packet on a Saturday I forget how I've had to sweat to earn it.'

'Ye're sixteen now, aren't yer, Bill?' Jenny leaned forward so she could see him. 'Yer'll be earning more than me, I only get seven and six a week.'

'I started on that, but I've had two rises since. It was me birthday a few weeks ago, and me pay went up to nine and six a week. Not bad, eh?'

'Not bad!' His sister's voice rose. 'It's blooming marvellous! Especially when me mam only takes five bob off yer, the same as she does me.' She squeezed Jenny's arm. 'He's a real mammy's boy, this one. She gives him all his own way, spoils him soft.'

'I pay me own fares out of it, and buy me own shoes.' Bill glared at his sister. Mammy's boy indeed. 'You'll get the same when ye're earning it.'

'I hope you two don't come to blows.' Jenny laughed. 'Yer've both got hot jobs and hot tempers to go with them.'

'It's his fault,' Janet said, as they turned into County Road. 'We should have left him at home.'

It wasn't long before Bill was himself wishing they'd left him at home. Why did they have to look in every shop window? Shoe shops, dress shops, jewellers, even blinking hat shops! And they didn't just glance in the windows, they spent ages pointing out a dress that they'd buy if they had the money. And those high-heeled shoes, well, they'd definitely be getting a pair like that, they were the last word in fashion. Blimey, he thought, it doesn't take much to make girls happy. Men now, they only ventured near shops when something wore out.

'I hate to break it up, girls, but it's starting to get dark and I think we should be making our way back. I don't want Jenny's mam telling me off for keeping her out late.'

There was a wicked glint in Janet's eyes when she turned to him. 'I bet yer've really enjoyed yerself, haven't yer? Think what yer'd have missed if yer'd stayed home.' She was turning her head when she spotted a familiar figure on the opposite side of the road. Giving Jenny a nudge, she pointed. 'Ay, am I seeing things, or is that your Laura over there? Yeah, it is, because she's got that horrible Cynthia with her.'

Jenny clamped her lips together when she saw her sister hanging on to a boy's arm and laughing up into his face. And behind them walked Cynthia, also engrossed in the boy she was linking. They looked like courting couples, but Jenny had never set eyes on the boys before. Her mam would go mad if she knew. She was always telling Laura that if she ever had a date the boy must call for her, so they could see him. And these weren't boys, either, they were men, much older than her sixteen-year-old sister. 'Don't let them see us. Yer know what our Laura's like for showing off.'

'Is she courting?' Janet asked. 'Is that her boyfriend?'

'I couldn't tell yer, she's never mentioned having a boyfriend.'

'If she has, she's two-timing him something rotten,' Bill said. 'I've seen her with loads of fellers, but I've never seen those two blokes before.'

Jenny peeped over her shoulder. 'They won't see us now, so let's go. Wherever our Laura's off to, I hope she keeps her eye on the time because she's got to be in by half ten.'

Bill decided to be daring. 'Let me walk between yer, then yer've got to let me join in the conversation. As long as it's not about dresses, shoes or flaming hats!'

This had the girls laughing and they kept it up all the way home. Funny incidents at work were remembered and exaggerated for maximum effect. And it was a happy trio who stood outside Jenny's front door. 'I've really enjoyed meself, it's been lovely seeing yer again, Jan. And you, Bill, of course.'

'I'll come round here tomorrow night, shall I?' Janet jerked her head at her brother. 'We can talk better without the queer feller with us.'

Jenny cocked an ear when she heard the lock turning. She just had time to whisper, 'Don't mention our Laura, please,' when the door opened.

Mary's face showed her pleasure. 'Janet, it's lovely to see yer again, I've missed that cheeky smile of yours.' Her gaze went to the boy with them. 'My God, Bill Porter, I didn't recognise yer! Ye gods, yer haven't half shot up.'

'It's me mam's dumplings and pies, Mrs Nightingale. I keep telling her I don't want two helpings, but she just keeps piling me plate high. She always makes too much, yer see, and to save her walking down the yard to the midden, she makes me eat it.'

'Well, whatever it is, son, ye're looking well on it. And you, Janet, yer look a treat, a sight for sore eyes.' Mary was happy to see her daughter's smiling face, and in the company of youngsters her own age. 'Has Jenny asked yer if yer'll go to the pictures with her one night?'

'She hasn't asked me yet, Mrs Nightingale, but yer see, we haven't said half what we want to because of big brother here. He's cramped our style something awful.'

'I'll take yer to the pictures, Jenny,' Bill said. 'If yer'll do me the honour.'

Jenny's clear laugh filled the night air. She was used to Bill pulling her leg, he'd done it for as long as she could remember. Many's the time she'd fallen for one of his jokes, but not now, she was wise to him. 'I'm too big for yer to pull me leg now, Billy, and I'm not daft enough to fall for that.'

Where he got the nerve from, Billy would never know, but out came the words he was thinking. 'It's because ye're big I'm asking yer, Jenny. I wouldn't want to take no girl in a gymslip to the pictures.'

'Ooh, er!' Janet started to giggle. 'The state of him and the price of fish! Take no notice of him, Jenny, he's acting the goat. He's always saying he can't stand girls. Oh, what he said was, God slipped up when He gave them mouths. They wouldn't be half bad if they didn't have that hole in their faces.'

Mary looked on with amusement. She wasn't so sure the boy was joking. It was dusk now, too dark to see her daughter's face clearly, but she'd bet any money that Jenny was blushing to the roots of her hair. She was soon to find out how wrong she was.

Far from blushing, Jenny found it so hilarious she couldn't stop giggling. Bill had always made her laugh, the things he came out with. It never entered her head he could be serious. 'If you didn't have that hole in yer face, Bill Porter, yer mam wouldn't have to slave over a hot stove all day. Just think of the money she'd save. And, you wouldn't be able to take the mickey out of people, as yer are now.'

Bill told himself it was best to quit while he was still ahead. After all, he hadn't thought of Jenny Nightingale for ages, until she walked into their house a couple of hours ago. And he'd be seeing a lot of her in future through his sister. 'I keep asking me mam to give me the money instead of the food, but she won't hear of it. I've reached the conclusion she's a sucker for punishment and likes slaving over a hot stove all day.'

'If you weren't so big, I'd hit yer!' Janet shook a fist in his face. 'Will yer keep yer mouth closed long enough for me and me mate to make arrangements to go to the pictures?' She watched as he stood to attention and saluted. She felt more like kissing him than hitting him. He was a good brother, always looking after her when she was little, protecting her when someone older than her picked a fight with her. He made sure she never came to any harm. Even now when she went out, he always asked where she was going and who with. You didn't get many like him in a pound. 'What night were yer thinking of, Jenny?'

'How about Saturday?' Jenny had her hands clasped under her chin. 'We could go to the first house, then yer could come back here and have a game of cards. That's if yer mam will have no objections.'

'She won't mind, the only thing is, she likes me to be in by ten o'clock. She doesn't like me being out in the dark on me own, either.'

Bill saw his opening. 'That's all right. I'll pick yer up at ten and walk yer home.'

Janet voiced her surprise. 'What! You go out every Saturday night! The highlight of yer week, that is. It takes yer ten minutes to flatten yer hair with Brylcreem and another ten minutes to polish yer shoes until yer can see yer face in them.'

Bill roared with laughter. 'A bit of an exaggeration, Jan, but I do have a lot of hair to flatten, and I do have big shoes to shine. Anyway, for your information, me and Johnny had decided not to go anywhere this Saturday because we're saving up to have a day in Blackpool. So as we'll be at a loose end, yer'll have two escorts home.'

'Yer can't ask fairer than that, sunshine,' Mary said. 'Grab the offer while yer can.'

'I'll come tomorrow night and we can see what's on that takes our fancy.' Janet didn't want to arrange things now because she had a feeling her brother was up to something. 'I don't want to go to the Atlas, though, 'cos Herbert Marshall's on and I think he's too old to be a heart-throb.' She linked her brother's arm. 'Come on, Bill, let's get going before yer open yer mouth again and we're here all night.'

Jenny stood on the step with her arm across her mother's

shoulders and waved them off. 'I'm glad I went round, Mam, it was lovely being with Janet again.'

'Bill's grown into a fine-looking boy,' Mary said, closing the door. 'Nice with it, too.'

'Yeah, he's a scream the things he gets up to.' Jenny smiled at her father who was hammering studs into the worn-down heel of one of his shoes. 'Still at it, eh, Dad?'

'Cheaper than taking them to the cobbler's, love. These will keep me going for a few months.' He brought the hammer down one more time before laying it on the floor. 'I bet Janet was glad to see yer.'

'Not half as glad as I was to see her. We're going to the pictures on Saturday night, I'm looking forward to that.' Jenny glanced at the clock. She didn't want to be here when Laura came in, didn't want to listen to her telling lies about where she'd been. 'I think I'll hit the hay, the long walk has tired me out.'

'Yer can sit down for five minutes, sunshine, and tell us about Janet's job and what she's been up to. It's only ten past ten.'

With her eyes keeping watch on the hands of the clock, Jenny gave them a much shortened version of the night's events. She ended with a giggle. 'I think Bill was sorry he signed 'cos he was bored rigid. He couldn't understand how me and Jan got a kick out of window shopping. I bet he never asks to come with us again.'

'He's no different to any other man, sunshine, they all hate shopping.'

'Too true!' Stan laughed. 'I tried it once, but never again. Yer wouldn't get me going to the shops with yer mam for a big clock.'

'I love it. I know I'll never be able to buy half the things, but I still like looking.' Jenny got to her feet. 'Anyway, I'm off to bed, I really am tired.' It was half past ten when she kissed her parents and she was praying her sister wouldn't come in before she got up the stairs. 'I'll see yer in the morning, Mam and Dad. Good night and God bless.'

'What time is it?' Laura had her back to the entry wall and she wasn't very happy with the way Jeff was mauling her. She wished she'd insisted on staying with Cynthia now, but the two lads had worked it so they were split up before the girls realised what was happening.

'Don't be worrying about the time, it's only early.' Jeff pressed his body closer and ran his hand down her back and over her buttocks. 'The night is young, yet.'

'It's not for me,' Laura said, trying to push him away. 'I told me mam I'd be in by half past ten. Yer've got a watch on, tell me what the time is.'

'It's too dark to see.' He had made sure they were at the very bottom of the entry, away from the gas-lamp and prying eyes. 'Anyway, why does a girl of eighteen have to be in at that ungodly hour?'

'Because I told me mam I was only going for a walk with me mate and I'd be in by then. She doesn't mind what time I come in as long as she knows not to wait up for me, but I didn't know I was going to meet you, did I?' Laura's worries were increasing by this time. This bloke was a lot older than her and far more worldly. She could handle young lads, they never wanted anything more than a kiss and a cuddle. And she was always in total control. She had the power to manipulate them, and this pleased and excited her. But Jeff, if that was his real name, was a different kettle of fish. He'd been around and wasn't going to settle for a kiss and a cuddle. 'Come on, Jeff, let go of me. Me mam will be worried stiff, not knowing where I am.'

'Yer weren't worrying about her when we picked yer up, were yer? Or when we took yer to the pub for a drink.' Jeff's mood was turning ugly. 'Me and Larry picked you and yer mate up because yer looked like good-time girls. And good-time girls don't have to go running to mammy at half past ten. Don't take me for a sucker, or I'll get angry, and I'm not nice when I'm angry. I didn't spend money on yer just to hold yer hand . . . understand?'

Laura had never been so frightened in her life. Her heart was thumping like mad, and a voice in her head was screaming that he could beat her up and no one would know. She could shout for help, but what if someone called a policeman? they'd ask questions and her mam and dad would find out. She could only try and talk her way out of it. 'Jeff, I know yer spent yer money on me, and I've really enjoyed meself. I do like yer, Jeff, honest. I could meet yer tomorrow night and make up for it. It wouldn't matter what time I got in, 'cos I can tell me parents I'm going to a dance. I could stay out until midnight, then. But if I'm late home tonight me dad will have the police out looking for me.'

It was the final sentence that had Jeff moving back. The last thing he wanted was to have the police after him. His wife wouldn't take kindly to that, and she was tough enough to beat the living daylights out of him. But if there was a chance of getting something back for his money, he was going to take it. 'Yer'll meet me tomorrow night? Is that a promise, or an excuse to get away?'

'No, I want to meet yer! How does eight o'clock outside the Rotunda suit yer?'

'Make it nine, it's nearly dark then. I've no money to be sitting in a pub for an hour.'

'Nine o'clock it is.' It was the last thing she wanted to do, but Laura kissed his cheek. 'I'll have to fly now.'

And fly she did. She couldn't even feel her feet touching the ground. She wondered briefly where Cynthia was, and if she was suffering the same fate, but her own troubles pushed all thoughts of her friend from her mind. Her chest was paining and she was gasping for breath as she neared her street. She paused by the chip-shop window to look at the time on the large round clock on the wall, and sighed with relief. Thank God, she was only going to be ten minutes late.

Before knocking on the front door, Laura ran her fingers through her untidy hair and straightened her rumpled clothing. She'd get upstairs as quickly as she could, her mother had very sharp eyes. And she'd have to watch her parents didn't get near enough to smell her breath.

'Buy yerself a watch, Laura,' Stan said when he opened the door. 'Then yer'll have no excuse for being late.'

Laura passed him with her lips clamped tight. She didn't speak until she was putting her handbag on the sideboard. 'I've been standing outside Cynthia's, nattering. I'm not that late, anyway.'

The red face and the smudged lipstick didn't go unnoticed by Mary. But she didn't want to upset Stan, so she kept her thoughts to herself. She'd have words with Laura tomorrow, and they'd be harsh words. And she'd keep on having harsh words with her until she got it through her daughter's head that her behaviour wasn't acceptable. 'Jenny's not long gone to bed, so if yer go up now it'll save yer disturbing her later.'

'Yeah, okay.' Laura turned her back on them and pretended to be searching in her handbag until the smile of relief left her face. It had been a close one, but she'd got away with it. And next time Cynthia gave the glad-eye to two passing men, she'd make sure they were young enough to be manipulated. 'I'll see yer in the morning. Good night.'

Stan waited until he heard her footsteps on the stairs, then asked, 'Can we believe a word she says? Or am I being bad-minded?'

'I don't know, love, I really don't. All we can do, as we've said before, is to hope she meets a nice boy and settles down. When she does that, you and I can settle down and enjoy a happy old age.'

Stan grinned. 'Blimey, love, I'm only thirty-nine – not ready for the scrap-heap yet. I've still got a lot of life left in me, and if yer want me to, I'll prove it to yer.'

'Yer'll prove it to me! How soft you are! If you want to make love to me, Stan Nightingale, yer'll do it because yer want to, not to prove ye're capable of it.'

'Playing hard to get, eh?' Stan patted his knee and opened his arms wide. 'Come here and I'll show yer how much I want to.'

* * *

Upstairs, Jenny turned her head on the pillow and sniffed up. 'You've been drinking!'

'Go to sleep like the good little girl yer are, and mind yer own business.'

Jenny turned her body over, dug her fists into the mattress and pushed herself up. She couldn't see her sister, but she could smell her. 'Anything that upsets me mam and dad *is* my business. How did yer get in a pub at your age?'

'Don't be stupid, I haven't been in a pub. I don't know why I'm bothering telling yer, 'cos ye're just a snotty-nosed kid, but I had a glass of sherry at Cynthia's. Now, if yer satisfied, can I go to sleep?'

'Have yer been in Cynthia's all night?'

'Why ye're so interested in what I do, is beyond me. But if it'll shut yer up, yes, I've been in Cynthia's all night. We had a game of cards.'

'Ye're a liar, our Laura, a bare-faced liar. And if I didn't know how much it would upset me mam and dad, I'd go right down and tell them.'

'Don't yer dare call me a liar, or I'll belt yer one. When I say I've been in Cynthia's all night, then that's where I've been. Now shut yer face and let's get some sleep.'

'I saw yer down County Road, Laura, so don't come that with me. You and yer dear friend Cynthia, linking arms with two men who looked old enough to be yer fathers. And I wasn't the only one who saw yer, either.'

There was silence for a while, then Laura said in a low voice, 'I suppose ye're going to snitch on me, are yer? Ye're a miserable little squirt, d'yer know that? Yer think because yer work in an office ye're better than anyone else.'

'I don't care what yer think or say about me, Laura. Yer can call me all the names under the sun if yer like, it won't bother me; it never has done.' Jenny wrapped her arms around her legs. 'I used to feel ashamed to say yer were me sister when yer were telling lies in school, or bullying the younger children into giving yer their sweets or pennies. But then I told meself it wasn't my fault if you were a bad 'un, and I kept away from yer. I don't care what yer do, yer can get yerself a bad name if that's what yer want. Why should I worry, yer've never been a proper sister to me. The only person yer think about is yerself. Yer don't even care about our mam and dad, and they're the best mam and dad in the whole world. But I care about them, and I'll do everything I can to stop yer from hurting them. I won't snitch on yer this time, but if I smell drink on yer again, or see yer picking up strange men, then I will tell them. Because they have every right to know what their daughter is up to.'

Jenny slid down under the clothes, turned on her side, and moved as far away from her sister as the bed would allow. But sleep was a long time in coming. Her mam and dad should know what Laura got up to, but she didn't want to be the one to tell them because she knew how hurt they'd be. What should she do for the best? If only she had someone she could confide in, someone who could advise her on what to do.

She heard Laura's gentle breathing and sighed. Here she was, too troubled to sleep, and the cause of the trouble didn't give a damn.

After seeing Stan out, Mary hovered near the kitchen door waiting for Laura to make a move. She was sitting at the table next to Jenny, and the silence between the sisters hung heavy. Breakfast was never the happiest of meals, but today there seemed more tension than usual. The two girls were acting as though they'd had a row and fallen out, but it couldn't be that because Jenny never rowed with anyone. But where was her smile this morning? What had happened to take it away?

Laura pushed back her chair and stood up. Without a word, she picked up her bag and made for the door. But Mary was quick and caught her as she was stepping into the street. 'Just hang on a minute, I want a word with yer.'

Laura's eyes rolled and she pulled a face. 'Not again! Won't it keep until tonight? I've got a job to go to, or had yer forgot?'

'The job will still be there in five minutes' time.' Mary couldn't believe she'd reared a child who would answer her back with such a brazen look on her face. And it was no use boxing her ears, she was too old for that and it would only make her harder. 'Where were you last night?'

'I told yer, I was at Cynthia's! If yer don't believe me, ask her.'

'Oh, and you and yer friend kiss each other, do yer?'

Laura looked at her mother as though she'd gone mad. 'Of course not! What d'yer think we are!'

'Then how did yer face come to be covered in lipstick?'

Laura was startled, caught offguard. But she quickly regained her composure. 'Oh, that! Well, Cynthia had bought three new lipsticks in different colours, and we were trying them out. We wiped our lips with a piece of rag and it must have gone all over the place. Cynthia didn't mention it, and she would have if she'd seen it. But then she wasn't looking for something to pick on me for, was she?'

'The one thing ye're good at Laura, is telling lies. If yer expect me to believe that load of garbage, yer must be crazy. But yer'll come a cropper one of these days, because liars always trip themselves up.'

Jenny came out and stood next to her mother. 'I poured yer a cup of tea out, Mam, and it'll be stiff if yer leave it much longer. Come in and sit down for five minutes, rest yer legs.'

'Yeah, that's right,' Laura sneered. 'Go and sit down and pull me to pieces.'

Jenny gently turned her mother around and pushed her into the living room. Then she looked down on her sister. 'I've got more to do with me time than pull you to pieces. Besides, I wouldn't waste me breath, ye're not worth it.' With her brows raised, she closed the door.

'How did yer get on last night?' Laura asked, when Cynthia opened the door. 'I had one hell of a time.'

Cynthia put a finger to her lips. 'Not a word,' she whispered, her eyes sending warning signals. 'I'll get me coat and we'll go for a walk.'

Arms linked, they walked down the street. When they reached the corner, Cynthia turned to the right, but Laura pulled her back. 'Let's go this way. I'm keeping clear of County Road, and Scotland Road. I promised to meet that bloke tonight by the Rotunda, but there's no fear of that, not after last night.'

Cynthia laughed. 'Got fresh with yer, did he?'

'He was all over me! I've never been so frightened in me life! I honestly thought he'd kill me if I didn't let him do what he wanted. How I talked me way out of it I'll never know.'

'Oh, I quite liked my feller. His hands were all over me, like yer said, but I don't mind that. I get a kick out of seeing them getting themselves all worked up, and their moaning and groaning excites me.' Cynthia's eyes swivelled sideways. 'I'd rather have an older man than the kids we've been going with, they're more experienced.'

'That's the trouble, they're too experienced. They want more off yer, and yer could end up in trouble.'

'No, Larry said there's no chance of that. He's been around, knows all the tricks.'

Laura gasped. 'Yer didn't let him go all the way, did yer?'

Cynthia laughed. 'I might have done, but some drunken man came down the entry and put Larry off his stroke. But I've promised to meet him tomorrow night.'

'Oh Cyn, he's too old for yer! Yer don't know him from Adam, he could be married with a gang of kids for all you know. Once he got what he wanted off yer, yer'd never see him again, and you could end up in the family way.'

'He said I won't come to no harm, he knows what he's doing.'

'Of course he knows what he's doing, every man knows what to do! He's having yer on, playing yer for a fool. I'm surprised at yer, Cyn, I thought yer had more sense.'

'Ooh, ay, listen who's talking! You've been down every entry in the neighbourhood with every boy in the neighbourhood! Now yer've suddenly gone all straitlaced because I've got meself a man.'

'I won't get meself into trouble with the boys I go with. A kiss, a cuddle, and a bit of groping, that's all. And yer can't get a baby doing that.'

'And yer think those boys are going to be satisfied with that? D'yer think they're not going to want more as they grow older?' Cynthia gave a snort of derision. 'One of these days someone will tire of yer leading them on, getting them all worked up and then leaving them swinging. They'll have yer knickers down before yer know what's happening.'

Laura shrugged her shoulders. 'I can look after meself with the lads we know. But I couldn't have looked after meself with that bloke last night. He made no bones about what he wanted and said he'd get angry if he didn't get it. That's why I had to promise to meet him tonight, but he can go and whistle. I wouldn't go through that again for a big clock.'

'Suit yerself, but I'm seeing Larry tomorrow night. So ye're on yer own, kid.'

'I won't be on me own long, don't worry. I can get plenty of fellers.'

'It's only for tomorrow night, I'll see yer on Thursday. I can't see Larry wanting to take me out every night, he won't have the money.' Cynthia sounded cocky. 'And if he doesn't take me for a few drinks first, there's no way he's getting me down a dark entry. What he wants he'll pay for in advance.'

Laura felt a flicker of envy for her friend's bravado. Cynthia was tough, she was afraid of no one. But with the memory of last night still fresh in her mind, Laura wasn't inclined to put herself in that position again. 'I just hope yer know what ye're doing, that's all. If he's anything like his mate, watch out.'

Chapter Nine

'Me mam said I can come here after the pictures on Saturday.' Janet was seated at the table and as she leaned forward the rich auburn shades in her hair were highlighted in the glow from the overhanging gas-light. 'Our Bill's going to pick me up at ten o'clock.'

'That's nice, sunshine, I'll look forward to it.' Mary smiled, remembering the days when this girl used to hold Jenny's hand as they walked to school. She was glad she was back in her daughter's life, she was a good friend to have. 'We're not playing cards for money, though, we're not gambling. So bring some matchsticks with yer.'

'I'll pinch some off me mam.' Janet's cute, pixie-like face was eager. 'She asked why don't yer come round to ours tonight, Jenny? Her and me dad like a game of cards, although I don't know why me dad does 'cos he never wins.' With her eyes twinkling, she rested her chin on her curled fist. 'I think he cheats, so me mam wins. He'll do anything for a quiet life, will my dad. It must be that, nobody could be as unlucky as he makes out.'

'Oh, yes they can, love.' Stan grinned. 'I don't very often have a flutter on the gee-gees, but yer can bet yer sweet life that when I do, my horse will come in last. In fact, me mate at work says he feels sorry for the horses I bet on, they don't stand a chance. He said I'm a jinx and the bookie's runner must rub his hands in glee when he sees me coming.'

'Yer not unlucky in everything, Dad,' Jenny said. 'Yer were lucky in love.'

Stan looked at Mary and grinned. 'Yeah, the luckiest man alive.'

'Is it all right if I go to Janet's for a game of cards, Mam? I'll be back for ten.'

'Of course it is, sunshine. But don't forget to take some matchsticks with yer.'

Laura, who'd been slouched in a chair filing her nails while wondering how Cynthia was getting on, now looked up with interest. 'I'll come with yer. I wouldn't mind a game of cards and it would get me out of the house.'

There was a stunned silence for a few seconds as glances were exchanged. Then Jenny spoke. 'You will not! You've got yer own friend, go down to hers if yer want to go out. Ye're not coming with us and that's all there is to it.' She stood up and jerked her head towards the door. 'Come on, Jan, let's go.'

Janet was off the chair like a shot. She'd been worried there for a minute because she didn't like Jenny's sister. Her mother didn't either, and she'd have laid a duck egg if Laura had walked in with them. And her mother wasn't one for mincing her words. If she thought it, she said it, and didn't care whether you liked it or not.

'Blimey!' Laura said, with a not very pleasant expression on her face. 'Anyone would think I had the flippin' chickenpox, listening to her.'

Jenny was pushing her friend towards the door. 'Yer can have the chickenpox, Laura, and I wish yer well with it. But yer can't have me friend.'

When they got outside, Janet puckered her lips and whistled. 'Me mam often says that some things improve with age, but your sister's not one of them, is she?'

'She's just a show-off, that's all.' Although Jenny agreed, she didn't want to start running her sister down. She linked her friend's arm. 'Ay, me mam got a lovely dress in the sales, and I was going to go into town in me dinner hour and get one. But I got talking to the women in the office and left it too late. I'm going tomorrow though, definitely.'

'I wouldn't mind one meself, but I spend me money as fast as I get it and I'm stony broke. I could try cadging a shilling off me mam, dad and our Bill, though. They're pretty good at slipping me money now and again.' Janet pressed her friend's arm. 'Ay, if they do, will yer come to town with us on Saturday afternoon?'

'Ooh, yeah! That would be great!' The excitement of going into town, shopping for the first time as grown-ups, thrilled them to the core. And they were so engrossed they failed to notice the two boys walking towards them.

'Good evening, Miss Nightingale.' Mick Moynihan's smile was wide, his dimples deep. 'Enjoying the night air, are yer?'

'Yer gave me the fright of me life, Mick, yer daft beggar. And you, John Hanley, why didn't yer whistle or something?'

'Shall we start all over again, then?' John asked, his face straight. 'Like we used to do in school when we were unlucky enough to be picked to play one of the wise men? Me and Mick will walk back six houses, then come towards yer. And if yer keep yer eyes where they should be, yer'll see us coming.'

'It's too late now, yer daft nit, we've already had the fright.' Jenny shook her head, sending her blonde hair swinging across her face. 'Anyway, yer know me friend, don't yer?'

'If me eyes are not deceiving me,' Mick grinned, 'it's little Janet Porter.'

110

'Ay, less of the little, if yer don't mind!' Janet managed to give a good impression of being indignant. 'I'm as tall as Jenny, and I'm a working girl, now.'

'Ye're both right, Mick,' John said, nodding as though he'd given the subject some thought. 'It is little Janet Porter, only she's got big, now.'

'And where are you two pretty maidens off to?' Mick asked.

'We're off to London to see the Queen, kind sir.' Jenny tried to keep the smile back, but out it came to light up her face. 'No, we're going to Jan's to have a game of cards with her mam and dad.'

'We'll walk that far with yer,' Mick said, 'and see yer come to no harm.'

'It's only two streets away, silly,' Jenny tutted. 'We're quite capable of walking that far on our own, yer've no need to bother.'

'Oh, it's no bother,' John was quick to say. 'We've got nothing else to do.'

The two girls began to walk, nudging each other and giggling. They didn't see the scuffle behind them as Mick and John fought to be the one to walk next to Jenny. 'I'm the one who said we'd walk them,' Mick said quietly but firmly, 'so it's only fair that I win. You can try yer luck next time, but yer'll have to be quick.'

So it came about that the two girls were being escorted for the first time in their young lives by two strapping young men. They thought it was a huge joke until John's nosy neighbour, Annie Baxter, came walking towards them. Blushing to the roots of their hair, they lowered their eyes, hoping she didn't stop them. But this little scene was just up Annie's street, too good to miss. She stepped in front of John, barring his path and bringing the line to a halt.

'Going out, are yer, John?'

'Oh, I'm not falling for that one, Mrs Baxter, I'm too old to have me leg pulled.'

Annie's beady little eyes almost disappeared. 'What d'yer mean? I only asked if yer were going out.'

'That's it! There's got to be a catch in it, because anyone can see I can't get any more out than I am now.' He looked along the line. 'All take two steps to the right and we're off.'

Annie Baxter scratched her head as she watched their retreating backs. There was something wrong with that lad, there had to be. Mind you, what could you expect? He was a Hanley and they were all tuppence short of a shilling. Especially the mother. Now if ever there was a headcase, it was Amy Hanley. There were people in the loony bin with a damn sight more sense than she had.

By the time they reached Janet's street, Jenny was feeling embarrassed that neither she nor her friend had opened their mouths. The boys must think they were stupid. So she said the first thing that came into her head – and could have bitten her tongue off afterwards. 'Me and Jan are going to the pictures on Saturday. First house, of course, 'cos me mam wouldn't like me to stay out late.' She groaned inwardly. Now they would think her and Jan were a couple of kids.

'Me and John are going dancing,' Mick said, then chortled loudly. 'I should say we're going to a dance, not that we're going dancing. Neither of us can put one foot in front of the other, so we'll be watching rather than taking part.'

'Ay, you speak for yerself.' John began to roll his shoulders. 'I'm pretty nifty on me feet, if I do say so meself. Yer should see me waltzing down our yard with me mam's brush as a partner. Me mam said I look like a crackpot, but she got her words mixed up. She really meant I looked a treat.'

'Don't yer dare bring that brush to the dance with yer on Saturday,' Mick said, 'even if it can do a nifty waltz.'

'Funny yer should say that.' John stuck his hands in his pockets and looked down at his shoes. ' 'Cos I did think about it. I even put a mobcap of me mam's on its head, and tried to tie a cardigan around it. But it was no good, the cardi kept slipping off. Anyway, me mam said I couldn't borrow it. She said it was a sad state of affairs when the only partner a son of hers could get was a yard brush.'

Jenny giggled. 'I always said yer were as daft as a brush, John Hanley.' Then a dreamy look came over her face. 'I'd love to be able to dance. I'm definitely going to learn when me mam says I'm old enough to be out late.'

'Me too!' Janet sighed blissfully at the thought. 'I'll come with yer.'

The boys exchanged glances. John got in first. 'Ask yer mam if yer can come with us one night. We go to Star of the Sea in Seaforth. It's only a church hall, but they get a good crowd there.'

'Yeah,' Mick wasn't going to be left out, 'they've got a feller on the piano and he can fairly make it talk. It's worth going just to hear him.'

Jenny shook her head. 'Me mam wouldn't let me. Don't forget, I'm only fourteen.'

'We're fourteen and five months, Jenny,' Janet reminded her.

Mick grinned. 'I used to count the months when I was your age. Me mam said I was wishing me life away. Now I'm seventeen, I don't even think about it.' His eyes slid sideways to look at Jenny. 'I'll give yer seven of my months, if yer like. That would make yer fifteen, and yer mam might think that's grown-up enough to come to the dance with us.'

They were standing outside Janet's house talking, when the door opened and Martha Porter appeared on the top step. 'Oh, aye!' she said, her hands on her ample hips. 'You two are starting young, aren't yer?'

112

John gave her a cheeky wink. 'Can yer think of a better time to start, Mrs Porter?'

'No, I can't, lad, but there's young and young. And these two have just come out from under their mother's wing. They're all right with you, I know that, but I didn't recognise yer voices and yer can't be too careful these days.'

'Yer never spoke a truer word, Mrs Porter.' Mick gave her a wide smile. 'We've just been telling the girls the same thing. We said that, if for instance they want to go to the dance at Star of the Sea in Seaforth, then they should go with someone they know, like me and John.'

'You fibber!' Janet said. 'Yer never said any such thing.'

'Well, if he did, he was right.' Martha was quivering with laughter. 'Don't ever go out with strange boys, always get them to call at the house for yer, so the family can give them the once-over.' She looked down as she smoothed the front of her dress so they wouldn't see the smile. 'Mind you, that won't be for a few years yet.'

'Ah, ay, Mam!' Janet was mortified. If her mother had her way, she'd wrap her in cotton wool until she was twenty-one. 'There's girls in work my age, and they go to local hops.'

'Yer live in Kirkdale, queen, and Seaforth's miles away. Yer can't call that a local hop, not by any stretch of the imagination.'

'There's not many places around here, Mrs Porter,' John said. 'Not nice ones, anyway. Unless yer go near town, to the Grafton or the Rialto. And they're more for grown-up experienced dancers. The small hops are better for learners.'

'We'll see when the time comes. Anyway, say good night, girls, or my feller will think I've run off and left him.' Martha Porter gave the boys one of her brightest smiles. 'Thank you for being concerned about the girls' welfare, it's much appreciated. But yer don't have to worry, 'cos the first few dates our Janet goes on, I'll be tagging along to make sure everything is above board.' The wink she gave was so exaggerated it contorted her face and her false teeth became separated from her gums. But Martha didn't mind, she wasn't a vain woman. 'Ta-ra lads, I'll be seeing yer.'

There wasn't a word spoken until she'd passed down the hall and into the living room. Then Mick said, 'I think things look hopeful for yer, Janet. Yer mam wasn't exactly enthusiastic, but she didn't sound dead against the idea.'

'Nah, you don't know me mam. She's frightened of the wind blowing on me. If I sneeze I've got a cold, if I cough I've got pleurisy, and if I say I'm feeling hot then I've definitely got pneumonia and should go to see the doctor.'

'Me mam's the same with our Edna, she doesn't half mollycoddle her. Me and our Eddy don't get a look-in.' John chuckled. 'If I sneezed me mam would tell me to blow me nose. If I coughed she'd tell me to take me germs elsewhere. And the only time I told her I felt hot she poured a cup of cold water all over me.'

Jenny hunched her shoulders as she giggled. 'I can just see your mam doing that. I'll have to remember never to tell her I'm hot.'

Janet pulled on her arm. 'Come on, Jenny, before me mam comes out again.' She smiled at the two boys. 'Ta-ra, we'll see yer.'

'Ta-ra.' Jenny was being tugged up the step. 'See yer soon.'

'Yeah, definitely see yer soon.' The boys waited until the door closed in their faces before walking away. They were quiet for a few minutes, then John said, 'Remember that conversation we had at the party, the Christmas before last?'

'Yer must be a mind-reader,' Mick said. 'I was just thinking about that.'

'Still feel the same about Jenny, do yer?'

'I hate to disappoint yer, John, but my feelings will never change. Jenny's the girl for me, if she'll have me.'

'Well, like I said at the time, all's fair in love and war. So it's a fight to the finish, mate.'

There was a smile on Mick's face when he turned to him. 'Pistols in the park at dawn, is that it? Or would yer prefer swords?'

John returned the smile. 'Words are my choice of weapon, mate. As long as we know where we stand, it's every man for himself.'

'It's not going to stop us being mates, is it?'

'No, of course not. But I've got to tell yer, Mick, I'm a very bad loser.' John punched his friend on the arm and laughed. 'Mind you, I'm not expecting to lose.'

'My God, ye're early this morning, Amy, I'm nowhere near finished me work.' Mary stood aside to let her neighbour in. 'I won't be ready to go to the shops for another hour.'

'I was up before the larks, girl, couldn't sleep. I had me living room done before Ben and the lads got up.' Amy pulled out a chair from the table and sat down heavily. 'I couldn't sit doing nowt until it was time for the shops. Not in that living room of mine – the bleedin' wallpaper gives me the willies. So I thought I'd come and give you the pleasure of me company, and I could sit looking at your wallpaper.'

'Yer'd want something to do to sit and look at that.' Mary waved her arm around the room. 'I can't even remember what the paper was like new, it's been up that long. All I do know is that the background used to be white, not the dirty beige it is now. And the brown flowers used to be a pretty pink.'

'Shall we nag our fellers into decorating, then? They can't moan 'cos it's flaming years since they were done.'

'I don't need to ask Stan, I can decorate meself. I've been using the extra money I get off Jenny to renew me crockery and bedding. And I was going to save up to buy a new fireside chair, that one's on its last legs. But now yer've made me take a good look at the wallpaper, I might do this room first.'

'I'm not as handy as you, I wouldn't know where to start. Anyway, Ben says he wouldn't trust me to put paper up 'cos I'd make a mess of it. He's right, too! Can yer imagine me on the top of a ladder? I'd have more wallpaper stuck to me than was on the wall.'

Mary grinned as she pinched her friend's cheek. 'Let Ben do it, sunshine, I wouldn't rest if I thought yer were perched on top of a ladder without a safety net. Anyway, seeing as yer've made yerself comfortable, I suppose I'd better put the kettle on.'

'I wondered when yer'd get round to it.' Amy followed her friend into the kitchen and leaned against the wall. 'I was just coming out of the door when misery guts came out of hers. I pretended I hadn't seen her, but the nosy cow called me. And yer'll never guess what she was so excited about.' Amy's tummy started to shake, and with it her whole body. 'Hang on till I get meself organised and I'll do the job proper.' She coughed, hunched her shoulders and folded her arms across her chest. Then narrowing her eyes and pressing her lips into a thin line, she put her face close to Mary's. ' "I didn't know your John was courting. He's a bit young for that, isn't he? And the girl only fourteen, that'll lead to trouble, mark my words".'

Mary was chuckling as she poured the boiling water into the teapot. 'That'll be our Jenny she's talking about.'

'Yeah, I saw her passing our window with her mate. And when our John came in he told me him and Mick had met the girls.'

'What did yer say to nosy Annie?'

'Well, I was ready for her, wasn't I, girl? I mean, I'd been pre-warned. So I said I was all in favour of child brides. I said I was hoping our John made me a grandmother by the time he was eighteen.'

Mary's mouth gaped. 'Yer didn't!'

'I bleedin' well did, girl! The nosy cow was asking for it. She wanted some gossip so I gave her some. Made her day, I did – she was over the moon.'

'It'll be all over the neighbourhood by tomorrow.'

'Nah, it won't take her that long. If everyone doesn't know by dinnertime I'll eat me flippin' hat. She couldn't get away from me quick enough. I bet she'd be at Lily Farmer's by the time yer opened the door to me.'

'Which hat will yer eat, sunshine? The one with the big green ostrich feather on, that curls right round under yer chin?'

'No, not that one, girl, I'm hanging on to that.' Amy's face was creased with deep laughter lines. Jokes about this imaginary hat had been going on for years. 'When I'm all on me lonesome, feeling sad and miserable 'cos nobody loves me and I've run out of people to pull to pieces, I put that creation on me head. The ostrich feather tickles me under the chin and in no time at all I'm laughing me bleedin' head off.'

Mary lifted the two cups of tea and nodded towards the door. 'Go on, and I'll bring these through. And I think I've just got two custard creams left.'

'Ay, this is the life, isn't it, girl? Ladies of leisure.' Amy picked up her cup by the handle as though it was delicate porcelain, and stuck her little finger out. 'This is how the posh people hold their cups, girl, did yer know?'

'I'll have to take your word for it, sunshine, 'cos I haven't got any posh friends.'

'Neither have I, girl, but yer know, it's funny how I seem to know how they behave. I think hundreds of years ago my ancestors must have been very rich because I've always felt I was destined for a better life than this.' Amy's chubby fingers were having difficulty holding the handle of the cup so she reverted to curling her hands around it. 'I wouldn't be surprised if they'd been of the nobility.'

'Somebody must have squandered all the money, sunshine, for you to end up in a two-up two-down terrace house in a cobbled street in Kirkdale.'

'I know, girl. Someone's got a lot to answer for, dragging me down from riches to rags. One of me great-great uncles must have been a bugger for wine, women and song, and spent me bleedin' inheritance enjoying himself.'

The two women looked at each other across the table and burst out laughing. 'Ye're two sheets to the wind, Amy Hanley, but if thinking these things keeps yer happy, then you just carry on,' Mary said. 'But can we forget yer fancies for now, and see what we can do to repair the damage yer've caused?'

'What damage, girl? I haven't done no damage.'

'I'm talking about Annie Baxter.'

'Annie Baxter! I didn't do her no damage, I didn't lay a finger on her.'

'Amy, will yer be serious for once? I know most people will take what she says with a pinch of salt, but there's some bad-minded folk around here who'd believe her because they want to.'

'Believe what, girl?'

Mary blew out her breath in frustration. 'What yer told her about yer wanting your John to make yer a grandmother by the time he's eighteen.'

'Is that what the cow is saying? Well, she's a bleedin' liar, and if I get me hands on her I'll break her scrawny neck.'

'But yer told me yer did say it.'

'Yeah, well, I told you 'cos ye're me mate. But I haven't told no one else. And if anyone mentions it, I'll say she's a bleedin' liar and I'll have her up for slander.'

'I give up on yer, I really do. Just don't get me involved, that's all. And don't yer dare mention it to your John, either. You might think it's funny but I don't think he'd appreciate being the butt of one of yer jokes. He's a nice lad and I wouldn't want to see him embarrassed or upset. He'd be frightened of showing his face in the street.'

Amy's face was dead serious. 'Yeah, well, it stands to sense he would be, if it was true.'

Mary stared, unblinking, for several seconds. Then she said, 'It's like leading a lamb to the slaughter, isn't it? Proper muggins, I am. But how was I to know that even you, with all the tricks yer get up to, would make up such a tale?'

'I didn't make it all up, girl.' Amy looked really put out. 'Annie Baxter did stop me, and she did say what I told yer. I only made up the bit about what I said to her to give yer a laugh. But ye're not laughing, are yer, girl?'

'I'll make up me mind when yer tell me what yer really did say to her. And can we have the truth, this time, please?'

'Oh, yeah!'

'Go on, then.'

'Go on what, girl?'

'So help me, Amy, I'll flatten yer in a minute. What did yer say to Annie Baxter?'

'I've just told yer!' Amy was red in the face. ' "Oh, yeah," that's what I said to the nosy bleedin' cow. Yer didn't think I was going to be all matey and hold a conversation with the woman, did yer? I can't stand the sight of her, she gets on me wick.'

'Well, before I split me sides laughing, can I just ask yer never to say anything like that in front of my girls? Or your kids for that matter.'

Amy's cheeks moved upwards and there was a glint of devilment in her eyes. 'Now, as if I would do that, girl.'

Jenny was bursting with excitement as she ran into the kitchen waving a paper bag. 'Mam, wait until yer see me dress, it's out of this world.'

Mary turned the gas low under the frying pan. 'Keep away from here, sunshine, the fat's spurting out all over the place. Let's go in the living room, otherwise yer dress will be ruined before yer've even had it on.'

'I knew as soon as I set eyes on it that it was the one I wanted.'

117

The words poured out as Jenny took the dress from the bag. 'I didn't look at any other, I really fell for this one.'

'Oh, sweetheart, what a beautiful colour.' Mary's heart filled with love and pride as her daughter held the dress in front of her, her eyes bright with happiness. In a shade of mauve, the dress had three-quarter sleeves, a plain round neck, was shaped to the hips then fell in soft folds. 'It'll go lovely with yer blonde hair.'

'I'm dead chuffed with meself, Mam, honest. The women in work were pulling me leg because I've had a smile on me face all afternoon.'

'That beats having a face on yer like a wet week, sunshine.' Mary smiled, delighted to see her daughter so happy. 'Yer did well, it's a lovely dress.'

'I can't wait to show it to Janet.' Jenny folded the dress carefully and put it back in the bag. 'I asked the woman who served me if they'd still have some on Saturday when we go into town, and she said it was more than likely.'

Laura stood in the hall listening. She'd come through the door Jenny had left open in her haste to show off her dress, and heard every word. Her top lip curled as, under her breath, she mimicked her mother's voice. 'Oh, sweetheart, what a beautiful colour. It'll go lovely with yer blonde hair.' They'd make you sick, fussing over a five and eleven dress. To listen to them talk, anyone would think she'd gone to Lewis's and paid a fortune for it.

Afraid that her father might come in and catch her, Laura pushed the living-room door open and walked through as though she'd just come in. 'Yer want to be careful in future, leaving that front door wide open. Anyone could walk in.'

'I must have forgot, I was in such a hurry.' Jenny smiled at her sister. 'D'yer want to see me new dress, Laura?'

As Jenny bent her head to open the bag, Mary caught the expression on Laura's face and felt a cold hand cup her heart. She'd always known her eldest daughter held no affection for her sister, but what she saw in the brown eyes that were staring at Jenny's bent head frightened her. She doesn't like her, Mary thought. Her own sister and she doesn't even like her.

'Don't bother getting it out,' Laura said, 'I'll see it when yer've got it on.' She ignored the hurt in Jenny's eyes and turned to her mother. 'Will the dinner be long, Mam? I promised to go down to Cynthia's early.'

'I'll put it out when yer dad gets in, and not before.' Mary felt like taking her by the shoulders and giving her a good shake. Why did she always put a damper on things when someone was happy? 'We eat together, not in dribs and drabs.'

Laura tossed her head. 'Well, I hope he puts a move on.'

118

'Whether he puts a move on or not, we wait for him.' Mary went into the kitchen and vented her sadness, anger and frustration on the pan lid. She'd bent over backwards with Laura to form the same loving bond there was between her and Jenny. Her youngest daughter always showed her love with spontaneous hugs and kisses, both to her and Stan. But Laura didn't welcome, or give, hugs and kisses. She didn't join in the light-hearted conversations that went on around the table when they were having their meals, and when she did smile there was no warmth in it.

Mary heard Stan's voice and reached up to take four plates from the shelf. And as she spooned mashed potato on to the plates, her mind went back to when Laura was a child. She'd been less than eighteen months old when Jenny was born, and although Mary had her hands full she'd always tried to share her time between the two children so Laura wouldn't think her nose was being pushed out. Stan made a great fuss of her for the same reason, but his over-indulgence was a source of worry and caused arguments between man and wife. Still, lots of children were spoilt by doting parents, but they didn't grow up to be surly, impudent and lacking in humour.

Stan came up behind her and put his arms around her waist. 'All right, love?'

She took a deep breath. There was no point in passing her anxiety on to Stan; it wouldn't solve anything and would only worry him needlessly. So when she twisted her head, there was a smile on her face. 'Everything's under control, sunshine.'

He tightened his hold, pulling her closer. Kissing her neck, he murmured, 'When I hold yer like this, I'm not in control.'

Mary slapped his hands which were laced together across her waist. 'Give over, soft lad.' Her eyes darted to the living-room door, afraid the girls might have heard. 'There's a time and place for everything, and this is neither.' She relaxed a little, her body enjoying the nearness of him. She loved him as much now as she had the day she'd walked down the aisle on her father's arm and Stan, standing in the front pew with his best man, had turned his head. His eyes had been full of admiration and love, and she recalled now how that look had chased away the butterflies in her tummy. So when she looked up at him, her eyes were bright and teasing as he nuzzled her neck. 'But if you've got the time, big boy, I know the place.'

He nipped her ear gently before releasing her. 'The girls have said they're going out at half seven. After that I'm all yours.'

Cynthia put a finger to her lips before closing the door behind her. 'Not a word until we're out of earshot.'

Laura linked her arm and contained her curiosity until they turned the corner of the street. 'Well, how did yer get on?'

119

'What d'yer mean, how did I get on?' Cynthia stared straight ahead. 'I met Larry and we went for a drink.'

'And after that, what did yer do?'

Cynthia shrugged her shoulders. 'Went somewhere dark for a kiss and a cuddle.'

'Oh, come off it, Cyn, yer got more than a kiss and a cuddle. He's not going to spend money on yer just for that. Yer did promise to tell me all.'

'Larry gave me a message for yer, from Jeff. He wants to see yer again. I'm meeting Larry on Friday night, and he's asked me to bring yer along one night to make a foursome.'

Laura pulled her to a halt. 'Not bloomin' likely! I'm not seeing him again, he frightened the life out of me. If I ever set eyes on him I'll run a mile.'

When Cynthia turned to her friend, there was a look of scorn on her face. 'Ye're not half childish, Laura. Yer let young lads kiss yer, but when it comes to a grown man, yer run scared, like a little rabbit.'

'That Jeff was after more than a kiss, and you know it. And that goes for his mate, Larry. Yer can't tell me he didn't try anything.'

'He didn't do anything I didn't want him to do, and that's all I'm telling yer. I'm still here, aren't I, and still in one piece. And if I didn't like it, well, I wouldn't be seeing him again. He's a real man, not like the kids we've been knocking around with.'

'Ay, yer didn't tell him where we lived, did yer?'

Cynthia shook her head. 'No, me dad would have a fit if he turned up on the doorstep. But I'm not stopping seeing him, I don't care what anyone says. And if you had any sense, yer'd come with us and make up a foursome, with Jeff. Start living, kid, instead of messing around with kids. Honest, yer don't know what ye're missing.'

Laura was torn. If she didn't go, she risked losing the only friend she had. But she didn't like the idea of being down a dark entry with Jeff. 'I'm not saying I'll come, like, but if I did, would we stay together? Not split up like we did last time?'

Cynthia turned her head so Laura didn't see the gloating in her eyes. She knew she'd be able to talk her friend round. Like she'd told Larry, Laura wouldn't want to miss out on anything. 'No, we won't split up.'

Still Laura wasn't convinced. 'I will come, but not for a week or two. I'll see how you get on first, and if ye're still seeing Larry in two weeks I'll come with yer. But I'll bet yer any money he's married with a few kids. He's too old to be single.'

'So what? I don't care if he's got dozens of kids, as long as I'm enjoying meself. From now on that's going to be my motto in life. Get as much out of it as I can and to hell with everyone.'

120

'Yeah, I agree with yer,' Laura said. 'That'll be my motto, too. So yer can tell Larry to pass the message on to his friend. I'll come with yer one night the week after next, as long as we all stick together.'

Chapter Ten

'Sixteen tomorrow, eh, Laura?' Stan smiled across the breakfast table. 'Ye're a young lady now.'

'Does that mean I can stay out later?' Laura spread the jam liberally on her toast. 'I'd like to go to second-house pictures, or go dancing, and yer can't do either when yer eyes are on the clock all the time.'

Mary came through from the kitchen with a fresh pot of tea. 'Me and yer dad have talked about this, and yer can stay out until eleven as long as yer tell us where ye're going.'

'Yeah, I'll do that.' Laura wagged her shoulders from side to side, looking very pleased with herself. 'That's the gear, that is.'

'Would yer rather we bought yer a present, or gave yer the money?' Mary sat down next to Stan, facing her daughters. 'It's up to you.'

'Ooh, I'll have the money, please.' Laura's green eyes were shining. 'How much?'

'Half-a-crown off me, half-a-crown off yer dad, and a shilling off Jenny. That's six bob, so yer should be able to buy yerself something nice.'

'Yer could try T.J. Hughes, Laura,' Jenny said, 'they might have some of those dresses left from the sale.'

Laura didn't bother turning her head to look at her sister. 'I'm going to save up for a winter coat. The one I've got is all right to go to work in, but I'd be ashamed to go anywhere nice in it. Cynthia's got a new one, and I look like a tramp next to her.'

Mary had seen Cynthia's mother at the shops yesterday, and if anyone looked like a tramp it was that poor woman. The coat she had on looked as though it had been a dark green at one time, but it was faded with age and frayed at the cuffs and pockets. While Cynthia was forever getting new clothes, her mother always looked shabby and down-at-heel. And she never spoke to a soul, not even to pass the time of day. Most of the neighbours had given up on her and never bothered to let on, but Mary felt sorry for her and never passed her without a nod or a smile of acknowledgement. However now wasn't the time to voice her thoughts on Cynthia's hard-done-by mother. She'd gone out of her way to be nice to Laura over the last week or so, and she didn't want to spoil things by criticising her

123

friend and chance a row developing. 'That's a very sensible idea, sunshine, because the winter is setting in now.'

'And I'm putting all me pocket-money away every week until I've got enough saved up.' Laura piled it on, thinking how easy it was to fool her parents. It would be no hardship to her to save her money, she never went anywhere without a boy paying for her. All she ever bought for herself was make-up, and she wouldn't be doing that for long. Staying out late meant she could go to dances and meet someone with enough money to buy her presents. 'Me and Cynthia are going to stay in every night, playing cards, or perhaps going for walks, so it'll only be a couple of weeks before I have enough saved for a coat.'

Stan raised his brows at Mary as he pushed his chair back, and she knew he was asking if this was the turning point, that their daughter was at last growing up. She answered with a smile, and a shrug which said not to bank on it, because only time would tell.

'I'm on me way, love.' Stan bent to kiss her cheek. 'Don't bother coming to the door with me, finish yer tea. I'll see yer tonight.'

'Don't forget, all three of yer, I want the dinner over as soon as possible tonight. I'm starting to scrape the wallpaper off, and Amy and Mrs Moynihan are coming to give me a hand. All the furniture has to be pulled away from the walls before they come.'

'Me and Janet will give yer a hand, Mam,' Jenny said. 'We're not going anywhere.'

'I'd offer to help,' Laura was thinking of her birthday money, 'but I've promised to see Cynthia and she'll expect me. If yer want me to, though, I could slip down and tell her I can't make it.'

'No, I want yer both out of the way. The place will be crowded as it is.' Habits died hard with Mary, and she couldn't let her husband go without seeing him to the door and waving him off. And as she followed him into the hall, she added, 'I'll have yer dad here, he'll be getting stuck in, same as the rest of us.'

Stan laughed as he stepped into the street. 'Yer don't really want me here, not with three jabbering women, do yer? Why don't I go for a pint with Seamus and I'll be out from under yer feet?'

'How soft you are, Stan Nightingale! Me and me mates slaving away, while you and Seamus Moynihan prop the bar up!'

'Okay, love, but it was worth a try.'

'I was only pulling yer leg, sunshine. Of course yer can go for a pint, as long as yer don't come staggering home, singing at the top of yer voice.'

Stan was chuckling as he walked away. 'That'll be the day.'

'Sure, I'll come and give yer a hand, so I will.' Seamus pushed his plate away and rubbed his tummy.' That was altogether a fine meal, me darlin', fit for a king and no mistake. Not another bite could I eat, I'm full to the brim.'

'I'll bet if anyone offered yer a pint, yer'd not be too full for that.' Molly gazed with satisfaction at her husband's empty plate. Clean as a whistle, it was. Sure, wasn't he a great man to feed, eating everything you put down before him? 'I'd like to see the day when Seamus Moynihan refused a pint.'

'I'd have to be offered one to refuse it, me darlin', and I don't hear yerself offering.'

'I'm not, no, 'cos I've got better things to do with me money. But Stan Nightingale has offered. According to Mary, he's terrified of being alone with a gang of women.'

'I'll not be blaming the man, for it's a frightening prospect, so it is. And I'll not be letting a mate down in his hour of need.'

Mick, who had been listening with interest, wiped the back of his hand across his mouth. 'That was really tasty, Mam, I didn't half enjoy it.'

'It does me heart good to know that, son.' Molly stood up and began to gather in the plates. 'I'll get these washed and then take meself over the road.'

'I'm not doing anything tonight, Mam, I could give a hand stripping the walls.'

'What! A young lad with a gang of old women? Yer'd be bored stiff in ten minutes, me darlin', so yer would.'

'Jenny's not an old woman, Mam.'

'Jenny! What's Jenny got to do with it?'

When Mick smiled, his eyes twinkled, his teeth shone and his dimples deepened. 'Well, it's like this, Mam. I'm waiting for her to grow up so I can ask her to be me girlfriend. And I just thought that rather than waste me time while I'm waiting, I could put it to good use by getting to know her better.'

Seamus let his head drop back and roared with laughter. 'It's good taste yer have, son, and it's right that yer don't let the grass grow under yer feet.'

Molly plonked herself down again. 'If Mary Nightingale could hear you two, she'd box yer ears for yer. The girl's only fourteen, for heaven's sake!'

'Fourteen and seven months, to be exact, Mam.' Mick's grin didn't falter. Nothing was going to put him off. 'I'm waiting until she's fifteen, then I'll ask her mam and dad if I can take her to the pictures.'

'D'yer not think it would be better to ask the girl herself, first?' Seamus asked, highly amused. 'Unless it's her mother yer want to take to the pictures.'

'Seamus Moynihan, don't yer be putting ideas into the boy's head. Jenny's a lovely girl and I'm very fond of her, but she's only fourteen.'

Molly leaned over and patted her son's hand. 'Bide yer time, sweetheart, let her grow up a bit first.'

'It's a short memory yer have, me darlin',' Seamus said, a loving smile on his face. 'Sure, how old were you when I started calling on yer?'

'I was older than Jenny is,' Molly said, blushing. 'Quite a bit older.'

'It's forgetful ye're getting in yer old age, me darlin', because yer were fourteen when we started walking out together. I remember it as clear as anything. My mother told me to wait, like ye're telling Mick, here. But I wasn't having any of that, indeed I wasn't. Yer were the prettiest girl in the village and I wasn't going to take a chance on another boy coming along and claiming yer for himself.'

Molly had a faraway look in her eyes as memories came flooding back. If the young, handsome Seamus Moynihan hadn't made the first move, sure wouldn't she have thrown all caution to the wind and made it herself? There'd been plenty of lads giving her the eye, right enough, but there was only one she ever wanted. The first time he'd looked into her eyes he'd stolen her heart, and it was still in his possession.

'Haven't yer always said, Mam, that I take after me dad?' Mick took advantage of the situation. 'Well, this proves how right yer were.'

Molly tutted as she pushed herself to her feet. 'So the two men in me life are taking sides against me, eh? Well, I'll have no part of it, me lips stay sealed.'

'Could yer not open them a little bit and put in a good word for me?' Mick grinned. 'Tell Mrs Nightingale I come highly recommended by yerself? Yer could drop little hints, like what a good bloke I am, and how handy I am around the house. I mean, yer could even go as far as to say I'd make someone a good husband.'

Molly was chuckling silently as she made her way to the kitchen door. There she turned, and said, 'Yer've cheek enough for anything, so yer have, Michael Moynihan. I'd not be surprised if yer didn't ask me to propose to Jenny for yer.'

'Oh, I've a long way to go before then, Mam. But I'll certainly bear yer offer in mind 'cos I might just need a bit of help. Especially as John Hanley has his eye on her as well, and he has the advantage of living next door to her.'

Molly put the dishes on the drainboard then stood for a while, deep in thought. They'd been pulling her leg and she'd fallen for it like a ton of bricks. She should have had more sense, knowing Mick was as bad as his father for acting daft. So she walked back into the living room with her hands on her hips. 'I've a good mind to turn the tables on yer, Mick Moynihan, and tell Mary all yer've said.'

'Oh yes, please, Mam! I knew yer wouldn't let me down. Yer see, if I don't pull me socks up, John will get in before me and I won't stand a chance.' Mick's grin was wide. 'For all I know, they might be tapping messages to each other through the bedroom wall.'

Molly shook her head. 'The joke's over now, me darlin', so let it rest. But yer had me going for a while, I have to admit.'

'Mam, it wasn't a joke, I've never been more serious in me life. I want Jenny Nightingale to be me girlfriend, and when we're older, I want her to be me wife.'

Molly looked across at Seamus. 'Is he having me on?'

'I'd say he was very serious, me darlin', and I have to say I'm altogether surprised that yer haven't noticed how often he stands at the window waiting for Jenny to put in an appearance. He's fair smitten with the girl, so he is.'

'He'll get fair smitten if Mary or Stan hear about it. And what's this about John? He's yer best mate!'

'I know he's me best mate, Mam, but not where Jenny's concerned. We've both agreed that it's every man for himself, and may the best man win. And I'm sure yer wouldn't like yer son to be anything but the best, would yer? I mean, there's such a thing as family pride, blood being thicker than water, and all that.'

'I'm fair flummoxed, and that's putting it mildly,' Molly said. 'Are yer telling me that John has his eye on Jenny, and he knows you do, too?'

'Yeah, I told him ages ago. In this very house, in fact.'

'And what did he say to that?'

'Told me to get in the queue.' Mick's laugh ricocheted off the walls. 'But I told him there was no queue, we stood side by side at the starting line.'

'I give up.' Molly glanced at the clock and tutted. 'I'm leaving you two to wash the dishes, I should be over the road by now, they'll think I'm not coming.' She got to the door and hesitated. 'Any boy who needs his mother's help to get a girl, Mick Moynihan, doesn't deserve her, and that's the truth of it.' With those parting words, she banged the front door behind her and hurried across the cobbles chuckling to herself. Sure, wouldn't she be the happiest woman in the world to have Jenny Nightingale for a daughter-in-law?

'Amy, for heaven's sake will yer be careful on that ladder?' Mary's heart was in her mouth as she watched the ladder swaying. 'Come on down and I'll scrape the top half while you do the bottom. I'm not getting anything done for keeping me eyes on you. Yer've got me a nervous wreck.'

'I'm all right, girl, honest!' Pressing a hand against the wall for support, Amy turned. With a broad grin on her chubby face, she winked. 'If I did fall, girl, I'd only bounce back up again.'

Mary screwed her eyes up tight and scratched her nose. 'Molly, will yer just look at the state of this one. Her face is filthy, there's bits of wallpaper stuck in her hair, the top button on her dress has come off and she's showing all she's got. It's a good job the men have gone out otherwise I wouldn't know where to put me face.'

Glad of the break, Molly came to stand next to Mary. 'Sure, if the men knew what they were missing, they'd be home like a shot, so they would. There's not many women got as much to show as Amy has, she's certainly well endowed, right enough.'

When Amy squared her shoulders the ladder swayed precariously and both women ran forward to steady it. 'What d'yer mean, Molly Moynihan, about me being well endowed?'

'She means yer've got a big bust, soft girl, and yer not half showing it.' Mary tugged on Amy's skirt. 'Come down and set me mind at rest.'

'The only thing that'll bring me down this ladder is a cup of tea.' Amy pursed her lips and nodded. 'Ye're a lousy boss, Mary Nightingale, yer don't look after yer workers proper.' Gripping the sides of the ladder like grim death, and testing each rung before putting her full weight on it, she came down slowly. 'Get that bleedin' kettle on, girl, before I clock yer one.'

'A fifteen-minute break, that's all we're having.' Mary wagged a finger in front of her friend's nose. 'Yer don't leave her tonight until all these walls are stripped.'

'Ye're a hard woman, Mary Nightingale,' Amy shouted after her. 'Ye're worse than the priest in Saint Anthony's – at least he only gives yer six Hail Marys. Ten minutes and yer've paid for yer sins and all is forgiven.'

'That's because yer only tell him the little sins. If yer told him what yer really get up to, yer'd still be saying yer prayers when they closed the church and yer'd be locked in.'

'Ay, now, girl, we'll have less of that! I may be big in the bust, but me lies are only ever little white ones.'

'I'll believe yer where thousands wouldn't.' Mary grinned as she made her way to the kitchen. And after striking a match under the kettle, she leaned against the sink and listened to her two neighbours.

'Ay, Molly,' Amy asked, 'does well endowed apply to all women with big breasts?'

'Well, now, me darlin', it doesn't only apply to them. People can be endowed in many ways. With a good figure, nice hair, caring nature and good sense of humour.'

'But it means big, doesn't it? Like my breasts?'

'I suppose yer could say that, me darlin', loosely speaking, of course.'

'Then my Ben is well endowed, too! He's—'

Amy's words were cut off when Mary's hand covered her mouth. She'd had a feeling her friend was going to come out with something outrageous and she'd shot out of the kitchen like a streak of greased lightning. 'Don't you dare, Amy Hanley, don't you dare.'

Amy's eyes were wide and innocent. Brushing her friend's hand away, she asked, in injured tones, 'In the name of God, girl, what's this in aid of? I haven't said nothing wrong.'

'No, but yer were going to. I know you, Amy Hanley, and I wouldn't trust yer as far as I could throw yer. D'yer want to shock Molly to the core?'

'I don't know what ye're on about, girl! All I said was that my Ben is well endowed. I can't see nothing in that to shock Molly – especially to the bleedin' core.'

'Well, just leave it at that, sunshine, 'cos we don't want to know how, when or where, your Ben is well endowed. Keep yer bedroom secrets to yerself.'

Amy's tummy was rumbling with laughter but she managed to keep a straight face. 'Oh, my Ben's not only well endowed in the bedroom, girl, he's the same everywhere he goes. I mean, I can't help it if I've got big breasts, no more than he can help what the Good Lord granted him. And fair's fair, girl, credit where it's due. There's not a man in this street who's got a bigger nose than my Ben.'

Amy's eyes went from Mary to Molly, waiting for their reaction. And when the laughter came it nearly lifted the roof. Mary held her tummy as she doubled up, tears running down her cheeks, while Molly, head back and loud guffaws coming from her open mouth, beat her fists on the arms of the chair. 'Glory be to God,' she gasped, 'have yer ever in yer whole life met a woman like her?'

'Ay, there's nowt wrong with me, Molly Moynihan, me mind's as pure as a baby's. But you two, well . . . yer've got minds like muck-middens. Dirty pair of buggers, that's what yer are. Just wait until I tell my Ben yer were making fun of his nose.'

Mary reached into the pocket of her pinny for a handkerchief. She gave her nose a good blow before saying, 'And just wait until I tell my Stan we couldn't get any work done for you talking the legs off us. We'll never get this room finished tonight.'

'Oh now, have faith, me darlin',' Molly said. 'You see to that pot of tea while me and Amy go at it like the clappers. These walls will be stripped before the men come home, so they will. Even if we die in the attempt.'

'Ooh, ay, I don't like the sound of that,' Amy said. Her lips were pursed as she shook her head, her legs dangling six inches from the floor. 'I don't mind going like the clappers, I'll pull me weight as good as the next one. But I don't fancy this dying in the attempt lark. I knew a woman once who said that, and d'yer know what happened to her? She died, that's what! And she stayed dead, into the bargain.

129

I don't fancy that happening to me, not when I've just joined the ranks of the well endowed.'

Mary jumped to her feet. 'Oh God, she's off again! Get cracking, Amy Hanley, and not another word out of you until we're finished.'

'Not even to say "thank you" for the cup of tea? If we ever bleedin' get one.' Amy winked. 'Okay, okay, I'm starting. And I'll work that bloody fast yer won't see me arms moving. You just watch, girl, I'll make Buster Keaton look as though he's standing still and the Keystone Cops are closing in on him.'

Cynthia closed the door behind her and linked her arm through Laura's as they set off down the street. 'Where shall we go?'

'*The Prisoner of Zenda* is on at the Atlas, and one of the women in work said it's marvellous. Thrilling, frightening and dead sad. We'd be in time for the big picture if we hurry.'

Cynthia pulled a face. 'I'm not in the mood for crying or sitting with me eyes closed all night. Couldn't we go and see a comedy?'

'It won't make yer cry, soft girl, it's only a picture. Anyway, we could stay on and see the shorts, there's bound to be something on to make yer laugh.'

'Oh, all right.' Cynthia gave in because she had other things on her mind. 'Ye're still coming with me tomorrow night, to meet Larry and Jeff, aren't yer?'

Laura took a deep breath. She'd been dreading this. 'I can't come with yer, not tomorrow, anyway. It's me birthday and me mam's making a little tea for me, just for a couple of the neighbours and John Hanley and Mick Moynihan.'

Cynthia pulled her to a halt. 'Yer gave me yer word that yer'd come! Ye're not backing out now, Laura Nightingale, or I'll never speak to yer again. I'd look a right fool, telling Jeff yer've gone to a kids' tea-party. He'll think we're giving him the round-around, and he won't be very happy – neither will Larry.' Her face like thunder, Cynthia began to walk away. 'If yer don't come with me tomorrow night, then we're finished. Please yerself.'

Laura hesitated for a few seconds before hurrying to catch up with her friend. What was the point of telling a lie to get out of something she didn't want to do, when she was going to have to tell another one next week? 'Cynthia, don't let's fall out over it.'

'You're the one that's falling out, not me,' Cynthia answered, keeping up the fast pace. 'Real friends don't make promises and then break them. And all for the sake of a stupid flaming party! What a lame excuse that is.'

'There is no party, that was a lie.'

The words brought Cynthia to an abrupt halt. 'So, ye're coming tomorrow night, after all?'

Laura shook her head. 'No, not tomorrow night nor any other night. I've tried to talk meself into it because ye're me mate and I didn't want to let yer down. But I don't want to see Jeff again because he scares me. He's too old for me, same as Larry is too old for you. They've both been around and are out for what they can get. A glass of sherry and then down a dark entry with any woman who's daft enough to go with them. On their way home to their wives and kids, they probably laugh themselves sick over how easy some girls are.'

'You speak for yerself, Laura Nightingale. Anyone would think yer were an angel, to hear yer talk. And I'm not just any woman to Larry; he really likes me, so there.'

'If he likes yer that much, he'd have told yer all about his family and where he lives. But I bet he hasn't.' When her friend didn't answer, Laura persisted. 'Well, has he?'

'What's it got to do with you? I don't have to tell you nothing.'

'No, yer don't, Cynthia. You do what yer want to do. If yer want to go out with Larry, then you do that. But don't expect me to go out with someone I don't like, just to please yer. All yer've got to do is to tell Jeff that I've got a boyfriend now. He can't argue with that, can he? And if he does get a cob on, so what? There's plenty of girls about, let him find one for himself instead of pestering me through you. I don't like him, I think he could be dangerous if he didn't get his own way, and he hasn't got a snowball's chance in hell of getting me down an entry ever again.'

'Well, I think ye're dead mean. It wouldn't hurt yer to come with me just this once, to save me looking a fool. I'd never ask yer again. Anyway, yer could tell Jeff yerself that yer've got a boyfriend and that would put a stop to him asking Larry all the time.'

'No, Cynthia,' Laura said, noting the petulant droop of her friend's lips. She was like a baby who couldn't get her own way. 'It's you that's mean, not me. Ye're trying to talk me into something yer know I don't want to do. I told yer how rough and bad-tempered Jeff was, and how he scared the life out of me, but ye're still trying to talk me into seeing him again. That's being selfish, that is, and not something yer'd do if yer were a real friend. So, if yer think more of Larry than yer do of me, then we'd better go our separate ways.' Laura wrapped her coat more tightly around her slim body to keep out the cold wind that was blowing in from the Mersey. 'Yer don't want to see *The Prisoner of Zenda*, so I'll go on me own and you can please yerself.' With that she set off down the street, the click of her high heels on the pavement breaking the silence.

'It's no skin off my nose,' Cynthia shouted after her. 'I don't need you to hold me hand, I'll be better off without yer.' But it was all bravado. She'd thought she could talk Laura around if she kept on at her, but it hadn't worked. And now she'd lost the only girlfriend she'd ever had. It was a stupid thing to fall out over, too! All because of Jeff, whom she didn't much like herself, either! He certainly wasn't worth losing a friend over.

Laura had turned the corner of the street when Cynthia caught up with her. 'It's daft to fall out over a feller, kid, there's none of them worth it.' She linked her arm through her friend's and pulled her close. 'Let's forget it, eh? I'll tell Jeff ye're courting strong and that's the end of the matter. You and me are still best mates, aren't we?'

'Yeah, of course we are.' Laura gave a sigh of relief. Being allowed to stay out until eleven meant she could go to places that were out of bounds to her before, and she'd set her heart on going dancing. But she didn't fancy doing it on her own. 'How about going somewhere exciting on Saturday?'

'Such as where?'

'I'd like to go dancing. Some of the girls in work go, and they don't half enjoy themselves. There's two or three dance halls not that far from here – a couple of stops on the tram, that's all. And it's only a tanner to get in, which includes tea and biscuits.'

'I can't dance for toffee, and neither can you!'

'There's a first time for everything, kiddo, and if we never try we'll never learn.' Laura's voice was filled with excitement. 'We can watch for a while, then have a go ourselves.' She chuckled as she squeezed her friend's arm. 'You can be the man.'

'How soft you are! You look more like a man than I do.' But Laura's excitement was contagious and Cynthia found herself warming to the idea. 'Yeah, we'll give it a whirl, eh? Who knows, we might get two fellers willing to teach us.'

'That is the general idea,' Laura said. 'The fellers will be older than the kids we've been hanging about with. I don't know about you, but I'm hoping for someone who is tall, blond and as handsome as a film star.'

'I want mine to have something more than that, kid. I want a man with loads of money who isn't too mean to spend it. Someone who'll show me a good time and take me places.'

'Yeah, me too.' Laura fished a silver sixpence out of her pocket as they neared the Atlas. 'I won't see yer tomorrow night, with yer meeting Larry, but I'll call the next night and we can talk about what we'll wear and how we'll do our hair.' She held out her hand for Cynthia's money and passed the two sixpences to the girl in the ticket kiosk. 'Two fourpenny ones, please.' As they entered the darkness of the cinema, she handed Cynthia's change over and whispered, 'I can't wait for Saturday to come, me tummy's turning over now, I'm that excited.'

They weren't to know that many tears would be shed before Saturday.

132

* * *

When Laura parted from Cynthia outside her house, there was a spring in her step as she carried on up the street. Oh boy, what a lot she had to look forward to. But she'd need some new clobber if she was to go dancing, especially silver dance shoes. Even if she couldn't dance, at least she could look the part.

As she neared her front door, she noticed two figures standing outside and the smile dropped from her face. It was their Jenny and Janet's brother, Bill. He always walked her sister home to make sure she arrived safe, but Laura thought it was stupid. What did they think could happen to her in the five-minute walk from the Porters' house? It must be his mother's idea, he certainly wouldn't do it off his own bat. He'd left school before she did, so he must be going on for seventeen, too old to waste his time on a fourteen-year-old. With his looks he could have any girl he took a shine to. Tall, broad, and not a pimple in sight.

Jenny was putting the key in the lock when Laura stopped in front of them. 'Hi-ya, Bill! What have you been up to with my kid sister? Me mam will have yer life, keeping her out until this time of night.'

'Permission for a late pass was requested and granted. Ten thirty yer mam said, and we're right on the dot.'

'I get to stay out later, after tonight. It's me birthday tomorrow, I'm sixteen.'

'Yes, Jenny told us. I hope yer have a happy birthday.'

Completely ignoring her sister, Laura went on, 'Me and Cynthia are going dancing on Saturday night and I'm not half looking forward to it. Do you go dancing, Bill?'

Jenny had had enough. Trust her sister to push herself forward and take over. 'I hate to break this up,' she said, 'but I'm going in. Thanks for walking me home, Bill, and I'll see yer soon. Good night.'

'I'm going meself now, Jenny. Up early for work tomorrow, and I need me beauty sleep.' Bill was too wise to walk into Laura's trap. 'I'll bid you good night, Jenny, and you, too, Laura. Sleep well.' With that he strode away, leaving Laura fuming that he'd given her the brush-off. Raging inside, she pushed Jenny roughly aside and made for the stairs. 'Tell me mam I've gone to bed, I'm tired.'

Using the light from the gas-lamp on the opposite side of the street, Laura began to undress. 'Who the hell does Bill Porter think he is?' she snarled as she pulled her dress over her head. 'God's gift to women, or something? Well, there are plenty more fish in the sea – and I'm going to start catching them at the weekend.'

133

Chapter Eleven

Laura came out of the factory gates with a huge grin on her face. In her hand she held the six birthday cards she'd got off the women she worked with, plus a pair of rayon stockings they'd clubbed together to buy for her. She was in a very happy frame of mind, declaring this to be the best birthday she'd ever had. There'd been two cards by her plate when she came down for breakfast, one from her mam and dad, and the other from Jenny, and on the top of them were two half-crowns and a shilling. And then the postman had knocked to deliver four more cards, from her grandad, Cynthia, Mrs Hanley and Mrs Moynihan.

'I'll see yer tomorrow, girls, and thanks again for me pressie and cards.' Laura waved before turning to make her way to the tram stop. She'd only taken a few steps when she heard her name called, and looking across to the pavement opposite, she saw Celia beckoning her. Looking both ways to make sure the coast was clear, she hurried over. 'This is a surprise. Are yer going somewhere?'

'No, I've been waiting for you. Yer grandad said it's yer birthday, so I've bought yer a little present.' Celia handed her a small parcel, nicely wrapped in pretty paper and tied with a piece of red ribbon. 'I hope yer like it, but if yer don't I can easy change it.'

Laura's eyes were agog. 'Ooh, that's the gear, Celia, ta very much.' She moved a few steps nearer the gas-lamp. 'Yer've wrapped it proper posh, I must say. I can't wait to see what's inside.'

'Open it and see, unless yer'd rather wait until yer get home.' Celia knew she was on safe ground saying that. She'd had Laura taped all along, knew she was too greedy to wait until she got home. 'Please yerself.'

Laura's mind was working exactly as Celia knew it would. Her mam wouldn't be very happy about this so she'd better keep it to herself. She could always say the girls in work bought it for her. 'I'll open it now, Celia, if yer don't mind. With you and me mam not really getting on, I don't think she'd like me taking a present off yer. So if I tell her I got it off me mates in work, yer wouldn't drop me in it, would yer?'

'Of course not, we're mates, aren't we? It'll be our little secret.' Celia was gloating inside. This was the first step in getting her own

135

back on that stuck-up daughter of her husband. 'I didn't let on to Joe that I was getting it, so there's only me knows, and I won't snitch.'

'Thanks, Celia.' Laura tucked the cards under her arm while she untied the ribbon and opened up the paper. Then she let out a shriek, and worries about her mother were forgotten as she lifted a lilac underskirt from the paper. 'Oh, it's gorgeous!' Fingering the white lace that adorned the bodice, she said, 'It's just what I wanted. Ye're a real pal, Celia, and I'll love yer for ever more.'

'I'm glad yer like it, kid. And don't worry, I won't tell anyone. Anyway, I'll have to scarper now because I left yer grandad's dinner in the oven on a low light.' The lie came easily to Celia; she was well versed in the art. There was no dinner in the oven keeping warm, she'd be buying chips from the local chippy on the way home, and if Joe didn't like it, he could lump it for all she cared. 'Eh, why don't yer come down one night and we could have a good chinwag?' She asked the question casually, as though she'd just thought of it. 'I enjoyed it last time. It was a change to have someone to talk to.'

'Ooh, I don't know.' Laura looked embarrassed. 'I got a good telling off.'

'Forget it then, kid, 'cos I wouldn't like to get yer into trouble.'

Laura looked down at the underskirt in her hand and felt really mean. 'I'd like to, I really would. But Grandad would be there and he'd be bound to tell me mam.'

'Then let's meet one night and go to the flicks! No one would know the difference then. What the eye don't see, the heart don't grieve after.'

Laura felt relieved. 'Yeah, we could do that, and no one would be any the wiser.' Then she frowned. 'But wouldn't Grandad want to know where yer were going?'

Celia shrugged her shoulders. 'I'll tell him I'm going with one of me old girlfriends. He won't think anything of it because I often go out on me own. What night suits you?'

Laura was in a dilemma. She was hoping to get a click at the dance on Saturday, and with a bit of luck the boy might ask her for a date. Much as she would like to please Celia after her buying such a nice present, a date with a boy was more to her taste. 'I'm going to a dance with Cynthia on Saturday, and I've promised to see her tomorrow so we can discuss what we're going to wear. But I could go tonight, if it's not too soon for yer?'

'Suits me, kiddo! Shall we say half seven at Everton Valley and we can decide then where to go?'

Little knowing she was being drawn into a web of deceit, Laura nodded. 'I'll have to put me skates on, but I'll be there. Ta-ra.'

Celia watched her for a while, then spun around and walked in the opposite direction. She was feeling very pleased her plan had worked so well and had a smug smile on her face. It was a pretty face at first sight, until the beholder looked more closely and saw the hardness and malice in her eyes. Especially now, when she was thinking that in the next half hour, Laura would have told her mother two lies. Those two lies, added to the other things she had planned, would one day be used to shatter Mary Nightingale's life. And that day couldn't come soon enough for Celia Steadman.

'Yer've done well, sunshine,' Mary said, having read the cards and been shown the presents. 'The underskirt is very pretty, it must have cost a pretty penny.'

'Ye're lucky, Laura,' Jenny said. 'I wish I had one as nice. Is the girl who bought it a special friend of yours?'

'I told yer, all the girls clubbed together for me presents,' Laura snapped, causing Jenny to widen her eyes at the sharp tone. 'They do it for everyone's birthday.'

'There's no need to bite me head off.' Jenny picked her knife and fork up and went back to the dinner that had been pushed aside when Laura came in. Why was her sister always so hostile towards her? She sometimes looked as though she didn't even like her, and Jenny couldn't understand the reason for it.

Mary's thoughts were also on her eldest daughter. She could read Laura like a book, and the guilty look in her eyes when Jenny had asked about the underskirt had Mary convinced that she was lying. But why lie? If she'd gone to the shops in her dinner hour, and bought the slip out of her birthday money, why didn't she just say so?

Stan finished his sausage and mash, wiped the back of his hand across his lips and pushed the plate away. He could sense a cooling in the atmosphere but couldn't figure out the reason for it. So he tried to lighten the mood. 'Twelve cards, eh, Laura? None of us have ever had that many before. Yer must be a popular girl, eh?'

The smile returned to Laura's face. 'Yeah, they're lovely, too. I was going to stand some on the sideboard and the mantelpiece, but there's not much point with the way the room is, they wouldn't be seen.'

'If yer don't want them to get dirty, yer'd be best putting them in yer bedroom,' Mary told her. 'Amy and Molly will be here in half an hour, we're going to wash the paintwork down, ready for Mr Moynihan and yer dad to start on the ceiling tomorrow night.'

'When are yer getting the wallpaper, Mam?' Jenny asked. 'Are yer getting something light and cheerful?'

Mary smiled. 'Shall I get one with clowns on?'

Jenny giggled. 'There's enough clowns in the house as it is.'

Laura gave her a sharp dig. 'Ay, you speak for yerself. There's only

137

one clown in this house and she's sitting right next to me.'

'Well, it certainly isn't you!' Jenny was stung into saying. 'Clowns are always happy. They laugh and joke and bring smiles to people's faces. You are a far cry from that. I've never seen yer really happy, yer wouldn't know a joke if it jumped up and hit yer in the face, and a smile from you is a rare sight.'

Laura was stunned into silence, but not for long. She curled her fist, and with her weight behind it, she punched Jenny in her ribs. 'Who the hell d'yer think ye're talking to? Don't come that with me or I'll give yer a good hiding.'

Stan banged his fist on the table. 'That's enough of that! Don't you ever raise yer hand again in this house, Laura, 'cos I won't have it.'

Laura's face was sullen. 'She started it, so why don't yer say something to her? Why is it always me what gets picked on?'

'Perhaps it's because yer haven't got a sense of humour,' Mary said. 'Yer don't see the funny side of anything. Jenny didn't mean you when she talked of clowns – it was just a joke.'

'Well, I didn't think it was funny.'

Mary sighed as she pushed her chair back and reached for the plates. Her eldest daughter was hard going, there was no doubt about it. There was just no pleasing her. 'Forget it, I don't want to hear another word on the subject. And both of yer put a move on, I want you out of here before Amy and Molly come.' With the dirty plates in her hand, she looked at Jenny. 'Are yer going round to Janet's sunshine?'

'Yeah, we'll probably have a game of cards.'

'And you, Laura, are yer going anywhere special to celebrate yer birthday?'

Laura lowered her head, appearing to concentrate on her clasped hands, where the thumbs were moving around each other in circles. 'Nowhere exciting, only the pictures with Cynthia.' The lie told, she raised her eyes. 'But we're going dancing on Saturday and I'm not half looking forward to that.'

Jenny saw her mother's shoulders slump as she walked into the kitchen. So for her sake, she tried once more with Laura. 'Which dance hall are yer going to?'

'I haven't got a clue,' Laura said airily, springing to her feet. She pushed her chair back under the table before bending down and whispering in Jenny's ear, 'And if I did, I wouldn't tell yer, smarty pants.'

With a shrug of her shoulders, Jenny went into the kitchen to help her mother with the dishes. 'You wash, Mam, and I'll dry.'

'There's no need, sunshine, I can have them done in no time. You go and get yerself ready to go out.'

'I'm not bothering to get changed, Mam.' Jenny didn't relish the thought of being in the bedroom with her sister because she knew she'd be subject to a load of sarcasm. And it would be a case of standing there and taking it, or answering back and starting a fight. 'I'm only going to Janet's and it's hardly worth it.'

When Laura came downstairs, all dressed up, Jenny took her time putting her coat on so they didn't leave the house at the same time. When she heard the door bang, she smiled at her mother. 'Half ten, Mam, is that all right?'

'Yeah, that's fine, we should be finished by then. Ta-ra, sunshine.'

'Ta-ra, Mam, ta-ra, Dad. Don't work too hard, now.'

Jenny could see her sister further down the street and expected her to stop outside Cynthia's. But Laura kept on walking and Jenny watched until she'd turned the corner of the street and was out of sight. 'What's she up to now?' Jenny asked herself softly. 'She's a mystery all right, yer can't believe a word she says. I don't care what she does, it's nothing to do with me, but I do care that she upsets me mam with her lies.'

Jenny was so deep in thought, she didn't see the two figures until they stood in her path. 'Yer frightened the life out of me, yer daft things.'

'Yer were talking to yerself, Jenny, and that's a bad sign, isn't it, John?'

'Yes, Mick, it's a very bad sign.' John had been walking with his hands deep in his pockets for warmth, but the sight of Jenny was as good as sitting in front of a roaring coal fire. 'They can cart yer off to the loony bin for it.'

'I wasn't talking to meself, I was singing.' They couldn't see properly in the dusk, so didn't see Jenny's blush of embarrassment. 'Anyway, what if I was talking to meself? Is there anyone better I can talk to?'

'Yeah, there's me,' said Mick, his white teeth flashing, 'I'm always available, and yer'll not get a better pair of listening ears than mine.'

'Oh yes, she will,' John chuckled. 'What about me? I can listen for hours without opening me mouth.' He put a hand on Jenny's arm. 'Don't ever take first offer, Jenny, always shop around for the best bargain.'

Not to be outdone, Mick put a hand on Jenny's other arm. 'Now just be careful yer don't end up with shopsoiled goods, Jenny. Yer want nothing but the best.'

John took up a boxing stance. 'Are yer insinuating that I'm shopsoiled, Mick Moynihan? If yer are, I'll set me mam on yer.' Realising his mate had the advantage over him now, with a hand still on Jenny's arm, he quickly relaxed his stance and put his hand where it wanted to be, touching Jenny. 'Yer heard that, didn't yer, Miss

Nightingale? Will yer be me witness when I take him to court?'

'Daft as brushes, both of yer.' Jenny's voice was full of laughter. They hadn't half cheered her up. 'Now, gentlemen, would yer kindly unhand me before *I* become shopsoiled goods? And tell me, pray, what are yer doing down here?'

'It's our night for jazzing and we're going for the tram.' Mick plucked up the courage to take hold of Jenny's arms and held them aloft. With exaggerated movements he spun her around, singing, 'Who's Taking You Home Tonight?'

Ho, ho, John thought, I'm not standing for that! Bare-faced cheek, that is. 'Excuse me,' he tapped Mick on the shoulder. 'Sorry, mate, but this is an Excuse Me waltz.'

Mick stood still but held on tight. 'Only if the young lady is willing.'

'To save any argument,' Jenny said, trying to free her hands, 'John can have three spins, and then ye're even. After that I'm on me way, 'cos Janet will wonder where I've got to.'

As John pushed him aside, Mick whispered, 'I don't wish yer no harm, mate, but I hope yer trip and break a flippin' leg.'

John winked in answer before he reached for Jenny, a look of pure bliss on his face. 'It was five spins he had, so don't be trying to short-change me, Jenny Nightingale.'

Jenny counted aloud and stopped dead on five. 'Now yer can walk down to me mate's with me.'

'I don't suppose, like, that yer could bring Janet out, could yer?' Mick ventured as they walked in line. 'Then we could have a dance in the street, save going all the way to Seaforth.'

'Some hope you've got, Mick Moynihan. Her mam would have yer life.'

'Yer could always ask her mam, too!' John was wishing the Porters lived the other side of Liverpool so the walk would last all night. 'She could chaperone yer, or even join in if she wanted.'

'Yeah, that's a good idea, mate!' Mick felt as though he was walking on air. 'I bet Mrs Porter can do a mean quickstep.'

Jenny was having a fit of the giggles. 'Why not ask the whole street and we could have a party? Mr Porter can knock out a tune on his comb, so we'd have music, as well.'

'And I'm pretty good at whistling,' John said. 'Mind you, yer wouldn't know whether to do a quickstep or a tango, but who cares?'

'I can hum, if that's any good.' Jenny was laughing when they stopped outside the Porters' house. 'And I can click me tongue, as well.'

Mick's laugh was loud. 'All we need is someone on the spoons and we've got a full orchestra. I bags being the conductor.'

'Oh no, matey, I've got yer down as the band's singer.' John's shoulders were shaking with laughter. 'I'll be whistling me head off while I'm dancing with Jenny, and you'll be on the stage belting out a nice smoochy song.'

'What's this about a smoochy song?' No one had heard the door open and they were surprised to see Martha Porter standing on the step, arms folded and a huge grin on her face. 'Come on, tell us about this smoochy song, I like the sound of it.'

'I think yer'd better ask me mate,' John said. 'He's the singer.'

'John Hanley, ye're a coward,' Jenny told him, wagging a finger. 'It was you what said it.'

Mick tilted his head to the side and weighed up Janet's mother, before saying, 'I said I bet yer can do a mean quickstep, Mrs Porter, am I right?'

'I've had me moments, lad, but they were a very long time ago. The best I could manage now would be a slow waltz.' Her laugh was loud and hoarse. 'In fact, it would have to be so bleedin' slow we'd be standing still.'

Janet's head appeared over her mother's shoulder. 'What's going on here?'

Jenny, the unpleasantness with her sister forgotten, was in a playful mood. 'The boys want to invite us to dance in the street, Jan. We've sorted the music out, with yer dad on the comb, you and me humming and clicking our tongues, John whistling and Mick singing. But we haven't got anyone to play the spoons.'

Martha doubled up. 'Oh dear, that's tickled me fancy.' She wiped her eyes and took a deep breath. 'Mr Wilkinson, down the street, he's got a ukulele, shall I go and drag him out?'

Bill towered behind his mother and sister, and when he saw Jenny standing with the two lads, he squeezed between them and joined the trio on the pavement. 'You ain't going anywhere, Jenny Nightingale. I've been waiting for yer so I could win back those ten matchsticks yer cheated me out of the other night.'

'You fibber! I never did no such thing! You're the one who cheats, hiding cards under the tablecloth so we won't see.'

'He's pulling yer leg, queen,' Martha said. 'Take no notice of him.'

'Yeah,' Janet agreed, 'he thinks he's funny but he's a pain in the neck.' She nudged her mother. 'Mam, didn't yer say I could go dancing with Jenny when we're fifteen?'

Martha tutted. 'Don't push yer luck, Janet. I said I'd think about it, as long as yer had someone to walk yer home.'

Mick and John spoke in unison. 'We'll walk them home, Mrs Porter.'

'That's all right,' Bill said. 'I'll go with them and make sure they come to no harm. I can't let me kid sister walk home in the dark.'

Mick and John exchanged glances which said it wasn't his kid sister's interest he had at heart, it was Jenny's. And the look wasn't lost on Martha. 'It's bad luck to plan so far ahead,' she told them. 'Something always turns up to throw a spanner in the works. There's a few months to go yet, so leave it be until then.'

'We'd better scarper,' Mick said, 'otherwise they'll be playing the last waltz by the time we get there.' The lads waved goodbye, then after a few steps, they turned. Mrs Porter and Janet had vanished indoors, and Bill had his hand on Jenny's elbow as she mounted the steps.

'I think we've got some competition there, Mick,' John said, 'and it's going to be stiff competition.'

'Ye're telling me!' If there had been a stone handy, Mick would have kicked it the length of the street. One rival was bad enough, but two? 'And he's got luck on his side being Janet's brother. It's a big plus, that is. We won't be in the meg specks.'

'I'd fight him, if he wasn't so big,' John said, hands dug deep in his pockets. 'But he's built like a flippin' house.'

'Oh, we've got no worries there, 'cos there's two of us. I'll hold him while you batter hell out of him.'

'Oh aye, soft lad! Put muggins here in front of him, while you stand behind, all nice and safe? You are definitely not on, mate! I'm as fond of me teeth as you are,' John chortled. 'Tell yer what, eh? We've got five months before Jenny's birthday, so it's you and me against Bill Porter. But the day she's fifteen, it's every man for himself.'

Celia was waiting at Everton Valley when Laura dashed up, out of breath with running. 'Have yer been waiting long?'

'Only about two minutes.' Celia linked arms. 'Where would yer like to go?'

'I don't mind, it's up to you.' Laura looked sideways and her heart dropped. Celia was dressed up to the nines, as though she was going somewhere special, and here was she in a tattered old coat. 'I don't want to go anywhere posh 'cos I'm not dressed for it. Me frock is all right, but this coat is shabby.'

'Laura, with a face and figure like yours, who the hell is going to look at yer clothes?' Celia gushed, smiling into her face. 'When yer've got the looks and the personality to go with it, kid, clothes don't matter.'

If Laura had been older, with a bit more experience, she might have noticed that the smile wasn't genuine, neither were the words. As it was, she believed what she wanted to believe and preened with pleasure. 'I'm saving up for a new coat, I should have enough in two or three weeks.'

'Anyway, where do yer want to go?' Celia asked. 'The pictures or a dance?'

'Ooh, I'd like to go to a dance, but don't forget, I've got to be home by eleven so I can't go too far away.'

'There's a dance at Spellow Lane, over Burton's, the Thirty Bob Tailor's. It's only a couple of stops on the tram, and if we leave at half ten, yer'll be home in plenty of time.'

'Yeah, okay. But I can't dance so I'll have to sit and watch.' When they had crossed the busy road and stopped by the tram stop, Laura eyed Celia up and down. 'Me grandad must be good to yer with money, yer always have something different on.'

'He's not a bad old stick. He knows I like going out, and as he's always too tired, he gives me the money to go where I want to.' Celia changed the subject. She wasn't going to tell Laura that the money Joe gave her was for housekeeping, but hardly any of it went on the house. She wanted clothes and enjoyment, and it was his own fault for not giving her more when she'd tried to wheedle it out of him. But the less said about that to his granddaughter, the better. She was trying to trap Laura, not the other way around.

When the tram came, Laura got her purse out to pay her fare, but Celia brushed her hand aside. 'This is my treat for yer birthday.' She handed the conductor the coppers and waited for him to turn the handle of the ticket machine which hung from his shoulders by a leather strap. With the tickets in her hand, she turned to Laura and asked casually, 'Would yer like to go for a drink before we go in? There's a pub right facing the dance hall.'

Laura shook her head vigorously. They were in Walton now, not that far from where her grandad lived, and it was too risky. He was the one person in the world she had any feelings for, and she knew in her heart she was doing wrong by seeing his wife behind his back. And if he found out and told her mam, she'd get a hiding. Anyway, look what happened the last time she went in a pub. That experience still gave her shivers when she thought of it. 'No thanks, Celia, I'd rather not.'

'I'm not fussy meself, kid,' lied Celia, who could drink most men under the table. 'Drink gives me a headache.' She felt disappointed that her plan hadn't worked, but there was plenty of time. She'd make a friend of Laura, use her until she had enough on her to shatter the life of the family-loving Mary Nightingale. At first Celia wanted to get her own back on Mary for the row they'd had, and for the slap on the face. But gradually she became obsessed, blaming Mary for everything that was wrong in her life. Like being married to a man more than twice her age who wasn't fun any more. She'd married him for a meal ticket, thinking he would be a soft touch, but the novelty had worn off. And because that man was Mary's father, then Mary was to blame.

'Isn't this our stop?' Laura asked, peering through the window of

143

the tram. 'The conductor has just shouted Spellow Lane.'

Celia, still deep in thought, stared at her blankly for a couple of seconds. Then she remembered where she was, and why, and scrambled to her feet. 'D'yer know, kid, I was miles away! If you hadn't been here I'd have ended up at the terminus in Fazakerly.'

'Me tummy feels as though it's full of butterflies,' Laura said, as they passed through the entrance and began to climb the stairs. 'Yer won't leave me on me own, will yer?'

'Of course I won't! Anyway, how can yer be on yer own in a hall full of people? And I've told yer, with your looks they'll be falling over themselves to dance with yer.'

Once again Celia pushed Laura's hand away when she tried to pay for her own ticket. 'The treat's on me tonight, kid.'

Shaking like a leaf, Laura followed Celia to the cloakroom. After handing their coats over they were given a ticket which Celia told her to hang on to until they were going home.

Then came the moment when Celia pushed open the door to the dance hall. It was crowded with couples dancing to the strains of a slow foxtrot, and some of the tension left Laura as she told herself she wouldn't be noticed in this crowd. She could just sit down and watch, and try to pick up a few points on how it was done. Then tomorrow night her and Cynthia could have a go.

Laura was walking ahead of Celia to where she had spied two empty chairs, when she heard someone saying in a loud voice, 'Hello there, sweetheart, where've yer been hiding yerself? I missed yer last week, it wasn't the same without yer.'

Turning her head out of curiosity, Laura saw a man with his arm around Celia's waist, smiling down at her. He seemed very familiar, as though he'd known her a long time. But he shouldn't be holding her like that, he must know she was a married woman.

Celia could feel herself being watched and waved a hand towards the chairs. 'Go and sit down, kid, I won't be long. Charlie's an old friend of mine.'

Before turning away, Laura glanced at the man's face and decided she didn't like him. Nor did she like the way he was looking down the front of Celia's low-cut dress. But it wasn't any of her business and she was probably being daft. You couldn't tell what a person was like just by looking at them. So Laura took her seat and turned her attention to the dancers. Some of the couples were really good, and it was a pleasure just to sit and admire. One day she'd be able to dance like that and the men would be fighting to dance with her.

The music came to an end and Laura noted how the couples clapped before leaving the floor. Some stayed with their partners, ready for the next dance, while others returned to their friends who were sitting on the chairs minding handbags. There were more girls

144

than boys, and that pleased Laura. Her and Cynthia wouldn't look out of place tomorrow night. But she'd have to buy a pair of proper dance-shoes, all the girls were wearing them. Most of them were silver, with thin straps and very high heels, and they didn't half look nice.

'I'm sorry about that, kid, but Charlie's a very old friend.'

Laura turned to see Celia sitting beside her. 'Yeah, it looked like it too, the way he had his arm around yer.'

'Oh, don't take no notice of that, Charlie's like that with all the girls.' Celia patted Laura's hand. 'He's a real ladies' man, but harmless enough when yer know how to handle him.'

'D'yer come dancing often, Celia, and are yer any good at it?'

'That's two questions in one, Laura. Let's see, which one shall I answer first?' Celia took her time answering, hoping the plan she'd hatched with Charlie worked before the questions got too personal. It was when the band struck up that she answered. 'I don't come very often and I guess me dancing is just about average.'

'Would yer take me for this dance, then? I wouldn't feel so daft about making mistakes if I was with you.'

Celia grinned. 'Yer don't need me, there's a boy making a bee-line for yer.'

Laura looked up in dismay when a male voice asked, 'D'yer want to dance?' The boy was about eighteen and not bad-looking. Any other time Laura would be fluttering her eyelashes, but right now she was worried about standing all over his feet and making a fool of herself. 'I'm sorry,' she croaked, 'but I can't dance.'

'Don't be stupid, kid!' Celia said. 'This is Gary, and he won't mind teaching yer a few steps, will yer, Gary? She's got to learn sometime.'

Gary grinned, showing a set of even white teeth. Charlie had asked him to dance with the girl as a favour, so he could be with Celia. And Gary had reluctantly agreed to have one dance with her. But looking down at her now, he realised he was the one getting the favour. She was a real good-looker, this one, it would be a pleasure teaching her to dance. 'Come on, the floor is crowded, no one will notice. I'll walk yer round until yer get used to it.'

Laura looked up at him and her apprehension began to fade. Tall, slim, blond and blue-eyed, what more could you ask for? She bent to put her handbag under the chair before standing up. 'Don't say yer weren't warned.'

There was a smile on Celia's face as she watched them take the floor, the smile of a victor. Good old Charlie had come up trumps once again. Now she could disappear for a while. But she'd have to be careful or the whole thing could backfire on her. So she waited until Laura's attention was focused on her partner's feet, then hurried

145

out to the foyer where Charlie was waiting. He was holding his overcoat ready to wrap around her shoulders, and grunted, 'I hope she's not with yer next week, this is bloody ridiculous.'

As she was hurried through the entrance door and into the street, Celia's voice was sharp. 'Hey, yer can cut that out. She's here for a purpose, and right now she's more important to me than giving you yer little bit of pleasure. So don't start yer moaning or I'll be back in that dance like a shot.'

'All right, sweetheart, keep yer hair on.' Charlie, hurrying her to the nearest entry, knew what a bitch Celia could be when she wanted, so he kept his voice soft. 'It's just that I want to be with yer as long as I can.'

'Gary said he'd keep her busy for ten minutes, so that's all the time yer've got.' Celia leaned back against the wall. 'So yer'd better get a move on, lover boy, hadn't yer? Otherwise I'll be leaving yer in the middle of the game, and yer wouldn't be a happy man if I did that, would yer?'

Laura didn't think anything of it when Gary asked her to stay on the floor for the next dance. In fact, she didn't think of anything, her head was in the clouds. He'd told her she was getting on really well, that she was a born dancer with natural rhythm and had the body to go with it. And Laura lapped it up. In no time at all she'd be as good as anyone on the floor.

When the music stopped, the singer with the band said there would be a five-minute break before the next dance, which would be a rumba. 'Ooh, I'm not even going to attempt that.' Laura cast her eyes around the room. 'Where's Celia got to?'

'She's probably gone to the toilet,' said Gary, who'd had his eyes peeled for the last five minutes. 'She won't be long, so stay and talk to me.'

When Celia did put in an appearance, quickly followed by Charlie, Laura was too full of her own importance to make a connection. 'I didn't half do well, didn't I, Gary?'

'Yeah, she was brilliant. Took to it like a duck to water.'

Celia smiled. 'Yer'll have to come again next week then, won't yer? Gary comes every Thursday, and now ye're getting on so well with him, ye're best sticking to the same partner.'

'Will yer be here next week, Gary?' There was excitement in Laura's voice. 'I'll come if yer are.'

Gary had taken a shine to her and would have told her that he came three times a week if Celia hadn't been glaring at him. She was the wrong one to make an enemy of, as many people in the hall had found out to their cost. The girls avoided her like the plague, but the men were around her like flies around a honey jar. 'Yeah, I'll be here.'

146

Gary wasn't the only one doing as he was told. Charlie, who was standing by the main door, had been ordered to keep his distance and he knew better than to disobey. But what he got in return for being a lap-dog was well worth it.

After the interval, Laura had two more dances with Gary, and then Celia said it was time to go. She made a show of being considerate, insisting she saw Laura on the tram so she'd know she got home in time. But she wasn't being considerate, she was being crafty. Laura had had a taste of Gary and would be only too willing to come back for more. And Gary would be ordered to toe the line until Celia gave him the go-ahead.

Chapter Twelve

'This is me very favourite meal, Mam,' Jenny said, gnawing at the bone she was holding between her fingers. 'Spare-ribs and cabbage, yer can't beat it. I could eat it every day and never get fed up with it.'

'Me too,' Stan agreed, 'especially when there's plenty of lean meat on the bones and yer can get yer teeth into it.'

'I'll have you know that sheet of ribs nearly started a war in the butcher's,' Mary told them, smacking her lips.' I noticed it hanging up in the shop window as we passed, and I could see how lean it was. But I didn't crack on to Amy, 'cos I thought she'd beat me to it.' Mary's titter turned into a full-blown laugh. 'Honest to God, that mate of mine will get me hung one of these days with her shenanigans. I asked Wilf for a sheet of ribs and pointed to the one I wanted. As he was hooking it down, Amy asked why that one was so special – what difference was there between that and the other sheets hanging on the iron bar in the window. I told her it was leaner, all the others had too much fat on them. Well, I bet Wilf cursed me up hill and down dale, 'cos she only made him lift every sheet down for inspection. She compared each one with mine and shook her head. "She's right, they are all fatty".'

Mary looked around the table to see Stan leaning on his elbows, his chin resting on his laced fingers, Jenny's eyes were wide with interest and even Laura was waiting for what was to come. 'Can anyone guess what happened then?'

'With Amy, anything could happen, love,' Stan said, 'so yer'd better tell us instead of keeping us in suspense.'

'Right, I'll show yer.' Mary got to her feet and cleared her throat. 'Now, pretend I'm Amy and I'm wearing a scarf around me head that keeps slipping down one side. Here goes.'

She pushed the pretend scarf back into place, folded her arms and sniffed up. ' "Yer've been very kind, Wilf, showing me all those sheets of bleedin' ribs. It's been real interesting. There's not many shopkeepers as obliging as yerself, especially when the customer isn't buying. We're having scouse for our dinner, so will yer cut me a pound of stewing meat up, please. And will yer do me the courtesy of letting me see it before yer take the knife to it, so I can be sure it's bleedin' lean?" ' Mary hitched up her bosom and narrowed her eyes.

' "What are yer standing there with yer mouth open for, Wilf? Yer'll not catch many flies in this weather".'

Stan guffawed and banged his fist on the table. 'She's a bloody hero.'

'I can just picture it, Mam, 'cos yer aren't half good at taking me Auntie Amy off,' Jenny said. 'But I wish I'd been there to see Wilf's face.'

Laura made no comment, but there was a smile on her face. In fact she'd had a smile on her face all day, still on cloud nine after last night. She'd done nothing but talk about it all day, adding little extras to spice it up a bit for the women she worked with. And she couldn't wait to get down to Cynthia's to go over it all again. She'd told the family she'd been to the dance with her friend instead of the cinema so she'd better watch what she said in case she let it slip.

'Come on now, the show's over,' Mary said briskly, knocking Stan's elbows off the table. 'Seamus is coming over to give yer dad a hand painting the ceiling and I want all the furniture covered with some old sheets.'

'Are yer getting the wallpaper tomorrow, Mam?' Jenny asked, following her mother into the kitchen. 'I can't wait to see the room finished, we'll be proper posh.'

'Well, I don't know about being posh, but it'll certainly be an improvement.' Mary grinned as she turned the tap on. 'Amy said she'd help with the papering, but I don't think me heart would stand it. Can yer just imagine the antics out of her? It would be a disaster.'

Laura popped her head in. 'I'm going down to Cynthia's, Mam, but I won't be late.'

'Okay, sunshine, but don't come back before half-ten, give the men a chance to get it all done and dusted.'

When she heard the door bang, Jenny asked, 'Where did our Laura go last night?'

'I couldn't tell yer, sunshine. She just said she'd been to a dance with Cynthia and I never thought to ask where.'

Jenny frowned as she reached for the tea-towel hanging behind the door. She was a dark horse, their Laura; you could never get to the bottom of her. She'd told a lie about last night, she hadn't been out with Cynthia, but why did she think there was a need to lie about it? If she was going out with a boy, their mam wouldn't mind, she'd be made up. In fact, Mary would welcome him with open arms if he was a nice bloke and good for Laura.

Jenny sighed. The best thing she could do was say nothing and hope it all worked out well in the end.

Laura ran down the street with wings on her heels. Wait until she told her friend where she'd been last night, and that she'd danced every dance with a bloke as handsome as any film star. Oh boy, Cynthia wouldn't half be jealous. But best not to tell her who she'd been with, in case it slipped out some time and got back to her mam. She couldn't say she'd been on her own because her friend knew she wouldn't have the nerve, so she'd have to say she'd been with a girl from work.

Cynthia was usually waiting for her and had the door opened before she'd finishing knocking. But that wasn't the case tonight, and Laura's face showed surprise when her mother answered her knock. 'Is Cynthia coming out, Mrs Pennington?'

'No, girl, she's been in bed all day, never went to work.'

Laura's spirits sank. 'What's wrong with her? Is she sick?'

'She said she's got a sore throat, a headache and pains in her tummy.' There was no sympathy in Fanny Pennington's voice. 'At least that's her story and she flatly refuses to get out of bed.'

'Can I go up and see her?' Laura was feeling desperate as her great plans came crumbling around her shoulders. 'I might be able to cheer her up.'

'Suit yerself, girl.' The door was opened wider. 'Yer know where her room is.'

Laura took the stairs two at a time. Cynthia often took a day off when she couldn't be bothered going to work, and her parents let her get away with it. At least her father did, her mother never had a say in it. But she'd never missed coming out at night.

'It's me, Cynthia.' Laura knocked lightly before pushing the door open. In the dim light coming from the candle standing in a saucer on a chest of drawers at the side of the bed, she could see her friend huddled in the middle of the bed, the clothes pulled up to her chin. 'What's wrong with yer, Cynthia? Are yer really sick, or just putting it on?'

'Close the door,' Cynthia's voice was muffled, 'and come and sit on the bed.'

Laura closed the door quietly then did as she was bid. 'Ye're not really sick, are yer?'

Cynthia struggled to sit up, groaning as she did so. 'I'm in agony, Laura, and I don't know what to do.'

'Have yer got pains in yer tummy?'

'I wish that was all it was.' Cynthia rocked back and forth, and when the tears came she covered her face with her hands to stifle the noise of the sobs that racked her body. 'It was terrible, Laura, I thought they were going to kill me.'

'What are yer talking about? Who did yer think was going to kill yer?'

'Larry and Jeff.'

151

'Larry and Jeff!' Laura's voice rose in surprise. 'What did they do to yer?'

'I can't tell yer. I couldn't tell no one.'

The springs on the bed were squeaking, and afraid that they would be heard downstairs, Laura put an arm around Cynthia's shoulders to try and calm her down. 'Yer mam and dad will be up if yer don't stop, Cynthia. Just take it easy and tell me what happened.'

'I haven't slept a wink, it's like a nightmare. I keep going over it in me mind and I feel like screaming.' She turned a tearstained face to her friend. 'They left me in a dark entry on me own, and I was terrified. All I could hear was them laughing as they walked away.'

'But what the hell were yer doing down a dark entry with the two of them! It was a pretty stupid thing to do, especially as I'd told yer how cruel Jeff was with me.'

'I had no choice, they dragged me. I thought Jeff would leave us when we came out of the pub, but he didn't! I wasn't worried because I was with Larry, and I thought we were walking in the direction of Jeff's home and he'd turn off any minute.' The sobbing started again and Cynthia pushed Laura's arm away. 'I can't tell yer any more, I get too upset and could scream the house down.'

'Shall I go and ask yer mam to make yer a cup of tea? I'll tell her yer throat's not as sore but it's dry.'

Cynthia's head shook vigorously. 'No, I don't want her to come in here, I don't want no one in here.'

'I'll stay down there until she makes the tea, so she won't have to come up. But in case she or yer dad asks if yer were out with me last night, what shall I say?'

'I told them I was going to the flicks with yer.'

'Okay, I won't be long.'

Fanny Pennington made the tea without a word, while Laura chatted with Dick, her husband. But when she passed the cup and saucer over, there was suspicion in her eyes. 'Tell her to drink it while it's hot.'

Walking up the stairs slowly so as not to spill the tea, Laura's mind was whirling. She couldn't imagine what had happened to upset Cynthia so much. She was always so sure of herself, and certainly capable of handling herself. And she had Larry with her, the man who was supposed to be in love with her. 'I just don't understand it,' Laura sighed as she pushed the bedroom door open with her foot. 'But I'll find out, even if I have to sit here all night.'

'Yer mam said to drink it while it's hot.'

Cynthia pointed to the chest of drawers. 'Put it on there for a minute and bring the candle over to the bed.'

Her brow furrowed, Laura held out the candle to her friend. 'Here yer are.'

'No, you hold it and sit on the side of the bed.' Cynthia was unbuttoning the neck of her nightdress. 'That's what they did to me.'

Laura stared in horror at the bruising around Cynthia's throat. It was yellow, blue and black, and it looked very sore. 'Did Jeff do that to yer? Where the hell was Larry when this was going on?'

Cynthia dropped her head in shame. 'Pass me the tea, then I'll tell yer everything.' She took a few sips, then said softly, 'Yer were right all along, Larry is just as bad as Jeff. In fact, he's ten times worse because he'd been leading me on for weeks now and muggins here fell for it hook, line and sinker.'

'I'm all mixed up, Cynthia, it won't sink in. So start at the beginning. Was Jeff with Larry when yer got to where yer were meeting him?'

Cynthia nodded. 'I told them yer couldn't come 'cos yer've got a steady boyfriend, and Jeff winked at Larry and said they weren't surprised, they had an idea yer wouldn't turn up. He said he'd come and have a drink with us and then toddle off home. I didn't think anything about it when we came out of the pub and he started walking with us, I thought he must live near there. Then, when we were passing an entry they each put a hand on me arms and, without any warning, they dragged me down it. That was when I started to get frightened and struggled to get away from them, but they were gripping me arms so tight, they were hurting.' She rolled up a sleeve of her nightdress and lifted her arm to show Laura the deep, angry bruising. 'The other arm's the same.'

'Why didn't yer scream yer head off? Someone might have heard yer, and anyway it would have frightened the fellers, they'd have run like hell.'

Cynthia shook her head. 'I've been thinking about it all night, going over every detail until I thought I was going mad. But I can see now they'd had it planned down to a fine art. They had it all worked out what they'd do if you didn't come. It was all done without one word being passed between them. And as for me screaming, how could I scream when Jeff had his hand over me mouth? They dragged me down to the darkest part of the entry and flung me hard up against the wall. Then Jeff held me there by putting his hand around me throat. I couldn't move or I'd have been choked to death. They were so rough, it was as if they wanted to really hurt me.' Cynthia shuddered as in her mind she relived parts of the nightmare. And when the tears began to flow she wiped them away with a corner of the sheet. 'If I live to be a hundred, I'll never forget last night.'

'I still don't get it,' Laura said. 'What kick would they get out of beating yer up? And why Larry? Yer hadn't done him no harm.'

Plucking nervously at the eiderdown, her eyes looking past Laura to a spot on the wall, Cynthia spoke almost in a whisper. 'If I tell yer something, yer won't breathe a word to a living soul, will yer? I want yer to swear on yer life that yer won't repeat it.'

'Of course I won't tell no one, I swear on me life. I'm yer mate, aren't I, and mates don't clat on each other.'

'While Jeff was holding me against the wall, Larry was pulling me clothes up around me waist and tugging me knickers down.' Cynthia heard Laura's sharp intake of breath and nodded. 'Oh yeah, it sounds terrible, docsn't it? Well, I can assure yer that the reality was far worse than just listening about it. I couldn't speak properly, but I was begging Larry to leave me alone. He didn't seem to hear me because Jeff was egging him on, telling him what to do. And the more he egged him on, the more excited Larry got and I think he'd have killed me if his mate had told him to.'

Laura was shaking her head in disbelief. 'And this is the Larry who was supposed to be in love with yer! What a joke!'

'Oh, he was in love with me all right.' There was venom in Cynthia's voice. 'He loved me that much he wanted his friend to have a share of me.'

Laura's hand flew to her mouth while her eyes widened in horror. 'Not him as well, kid? Yer not saying they both . . . er . . . yer know what I mean?'

'Oh aye, I have good reason to know what yer mean. When Larry had finished, he took over from Jeff in keeping me quiet while his mate had his bit of fun. That's all I was to them, something they could satisfy themselves with, then throw away. And that's just what they did. Used me, then knocked me to the ground, crying me eyes out while they walked away laughing. I could have been dead for all they knew, or cared.'

The horror of it all was slowly sinking in with Laura. If she'd let her friend talk her into going with them last night, the same thing could have happened to her. It didn't bear thinking about. 'I don't know what to say, Cynthia, I've never heard anything like it. They should be sent to prison for what they did.'

'Yer don't know the half of it. The bruises on me throat and arms are nothing compared with the ones at the top of me legs. I walked all the way home because I knew I must have looked a mess, with me clothes all dirty and me eyes red from crying. And every step I took was pure agony.'

'What did yer parents say?'

'They didn't see me. Me mam opened the door and I told her I must be in for a cold 'cos I had a sore throat and a headache. I came straight upstairs and got into bed. Me dad came in to see me this morning before he went to work, but I kept meself well covered and told him I didn't feel well. Yer know how soft me dad is with me, he told me to stay where I was until I felt better.'

154

'And when is that going to be?' Laura asked. 'If yer stay there too long they'll think ye're really sick and send for a doctor.'

'I can't go out looking like this, not with me bruises showing. Anyway, I'm in too much pain to walk.'

'There's only yer throat showing, and a scarf would cover that. We could go for a little walk tomorrow afternoon if yer like. Just around the shops for half an hour, it'll do yer good. Yer'll be in the fresh air and it'll help to get yer legs moving.'

Cynthia eyed her friend through lowered lashes. 'Are yer still going dancing?'

Laura had been so looking forward to tomorrow night and was bitterly disappointed. But she had no one to go with now, and she didn't have the nerve to go on her own. And anyway, Cynthia was her best mate, she couldn't let her down. 'No, I wouldn't go without you. There's always next week.'

'Will yer tell me mam I'm going out with yer tomorrow afternoon, just for a bit of fresh air? I've got a scarf in one of the drawers, so I'll do what yer said.'

'Do yer feel a bit better, now yer've talked about what happened?'

Cynthia nodded. 'Yeah, I do, kid. But I'll never forget it, and I'll get even with them if it's the last thing I do. I've been meeting Larry on a Tuesday and Thursday, so they must be their nights out. I'll haunt Scotland Road on those nights until I come across them. They won't see me but I'll follow them until I find out where they live. And then I'll think of a way to get me own back. They won't get off scot-free, not after what they did to me.'

'Don't do it, Cynthia, yer might get yerself in a load of trouble. They're bad men, I wouldn't tangle with them if I were you.'

'It's easy for you to talk, it didn't happen to you. I'm the one who's in pain, the one who's going to have to live with the memory of it all me life. But I'll live with it easier if I have the satisfaction of knowing they're suffering too.' She saw the apprehension on Laura's face and added, 'Don't worry, I won't involve you. I'll do it all meself and take great satisfaction from it.'

'Did yer say seven rolls of paper, Stan?' Mary sat at the table with a pencil and a scrap of paper. 'Are yer sure that's enough?'

'I say seven, and Seamus and Ben say the same. We can't all be wrong, can we?'

'I didn't say yer were wrong, sweetheart, I was only asking to make sure.' Mary made a note on the paper. 'And don't tear yer hair out when I ask if it was sixteen yards of border?'

Stan grinned. 'I wouldn't tear me hair out no matter what yer said, love, 'cos I haven't got much as it is.' He bent his head so she could see the bald patch at the top. 'That spot seems to be growing bigger every day. If it keeps up at this rate, I'll be as bald as a billiard ball by this time next year.'

When Jenny came through from the kitchen she was giggling helplessly. 'Mam, get an extra roll of paper and do me dad's head. He'd blend in with the walls, then.'

'Don't be so cheeky, young lady.' Stan's smile was wide. 'Anyway, I've got a better idea and it's cheaper. Yer mam can put a tin of black Cherry Blossom shoe polish on her list – that should do the trick. When I'm polishing me shoes I can rub the brush over me bald spot'

'Yer'll not be sleeping on my pillowcases then, sunshine. It'll be the coal-hole for you.'

When the knock came, Jenny made a bee-line for the door. 'This'll be me grandad.'

Mary cocked an ear and grinned across at Stan when they heard Jenny's peal of laughter. 'Grandad, yer haven't had a shave and yer whiskers are tickling me.'

Joe's voice boomed, 'A tickle is better than a slap any day, queen.'

Mary got to her feet to greet her father with a big hug and a kiss. 'Yer cheeks are not half cold, Dad, I didn't think it was that bad out.'

'I think I'd be right in saying it was parky, what do you say, Stan?'

'I'd say we're in for a bad winter, Joe. It's only the end of October and it's bitter.'

Mary studied her father's face. He looked gaunt, but then who wouldn't if they weren't getting the right food inside them. 'Take yer coat off, Dad, and sit by the fire. I've put a dinner in the oven to keep warm for yer. We got ours over early, 'cos I'm going to the shops for wallpaper and paint.'

Joe handed his coat to Jenny before standing in front of the fire with his hands spread out near the flickering flames. 'I'll come with yer, sweetheart, to give yer a hand. Tins of paint can be very heavy.'

'No thanks, Dad, I've got me two mates coming with me. You stay in the warmth and keep Stan company.'

Laura stood at the top of the stairs listening. She'd hoped to be out before her grandad came, and she would have been if he'd come five minutes later. Not that she didn't want to see him, she did. He was always nice to her, and all her life she'd had a sneaking feeling that between her and Jenny, she was his favourite. The only reason she didn't want to see him now was because she was afraid his wife might have mentioned the birthday present or the dance. After all the lies she'd told, she had visions of walking into the room and being asked if she'd liked her present and did she enjoy the dance. She wouldn't know where to put herself, being found out in all those lies in front of the whole family. Celia had promised not to tell, but deep down, Laura didn't quite trust the girl her grandad had married. Oh, she was nice and friendly, fussed over Laura as though

156

she was someone special. And she was generous, no doubt about that. It was just a little niggle, something that didn't quite click with Laura that she couldn't put her finger on.

'I'd better go and get it over with,' she muttered, holding on to the banister for support as she stepped down the narrow, steep stairs. 'It's got to come sometime, I can't keep hiding from me grandad.'

Joe gave her a warm welcome. 'There yer are, sweetheart, I was wondering where yer'd got to. Come and give yer old grandad a big kiss. I'm sorry I missed yer birthday, but I didn't call because I thought yer'd be out celebrating. I did think about yer, though, and there's a slab of chocolate in me pocket for yer.'

Laura was so relieved she rained kisses on his face. 'Thank you, Grandad, ye're a little love, that's what yer are.'

'Being sixteen is an important milestone in yer life, sweetheart, one yer'll look back on when yer get old and grey, like yer grandad. So I hope yer did something that yer enjoyed and will look back on with pleasure.'

Laura knew her mam and dad were looking on with interest and contented smiles on their faces. They'd believe anything she said. But it was the look on Jenny's face that unnerved her. It was almost as if her sister knew everything and was saying, 'Go on, let's see yer lie yerself out of that.'

Deliberately snubbing her sister by turning her back on her, Laura did the only thing she could, she brazened it out. She'd got herself in so deep now there was nothing else for it. 'I got loads of cards and presents, Grandad, they were brilliant. And me and me mate went to our first dance. I would have enjoyed that but Cynthia didn't feel well and we had to leave early.'

'Oh, what's the matter with her?' Mary didn't like Cynthia, but she wouldn't wish the girl any harm. After all, she'd been Laura's friend since they'd started school and as far as Mary knew, they'd never had a quarrel. 'Got a cold, has she?'

'Yeah, she had a sore throat and everything. She stopped off work yesterday and was in bed all day. I'm going down there now to see if she wants to go for a walk for half an hour, then I'll stay in with her.'

'Yer'll stay in all day with her?' Mary's voice was high, showing her surprise. My God, this was a turn-up for the books. Her daughter actually putting herself out for someone . . . it had never been known before. 'Yer mean yer won't go out tonight?'

Laura shook her head. 'I don't mind for one night. We'll listen to the wireless or play cards.' She took her coat down off the hook and shivered as her arms came into contact with the cold lining. 'I won't be in for tea, Mam, I'm having a bite at Cynthia's.' She gave Joe a big hug. 'Ta-ra, Grandad, I'll see yer soon.' With a wave of her hand she was gone.

157

'That's one out of the way,' Mary said. 'Can't you get yerself an invite somewhere for tea, sunshine, 'cos it'll be pot luck here.'

Jenny shook her head. 'It's too cold to go out just for the sake of it. I'll be going to Janet's about seven, but right now I'll stay in with me dad and Grandad and make a nuisance of meself.' Then her face lit up. 'I've got an idea! Why don't I go and get some meat pies for our tea? They'd be quick, easy, and there'd be no washing up after 'cos we could eat them in our hands.'

'That's a brilliant idea, sunshine. But first, while I'm getting meself ready, will yer fetch Grandad's dinner out of the oven before he starves to death? I can hear his tummy rumbling from here.'

Mary was walking between her two neighbours as they neared the wallpaper shop, and instinctively put her arm out to bar Amy from walking into the shop first. 'Hang on a minute, sunshine, let's get this straight. Just for once, can we go in a shop without you causing ructions and having the place up?'

Amy spread her arms wide and appealed to Molly. 'What would yer do with her? Any stranger listening to her would shy clear of me, thinking I was a troublemaker with a mouth on me yer could hear the other side of the Mersey. Me real friends and neighbours wouldn't think that, like, because they know I'm the quietest, most docile woman in the street. I never raise me voice or finger to anyone.'

'Oh I know, I know, me darlin',' Molly sympathised, 'it's always the wrong ones what get the blame. I've noticed it meself, so I have, and isn't it the same the whole world over?'

'Would you two like to stay out here and pay each other compliments while I go and choose me paper?'

Amy sprang to life and pushed Mary out of the way. 'Not bleedin' likely! I see as much of yer wallpaper as you do, so I think I'm entitled to some say in what I have to feast me eyes on every day.' She huffed with disgust. 'The bloody cheek of yer, Mary Nightingale, thinking about yerself as usual. I've a good mind not to visit yer any more.'

'Amy, sunshine, yer don't visit me, yer practically live with me. Sometimes, without thinking, I even set a place for yer at the table.' Mary gave Molly the nod and they each took an arm of Amy's and frogmarched her into the shop. 'Now behave.'

As soon as Amy was in the shop she came over all sweetness and light. 'Hello, George, how's the world treating yer?'

The man behind the counter scratched his head. 'My God, are me eyes deceiving me, or is it really Amy Hanley?'

Amy smiled, straightening her scarf and throwing her shoulders back. 'In the flesh, George, in the flesh.'

George kept his face straight. 'I must say ye're wearing well, Amy.

I expected yer face to be all wrinkled and yer hair snow-white, by now.'

Amy considered this carefully. She liked the bit about her wearing well, but wrinkled and snow-white hair? That didn't sound like a compliment. 'What the hell are yer on about, wrinkles and snow-white hair? It's not that bleedin' long since I saw yer, only since the last time we decorated.'

'And that's about four years ago!' Still there was no smile on the shopkeeper's face. 'It's a wonder the paper hasn't walked off yer ruddy wall in disgust. Yer've certainly had yer money's worth out of it.' George was warming up to it now. A set-to with Amy Hanley was as good as a pint of bitter any day. 'How d'yer expect men like me to make a living while there's skinflints like you around? Yer'd take the crust out of a baby's mouth, ye're that tight.'

Amy's hackles rose to the occasion. 'Listen to me, yer moaning, miserable sod. I brought me mate here for all the material to decorate her room, and that's a whopping big order. But after what yer've just said, I've a good mind to take her to the shop in Stanley Road and give them the custom.' Hitching her bosom up and giving little nods of her head, she went on: 'I was passing there last week, quite by accident, like, and they had a paper in the window that my friend would love. It was sky blue pink with a finny-haddy border.'

Mary gave Molly a nudge. 'Yer can talk to her until ye're blue in the face, but she never changes.'

'Now would yer be wanting her to change, me darlin'?'

'Would I heckerslike! I know which side me bread's buttered on, Molly. She saves me a fortune in not having to go to the pictures. I've never seen a film yet that can make me laugh as much as my mate can. She saves me money in other ways, too. You just watch her haggle with George. I bet she'll get a ha'penny knocked off a yard of border, a penny off a roll of paper, and if she's in good form I'll get coppers knocked off the tins of paint.'

'Sure, it's crafty yer are, Mary Nightingale.'

'Sure, and don't I know it, Molly Moynihan?'

Chapter Thirteen

'Ye're late,' Mary said, wagging a finger at Amy. 'I've been standing with me coat on since yer knocked on the wall, and that's a quarter of an hour ago. I suppose yer've been jangling, as usual?' Her tone changed to one of concern when she noted her friend's red face and heaving chest. 'Yer look all flustered, sunshine, is anything the matter?'

'I've been running and me heart's going fifteen to the dozen.' Amy, her palms flat on the table, inhaled deeply and blew out the breath through puckered lips. 'I'd just closed me front door after me, when I heard a cry. And when I looked to see where the noise came from, I saw old Lizzie lying on the ground outside her house. It gave me a fright, I can tell yer, I thought she'd dropped dead. The poor bugger had fallen down the steps and hurt herself. I tried every which way to pick her up, but every time I touched her she cried in pain. Yer'll have to come with me, girl, and see if we can manage her between us.'

'Oh, dear God, d'yer think she's broken anything? If she has, we shouldn't move her in case we do more harm. Best get an ambulance.'

'Will yer stop thinking the worst until we know for sure? I've got to say, girl, yer can be a right misery guts at times. Yer'll have her dead and buried before we know it. If she does peg out, it'll be from being left to lie on the ground, in freezing weather, and catching pneumonia while we're standing here playing guessing games.' Her wide hips swaying, Amy made for the door. 'Get a move on, girl, or yer'll be too late for the bleedin' funeral.'

As she stepped down on to the pavement, Mary said, 'I'll give Molly a knock, she's usually good at times like this.'

'Okay, but make it snappy.' When Amy looked to where she'd left Lizzie Marshall, who should she see standing over the frail figure, but her nosy neighbour, Annie Baxter. 'Wouldn't yer just know it! There's never a bleedin' show without Punch!' Not bothering to lower her voice, she went on as she hurried along, 'Never misses a trick, the nosy old cow. I bet she's licking her lips at the thought of knocking on every door in the neighbourhood with the news.'

'I'm glad ye're back, queen.' There was pleading in Lizzie's faded blue eyes. Annie Baxter was not a favourite of hers and was the last person in the world she'd want to accept help from. 'Is Mary coming?'

'Yeah, she's knocking for Molly Moynihan. Between us we'll get yer back in the house and make yer comfortable before we see what yer've been and gone and done to yerself.'

'I offered to help her up,' Annie said, fussing as she tried in vain to get in front of Amy. She wanted a ringside seat so she didn't miss anything. 'But she wouldn't let me.'

Amy's eyes travelled the length of her neighbour. 'I see yer haven't got yer jungle drums with yer today, Annie. Or are yer using smoke signals, like Big Chief Sitting Bull?'

'Don't be so bleedin' funny, Amy Hanley. I'm just as concerned about Lizzie as you are, yer sarcastic mare.'

Lizzie stepped in before war was declared and Amy lost her temper and landed one on her neighbour. 'It's very kind of yer to be concerned, Annie, but there's no need. I'll be as right as rain when me friends get me inside.'

But Annie Baxter wasn't going to be dismissed so easily. She had as much right to stand in the street as that fat nosy cow from next door had. And with her thin arms crossed over her thin chest, and her thin lips clamped together, she stood her ground. Even when Mary and Molly came dashing down, she didn't move an inch, even though she was preventing them from seeing to the old lady. Amy stood it for so long, then decided enough was enough and grabbed her arm. She turned her towards the top of the street, saying, 'That's the way to Lily Farmer's. She's usually first on yer list so yer may as well stick to yer routine. And if yer want to spice yer story up a bit, yer can say Lizzie was wearing bright red fleecy-lined knickers with a pocket in. She's not, of course, but yer mate won't know that, and I won't snitch.'

If looks could kill, Amy would have been a dead duck. 'Anyone would think yer owned the bleedin' street, the way yer carry on. But ye're only the monkey, not the organ grinder.'

'Go away, will yer, missus, before I lose me temper. If yer fancy lying beside Lizzie on the bleedin' ground, just say the word because me hands are itching to thump yer one.'

Annie waited until she was far enough away for safety, before calling, 'I'll tell my feller about you, Amy Hanley. He'll be round to see yer.'

'I'll look forward to that, Gabby Annie! Tell him I'm free next Tuesday night.'

While this exchange was going on, Mary had opened Lizzie's front door, while Molly scooped up the old lady and cradled her in her arms like a baby. 'I don't think yer've broken anything, me darlin', or yer'd be screaming in pain, so yer would. But let's get yer inside and give yer the once-over.'

Lizzie Marshall was a spinster. She'd lived in the street since her parents died, many years ago. She'd been forced to move out of the three-bedroomed house that she'd been born in, because with just her wage coming in, she couldn't afford the rent or the upkeep of it. She was small and frail now, with wispy white hair, faded blue eyes and deep wrinkles on her face. Living on a pittance, she managed to keep her house spotlessly clean and there was never a moan out of her.

'Put those two cushions together for her head,' Molly said, laying the old lady down as gently as if she was a piece of Dresden china. 'There yer go, me darlin', we'll soon have yer as snug as a bug in a rug.' She turned to Mary who was standing wringing her hands. 'Nip up and get a blanket off the bed, she's shivering with cold.'

'I'll put the kettle on,' Amy said, springing into action. 'A cup of weak, sweet tea is the best medicine for shock. And yer could do with a few more cobs of coal on the fire.'

'I'm not cold,' Lizzie said quickly. She could only afford one bag of coal a fortnight but was too proud to say so. 'I haven't got much coal until the coalman comes, so I'm having to eke it out.'

Mary came into the room at that moment, and glanced from Molly to Amy. It was only three days since the coalman was round; there was no way Lizzie could have used it all in a couple of days. Unless, of course, the old lady couldn't afford to buy any. 'We'll all lend yer a bucket of coal, Lizzie, so don't be worrying. The main thing is to get you warmed through to the marrow before yer get pneumonia.' She shook the folded blanket she'd brought down with her and tucked it around the shivering woman. 'I'll tell yer what, sunshine, yer house is a credit to yer. Yer put the three of us to shame.'

'You ain't kidding,' Amy said, coming back after putting the kettle on. 'Yer could eat yer bleedin' dinner off the floor out there.'

Lizzie smiled with pleasure, even though every part of her was hurting. 'I do me best. I've never forgotten what my mother used to tell me. "Never let housework get on top of yer. Do a bit every day, then yer'll never have a dirty house".' A look of sadness came to the faded blue eyes. 'It's thirty years since she died, but I've never forgotten her, or me dad. They were wonderful parents.'

'Sure, wouldn't they have to be, to have brought a lovely lady like you into the world?' Molly sat down on the edge of the couch and lifted one of the thin hands. 'Will yer let me run me hand up yer arm, me darlin'? I'll be as gentle as I can, but shout out if I hurt yer.'

Lizzie nodded. 'I trust yer, Molly.'

The kettle began to whistle and Amy jumped to her feet. 'I'll pour

163

the water into the pot and leave it to brew for a while.'

When Lizzie shuddered, Molly quickly took her hand away. 'Does that hurt, me darlin'?'

The old lady nodded. 'It's very painful.'

'Right, we'll have a cup of tea then take yer jumper off to see what's what.' Molly smiled into the lined face. 'Yer haven't broken anything, sweetheart, so that's a blessing.'

Mary glanced towards the kitchen. 'Amy Hanley, have yer gone to China for that ruddy tea? We're all spitting feathers in here.'

'Ay, I'm seeing to the invalid.' Amy appeared, carefully carrying a cup and saucer. 'You can see to yer ruddy self, ye're ugly enough.' She handed the saucer to Molly. 'You hold it, girl, in case Lizzie spills it on herself.'

The old lady looked flustered. 'I've only got a drop of milk, I was on me way to the shops to get some when I fell.'

'That's all right, sunshine, we're not dying of thirst.' Mary felt sorry for the proud old lady who'd never been known to borrow or cadge off anyone. 'We'll see to yer bit of shopping, so don't worry.'

The drink seemed to perk Lizzie up. She licked her lips and said, 'That's the best cup of tea I've ever had.'

Molly took the cup from her and handed it to Amy, who was hovering by the end of the couch. Then she stroked Lizzie's cheek. 'Lean forward, me darlin', and I'll roll yer jumper up from the back. It'll be over yer head in the blink of an eye, so it will.'

Lizzie was covered in bruises, particularly down the right side, where she'd landed. They were only just beginning to colour, but as Molly said, 'Tomorrow they'll be black and blue, me darlin', and very sore. Best if yer stay in and rest for a few days.'

'I wouldn't be able to go out, Molly, 'cos I think I've broke me ankle.'

'I don't think yer'll have broken it, sweetheart, or they'd hear yer screaming down at the Pier Head. But yer may have sprained it when yer fell. Let's take yer shoes and stockings off and have a gander.' Molly sat nursing the painful foot. 'It's not broken, me darlin', or it would be swelled up like a balloon. But yer've sprained it all right and yer won't be able to walk on it for a few days.'

'How's she going to get up the stairs to bed, then?' Amy wanted to know. 'Or down the yard to the lavvy?'

'With our help, that's how,' Mary said. 'We'll make up a bed on the couch so she's nice and comfy, and we'll give her an arm to lean on while she hops down the yard.'

Molly saw the worried frown on Lizzie's face and patted her gently. 'It's only for a few days, me darlin', and won't it be nice to be waited on hand and foot?'

'I'm going to be a nuisance to yer, I'm sorry.'

'Don't be so daft!' Amy felt like picking the old lady up and taking her home, where there was a nice fire roaring up the chimney. 'There's three of us, we'll take turns looking after yer.'

'Then let's start now,' Molly said briskly. 'Mary, if Lizzie doesn't mind, will yer see to the bedding? Oh, and bring a nightdress and something to wrap around her shoulders. And Amy, will you bank the fire up, me darlin', then make Lizzie another cup of tea?' The Irishwoman winked at Amy. 'Sure, I can see in yer eyes what yerself is thinking, Amy me darlin'. So I'll answer yer and save yer the trouble of asking. I'm off home to get a bucket of coal to fill the scuttle and some milk to keep Lizzie in drinks until one of us goes to the shops.'

The small house became a hive of activity and Lizzie began to enjoy herself. It was nice to have people for a change, to hear a human voice instead of just the steady ticking of the clock. She never had visitors and sometimes felt very lonely as each dreary day dragged on to another dreary day. But the house was ringing now with the sound of Mary's laughter and Amy's antics, and although she was in pain, the old lady was thinking her fall was a blessing in disguise.

When Molly came back with the coal and milk, it was to see the old lady looking much brighter and contented. She had a clean nightdress on, with a maroon cardi over her shoulders, and her head was resting on three feather pillows.

'Well, now, don't you look the posh one? Sure 'tis the life of Riley himself yer'll be having for the next few days.' Molly placed a jug of milk on the table before emptying the bucket of coal into the brass coal scuttle at the side of the hearth. 'That should keep yer going until tonight.'

'I'll send our John down with another bucket when he's had his dinner,' Amy said. 'He'll bank the fire up so it lasts all through the night and keeps the room warm.'

'There's no need,' Lizzie said, afraid she'd never be able to pay these women back. 'I don't feel the cold.'

'While ye're lying there, Lizzie Marshall, yer'll do as ye're told. I'll ask our Jenny to come down and sit with yer for an hour, keep yer company. And when it's time for bed, one of us will come and help yer to the lavvy before settling yer down for the night.'

Molly turned her head away so they couldn't see the grin on her face. John and Jenny coming here tonight, eh? Didn't that give Amy's son an unfair advantage? She'd have to pass that bit of information on to Mick, so she would, otherwise he'd be left at the starting post.

'Look, Mary and Amy, you two go and get yer shopping done. I'll stay with Lizzie until dinnertime, then one of you can take over.'

'Are yer sure, Molly?' Mary asked. 'I feel a bit mean, leaving yer.'

165

'Nonsense!' Molly shooed them out of the room. 'I couldn't pass me time in better company than Lizzie's. We'll have a great time, altogether, pulling everyone to pieces.' But her face became serious when she was showing her neighbours out. 'She seems fine, but I think we should keep our eyes on her for a few days. I'm not worried about the bruises, they'll not kill her. But Lizzie is eighty years of age, so she is, and a fall can be a terrible shock to the system.'

'Yeah, I've been thinking of that meself.' Mary sighed as she linked her arm through Amy's. 'We'll get her a few groceries to keep her going, and go half each with the cost. Is that all right with you, sunshine?'

'Yer've no need to ask, girl, yer know that.' Amy's voice was choked. 'She's a ruddy hero, that old lady, d'yer know that? She keeps her house beautiful, like a little palace. But her cupboards are bare. There's nowt to eat in the kitchen, not even a crumb to give to the birds. It's no wonder she fell, she must be as weak as a kitten and light-headed with hunger.'

'We'll feed her up in the next few days,' Molly said, 'and watch out for her in future. But we'll have to be careful how we do it. She's a proud old lady and would be offended if she thought we were doing it out of pity.' She began to close the door. 'I'll get back to her now and see if she wants to spend a penny.'

In the Nightingale house, the family were seated around the table eating their dinner as Mary told of the day's events. 'Honest to God, there's not a pick on her, she's as thin as a rake. Molly picked her up as though she was a baby. But what a little love she is. I felt like hugging the life out of her.'

'Yeah, she's a nice little thing, always got a pleasant smile for yer,' Stan said. 'And she does well for her age, her windows and step are always the cleanest in the street.'

Jenny's eyes were full of concern. 'I hope she wasn't hurt bad, Mam? I think she's lovely, like a little doll.'

'She's full of bruises, and they must be sore because she's got no flesh on her. But a week's rest, staying in the warmth, should see a great improvement.' Mary pushed her plate back and rested her elbows on the table. 'I want one of yer to sit with her for a few hours tonight, just to keep her company so she's not dwelling on things.'

For the first time, Laura showed interest in the conversation. It was Thursday, her night for Barlow's Lane and Gary. She hadn't seen him since last week and she was going tonight come hell or high water. 'Ah, ay, Mam! I'm going dancing tonight – I've made arrangements! Anyway, I don't want to sit with an old woman, I wouldn't know what to talk about.'

'I'll go, Mam,' Jenny said quickly, before her mother could speak.

166

'Me and Janet will sit with her – we'd like that.'

Mary sighed as she looked at her eldest daughter. Selfish to the core, as usual. There was only one person she cared about and that was herself. But angry words wouldn't change her so what was the point in getting herself all worked up for nothing? So Mary smiled at Jenny as she thanked God that both sisters were not alike. 'Thanks, sunshine, I might have known yer wouldn't let me down. I've got Miss Marshall's key and I told her someone would be there about seven. So get yerself ready and go round for Janet.'

Jenny's chair scraped back. 'I'll wash the dishes first.'

'No, yer won't,' Stan said, 'Laura will wash the dishes.'

Laura's face was like thunder and a sharp retort was on the tip of her tongue. But it stayed there, because her father's face told her he would brook no argument. So it was with ill-grace she collected the plates and made for the kitchen.

In the house next door sat the Hanley family, and Amy had just finishing telling them the news. Mealtimes in the household were usually lively, with the house ringing with laughter. But tonight was different, as Miss Marshall was well liked by them all. The two boys, John and Eddy, were remembering that when they were younger, never once had the old lady chased them when they were playing footie outside her house. Never shook a clenched fist at them nor threatened to tell their mother like the other neighbours did. And Edna was thinking of the times Miss Marshall had given her a ha'penny for going on a message.

'Is the old girl going to be all right?' Ben asked. 'Shouldn't she have a doctor?'

'We decided to wait and see how she is tomorrow.' Amy cupped her chin in her hand. 'I'll tell yer what, that Molly Moynihan is as good as any doctor. Like Florence Nightingale she was. Me and Mary wouldn't have had a bleedin' clue what to do, but Molly did.' She gave her eldest son a dig in the ribs. 'By the way, I want yer to take a bucketful of coal over and bank the fire up for Lizzie.'

'I'll go now then, 'cos I'm going out later.'

'It's no good going before seven 'cos yer won't get in. Mary took the door key so one of the girls can let themselves in to sit with Lizzie for a couple of hours. It'll probably be Jenny – I can't see the other selfish so-and-so helping out.'

John's spirits lifted. He'd get there for seven and pull a fast one on Mick. 'Okay, I wasn't going anywhere exciting, anyway.'

In the house opposite, the Moynihan family were discussing the same subject. 'So, with one thing and another, it's been quite a day,' Molly said. 'But, thanks be to God, she'd only just fallen when Amy

167

saw her. If she'd been left to lie on the ground for long, in this weather, she'd have died of cold, and that's the truth of it.'

'Is there anything I can do, sweetheart?' Seamus asked. 'Sure, haven't I always had a soft spot for the dear old soul? I bet there's never been an angry word passed her lips, nor a swearword; she's too much of a lady for that.'

'We're sorted out for today, everything's under control. Amy's sending John down with coal and he's going to bank the fire up to last through the night. And Mary's going down last thing to take Lizzie down the yard.' Molly was facing her husband but her eyes were looking sideways to where her son was sitting. 'Oh, and young Jenny is going to sit with Lizzie for a couple of hours to keep her company.'

Mick stopped chewing and his mouth fell open. But he quickly recovered when the implication of what his mother had said hit home. He swallowed the food in his mouth and put down his knife and fork. There were more important things at stake than food. He racked his brain to think of something that would put him on a level pegging with John, but his usually sharp mind was lacking in ideas. 'I'll take her some coal, as well, to save you ladies having to lug it down tomorrow.'

Molly kept her face straight. 'I've told yer, me darlin', John's taking a bucketful. If you turn up with another, the old lady will have a fit, so she will.'

'Well, I'm going down with something, I'm not letting John Hanley have a clear field.' Mick nodded his head for emphasis. 'I bet he's laughing sacks, having it handed to him on a flamin' platter.'

Seamus felt his wife kick him gently on the ankle, and turned to see the laughter in her eyes. 'You could go down tomorrow night, son, that would make it fair. Anyway, aren't yer supposed to be going out with John? So he won't be spending much time there, will he?'

'Huh! Yer don't think he'll be thinking of me, do yer? Not on yer blinking life, he won't. If Jenny's there he'll stay put. Not even Jean Harlow would get him out.' Mick glared at his mother. 'Why didn't yer say I'd take the coal down?'

Molly leaned across the table and gave him a broad wink. 'Well, yer see, me darlin', I thought Miss Marshall would appreciate a homemade custard instead.'

When the words had sunk in, Mick's eyes shone and his dimples appeared. 'D'yer mean yer've made her a custard?'

'I have that, me darlin'. And although I say it as shouldn't, it looks very appetising, so it does. Lovely golden brown, with a pinch of nutmeg on the top.'

'Mam, ye're an angel. And a clever one at that.'

'Perhaps devious would be a better word. But, sure, I couldn't stand back and see me only son and heir left out in the cold.'

Mick jumped to his feet. 'I'm going to get washed and put a clean shirt on.' He got halfway up the stairs, stopped for a second then turned and came down again. Poking his head around the door, a wide smile on his handsome face, he asked, 'Would yer say that a custard was a better present than a bucket of coal?'

Seamus dropped his head back and roared with laughter. 'Sure, now, that would mightily depend upon whether yer were hungry or cold.'

When they were alone, the big Irishman put his arm around his wife's shoulder. ' 'Tis a bit of the divil himself yer have in yer, Molly Moynihan, and that's a fact.'

She met his eyes and the love she had for her husband was there to see. 'I've two men in me life, Seamus Moynihan, and if they need a little help from me, then I'll always do me best. But, sure, I'll not be making friends with the divil to do it.'

Jenny pulled two of the wooden chairs away from the table and set them in front of the couch. 'There now, we won't have to raise our voices to hear each other.'

Lizzie Marshall smiled. 'It's very kind of you to come and sit with an old woman. But young girls should be out enjoying themselves. Haven't yer got boyfriends?'

Jenny got a fit of the giggles. 'We're too young to go out with boys, Miss Marshall.' She turned to her friend, who was blushing to the roots of her hair. 'Anyway, no one will have us, will they, Jan?'

'They will when we're a bit older.' Janet was quite indignant. 'Another few months and me mam said I can go dancing.' She narrowed her eyes. 'Have you asked yer mam yet if you can come with me?'

'Not yet, but I think I could get round her. Especially if I'm going with you.'

Lizzie was visibly startled when there was a loud ran-tan at the door. 'Oh dear, I wonder who this can be at this hour?'

'It'll only be John Hanley, Miss Marshall, don't be frightened. Me mam told me he was coming with some coal. I'll let him in.'

But when Jenny opened the door it was to see Mick standing there with a plate in his hand, covered by a pure white cloth. 'Me mam thought Miss Marshall might fancy this for her supper.'

'Oh, I thought it was John knocking.'

Mick feigned surprise. 'Why, is he coming over?'

Jenny nodded as she held out her hand. 'I'll take it, shall I?'

But Mick wouldn't have parted with the plate for all the tea in China. After all, she wouldn't be asking John to hand a bucket of coal over, it would be too heavy. 'No, I'd like to give it her meself, and ask how she is. It would be bad manners not to pay me respects. And me mam is red-hot on respect. If I went home and said I'd just handed the plate in and didn't see the invalid, I'd get a clip around the ears for not being polite.' His white teeth shone in the darkness. 'And yer wouldn't like me to get a clip around the ears, would yer, Jenny Nightingale?'

Jenny's peal of laughter rang out in the deserted street. 'Mick Moynihan, has anybody ever told yer that yer talk too much?'

John Hanley had just closed the door behind him when he heard Jenny's laughter. A smile came to his face but quickly disappeared when he saw Mick standing outside Miss Marshall's house with a plate in his hand. Then he started to leg it across the cobbles. There was some dirty work at the crossroads going on here – his mam hadn't mentioned anything about Mick. The bucket was banging against his leg, but he didn't slow down, even though he had his best pair of kecks on. The only thing on his mind was to stop his rival from setting foot in that house. But he was too late. Mick was already mounting the step when he reached the pavement opposite. 'Don't close the door, Jenny,' he shouted. 'This bucket is heavy.'

Mick stood in the tiny hall and feigned surprise at the sight of his mate. Jenny had gone inside with the plate, so she wasn't there to hear him tell fibs. 'Well, well! Fancy seeing you here, mate.'

'I'm supposed to be here, you're not!' Although John was none too pleased that things hadn't gone according to plan, he secretly admitted he was being underhanded as well, so he was as guilty as his friend. Changing the bucket over to the other hand, he asked, 'How did yer pull it off, yer devious swine?'

Mick tapped the end of his nose with a finger. 'That's for me to know, and you to find out. But I don't put a foot outside this door until you do. Now, shall we make our presence known, or have yer become attached to that bucket of coal?'

'I feel like throwing it over yer, if yer want to know. I've got me best trousers on and they'll be as black as the hobs of hell.'

Lizzie, who never had a visitor, had seen so many people in her house today she was dizzy. But oh, wasn't it lovely to have company? Particularly in the evening, which was the loneliest time of the day. 'Well, two pretty girls and two handsome lads, aren't I lucky?'

'I can see the two pretty girls, Miss Marshall,' Jenny said, nudging Janet and giggling, 'but where are the handsome lads?'

John was quick to reply. 'She doesn't recognise me, 'cos I'm covered in coaldust.' He took out a hankie and wiped a cheek. 'There yer are, Jenny, it's me.'

'I know it's you, soft lad, but I want to know where the handsome lads are.'

'I'm saying nothing,' Mick said. 'It doesn't do to blow yer own trumpet.'

'Well, I think ye're both very handsome,' said Lizzie, 'and if I wasn't seven times older than yer, I'd be fluttering me eyelashes and going all coy.'

John, still lumbered with the bucket, asked, 'Shall I put this in the kitchen and bank the fire up before I go, Miss Marshall?'

'You've got a date, haven't yer, John?' There was a mischievous twinkle in Mick's eyes. 'So there's no need for you to stay, I'll see to the fire.'

'Over my dead body, mate. When I go, you go.'

'Oh, ye've both got dates, have yer?' Jenny said, before turning to her friend. 'Yer see, Jan, there'll be no fellers left by the time we're fifteen. Just our luck, eh?'

'Neither of us have got dates,' Mick said, turning the corners of his mouth down in an expression of self-pity. 'No girls will have us 'cos we're too ugly.'

'Ah, yer poor things.' Jenny put a hand to her heart in a show of sympathy. 'I don't think ye're that ugly, do you, Jan?'

Janet thought they were two very handsome lads but was enjoying the leg-pull. 'No, not really ugly. I mean, in the dark they could be mistaken for Cary Grant and Gary Cooper.'

'That's where we're going wrong, John,' Mick said. 'We should stay indoors during the day and only come out at night, like Dracula.'

Lizzie was taking all this in and thoroughly enjoying herself. She wasn't missing anything, either. Unless she was very much mistaken, both boys had their eyes on Jenny. It was understandable because she was a lovely girl, in looks and in personality. But both boys couldn't be winners, so it would be interesting to see what happened in the next year or so.

'Can I put this bucket down, Miss Marshall?' John asked. 'Otherwise I'll have one arm a yard longer than the other.'

'Put it in the kitchen, dear, and then you and Mick sit down and keep us company.' Lizzie had a hard time keeping her laughter at bay as she watched Mick take advantage of John's brief absence. Within seconds he had pulled a chair from the table and plonked himself next to Jenny. And John's face when he returned was a study, as he tried to think of a way to usurp his mate. She could almost hear him thinking, and when his face lit up she knew he'd found a solution.

'I know, let's have a game of pass the parcel. And the one what gets left with the parcel, has to do a forfeit.' John thought his idea was brilliant. 'We'll have to spread out, though, so let's put the chairs back around the table.'

Lizzie gave him ten out of ten for initiative. Nevertheless, the idea didn't appeal to her. 'I'm too long in the tooth to be doing forfeits, John.'

'Yer wouldn't have to, Miss Marshall, you could be referee. Yer just turn yer head away, so yer can't see, and clap yer hands when yer want us to stop.'

Mick wasn't about to be moved from his prime position so easily. 'Where are yer going to get a parcel from?'

'It doesn't have to be a proper parcel,' said John, equally determined. 'A piece of coal wrapped in paper will do.'

'Oo, er, what kind of forfeit?' Janet wanted to know. 'I can't sing or dance, and I don't know any jokes.'

'Don't be so miserable, Jan!' Jenny thought it was a good way of entertaining Miss Marshall. 'Yer know nursery rhymes, don't yer?'

Janet looked relieved. 'Is that all I have to do?'

They were being too longwinded for John's liking. At this rate Mick would still be sitting pretty next to Jenny when it was time to go. He took hold of Janet's arm and lifted her from the chair. 'That's all yer have to do, Janet, so sit at the table and Jenny will sit next to yer. Me and Mick will sit the other side.'

For the next two hours, Lizzie Marshall laughed more than she'd ever laughed in her life. The two boys were really comical as they tried to outdo each other. When Mick got caught with the parcel, he chose to sing a song. He had a fine voice, too, but it was drowned out when John decided his whistling would make a fine accompaniment. And when it was John's turn to pay a forfeit, Mick used the table as a set of drums while Jenny and Janet hummed completely out of tune.

The girls didn't get off scot-free, either. While Jenny was reciting *Goldilocks and the Three Bears*, the boys were doing all the actions in such an exaggerated way everyone was reduced to fits of laughter. But Janet's contribution, *Jack and Jill*, had John shaking his head vigorously. 'You can get the pail of water, Mick. I'm not lifting that ruddy bucket again for no one, never mind running up a hill with it.'

Mary had her hand on the knocker when she heard shrieks of laughter. 'In the name of God,' she muttered, 'what's our Jenny thinking about! Lizzie is supposed to be resting, not having a flaming party!' When there was no response to her knock, she rapped on the window and had a sharp rebuke on her tongue when the door opened.

'Mick Moynihan, what the hell's going on here? Just wait until I see our Jenny, she should have more sense.' She brushed the startled boy aside and entered the room, ready to do battle. But when she saw Lizzie wiping tears of laughter from her eyes, and looking happier than she'd ever seen her, Mary had the rug pulled from under her feet. 'Well, I declare!'

172

'Oh Mary, yer should have been here, yer don't know what yer've missed.'

'Aren't you supposed to be sick, Lizzie Marshall, with pains everywhere?'

'Oh, I've still got the pains, worse than ever.' The faded blue eyes twinkled back at Mary. 'But how can yer lie still when ye're doubled up with laughter? I've got pains now where I didn't have them before. But isn't it better to be in agony when ye're happy, than be in agony when ye're on yer own and feeling miserable? I've had the time of me life tonight, Mary, thanks to these four young people.' She grinned as she added, 'Oh, and a bucket of coal.'

'I've been keeping me eye on her, Mam,' Jenny said. 'I made sure she wasn't doing anything to hurt herself.'

'I've been keeping watch, too!' Mick said.

'I made her a cup of tea, Mrs Nightingale,' came from John.

Mary was beginning to see the funny side of it. She looked at Janet and asked, 'What about you, Janet, what have you got to say for yerself?'

Janet was surprised by the question. 'Er . . . I enjoyed meself, Mrs Nightingale.' And she was even more surprised by the burst of laughter. She didn't think she'd said anything funny, but joined in, anyway.

Mary looked at the clock. 'Right, time yer were on yer way so I can get Miss Marshall settled for the night. Jenny, you and Janet tidy up while John sees to the fire.'

Wanting to curry favour with the woman he hoped would one day be his mother-in-law, Mick asked, 'Have yer got a job for me, Mrs Nightingale?'

Before Mary could answer, John said, 'I have, mate. Yer can get that bucket of ruddy coal. And if yer can manage it, bang it against yer leg a few times so yer kecks are as black as mine.'

When they were leaving, Jenny was the first to kiss Lizzie. The other three looked uncertain, until Mick bent and kissed her cheek, then they all followed suit. The smile on the old lady's face couldn't have been wider. 'Thank you for giving me a lot of pleasure. And seeing as the girls can't get boyfriends because they're too young, and the boys can't get girlfriends because they're too ugly, there'll always be a welcome here if ye're ever at a loose end.'

Mick got in just before John. 'How about tomorrow night?'

'Ay, two nights on the trot is too much, Mick Moynihan.' Mary herded them towards the front door. 'She seems to have enjoyed herself, and I thank yer for that, but let's wait and see how she is tomorrow. It might prove to have been too much for her.' She was about to close the door, when she remembered. 'Oh, and make sure Janet gets home safely.'

'We'll make sure the two girls get home safe and sound, Mrs Nightingale,' Mick said, 'so don't be worrying.'

John thought his mate was getting all the action, so he added his twopennyworth. 'Yer can rely on us.'

Jenny and her friend linked arms and started walking back to Janet's house, unaware of the jostling for position that was going on behind them. Apart from splitting the girls, there was no way they could both walk beside Jenny. So John said, through gritted teeth, 'You go first, but we swop over halfway, d'yer hear?'

'Anything yer say, pal.' Mick's mind was elsewhere. Could he talk his mam into making another custard tomorrow?

And as John fell into step beside Janet, he was telling himself to keep his working trousers on tomorrow night when he took the coal over.

Chapter Fourteen

Laura gave a quick glance at her friend's house as she passed it on the next Thursday evening, wondering if Cynthia was getting ready for one of her twice-weekly visits to the Scotland Road area. Laura never thought for one minute that she'd keep it up, but this was the fourth week and her friend was more bitter and determined than ever. Every Tuesday and Thursday she left the house in flat-heeled shoes, wearing her working coat and with a scarf in her pocket to wrap around her head as soon as she neared her destination. She hadn't seen hide nor hair of Jeff or Larry, but she insisted she'd keep on looking until she spotted them, even if it took her a lifetime.

Laura hopped on to the platform of the tram and made her way to a seat. She missed going out with her mate on a Tuesday night, but not on Thursday, her night for the dance at Spellow Lane. Her dancing had come on in leaps and bounds, thanks to Gary. He partnered her for every dance, was attentive to her, and really seemed to like her. Yet he'd never asked her for a date, and she couldn't understand this. Unless it was because Celia insisted on leaving with her at half-ten – this was enough to put any boy off. He probably thought she wasn't capable of looking after herself. There were times when Laura regretted ever getting involved with her grandad's wife, then she'd remind herself that if she hadn't, she'd never have met Gary.

Her heart beating with anticipation, Laura ran up the flight of stone steps and pushed open the door to the foyer of the dance hall. The first person she saw was Celia, leaning with her back to the wall and deep in conversation with Charlie. But as soon as she saw Laura, she hurried towards her and made a big show of greeting her with a hug and kiss. 'Hi-ya, kid, it's good to see yer.'

This fussing every week was beginning to grate on Laura. There was no need for it; girls didn't kiss each other, it was soppy. She'd known Cynthia all her life, but never once had they kissed each other. Bringing her friend to mind gave Laura an idea: she'd coax Cynthia to come with her next week, then there would be no reason for Celia to stick to her like glue.

'I'll just put me coat in the cloakroom.' Some of the girls folded their coats and put them under chairs, but not Laura. She'd only had this coat two weeks and didn't want it to get creased or dirty. 'You go in, I'll see yer inside.'

Gary claimed her as soon as she walked in the dance hall. 'Just in time for a slow fox, babe, come on.'

Laura scanned the faces around them. 'Where's Celia? She can mind me bag.'

'Hang it over yer arm for now, the dance will be ended soon.' As they were twirling past the stage, Gary took the bag from her and placed it near the pianist. 'Keep yer eye on that for us, Tommy.'

When the dance came to an end, he kept hold of her hand and walked her to the edge of the dance floor. 'There's no point in sitting down, we may as well stay up for the next dance. It should be a waltz or a rumba.'

With a handsome boy holding her hand, Laura was flushed with pleasure. He must like me, she thought, or he wouldn't want to be with me all the time. There's plenty of unattached girls he could take his pick from, but he's only interested in me. Perhaps tonight was the night he'd ask her for a date. They laughed and joked their way through three more dances, then Laura called a halt. 'I'll have to look for Celia, I haven't seen her since I came in. She'll think I'm terrible, not going near her.'

'I wouldn't worry about that,' Gary said. 'Celia is more than capable of looking after herself, believe me.'

Laura thought there was a funny look in his eyes, but it was soon gone and she put it down to her imagination. 'Still, I think I should put in an appearance.'

'Suit yerself. I'll have the next dance with Dorothy then. I've been neglecting her since you came on the scene.'

Laura pulled him back. 'Oh no, yer won't have the next dance with Dorothy, whoever she is. I'll find Celia in the interval. Mind you, I've been keeping an eye out for her and haven't seen sight nor light of her since I came in.'

'She's probably sitting down somewhere, talking to Charlie.'

This gave Laura the opportunity of asking something that had been puzzling her for the last four weeks. 'Is Charlie a very good friend of hers?'

Gary averted his eyes as he shrugged his shoulders. 'Charlie's a friend to everyone, especially if they happen to be female. He's got an eye for the girls.'

It was on the tip of Laura's tongue to ask if that included married women, but she thought better of it. After all, Gary was a friend of Celia and Charlie; he might repeat anything she said. 'Yeah, I gathered he was fond of women.'

'I think there's only one more dance before the interval, and she'll probably come looking for you then.'

176

Gary was right. But then he would be, because he knew full well where Celia was. He'd been given his instructions to keep Laura occupied for at least half an hour. They were walking off the dance floor, hand in hand, when Celia came through the door, followed by Charlie who was straightening his tie. She spotted them right away and made directly for them, leaving Charlie to stand just inside the door where all the men congregated during the interval. 'There's a couple of empty chairs over there, kid, let's grab them quick.'

'You go ahead,' Laura said, 'I want to get me handbag off the stage.' On her way back, skirting the people standing around in groups, her eyes lighted on Gary. He stood out in the crowd because of his light-blond hair. Then she saw him bend towards Celia and the expression on the woman's face halted Laura in her tracks. There was no smile now on the heavily made-up face, and the words pouring from her mouth appeared to be angry ones. I wonder what she's on about, Laura thought. She's giving the pay-out about something.

Laura approached them from the side, hoping to hear something that would give her an inkling about what was going on. But Gary saw her coming and straightened up. 'Yer didn't have to worry about yer bag, babe, Tommy would have kept his eye on it.'

'He'd have a job, seeing as the band have left the stage. All me worldly goods are in this bag. I wouldn't even have the fare home if it got pinched.'

'I wouldn't see yer without, love, yer know that.' Celia patted the seat of the empty chair next to her. 'Come on, park yer carcass.' Smiling sweetly, she took a cigarette out of the packet on her knee. After lighting it, she asked, 'Don't yer smoke, Laura?'

'No, I'm too young,' Laura said, 'and anyway, me mam would kill me.'

'Yer mean yer work in the tobacco works, and yer don't smoke! I thought everyone got an allowance of free ciggies there. What d'yer do with them?'

'I give a packet to me dad and the rest to me mate, Cynthia.' Laura was lying. She sold her free cigarettes to a woman in work whose husband smoked like a chimney. 'Me mate's parents don't mind, but mine would.'

'Well, yer parents are not here, kid, and what the eye don't see, the heart don't grieve.' Celia held the open packet towards her. 'I was younger than you when I started smoking, it's the fashion these days. Go on, be daring.'

Laura could feel Gary's eyes on her, but she didn't look up. If she had, she would have seen the slight shake of his head and acted differently, knowing he was on her side. She didn't want to smoke, but was afraid of being thought old-fashioned. She hesitated, then reached out to take one of the cigarettes and held it awkwardly between her fingers.

There was a gloating expression on Celia's face as she struck a match. But as she was about to hold the flame to the cigarette now dangling between Laura's lips, Gary bent down and stayed her hand. 'Don't breathe in deeply, Laura, or yer'll feel sick and go dizzy. Just take a little puff, and if yer don't like it then don't smoke it.'

'Don't be a misery guts, Gary.' There was a warning in Celia's eyes as she blew out the match which was threatening to burn her fingers. If she could hook Laura on to smoking, it was another thing to add to her list. 'Leave the girl alone and go and amuse yerself elsewhere.'

Gary nodded curtly. 'I'll go to the gents, but I'll be back for the first dance, babe.'

Celia struck another match. 'Gary's right, just a little puff to begin with.'

Laura coughed when the smoke hit the back of her throat and wafted into her eyes, making them water. 'Ooh, I don't like it.'

'Yer haven't given it a chance, kid! Leave it for a minute and then have another go,' Celia coaxed. 'The first cigarette always makes yer feel like that. I remember going down an entry to have my first, with one of me mates. We were only fourteen and we'd bought a packet of five Woodies between us. We had to smoke the five because neither of us would take them home with us in case our mothers found them. I remember we both staggered out of that entry and our faces were green. But next time we tried, it was all right. I don't know about me mate, Sally Greenfield, but I've been smoking ever since. I think a girl looks sophisticated with a cigarette in her hand, particularly if it's in a holder. I've got a long ebony holder and I feel like the pig's ear when I use it.' A sneer crossed her face. 'Mind you, if I used it here they wouldn't know what it was. They haven't a clue about fashion, or how to look glamorous.'

Laura held the cigarette upright between finger and thumb and watched the smoke spiralling upwards. What harm would it do? Most of the women in work smoked, and her dad did too! And after all, she didn't need to have another one after this, not if she didn't want to. So she lifted the cigarette to her lips, but was careful this time not to inhale the smoke. 'I've been thinking, Celia, it's daft you leaving early every week because of me. I'll get Cynthia to come with me next week and we can go home together.'

'No, you mustn't do that!' The words shot from Celia's lips. 'If she lets slip that yer meet me here, yer mam will find out and the sparks will fly. She'll know yer've been telling lies about everything and yer'll land yerself in a load of trouble. So forget the idea, kid, 'cos I don't want to find myself in the middle of a family row.'

Laura was taken aback. 'But Cynthia wouldn't say anything, she's me best mate! And we could always say we'd met yer here by chance.'

'I said nothing doing, kid. You bring yer mate here and I'll find another dance to go to. And Charlie and Gary will come with me.'

Laura was about to blurt out that it wasn't fair! If Cynthia wanted to come here, no one had the right to stop her. But one look at Celia's angry face told her the older woman meant every word she said. And that in turn meant she wouldn't see Gary again. She couldn't care less about Charlie, she'd never exchanged more than a dozen words with him and she didn't like the man anyway. But she did care about Gary. And although she couldn't fathom out why he should do as Celia told him, she knew without doubt that he would. The same as she was going to do. It seemed as though Celia had a hold on each of them. 'Okay, I won't mention it to Cynthia just in case.'

'That's a good girl.' Celia's face relaxed into a smile. 'Yer see, it wouldn't only be you in trouble, but me as well. I don't tell yer grandad about our Thursday nights, and he'd be mad if he found me out in a lie.'

Laura turned her head away. There were a few things her grandad would go mad about, and Charlie was one of them. There was something fishy going on there, but she was best not to get involved. It wouldn't do to cross swords with the woman her grandad had married.

The band were tuning up for a slow foxtrot when Gary re-appeared. He held his hand out to Laura. 'Come on, babe, let's be first on the floor.'

'Ooh, I'm not that good yet, I'll make a holy show of meself.'

Celia put a hand in the middle of Laura's back and pushed her forward. 'Go on, kid, ye're as good as most, so get up and enjoy yerself. Ye're prettier than any of them, too.'

As they dipped and twirled, Laura was thinking how suited her and Gary were as dancing partners. They got on so well together on the dance floor, yet she didn't know a thing about him. He didn't mention his family, where he worked, or where he lived. And he knew as little about her because he never asked questions.

Laura was the first to break the silence. 'It's only four weeks to Christmas. Are yer looking forward to it?'

Gary looked down at her and pulled a face. 'Nah, I think it's boring. It's all right for kids, but there's nothing to do for grown-ups. This place doesn't open Christmas week, none of the dance halls do, so it's a case of lounging around the house for two days.'

Laura tried to draw him out. 'I love it. The tree with the surprise presents underneath, and lots to eat. Me mam has a party on Christmas night and invites some of the neighbours. We have a whale

179

of a time. I'm surprised that you don't have any parties to go to.'

'Oh, there's parties I could go to, but I'm not interested.'

Laura took the plunge. 'I'll ask me mam if yer can come to ours, if yer like?'

'I'd rather not, babe, but thanks all the same. I'm not one for mixing with strangers – I never know what to talk about.'

'Yer could talk to me, I'm not a stranger.'

Gary averted his eyes so she wouldn't see the wistful expression in them. 'No, honestly, babe, I'd rather not.'

Laura felt herself blush with shame. She'd practically asked him for a date and he'd turned her down. But why? If he wasn't interested in her, why did he dance every dance with her? Why was he always holding her hand and calling her 'babe'? Then she felt a ray of hope surface. Perhaps he was shy. Yes, that would explain everything. She shouldn't have mentioned the party, she'd jumped the gun. She should have waited until he'd asked her for a date, because he would ask her, she was sure of that. She crossed her fingers, hoping tonight would be the night.

But Laura's heart was heavy when Celia said it was time to go, and the tall blond boy she'd fallen for just squeezed her hand and said, 'I'll see yer next week, babe.'

'Go on, I dare yer,' John said, leaning against the street-lamp almost outside Miss Marshall's house. 'You're the one that suggested it, so go on, show how brave yer are.'

'Ay, pal, I didn't suggest no such thing.' Mick's hands were dug in his pockets and the collar of his coat turned up to keep the icy wind from numbing his ears. 'All I said was, that I'd seen Jenny and Janet going into Miss Marshall's, that's all. I never mentioned doing nothing that would earn me a medal for bravery.'

'Don't yer want to see Jenny, then?'

'Of course I do. And don't forget Janet.' Mick grinned at what he was about to say. 'She's a nice girl is Janet, and anyone can see she's got her eye on yer. She'll make yer a good wife one day, you lucky man.'

'I'll give yer a thick lip if yer keep saying things like that.' John kicked the lamp-post to show he was in earnest. 'And if yer ever say it in front of her, I'll give yer a cauliflower ear to go with yer thick lip.'

'Generous, aren't yer, mate? And what am I going to be doing while ye're bashing me about? Twiddling me ruddy thumbs?'

'We're wasting time here,' John said. 'It'll soon be too late to knock on an old lady's door to ask how she is.'

'Particularly as we know she's been up and about for two weeks now. And more particularly since we asked her the same question last night, and the night before. She'd be telling us to change our tune if she wasn't so polite.'

'I know what we'll do, we'll toss a penny. If it comes down heads, you knock on the door; tails, I knock.'

'I keep telling yer I wasn't born yesterday, why don't yer believe me?' Mick thrust his face nearer until their noses were only an inch apart. 'Have yer forgotten yer showed me the two-headed penny yer had in yer pocket last week?'

John looked equally as fierce. 'So yer think I'm a cheat, eh? Use one of yer own flaming pennies then, if yer don't trust me.'

Inside Miss Marshall's house she was being entertained by Jenny, who was doing a very good impersonation of the woman who came round the factory morning and afternoon, with the tea urn. Suddenly the old lady cocked an ear. 'Shush.' With a finger to her lips, she crossed over to the window and peeped through the side of the drawn curtains. 'Just come and listen to this, but don't let them see yer.'

Jenny stood on tiptoe, looking over the old woman's shoulder, while Janet crouched down to see through the crook of her arm. Jenny suppressed a giggle when she saw the stance of the two boys. 'Yer wouldn't believe they were best mates, would yer? Anyone would think they're about to knock spots off each other.'

'It's very naughty of us to eavesdrop on them,' said Lizzie, with a twinkle in her eye, 'but I'd never sleep tonight if I didn't know the outcome. So let's listen and watch.'

John pushed Mick away. 'Come on, mate, get yer penny out. But I want to inspect it first to make sure it's not a dud one.'

'Everyone knows their own tricks best, pal.' Mick fished in his pocket and brought out a penny coin. 'And in case yer accuse me of cheating, I won't catch it in me hand, I'll let it fall on the ground.'

The coin spun through the air and they heard it hit the ground. 'Where did it go?' John asked. 'I heard it land but didn't see it.'

'Ye've got eyes in yer head, pal, so help me look for it. But whoever finds it, don't touch it. Let's keep it all above board so I don't have to listen to yer moaning.'

The two boys searched for several minutes, but in the dim light of the gas-lamp it wasn't easy. So they bent their knees and squatted, searching while keeping an eye on each other.

'It's like looking for a needle in a blinking haystack,' Mick growled. 'If it wasn't my penny, I'd let yer get on with it.'

John gave a cry of excitement. 'I can see it – it rolled in the gutter.'

'Leave it! I wouldn't trust you as far as I could throw yer.'

They stood looking down at the coin which was now half-covered by a piece of paper, blown there by the breeze. 'I can't see properly,' John said. 'Is it heads or tails?'

181

'I'm blowed if I know, mate.' Mick stuck his hands back in his pockets. 'But seeing as it's my penny, I think it only fair that I win.'

'Yeah, okay, I'll let you win.' John chuckled, 'I'll let you knock at the door.'

'You can go and take a running jump, mate. That wasn't the bet, and well you know it.' Mick took his hands from his pockets and hunched his shoulders, ready for action. 'The one to pick it up is the winner.' He was off the mark before John had time to think. Holding the penny aloft, he chuckled, 'Behold the winner.'

'Behold the cheat, yer mean. That was below the belt, Mick Moynihan, and I'm surprised at yer. Like kicking a man when he's down, that was.'

'Yeah, it wasn't fair,' Mick agreed. And without further ado, he lifted the knocker.

Jenny wiped her eyes before opening the door. 'Lost the toss, did yer, Mick?'

Both boys stood with their mouths gaping. Mick couldn't think straight because the sight of Jenny, her pretty face alive with humour, chased everything else from his mind. The older she got, the more beautiful she became, and he'd move heaven and earth to win her hand. 'We were only acting daft, Jenny, that's all.'

'Yeah, yer know what we're like,' John said, his thoughts going down the same path as his mate's. 'At least, yer should know by now.'

Jenny opened the door wider and jerked her head. 'Come on in, Auntie Lizzie is expecting yer.'

'Auntie Lizzie!' The boys echoed. 'Since when has she been yer auntie?'

'Since the last half-hour.' Jenny waited until they were squeezed into the tiny hall, then said, 'I can't call her Lizzie, that wouldn't be respectful, and I can't keep on calling her Miss Marshall, it doesn't sound friendly. So she said she'd be thrilled to bits if we call her Auntie Lizzie. Me and Janet are made up.'

The old lady was grinning when they entered the room. 'The same goes for you two, if yer want to.'

'Ooh, yeah, that would be great!' Mick's dimples deepened as his grin spread from ear to ear. 'How are yer today, Auntie Lizzie?'

'I'm fine, thank you. And all the better for seeing my two handsome boyfriends.'

'I'm glad to hear ye're fine, Auntie Lizzie.' John elbowed Mick out of the way, thinking he'd hogged the limelight long enough. 'And it is my sincere wish that you continue to be fine.'

'How come yer never ask me how I am?' Jenny asked.

'We can see how you are, Jenny,' Mick wished he could say what he really thought. 'Ye're always in tip-top form.'

182

'Yeah.' John was going weak at the knees just looking at her. 'Prettier than a fiddle, but as fit as one.'

Janet coughed. 'Excuse me, but in case yer hadn't noticed, I'm here.'

Mick lifted his hands in mock surprise. 'Ah, Miss Porter! As lovely as ever, I see.'

John decided to go one better. 'It's a delight to see you, Miss Porter. And a sight for sore eyes, as usual.'

Janet's face glowed with pleasure. She was betwixt and between with the two boys. One night she favoured Mick, the next it was John. Perhaps she should wait for her birthday before making up her mind. Her mam had told her she'd have more sense when she was fifteen.

Lizzie gestured to the chairs around the table. 'Sit yerselves down and tell us what yer were up to, out there.'

As they were pulling the chairs out, John and Mick grinned at each other. What excuse were they going to come up with this time? John ran his hands through his hair and pulled a Stan Laurel face. 'Another fine mess yer've got me into, Ollie.'

When the hoots of laughter had died down, Mick said, 'Listen who's talking? You were the one with the bright idea of tossing a coin.' He smiled across at Lizzie. 'Neither of us liked knocking on yer door in case yer were fed up with us, so we dared each other. As yer must have seen, we both ended up on our hands and knees, all over a ruddy penny. Mind you, it was my penny and it had come from a good home.'

'I told yer they were as mad as hatters, didn't I, Auntie Lizzie?' Jenny winked at her. 'One on their own is bad enough, but two together is a recipe for trouble.'

'Well, they don't ever have to worry about knocking on my door – all four of yer will always get a welcome. I've slept soundly every night since yer've been coming and keeping me company, and that's something that never happened before. I used to toss and turn for hours before I could drop off.' Lizzie shook her head to dismiss the memories of all those lonely nights, lonely days, and lonely years. 'Anyway, instead of crawling on the ground in the cold, yer should have come straight in and yer'd have seen Jenny amusing us. She takes after her mam for impersonations, and she had us in stitches.'

Mick leaned back on the wooden chair. 'Come on, Jenny, me and John could do with cheering up.'

'Promise yer won't make fun of me?'

'He won't make fun of yer, Jenny, I won't let him.' John was chuckling inside. 'If he does, I'll break his nose, to go with his thick lip and cauliflower ear. He wouldn't be a pretty sight when I'd finished with him.'

'Oh, aye!' Mick pretended to be angry. 'You and whose army, mate?'

'See what I mean, Auntie Lizzie? They can't be quiet for one minute.'

'I'll be as good as gold,' Mick told her, while John promised to be as quiet as a mouse.

Jenny stood up for effect. 'Well, there's this woman who works in the factory as a cleaner, and she also makes tea for the workers in the morning and afternoon. She comes around with a big tea urn on a trolley and fills the men's mugs. Now if I describe her to yer, it'll give yer an idea of why I think she's so funny.' Jenny brought the actions into play now. Holding her hands out in front of her chest, she said, 'She's out here on top, and her backside's as big as the back of a tram. Her hair is dyed and it's a horrible orange colour. She doesn't talk, she bawls, and she's always got a cigarette dangling out of the side of her mouth. That cigarette is never taken out until it starts to burn her lips, and then she lights another one from it. Sometimes the ash on it is inches long and we all wait with bated breath to see where it lands. Usually it's in the tea urn or in the men's mugs. Honestly, she's like a gangster's moll. The men are terrified of her because she's built like a house and could pick any of them up with one hand.'

Jenny stopped to take a deep breath. 'Have yer all got the idea of what she's like?'

John nodded. 'I can see her as plain as if she was standing next to yer.'

'I'm glad I'm not standing next to her,' Mick said, trying to look solemn. 'She sounds a right nasty piece of work.'

'Why don't the bosses sack her?' Lizzie asked. 'They don't have to put up with that, there's plenty of women who'd be glad of the job.'

'None of them have got the guts.' Jenny laughed at the idea. 'Anyway, I'm coming to that. One day, her whole cigarette fell into one of the men's mugs. She didn't pass him any compliment, just stood there and brazenly lit another one before carrying on to the next man. The poor bloke stood staring down at the cigarette floating on top of his tea, and when she was well out of sight, he called the floorwalker over. "I'm not putting up with this, it's bloody ridiculous. She should have been kicked out on her backside long ago." The floorwalker is a small, slightly built man, and he asked, "Would you like to have the honour of sacking her, Nobby?" ' Jenny bent double as she pictured the scene. 'Nobby's face was a picture. "I don't get paid to sack people, that's your job." The floorwalker thought for a minute then took Nobby's mug from him. "I don't get paid that much, Nobby, but I know a man who does".'

Jenny scanned the faces listening with interest. 'It's a long story.

184

I'll pack it in if ye're fed up with the sound of me voice.'

'Don't you dare pack it in,' Mick said, 'even if it takes all night.'

There were sounds of approval, so Jenny continued. 'The mug was taken to the office of the manager, Mr Grearson. There's glass windows in his office, and we all stopped work to see what his reaction was. We couldn't hear what was being said, but after what seemed a heated argument, the floorwalker, Phil, went in search of the cleaner. She stood as bold as brass in front of Mr Grearson and as far as we could see, he could hardly get a word in. She stormed out of his office and deliberately stood facing the window and lit up another cigarette!'

'So he did sack her?' Lizzie said. 'Quite right, too.'

Jenny shook her head. 'He didn't sack her, just told her to pull her socks up or the men would mutiny and she'd be out of the door. We had to wait for Phil to tell us what went on in the office, and he said she told Mr Grearson she didn't know what all the fuss was about. After all, she'd only charged Nobby for his tea, she didn't charge him for the cigarette which, after all, was still in his possession.'

Mick was the first to roar with laughter, followed quickly by the others. 'I'm beginning to like her! Mind you, I wouldn't want to share a cup of tea with her.'

'I'll tell yer what I think is the funniest. I've described her to yer, except to say that she's as common as muck and has a filthy mouth on her. But guess what her name is?'

John was first off the mark. 'Mae West?'

'Yer'll never guess, so I'll tell yer. It's Philomena Dorothea Victoria Anastasia Smith.'

They were still laughing about it when the two boys walked the girls round to Janet's to make sure she got home safely. Then on the way back, with Jenny walking between them, their laughter had nothing to do with Philomena Dorothea Victoria Anastasia Smith. It was all to do with Jenny, and their laughter was that of happiness.

Chapter Fifteen

Amy put her arms flat on the table and leaned forward. 'Ay, girl, is it the same as usual this Christmas? Christmas night here, and New Year's Eve over the road at the Moynihans'?'

Mary gasped, or at least pretended to. 'You've got a ruddy cheek, you have, Amy Hanley, the way yer take things for granted. Me and Molly haven't mentioned anything about having no party.'

'I know yer haven't, girl, that's why I'm asking. Ye're that bleedin' slow about it, yer've got me worried. Talk about having no consideration for others, isn't in it! I mean, like, I'll have to make other arrangements if me two best mates are too tight, and too miserable to have a party to celebrate Christmas.'

'Ooh, er! The state of you and the price of fish!' Mary knew how all this was going to end because never a day past without her friend going through some sort of rigmarole. But it always ended up in a laugh and a bit of fun never did no one any harm. So with a look of anticipation on her face, she asked, 'When yer say yer'll have to make other arrangements, does that mean yer might think of having a party in *your* house?' She clapped her hands in glee. 'Oh, I can't wait to tell Molly, she'll be over the moon.'

'Ay, just you hang on a minute, girl, I haven't said nothing about having no party in my house.' Amy was pinching the fat on her arms. 'I only said I'd have to make other arrangements, 'cos yer can't expect me not to celebrate just because you're not in the mood. No, what I mean is, I'll have to go to a party in one of me other friends' houses.'

'Oh, aye, such as?'

'I've got other friends beside you, yer know, girl. I know loads of people who'd be honoured to have me.'

Mary was chuckling silently. 'Name them.'

'Huh! No bleedin' fear! How soft you are! If I tell yer their names yer'll try and wangle an invite for yerself. Find yer own party, Mary Nightingale.'

'I don't need to, I'm all sorted out. But I'll tell Molly what yer said, so she won't expect yer.'

Amy banged on the table with the flat of her hand, her chubby face creased in a wide smile. 'I knew all along yer were having me on, yer know, girl. I just went along with yer for the ride. But I'd better not say what's in me mind in case yer take yer invite back.'

'I haven't given yer an invite, yet! I'll see how yer behave yerself over the next few days, then I'll decide.' Mary narrowed her eyes in suspicion. 'What did yer mean before when yer said yer wouldn't tell me what was in yer mind?'

'I'm not telling yer until I'm certain I've got me invitation and yer won't take it back.'

Mary tutted. 'Yer've got yer invitation, sunshine, so spit it out.'

'Well, I was thinking yer were the world's worst bleedin' liar. Our cat can tell a lie better than you.'

'Yer haven't got a cat, Amy.'

'Ye're right, girl, but I'm saying if I did have one, he'd be a better liar than you.'

'Telling lies is not something to be proud of, sunshine, and it's certainly nothing to go round bragging about. It's one of the Ten Commandments, or have yer forgotten yer Catechism?' Mary saw the gleam of merriment in Amy's eyes and clicked her tongue. 'You'll never go to heaven when yer die, that's for sure.'

'Ay, I've no intention of bleedin' dying, girl!' Amy said, moving her fingers to the dimples in her elbow. 'Not until after the parties, anyway. I'll tell yer what, if I died before then and missed all the fun, I'd ruddy kill meself.'

'Amy Hanley, how you can sleep at night after all the things yer say, I'll never know. If it was me, I'd be seeing the Grim Reaper standing at the foot of me bed, biding his time.'

'Nah! My Ben wouldn't allow another man in the bedroom. Especially since I told him what Molly said about me being well-endowed. He thinks I'm someone special now, treats me with kid gloves.'

'It's boxing gloves he needs, not kid gloves. My Stan would wonder what hit him if he was married to you. He doesn't know he's born, the care I take of him.'

'Ah, but does he have as much fun, girl? That's the question yer've got to ask yerself.'

'I beg your pardon? What makes yer think your Ben has more fun than my Stan?'

Amy closed one eye and squinted at her neighbour. 'Well, from where I'm sitting, ye're not particularly well-endowed, are yer, girl?'

Mary's mouth dropped open. 'That's nice, I enjoy getting insulted in me own house. And if we're on yer favourite subject of bedroom games, I'm going to get on with me washing, which you rudely interrupted.'

Amy held up her two hands in surrender. 'Not another word about bedrooms will pass me lips, Scout's Honour. We'll talk about the parties instead. The only reason I brought it up in the first place is because I want to prepare me costume for my party piece. Like all professional entertainers, girl, I put a lot of thought into me costume.'

'It's a pity yer don't put as much material into them as yer do thought, then. Wear something that covers yer body, sunshine, not one that shows everything yer've got. The kids are getting too old now to see yer half-naked. Don't forget, Mick's just on eighteen and your John's not far off it.'

'Ay, talking about kids, girl, I was worried about our Eddy and Edna. I couldn't leave them on their own on Christmas Day, it wouldn't be right. I didn't mind when they were younger 'cos they went to bed early. I thought of asking yer if they could come, too?'

'Some hope you've got, Amy Hanley! That would be five from your house, three from the Moynihans', four from here, and I've asked Lizzie to come, as well. This room wouldn't hold that many – it would be bursting at the seams.'

'It would if yer scraped yer new wallpaper off.' Amy's face was straight. 'That would give yer a bit more room. We could take it off careful, like, and stick it back on the next day. But yer won't put yerself out for no one, will yer?'

'Don't even think of it, sunshine, I'm not having thirteen people in this house, not for you nor anyone else.'

'Where d'yer get the thirteen people from, girl?'

'Oh, not again! I've just told yer! Four from here, three from the Moynihans', Lizzie and your five.'

'Ye're lousy at adding up, girl. I know yer know a lot of big words, but when it comes to adding up, ye're bleedin' hopeless. There's only three from our house. Me, my Ben and our John. When I went to school, that came to three.'

'What about your Eddy and Edna?'

Amy put on her surprised face. 'Oh, they're not coming. They've both got parties of their own to go to.'

'Holy suffering ducks, Amy, what have we gone all through that for! Yer were even talking of stripping me wallpaper off to make room for them!'

'Ah, ay, now, girl! I only said I *thought* I was going to have to ask yer if they could come. That was before they got fixed up. And as for yer wallpaper, that was only supposing. You know, like, supposing I had to ask yer. But I might have known yer wouldn't strip yer paper off, not for no one. It comes between you and yer bleedin' sleep, that wallpaper. Every time I come in I expect yer to hold yer hand out for me admission fee.'

Mary chuckled. 'Jealousy gets yer nowhere, sunshine. I told yer we'd all give yer a hand to decorate your room if yer wanted, but ye're too ruddy slow to catch cold. Either that or too mean, one or the other.'

'A bit of both, girl, a bit of both.'

There was deep affection in Mary's eyes as she studied her friend. How dull life would have been over the years without her. 'Yer've been a good mate to me, Amy Hanley, and I love the bones of yer.'

The chubby cheeks moved upwards and Amy's eyes almost disappeared. 'Ay, girl, couldn't yer love me fat, instead of me bones? Yer see, in case yer hadn't noticed, I've got a lot more fat than bones.'

Mary turned her head as she laughed, and through the window she saw Molly hurrying across the cobbles. 'Oh, I forgot to mention that Molly would be coming over to see if we felt like going to the pictures with her tonight. She's on her way over now, I'll let her in.'

Molly came in rubbing her arms briskly. 'It's a cold one, today, so it is. Sure, if I had the sense I was born with I'd have slipped me coat on.'

Amy grinned at her. 'Ye're in luck, Molly, we haven't had our cup of tea yet. Mary was just about to put the kettle on, and I'm sure I heard her say she had some custard creams. So yer timed it nicely, girl.'

Mary shouted as she made her way to put the kettle on. 'I haven't got no custard creams. I'm sorry, but would yer like a cracker with cheese on?'

'Oh, my God, it must be someone's birthday!' Amy winked at Molly before calling back, 'Cream crackers and cheese, on a week-day? It's never been known.'

'Not crackers, sunshine, just cracker. Singular.'

Molly saw the frown on Amy's face. 'Mary means ye're only getting one cracker, me darlin'.'

'Yeah, I understood that bit. But what's her singlet got to do with it?'

While Molly's loud guffaw filled the room, Mary came to the kitchen door and doubled up. 'She's priceless, isn't she?'

Amy looked from one to the other. 'Have you two lost yer bleedin' marbles? I'm blowed if I see anything funny in a singlet.'

'I said "singular", sunshine, not singlet. And as Molly rightly said, that means ye're only getting one cracker.'

'You're too bleedin' clever for yer own good, d'yer know that? But yer'll come unstuck one of these days, mark my words.' Amy's chins danced in tune with her nodding head. 'I'm going to root a dictionary out when I go home, and I'll find the longest word in it. Then I'll baffle yer with bleedin' science in the morning.'

'Make sure yer read what it means, sunshine, or it might be you what comes unstuck.' Mary cocked an ear. 'That's the kettle boiling, I'll brew the tea.'

190

As she reached to take three cups down from the hooks on the shelf, Mary could hear her neighbours talking. 'What picture did yer have in mind, Molly?'

'Charles Laughton's on at the Atlas, he's usually in a good picture.'

'Ah, no, I hate him! He's as ugly as sin! I don't fancy sitting for two hours looking at his ugly mug. I'd be just as well sitting in me own warm house and looking at my feller's ugly mug.'

Mary wet the tea and carried the pot through. Setting it in the middle of the table, she shook her head at Amy. 'That's a terrible thing to say about yer husband. I'm going to tell Ben next time I see him.'

'Oh, yer don't need to bother, girl, 'cos he knows. He sees himself in the mirror every morning when he's getting shaved.' Amy shuffled to the edge of the chair. 'Will yer get the bleedin' cups, girl, 'cos me and Molly are spitting feathers. And when ye're cutting the cheese, let yer hand slip, will yer? Don't be cutting it so thin we can see through it.'

Molly was chuckling as she poured the tea out. 'Sure, haven't I lost interest in going to the pictures, now? Why don't you both come over to ours and we can have a laugh. I'll get Seamus to mug us to a few bottles of stout, then send him to prop the bar up at the pub for a couple of hours.'

'That's the most sensible thing I've heard since I got out of bed, Molly.' Amy's face was beaming when she looked at Mary. 'I'll knock for yer at eight, girl, okay?'

'That's fine, sunshine, and bring yer dictionary with yer, just in case.'

Laura could sense Cynthia's excitement as they linked arms. And the smile that had been missing for weeks, was back on her face. 'You seem in a happy frame of mind. Has something nice happened?'

'I saw them last night, both of them.'

Laura stopped in her tracks. 'Go 'way! Are yer pulling me leg?'

Cynthia tugged on her arm. 'Keep walking in case me dad comes out. He was getting ready to go to the pub when I left.'

When they were well away from their street, Laura could contain her excitement no longer. 'Go on, Cyn, tell us what happened. Did they see yer?'

'I'd been giving it a lot of thought over the weeks while I've been keeping an eye on the pub they took us to. And I began to realise they must have been giving it a wide berth in case I turned up and caused trouble. So last night, I walked back in the direction they were coming from when we met them. I stood in a shop doorway for ages, and it was freezing cold. I was almost giving it up as a bad job when the pair of them came swaggering along on the opposite side of the road.'

'Oo, er, I don't know how yer had the nerve,' Laura said. 'I'd have been shaking in me shoes in case they saw me.'

'Yes, but it didn't happen to you, did it?' Cynthia came to a stop and faced her friend. 'Yer have no idea what I went through, Laura, 'cos I didn't tell yer the half of it. On top of the pain I had, and the raging torment in me mind and the terrible nightmares every single night, I had an even bigger worry that I bet you never even thought of. What if one of them had made me pregnant? For three solid weeks I was out of me mind with fear. I even thought about running away from home, 'cos I couldn't have faced me parents. But I was lucky, and when me period came on, I thanked God from the bottom of my heart.'

Cynthia sighed as she linked arms with Laura and began to walk. She couldn't expect her friend to understand the horror and torment, no one would unless they went through it themselves. 'Anyway, that's why I've been so determined to find them. And now I know which pub they go to, I'll make it me business to find out where they live. And then I'll make them pay heavily for what they did to me.'

'Yer mean to say that yer followed them?' Laura's tummy was churning over as she thought of the risk her friend had taken. 'It's a wonder they didn't spot yer.'

'They wouldn't have recognised me. I had me old clothes on and a scarf pulled low over me forehead. Anyway, if they had spotted me, they'd have been the ones to get a fright. But I don't only want to give them a fright, I want to ruin their lives for them. And I swear, Laura, that's what I'll do. More so, after what I saw last night.'

'Why, what happened after yer followed them?'

'I crossed the road and followed them from behind. When they turned into a pub, I was in two minds whether to wait for them or go home, 'cos I was frozen. I decided to stick it out for a little while, and I was glad I did. They weren't in the pub long, and when they came out they were with two women. Or girls, I should say – they looked about eighteen or so. Jeff and Larry were full of the joys, laughing and joking, and I felt like walking up to them and scratching their eyes out. But I thought, no, I'll bide me time and do the job properly. So I followed them, keeping well into the wall. And guess where they went – down an entry.'

Laura sucked in her breath. 'They want a damn good hiding, they do. Someone should sort them out.'

'Oh, I intend to, believe me. Now I know the pub they go to, and roughly what time they get there, I'll be waiting for them on Thursday. I won't go as early, 'cos it's too cold to hang around, but I'll be there.'

'I still don't see what yer can do to pay them back.' Laura shivered and moved in closer to her friend. 'I mean, we don't know any fellers that would knock the living daylights out of them.'

'I've got a plan in me head, but I'm not telling yer about it in case it doesn't come off. When the time comes, I might get cold feet. I can't see it, not the way I feel, but I'd rather say nowt until I've accomplished what I set out to do.'

'I'll be glad when it's all over and yer get back to normal.' Laura squeezed her arm. 'Yer haven't been the same girl since the night it happened.'

'I'm seeking retribution, Laura, and if I get that I might be able to get on with me life. I don't like being miserable, but what happened that night is in me mind all the time, like a nightmare repeating itself over and over again. The only way to rid meself of it, is by paying them back in some way.'

'I wish I could help yer, Cyn, but I'm not as brave as you. I'm a coward and would run a mile if I set eyes on them.'

'This is my fight, Laura, and one way or another, I'll win it.' Cynthia was well aware that getting even with Larry and Jeff had become an obsession with her, but she couldn't help it. For what they put her through that night, down a dark entry with no one to call to for help, they deserved to be punished. She gave a deep sigh. 'Anyway, kid, how are yer getting on with this Gary feller?'

Laura pretended to have a coughing fit, giving herself time to think of an answer. When her friend was feeling better, she'd want to come to the dance with her, and that was out of the question. But she couldn't tell her that. 'We get on fine together. He's a nice bloke, Cynthia, and not half handsome. He's taught me all the dances, even the tango.'

'Has he asked yer for a date, yet?'

'He's hinted that we should go to the pictures one Thursday, instead of meeting at the dance hall, but I've been too keen to learn how to dance. Perhaps after Christmas we'll go out together.'

'Is there romance in the air, kid?'

Laura laughed it off. 'Ask me again when I've had me first kiss off him.'

'My God, you're slow, aren't yer? All these weeks and he's never even kissed yer?'

'He's not like the boys we used to knock around with, they were only kids. Gary's not the type to kiss a girl when he's only just met her, he's more of a gentleman. And I won't let him bring me home because I have to leave the dance at half ten to be home by eleven, and it wouldn't be fair on him. But it'll be different when we go out on a date and we're on our own.' Laura tittered. 'I only hope he's not a sloppy kisser or I'll go right off him.'

'Ay, don't be so big-headed,' Cynthia said. 'He might go off you!'

'No, he really likes me, Cyn, honest. He dances every dance with me, holds me hand and calls me "babe".'

'I'll have to meet this he-man, and see if I approve.'

'Oh, yer will meet him sometime, Cyn, that's for sure.' Laura crossed her fingers. 'In a couple of weeks, eh?'

'I'm glad we've got the pleasure of yer company again, sweetheart, 'cos we've missed yer.' Martha Porter waited until Jenny had slipped her coat off, then took it from her to hang up. 'But why aren't yer going to sit with the old lady? I asked our Janet, but she didn't seem to know. Did the old girl get fed up with yer?'

Jenny laughed as she took a seat at the table, opposite Bill. 'No, it was me mam that said it was too much for her, four of us there every night. So me and Janet are going one night, and the lads the next.'

No one was more pleased to see Jenny than Bill. 'About time, too! The six matches yer owe me from the last game of cards has gone up to ten. I'm charging yer interest 'cos yer've owed it for so long.'

'Some hope you've got, Bill Porter!' Jenny winked at her friend. 'I didn't know yer brother was a moneylender, Jan.'

'He's tight enough to be one,' Janet said. 'He wouldn't give yer the skin off his rice pudding unless yer paid him for it.'

'Now, now, that's enough.' Her father laid his newspaper down. 'I'm not having two women ganging up on me own son without coming to his aid. What about the time you had the measles, Janet, and yer wouldn't even give him a spot? He cried his eyes out, but yer wouldn't budge. Not one spot would yer part with, even though yer were covered in them.'

'She was generous enough with her colds, though, wasn't she, Dad?' Bill was feeling happier than he'd felt for weeks. It was so good to see Jenny's pretty smiling face sitting opposite to him. 'Remember that time she sneezed all over me, and I had a runny nose for weeks after?'

Martha joined in now. 'That was because yer were bending over her, trying to pinch one of her jelly babies. It served yer right, that did.'

Jenny wagged her head from side to side, her eyes sparkling. 'We never have no rows like this when we're sitting with Auntie Lizzie, do we, Jan? All we do is act daft and laugh and joke the whole time.'

Janet giggled. 'Mick and John act daft, we just sit and laugh at them.'

'Yeah,' Jenny agreed, 'I wonder how they're getting on?'

'Never mind about them.' The last thing Bill wanted to do was talk about the two lads he saw as rivals for Jenny's affection. 'All ye're doing is changing the subject, hoping I'll forget about the matchsticks yer owe me. And the number has gone up to eleven, by the way.'

'I've only got ten with me. I couldn't take any more because the box was nearly empty, and I couldn't leave me mam short or we'd have got no breakfast.'

'Then yer'd better have a winning streak tonight, or yer'll be in debt to me for the rest of yer life.' What a lovely thought, Bill told himself. A whole lifetime of Jenny being in his debt. 'Get the cards out, Janet, there's a good sister, and we'll start.'

'Mr Porter, before we start, can I ask yer to forget ye're a man, and be on my side for a change? I need all the help I can get to make sure yer son doesn't cheat. If we've all got our eyes on him he'd have a job to hide cards on his knee, covered by the tablecloth. He thinks I haven't seen him, but I have, loads of times.'

Vincent roared with laughter. 'Okay, I'll join the girls. In fact, so I look the part, I'll borrow Martha's pinny.'

Bill wagged a finger at Jenny. 'You are one big fibber, Jenny Nightingale. I never hide cards on me knee.' A smile lit up his face. 'I slip them down the side of me shoe.'

By the end of the night, when it was time for her to leave, Jenny had paid the matchsticks back that she owed, and was three in hand. She was over the moon, and holding the matchsticks in an open palm, she held them under Bill's nose. 'How about that, then, old clever clogs?'

'Sheer fluke, that's what it was.' Bill gathered the cards in and slid them back in the packet. 'And the help yer got from me dad did yer no harm. I saw him pass yer the six of diamonds in that last game.' He put the cards in the drawer of the sideboard. 'I'll walk yer home, even though yer cheated and cleared me out.'

'There's no need, Bill, I can be home in five minutes if I run all the way.'

Bill wasn't about to let that happen. 'I'll run all the way with yer, so I should be back home in ten minutes.'

'It's no good arguing with him, Jenny, he'll have his own way if it kills him,' Janet said. 'I'll see yer out and go straight up to bed. I'm up earlier than you, 'cos I don't have a cushy job sitting on me backside all day.'

When the youngsters had left, Martha and Vincent exchanged amused smiles. 'Isn't it funny that our Bill goes out every single night when Jenny's not here?' Martha took the poker from the brass companion set and lifted the coals in the fire, hoping the draught would inject a bit of life back into it. 'Anyone would think he fancied her.'

'I don't only think it, love, I know it! It's sticking out a mile, the way he looks at her.' Vincent chuckled. 'The only one who can't see the cow eyes he makes when he looks at her, is Jenny herself. But yer can understand the lad, 'cos she's a right bonny lass.'

'She'll be bonnier still, in another year or so. Our Bill will have a run for his money, believe me.' Martha hung the poker back in the companion set. For all the good she'd done she might as well not have bothered. The fire was on its last legs and wouldn't be coaxed. 'Our Janet's a pretty girl, too, but we don't notice because we see her every day. She hasn't got Jenny's humour, but there's plenty of time for her to come out of her shell, she's still only a kid.'

Vincent reached for his cigarette packet with one hand, and smacked his wife's bottom with the other. 'The next year or so could be very interesting, love. I'm looking forward to it.'

Mick put the dominoes back in the box and grinned at John. 'That's a tanner yer owe me, pal. But I'll wait until yer get yer wages on Saturday.'

'Yer can wait until the cows come home, mate, 'cos we weren't playing for money, it was only pretend.'

'We'll have no fighting, now, lads,' Lizzie said. 'John's right, it was only pretend. Playing for money is gambling, and I don't hold with it.'

'Don't take anything we say seriously, Auntie Lizzie, we're always having each other on.' Mick swivelled in his chair and placed the domino box on the sideboard. When he turned back, he asked the question he'd been dying to ask for weeks. 'Did yer never think of getting married, Auntie Lizzie? I bet yer had plenty of chances, 'cos I can see yer must have been very pretty when yer were younger.'

John glared at his friend. 'What d'yer mean, when she was younger? That's a back-handed compliment if ever I heard one. Auntie Lizzie is still pretty.'

'Of course she is! Just like Janet is very pretty, but yer don't seem to see that! She hasn't half got her eye on you, pal, so yer'd better watch out.'

'Say that once more, mate, and yer'll be missing two of yer front teeth. If yer'd wear yer glasses, yer'd see it's you she's got her eye on, not me.'

'I didn't know yer wore glasses, Mick,' Lizzie said. 'I've never seen yer in them.'

The two boys looked at each other and burst out laughing. 'I don't wear glasses, Auntie Lizzie, that's John's idea of a joke. The same as when he says he's going to separate me from me two front teeth. It's just wishful thinking on his part.' Mick's eyes were tender as he looked at the old lady. 'Now to me question. Did yer never think of getting married?'

'Oh, yes! I had quite a few boyfriends when I was a girl, but there was only one lad I ever loved enough to marry. He joined the Army in 1914, and before he went away we got engaged. We wrote to each

196

other every day, and he got a week's leave before he was sent overseas. We were going to get married when he came home, and I started buying things for me bottom drawer. But I never saw him again; he was killed in action in 1916.'

When Mick saw a tear glistening in the faded blue eyes, he cursed himself. 'I'm sorry, Auntie Lizzie, I shouldn't have been so nosy. Now I've gone and upset yer.'

'No, yer haven't, son, I'm glad yer asked. I often think about him – his name was Bill Furlong – but I never talk about him because there's no one to talk to. So it's good for me to be able to say his name. I've still got me engagement ring, and every letter he sent me is in me drawer upstairs, tied with blue ribbon.'

John swallowed hard to remove the lump in his throat. 'That's a real love story, Auntie Lizzie. Yer must have loved him very much to have remained true to him.'

'I never looked at another man after he was killed,' Lizzie told them. 'I've lived with me memories all these years.'

'I hope I find a love like that.' Mick rounded the table and hugged her. 'You are one lovely lady. I can see why your Bill fell for yer.'

'I'm a lucky lady, to have young people around me at my age. Yer've brightened my life for me and I do appreciate it.' There was a glint in her eyes as she smiled at him. 'But we've all missed the girls tonight, haven't we?'

'Yeah.' Mick returned her smile. 'I'll have to have words with Mrs Nightingale, see if I can work me charm on her.'

'Yer'd better let me do that,' John said. 'I mean, it's a well-known thing that I've got heaps more charm than you.'

'In yer dreams, pal, in yer dreams. Yer might stand a chance charming a snake, but when it comes to Mrs Nightingale it's a different kettle of fish. A real expert is called for, and that's yours truly.'

'If you two don't stop messing around, yer'll miss Jenny,' Lizzie said. 'She'll be on her way back from Janet's about now.'

John gave his friend a dig in the back. 'Yer talk too much, mate. Move yerself before it's too late.'

'Right, it's all hands to the pump, then.' Mick pointed to the fire. 'You bank that down while I fill Auntie Lizzie's hot-water bottle.'

Five minutes later the boys were standing in the street listening for Auntie Lizzie to shoot the bolt on the door. When they were satisfied she was safe, they turned just in time to see Jenny passing on the opposite side, with Bill by her side. 'Oh,' John groaned, 'she's got that long streak of misery with her.'

'Let's spoil it for him, eh?' Thinking all was fair in love and war, Mick called, 'Hang on a minute, Jenny.'

Jenny was grinning as she watched them cross the cobbles. 'How did it go?'

John got in first. 'We've had a very interesting night, especially the last half-hour.'

Oh, he's not stealing my thunder, Mick thought. I was the one who asked Auntie Lizzie about her life and now he's trying to cash in on it. 'She told us all about herself, when she was young, and it wasn't half sad.'

Jenny looked up at Bill. 'Thanks for walking me home, Bill, but yer may as well go now, it's no good standing here freezing.'

Bill wasn't very happy about that. 'I said I'd see yer home, and that means seeing yer get safely inside yer house. I don't mind waiting.'

'That's daft, that.' Mick couldn't help himself. If this bloke was going to walk Jenny home every other night, they'd be courting in no time. 'This is John's house, Jenny's is next door and I live in that house opposite. We'll see she gets inside safely, so it's no good you getting yer death of cold.'

Bill was now becoming irritated. 'Aren't you frightened that *you* might catch *yer* death of cold? It strikes me that yer stand as much chance as I do.'

'Yes, but you've got that walk ahead of yer, Bill.' Jenny hadn't a clue that there was a fight for supremacy going on under her nose. 'Anyway, I'm freezing meself so I won't be hanging around for long. I'm certainly not standing listening to a long drawn-out tale from these two. So you make tracks, Bill, and tell Janet I'll see her tomorrow night.'

Unless he wanted to make a fool of himself, there was little Bill could do. He knew what he'd like to do, and that was punch these two blokes on the nose for cramping his style. But that wouldn't go down well with Jenny. So with as much sincerity as he could muster, he bade them good night, and with his shoulders hunched, walked away. They'd pulled a fast one on him tonight, but if they tricked him like that again, he'd marmalise them.

Thinking they'd put paid to the enemy, Mick and John were standing with grins on their faces. 'D'yer think yer mam would like to hear about what Auntie Lizzie told us?' John asked, hopefully. 'It's not half sad.'

'Would she heckerslike!' Jenny was thinking her mother would have a fit if these two walked in and she was sitting with dinkie curlers in her hair and a nightdress on. 'It's half-past ten, yer daft nit, yer don't go visiting at this time of night. Anyway, I'm too cold to stand here any longer, I'm going in. Auntie Lizzie can tell me the story herself, tomorrow night.'

Left on their own, the pals looked at each other and shrugged their shoulders. 'The only good thing about that, pal,' Mick said, 'was we put a halt to the queer feller's gallop. I only hope he hasn't put a death wish on us.'

'If he does, the one I'm putting on him will cancel it out.' John felt in his pocket for the front-door key. 'Don't worry, mate, there's always tomorrow. We've got an excuse to call and see Auntie Lizzie, I've made sure of that. I dropped me comb on the floor under her table, accidentally on purpose, like. So who's a genius, eh?'

'I only hope the genius hasn't dropped his comb on top of my handkerchief.'

Inside the Nightingales' house, Mary shook her head when she heard roars of laughter outside. 'Just listen to them! I'm laughing with them, but I haven't a clue what I'm laughing at. I don't know which one of them is the funniest.'

'They're both cracked, Mam,' Jenny said. 'But in a nice way.'

Chapter Sixteen

Cynthia huddled in the shop doorway, stamping her feet to try and get some feeling back in them. They were like blocks of ice and she'd probably get chilblains after this. And for what? If Larry and Jeff didn't put in an appearance she'd have wasted her time and frozen to the death in the process. She folded her arms and stuck her hands under her armpits for warmth. This was the coldest night she'd known, and if the people hurrying by knew why she was there they'd think she had a screw loose. The best place on a night like this was home, in front of a fire roaring up the chimney.

Thinking of home, Cynthia's mind took her to her parents. Her dad never questioned where she was going or who with. All he'd said when he'd seen her going out in the old coat and shoes was, 'What are yer wearing that old coat for? Surely yer've got better than that?' But when she'd told him she was saving her best coat for Christmas, he seemed satisfied. Her mam, though, never said a word, but Cynthia knew she was thinking plenty. She could always tell when her mam knew she was lying, you could see it in her eyes. What a shock they'd both get if they knew what she was up to, and why. Her dad would go stark raving mad and want to find the blokes who had harmed his beloved daughter. He would want to kill them with his bare hands. But her mother would stay silent. Only her eyes would speak, and they would say she wasn't surprised because her daughter was a wayward girl who had probably contributed to what had happened.

Cynthia bent down to press on her toes, which were giving her gyp. And she would have missed the two men passing by on the opposite side of the road if it hadn't been for Jeff's burst of loud laughter. Instantly she was alert, the cold and her pains forgotten as her heart thumped in her breast like a drum. She let them walk a safe distance before crossing the road and following them. And as she pulled her scarf low over her forehead, she vowed she'd stay with them until they made their way home. She was determined that tonight she would find out where they lived, and put a stop to this twice-weekly vigil. Once she had their addresses she would work out how to make the best use of the information. It was only two days to Christmas so there was little she could do before then. What she had in mind had to be planned right down to the last detail if it were to be successful.

There were fewer people on the road now, and Cynthia, afraid of one of them turning, moved in closer to the wall. They wouldn't recognise her as the well made-up, fashionable girl they knew, but if they noticed a lone woman walking behind them for too long, they just might get curious. They'd covered some distance by now, and Cynthia's toes were so sore every step was an effort. It was sheer willpower that kept her going. Then the two men were no longer in front of her, and she hurried to the spot where she'd lost them to find it was a corner pub. That meant she'd have at least half an hour's wait, but even though her nose and eyes were running with the cold, she told herself she couldn't give up now, not after coming so far. So she looked for a safe place to hide, one where she'd be sheltered from the wind. There was a block of shops opposite and she quickly made up her mind that in the shelter of one of the doorways she'd be out of the wind and have a good vantage point.

When Larry and Jeff came out of the pub they were closely followed by a woman. They were all laughing as the woman linked their arms and the trio set off, not in the direction the men had come from, but towards Liverpool centre. Cynthia's instincts told her that if the men ran true to form, they wouldn't be walking very far. As she waited for them to cover a safe distance, she made a mental note of the woman's appearance. Probably about twenty years of age, slim figure, reddish hair, and dressed in a dark green swagger coat. This information would be written down when she got home, under the details of the two girls she'd last seen them with. Times, dates and places were also noted.

When she saw them stop at the top of an entry, Cynthia held back. She was thinking how easy it was for Larry and Jeff to pick girls up, when she heard the woman's raised voice and saw her struggling. Then to her horror, she saw the men pull the same trick they'd pulled on her. She saw them grab the woman's arms, and just before they were lost to view, Jeff's hand was muffling her screams. Cynthia couldn't move, she felt as though she'd been turned to stone. Then memories came flooding back, memories of pain, horror and humiliation. This had the effect of setting her in motion. They'd not get away with putting some other poor woman through what she had suffered. Galvanised into action, Cynthia flew across the road and made for the entry. She didn't know what she could do, but she couldn't stand by and do nothing.

'Oh, thank God,' Cynthia cried with relief when two men rounded the corner of a side street. 'Please mister, will yer help? I've just seen two men dragging a woman down that entry. She was crying and struggling but they wouldn't stop. Yer've got to help her, please.'

The two men didn't even stop to think, they moved like greased lightning. And as they ran down the dark entry, one shouted, 'The bastards, I'll kill them.'

Cynthia knew if she had any sense she'd make herself scarce, but she couldn't go, not until she knew what happened. She moved closer to the entry and could hear roars of anger, then Jeff's voice, shouting, 'What the hell's it got to do with you?'

'I'll show yer what it's got to do with me.' This came from one of the men Cynthia had asked to help. 'Yer dirty buggers, I'll flay yer alive.' There was the sound of scuffling and cries of pain as fists landed on their target. After a minute, the same voice shouted, 'You make a run for it, love. We'll sort these two out, they'll not bother yer again.'

Cynthia flattened herself against the wall as the woman rounded the corner. Her hair and clothes were dishevelled, and her eyes red-rimmed with tears. 'Are yer all right, love?' Cynthia stepped from the shadows. 'I saw what happened and asked those two men to help.'

'Thank God yer did.' The woman ran the back of her hand across her eyes. 'They're beasts, those two are. If you hadn't got help for me, I don't know what they'd have done to me. I honestly thought I was a goner.'

'D'yer know them?' Cynthia asked.

'I've never seen them in me life before.' The woman was shaking like a leaf. 'They came in the pub I go to, and they seemed nice and friendly. So when they asked me if I'd like to go to another pub they know, I didn't think anything of it.'

'I think yer should go on home, love, before they come out.' Cynthia was thinking that she too should put a distance between them and herself. Heaven alone knew what was going on in the entry, there were still sounds of fighting. 'Go on, love, take my advice and scarper.'

The woman took a few steps, then turned. 'I don't know how to thank you; yer saved me life.'

'That's all right, love. I might need help meself some time, yer never know.' As she watched the woman running as quickly as her high-heeled shoes would allow, Cynthia was glad she'd been able to get help for her before she was put through the nightmare she herself had endured. And she was taking great satisfaction from knowing she'd upset the apple-cart for Larry and Jeff. But what was happening in that dark entry? Were Larry and Jeff getting their just deserts, or were the Good Samaritans being punished for their act of kindness? She couldn't go home without knowing.

Ten minutes passed, then the two strange men who would forever be heroes in her mind, came out of the entry dusting their hands as though they'd touched something unpleasant. And Cynthia, huddled in the shop doorway opposite, gave a sigh of relief. They didn't appear to be hurt, in fact just the opposite. She could hear them talking and they seemed in high spirits.

'That sorted the dirty buggers out.'

'Aye, they'll not be going down an entry for a very long time. Serves the sods right.'

'Let's hope it's taught that young woman a lesson. As my old ma used to say, "Never trust a man until yer've met his family".'

Their voices faded as they walked away, and Cynthia was left to consider her position. Nothing would drag her away until she'd seen Larry and Jeff and satisfied herself that they'd been taught a lesson. But after that, what should she do? Go home and put the whole thing out of her mind? Going home would be the sensible thing to do because she was so cold her teeth were chattering. But in the darkness of the doorway, she shook her head. She didn't want to be sensible; she wanted to accomplish what she'd set out to do. Those two evil devils might have got a hammering tonight, but it would be nothing to the terrible things they'd done to her. Acts so terrible, she'd never tell anyone, not even Laura.

Cynthia felt her body stiffen. A man had emerged from the entry and she could tell by the colour of his hair that it was Larry. Her precious Larry, who was forever telling her he loved her. And she'd been fool enough to believe him. He was doubled up, with one arm across his tummy and the hand of his other arm holding his face. And she could hear his groans from where she stood. A grim smile came to her face. It serves you right, she thought, you dirty, wicked, evil monster. I hope you're in agony, and that it lasts a hell of a sight longer than mine will.

Thinking she couldn't be seen, Cynthia had edged herself forward, but when Jeff appeared she stepped back sharply. He too was holding his tummy and his face as he staggered to where his friend was. In the stillness of the night, their voices carried across the road.

'Where the bleedin' hell did they come from?'

'I dunno, but one of them has broke me flaming nose.' This came from Larry. 'I'm in agony and I'm covered in blood.'

'I think my nose is bust, too, I can't bear to touch it. And I feel as though the bastards have kicked the inside out of me. They wouldn't have got away with it if they hadn't taken us by surprise. Someone must have tipped them off.'

'Grow up, will yer, Jeff? The bitch was making enough noise to wake the neighbourhood. The stupid cow.' Larry was a very unhappy man. 'We can't go home like this, so what shall we do?'

'We've got to go home, there's nowhere else we can go. Unless we go to the hospital to get seen to. We can say a gang of drunks set about us and we didn't stand a chance.' Jeff put a hand to his head and groaned. 'I don't know which hurts the most, me nose or me insides.'

'I'm not going to no hospital,' Larry said, 'I'm going home and getting it over with. I'll tell Doreen the one about a gang of drunks. She won't believe me, but she can't prove otherwise.'

'I'll tell Iris the same, and I don't care whether she believes me or not. The way I feel, she can sod off for all I care. We'll walk to the tram stop and catch a twenty-two.'

'Are you crazy? We can't get on a tram looking like this, we're both covered in blood!' When Larry tried to straighten up, he groaned and fell back against the wall. 'Even if I have to crawl home, I'm not getting on no tram.'

'Have it yer own way,' Jeff growled. 'But we'll have to take it easy because I feel as though every bone in me body's been broken.'

Cynthia stepped from the shadows on to the pavement. There went two men who didn't like getting a dose of their own medicine. And if she had her way, there was a worse fate in store for them.

As she was passing a pub, Cynthia glanced at her watch. She was surprised to see it was only ten to ten. So much had happened she thought it was much later. She'd been trailing Larry and Jeff for miles, crossing from one side of the road to the other, so as not to arouse their suspicions. They'd started out in Scotland Road, and were now halfway along County Road. They certainly didn't play in their own neck of the woods, that was for sure. It was no wonder they'd never been caught out; they went far afield for their pleasures. They were walking one in front of the other, with their heads turned towards the shops and pubs so they wouldn't be recognised by passers-by. And it was plain to see they were in great discomfort.

Cynthia pretended to be looking in a shop window when the two men came to a halt. They began talking, looking around furtively as they did so. They must be nearly home, she thought, and were getting their story ready to tell. Her excitement mounted at the thought of being so near her goal. And when the men turned the corner of the next street, her footsteps quickened. It was crucial she didn't lose sight of them at this point. Pretending to be arranging her scarf, she stood at the corner of the street and saw Larry mount the step of a house about five dwellings down, while Jeff crossed to a house opposite. Keeping her eyes fixed on the spot, Cynthia took a chance and began to walk slowly towards it, giving Larry time to let himself in. She appeared to be looking straight ahead, but her eyes swivelled towards the front door and noted the brass plate with the number fifteen outlined in black. Then she calmly turned and walked to the main road, to catch a tram that would take her home.

★ ★ ★

Jenny opened the door with the key her mother kept in case Lizzie ever took bad and they needed to gain entrance. 'You stay here,' she said to Janet and the two boys, 'while I tell Auntie Lizzie she's got the four of us again.'

However, Lizzie had sharp ears. 'Don't leave them standing in the cold, let them come in. I knew yer were all coming, 'cos yer mam told me.' Her eyes were bright with pleasure when the four of them trooped in, one after the other. 'I've been sitting here waiting for yer.'

Each of them gave her a kiss before making for the fireplace. 'It's not half cold out, Auntie Lizzie,' Mick said, rubbing his hands together in front of the fire. 'I wouldn't be surprised if we had snow.'

'Ooh, I hope so.' Jenny's cheeks were a rosy red, matching the beret she was wearing at a saucy angle on top of her long blonde hair. 'It would be lovely to wake up on Christmas morning and see everywhere white.'

'Yeah, like last Christmas,' John said. 'It was the gear.'

'It's very pretty to look at through the window, son, but not very nice if yer have to walk far in it.'

Mick, warmed through now, moved away from the fire and pulled out a chair. 'If there's snow on the ground on Christmas Day, Auntie Lizzie, I'll give yer a piggy-back over to the Nightingales'.'

John wasn't to be left out. 'And I'll give yer one back. Even if it's not snowing I'll carry yer, just in case yer have too many bottles of stout and yer get a bit tipsy.'

'The day has yet to come when Lizzie Marshall gets tipsy, son.' The old lady giggled at the thought. 'But it's a very kind offer and I'll bear it in mind.'

Mick pouted his lips. 'Wasn't my offer as kind as his?'

'Of course it was, son. Ye're two very kind lads.'

Jenny tutted as she placed her mother's basket on the table. 'Don't start that lark. We came here to make decorations, remember?'

'I was only putting the record straight.' Mick winked at Lizzie. 'It doesn't take much for Jenny to get on her high horse, does it? Best thing to do is humour her, that's what I've found.'

'And I've found the best way to deal with you and John is to ignore yer.' Jenny delved in the basket and brought out some packets of crêpe paper. 'We bought a packet each, Auntie Lizzie, so there's two red and two green. We're going to cut them into strips and make paper chains to go around the picture rail.' Once again her hand went into the basket. 'Me mam mixed some flour and water for us to stick them together with, and she put it in this basin so we can all reach it to dip our fingers in.'

Janet pulled a face. 'I don't fancy putting me fingers in that. Haven't yer got any brushes we can use?'

206

'No, we haven't, so it's no good yer pulling faces. We used to make them in school and I never heard yer moaning to Miss Harrison about getting yer fingers sticky. If yer had, it would have been three strokes of the cane.'

'I'm not pulling faces, Miss Nightingale, and I don't mind getting me fingers sticky at all.' Even Jenny had to laugh at the look of innocence on John's face as he held his hands out, palms upward. 'I'll do anything yer say, Miss, but I don't want no cane.'

Mick guffawed. 'He used to do that in school. Proper crawler, he was.'

John glared. 'How do you know? Yer weren't in my class.'

'Well, I just happened to be passing your classroom one afternoon and I saw yer on yer knees in front of the teacher's desk, begging for mercy. I remember thinking what a pathetic little creep yer were.'

'Isn't it funny how things come back to yer?' John's face was one big grin. 'I remember that afternoon, I saw yer go past. One of the lads told me afterwards that yer'd been to the headmaster's office for six strokes of the cane. If my memory serves me right, it was for giving cheek to Mr Johnston.'

'No, no, yer've got it all wrong,' Mick said. 'I didn't get the cane for giving Mr Johnston cheek, I got it for tripping him up.'

While the others roared with laughter, Janet's face was serious. 'Did yer trip Mr Johnston up on purpose?'

The laughter increased with her words, until Jenny called a halt. 'Auntie Lizzie wants these decorations for this Christmas, not next.'

'Your word is our command, Jenny,' Mick said. 'Just tell me and John what to do and we'll start.'

'Yer cut the paper in two-inch strips, first. Then yer cut those strips into four inch ones. We've only got two pairs of scissors between us, so I'll cut a couple of strips first and me and Jan can start making the chains.'

Lizzie sat back watching, her cheeks stiff with laughing so much. It was like something out of a comedy picture. The two boys were hilarious, they talked incessantly.

'That's not two inches, mate,' John said. 'More like three.'

'That is dead on two inches, pal,' Mick answered. 'Why didn't yer bring yer flaming specs with yer? If yer had, yer'd know that those strips you're cutting are nowhere near four inches.'

Lizzie's eyes went to the girls. Jenny was quick and efficient. All the time she was geeing the boys up if they kept her waiting. Janet, on the other hand, was taking the job very seriously. With her tongue sticking out of the side of her mouth, she weighed each piece of paper up carefully before linking it through the last piece. And the look of distaste on her face when she stuck her finger in the basin was a picture no artist could paint.

'Have yer brought the drawing pins, Mick?' Jenny asked as she eyed the long paper chain she was working on. 'I think this strip will do one of the walls.'

'Now, would I let yer down?' Mick brought a box out of his pocket. Then, with a look of pretend concern on his handsome face, he passed them over the table and said, 'Yer'll have to be careful, Jenny, it's very high.'

'I'm not putting it up, yer daft nit!' Jenny's voice was indignant. 'That's your job, or John's.'

The expression that came to John's face was pure bliss. 'I'll do it for yer, Jenny. As long as you hold the chair and catch me if I fall off.'

Mick pushed his friend down in his chair. 'This is a private conversation, pal, so keep yer nose out before I put it out of joint.'

'I think I'm an inch taller than you, mate, and that inch might make all the difference.'

'Are you heck! Anyway, I can always stand on me toes.'

Janet studied them both before coming out with one of her gems. 'Isn't it funny, I've never noticed yer were an inch taller, John. Yer both look the same height to me. Stand back-to-back and let's see.'

Jenny banged a fist on the table. 'Don't you dare! Don't you flamingwell dare! Ye're both so big-headed it's a wonder yer can get through the door. I bet as soon as yer get home yer'll have a tape-measure out. *And* I bet ye're vain enough to stand in front of a mirror while yer measure yerself. But yer came here to do a job, and if yer don't want to do it, then yer can both scram. Me and Janet will make the chains on our own, and I'll ask Bill if he'll put them up for us tomorrow night.'

That did the trick. Within an hour the chains were made and hanging gaily from the picture rail, brightening the room and making it look Christmassy. The two boys gazed at it with pride, their chests sticking out a mile. 'How about that, Auntie Lizzie?' Mick asked. 'Not a bad job, even if I do say so meself.'

'Yeah,' John said, 'when we put our mind to it, we can go like the clappers.' He punched Mick playfully on the back. 'We make a good team, don't we, mate?'

Lizzie coughed. 'Yer've done a fine job, without a doubt. But what about the girls – don't they get a mention? After all, they had to make the chains for you to put up.'

'Thank you, Auntie Lizzie, I'm glad someone noticed us.' Jenny was feeling very happy inside but wasn't going to let the lads get away with all the glory. 'Listening to these two big-heads, I was beginning to think I'd only dreamt that me and Janet had made all those links. It was the hardest job of the lot, sticking them all together.'

Janet nodded her head. 'Yes, and we've got all our fingers sticky.'

'Ah, yer poor things.' Mick put his arm across Jenny's shoulder. 'You do all the work and we take the credit. I humbly apologise, Miss Nightingale.'

Janet looked at John. 'Aren't you going to apologise? Yer should do, 'cos, as Jenny said, we did all the hard work.'

John gave Mick a dirty look before putting his arm across Janet's shoulder. 'Yes, yer worked very hard, and I do apologise. I'm sorry about yer sticky fingers, as well.'

Jenny clapped her hands. 'Now that's been settled to everyone's satisfaction, let's clear this mess off the table and put the chenille cloth back.' She spied the old lady looking up at the decorations. 'They look nice, don't they, Auntie Lizzie?'

'They look lovely. The room seems bright and cheerful, now.' She caught hold of Jenny's hand. 'You know, lass, it must be all of thirty years since this room saw a Christmas decoration. Yer see, yer don't bother when yer live on yer own, it doesn't seem worth it.'

'Well, ye're not on yer own now, Auntie Lizzie, 'cos yer've got us. We're here to stay whether yer like it or not. We all love the bones of yer.'

Lizzie grinned. Jenny didn't only look like her mother, she had the same sense of humour and had picked up all her sayings.

By the time the foursome were ready to leave, Lizzie was sitting comfortably on the couch with her hands curled around a cup of cocoa. The fire had been damped down and the fireguard put in front for safety. And her bed was being warmed by a hot-water bottle. She was being spoilt in her old age and loving every minute of it. These four youngsters were very considerate and a credit to their parents. She wished things could stay this way until the end of her days, but knew it wasn't possible. They were coming to an age when they would meet someone and start courting. It was surprising the boys didn't have girlfriends already, they were old enough. Even as she thought it, Lizzie knew the answer. It was as plain as the nose on her face that they were both waiting for Jenny, but the girl herself didn't favour one nor the other. They were both mates to her.

'We'll leave yer in peace now, Auntie Lizzie.' Jenny kissed her cheek. 'You go and snuggle up in yer warm bed, and have sweet dreams.'

Lizzie held her face for the other three kisses. 'Yer've been angels, the four of yer. If yer didn't have mams and dads, I'd adopt the lot of yer.'

Mick was the last to wave goodbye and when he heard Jenny's familiar peal of laughter, he hurried down the hall. 'What's going on?' Then he saw her standing on the pavement, her arms outstretched and her head back, catching the snowflakes as they fell. 'Well, yer've got yer wish, Jenny.'

'Oh, I'm so happy!' Jenny was clapping her hands and spinning around. 'I hope it sticks and we have a white Christmas.'

'It's sticking now, and it's coming down thicker,' John said. 'Look at the size of the flakes, they're like big white feathers.'

Laughing with happiness, Jenny bent down to gather a handful of snow from the pavement. It wasn't thick enough to make a decent snowball, but she'd just managed enough to fill her hand as Mick decided she was so pretty he wanted to be by her side. The devil in Jenny couldn't resist, and the snow ended up on Mick's face. Blinking rapidly, he wiped the snow away, growling like an animal. 'Ye're not getting away with that, Jenny Nightingale.' He scooped her up in his arms and laughed as her arms and legs thrashed about. 'Get me some snow, John, and I'll give her a taste of her own medicine.'

This wasn't to John's liking at all. He felt like kicking himself for not thinking of it first. 'Not on yer life, mate. I don't mind holding her for yer, though, so pass her over.'

'Pass me over!' Jenny stopped thrashing about to shake a fist. 'I'm not a sack of flaming spuds, John Hanley. Now let me down from here, if yer know what's good for yer.'

'She means it, mate,' John was happy to say. 'If I were you I'd drop her, quick.'

'I think she's too fragile to drop, so I'll either put her down gently or carry her all the way to Janet's so her feet won't get wet.'

'There yer go, big-head again.' Jenny wasn't struggling now; she'd hit on an idea to take him down a peg or two. Never in a million years did she think he could do it. He might get as far as the corner, but that was all. 'There's no way you could carry me all the way to Janet's.'

'No? Well, just watch me.' Mick began to walk down the street, his back straight and no sign of strain on his smiling face. In fact, he was in his seventh heaven. 'Yer wouldn't like to bet on it, would yer?'

'I'll bet yer don't make it all the way to Janet's. But I'm not betting with money.'

'How about a kiss, then?'

'You cheeky beggar, Mick Moynihan, I'm going to tell yer mam on you.'

'Just a peck on the cheek?'

'Oh, all right.' Jenny thought she was safe in saying that 'cos he'd never make it.

John, walking behind with Janet, was filled with envy. 'If he does manage it, Jenny, I'll have to carry yer back, just to prove I'm as strong as him.'

'You can carry me, if yer like, John,' Janet said. 'That will prove ye're as strong as Mick is. And it'll save me getting me feet wet.'

John was filled with dismay. 'Ah, I can't do that, Janet! I wouldn't have the energy left to carry Jenny home. And it's her we're betting on.' He saw her face fall and felt a heel. But there was a lot at stake here. 'I'll tell yer what, though, I'll carry yer tomorrow night. How does that suit yer?'

Janet nodded, but there was still disappointment showing on her face. 'Yeah, that suits me fine, John. Thank you.'

John felt like crawling under a stone. 'Oh, what the hell, come on, I'll carry yer.'

Janet's face lit up. 'I'll let yer kiss my cheek, John, as long as me mam doesn't see yer do it. If she did, she'd hit yer on the head with the rolling pin, and I wouldn't want yer to get hurt.'

John saw the funny side and his laughter joined Mick's. 'Oh, does it hurt when yer get hit on the head with a rolling pin? I didn't know that.'

Down at the bottom end of the street, Laura was standing on Cynthia's step when they heard the laughter. 'That's our Jenny, the stupid nit. Anyone would think she'd never seen snow before. It's about time she grew up.'

'I could never understand why ye're so against yer sister,' Cynthia said. 'I've always thought she was a nice kid.'

'Nah, you don't have to live with her. She's a real little mummy's girl, never does nothing wrong. She gets on me wick, with that smile pasted on her face all the time. Too flaming good to be true, that's our Jenny.'

Laura could feel the wet of the snow seeping into the thin soles of the high-heeled shoes she was wearing, and she shivered as she wrapped her coat tighter around her body. 'Anyway, it wasn't half exciting listening to what yer did last night. Yer were very brave, Cynthia – I couldn't have done it. Fancy yer catching them in the act and having the nerve to ask those two men for help! I would have wet me knickers and run like hell. But I really hope Larry and Jeff did get their noses broken, it's what they deserve. And fancy you following them all that way. That took some guts, that did.'

'I had to follow them to find out where they lived. Now I know, I can take it from there. The hiding they got last night will be nothing compared to what their wives will do to them when they learn what their husbands get up to every Tuesday and Thursday. I'm going to blow those two sky high, and take great delight in doing it.'

Chapter Seventeen

'Come on, Amy, get a move on, will yer?' Mary sounded impatient. 'The flaming shops will be crowded and there'll be nowt left by the time we get there.'

'Keep yer hair on, girl, I'm being as quick as I can.' Amy waddled into the hall and reached to lift her coat from one of the pegs on the hallstand. 'I don't know what the big rush is for, anyway, seeing as Wilf's put our turkey aside, the greens have been ordered and will be ready for us to pick up, and the Maypole will have our order ready.' She slipped her arms into her coat. 'Ye're a proper bleedin' worry-wart, girl, and yer'll have me nerves wrecked the way ye're going on.'

Mary tutted. 'Who, please, said last night that we'd better get to the shops early so we wouldn't get trampled in the crush?'

Amy grinned as she picked up her basket. 'Aye, well, that was last night. Things look different when ye're lying in bed all nice and warm. It was a real struggle to get me legs over the side of the bed, I can tell yer. They took one look at the snow on the window sill and decided to stay put. I gave them a good talking to, explained that you were coming early, but they wouldn't budge. In the end I had to resort to playing dirty, and I threw the bedclothes back when they weren't looking.' She slipped her keys into her coat pocket and shook her head at her neighbour. 'I don't know why ye're standing there yapping yer head off when we've got stacks to do. Have yer forgotten it's Christmas Eve?'

Mary rolled her eyes before looking down at her neighbour's feet. 'I hope yer've got sturdy shoes on, the snow is inches deep.'

'These are the only shoes I've got, girl, apart from me best ones. They wouldn't be a ha'porth of good in this weather, so it's Hobson's choice, I'm afraid.'

The two friends walked briskly down the street. With each step, Mary was pushed closer to the kerb as Amy clung to her arm in an effort to keep her feet on the slippery ground. 'Careful, Amy,' she said, as a car went past and sprayed her with slush, 'otherwise I'm going to end up in the gutter.'

Amy chuckled. 'Now I wouldn't say it, being yer mate, like. But there are those who would say they weren't surprised that yer ended up in the gutter.'

213

'Now why would they say that?'

'Well, you know, anyone that's always bragging and swanking, that's where they usually end up,' Amy told her, straightfaced.

'You wouldn't say that, though, would yer, sunshine?'

'Not on yer life, I wouldn't! And I'd flatten anyone that did! I mean, you and me have been mates for nearly twenty years now, and if we ever fell out I wouldn't know what to do with meself.' Amy gave what Mary called one of her dirty laughs. 'Especially on Christmas night.'

'Ye're a corker, Amy Hanley, it's a good job I don't take a blind bit of notice of yer.' Mary pushed her friend into the butcher's shop. 'My God, Wilf's doing some business today. I see he's got his wife in helping.'

'We shouldn't have to wait, we've paid for our bleedin' turkeys. All he's got to do is hand them over the counter.'

'Amy, yer can't expect Wilf to serve yer before all these other people. He'd have a mutiny on his hands if he did.'

'Sod off, girl.' Amy stood on tiptoe to see over the shoulders of the women in front. 'Good morning, Wilf,' she called out. 'I see ye're coining it in as usual. I bet when Father Christmas comes down your chimney, he'll find yer counting yer money. He won't leave yer nothing 'cos he'll think yer've got enough.'

Wilf, red in the face after being on the run since he opened the shop at eight o'clock, looked up and groaned. 'Oh, dear Lord, haven't I got enough trouble without sending me the biggest troublemaker in the neighbourhood?'

Every head in the shop turned. Those who knew Amy smiled; those who didn't tutted impatiently. If the little fat woman thought she was going to jump the queue, she had another think coming. And Wilf's wife, Irene, didn't know whether to laugh or cry. She'd been the butt of Amy's jokes a few times and, not having her husband's sense of humour, she hadn't thought them very funny. She'd make sure she didn't serve her, she'd leave that to Wilf.

Amy, bobbing up and down like a rubber ball, stuck her hand in the air. 'I'm not going to cause no trouble, Wilf, I can see ye're busy. So if yer'll just pass over the turkeys that me and me mate chose and paid for yesterday, we'll leave yer in peace to make yer fortune.'

There was muttering amongst the crowd and dark looks were aimed at the two women 'Yer'll have to wait a while, Amy, I can't serve yer now. I've only got one pair of hands, and some of these ladies have been waiting a long time.'

Mary was beginning to feel uncomfortable, but Amy was undeterred. 'Then they should have done what we did, instead of leaving it until the last minute. This means that me and me mate have got to queue twice for the same bleedin' turkey, and yer can sod that for a lark.'

214

'Yer may as well serve her, Wilf,' said one of the neighbours from their street, 'otherwise she'll carry on something shocking.' The woman said it with a smile on her face, hoping to do Amy a favour, but it didn't go down well with some of those waiting.

'She's not going before me,' said one.

'Let her wait her turn like the rest of us,' said another.

'Ay, missus, I waited me bleedin' turn yesterday. I was stood here so long with me eye on this flaming turkey, that I got real friendly with it. I even gave it a blinking name. I christened it Ben, after my feller, 'cos I always have to wait for him, as well.' Smiles were appearing on faces now, and Amy was encouraged. 'I'll lay odds that when that turkey sees me, it'll run to me shouting "Mammy".'

If Wilf had had the time, he'd have taken his hat off to her. The smiles had turned to titters and even a couple of full-blown laughs. 'Come to think of it, Amy, it does look like you. There's definitely a family resemblance.'

'I'll take that as a compliment, Wilf Burnett, because if I didn't, I'd be round that counter to give yer a fourpenny one. And now, will yer do the gentlemanly thing and reunite me with me baby, so I can take it home and put it to bed in me roasting tin.'

Wilf had served two customers while all this was going on. He'd weighed and wrapped two turkeys which were now lying on the counter. The customers didn't know he was waiting to be paid, they'd turned around to watch Amy. 'Ladies, can I have yer money, please?'

One of the women took a pound from her purse. 'Here yer are, take for both of them and I'll get Lucy's money off her later.' When Wilf came back with her two bob change, she said, 'Give that woman her turkey, she deserves it.'

Wilf gave his wife the eye. 'There's two bags on the floor out there, love, with Hanley and Nightingale on. Pass them over, will yer, so we can have a bit of peace?'

Amy wasn't going to go quietly, though. 'I just want to make sure yer've not pulled a fast one on me and given me the wrong bird.' She pulled the turkey out by its legs and held it high. 'Ay, Wilf, has this bird been on night-shift?'

'Not that I know of, Amy, but then I've been working most of the night and haven't had much time to get acquainted with it. Why?'

'I think yer've been working this poor bleedin' thing all night, too, 'cos it's only a shadow of its former self. Look, it's got no bleeding meat on its legs! I've heard of sparrow legs, but this is ridiculous! And another thing, Wilf Burnett, how could yer notice a family resemblance when it's got no bleeding head?'

'It was while I was cutting its head off, I thought of you. I remember wishing something when I brought the chopper down, but I can't for the life of me think what it was.'

215

Amy's laugh was the loudest as she put the turkey back in the bag. 'Nice one, Wilf. I'll get me own back after Christmas. After all, this is one time of the year it's a slap on the back and goodwill towards all men. So have a nice Christmas, Wilf, and you Irene. Don't be spending all yer time counting yer money, try and enjoy yerself.' Being pulled out of the shop by Mary, she yelled, 'Merry Christmas, ladies. And don't yer be doing anything I wouldn't do if I got half a chance.'

Once outside, Amy turned to Mary, her lips pursed. 'If ye're going to talk that much in every shop we go to, we'll never get finished. So keep yer trap shut, girl, and try and behave yerself.' Waddling ahead, she muttered, 'Honest to God, I've never known anyone like yer for yapping. Yer'd talk the hind legs off a donkey – that's if yer knew a donkey, and providing it had hind legs.'

When they got to the greengrocer's, Mary made Amy stand outside. 'The shop's full, and I'm not putting up with any more shenanigans from you. So you stay right there and I'll bring yer things out to yer.'

Billy Nelson was rushed off his feet, even though he had his wife and son helping. But he still had a smile on his face and a joke on his lips. He spotted Mary as he was weighing potatoes and called, 'Where's the queer one, then?'

Mary jerked her thumb towards the door. 'I've made her wait outside. She's just caused ructions in the butcher's, and I couldn't go through that again.'

'Go 'way, I bet she had them in stitches.' Billy grinned as he emptied the potatoes from the scale into a woman's basket. 'I gave yer good measure, Mrs Gillespie, seeing as it's Christmas.' He put the scale back on the big iron weighing machine that hung from the ceiling. 'I'll be with yer in two shakes of a lamb's tail, love. I just want to show Mrs Nightingale where her order is.'

'Finish serving her, Billy, I can wait.'

'No, these two boxes are your orders, and I'll be glad to get them from under me feet.' He lifted a wooden box and placed it in Mary's outstretched arms. 'That's Amy's, and the bill's inside. If yer take it out to her, I'll follow with yours.'

Amy took one look at the box and shook her head. 'I'll never be able to carry that! Who d'yer think I am, Billy Nelson, King bleedin' Kong?'

'It's what yer ordered, Amy, so don't blame me.'

'Put the turkey on top, Amy, and take the ruddy box off me,' Mary said. 'Billy's got a shop full of people to see to.'

Amy held her arms out and pretended to buckle under the weight. 'If I do meself an injury, Billy Nelson, my Ben will have something to say to yer.'

After passing Mary's order over, Billy bent to smile into Amy's face. 'I've got yer where I want yer now, haven't I? If I wasn't so busy, I could do what I like to yer and yer wouldn't be able to do a thing about it.'

'No, lad, I wouldn't. But whatever yer were doing, yer wouldn't be enjoying it, 'cos I'd have dropped this box on yer bleedin' foot and broke all yer toes.'

Roaring with laughter, Billy made his way through the shop doorway, calling over his shoulder, 'Yer can pass the money in later, ladies.'

Amy looked down at herself with dismay. 'Sod this for a lark, girl, all me well-endowments are getting squashed to blazes.'

Mary didn't want to laugh, but laugh she did. Amy's mountainous bosom was a definite drawback to carring a box in her outstretched arms. If she carried it high, her breasts would be squashed, if she lowered her arms and carried it low, her tummy would suffer the same fate. 'D'yer know what I think, sunshine? Being so well-endowed isn't all it's cracked up to be, is it?'

'Never mind all that now, girl, how am I going to get home? How am I going to carry all this, and me basket?'

'Where is yer basket?'

'Between me bleedin' feet! I suppose I could ask someone to put it over me head, and let everyone have a good laugh at my expense. But somehow I don't fancy that.'

'Well, let's not get excited. I've got my basket on me arm, so if I could pick yours up I could hang it on me other arm.' Very gingerly, Mary bent her legs and lowered herself down. 'Open yer legs, sunshine.'

'Ah, not tonight, Ben, I've got a headache.'

Mary nearly lost her balance with laughing. No matter what the problem, Amy could always find a joke in it. 'If you don't stop making me laugh, Amy Hanley, I'm going to end up on me backside with me turkey and potatoes around me. Now, behave yerself, if yer know how.'

The main road wasn't too bad for walking because the shop-keepers had cleared the snow away. But the side streets were very hazardous, and the friends walked with great care. They were just six houses away from their own homes when Amy said, 'I'm dying to go to the lavvy, girl, I'll have to move. It must be the cold weather.'

'Amy, for heaven's sake be careful or—' Mary watched with horror as Amy's foot slipped on the ice, and unable to use her arms to balance herself, she went flying. She fell on her back and all around her were scattered the contents of the box. Mary could see apples and oranges flying in all directions, but her concern was for the inert figure lying on the ground. 'Oh, dear God, let her be all right.'

217

Throwing everything down, Mary ran towards her friend. Never very good in an emergency, her heart was pounding in case Amy had really hurt herself and needed the kind of help she didn't know how to give. Taking a deep breath, she looked down.

'I don't need to go to the lavvy now, girl, I've used the public toilet.' Amy's smile turned to a grimace as she tried to move. 'I've certainly come a cropper, haven't I?'

'Don't you try to move, Amy Hanley, it's no joke.'

'Oh, I know that, girl, no one better. But I thought yer might be worried about me wanting to spend a penny. So it's one worry less for yer.'

'I'm going to see if Molly's in, 'cos I'm as much use as that ruddy turkey.' With tears in her eyes, Mary crossed the snow-covered cobbles, praying that Molly would be home. And her prayers were answered when the Irishwoman opened the door.

Molly took one look at Mary's face and her smile vanished. 'What is it, me darlin'?'

'It's Amy, she's fallen over and I don't know what to do.'

Molly put the catch on the door so she wouldn't lock herself out, and hurried after Mary. 'Glory be to God, Amy, what have yer done to yerself?'

'If yer'll give Mary a hand to lift me up, girl, I'll tell yer whether or not I'm still in one piece.' There was much grunting and groaning from Amy as her friends lifted her to a sitting position and dusted the snow from her coat. 'So far, so good, girls – at least there's nowt broke. I'll have a few bruises, but what's a bruise between friends? It's me backside that hurts most, and the bottom of me back. But don't worry, I'll live. Now, if yer can manage it, would yer lift me to me feet?'

It was obvious Amy was in pain when they tried to stand her upright. 'Let me bend for a while, till it eases off.'

Molly nodded to the empty box. 'Mary, me darlin', would yer pick up all the groceries, please? If yer take them inside, sure that'll be a big help, so it will. Amy will move in her own good time, won't yer, me darlin'?'

'It's me own stupid fault, I'm a crackpot. I started to run because I wanted to go to the lavvy, yer see. I don't want to go to the lavvy now, like, but I did then.'

Mary, throwing fruit and vegetables into the box, winked at Molly. 'The woman has no modesty whatsoever.'

Amy tried to stand upright to have her say, but the pain was so sharp she contented herself with raising her voice. 'What the bleedin' hell is the good of trying to be modest when yer've got an orange stuck in yer mouth and there's a ruddy dead turkey lying on yer chest? To hell with modesty, girl, that's what I say.'

When Amy insisted that all the shopping be taken into Mary's house, Molly tried to reason with her. 'But, me darlin', wouldn't it be better altogether if the shopping, and yerself, went straight into yer own house? Sure, wouldn't it save yer the trouble of doing more walking than yer need to? Yer could settle yerself on the couch with a pile of pillows to try and ease the pain. It would make things a heck of a sight easier all round.'

It would have been the sensible thing to do, but then Amy never did anything because it was sensible. It took her all her time to mount the front steps, but grunting and groaning, and using every swearword she could think of, she finally made it. 'I'd rather get me ease on Mary's couch, it's much more comfortable than mine. Besides, I can lie and look at her nice wallpaper instead of the miserable bleedin' stuff I've got on my walls. It's enough to give yer the willies.'

'I've got to go out again for the rest of our shopping, sunshine, so it means yer being on yer own.' Mary looked at the clock and groaned. There was so much to do and time was marching on. 'Ye're as stubborn as a mule, Amy Hanley; yer'll have yer own way if it kills yer. So don't go blaming me if yer find yer can't walk at all and ye're stuck on my couch all over Christmas.'

'I'll be walking, girl, don't you worry yerself about that. If you think I'm going to let a few aches and pains stop me from coming to yer party, yer've got another think coming. I've spent weeks getting me party piece ready and I'm going to show off come hell or high water.'

Molly shrugged her shoulders at Mary. 'You go and get yer shopping done, me darlin', and I'll stay with her. I'll have a look at her bottom and back, make sure she hasn't done herself any real harm.'

Amy, who was perched on the arm of the couch, looked at Molly as though she'd gone mad. 'Listen here, Florence Nightingale, nobody has seen my backside since the midwife delivered me. Except for my Ben, of course, but then he'd paid seven and six for the marriage certificate, so he was entitled. But I ain't pulling me knickers down for no one else.' Her head and chins wagged. 'The very idea, indeed!'

Molly's body shook with laughter. 'Well, me darlin', I've got to admit I wasn't looking forward to it meself, and that's the truth of it. Not particularly because it's your backside, which I'm sure is exactly the same as me own, but because it's not the most attractive part of the body. But I'll not be criticising the Good Lord for giving us one, 'cos if He hadn't, sure, we'd have nothing to sit on.'

Imitating Molly's Irish accent, Amy said, 'Sure, it's a foine way with words yer have, Mrs Moynihan, and that's a fact. Wouldn't I even go as far as to say that you and I are on a level when it comes to making interesting conversation?'

'Then I'll leave yer to get on with educating each other,' Mary said, 'while I go to the Maypole and pick up our orders. Then there's only the bread to get in.' She shook her head at Amy. 'Yer certainly picked a fine time to take up skating, sunshine, I'll say that for yer. Only the busiest day of the year.'

Amy's face, which had drained of colour from the shock of the fall, was now showing traces of pink in her chubby cheeks. 'Take no notice of her, Molly, she's only jealous 'cos we're more cleverer than she is. Yer see, she doesn't know her arse from her bleedin' elbow.'

'Considering ye're supposed to be in agony, Amy Hanley, it certainly hasn't affected yer mouth, has it? Now, when I come back from the shops I expect to see yer walking around this room. D'yer hear me?'

'The whole bleedin' street can hear yer, girl! Yer've got a mouth on yer like a fog-horn when yer start. But I'll be walking, have no fear, 'cos we're all going to Midnight Mass, aren't we? I promised to go and I'll keep me promise.'

Mary put her basket in the crook of her arm. 'The church will probably fall down when you walk in. I've never known yer go to Midnight Mass before.'

'Well, yer see, girl, it was our John who taught me the error of me ways. He said you and Stan were going with Jenny, and all the Moynihans. He said he was going with yer whether I came or not. So I couldn't let me eldest born think his mother was a heathen, could I?'

Molly turned her face to hide a smile. John and Mick would go to any lengths to spend time with Jenny. Her son had even asked Seamus not to have too many pints because he didn't want to be ashamed of his father smelling of drink in church. And would he kindly refrain from singing at the top of his voice.

'I'll be back in an hour,' Mary said, putting her arm around Amy. 'If it hurts yer to walk, sunshine, then don't walk. Take no notice of me, I was only joking.'

'It's been a right day, I can tell yer. I certainly wouldn't want another one like it.' They were sitting around the table having their meal and Mary had gone over the day's events. 'Yer know what I'm like in an emergency, I'm about as much use as a wet fish. I always think the worst, and when Amy was lying so still, I thought she'd broken her neck.'

'Won't Auntie Amy be coming to church with us?' Jenny asked. 'I was looking forward to all of us going together. Janet and her brother are coming round to walk there with us.'

'I don't know about Auntie Amy, sunshine, we'll just have to wait and see. Me and Molly got her home between us, one holding each

220

of her arms. She said she's coming, and yer know what she's like when she sets her mind to anything. She'll probably get Uncle Ben to give her a piggy-back.'

'I know I shouldn't laugh, love, 'cos it's not funny,' Stan said. 'But I've got this picture in me head of all the potatoes and everything flying in the air and landing all over the place.'

'Oh, when I got back from the shops we all had a laugh over it. And the one that laughed the loudest was Amy! Even though she was in pain, she thought it was hilarious. She said it was a pity no one had a camera because it would have made a good snap.' Mary looked across the table to where Laura sat. Her eldest daughter hadn't opened her mouth since they'd sat down. 'Are you coming to church with us, Laura?'

'No, I'm going down to Cynthia's.' Laura's mind was on Gary. She wouldn't see him for a week, and to her a week was an eternity. 'If she's going, I'll go with her.'

'Before yer go anywhere, yer can help Jenny to finish decorating the tree. I'll wash up and then I've got the turkey to clean and the stuffing to make.'

Jenny collected the empty plates and carried them out to the kitchen. Looking through the window, she could see the snowflakes falling and a smile lit up her face. 'Mam, it's snowing heavy, we're going to have a real white Christmas. Ooh, I'm made up.'

The smile on her face annoyed Laura. She herself had nothing to smile about, and she couldn't bear to see anyone else happy. 'I don't know why ye're getting so excited about snow. It's horrible to walk in, sloshing through it, getting yer feet all wet. I can't see anything nice about it and I think you need yer head testing.'

Mary opened her mouth to say something, but Jenny got in before her. 'It makes everywhere look pretty, but you wouldn't see that, would yer, Laura? I've never yet heard yer say anything was nice. I feel sorry for yer really, but if you want to be miserable, that's your affair. Just don't expect everybody else to be miserable with yer.' All the time she spoke, Jenny kept the smile on her face. 'I'll finish the tree on me own; you hurry out before the snow gets too thick and yer poor feet get wet.'

'Right, that's enough,' Stan said. 'This is supposed to be a happy time, so we'll have no arguments in this house, if yer don't mind.'

Only her father's intervention stopped Laura from striking her sister. She pushed her chair back and glared. 'I'll leave you to the tree, then. They say small things amuse small minds.'

'Is that what they say?' Jenny never batted an eyelid. 'It should follow then, that anyone who is never amused, has no mind at all.'

When Stan saw Laura make a dive towards Jenny, he banged his fist hard on the table and stopped her in her tracks. 'I've warned yer once and I'll not do it again. Any more of this and there'll be no presents under that tree in the morning. And don't make the mistake of thinking I don't mean it, because I damn-well do.'

As the sisters moved in different directions, their emotions were poles apart. Laura was filled with anger as she bounded up the stairs. She'll not get away with making fun of me, the little upstart. One of these days, she vowed, I'll knock that smile off her face.

Jenny was angry, too, but the anger was directed at herself. She should have kept her mouth shut instead of letting Laura get to her. Now, between them, they'd spoilt the night for their parents. But for years she'd put up with her sister's sarcastic remarks and taunts, and there had to come a time when she gave back as good as she got. She wasn't a child any more, nor was she worthless as Laura tried to make out. But she shouldn't have made her stand tonight, in front of her parents. Her mam had had a trying day as it was, without her daughters adding to the pressure.

As Jenny hung a silver ball on the tree, she glanced over at her father, who was reading the *Echo*. He didn't look relaxed, or at ease with himself, and Jenny knew she was partly responsible for putting that look on his face. And it wasn't fair, he was a good father and didn't deserve to be upset. The least she could do was try and make amends. She crossed to where he was sitting and knelt in front of him. 'I'm sorry, Dad, I shouldn't have taken off like that. It was childish of me.'

Stan lowered the paper and put out a hand to stroke the long blonde hair. 'You had reason to, sweetheart. Laura would try the patience of a saint.'

'I know, but I should be used to it now and ignore her. When I stand up to her, it makes matters ten times worse. So I'll take anything she wants to throw at me, at least until after the Christmas holiday.' Jenny scrambled to her feet and kissed his forehead. 'I'll go and say sorry to me mam, then get back to the tree. We can't have Father Christmas coming down the chimney and the place not ready for him. He'd take all our presents back.'

When Mary answered the door to John, he came in rubbing his hands. 'I've come with a message from me mam. Actually she gave me two messages, but I told her one was too cheeky, and I wouldn't pass it on in case yer slapped me face.'

'She's not coming to Midnight Mass?'

'Oh yeah, that's one of the messages.' John nodded to Stan and gave Jenny a wide smile. 'Her and me dad have gone on, so she can take her time walking.'

'She's as stubborn as a mule, your mam,' Mary laughed. 'But I'm glad, because it wouldn't have been the same without her.'

Jenny noticed John was shivering and she pointed to the fire. 'Get a warm, John, yer look like a block of ice. How come yer got so cold coming from next door?'

'I walked down to the bottom of the street with me mam, to make sure she was all right. Me and me dad took an arm each and half carried her. She'll make it, because our Eddy took over from me, and our Edna's with them, as well.'

Mary narrowed her eyes. 'What was the other message, sunshine?'

John's chuckle was loud. 'Promise yer won't hit me?'

'I'll try not to, sunshine, so spit it out.'

'Me mam said will yer leave a decent fire going, and a full kettle on the hob so there'll be a cup of hot tea for everyone when we get back from church.'

Mary's mouth gaped. 'Holy suffering ducks! That's cheek for yer, even by yer mam's standards. D'yer know there'll be about twelve people? I don't have enough cups for that many! Does she think I've got a ruddy cafe?'

John moved to stand beside Stan's chair. 'I'm keeping out of yer way while I pass on the rest of the message.' With his whole body filled with laughter that was yet to come, he went on. 'So help me, Mrs Nightingale, this is word for word. Me mam said if yer moaned about not having enough cups, I was to tell yer she'd lend yer some out of the goodness of her heart. Only ones with cracks and chips in, though, 'cos she knows how rough some of yer friends are and she's not having none of her best china broke by no hoodlums.'

The room filled with laughter. Stan was beating his fists on the arm of his chair, Jenny's arms were holding her tummy as she bent double, and Mary made no attempt to wipe the tears away. Even when she wasn't here, her mate Amy had the knack of filling her heart with happiness. 'She is one corker, your mam.'

'She is that, Mrs Nightingale. The best mother anyone could have, and that's why we all love her to bits.' John suddenly snapped his finger and thumb. 'Oh, I almost forgot. She said something about custard creams.'

'Are we all present and accounted for?' Seamus asked as Mary banged the door behind her. 'I hope ye're all well wrapped up, 'cos it's a night the divil himself wouldn't venture out in.'

'Amy went on early to give herself plenty of time to walk there slowly. But Jenny's friend and her brother haven't arrived yet.'

'It's no good hanging around waiting for them,' Stan said. 'They may have gone straight there with it being so bad underfoot.'

'But I promised them,' Jenny said, 'and I'd feel mean if they came all the way around here and we'd gone without them.'

'If we leave it any longer, sunshine, we'll not get seats.' Mary linked her arm through Stan's. 'I'm not going without yer, and it's their own fault for not being here on time. So come on, grab hold of John and Mick so yer don't slip.'

The boys had always liked Mary, but right now they thought she was wonderful. Taking up positions either side of Jenny, they bent their elbows. 'Stick yer leg in, Jenny,' John said, feeling very grown-up and protective. 'We'll make sure yer stay upright.'

'Yeah.' Mick felt a thrill run through his whole body as Jenny slipped her hand through his arm. This was a mighty step forward in his quest and he wanted to jump for joy. 'Yer've got two escorts tonight and I hope yer know how lucky yer are. There's not a girl in the neighbourhood who wouldn't swap places with yer right this minute.'

John ground his teeth. He's talking too much, he is. If he keeps that up I'll never get a word in edgeways. 'It's true, Jenny, me and me mate are very much sought after by every beauty from here to Glaxton.'

Mick looked over Jenny's head. 'Where's Glaxton when it's out? I've never heard of the flippin' place.'

'Ah well, yer see, that just shows how far our reputation has spread. If yer've never heard of the place it must be hundreds of miles away.'

The grown-ups, walking ahead, were listening to the two lads with smiles on their faces. Now Seamus decided to add his two-pennyworth. 'If I'm not mistaken, John, I've seen the name Glaxton on the map. And if me memory isn't playing tricks on me, it's in South Africa.'

'Oh well, that puts those girls out of the running, doesn't it? I feel sorry for them, 'cos they'll be really heartbroken. But, sadly for them, yer can't get to South Africa on the twenty-two tram for tuppence.'

Mary turned her head. 'Here's Janet and her brother, Jenny.'

'I'm sorry we're late, Jenny,' Janet said breathlessly, 'but the clock was slow.' She smiled at John. 'Can I walk beside me mate?'

By silent, mutual consent, John and Mick put their hand over Jenny's and held it tight. Oh no, this was their night, they'd put a lot of organisation into it. So neither Janet nor her big brother were going to spoil it. 'Ah, not now, Janet,' John said, returning her smile. 'We're just nice and comfortable.'

'Go on, yer big soft nit, let me next to her.' When there was no move made to accommodate her, Janet appealed to her friend. 'Make him move, Jenny.'

But much to Jenny's surprise, she found she was enjoying having a boy either side of her holding her hand. Especially when those two boys were making her laugh. 'Leave it for now, Jan, I'm all nice and warm and these two are making sure I don't slip.'

'You hang on to me, Jan,' Bill said, not liking the situation any more than his sister did. 'We can swap over on the way home.'

Mick's lips were moving as he talked to himself. 'On yer bike, pal, this is definitely not your night.'

While John muttered silently, 'What a hope you've got, mate. This is one night ye're not walking Jenny home. I know it's Christmas, but ye're not getting a present off me!'

Janet, oblivious to the thoughts of the three boys, linked one arm through her brother's and the other through John's. 'There yer are, we'll all be nice and warm now. All pals together, eh, isn't that nice?'

Chapter Eighteen

They'd just finished their dinner when the knock on the door came, and Mary tutted loudly. 'Just look at the state of the place; what a time for visitors to come.' She pushed her chair back. 'Jenny, will you clear the plates away, and you, Laura, pick up all the wrapping paper? Be quick!' As she walked to the door, she muttered, 'I hope it's no one important – the room looks like a pigsty.'

'I don't know what ye're worrying about, love,' Stan called. 'Every house in the country will look the same – it's to be expected.'

When Mary opened the door her misgivings fled. 'Dad! Oh, it's lovely to see yer.' They held each other close and didn't speak for a while. Then, after wishing each other the compliments of the season, she said, 'I expected yer last night, same as usual. We waited until half eleven and then had to leave. I was worried when yer didn't come because it's not like you to miss Midnight Mass. I thought yer were ill or something.'

'No, sweetheart, I went for a few drinks with the men from work and by the time I got home the weather put me off going out again.'

Mary pushed the living-room door open. 'Come in and get a warm.'

Stan jumped to his feet, his face beaming, and shook his father-in-law's hand. 'It's good to see yer, Joe, all the best.'

Jenny ran in from the kitchen and took a flying leap to put her arms around Joe's neck. 'Grandad, a Merry Christmas.' She rained kisses on his cheeks. 'I'm glad yer've made it, 'cos me mam was worried when yer didn't come last night. I told her I'd walk to yours this afternoon to see what was wrong.'

Laura watched with the fear she always felt when her grandad came these days. She wouldn't put it past Celia to let the cat out of the bag if she got in a temper. But today, mixed with the fear of being caught out, was another emotion – one of guilt. She knew the woman he'd married wasn't a nice person, and that Celia was cheating on him.

'What's wrong with yer, sweetheart, have yer fallen out with yer old grandad?' Joe bent to look in Laura's eyes. 'I thought yer'd be glad to see me.'

Laura dropped the papers she'd been picking up and walked into his arms. And as he hugged her tight and kissed her, she kept telling herself it wasn't fair, it just wasn't fair. And she was as much to blame for deceiving him as Celia. In fact, she was more to blame because he was her grandad. He'd always loved her and it would kill him if he knew what she'd been doing behind his back.

'Come on, break it up.' Mary slapped her daughter's bottom. 'Anyone would think yer hadn't seen yer grandad for years.' She plumped a cushion on the fireside chair facing Stan, the one that she usually sat in. 'We've just finished our dinner, Dad, and there's plenty over. So sit yerself down while I rustle a meal up for yer.'

'Give me yer coat, Grandad and I'll hang it up for yer,' Jenny said, smiling up into his face. 'Then yer'll look as though ye're at home.'

'Wait until I empty me pockets, sweetheart, I've got some presents for yer. They're not much, mind, but it shows I was thinking of yer.'

Mary watched him take the badly wrapped packets from his pocket and sighed. Who would have thought her dad would come down to this? He'd lost so much weight his shirt collar was miles too big for him, and the shirt looked as though it had never seen an iron. And she'd noticed when she followed him in from the hall that he had a hole in the heel of his sock.

Joe handed the girls a packet each, gave Stan his, then with a smile that held a tinge of sadness, he offered the last one to Mary. 'As I said, sweetheart, they're not much. I haven't been getting any overtime in, so I haven't been exactly flushed for money.'

'Dad, I wouldn't care if there was only fresh air in this paper, as long as you're here. That's all the present I want.'

Laura was thoughtful as she began to unwrap the paper. No wonder her grandad had no money; his wife spent it all. Celia never seemed short, and she had something new on nearly every week. And Thursday night wasn't the only night she went out, either. Laura had heard Charlie talking to her when they were leaving the dance one night. He'd said, 'I'll see yer tomorrow night, my lovely, and we'll have more time on our own.'

Jenny's shriek of delight brought Laura away from her thoughts. 'Oh Grandad, it's beautiful! Look, Mam, a bracelet with red stones in.' She rushed to her grandfather and knelt in front of his chair. 'It's the best present I ever had and I love it. I love you, too, ye're the best grandad in the whole world.'

Laura looked down at her hand and nestling in the palm was a bracelet identical to the one her sister was holding high, except the stones in hers were blue. The guilt she felt almost brought tears to her eyes. They weren't good bracelets, they probably came from Woolworth's, but he must have left himself skint to buy them. 'Move over, Sis, give someone else a chance.' She pushed Jenny out of the

228

way and took her place. 'Thank you, Grandad, it's lovely. I haven't got any jewellery worth speaking of, so I won't half swank with this on me wrist. Just wait until Cynthia sees it, she'll be green with envy.'

'Yer did well all round, Dad,' Mary said. 'The girls are over the moon, I'm always glad of a pair of stockings and Stan's already opened his packet of ciggies. Now while I see to some dinner for yer, the girls will get your presents off the tree.'

Mary spooned potatoes and carrot and turnip on to a plate, and covering it with another plate, she put it in the oven to heat up. Then she lit the gas under the pan of gravy and gave it a stir before picking up the carving knife. As she cut into the turkey, Mary's sadness turned to anger. Not for one moment did she believe her dad's story about not working overtime. For as long as she could remember, he'd always worked late at least three times a week. He wasn't on a bad wage, so why was he still wearing the same shabby overcoat and shoes that were down-at-heel? She sighed and said softly, 'Do I really have to ask that question? It's that bitch he's married to, she probably bleeds him dry. And if this was a three-bedroomed house, I'd persuade him to leave her and come and live with us. No one would blame him. She's not a proper wife, never has been and never will be.'

Jenny came skipping into the kitchen. 'Me grandad's made up with his presents, Mam. He said they're just what he wanted.'

'They'll come in useful, sunshine, especially in this weather.' When Mary had bought her father the warm scarf, gloves and thick woollen socks, she'd told herself that when he went out to work on these cold mornings, at least parts of him would be warm. 'He needs looking after, he's not getting any younger.'

Jenny held her wrist out and twisted it around. 'Isn't that lovely, Mam? I'm going to wear it at the parties.'

'All the boys will be after yer, sunshine, yer'll be the belle of the ball.'

Jenny giggled. 'All the boys – there's only John and Mick.'

'Well, they're boys, aren't they? If they're not, they shouldn't be wearing trousers.'

'Yeah, but they're me mates, I wouldn't swank in front of them. I'd get me leg pulled soft if I did.'

Mary opened her mouth, then decided not to say what was in her mind. If she told her daughter that she didn't think the two boys thought of her as a mate, she might put Jenny off and she didn't want to do that. Best to let nature takes its course. 'Set the table for yer grandad, sunshine, and I'll bring his dinner through.'

Jenny hesitated as she got to the door. And when she spoke, her voice was low. 'Mam, his wife doesn't look after him proper, does she?'

Mary was surprised, but she kept her voice light. 'What makes yer say that?'

Jenny shrugged her shoulders. 'I don't know, he doesn't look as though anyone cares for him. And sometimes he looks so sad I could cry for him.'

'Yer all know there's no love lost between me and Celia, sunshine, I've never tried to hide it. But it's not up to me to interfere in yer grandad's life, much as I'd like to.'

'Well, I love me grandad, and I hate her for not looking after him proper.'

'Keep that to yerself, sunshine. Don't say anything that will upset him.' Mary picked up a tea-towel to take the plates from the oven. 'Get that table set, there's a good girl.'

While Joe was tucking into his dinner as though he hadn't eaten for a week, Mary said casually, 'We're having the gang here tonight, Dad, for a bit of a party. Why don't yer stay and have a good laugh. That is, of course, if yer haven't got something else on.'

Joe chewed slowly on the food in his mouth, buying himself time. When he'd left the house this morning, Cynthia had still been in bed. But she must have heard him unbolt the front door, and she shouted down to him. 'I'm going to a party at one of me mates' tonight, so don't worry if I don't come home, I might sleep there.' Then, with sarcasm dripping from her words, she added, 'It would be no use you coming, they'll all be young people.'

'I haven't got anything else on, sweetheart, but yer don't want an old man at yer party.'

'Who's the old man, Joe?' Stan asked. 'I hope ye're not referring to me.'

'Go on, Grandad, say yer'll stay,' Jenny pleaded. 'Yer'll be the most handsome man at the party.'

Laura looked up from admiring her bracelet. 'Yeah, go on, Grandad, stay. Yer'll enjoy yerself.'

Mary's brow shot up. 'Don't tell me you're staying in? That would be a change, a real turn-up for the books.'

'I'm going down to Cynthia's to see what presents she got, but I'll be back in time.' Laura lowered her eyes. 'I don't suppose yer'd let her come back with me for an hour, would yer?'

Mary exchanged glances with Stan. This was the first time their eldest daughter had ever asked if she could bring a friend home; they couldn't refuse. 'Of course yer can, sunshine, but warn her that there'll be no room to breathe.'

Laura looked both surprised and pleased. 'She won't mind that, Mam. It'll be better than sitting at home twiddling her thumbs.'

Joe wiped the back of his hand across his mouth, pushed his plate away and rubbed his tummy. 'Well, seeing as there'll be so many lovely girls here, I'll stay meself. But not till too late, mind, 'cos there's no trams running and it's a long walk.'

Amy sat on Mary's couch, cushions beneath her and pillows at her back. 'I must have come a real cropper, 'cos me backside and me back are every colour of the rainbow.'

'How d'yer know that, Mam?' John asked. 'Yer'd need eyes in the back of yer head to see that part of yer body.'

'Don't be looking at me,' Ben said, shaking his head and holding his hands out. 'I did offer to have a look, but was told if I went near her she'd give me a go-along.'

'I should think so, too!' Amy huffed and puffed. 'A girl's got to have a bit of privacy. So yer'll just have to take my word for it, won't yer?'

'Have yer a mirror in yer bedroom, Amy?' Seamus had a grin on his face and a pint glass of beer in his hand. 'Is that how yer did it, me darlin'?'

'Don't yer be so personal, Seamus Moynihan, or I'll set my feller on yer.' Amy turned to Joe, who was sitting next to her on the couch, looking more relaxed and at ease than he'd looked for a long time. 'Wouldn't yer think they'd show a bit of sympathy for someone who nearly broke their neck? They've got no bleedin' hearts, none of them.'

'Ye're telling fibs, Mam,' John said. 'I did tell yer that me heart was bleeding for yer.'

'Yeah, and yer were laughing all over yer bleedin' face when yer said it.' When Amy looked at Joe, her chubby cheeks were almost hiding her eyes. 'I was laughing me own head off, Joe, but because I'm the one with the pains, I'm entitled to that privilege, aren't I? And seeing as I'm the only one in the room with a backside the colours of the rainbow, I'm one up on all of them.'

Joe grinned. 'Take a little bit of advice, Amy. If they ask yer to play truth or dare, just flatly refuse.'

Amy looked puzzled for a few seconds, then the light dawned. 'Oh yeah, I get yer, Joe! That's just what the buggers would do, an' all, the cheeky sods.'

Jenny was standing between John and Mick, looking very pretty in the new jumper and skirt she'd got for Christmas. And her hand kept going to her cheek so she could show off the new bracelet she was so proud of. 'Your mam's a scream, John. I've never yet known her to be down in the dumps.'

'Oh, she has her moments. But if she ever does get in a bad temper, it never lasts long because all me dad's got to do is tell her to look in the mirror and see the gob on her.' He took a deep breath and then said what was in his heart. 'Yer look really pretty tonight, Jenny.'

Mick had been all ears, listening to every word. 'Yeah, yer do, Jenny. Yer look good enough to eat. I bet yer'd taste better than me mam's Christmas pudding. And that's saying something, 'cos the pudding was delicious.'

Any other time, Jenny would have told them to stop acting daft, they were making her blush. But last night, as they were holding her hands, she suddenly became aware that what they were doing was flirting with her. It was a new experience for her, and one she enjoyed very much. So now she gave a little curtsy and said, 'I thank you, kind sirs.'

Molly, who had been watching, nudged Seamus. Nodding to where the youngsters were standing, she said softly, 'I wonder what's going to happen there? Sure, there'll be a heart broken somewhere along the line.'

'There's many hearts broken every day, me darlin', but people survive. Isn't it a fact that yer can't put love in anyone's heart; it has to grow and blossom of its own free will.'

'I know, me darlin', but I'll say an extra prayer every night to help it along.'

'As Amy's a friend of yours, wouldn't it be altogether the act of a friend to tell her to say an extra prayer every night, too? After all, the lads have been mates for years and both deserve the same chance. Would yer not be thinking that was right, me darlin'?'

But a knock on the door saved Molly from telling him that he was speaking as a father, not a mother.

Mary was expecting the newcomers to be Laura and Cynthia, and she nearly fell over backwards when she opened the door to find Janet and her brother standing there. Oh my God, she thought, yer can't move in there as it is. But she managed a smile. 'I wasn't expecting you, Janet.'

'We're not staying, Mrs Nightingale.' It was Bill who spoke. 'We only came around to see if Jenny would like to come to our house tomorrow night. Me mam said we could have a bit of a do. Just a few friends, like.'

Mary held the door wide. 'Come in and ask her. That's if yer can get in, the room is pretty crowded.'

'We won't stay.' Even as he was speaking, Bill was ushering his sister into the hall. A few minutes with Jenny was better than nothing. 'We'll have a word with Jenny, then make ourselves scarce.'

Jenny gave a shriek of delight when she saw her friend. 'Janet!' She dashed forward and missed the dark looks John and Mick exchanged when they saw Bill. Mick leaned towards his friend and whispered, 'We'll have to find a way of getting rid of him, he's beginning to get on me nerves.'

'Yeah, I know,' John whispered back. 'I believe arsenic is the best

232

thing for getting rid of people.' His shoulders began to shake and his laugh came out the same time as Mick's. 'It doesn't leave no blood, either, so we wouldn't ruin our kecks.'

'You'll have to have a drink while ye're here, Bill.' Mary was determined to be a good hostess, even though she wasn't sure they had enough glasses. 'After all, it is the festive season. Will yer have a beer, and I'll give Janet a glass of lemonade with a drop of port in?' Her hand went to her head when there was another knock. 'Oh dear, this will be Laura and her friend. I think we've got what yer'd call a full house.'

As Mary walked to the door, Amy shouted after her, 'Ay, girl, have yer been selling bleedin' tickets for this do?'

Mary was smiling as she opened the door. 'Come in, girls, but take a deep breath, the room is at bursting point.'

'We'll put our coats on the bed, Mam,' Laura said, leading the way upstairs. 'We'll be down in a minute.'

Bill tried to get Jenny on her own to invite her to their house the next night, but he hadn't reckoned on his sister. 'John and Mick can come, too, can't they, Bill?' Janet asked in all innocence. 'They're our mates, we can't leave them out.'

Oh, I could leave them out with pleasure, Bill thought. But there was no way he could refuse, so he said grudgingly, 'Yeah, they can come. That's if they want to.'

'Of course they'll come.' Jenny's face was flushed with excitement. And it ran through Mick's mind that she looked better than the Christmas pudding and the Christmas cake put together. 'I'll make them come so they can walk me home.'

John bowed from the waist. 'I'd be honoured.'

Mick did likewise, saying, 'I'd be delighted.'

Bill was grinding his teeth when the door opened and Laura came in, followed by Cynthia. He stopped grinding his teeth and his eyes widened. That couldn't be Cynthia Pennington, surely? The wild girl who, like Laura, was always in trouble when she was young and who had gained a bad reputation since she left school. It must be her, seeing as she was here with Laura, but what a change! She looked very glamorous in a sage-green, soft wool dress which clung to the curves of her body. She was a bobby dazzler, no doubt about that.

'Jenny, d'yer think your Laura would like to come to our party?' The words were out before Bill knew he was going to say them. His mother would go mad because of the reputation the two girls had, but he was willing to risk that. Cynthia had taken his eye and his interest. 'It's only for young ones, me mam's not asking any of the neighbours.'

Jenny shrugged her shoulders. 'I think yer'd better ask her yerself. If I asked, she'd tell me to get lost.'

233

Mick had seen the change come over Bill when Cynthia walked in, and it entered his head that perhaps they wouldn't need to resort to arsenic after all. It just needed a push in the right direction. 'I'm sure she'd come if you asked her, Bill. Go on, she can't eat yer.'

When Bill looked uncertain, John thought it was time he gave a helping hand. After all, the more girls at the party, the more likely it was that they'd have Jenny to themselves. 'Would yer like me to come with yer?'

That was testing Bill's pride and he shook his head. 'I think I'm capable of doing it on my own, thanks.' Without further ado, and with a glass in his hand to boost his courage, he made his way to where the girls were standing. 'Laura, I'm having a party tomorrow night and I wondered if yer'd like to come? And the invitation is extended to yer friend, if she'd be interested.' Without waiting for Laura to reply, he turned his gaze on Cynthia. 'I've been puzzling me brains since yer walked in, and it may sound rude, but aren't you Cynthia Pennington?'

'Yer know damn well I am, Bill Porter, I haven't changed that much.' Cynthia smiled for the first time since she'd entered the room. She knew what most of the neighbours thought of her, and though it wouldn't have worried her at one time, it did now. 'You have, though. Yer've grown into a giant.'

Bill didn't want to take his eyes off her, but knew he was being watched and turned to Laura. 'How about it, Laura? Are you and Cynthia game for a party?'

'What d'yer think, Cyn? D'yer want to go?'

'Yeah, I'd like to. Thanks for the invite, Bill.'

'Right, I'll see you both at ours, about eight o'clock.' Bill pulled a face. 'Me and Janet will have to go now, Mrs Nightingale's got enough on her plate without us gatecrashing her party. But I'll look forward to seeing yer tomorrow.' He handed his now empty glass to Laura. 'Will yer be a pal and take this off me hands?'

By the time Bill and Janet left, enough beer had been drunk to put everyone in a party mood. And Seamus started the revelry with *Phil the Fluters' Ball*. Mick took hold of Jenny's arm and pulled her into the middle of the floor. Then John, having no intention of playing wallflower, joined them. Jenny was embarrassed at first, but when she saw Laura and Cynthia take to the floor, she threw her shyness out of the window and joined in the merriment. But Amy was the one who had the rafters ringing with laughter. She couldn't get up, but wasn't going to be left out. One leg after the other was kicked out and the hem of her skirt was lifted to shake to the tune of the jig. She winced with every movement, and the contortions of her face were enough to send everyone into pleats.

When Seamus stopped singing, Amy sat back and said, 'By, I did enjoy that. It did me more good than the dose of salts I had this morning.'

Laura and Cynthia clung to each other, gasping for breath. 'Oh dear, I've never laughed so much in all me life,' Cynthia said. 'I'm glad yer mam asked me to come.'

'Yeah, it's great, isn't it?' Laura looked over at Amy. 'Yer know, I've always thought me Auntie Amy was crackers. But she's dead funny really, isn't she?'

Stan was standing by the kitchen door, ready to refill glasses, and Mary went to join him. 'Have you ever seen our Laura laugh so hearty before, or let herself go?'

He put his arm around her waist and pulled her close. 'Two great minds think alike, love, I was just thinking the same thing. And that Cynthia's turned out to be a surprise. She's not as forward or hard-faced as I expected.'

'Ay, out,' Mary said, 'Mick is going to sing.'

Mick cleared his throat. 'Yer must be fed up with Irish songs, so I'll do one of Al Jolson's. I'm telling yer it's him I'm doing, 'cos yer won't recognise it otherwise.' He knelt down on one knee and with all the great singer's facial expressions and hand movements, he began to sing 'Mammy'. He did it so well, not even Amy dared to join in. Then he went straight into 'Toot-Toot-Tootsie, Goodbye' and the room erupted.

Cynthia nudged Laura in the ribs. 'Ay, he isn't half handsome, isn't he? Get a load of those eyes and dimples.'

'Yeah, he's not bad I suppose,' Laura said, 'but I prefer blonds.'

'And the other one, John Hanley, he's not to be sneezed at either. It's hard to think of them as the kids who used to play footie in their short trousers. Still, they probably think the same about us. We've all grown up, and changed. I got a shock when I saw Bill Porter – he's grown into a real he-man.'

'Yer can keep them all – for me, I'll stick to my Gary. He knocks spots off any of them for looks.'

'We've only got your word for that, Laura, and everybody has different ideas on what is handsome and what is not. As they say, beauty is in the eye of the beholder.' Cynthia studied her friend's face before saying, 'At the moment I'm off men, I feel uncomfortable with them and wouldn't trust them an inch. That is what those two thugs have done to me. But I'm hoping that when I'm even with them, I'll get back into the swing of things. That's if they haven't put me off men for life.'

'Yer'll be all right, kid, I know yer will,' Laura said. 'All fellers are not the same.'

Cynthia shook herself mentally. It would be a long time before she trusted herself with a man, she knew that. But she was only sixteen, for heaven's sake, so she had to try and put the past behind her and get on with her life. 'When am I going to meet this Mr Wonderful of yours? I can't wait to see if he's all yer've cracked him up to be.'

'Oh, he is, and more. Yer'll meet him soon, Cyn, but I want to get to know him a bit better meself first. After I've been out on a few dates with him, eh?'

Martha Porter faced her son across the table. 'You've what! Have yer lost the run of yer bloody senses? If you think I'm having those two tarts in this house, yer've got another think coming, me lad.'

'Oh, come on, Mam, be reasonable.' Bill had expected opposition but nothing like this. 'You haven't set eyes on them for years, so how can yer talk about them like that?'

Janet's brow was furrowed. She couldn't understand why everything had suddenly gone wrong. Her and Bill had been so happy walking back from the Nightingales', talking and laughing about what games they'd play at the party. And now there was all this shouting. 'What d'yer mean, Mam, about them being tarts?'

'You keep out of it. Your brother knows damn well what I mean.' Martha's face was red and her nostrils flared. 'I will not have those two trollops in my house, and that's the end of it. So yer can just take yerself back there and tell them the party's off.'

'Calm down, Martha,' her husband said, 'before yer burst a blood vessel. If Bill's invited Jenny and the other two girls, yer can't just un-invite them.'

'Oh, can't I? Well, just you wait and see whether I can or not. If he doesn't turn around and go back right this minute, I'll go meself.'

'Martha, I said calm down, and I mean it. Now sit down in that chair and let's talk like reasonable adults, instead of bawling at each other.' When his wife stood her ground, he pointed to the chair. 'I said sit down.'

Martha was taken aback. It was very seldom that her husband raised his voice, never mind used that tone to her. So she turned towards her chair. And when her back was to them, Vincent gave a slight shake of the head, to indicate to his son that he stay out of it.

'Don't think ye're going to change me mind for me, Vincent Porter,' Martha had no intention of giving in, ' 'cos ye're not.'

'Let's talk it through, shall we, just to clear things in me mind.' Vincent leaned forward and rested his elbows on his knees. 'Yer can't go around calling people tarts and trollops, love, unless yer've got good reason to. And as I only know these girls by sight, I'm at a loss as to what yer reason is.'

'Oh, come off it, Vincent Porter! Everybody knows what Laura Nightingale and Cynthia Pennington are like.'

236

'I don't,' Vincent said quietly. 'So tell me.'

'They're impudent, hard-faced little madams, that's what. And they're a holy terror for the boys. Anything in trousers, they're not fussy.'

'And this is first-hand knowledge, is it, Martha, not gossip? They've given you cheek, and with your own eyes you've seen them fooling around with boys?'

'Well, no, not me personally,' Martha blustered. 'But you ask anyone in their street, they'll tell yer what they're like.'

'So yer'd blacken their names on the word of gossip-mongers? I'm surprised at yer, Martha Porter.'

Bill couldn't let this go on, it wasn't fair to his mother. 'Me mam's not wrong altogether, Dad. The two of them were terrors at school, I know that even though I wasn't in their class. And they did have a bad reputation in their street for giving cheek. But they've grown up now, they've been working for over two years.'

There was suspicion in Martha's eyes. 'Have you been out with either of those girls on the sly?'

'No, I haven't, Mam! In the last year I've seen Laura a couple of times when I've walked Jenny home, but we've hardly exchanged half-a-dozen words. And tonight, in the Nightingales', I saw Cynthia for the first time in years. I only invited them to make the numbers up 'cos we were short of girls. Jenny's coming with Mick and John, and I asked me mate, Gerry. That means two girls and four boys.' In an effort to put a smile on his mother's face, he asked, 'How would you like it, Mam, if yer were playing Postman's Knock, and the chances were fifty-fifty that yer'd get to kiss yer sister?'

When Martha heard her husband chuckle, she knew she'd lost the fight. But she wasn't going to just cave in. 'You haven't had much to say for yourself, Janet. What do you think?'

'Mam, I only wanted a party, I didn't want all this shouting and falling out.'

Martha threw her hands up. 'Okay, okay, you win. But I warn yer, if I see either of those girls messing around with the boys, or snogging, they'll be out of that door so quick they won't know what's hit them.'

'Fair enough, Mam,' Bill said, throwing his father a look of gratitude. 'Now, can me and our kid take our coats off and get a warm by the fire?'

Chapter Nineteen

When John and Mick called for Jenny on Boxing Night, they found Lizzie Marshall sitting in Stan's fireside chair looking warm and happy. They made straight for her, and standing either side of her chair they bent to kiss her cheeks. 'Yer should have come last night, Auntie Lizzie,' John said, 'it was a cracking party.'

'Yeah, yer missed a good night.' Mick's dimples deepened. 'Most of all, and yer'll kill yerself when I tell yer this, yer missed me doing me Al Jolson impersonation.'

Lizzie, her cheeks pink from the warmth of the fire, smiled up at them. 'I did miss a treat then, didn't I? But I knew there were going to be a lot of people here and I'm getting too old now for noisy parties. Tonight will suit me fine, with Amy and Molly and their husbands coming. Seamus has promised to sing *Rose of Tralee* for me, and yer never know, after a glass of port I might even give a song meself.'

'Oh aye, Auntie Lizzie,' John fingered a wisp of the fine white hair, 'yer've got hidden talents, have yer?'

Lizzie tapped her nose. 'Ah now, that would be telling.'

'If yer did happen to have a drink over the eight, Auntie Lizzie,' Mick said, dropping on his haunches so he could look into her face, 'and yer did sing a song, what would it be?'

'My very favourite, son – "Just A Song At Twilight".'

Mary shuffled to the edge of the couch and tapped Mick on the shoulder. 'Do yer know it, sunshine?'

'Mrs Nightingale, there isn't a song I don't know. I've been listening to me mam and dad singing since the day I was born.'

'Would yer sing it for her? Our Jenny and Laura are upstairs getting ready, so yer've got plenty of time.'

Stan leaned forward now. 'Go on, son, it's one of my favourites, too.'

Mick looked up at John. 'If you make fun of me, pal, I'll crack yer one.'

'I won't make fun of yer, mate, not when it's for Auntie Lizzie. If I can get the hang of the tune, I'll whistle along with yer.'

So it was when Jenny opened the door, she heard the pure clear sound of Mick's voice. She stood quietly by the door so as not to disturb them, and wondered at a boy from a small two-up two-down house, having the voice of an angel. And then she saw John curl a hand around his mouth and soon his tuneful whistling joined Mick's voice. The words of the song always made her feel sad, but it was the sight of the two boys that had her sniffing the tears away. They'd been mates all through school and had remained firm friends. Just like her and Janet.

'Oh, that was beautiful.' Lizzie wiped a hand across her eyes. 'I wouldn't have the nerve to sing it after hearing that. Anyway,' she smiled up at John, not wanting to praise one and leave the other out, 'I wouldn't have the marvellous accompaniment that you had.'

Mick straightened himself out. 'We usually charge, yer know, Auntie Lizzie, but not those we love.' He turned to Jenny. 'I knew yer were there. I always know when ye're there, even if I can't see yer.'

Lizzie smiled, while Mary and Stan pulled surprised faces at each other. John, on the other hand, was trying to think of a way to get even. 'The only way yer'd know that, mate, would be if Jenny ponged. And I can't smell nothing.'

Jenny roared with laughter. 'Will you two ever grow up?'

'Not unless we're forced to,' Mick said. 'We like acting daft and yer can't get away with it when ye're grown-up.'

'Well, try and act grown-up tonight, please. Remember, it's me mate's house we're going to.' Jenny slipped into her coat and asked, 'What time d'yer want me in by, Mam?'

'It's work tomorrow, sunshine, so I think eleven is late enough.' Mary cocked an ear. 'Isn't Laura going with yer?'

'Yeah, but she's calling for Cynthia first.' Jenny blew a kiss. 'Enjoy yerselves and don't get too drunk.'

Martha Porter was looking for something to fault the two girls, but so far they hadn't put a foot wrong. They were friendly without being pushy, polite, well-dressed, and their faces weren't caked with make-up. And far from running after the boys, they were sat side-by-side on the couch while Bill and his mate Gerry were doing their damnedest to chat them up. They weren't getting very far, either, from what she could see. It was going to be a very quiet party from the looks of things. If it wasn't for Mick and John, it would be dead boring. They had Jenny and Janet in stitches the whole time. When Mick cracked a joke, John had one ready to throw back at him, and vice versa. They seemed to bounce off each other. And they were keeping Vincent amused, too. Her husband never had a smile off his face.

'Why don't yer put a record on, Bill?' Martha asked. 'Liven the place up a bit.'

Laura showed her interest. 'Ooh, have yer got a gramophone?'

240

Martha proudly lifted the lid of a wooden cabinet standing next to her chair. 'Yes, and we've got some records.'

'Do yer dance, Cynthia?' Bill asked hopefully.

Cynthia seemed to sink back further on the couch. 'No, I've never been to a dance, but Laura can. I'll be quite happy to sit and watch.'

'What shall I put on, a waltz or a quickstep?'

Gerry, who thought he was God's gift to women, stuck out his chest. 'It doesn't make no difference to me, Bill, I can dance to anything.'

Laura, thinking the night wasn't going to be a complete waste of time, was eager to show off her prowess on the dance floor. It was a pity somebody hadn't told her that Gerry was the biggest liar in Liverpool, and the worst dancer. But she was about to find out the hard way. He couldn't wait for her to stand upright before pulling her into his arms, gripping her left hand tight and thrusting their arms out as far as they would stretch. If anyone had been standing near, they would have either lost a few teeth or been sporting a black eye. He started off with the wrong foot and his size ten shoe landed down hard on Laura's toes. She let out a cry and her face crumpled with the pain, but Gerry soldiered on regardless.

Mick and John looked on with amusement. 'She'll have no feet left by the time this record's over,' Mick spoke out of the side of his mouth. 'He's like a walking plank.'

'Yeah,' John agreed, 'as stiff as a board.'

'Ay, Jenny, d'yer want to have a go? Yer couldn't be any worse than that bloke.'

Jenny shrank back. 'No, thanks, Mick, I've never danced in me life.'

'I'll show yer how, eh? If I excuse yer sister, saving her from a fate worse than death, you could watch what she does with her feet, and then have a go with me when they put the next record on.'

John was certain Mick wouldn't excuse Laura. Even if he liked her, which he didn't, he wouldn't have the nerve. 'Go on, mate, I dare yer. In fact, I double dare yer.'

Mick looked down into eyes as blue as the sky on a summer's day. 'How about it, Jenny, are yer game?'

'Ooh, I don't think so, Mick, I'd be frightened of making a fool of meself.'

'I'll dance with yer, Mick,' said Janet, who was on home territory and didn't care if she did make a fool of herself. 'I'd like that.'

Mick's heart plummeted, but he didn't let it show. 'Okay, Janet, ye're on.' With that he stepped forward and touched Gerry's arm. 'Excuse me, please.'

The relief on Laura's face was obvious. And when Mick began to twirl her around like the experienced dancer he was, she was delighted. 'Thanks, Mick, I owe yer one. That bloke was flaming hopeless.'

Too quickly the record ground to a stop. 'Ah, I was enjoying that,' Laura said. 'Ye're a good dancer, Mick. If I get lumbered again, will yer come to my rescue?'

Mick grinned. 'I've promised the next dance to Janet, but John's a good dancer, better than me. He can come to yer rescue next time.'

Martha turned the record over and the strains of another waltz filled the room. 'Take yer partners for a waltz,' she said, sitting back and folding her arms. Then with a wink at Laura, she added, 'And it's an "excuse me".'

Mick bowed from the waist before extending a hand. 'This is my dance, I believe, Miss Porter.'

Janet was willing and eager. 'Don't twirl me around, though, Mick, not until I've found me dancing feet proper.'

'I'm not that daft, Janet.' Mick led her into the middle of the room. 'I'll put me hands on yer waist, and that way yer can see me feet better.'

Cynthia saw Gerry rub his hands together and look at Laura. Sitting next to her, perched on the arm of the couch, was Bill. She tapped his arm. 'Get Laura up quick, before soft lad gets to her.'

Bill bent towards her ear and whispered, 'Only if yer promise to come out with me one night.'

'We'll talk about that later, now get moving.'

Laura was happy because Bill was a good dancer, and Janet was deliriously happy because, under Mick's tuition, she was mastering the basic steps of the waltz. Her face was animated and she'd never looked so pretty.

'Ye're doing well, sweetheart,' Martha called, 'I'm proud of yer.'

When the dance ended, Mick passed her over to John. 'You can give Janet her second lesson now, while I give Jenny her first.' He saw Jenny was about to object and got in before her. 'Don't forget, I let me mate double dare me so I could dance with yer.' He stood in front of her and put his hands on her waist. 'There's only three basic steps in a waltz, so let's try. You go back with yer left foot, to the side with yer right foot, then bring them together. See, do it again. There yer go, it's as easy as falling off a bike.'

Jenny was feeling quite pleased with herself. At least she'd got over her shyness, and those three steps were easy enough. So when Mick said they should hold each other properly now, she did it without hesitation or thought. And she was too busy keeping tabs on her footwork to notice the strange expression on his face. He was experiencing feelings he'd never felt before, like his spine and legs had turned to jelly, and there were shooting stars in his head. He put his lips close to her hair and whispered, 'Grow up quickly, Jenny.'

242

She pulled back a little. 'What did yer say, Mick?'

'Oh er, the time's going quick.'

Janet watched them for a while, then looked up at John. 'Mick's holding Jenny different to what we are. Why can't we hold each other proper, like?'

John chuckled. 'What about yer mam and her rolling pin?'

Not for one moment did he think she'd take him seriously. And he blushed to the roots of his hair when she called, loud enough for everyone to hear: 'Mam, if John holds me proper, yer won't hit him on the head with the rolling pin, will yer?'

It was hard to say who laughed the longest, but the loudest definitely came from Mick, with Cynthia a close second. And Martha had to get hers under control before she could answer. 'As long as he leaves a space of three inches between yer.'

'Did yer hear that, John?' Janet lifted a hand and measured with her thumb and forefinger, what she thought was three inches. 'That's about it.' She looked so innocent, he thought, Ah, God bless her, and he felt like hugging her, as he would a baby.

For the rest of the evening, in between having something to eat and drink, the two boys were very fair with each other and swapped partners for every dance. That is, all except for two dances which the girls had with Gerry, who they felt sorry for. The fact that they were beginners didn't make any difference to him; he plodded on in his own way anyhow.

They were enjoying themselves so much, Jenny was sorry when she saw the time was a quarter to eleven. 'I'll have to go, Jan, I promised me mam I'd be home by eleven.'

'Yer don't need me to walk yer home tonight, then Jenny?' Bill asked, thinking she was still the nicest-looking girl he knew. But he was attracted by the mystery and intrigue which Cynthia wore like a cloak. She was very polite, but kept him and Gerry at a distance, as though they held no interest for her. And although his mate might be a lousy dancer, he was a fine figure of a man and had no trouble getting girls. So if this girl sitting on his mam's couch was the real Cynthia, then she certainly hadn't earned her reputation as a man-eater. Either that or she was a ruddy good actress. This was the mystery he wanted to solve.

Mick was holding Jenny's coat when she replied, 'No, I've got two escorts tonight. But the other girls will need to be walked home.' She shook Martha and Vincent by the hand. 'Thank you for a lovely party, I really enjoyed meself.' Her infectious giggle brought a smile to all the faces, even that of her sister. 'And I got free dancing lessons into the bargain, so all in all I'd say I hopped in lucky.'

'Ye're welcome here any time, queen, yer know that,' Vincent said. 'Our door is always open to yer.'

243

Martha gave her a hug. 'A second daughter to us, that's what yer are.'

Janet showed them to the door. 'Are we going to Auntie Lizzie's tomorrow night?'

She was looking at Jenny, but it was Mick who answered. 'Yeah, we'll all go. We won't stay long, just keep her company for an hour or two.'

'Oh, yeah.' Janet was childlike in her pleasure. 'We can show her how we've learned to do the waltz.'

Jenny put a hand through each of the boys' arms. 'We'll do that, Jan, and give her a good laugh. Thanks for inviting us to yer party, and good night and God bless.'

Back in the living room of the Porters' house, Cynthia and Laura were on their feet. 'We'll be on our way, 'cos it's back to the grind tomorrow.'

'We'll see yer home,' Bill said. 'Just in case there's any drunks around.'

'Yer've no need to, Bill,' Laura said. 'We can look after ourselves.'

'I've no doubt yer can, but we'll still come with yer, even if it's only to stop yer from falling over on the ice.'

'Yeah, it's bad out,' Janet said. 'Yer'd be best linking each other, like Jenny and the two boys.'

They took their leave after thanking the Porters for a lovely evening. And they left Martha looking sheepishly at her husband. 'It just goes to show, doesn't it, that yer can't believe everything yer hear? They seem like two nice girls to me, and if anyone tells me otherwise, I'll clock them one.'

Having been asked to do so as a favour to his workmate, Gerry took Laura's arm and walked in front. 'Do you and yer friend live near each other?'

'In the same street.' Laura was glad of his supporting hand because the slush had hardened and it was very slippery underfoot. 'I live at the top end, and Cynthia at the bottom.'

'How come you can dance and she can't?'

'Because I go dancing with me boyfriend.' Laura thought a little white fib would nip in the bud any ideas he was harbouring. 'He's a smashing dancer.'

Bill allowed the distance between the couples to grow. He wanted to talk to Cynthia without being overheard. 'I asked yer earlier if yer'd come out with me one night, but I never did get an answer.'

Cynthia knew she had nothing to fear from Bill, he was a different breed to Larry and Jeff. But still she couldn't bear the thought of a boy even touching her. Perhaps after next week, when she'd completed the task she'd set herself, she might feel different, be more settled in her mind. And with Bill Porter she'd be as safe as houses. 'I'll come out with yer one night, but it won't be for a couple of weeks.'

'Why is that? Have yer got a boyfriend?'

'No, it's just that I'm tied up for a few weeks, that's all.'

'Yer haven't got a boyfriend, but ye're tied up every night?' Bill raised his eyebrows questioningly. 'And I've got to wait two weeks for a date?'

'That's the way it is, Bill, I'm sorry. I'm not playing hard to get, if that's what yer think. I've got something important on and I can't cancel it. If yer'd rather leave it, then I'll understand. We'll probably bump into each other some time.'

'I'll wait, but give me a date now, so I'll know yer mean it.'

Without hesitation, Cynthia said, 'Two weeks tonight, and yer can call for me.'

With that Bill had to be satisfied. As he had to be satisfied when she would only allow him to give her a good-night peck on the cheek. He kept telling himself to be sensible, she was just another girl and there were plenty of them around. But her very coolness fired his interest in her and he knew the next two weeks were going to be the longest he'd known.

'What are you doing with yerself tonight, sunshine?' Mary asked. 'Are yer coming to the Moynihans'?'

Laura shook her head. 'No, I'm going to the dance. They didn't have one last week with it being Christmas, but it's open tonight. I don't know whether they'll finish at eleven, like they usually do, or if they'll carry on to let the New Year in.'

'Well, if ye're not too late, Mrs Moynihan won't mind if yer call in. Yer don't want to see the New Year in on yer own, do yer?'

'I'll see how it goes.' Laura had big hopes for tonight and wasn't expecting to be going across the street. She'd made up her mind that no matter what Celia said, she was staying until the end. Surely Gary, on this special night, would ask to walk her home. And she should get her first kiss, 'cos at midnight everybody would be kissing everybody else – even strangers. Then a thought entered her head that took some of the pleasure away. Her grandad wouldn't be getting a kiss; he'd be all on his own. Unless, with a bit of luck, his wife stayed in with him. If she did, she'd be doing everyone a favour.

'Is Auntie Lizzie coming to the party, Mam?' Jenny asked. 'Or does she think it'll be too noisy for her?'

Mary chuckled. 'It will be too noisy for her, sunshine, without a doubt. Especially as Auntie Amy's back in fine form and raring to go. I don't know what she's got up her sleeve for us tonight, but she's had a sly smile on her face all day.'

'Oooh, I can't wait.' Jenny's eyes were sparkling with excitement. If there was any dancing tonight, she'd definitely have a go. 'Can I get washed at the sink, Mam, before we start the dishes? Then I can take me time getting ready.'

'I was going to ask that,' Laura said. 'Let me go first, 'cos I've got a long way to go. You've only got to go across the street.'

'Yeah, okay, but don't make a meal of it. There's others in the house beside you.'

When Laura was leaving, her dance shoes tucked under her arm, Mary asked, 'Yer won't be coming home on yer own at that time of night, will yer?'

'No, I'll be with Cynthia.'

'Even so, just take care. There'll be a lot of people out on the street and most of them will be blotto.'

'Mam!' Laura shook her head and rolled her eyes. 'We can take care of ourselves, we're not kids.'

'Yer mam's only warning yer,' Stan said, 'so think on.'

Jenny watched her sister leave the room and she felt worried inside. She didn't know where Laura got to on a Thursday night, but wherever it was, she certainly didn't go with her friend. Jenny had seen Cynthia a few times when she'd been coming back from Janet's, and it was too early for her to have been to a dance. Besides, she was always on her own and wearing her working clothes.

Jenny sighed as she went upstairs for her best shoes. I wish our Laura wouldn't lie to me mam, she thought. And I wish I didn't know she was lying because it makes me feel guilty. If she gets herself into trouble, and me mam and dad find out I knew there was something going on, they'd say I was as bad as her for not letting on. But I just can't bring myself to snitch on my own sister.

'Come on, sunshine,' Mary shouted up the stairs. 'Me and yer dad are ready and waiting.'

'I'm coming, Mam.' Jenny sighed before saying under her breath, 'I'm not going to let our Laura spoil the party for me. She's probably having a whale of a time, wherever she is, so why shouldn't I enjoy meself?'

Laura pelted around the corner of Burton's shop to the side entrance of the dance hall. All the time she was chanting over and over, 'Let him be there, let him be there.' She took the stone steps two at a time, and when she pushed open the door at the top her heart flipped when the first person she saw was Gary. She could tell by the way his face lit up that he was as glad to see her as she was to see him. Even the presence of Celia and Charlie couldn't dim her happiness.

'I've been waiting for yer.' Gary reached for her hand. 'I was worried that yer weren't going to come.'

246

'Just as if.' Laura nodded to Celia and Charlie. 'Hi-ya. I'll put me coat in the cloakroom, I won't be a tick.'

Celia followed close on her heels. 'Come to the toilets with us, I want a word with yer.'

Looking in the spotted mirror over a sink, Laura wet a finger with her tongue before running it over her eyebrows, making sure every hair was in place. She wanted to look her best tonight. 'What d'yer want to have a word with me over?' she asked Celia's reflection in the mirror. 'I can't wait to get on the dance floor.'

'The dance is going on until twelve o'clock tonight, but it wouldn't be a good idea for you to stay until then. I think eleven is more like it.'

Laura spun round, eyes wide with astonishment. 'What a hope you've got! I'm not leaving at eleven! I've told me mam I'll be late, so it's all right.'

'Have yer told yer mother ye're with me?' There was a sly look on the older woman's face. Her voice was as sweet as honey, but there was a threat in her words. 'I bet yer haven't.'

'No, I told her I was with Cynthia. But what's that got to do with anything? I'm not leaving early, and that's that. I'm staying right to the end.'

Celia leaned against the tiled wall and lit a cigarette. She watched the smoke ring spiral upwards until it broke apart. 'What d'yer think yer mother would do if she knew yer were with me? She wouldn't like it, would she?'

Laura was stung into saying, 'No, she wouldn't like it at all. But seeing as she won't find out, I don't see what it's got to do with anything.'

'She might find out. I might have a row with yer grandad one day and it might all come out in the open. I wouldn't do it on purpose, like, but yer know how it is when yer get in a paddy, yer'll say anything in the heat of the moment.' Celia pushed Laura out of the way so she could stand in front of the mirror. Spitting on a finger and thumb, she took a strand of hair and twisted it into a kiss-curl. 'And I'd have to explain how the Thursday meetings came about, wouldn't I? That means yer mam finding out I gave yer the underskirt for yer birthday.'

Laura sucked in her breath. 'Yer wouldn't be that mean, would yer?'

'Not while we're friends I wouldn't, of course not. And we are friends, aren't we?'

She's blackmailing me, Laura thought, as she stared into eyes that were as cold as steel. And there's nothing I can do about it because she's spiteful enough to carry out her threat. 'I never said we weren't friends, did I? But I still don't see why I have to leave the dance early. What difference does it make to you?'

'Well, yer see, kid, I'm going on to a party with Charlie at eleven, and we're taking young Gary with us. So yer'd be all on yer lonesome and I'd worry about yer getting home.'

Would you heckerslike worry about me, Laura said silently. The only person you worry about is yerself. But she knew better than to voice her thoughts. She'd got herself involved with a really bad woman who wouldn't think twice about getting her into serious trouble. 'Why is Gary going to the party with yer? Why can't he stay here with me?'

'I promised me friend I'd bring him 'cos they're a few fellers short. And when I asked Gary, he jumped at the chance.'

Laura's heart slumped as she gazed down at the floor. She'd been looking forward all week to this night, and now it had all gone wrong. But what she couldn't understand was, while Gary's eyes and smile, and his obvious delight at seeing her, told her one thing, his actions told her another. If he had any feelings for her, he wouldn't leave her, not tonight of all nights, to go to a party.

When Laura raised her head, it was to see a gloating expression on Celia's face. And this angered her. 'I'm going to ask Gary to stay with me. I bet he will if I ask him.'

'I wouldn't do that if I were you, kid. He's already said he'd come with us and you'd only put him on the spot if yer asked him to let us down.'

Laura flounced towards the door. 'I'm going into the dance, that's what I came for.'

Gary was waiting and put his hand out to her. 'What the heck have yer been doing? I was beginning to think yer'd flushed yerself down the lavatory.'

She pulled him through the double doors of the dance hall. 'Let's dance.'

'Don't yer want to put yer handbag down?'

'No, I'll do it later.' Laura's tummy was churning over as she followed Gary's steps in a slow foxtrot. 'I've been looking forward to tonight.'

'Yeah, me too, babe. I missed yer last week.'

'Then why have yer promised to go to a party with Celia, leaving me on me own?'

Gary slowed down, a surprised expression on his face. 'What did yer say I've promised to do?'

'Don't come that with me, Gary, yer know what I'm talking about. Celia said she invited yer to a mate's party and yer jumped at the chance.'

Gary kept on dancing, his eyes looking over Laura's shoulder. 'Oh, that? I wasn't fussy, but she talked me into it. She said you'd be leaving early, anyway.'

'She had no right to say that, she's not running me life for me. I asked me mam if I could stay till the end, and she said I could. I wouldn't have bothered if I'd known you weren't going to be here.' Laura was near to tears. 'Why d'yer always have to do what Celia tells yer, anyway? She doesn't own yer.'

'I owe Celia a favour and I'm obligated to her.'

'Yer don't have to jump every time she pulls the strings! Can't yer, just for once, tell her to get lost?'

'Can you tell her to get lost?'

'No, I can't,' Laura admitted, 'because she can make trouble for me.'

'Celia can make trouble for a lot of people, babe, believe me. We'll leave it at that for now, but one day I'll tell yer the whole story.'

Laura was thoughtful for a while. And troubled. What had she let herself in for with Celia? Oh, how she wished she'd never seen her outside the factory gates that night. Then none of this would have happened. 'Can I ask yer something, Gary?'

'Go ahead, babe.'

'Do you like me? Yer know, really like me?'

'Of course I like yer.' He pulled her closer. 'I would have thought that was obvious to anyone.'

'And if it wasn't for Celia having some sort of hold over yer, would yer like me more?'

'Listen, babe, this conversation is just between you and me. Don't ever repeat it to anyone. Celia is not a woman to be crossed, she's dangerous. I go along with her because she could bring trouble to me door. One day I'll tell yer the whole sorry story, but just for tonight, for the few hours we've got, let's enjoy ourselves, eh?'

'And you're still going to the party with her and Charlie?'

'If I don't, I won't be the only one in trouble. She'll crucify you and yer family. And don't think I'm exaggerating because I've seen it happen to people who crossed her path.'

Laura pulled a face. 'So I won't get me New Year's kiss after all? That's all I've thought about all week.'

Gary smiled down at her. 'I think we can manage that, babe. When Charlie and Celia go out for their usual half hour, we'll find a dark corner somewhere.'

'Where do they disappear to, Gary?'

'I think I've said enough for tonight, babe, so let's dance.' He lowered his head and spoke into her hair. 'I like you very, very much, babe. And I mean it.'

After the interval, a spot waltz was announced. And with the whole room in darkness except for the light moving over the dancing couples, Gary led Laura to a quiet corner and put his arms around her waist. 'Happy New Year, babe.'

Laura smiled up at him, wishing this moment could last for ever. 'Let's make a wish before we kiss, eh? Let's wish that something happens to Celia and we don't have to see her ever again.'

'I've been wishing that for the last eight months, babe, but me wish hasn't been granted. I keep telling meself she'll come unstuck one day, and she will. She can't go around bossing people and threatening to ruin their lives.' He pulled her close. 'Can I have me kiss now, before the lights go up?'

When his lips came down on hers, Laura felt as though all the breath had gone from her body and her head was spinning. If his arms hadn't been holding her tight, she would have fainted. She had never in all her dreams imagined such a sensation. And when he finally lifted his head, she could hardly speak. 'I think I'm going to pass out.'

'I feel the same, babe, but don't pass out before I have another kiss.'

They broke apart when the lights went up. 'Yer'd better wipe yer lips,' Laura said shakily. 'Ye're covered in lipstick.'

'All these wasted weeks, when I didn't know what I was missing,' Gary grinned as he took a hankie from his pocket. 'I can't wait for the spot waltz next week.'

'Why do we have to wait until next week? Why don't we just tell her to go to hell?'

The smile vanished from Gary's face. 'She wouldn't go to hell, she'd go straight to your mam. From what I've heard, she's got it in for yer mother. She said she's a stuck-up bitch and one day she'll pull her down a peg or two. And you're the one she's going to use to do it. What I can't understand is how she gets away with it with her husband. He must be as soft as a brush to let her gad around the way she does. And it's an uncle of yours she's married to, isn't it?'

'What? No! She's married to me grandad!'

Gary shook his head as he looked at her with disbelief. 'Yer *grandad*? But yer grandad must be an old man!'

'He's not an old man, he's lovely. And she treats him terrible, gives him a dog's life. I hate her, she's wicked.'

'She's a bigger liar than I thought,' Gary said. 'She tells everybody she's married to this handsome bloke who's got a good job and gives her everything. They both like a good time and have agreed to give each other a lot of freedom. She goes her way, he goes his.'

'Me grandad's a nice-looking man, even though he's nearly sixty. But he doesn't have a lot of money and never goes anywhere except to work or to our house. He doesn't give her everything, she takes it and leaves him skint.'

Gary saw Celia and Charlie come through the door, and he touched Laura's arm. 'That's the end of the conversation for now, babe, the enemy approaches. We'll talk more next week, and there's always the spot waltz.'

'I liked the way yer kissed me, Gary.'

'And I liked the way yer kissed me back, babe. Roll on next week.'

Chapter Twenty

Mary and Stan crossed the slippery cobbles with great care. Mary was carrying a plate of fairy cakes to help out with the food, and Stan was gripping three pint glasses in one hand and three sherry glasses in the other. 'I've got a couple more if they're short, but Seamus said three of each would do.'

'There's not a sound,' Mary said as she knocked at the door. 'We must be the first.'

Stan chuckled, 'If it's quiet, that means Amy hasn't arrived yet.'

'Come on in out of the cold.' Molly opened the door wide. 'Sure, it wouldn't surprise me if we had another fall of snow, the sky's been heavy all day, so it has.'

'I hope not, Molly. This week's been murder trying to get around.' Mary handed the plate over. 'They're not much, sunshine, but they'll help out.'

Seamus greeted them warmly. 'Let me have yer coats, then take a seat near the fire.'

'I'll see if Molly wants any help before I sit down,' Mary told him. 'An extra pair of hands are always welcome.'

'Sure, there's no need, me darlin'. Hasn't my dear wife got everything under control, as usual? And hasn't she had me and Mick running around like blue-arsed flies?'

They heard footsteps clattering down the stairs and then Mick appeared. He was wearing a smile until he saw there were just the two of them. 'Where's Jenny?'

'Her and Janet were upstairs titivating themselves up when we left, but they should be here any minute.' Mary grinned. 'Anyone would think they were going to Buckingham Palace, the time they're spending on themselves.'

'Jenny doesn't need to titivate herself up,' Mick said. 'She always looks pretty.'

Seamus let out a hearty guffaw. 'Keep an eye on yer daughter, Mary, or me son will be stealing her from yer.'

'Not while she's only fourteen he won't, Seamus. I'll be tanning his backside for him if he tries.'

Although Mick smiled at her, his deep blue eyes were serious. 'She'll be fifteen in three and a half months, Mrs Nightingale, and me and John were going to ask yer if she can come to the dance with us? Mrs Porter has already said Janet can come with us.'

'Oh well, if Mrs Porter has already agreed, what can I say?' Mary was shaking inside with laughter. 'If I refused, I'd be the worst mother in the world, wouldn't I? Or like the wicked step-mother in *Cinderella* who wouldn't let her go to the ball, and made her stay home to sweep the floor and wash the pans.'

Mick's dimples appeared. 'I'd go along with that, Mrs Nightingale, as long as I can find out how to get hold of Cinderella's fairy god-mother.'

They heard Amy's loud voice outside. 'Take yer bleedin' hands off it, Ben Hanley. I've carried it this far without your help.'

Then came Ben's voice. 'What's in it, anyway?'

'Mind yer own bleedin' business. And take yer hands off before I brain yer.'

They then heard John. 'Mam, do yer have to shout so loud? The whole flippin' street can hear yer.'

'Sod the whole street, if they've nothing better to do. Now knock on that bleedin' door before I freeze to death.'

Mick, who had been standing behind the door, had it open in a flash. 'I don't know what *it* is, Mrs Hanley, but I promise I won't put me bleedin' hands on it.'

Amy chuckled as she brushed past him. 'You can sod off, too, Mick Moynihan. Ye're as bad as yer old man.' She entered the room with a beaming smile on her face and carrying a battered suitcase in her chubby hand. 'Good evening to yer, Molly, and you, Seamus.' She narrowed her eyes at Mary. 'I might have known yer'd be here first, so yer could have a few sly drinks before anyone else arrived. It's no wonder everyone in the neighbourhood calls yer "those bleedin' scroungers, the Nightingales". They've all got yer taped, girl.'

'I've often wondered what people were saying behind their hands when I pass. Well, I need wonder no more 'cos me mate has solved the mystery.' Mary nodded to the suitcase. 'What have yer got in there, sunshine?'

'Seeing as yer all dying of curiosity, even my feller, I'll tell yer. I am a professional artiste, as yer all have reason to know, and inside here,' she lifted the case that had seen better days, 'is the costume I'll be wearing to entertain my adoring public.'

Ben, as funny as his wife in his own way, put on the downtrodden, henpecked husband face. His hand to his forehead, and looking down at the floor, he said, 'She's wicked is my wife. She lifts yer up one minute, then knocks yer down the next. When she came down with that suitcase, me heart filled with joy. I could even hear birds singing. And that should tell yer how happy I was, when there isn't a

254

tree within miles of us. I really thought she was leaving home.'

When there was a roar of laughter, Ben shook his head sadly. 'No, folks, it's no laughing matter. There I was, floating on air, and she tells me it's her ruddy costume in the case. I came down to earth with a bump, I can tell yer.'

'Ho, ho, very funny, I must say.' Amy's face was set, but everyone could see her tummy shaking. 'Listen to me, buggerlugs, there's only room for one comic in the house and it ain't you. So don't be trying to get in on the act.'

John peeped in the kitchen. 'Where's Jenny?'

'Oh, my God, will yer listen to this son of mine?' Amy was nodding and shaking her head at the same time, which confused her layer of chins. They didn't know whether to sway sideways or go up and down, so they stayed where they were. 'His mam and dad are nearly coming to blows, and he wants to know where Jenny is.'

'It's all right, Amy, we've been through this with Mick. Our Jenny and Janet will be over in a minute, they're dolling themselves up.'

'I don't know why me son and Mick bother.' Amy shifted the suitcase to her other hand. 'Jenny told me she's got her eye on a feller at work.'

When Mary saw the look exchanged between the two boys, she could tell they didn't think it was funny. 'Ye're a lying hound, Amy Hanley. One of these days someone's going to take ye're serious, and then yer'll be in trouble.'

Amy bent down and glared into her face. 'Is it my fault they can't take a bleedin' joke?'

Seamus held out his hand. 'Let me put the case down for yer, me darlin', before yer hit someone with it.'

Amy came over all sweetness and light. 'It's a kind man yer are, Seamus, and I really do appreciate it. But no one gets their bleedin' hands on this case but me, so there.'

'Come with me, me darlin',' Molly said. 'Yer can hide it at the back of the pantry where no one will get at it. Yer have my promise, I'll guard it with me life, so I will.'

The two boys had been eyeing the clock with growing impatience, and when the knock finally came they moved as one. Elbows and feet were being used, and as neither would give way to the other, they ended up getting stuck in the doorway. Ignoring the laughter behind them, Mick said, 'Okay, pal, let's be sensible about this. I'll open the door and you bow them in. Okay?'

'Oh, no yer don't, mate! This might be your house, but fair's fair. I'll open the door and you bow them in.'

Mick knew this would happen and was delighted. When the door was finally opened he was in full view, while John was stuck behind it and all you could see of him was his face.

'Yer look very pretty tonight, Jenny.' Mick didn't care that everyone was listening. He had three months to get in the lead and he didn't intend wasting any time.

John, nearly tripping over his feet, rushed to Mick's side. 'Yes, yer do, Jenny, very pretty indeed.'

Not noticing that all the grown-ups had their hands in their mouths to keep the laughter quiet, Janet tugged on John's arm. 'Don't I look pretty, John?'

John looked into her face and felt ashamed. They shouldn't make such a fuss of Jenny and leave her friend out, no matter how they felt. 'Janet, yer look lovely. Doesn't she, Mick?'

'She certainly does,' Mick agreed. 'Nice enough to be on the lid of a box of Cadbury's chocolates.'

Amy put her hand to her stomach and made a gurgling sound. 'Seamus, if yer don't put a glass in me hand this minute, I'll be sick all over yer floor. And put those four outside, while ye're at it. Sloppy beggars.'

'Now, me darlin', were yer not young yerself once? It's a long time ago, I'll grant yer that, but sure, yer must have some memories of being flattered and courted.'

Amy caught her husband's eye and jerked her head. 'Go on, you tell them how yer flattered and courted me.'

'You tell a better tale than me, love,' Ben said. 'And ye're a better liar than me.'

Amy, her chubby hands around a glass of stout, was in her element. 'Well, when my Ben used to call for me, I'd open the door and he'd say, "Are yer ready, girl?" Then we'd walk down the street with him on the inside and me on the outside near the kerb. I always took me own quarter of wine gums, 'cos I knew he wouldn't dream of buying me sweets. We'd sit in the dark of the picture house, chewing on MY wine gums, without a word being spoken. If James Cagney and Pat O'Brien were on, and it came to an exciting bit, Ben used to close his eyes and I'd have to tell him when it was safe to look. Then when we came out of the pictures, I used to walk him home 'cos his mam didn't like him being out on his own in the dark, and when we got outside his house he'd tap me on the arm and say, "Ta-ra, girl, see yer tomorrow". If I was quick, I'd have a chance to kiss him on the cheek before he had time to put his key in the lock.'

Amy took a long swig of stout before gazing around the rapt faces. 'I knew I'd always have to buy me own wine gums and walk in the gutter, but yer see, although yer wouldn't think so now, he was dead handsome, was Ben. A real he-man, he was, knocked spots off the likes of Clark Gable. Sometimes, when we were walking, our hips would touch and I'd swoon with rapture. He'll tell yer himself the number of times he had to lift me up out of the gutter.'

Ben, who had enjoyed the tale of fantasy more than anyone, cocked an eyebrow. 'Yer were lying in the gutter the first time I set eyes on yer, love. Yer were dead drunk and slobbering. And I remember saying to meself, as I picked yer up, "This is the girl for me".'

Amy grinned. 'There yer are – didn't I tell yer he was dead romantic?'

The laughter increased ten-fold when Janet said, 'I don't think he was dead romantic. Fancy him making yer buy yer own wine gums!'

Amy, the chair creaking beneath her, looked at her son. 'John, spell it out for her, will yer? Or, better still, draw her a picture.'

'Mam, she doesn't know yer well enough yet. How was she to know that every word yer spoke was a lie? Janet's mam's not as daft as you.'

'Ooh, er!' There was a look of amazement on Janet's face. 'Yer mean that was all lies, Mrs Hanley? Well, why was yer husband laughing?'

'Because he's sitting on a feather, girl, and it's tickling his fancy.' Then Amy felt sorry for her. 'It was all a joke, girl, just to make people laugh. I often come out with these weird and wonderful tales, but they're all in fun.'

Janet's face broke into a wide smile. 'In that case, Mrs Hanley, it was very funny. But will yer tell me in future, so I can enjoy the joke?'

'Listen, sunshine,' Mary said, 'just treat everything me mate says as a joke and yer can't go far wrong. She never gives a warning because she doesn't know herself what she's going to come out with.' Mary chuckled. 'Come shopping with us one day, Janet, and yer'll find out what I mean.'

Janet put her hand on John's arm. 'Your mam is very clever, John, to be able to make up stories like that.'

Amy was delighted. 'A girl after me own heart. She'll make someone a good wife.'

'All right, Mam.' John felt it was time to shut his mother up before she said Janet would make a good daughter-in-law. The trouble with his mam was, she didn't expect people to take to heart what she said. 'Yer've hogged the stage for long enough, give someone else a chance.'

'Ye're right, son,' Amy said. 'I should be concentrating on me big performance later on. We artistes are very highly strung and temper – er, tempora –' she glanced at Mary. 'What's the word I'm looking for, girl?'

'Temperamental, sunshine.'

'That's what I am.' Amy nodded. 'So I'll save meself for the big moment.'

257

And the big moment came at half-past eleven, after much beer and port had been drunk, songs sung and jigs and reels danced. Amy made her way into the kitchen and closed the door, telling Molly not to let anyone out there, even if they were desperate for the lavvy. 'Tell them to cross their legs,' she said.

While the adults were engaged in conversation as they waited for the star of the show, Mick said to Jenny, 'Yer mam said yer can come to the dance with us after yer birthday.'

'Did she? Oh, won't that be great!' Jenny's pretty face was animated and flushed with all the laughing. 'I'm really looking forward to it.'

'Yeah, me too.' Mick thought that was putting it mildly. He was counting the days. 'We'll have some fun.'

'You bet,' John said. 'We'll be that good we'll be able to enter in competitions.'

'Will yer teach me to dance proper, John?' Janet asked. 'You know, like they do in the movies?'

Why does she always ask me things, John asked himself. Why doesn't she ask Mick? 'Yeah, me and Mick will both teach yer. We'll take turns apiece with you and Jenny until yer can do all the dances.'

There came a thumping on the kitchen door. 'Molly, as yer've taken over as me manager, it's up to you to introduce me and make sure the audience don't get rowdy. This act I'm doing tonight is a real class act, and I won't put up with any whistling or bawling. So if ye're expecting to get paid for the job, get cracking and give me an introduction worthy of me many and varied talents.'

'Oh dear,' Molly said, 'would somebody else like to be her manager? I'm out of me depths, so I am, and haven't a clue what to do or say.'

There was a lot of pulling of faces and shaking of heads. No one wanted to be Amy's manager when they didn't know what she was going to look like when she came through that door. Oh, it was all in fun, a great big joke to Amy. And the person opening the door for her big entrance could end up in tears of laughter. But they could also end up with a very red face and wishing the floor would open and swallow them up. 'Seamus,' she pleaded, 'will yer not be helping me out?'

Seamus was shaking with laughter. 'With the best will, and all the love in the world, me darlin', I'll not be taking that chance. If Amy comes in here in her birthday suit, wouldn't it be me being chased up the street by yer dear self, with the stiff brush in yer hand?'

Amy was getting impatient. 'What the bleedin' hell is going on in there? I've got me own flippin' legs crossed now, yer've been that long.'

Molly breathed out through her teeth before opening the kitchen door slowly. Then, with a sigh of relief and a smile on her face, she announced, 'Here she comes, for your entertainment, the one and only – *Amy Hanley*!'

When the laughter erupted, it was like an explosion. Amy was wearing her husband's working clothes, right down to the dirty old cap, collarless shirt and braces. Now Ben was a big man, and his wife was swamped in his clothes. The jacket came down to her knees, the trouser legs had been rolled up and secured with large pins, and the waist was tied with a piece of strong string, knotted above Amy's tummy. The sleeves had also been turned up half-a-dozen times to fit. It was the dirty old cap that had everyone rolling about. It came down over her ears and almost covered her eyes. All you could see was her chubby cheeks and the wide smile which told of her delight in the reception.

'In the name of God, love, how did yer do that?' Ben asked. 'I had those clothes on for work today!'

'I know, and I thought I was going to have to drag the bleedin' things off yer, yer were that slow getting changed. Anyway, on with the show. Nobody join in till I tell yer, 'cos some of yer are tone deaf and yer put me off me stroke.' With a thumb hooked each side of the braces, and a swagger to her walk, she began. 'Anytime ye're Lambeth Way . . .' She'd told them not to join in, but the song was so catchy they had to do something, so they clapped their hands and stamped their feet.

What a sight Amy looked, a real scream. And there wasn't a soul in that room who didn't feel like giving her a big hug. One song followed another, all with a Cockney theme. 'Any Old Iron' was followed by 'Maybe It's Because I'm A Londoner'. And as she sang, her legs and feet were never still. Till in the end, with sweat running down her face and her breathing laboured, she called it a day. 'That's all for now folks, I'm all in.'

There were shouts of, 'Encore!' and, 'Bravo!' but Amy shook her head. 'I need two glasses of stout to catch up with the rest of yer. And until I get that, my backside stays on this chair.'

John, his mother's biggest fan, looked across at her and said, 'I don't half love me mam, she's a real corker.'

'I love yer mam, too, John.' Janet nodded her head. 'I think she's brilliant.'

'We all love Auntie Amy,' Jenny said. 'Yer couldn't help but love her.'

Although Mick agreed with their sentiments, he wasn't very happy about it. If Jenny loved his mother, it gave John a head start. 'I love Mrs Hanley, she's great. But doesn't anybody love my mam?'

'Of course we do!' Jenny giggled. 'I always think of my mam, Auntie Amy and Auntie Molly as The Three Musketeers. They're one for all and all for one. If a helping hand is needed, it is quickly offered. They've been friends for as long as I can remember, and I love the bones of the three of them.'

Mick and John were very happy with that statement. But it left Janet wondering whether they lived too far away for her mam to join the friends, so she could be loved by everyone. 'Yer can't have Four Musketeers, can yer?'

'Nah,' John said. 'It doesn't have the same ring to it, somehow.' He looked at Mick and knew his friend was trying to figure out the same thing as him. Was Janet really as daft as she made out, or was she, in her own way, as funny as his mam?

It was a Monday morning, ten days into the New Year, when Cynthia decided to put her plan into action. She left for work as usual, in her old coat, scruffy shoes and a scarf over her head. In her handbag was the letter she'd written and an old pair of her father's reading glasses. She worked through until the dinner break, then asked the supervisor if she could go home as she wasn't feeling very well.

As she walked through the factory gates, Cynthia's nerves were as taut as a violin string. The only thing that kept her going was the knowledge that if the letter had the desired effect, she'd finally get the revenge she sought. Larry and Jeff had made her life a hell, and she hadn't asked for it. She may have been stupid to have taken up with Larry in the first place, but she didn't deserve what he and his friend had done to her. Nobody deserved that. And it wasn't only herself who had suffered at their hands, but others, too. They couldn't be allowed to carry on; they must be punished and have their lives made a hell on earth.

Cynthia could feel sympathy for their wives, for she had no doubt they were married, but they had to know. They were the only ones who could put a stop to it. None of the women they forced into having sex would go to the police, because they'd be too ashamed to put into words what had happened to them. And too ashamed of their families and neighbours finding out. There was always one who would say, 'I bet she asked for it. There's no smoke without fire.'

Cynthia hopped on a tram at Everton Valley and took a seat by the window. And as she swayed with the movement of the tram, the shops and buildings that flashed by were just a blur. She was deep in thought, going over and over her plan. She'd worked it out to the last detail, but would it be as easy in reality? It had to be; she desperately needed it to be successful so her mind would be cleansed and she could put the whole incident behind her. She'd never forget, but it wouldn't be nagging away in her head every day and night. And she wouldn't be looking at every boy with suspicion.

'Walton Church next stop,' the conductor called as he rang the bell.

Cynthia stepped down from the tram and began to walk back to the street with a pub on one corner and a sweet shop on the other. She stopped before she reached the corner and put on her father's glasses before pulling the scarf down to cover her hair. No one would have given her a second glance; she looked like a dowdy, middle-aged housewife. She couldn't see out of the glasses clearly so she bent her head and peered over the rims as she turned the corner of the street. She glanced briefly up at number fifteen as she passed, noting that the house seemed well-kept, with bright windows and clean steps, but kept on walking until she came to number fifty-five. Then, settling the glasses straight on her nose, she lifted the knocker.

The woman who opened the door was middle-aged with a happy face and ginger hair. 'Yes, can I help yer?'

Her eyes squinting, Cynthia asked, 'Is Larry in, please?'

'There's no Larry here, queen, yer've got the wrong house.'

'Oh, I'm sure me dad said fifty-five.' Cynthia held the envelope out. 'He asked me to bring this letter, but he hasn't put the address on. It's just got Larry on the front.'

'I've got it now,' the woman said, smiling. 'It'll be Larry Langton, he's the only Larry I know. He lives up the road at number fifteen. But he won't be in now, he'll be at work.'

'Perhaps his wife will be in?'

'She'll be at work, queen, and the kids are at school. If yer come back tonight, they'll all be in.'

'I couldn't do that, I've come all the way from Bootle.' Cynthia lifted the glasses and pinched the bridge of her nose. 'I've got a splitting headache with these glasses. I need new ones but I can't afford them.'

'Why don't yer pop the letter through their letter box, queen, save anyone having to make that long journey?'

'I don't think me dad would like that. He said to be sure to give it to Larry or his wife. In fact, he thought Larry would be at work, and he told me to give it to his wife. If I tell him I went to the wrong house in the first place, and then put it through a letter box, he'll have me guts for garters.'

'Then give me the letter and I'll nip up with it when Doreen gets in. That's his wife, and she works until three o'clock.' The woman held out her hand. 'My name's June Lawson, by the way, queen. What's yours?'

'Ooh, isn't that funny, my name's June, too!' Cynthia was thinking fast as she passed the letter over. 'June Hardcastle.'

'Right, I'll let Doreen know yer called and she can tell Larry. Yer can promise yer dad he'll definitely have the letter in his hand as soon as he gets home. Is there any other message, queen?'

'No, I don't even know this Larry, it's me dad what knows him.'

Cynthia turned to walk away. 'Thanks very much, yer've saved me life.'

'Think nothing of it, queen, ye're welcome.' June Lawson watched her walk away. A spinster from the looks of her, she thought. And a downtrodden one at that. Seemed her father had the whip hand. She closed the door and gazed down at the envelope. Why the hell couldn't the old man have posted it, save putting his daughter to all that trouble? Whatever was in the ruddy letter couldn't be that important.

When Cynthia heard the door close, she speeded up her steps. The glasses were discarded and thrust in her pocket. The deed was done now and the sooner she got away from here the better. By tonight, Larry's wife, and Jeff's too, with any luck, would know what their husbands got up to. For Doreen was sure to do as Cynthia expected and open the letter as soon as she got in. After all, she wouldn't see any harm in reading a letter that had been hand-delivered, and curiosity would be bound to get the better of her. However, what she would find inside would shake her to the core. First was the date when her husband and his friend had picked up two young girls in a pub and taken them down an entry. The pub was named and a description of the girls given. Then Doreen would read about the woman who was dragged struggling down an entry by her husband and Jeff, and how they were in the act of raping her when two men who were passing came to her aid. This was the night their husbands had come home badly bruised and beaten up. Their injuries had been inflicted by the two men who didn't take kindly to rapists. Again the date was given and the name of the pub.

Cynthia had not given details of her own ordeal for fear of being found out as the writer of the letter. But she had written that the incidents mentioned were only two of many, and that Larry and Jeff were nothing but evil bullies and rapists, unfit to be members of the human race.

While Cynthia was waiting at the tram stop, she told herself it was too early to go home without awkward questions being asked. She'd go into town and have a cup of tea at the Kardomah. She realised with surprise that the tension had left her body and her heart felt lighter than it had done in months. Please God it would stay like that and the dark moods were a thing of the past.

When the tram came and she jumped on board, the conductor was standing on the platform talking to the driver. He held out his hand, asking, 'Where to, love?'

She smiled as she handed him two pennies. 'A single to Church Street, please.'

Doreen Langdon closed the door on June and looked down at the letter in her hand. 'I bet he's been backing the gee-gees and owes the bookie money.' She walked through to the living room and stood the letter up on the mantelpiece. She was alone in the house, the children wouldn't be in from school for another half-hour. 'I'll break his bloody neck for him, if that's the case. What's the point in me going out to work to earn a few bob if he's going to squander it on bloody horses?'

It was anger and curiosity that had her reaching for the letter. 'He's not likely to tell me,' she muttered, her finger slitting the top of the envelope, 'so I'll find out for meself.'

As the words on the paper sunk in, Doreen began to sway and held on to the table for support. Her face drained of colour, she read the letter again to make sure her eyes weren't deceiving her. Then, her voice choked, she cried, 'My God, they could go to prison for this! The bastards! The no-good bleedin' bastards!' Her mind whirled as she gazed around the room. Perhaps it wasn't true. It was someone's idea of a joke. But even as she thought it, she knew it was no joke. Her husband and his mate were selfish swines, they thought only of themselves. Her and Iris, Jeff's wife, could be skint through the week, with no money for food, but the two men made sure they had their beer and ciggie money, and a few bob for the gee-gees.

Doreen looked down at the sheet of paper in her hand. Her husband had pulled some stunts in their married life, but nothing had prepared her for this. If the police found out, he and his mate would spend the rest of their lives in prison. And what shame that would bring on the family. She wouldn't be able to look anyone in the face. The best thing she could do would be to go over and show the letter to Iris before anyone else told her what their husbands got up to.

Iris had a smile on her face when she opened the door. 'This is a surprise, I wasn't expecting yer.'

'I've got a bigger surprise for yer, kid, and it's not a pleasant one.' Doreen brushed past her and walked into the living room. 'Are the kids home yet?'

Iris shook her head. 'Another ten minutes or so.'

There was no time to spare, so Doreen just handed the letter over. 'Take a grip of yerself and read that.'

The silence lasted just a few seconds, then all hell broke loose. 'I'll break his bleedin' neck for him.' Iris was beside herself. 'I won't even bother to ask him if it's true because I know it is. The number of times I've smelt powder or scent on him, and he's always laughed it off. Well he'll not laugh this off, 'cos I'll bleedin' kill the swine.'

'Calm down, Iris, and let's talk before the kids come in. We don't want them to know about things like this.' Doreen put her arm across her friend's shoulder. 'What I'm worried about is that whoever wrote

263

that letter might not be the only one who knows what they get up to. It might only be a matter of time before the police find out. And I'm not staying around to be shamed in front of all the neighbours. So first thing tomorrow I'll be looking for somewhere else to live, well away from here.'

'And what are yer going to do about Larry?' Iris had a quick temper at the best of times and right now it was ready to boil over. 'I'll kill my feller when he gets in.'

'I won't do anything until the kids are in bed. Then I'll give him the hiding of his life to get this hurt and anger out of me system, and to pay him back for what he did to those girls. After that, if he's capable of listening, then I'm going to lay the law down. The Tuesday and Thursday nights out are a thing of the past. I want extra housekeeping money off him. I will not sleep in the same bed as him, I'll sleep with the kids. And if he doesn't want to move to another area, I'll go on me own with the kids. I can get a full-time job to keep us.' Doreen waved the letter under Iris's nose. 'And all the time this letter will be in me hand. I'll put the fear of God into him by saying I'm so disgusted it wouldn't take much for me to go to the police and turn him in.'

They heard children's voices and Doreen quickly folded the piece of paper. 'Keep yer temper in check until the kids are in bed. It wouldn't be fair on them to hear you and Jeff having a slanging match.'

Iris nodded. 'I'll come down with yer tomorrow to the landlord's office and we can ask for a transfer. We shouldn't have any trouble because we've always paid our rent on time. We've been good tenants.'

Three weeks later the two families moved out. And they didn't leave a forwarding address.

Chapter Twenty-One

'Spring is in the air, girl,' Amy said cheerfully as she linked Mary's arm. 'The first day of April, the sky is blue and the sun is doing its best to come out.'

'I'm not sorry to see the back of the bad weather, it's been a hard winter. We needn't light the fire first thing in the morning soon, so we'll save a few bob on coal.'

Amy pretended to smooth down the front of her coat before pulling Mary to a halt. 'Ay, girl, has the elastic gone in yer knickers? They're hanging down.'

Mary's mouth dropped open in horror. She looked down at her legs, front and side, and frowned. 'I can't see nothing.'

Amy's cackle could be heard from one end of the street to the other. 'Ever been had, girl? April fool!'

'Oh God, I fell for it again. Every year yer do it, so wouldn't yer think I'd have learnt by now? The best of it is, I was going to tell yer something when we left our house, but I better not say anything now because yer won't believe me.'

'Why won't I believe yer, girl?'

'Because yer'll think I'm pulling ycr leg.'

'Nah, I wouldn't, girl, 'cos ye're not quick enough to catch me out.'

'Well, yer've got a flaming big hole in the heel of yer stocking and it's got about ten ladders running from it, right up yer leg.'

Amy leaned heavily on Mary's arm as she bent one leg backwards, then the other. 'I'm blowed if I can see anything. Yer must be imagining things, girl.'

'I'm not imagining I've just made an April fool of yer, sunshine.'

'Well, I'll be buggered! First time, eh, girl?'

'I'm a bit slow on the uptake, sunshine, but I get there in the end.' Mary pressed on her friend's arm and they carried on walking. 'I hope yer don't start any shenanigans in the shops, with yer April fool. Not everybody appreciates your humour.'

'Stop yer worrying, girl, it gives yer wrinkles and puts years on yer.'

While Mary entered the butcher's shop with trepidation, Amy was full of the joys of spring.

'Good morning, Wilf, I hope we find yer hale and hearty on this lovely day?'

'I'm fine, thank you, ladies. Whether I'll be fine by the time you leave, well, that remains to be seen.'

'Have yer got a pound of beef sausage, Wilf?'

The butcher leaned in the window and lifted a string of sausages. He counted out how many he thought would be the right weight, cut them free from the rest and threw them on the scales.

Mary was growing uneasy. 'Yer told me yer were having brawn tonight,' she whispered in Amy's ear, 'with egg and chips.'

'That's wasn't no lie, girl, that's what we're having.'

'Well, why have yer asked for a pound of beef sausage?'

Wilf heard what was said and his hand hovered over the scale as he waited for the bane of his life to answer.

'I didn't say I *wanted* a pound of beef sausage, girl, I only asked if he *had* a pound of beef sausage. Just taking an interest in his business, like, yer see.'

It was Mary who thought an apology was in order. 'I'm sorry about that, Wilf, but if it's any consolation she caught me out, too.'

'That's all right, Mary.' Wilf threw the sausages back on the tray in the window. 'I wasn't doing anything, anyway. Before you came in I was just standing here catching fleas.'

Amy couldn't speak for laughing. She banged on the counter as she roared her head off. 'Nice one, Wilf. Ooh, I like that! Just standing catching fleas. I'll have to remember that one. Wait until I tell my Ben, he'll laugh his little cotton socks off.'

'I would prefer yer not to repeat that, Amy,' Wilf said. 'Some of my customers wouldn't see the joke and it'd be around the neighbourhood in no time that I had fleas.'

The floorboards began to shake with the weight of Amy's heaving body. Mary and Wilf looked on with smiles on their faces, wondering what she was going to come out with that was so funny she couldn't stop laughing. Eventually she drew herself up to her full four feet ten and a half inches, sniffed up and wiped a hand across her eyes. 'Ooh, it did me a power of good, that. Better than a dose of salts any day.'

'Aren't yer going to let us in on the joke?' Mary asked. 'It's not like you to keep things to yerself, more's the pity.'

Amy looked at the smiling butcher. 'Are yer sure yer want to know, Wilf?'

'If I couldn't take a joke, Amy, I wouldn't last five minutes behind this counter.'

'I was going to say that if yer catch a flea, put it away for us till the weekend. It would probably have more meat on it than that bleeding chicken yer sold me on Saturday. It couldn't have less, that's a dead cert.'

266

Mary's cheeks were stiff with laughing. 'What would yer do with her, Wilf?'

'Actually, Mary, she comes in very handy for me sometimes. Whenever me missus gets ratty and is moaning her head off, I think of Amy and realise how lucky I am.'

Amy got on her high horse. 'Well, actually, Wilf Burnett, my Ben thinks he's the luckiest man in the world. He wouldn't swap me for all the gold in China.'

'The tea in China, sunshine.'

'What did yer say, girl?'

'I said the tea in China.'

'What about the tea in China, haven't they got none?'

Mary threw out her hands. 'I give up! Wilf, I'll have three-quarters of brawn, please. And when we left the house, me mate was having the same. But if I were you, I'd take her money before yer start weighing it.'

When they got outside the greengrocer's, Mary stood firm. 'You can get me five pound of spuds, I'll wait here for yer. I wouldn't go through another performance for a big clock.'

'I won't do nothing, girl, cross my heart and hope to die.'

'Then go and do nothing on yer own, sunshine, 'cos I ain't going in with yer.'

Amy walked away looking down in the mouth. But it didn't last long. She'd no sooner disappeared inside the shop, when Mary heard her shout: 'Top of the morning to yer, Billy. Have yer got a pound of those soft tomatoes?'

Mary could feel herself cringe inside. How her friend could do it, she didn't know. And she got away with it. Nobody ever fell out with her, only her neighbour, Annie Baxter. But Annie didn't count, 'cos she was as miserable as sin, anyway.

The next thing, Mary heard Billy Nelson roar his head off. 'Yer what! I've a good mind to throw the bleedin' things at yer. In fact, it would be worth losing the tuppence to pelt yer with them.'

Then came a voice Mary didn't recognise. 'She's a big enough target, Billy.'

There was no mistaking the next voice. 'Oh, ye're there, are yer missus? Well, why don't yer try minding yer own business? And when yer get home, if yer've got a mirror that isn't already cracked, take a good look in it and see the gob on yerself.'

That's it, Mary thought, I'll be here all day at this rate. So she marched in the shop, took the basket from Amy and plonked it on the counter. 'We just want two lots of spuds when ye're ready, Billy.' She turned to say something to Amy and saw her friend and another woman eyeing each other up. Oh Lord, she groaned, these two are going to be at each other's throats any minute now. 'I'll

267

wait for the potatoes, sunshine, you go and get our bread.'

Amy's eyes never wavered. 'You get the bread, girl, I'm comfortable where I am.'

Billy weighed five pound of potatoes and threw them in the basket. He'd be best serving them first, for the sake of peace and save his shop from becoming a boxing ring. He covered the potatoes with a newspaper, and weighed out another five pound. Then he had a brainwave. 'Ye're the only one that caught me out today, Amy.'

Amy pricked her ears. Praise was something she never ignored. 'Oh, yeah?'

'Yeah.' Billy passed the basket to Mary and took her four pennies. 'Six of them tried it on, but you were the only one I fell for.'

The woman showed she was curious. 'What did they try on, Billy?'

'It's April Fool's day, Mrs Chambers.'

'Oh.' The woman looked sheepish. 'I didn't know.'

'Well, you wouldn't, would yer, missus? It's just another day to you.' Amy turned when Mary pulled on her arm. 'What is it, girl?'

Mary thrust the basket at her. 'You can carry this, me arm's dropping off.' She waved to the shopkeeper. 'Ta-ra, Billy.'

'Ta-ra, Mary! And you, Amy, my little flower, be careful how yer go.'

When they were outside, Amy said, 'I could have hit that bleedin' woman. Billy took it all in good fun and was laughing his head off until she stuck her nose in. Cheeky cow.'

'All right, sunshine, let's forget about it now, eh? We'll get the bread and then go home for a nice cuppa. If yer can manage to keep yer trap shut in the bakers, I'll mug yer to a cream slice. Is that a deal?'

'It sure is, girl, it sure is.'

Half an hour later the two friends sat facing each other with a cup of tea in front of them and a plate with a cream slice on. The slice had pink icing on the top and cream oozing out of the sides. Amy ran her tongue over her lips. 'I know it's manners to wait until ye're asked, girl, but I haven't got no manners so I ain't waiting.' She picked up the slice and ran her tongue down one side. 'Heaven.' Her eyes were closed as she savoured the luxury. 'Pure, bleedin' heaven.'

'Yeah, yer could get used to being rich, couldn't yer?'

'Sure could, girl, sure could. We should have married men with money, that's where we went wrong.'

'The trouble is, if yer could have them every day, yer wouldn't appreciate them. People who are loaded, they don't have anything to look forward to. They've been everywhere, seen everything and can have anything in the world they want. I wouldn't swap places with them because half the pleasure of getting something yer really want,

268

is the saving up for it, the anticipation. Then yer really appreciate it.'

Amy licked each finger in turn, not missing a speck of cream. 'Changing the subject, girl, have yer any bright ideas on what I could buy Jenny for her birthday?'

'Anything at all, sunshine. She's not expecting anything, so whatever yer buy she'd be over the moon about it.'

'How about an underskirt?'

'Fantastic, she'd be delighted. It's her birthday next Wednesday, and Janet's is on the Friday, so we're having one party for both of them. I'll have to ask the Porters because they offered to have the party, but Jenny said she'd rather have it here.'

'Is Bill Porter going out with that friend of Laura's from down the street? I've seen them together a few times.'

'I couldn't tell yer, sunshine. I know he goes out with Cynthia, but whether they're courting is anyone's guess. Our Laura is not very forthcoming about her friends.'

'I often wonder about your Laura. She seems to have calmed down a bit, but she's still a mystery to me. I mean, with her looks, yer'd think she'd have boys knocking on the door every night.'

'She could have a boyfriend for all we know, she never tells us anything. We don't know where she goes, or who with. I've given up worrying about her, it doesn't get me anywhere.'

'Your Jenny's a different kettle of fish. If she had a boyfriend, she'd bring him home to see yer on the first night. Mind you, she's got two boys right on her own doorstep who are crazy about her. I think it'll be a fight to the death with them two.'

'I suppose ye're talking about John and Mick? I'm keeping out of it, it's up to Jenny who she chooses for a boyfriend. But I've got to say I'd be very happy if she chose one of them. I'm very fond of both of them.' Mary reached for Amy's empty cup. 'Now, missus, will yer go home so I can get on with some work?'

'I'm going round for Janet, Mam.'

'I thought yer were sitting with Lizzie tonight? Surely Janet can find her own way without you walking round there?'

'I enjoy the walk, Mam, after being sat in an office all day. I enjoy stretching me legs and breathing in the fresh air.'

'Are the boys going, so one of them can walk Janet home?'

'We never make arrangements, Mam. They either turn up or they don't.'

'Well, it's not as dark these nights – she'd be all right walking back on her own. Don't stay too late at Lizzie's or yer'll tire her out.' Mary walked to the door with her daughter. 'Will Bill be coming to the party?'

'I've invited all the family, but I'm not sure about Bill. He's been

269

going out with Cynthia off and on, but according to Janet they're always falling out, so yer wouldn't know what was going on. We'll just have to wait and see.'

Jenny walked with her head bent, deep in thought. Laura was still a source of worry to her. Although her sister wasn't as hard-faced as she used to be, she remained aloof and secretive about her life outside her home. She still went out with Cynthia a few nights a week, and it wasn't unusual now for her to have a night in to wash her hair. But there was still a big question mark about what she got up to on Thursdays. She claimed she was going to a dance with Cynthia, and her parents had no reason to doubt her. But Jenny knew it wasn't true and had this terrible nagging feeling that one of these days Laura would be up to her neck in trouble and would bring it home with her.

Janet was waiting for her with the door open. 'Me mam and dad said to tell yer hello and they're looking forward to the party.'

Jenny waited for her friend to fall into step beside her before saying, 'Me mam needs to know the numbers for the party so she'll know how much to get in. So will your Bill be coming, or not? And if he is, will Cynthia be with him?'

'Your guess is as good as mine, Jenny. I would say they're not on speaking terms at the moment because he's sitting in the house with a face on him like a wet week.'

'Oh, well, if he turns up and there's not enough to eat or drink, it'll be his own fault. Me mam's not a mindreader, she can't cater if she doesn't know how many to cater for.'

Janet was eyeing her friend. 'Yer've done yer hair different again, Jenny. I wish I could do mine like you do – I'd have a different style every week.' Then she suddenly reverted back to the babyish voice she'd got into the habit of using. 'I bet John would like to see me hair done different. He wouldn't half get a surprise.'

Jenny put a hand on her friend's arm. 'Jan, this is Jenny – remember me? We used to sit next to each other every day in school. And yer were pretty clever in school, always in the top ten of our class. Can yer remember all that?'

'Of course I can, I'm not daft.'

'Then why do yer act daft? Yer never used to.'

There was a merry glint in Janet's eyes. 'I have me reasons, Jenny, and I'll tell yer them on me birthday. I'm going to grow up that day.'

'I don't get it, Jan, yer've lost me. Why would yer go on letting people think ye're stupid when it's only a game to yer? I don't know what yer hope to gain by it.'

'I might not gain anything by it, but there's a method in me madness. You'll see, on me birthday, I'll be all grown-up and not act daft no more. If I haven't done what I set out to do by that time, then

270

I never will.' Janet eyed the blonde hair bouncing on Jenny's shoulders. She had it in a page-boy bob tonight, a style that was all the rage, and it suited her. 'On the night of the party, would yer do something with my hair for me?'

'Yeah, of course I will. How would yer like it?'

'I'll leave that to you, whatever yer think suits me. But I would like to look glamorous, Jenny, if yer could manage that.'

'Yer could manage it yerself if yer put yer mind to it! Yer hair's lovely and thick, and the auburn chestnut colour is beautiful. I'll do yer up like a dog's dinner for the party.' Jenny giggled. 'If yer intend growing up that night, yer hair may as well grow up with yer.'

'Is Cynthia in, Mrs Pennington?' Bill shuffled his feet in embarrassment. He'd sworn he wouldn't be the first to give in this time, yet here he was coming cap in hand. He did it every time they had a fall-out, he couldn't help himself. If Cynthia wasn't so indifferent towards him he probably would have lost interest by now, but as it was he was still fascinated by her.

Fanny Pennington smiled at him. She could feel his nervousness and felt sorry for him. He was a nice lad, her daughter could do a lot worse. But then, her daughter was a law unto herself. She pleased herself what she did, regardless of anyone's feelings. Like this lad here; he shouldn't have to come crawling, he was too good for that. 'I'll ask her to come to the door, son, I think that's best.'

Cynthia came along the hall with her arms folded and a slump to her shoulders. 'Hello, Bill. I'm sorry I look a sight, but I'm not in the mood for getting dolled up.' She leaned against the hall wall. 'Did yer want something?'

Bill let out a sigh of exaggeration. 'I want to have a talk to yer. Can't yer slip a coat on and come for a walk?'

'What is there to talk about? Every time I see yer, we fall out.'

'You fall out, not me.' Bill couldn't go through another sleepless night, so his voice was insistent. 'Put a coat on, Cynthia, and let's talk. Yer owe me that much.'

'Wait there, I won't be a minute.' Cynthia took her coat from the hallstand and opened the living-room door. 'I'm going for a walk with Bill, Mam, I won't be long.'

Dick Pennington looked over his newspaper. He'd noticed the difference in his daughter but put it down to her age, and women's trouble. That was why she was on better terms with her mother, he thought, because it was easier for her to talk to a woman than a man. 'Why didn't yer ask the lad in?'

'It's all right, Dad, we'd rather go for a walk.'

Bill cupped her elbow. 'Is there anywhere yer'd like to go? The pictures, perhaps?'

271

Cynthia shook her head. 'You wanted to talk, so let's talk.'

'I'll get what I've got to say off me chest first, shall I?' Bill looked sideways at her, but her face gave nothing away. 'This has been going on for months now, and I can't understand yer attitude. We seem to be getting on fine one minute, then the next it's as if I'm a stranger to yer. I can't hold yer hand, can't put me arms around you or kiss yer. If that's the way yer feel about me, why don't yer come straight out with it and tell me to get lost, instead of going all quiet and backing off from me. Do yer like me or not, Cynthia?'

'Of course I like yer.' Cynthia's voice was husky. 'But ye're rushing things too much and I don't want to be rushed.'

'Rushing things! Blimey, I've been more patient with you than any other girl I've been out with! Holding hands with a girl ye're out on a date with, or giving her a kiss, that isn't rushing things, Cynthia, that's normal. That's what all young fellers do when they're out with their girlfriend. It's normal and healthy, Cynthia – no harm in it at all.'

It was time for an explanation, Cynthia knew that. She couldn't expect him to put up with her attitude without having a reason for it. She pulled him to a halt by a shop doorway. 'I had a bad experience with a feller, and it scared me. I can't help feeling the way I do, and I'll be all right if I'm given time. It's nothing to do with you, Bill, I swear.'

'What d'yer mean about a bad experience? Who was this bloke, and what in the name of God did he do to yer?'

Wild horses would never drag the truth from her. She'd be ashamed to tell him, and afraid of his reaction. He would probably run a mile on learning how she'd been violated by two men whom she hardly knew. No decent lad would touch her with a barge-pole unless they were like Larry and Jeff. No one would want her for a girlfriend, someone they could take home to meet their parents. So what she told him was; 'I was going out with this bloke for a few weeks, and yes, we did kiss and cuddle. But one night he tried to force himself on me and I was terrified. He was like an animal and I couldn't go through that again for anyone.'

In the dim light of the street-lamp, she could see Bill was thinking deeply. Then he asked, 'What do yer mean by he tried to force himself on yer?'

'He tried to make me do something I didn't want to do, Bill, and don't ask me any more 'cos I've had enough nightmares about it.'

'And ye're afraid I might try the same thing? He was a rotter, Cynthia, and I can't believe yer have so little respect for me that yer think I might turn out to be the same.'

She put a hand on his arm. 'Never for a moment did the thought enter me head, Bill. If it had, I'd never have even looked at yer. I

272

know ye're a nice, decent bloke, and yer deserve better treatment than I've been dishing out to yer. I've told yer now why I've behaved the way I have, and I hope yer understand. If yer don't, then we'll call it a day with no hard feelings on either side.'

Bill spread his arms in a gesture of hopelessness. 'What am I supposed to say or do, Cynthia? I feel like putting me arms around you and comforting yer, but if I were to touch yer, yer'd run a mile. And that's what hurts the most – yer lack of trust in me.'

'I do trust yer, Bill, but can't we take things slowly? Like this.' She put her arms around his waist and rested her head on his shoulder. 'A little comfort and tenderness to start off with.'

Bill held her, but not closely. He was so relieved, and so blissfully happy, he didn't want to spoil things. He'd wait and give her the time she needed. 'I'll do what the song says, eh, Cynthia? I'll Try A Little Tenderness.'

They walked home slowly, arm in arm, relaxed and contented. 'Will yer come to our Janet's birthday party with me?' he asked. 'It's in the Nightingales' 'cos it's Jenny's birthday too, so they're having a party between them.'

'Will your parents be there?'

'Yeah, but what difference does that make? They know I've been going out with yer and me mam will be made up to see us together. She'll tell yer I've been like a bear with a sore head whenever we've had a tiff.'

'Okay, I'd like to come to the party. Shall we buy the girls a present each between us? It would look lousy to turn up at a birthday party without presents.'

'You get them something, will yer? I wouldn't have a clue what to buy for girls.'

'I dunno, that's typical of a man. Talk about act soft and I'll buy yer a coal-yard, isn't in it.'

They stood outside Cynthia's house holding hands. 'Can I call for yer tomorrow night?' Bill asked. And when she nodded, he raised his brows. 'How about a peck on the cheek?'

Cynthia leaned forward and kissed him briefly on the lips. 'I'll look forward to it.'

Fanny Pennington was putting the fireguard in front of the hearth when her daughter came in. 'Yer dad went to bed early, he was feeling tired.'

As Cynthia gazed at her mother, her mind went back over the years. She'd been a bitch to this woman who had brought her into the world. The woman who had kept the house spotlessly clean, did the washing, ironing and cooking, and never been given a word of thanks or kindness. Well, the time had come to try and make amends, and Cynthia hoped she hadn't left it too late. 'I'm going to a party at the Nightingales' on Saturday with Bill, Mam, and I've got to buy presents for the two birthday girls. Have yer any idea what I could get?'

Fanny knew an olive branch was being offered and she grasped it with both hands. She'd been concerned for her daughter over the last few weeks but knew better than to ask what was wrong. Her motherly instinct told her something drastic had happened to change the girl's whole personality, and she worried what it was. When Bill had come on the scene she was delighted because he was a nice lad. But even that friendship seemed to be floundering. 'I wouldn't know what to suggest, love. Why don't we make a list of everything a young girl wears or uses, and pick the one yer fancy most?'

'That's a good idea, Mam, we'll do it now. I'll get a piece of paper.'

So for the very first time, mother and daughter sat together in friendship. Each hoping this closeness would grow into the love that had been missing from their lives. 'Now, let's see,' Cynthia said. 'We'll start on what we wear that nobody can see, and work our way out. Then we'll go on to what they'd use, like lipstick or powder. See if we both pick the same thing.'

'Where's Celia got to?' Laura asked, as Gary spun her around in a foxtrot. 'Apart from seeing her outside when I came in, there hasn't been sight nor sign of her since.'

'Don't worry about her, babe, let's just enjoy ourselves. The less we see of her the better it suits me.'

'I'm not worried about her, I'd be made up if I never clapped eyes on her again.' Laura was trying to pluck up courage to ask something, but the fear of refusal kept the words from being said. 'Just think, if it wasn't for her, me and you could be sitting on the back row of the picture house, holding hands.'

'We're holding hands now, babe, or hadn't yer noticed?' Gary smiled down at her. 'I know I'm holding your hand because I've got that thrill running up and down me spine. The one I get whenever I see or touch yer.'

'I feel the same way about you, Gary, but the difference is, I'm prepared to do something about it, and you're not. I've had enough of Celia telling us what we can or can't do, I'm fed up with it. How long is it going to go on for? For the rest of our lives, until we're old and grey?'

'I've told yer, babe, that if it was only me, I'd tell Celia to sod off. It's me mam I'm frightened for. She's been good to me, me mam. When me dad died, she was left to bring me up on her own, and she had a hard time. I wouldn't burden her with trouble for all the money in the world.'

'I can't imagine yer doing anything so bad that Celia could go running to yer mother telling tales. Ye're not a bad person, Gary.'

'No, babe, I'm not a bad person. And what I did wasn't that bad. Wrong, yes, but not bad. It's what Celia would add to it that makes me afraid. If she ever spills the beans on you, it won't be the truth as you know it, but a pack of lies.'

'I was going to ask yer if, just for once, yer'd take a chance? It's our Jenny's birthday party on Saturday, and I'd love yer to come and meet the family. I know they'd make yer welcome and yer would like them.'

The dance came to an end and Gary cupped her elbow to lead her off the floor. 'Would yer like to go outside for a breath of fresh air?' he asked. 'It's not cold out.'

Laura agreed eagerly. If there was no one else out there, they could steal a few hugs and kisses. Then in her mind, she asked herself was she satisfied with stolen kisses? After months of knowing Gary, caring for him and knowing he cared for her, all she'd had was a few stolen kisses. It was ridiculous to let one woman keep them apart. 'Why don't we both tell our mothers and get it over with – beat Celia to it? She'd have nothing on us then. We could do whatever we wanted, when we wanted.'

'Since I met you, babe, I've thought of doing that many times. Then I picture me mam's face and know I couldn't go through with it. Wouldn't your mam be hurt if she knew yer'd told her lies?'

Laura hung her head. 'I'm all mouth, Gary, all talk. I could no more look my mam in the face and tell her what I've done, than fly.' She looked up at him. 'You know what Celia's got on me, but yer won't tell me why she can wrap you around her little finger. I think yer should tell me – it's only fair.'

Gary gave a deep sigh. 'Yer might be sorry, babe, it might put yer off me.'

'There's no chance of that, unless yer've murdered someone.' Her eyes widened in alarm as a thought entered her head. 'Yer haven't got a girl into trouble, have yer?'

'Certainly not! What d'yer take me for? No, it's nothing like that.' Gary stared up at the stars, too afraid to look her in the eye as he explained the hold Celia had over him. 'When I left school at fourteen, I got a job in a grocery shop. Celia was a customer there, that's how I came to know her. One day she asked me for what shopping she needed, then when I added it up and told her what she owed, she said she was threepence short, and could she pass it in later. I was green, I'd only been there a few days. The manager was serving someone, and as I believed her, I said it would be all right.' This time the sigh came from his very soul. 'I wish I had me time over again, I'd have acted different. She never came back that afternoon and I was a nervous wreck in case me boss found out.

Then when I came out of the shop and started to walk home, she came up to me. She said she was sorry she hadn't made it in time, but she'd definitely be in, in the morning to pay her debt. "This is for yer trouble," she said, slipping a penny in me pocket. And once again I was a fool to believe her. For that was the start of a nightmare. She came in the next day all right, and gave me her order. It came to one and eleven, and I thought she'd give me the threepence she owed from the day before. But she passed one and six over, saying, "We'll stick to our little arrangement, love, and I'll meet yer outside tonight with your cut".'

'The hard-faced bitch!' Laura was beside herself with temper. 'Why didn't yer just call yer boss over?'

'Because I was fourteen, babe, as green as grass. There was a look in her eyes that told me she'd lie through her teeth, and I'd be the one in trouble. I couldn't afford to get the sack because me mam needed me wages to help out with the bit she got from a cleaning job. Celia certainly knew who to pick on; a fourteen-year-old who was too frightened of not being believed and terrified of facing his mam and saying he'd been sacked.'

'Yer don't still work there, do yer?'

Gary shook his head. 'I'd have left the next week if I'd had a job to walk into, but it took me six months to get out of the shop and out of her clutches. One of the neighbours in our street worked in a ship-repairers down at the docks, and he got me a job as an apprentice. That's where I still work.'

'I can't believe anyone is that wicked. Ye're eighteen now, and ye're saying she still has a hold on yer?'

Gary nodded. 'She's quite brazen about it. If she doesn't get her own way she threatens to go and tell me old boss at the shop that I gave her stuff for half price and took some money off her in return, and she'd also tell the firm I work for now. And there's little I can do because it's my word against hers.'

'I could scratch her eyes out for doing that to yer.' Laura felt like crying for him. 'We've got to get away from her, somehow.'

Gary pulled her close and ran a hand up and down her back. 'I'm sorry about not coming to yer sister's party, babe, honestly. And I'd love to meet yer mam and dad. I give me word that I will meet them in the not-too distant future, and that's a promise.' He ran his fingers through her thick mop of rich, dark hair. 'I'm going to tell yer something I shouldn't, until I'm really sure it's true. But I want to take that sad look off yer pretty face and give yer some hope. I want yer to promise not to ask me any questions, and not to breathe a word to a soul. Will yer do that, babe?'

'Of course I will. I've let a lot of people down in my life, but I would never, ever, let you down. I think too much of yer.'

276

'D'yer remember me saying that Celia would come unstuck one day? Well, if what I've heard tonight is true, that day has arrived. She's come unstuck in a big way. Unfortunately, babe, it might affect your family and there could be hell to play. On the other hand, she might just get away with it, as she's been doing for years. They say the devil looks after his own.' He put a finger on her lips. 'No, don't ask questions because I can't answer them. It'll all come out very soon.'

Chapter Twenty-Two

'Do I look all right, Jenny? They won't laugh at me, will they?'

'Jan, yer look like a million dollars, honest. Yer'll bowl everyone over.'

'I don't want to bowl everyone over.' Janet smiled as though she had a secret and wasn't going to share it. 'Just one or two, perhaps, and I'll be happy.'

Jenny had spent half an hour in the kitchen with her friend, curling her hair with the aid of Laura's curling tongs. There was nobody in the house except her mam and dad, so no one had yet seen the difference the new style had made. They were in the bedroom now and Jenny had just put the finishing touches to it. 'Even if I do say it meself, Jan, I've made a really good job of it. I think I should have taken up hairdressing.' Laughing, she held out her hand. 'That will be one shilling, madam.'

'It's all right for you, Jenny, your hair always looks nice.'

'That's because I look after it, soft girl. And that's what you should do.' Jenny smiled at her friend, who was looking really nervous. 'Come on, everyone's here, they'll wonder what we're doing. After all, it is our party.'

'Yeah.' Janet gave her a big hug. 'We'll always be friends, won't we, Jenny?'

'Of course we will. Now, get going.' Jenny deliberately let Janet go down the stairs before her. She didn't want to spoil her big entrance. The girl walking ahead of her now looked nothing like the girl who had been standing on the step when Jenny had opened the door to her two hours ago. That girl had had her hair parted down the middle with a deep fringe. And although there was a natural curl to it, it hung down to her shoulders looking dull and uncared-for. It was the same style Janet had worn since leaving school – and it didn't do a thing for her appearance. But oh, what a difference now! Her hair had been brushed until it shone before Jenny took the curling tongs to it, bringing out the richness of the colour. And it now looked as if it had been styled by a professional, and was a mass of bouncing curls.

The sound in the room was deafening, as there were half-a-dozen conversations being conducted at top volume from one side of it to

279

the other. The atmosphere was lively, with everyone in the party spirit, when Janet opened the door and stood just inside the room. Nothing happened at first, then slowly the noise died down as all eyes were fixed on the young girl who looked as though she wanted to turn tail and run.

Mary was the first to move. 'Oh, sunshine, don't yer look beautiful! I didn't recognise yer for a minute.'

Every voice was raised in surprise and praise, and Martha and Vincent Porter, sitting next to each other on straight-backed wooden chairs, looked as proud as peacocks. 'By, love, yer look like a flippin' film star,' Martha said with a catch in her throat. 'When yer said Jenny was going to do yer hair, I never expected nothing like this.'

Janet, her courage strengthened by the praise, looked to where Mick and John were standing. Wide-eyed, their mouths agape the boys looked as though they couldn't believe what they were seeing. 'What's the matter with you two, has the cat got yer tongue?' Janet's eyes were dancing with pleasure. 'Don't yer think I look nice?'

John's Adam's apple moved up and down as he swallowed hard. 'I'm trying to think of the words, Janet, but the only ones that spring to mind, are "bobby dazzler".'

'That'll do to be going on with.' Janet turned her attention to Mick. 'You're not usually short of a few hundred words, Mick Moynihan, so what have you got to say?'

'Yer look a real humdinger to me, Janet.'

Bill, standing between Cynthia and Laura, couldn't get over the change in his sister. 'I think yer look a belter, our kid.'

'A little cracker,' was Stan's opinion.

Seamus Moynihan scratched his chin. 'I'm not familiar with any of these new-fangled words, me darlin', so I'll just say yer look as pretty as a picture.'

Jenny stood by the door smiling. She was delighted for her friend. 'Jan, tell them what yer've done today, apart from changing yer hairstyle.'

Jan turned and winked at her before saying, 'I've grown up today. Me mam was always telling me I'd grow up when I was fifteen, so I have. Really, I grew up a few months ago, but I wouldn't like me mam to be wrong, so I waited until today.'

There was a burst of laughter and applause. 'Welcome to the world, girl,' Amy said, before giving her husband a dig in the ribs. 'Go on, slowcoach, tell her how nice she looks.'

Ben raised his eyes to the ceiling, searching for inspiration. Then he sighed. 'This puts me in a bit of a pickle. If I said she looks adorable, which is about the only word that hasn't been used, I'd cop it off you when we got home because I've never said you looked adorable. In me own defence, though, it wasn't that yer never looked adorable, yer understand, but we never used fancy words like that when we were young.'

Amy gave him daggers before saying to Janet, 'D'yer want time to thank him, girl, before I take the poker to him? Huh! Have yer ever heard the likes of it? "Never used fancy words like that when we were young"! What a bleedin' lame excuse that is.'

'Auntie Amy,' Jenny called across, 'we'll have no fighting at my party if yer don't mind. Wait until yer get home.'

'Yeah, okay, girl, I'll do that. I'm better off in me own home when I come to think of it, 'cos I'm used to me own poker. It's all bent, yer see, with me hitting my feller so often, and his head just fits nicely into the bend.'

'Well now, hasn't that just solved a mystery for me?' Seamus shook his head knowingly. 'Haven't I spent many a sleepless night wondering how Ben got that dinge in his head? Sure, I can sleep peacefully now, knowing it was Amy's poker that did it.'

Glasses were replenished and conversations re-started. In another hour the house would be heaving with songs, laughter and dancing. As Molly was heard to say, 'Sure it's a miracle, so it is, what a few bottles of stout will do for yer.'

Jenny and Janet were standing with the boys when Mary came up behind them. 'Are yer going to open yer presents now, so everyone can see what yer got?'

'Where are they, Mam?'

'On the sideboard, sunshine, there's stacks of them.'

'I'll help yer, Jenny,' Mick said. 'I'll open them and you can hold them up for everyone to see.'

'John will help me, won't yer, John?' Janet didn't know there was such a word as coquettish, and even if she did she wouldn't have understood its meaning. But it was the right word to describe the look in her eyes. 'Say yer will, John?'

John was cursing Mick in his head for having stolen Jenny away from him. But when he looked at Janet he realised it was no big deal. It would be a pleasure to help open her presents and see the delight on her face. She was such an easy kid to please. And he'd have Jenny all to himself later, when Mick was singing and they were dancing.

The two girls were like children after Father Christmas has been. They shrieked with delight as each present was unwrapped. And their families and friends had made sure they each got the same gift. Stockings, underskirts, slippers, blouses, and brush and comb sets. There were two presents they particularly liked, but didn't say so for fear of offending. One was the gift off Laura – a tortoiseshell comb, studded with diamond-like stones. This surprised and pleased Jenny so much she felt choked. She hadn't expected anything off her sister. And the last present to be opened had the girls hugging each other

281

in delight. A bottle of Evening In Paris perfume in its famous dark-blue bottle. Well, this showed they really were grown-up now.

There were hugs and kisses all round, and the pleasure on the two pretty faces was enough to lift everyone's heart.

'Clear all the paper away now,' Mary said, 'so we can get on with the party.'

'Me and Janet will take the presents upstairs, Mam, and put them on the bed. Mick and John will clear away, won't yer, fellers?' Jenny got to the door and turned. 'Yer've been good helping us with the presents, thanks.'

'What are yer thanking us for?' Mick asked. 'Yer haven't had our present yet.'

Jenny didn't know how to take this, knowing what jokers the boys were. Then she decided they were having her on. 'Stop acting daft and clear up for us.'

John caught her arm. 'No, Mick's not kidding, we got presents for both of yer.' Still holding on to her tight, he called, 'Mrs Nightingale? Where the heck are yer?'

Mary worked her way round to them. 'What is it, son?'

'They haven't had our presents yet.'

Mary's hand went to her mouth. 'Oh, I'm sorry, boys, I clean forgot with all the running around. I put them in the sideboard cupboard for safety, so Jenny wouldn't see them. I'll get them for yer.'

When Mary came back she was carrying two parcels, and she handed one to each boy. 'I think yer should hand them over yerselves.'

'Which one's which, Mrs Nightingale?' Mick asked. 'We don't want to give the wrong ones.'

Janet dropped her presents on the bottom stair. 'Ooh, isn't it exciting, Jenny? It's the best birthday I ever had.'

Mary looked at the parcels closely. 'That one is for Janet, and this one's Jenny's.'

Amy and Molly had spread the word and the whole gang moved towards the door. 'Go on, girls, open them up.'

Jenny suspected the boys were playing a prank and tried to feel what was inside the parcel. Whatever it was felt hard, and this added to her suspicion. 'You open yours first, Jan.'

Janet didn't need telling twice. She ripped the paper off and was so stunned she couldn't speak. In her hands were a pair of dancing shoes in black patent leather, with a narrow ankle strap and a two-inch heel. Her mouth was moving but no sounds were coming from her.

Jenny looked up to find Mick's eyes on her. 'Go on, Jenny,' he begged. 'Open it up.'

The shoes were the same as Janet's, except for the size, and Jenny was so thrilled she didn't know where to put herself because she felt like bawling her eyes out. She knew she was going to make a fool of herself, so she quickly kissed Mick on the cheek, said, 'I love them,' and fled into the hall. Stepping over Janet's presents she took the stairs two at a time.

When Janet came down to earth it was John she kissed. 'They're the bestest present I've ever had. And when me and Jenny have had a little weep, we'll be down to dance the night away in our new shoes.'

Mary went out to the kitchen to take the cloths off the plates of sandwiches, ready for handing them out, and Stan followed her. 'The girls have done well, haven't they?'

'They certainly have,' Mary smiled. 'They'll be wanting a birthday every week.'

'Our Laura's very quiet.' Stan sneaked one of the sandwiches before leaning against the sink. 'I can't make her out. She's as good-looking as any of them, yet she hasn't got a boyfriend. At least, not one that we know of. Her mate, Cynthia, she seems to be settled with Bill Porter; he can't take his eyes off her.'

'At the moment, Stan, I'm more worried about me dad than I am about anyone else. He should have been here ages ago. He said he was definitely coming and I know he wouldn't miss one of the girls' birthdays unless it was something serious.'

'He might turn up yet, love, it's not that late.'

'I hope so. I do worry about him.'

If Mary had known the real reason for her father's absence, she would have been heartbroken.

Joe Steadman was sitting on the edge of his chair, his elbows on his knees, his hands covering his face. Over the last three years the young woman he'd taken as his wife had humiliated him, shamed him and made him a laughing stock. He was living in a filthy house, slept between sheets that were seldom washed, and wore clothes that were old and shabby. The only decent meal he ever got was when he went to his daughter's, and he seldom had money in his pocket because, as his wife was fond of reminding him, he was an old man who never went anywhere and didn't need good clothes. He'd thought there was nothing more she could do to hurt him, thought it wasn't possible for her to drag him any lower, but how wrong he'd been.

Celia was standing in front of him, her hands planted on her hips, a brazen look on her face and defiance in her eyes. 'Well, haven't yer got anything to say?'

Joe slowly took his hands from his face and forced himself to look at the woman he regretted ever setting eyes on. 'Who's the father?'

Celia's lip curled in scorn. 'You are, of course.'

Joe rolled his hands into a ball. He wasn't a fighting man, had never hit anyone in his life, but right now the urge to knock that sneer off her face was overwhelming. 'I am not yet in my dotage, Celia, so give me the credit of having some intelligence. It is impossible for me to be the father, we both know that. Nor would I want to be. So who is the father?'

'What difference does it make? Yer wouldn't know him if I told yer.'

'Perhaps yer don't know yerself, is that it? Nothing would surprise me about you, Celia, ye're bad through and through.'

'Call me what yer like, it doesn't mean a thing to me. As far as I'm concerned, you are the father of this baby. That's what the neighbours will think, and I can't see yer telling them any different. Nor that precious family of yours. Think how stupid yer'd look if yer told them I had a bun in the oven but yer don't know who put it there?' Celia's smile was unpleasant. 'I'd give anything to see the look on the face of that daughter of yours. My, my, my, how the mighty have fallen.'

'Don't push me too far, Celia, I warn yer. Take that smirk off yer face and sit down. Yer seem to forget this is still my house. Your name was never put on the rent-book, so I'd be in my rights to throw yer out.' He waited until she was seated, then asked, 'The man who is the father, does he want the baby? Yer could always set up house together and we could get a divorce. It would take years, but if the man loves yer he wouldn't mind waiting, I'm sure.'

'Forget it! Ye're not getting rid of me that easy. I'm staying put, whether yer like it or not, so get that through that old head of yours.'

'I wonder why I get the feeling that yer've been very free with yer favours and yer don't know who the father is?' Joe spoke calmly, but inside he was filled with mixed emotions. He was sick in the tummy and worried and angry in his head. 'Well, is that true?'

Celia's hard eyes bored into his. 'You are the father of this baby and I'm sticking to that. If yer tell anyone different, I'll tell them ye're lying because ye're ashamed of fathering a child at your age. I'd get a real kick out of telling yer daughter, and that bleedin' cow next door who looks down her nose every time I see her.'

Joe looked down at his clasped hands. He should be at his granddaughter's birthday party, and he'd been looking forward to it. Instead, fate had dealt him a blow he couldn't see any way out of. Mary and her family were all he had in life, and he'd let them down. If he didn't go along with Celia's story, he'd bring more trouble to their door. Because not for one second did he doubt that his wife would carry out her threats, and take great delight in doing so. The woman he'd married was capable of great wickedness.

284

Joe pushed himself out of the chair. 'I'm going for a pint and a breath of fresh air. The air in here is putrid.'

Celia knew she'd won, but then she'd never had any doubt. Still, she wasn't satisfied with hurting him, she had to turn the screw tighter. 'What, are yer not going to yer granddaughter's birthday party? I would have thought yer'd like to celebrate with yer mates. It's not every day yer find out ye're become a father.'

Joe looked down at her. 'D'yer know, I feel sorry for the baby. Boy or girl, it's going to have a lousy start in life.' With that he turned on his heel and left, to go down to the pub on the corner. He found a quiet alcove, and with a pint in front of him, he tried to sort out his thoughts. He'd have to go down to Mary's tomorrow, he couldn't let Jenny's birthday go without a word. Besides, he had a present for her and was dying to see her face when he gave her a necklace that matched the bracelet he'd given her for Christmas.

Joe picked up his glass and drank deeply. That would be one solution, to get drunk and forget what he'd been told in the last hour. But although the prospect was appealing, it wasn't the answer. He'd be sober tomorrow with the problems still facing him. Better to sit quietly and get things sorted in his mind now. He had two choices. He could tell Mary and the family, and his neighbours, that he and Celia were expecting a baby, and leave it at that. He'd be embarrassed at his age to admit to it, but it would keep his wife quiet. Or he could tell the truth. That he and his wife hadn't been on intimate terms for eighteen months, so the baby couldn't possibly be his. And let Celia do her damnedest.

When he left the pub, Joe's mind was still in a daze. He didn't know what to do for the best. The best for his family, not for Celia. So he went home to bed, to lie staring at the ceiling for hours while asking God to help him do the right thing.

Celia didn't come home all night, but he no longer cared.

'Grandad's just passed the window, Mam.' Jenny shot out of her chair. 'I'll open the door for him.'

'Good, he's just in time, I'm dishing the dinner out.' Mary was wiping her hands on a towel when she came through to the living room. She grinned when she saw Joe being hugged by Jenny, with Laura waiting for her turn. 'Yer've got a good sense of smell, Dad, the dinner's ready.'

'I could smell it from the top of the street.' Joe smiled as Laura let go of him and Mary's arms came around his neck. 'I felt like one of the Bisto Kids, with me nose following the smell.'

'Where did yer get to last night? Yer had us worried to death.'

'I knew yer would be, sweetheart, but there was no way of letting yer know.' Joe felt the lie sticking in his throat. But what else could he do with the two girls there? 'The boss asked me to stay on until four, to get a job finished. By the time I got home I was whacked.'

Jenny's squeal brought Mary spinning round. 'I don't believe it! I don't believe it! Look, Mam, what Grandad bought me.' Jenny was holding up the necklace and her face couldn't have been happier. 'Yer've got to be the most wonderful grandad in the whole world, and I love you, I love you, I love you!'

Laura held out her hand for a better view. 'I'll be borrowing this.'

Jenny didn't answer at once, then she said, 'Yeah, okay, yer can borrow it if yer take good care of it.'

Mary clapped her hands as she bustled out to the kitchen. 'Come on, set the table before the dinners go cold. Give yer dad a shout, Jenny, he's down the yard.'

Joe was struggling to get his dinner down, for he had no appetite. And Mary watched him anxiously. He looked dreadful, really tired and worn out. But what could you expect when he was working such long hours? He should be letting up a bit now, instead of working all the hours God sends. It wasn't as though yer could see where the money was going; he never looked as smart as he used to. When her mam was alive, she always made sure he was well turned out. Always a pure white collar and shirt, neatly tied tie, shoes so highly polished you could see your face in them, and the creases in his trousers always ironed to perfection. But then her mam had idolised him. She'd have worked her fingers to the bone for him if it had been necessary. What a far cry from the woman he was married to now.

'I couldn't eat any more, sweetheart, I'm bloated.' Joe put his knife and fork down and pushed the plate away. 'I had a lie-in and it's not long since I had me breakfast.'

'That's all right, Dad, at least yer've eaten half of it.' Mary smiled at her daughters who had polished their dinners off in no time. 'Yer dad's nearly finished, so be a pair of angels and start taking the dishes out.'

'We'll wash them for yer, Mam,' Jenny said, touching the necklace which was now her proudest possession. 'I'll wash and our Laura can dry.'

'Come on, Joe, sit yerself by the fire,' Stan said, taking the Sunday paper off the seat of the fireside chair. He couldn't put his finger on it, but there was something not quite right about his father-in-law. He reminded Stan of a little lad who'd broken a neighbour's window playing footie and was terrified of telling his mam. 'Let's leave the work to the women.'

Mary watched with interest as Laura helped clear the table before standing by the side of the sink to dry the dishes as Jenny washed them. That's a change, she thought, not a murmur out of her. And Jenny was doing her best to improve relations between the two of them. Look how she'd offered to lend Laura her new necklace; not many girls would do that for a sister who barely passed her the time of day. That was definitely extending a hand of friendship. I'm not going to knock it either, Mary thought. I just hope it lasts. She cocked her ears when she heard her husband talking to her father.

'How's life treating yer, Joe?' Stan asked. 'Everything okay?'

'Just so-so, Stan, same as everybody else. We all have to muddle along as best we can, I suppose.'

Laura came through rolling her sleeves down. 'I'm going to Cynthia's, Mam, and I might stay there for me tea.'

'She's not seeing Bill, then?'

'No, not tonight. We're having a game of cards with her mam and dad.'

Jenny's head appeared over her sister's shoulder. 'I'm going to Jan's. I promised to comb her hair for her before we take our presents over to Auntie Lizzie. She didn't want to come to the party but she said she'd love to see what we got.'

'Are the boys going, or don't I need to ask?'

'Yeah, they said they were. And I better warn yer, Mam, they're coming to see yer one night to ask if they can take me and Janet to a dance. It's not a big dance hall, just a little place belonging to a church.'

'Do yer want to go?' Stan asked, trying to hide a smile at his daughter's naivety. 'It's no good me and yer mam wasting time spending hours in discussion over this serious matter if yer don't want to go.'

'Oh yes, Dad, I'm dying to go. Especially as I've got those lovely shiny dancing shoes. I've been walking up and down me bedroom in them, to get used to the high heels. I don't want to fall flat on me face in them, do I? Not if I'm dancing with Mick or John, 'cos I'd never hear the end of it. And yer know they'd both take good care of us.'

'Don't worry, sunshine,' Mary laughed. 'Yer wouldn't be allowed to go with them if I wasn't sure about that. I have complete trust in both those lads.'

They could hear Jenny humming as she ran up the stairs, then her voice saying, 'Wait for me, Laura, I'll walk out with yer.'

Joe's nerves were taut; he couldn't sit still. He clasped and unclasped his hands, ran his fingers through his hair and fidgeted with the buttons on his cardi. He'd get it off his chest as soon as the girls went out. He couldn't stand the strain much longer or he'd crack.

Laura gave him a kiss. 'Ta-ra, Grandad. Yer'll be gone by the time I get in, so I'll see yer through the week.'

Jenny kissed him as well, even though she said, 'I'll see yer later,

Grandad, 'cos I'm coming home for me tea.'

Mary and Stan watched the two girls pass the window and smiled when they saw Jenny talking to her sister. Her face was animated and the words were pouring from her mouth fifteen to the dozen. It was a rare sight, but a very welcome one.

'Jenny loves her present, Joe,' Stan said. 'Yer couldn't have chosen anything better.'

'I'm lucky – one of me mates in work has a daughter roughly the same age. It was his wife's idea to get the bracelets at Christmas, and as they went down a treat I asked if she'd help me out again.'

'Are you feeling all right, Dad?' The more Mary looked into her father's face, the more concerned she became. 'Yer don't look yerself today and I think ye're working too hard. Cut down on the overtime – I'm sure there's plenty of fellers would be glad of it. Don't forget, ye're not getting any younger.'

Now is the right time, Joe thought, curling his fists and digging his nails into his palms until he could feel the pain. And with the pain came the courage to speak the words which would devastate his daughter. 'Celia's expecting a baby.'

Mary gripped the narrow wooden arms of her chair and pressed until the skin on her knuckles was stretched to show blue veins standing out in stark relief. She felt as though her heart had stopped beating, and the room was starting to spin around. No, it's not true, a voice in her head kept repeating. My dad wouldn't do that to us! I'm older than his wife, for God's sake, and he's got grown-up granddaughters! We'd all be a laughing stock! And how would she tell the girls? She couldn't, she'd die of shame.

Then Mary looked at her father's face, and the pain etched there. And all thoughts of shame vanished. He looked like an old man who had the troubles of the world on his shoulders. He was her father, she loved him dearly, and he needed her now more than he'd ever needed her. She left her chair to kneel before him and they wrapped their arms around each other. With tears streaming down her face, she sobbed, 'I'm sorry, Dad, I really am, but I've got to be truthful and tell yer I'm not happy about it.'

There were tears in Joe's eyes as he stroked her hair. 'I didn't expect yer to be, sweetheart. I didn't want it meself, but these things happen.'

Stan had had time to recover from the shock, and looking at his father-in-law, he felt heartily sorry for him. He was too old to be starting a new family, especially as his wife couldn't look after him, never mind a new baby. But as Joe said, these things happen and you couldn't do anything about it. It was sad, though, because the old man looked anything but overjoyed about the situation himself.

'Come and sit down, love. It's no good crying, it doesn't solve anything.' Stan cupped his wife's elbows and raised her up. 'What's done is done, and nothing can change things.'

Mary ran the back of her hands across her eyes. 'I'm sorry for upsetting yer, Dad, but I don't think it's right and there's no use pretending otherwise. And I've got to speak me mind. Apart from yer being too old to start again with all the work a baby brings, that wife of yours is not fit to be a mother. The child will never get the love and care it needs.'

Joe felt like blurting the truth out, but knew the consequences would bring more hurt than his daughter was feeling now. Because anger would take over all the other emotions and she'd want to have it out with Celia. And Joe would die rather than see his beloved daughter getting into a fight with a woman who wouldn't fight fair. She was good at biting and scratching was his wife, as he knew from experience. So he had to stick with the lies and the pretence. 'I've had words with Celia, and there's going to be a lot of changes. I'm going to come down hard on her if there isn't.'

Mary sighed, thinking, Aye – and pigs might fly. 'And how d'yer think I'm going to tell the girls, Dad? I don't think I could.'

'Don't tell them yet, sweetheart, it's still early days.' Joe was certain his wife was pregnant, she wouldn't make up a tale like that. But he was hoping against hope that whoever the father was would turn up and take her off his hands. 'And don't forget, I've got to face them, too.'

Stan got to his feet. 'I'll stick the kettle on, we could all do with a cuppa.' And in his mind he added, 'especially Joe.' His father-in-law looked as though he would like nothing better than to curl up and die, leaving his pain and worries behind him.

Jenny steadied herself by holding on to the walls on either side as she tottered along the hall of Lizzie's house in her two-inch heels. Giggling as she went, she called back over her shoulder, 'I can't even walk in them, never mind dance.'

She opened the door to see two beaming, happy faces. 'Yer'll be all right when ye're dancing, Jenny,' Mick said, ' 'cos I'll be keeping tight hold of yer.'

Cheeky beggar, John thought. He's always got to get in first. 'And when he's not, I'll be holding yer tight, Jenny.'

'Close the door after yerselves.' Jenny tried the journey back with just one hand on the wall, and when she reached the living-room door she became daring and walked into the room unaided. 'See, Jan, it's easy when yer know how.' She held her arms slightly away from her body, and much to the amusement of the two boys, swayed over to Auntie Lizzie like a mannequin. 'D'yer think I'll get a feller, Auntie Lizzie?'

289

The old lady laughed. 'Yer've already got two, how many more d'yer want?'

'No, I've got two mates. I mean a feller of me own. Yer know, like a boyfriend.'

'I'll be yer boyfriend, Jenny,' Mick said. 'I'd be honoured if yer'd have me.'

'And me.' John gave his mate a look to kill. 'I'll be yer boyfriend and I'd be more honoured than Mick would be. He's not very good at being honoured.'

'Excuse me,' Janet said huffily, 'I'd like a boyfriend, too.'

John grinned at her. 'Hello, curly top. I see Jenny's been busy with yer hair again. It doesn't half suit yer.'

'Ooh, er, I've come down in the world, haven't I? I was a bobby dazzler last night, Auntie Lizzie, and now I'm just curly top.'

'Ye're still a bobby dazzler, Janet.' Mick put a finger in one of her curls and smiled when he let go and it bounced back into place. 'And a humdinger.'

Mollified, Janet said, 'I'll let yer off. Anyway, we've shown Auntie Lizzie all our presents, and we're agreed that the shoes were our best present. Except that Jenny's a lucky beggar, she's got two best presents.'

Jenny put her fingers under the necklace and lifted it from her neck. 'Me grandad gave me this, isn't it gorgeous?'

She was fifteen now and Mick was in for the kill. 'It's not half as gorgeous as you.'

John, whose thoughts were running on the same track, was right behind him. 'You put it in the shade, Jenny.'

Jenny stamped her foot. 'Will you two stop acting the goat? If we're going to the dance with yer on Wednesday, I don't want everyone thinking we're raw beginners. So will yer behave yerselves for once, and teach us a few steps?'

'Did yer mam say yer could come with us?' Both boys spoke as one, then turned to grin at each other. Rivalry hadn't spoilt their friendship or their sense of humour. 'That's the gear!'

'Me mam hasn't said I can, but she will when yer ask her.' Jenny raised her brows in a haughty expression. Indeed, with her beautiful necklace and bracelet, and such posh dancing shoes, she was feeling haughty. 'As long as yer ask politely.'

'The boys are always polite, Jenny,' Lizzie said. 'I've never known them to be anything else but polite.'

Jenny turned her head to look at the old lady, and her wink was so broad her whole cheek moved upwards. And there was a mischievous twinkle in her eyes. 'Yes, they are always polite, Auntie Lizzie, when they're not acting the fool. But if me and Janet have got to act like grown-ups now, then these two have, as well.'

'Oh, I am grown-up, Jenny,' Mick said, his dimples beginning to deepen. 'In fact, everyone says I'm old for me age.'

This set Janet thinking. 'How can yer be old for yer age? I mean, like, if I'm fifteen then I'm fifteen, I can't be any older. Same as if I was twenty, I couldn't say I was fifteen.'

'Yer could say yer were young for yer age.' John thought she was hilarious. She reminded him of his mam, but whereas his mam knew she was funny and made the most of it, Janet didn't. 'One of my mates in work is twenty, and he's young for his age.'

'Then he's telling fibs, isn't he?' Janet poked a finger in his chest, her face really serious. 'You should tell him it's a sin to tell lies.'

John took her finger and kissed it. 'D'yer know, Janet, I don't know half the time whether ye're having us on or not. But whatever, yer look very pretty when ye're doing it.'

Jenny giggled. Her friend hadn't stayed grown-up very long. But John was right, she did look very pretty. 'When ye're ready, will one of yer teach me how to dance.'

Mick was by her side in a trice. He picked up her hands, put one on his shoulder and gripped the other. 'Here I am, Jenny – ready, willing and able. Auntie Lizzie can watch and give us points on our performance.'

'Ooh, er,' said Janet, 'yer better dance good, John, so *we* get some points. Don't be relying on me 'cos I'm only a learner.'

Lizzie smiled. Janet might be a learner when it came to dancing, but she had her head screwed on the right way. Although John didn't know it, he was being wooed. Would he succumb, or would his heart stay with Jenny?

Mick sang *Girl of My Dreams* as he took Jenny slowly through the steps. He thought the song was very appropriate because she was, and always would be, the girl of his dreams. To John, the dance was more fun than anything. Every time he looked at Janet's face he doubled up and missed a step. She looked so serious, with her tongue peeping out of the side of her mouth. And when he did miss a step, she'd say, 'Never you mind, John, even I make a mistake sometimes.'

Lizzie awarded the girls ten points each. In her head, Jenny's points were for her ability to learn quickly, and Janet's for her novel way of catching a boy without him knowing.

Chapter Twenty-Three

'I'm all on edge, Mam – me tummy's doing somersaults.' Jenny was pushing a potato around her plate. Her appetite had deserted her tonight, she was far too excited to eat. After all, going to her first dance was a big event in a girl's life. 'I hope me dress doesn't look out of place.'

'Of course it won't, sunshine, yer'll be fine,' Mary assured her. 'Yer'll be with Janet, and her dress is no nicer than yours, is it?'

Laura glanced sideways at her sister. 'It's not a proper dance, yer know.' There was no malice or sarcasm in her voice, as Mary was quick to note – perhaps just a trace of impatience. 'They won't be all dolled up.'

'It's still a dance, though, isn't it?' Jenny said firmly. She wasn't going to let anybody dampen her expectations. 'I mean, it's no use taking our dancing shoes if we're going to spend the night sitting down.'

'It's only a fourpenny hop,' Laura said. 'There won't be a band there, yer dance to gramophone records. It's where beginners go to learn, before they go on to the big dance halls.'

'Oh well, we'll be in good company, won't we? If I fall flat on me face there'll probably be half-a-dozen people stretched out beside me.'

Stan chuckled. 'I learned to dance at a church hop, but it was only tuppence in those days. I can laugh now when I look back, but we didn't half enjoy ourselves. Me and me mate, Ginger Lunt, we really thought we were the bees-knees. We used to swagger down the street with our dance shoes tucked under our arm, without a care in the world. We were seventeen when we went on to the Grafton, and I can tell yer that what we learned at that tuppenny hop stood us in good stead; we could hold our own with anyone.'

Both girls listened with interest. Their dad had never told them he went dancing, and they'd never heard of Ginger Lunt. 'Go on, tell us some more, Dad,' Jenny asked eagerly. 'What happened to yer mate, Ginger?'

'The same as happened to me, love. We were eighteen when we went to the Grafton one night, and I saw this blonde girl dancing with some feller. And could she dance? I'll say she could. It was an "excuse me" quickstep, so I did no more than pinch her off her partner. But she got her own back on me, 'cos she pinched something of mine.' Stan stretched his hand to cover his wife's smaller one. 'Her name was Mary Steadman and she stole my heart.'

Jenny's eyes were bright. 'Oh Dad, that's a lovely story. So romantic! But what happened to Ginger?'

Laura didn't speak, but she was feeling emotional. Gary was eighteen, and she knew he'd fallen for her, like she'd fallen hook, line and sinker for him. Why couldn't they be like her mam and dad? The answer to that was easy: her name was Celia.

'Ginger met a girl the same night; she was called Nancy. We went out as a foursome for a couple of weeks, then we started courting seriously. I wanted yer mam all to meself, yer see, 'cos I loved her so much, and still do.'

Jenny's eyes were moist with tears. 'I hope I find someone who loves me as much as you love me mam.' She turned to her mother and was surprised to see she looked sad. 'What's the matter, Mam, are yer not feeling well? I've noticed yer've not been yerself for a few days. Are yer sickening for something?'

Laura pricked her ears, remembering Gary saying the bubble had burst for Celia, and her family could be involved. There'd been no hint of trouble, but her mam had been quiet and that wasn't like her. She was always happy and joking.

'I'm all right, sunshine – a touch of the blues, that's all. It'll wear off in a day or two, you'll see.' Mary looked at the clock and raised her brows. 'Hadn't yer better start getting yerself ready? It's a special night tonight, yer want to look yer best.'

When Jenny had hot-footed it from the room, Laura said, 'I'm not going out, so I'll wash the dishes for yer. You sit down and rest, Mam, if ye're feeling off-colour.'

'Thanks, sunshine, I'll do that.' Mary hadn't slept well for the last three nights. Even when she did manage to drop off for half an hour, she tossed and turned restlessly. Her father's news had devastated her and she couldn't see her life ever being normal again.

Mick and John looked so happy walking down the street with Jenny between them, anyone would believe they'd come up on the pools. They didn't do the pools, mind, but if they did, and they'd won, they couldn't have looked happier. John carried her dancing shoes so she could link them, and you'd have thought he was carrying the crown jewels.

'Yer look nice, Jenny, and yer smell lovely,' Mick said. 'Yer smell like a rose garden.'

'Yeah, yer do, Jenny, but I think the smell is more like sweet-peas.'

'It's Evening In Paris perfume, I'll have you know.' Jenny tossed her head, sending her blonde hair swishing around her cheeks. 'I put a dab behind each ear, and a tiny little dab on me throat. It's only a little bottle and I don't want to use it up too quick, 'cos one of the women in the office said it's quite expensve.'

'We thought about that, didn't we, Mick?' asked John, whose head the thought had never entered. But Bill Porter wasn't going to go one better than them, even if he did seem to be out of the scene just now. 'Didn't I say "Shall we buy her Evening In Paris?".'

'Yer certainly did, pal! And we were in two minds about it, as well. But after much consideration, we decided Jenny would rather have the dance shoes.'

'You are two of the biggest fibbers in the world.' Jenny giggled and squeezed their arms. 'But if I'd been asked, I would have chosen the shoes.'

Martha Porter answered their knock and her eyes went to the heavens as she said, 'Yer'd better come in, there's been a slight mishap.'

'Is Janet all right?' Jenny asked, mounting the steps. 'She's not done anything silly like catching a cold, has she?'

The smell that met them as they crowded into the hallway was sickly and overpowering. They sniffed up and looked at each other, but no one liked to comment for fear of upsetting Mrs Porter. Janet's mother, however, was forthcoming. 'That smell ye're all afraid to mention is half a bleedin' bottle of Evening In Paris, if yer don't mind. The silly cow doused herself in it and it's stinking the ruddy house down. She couldn't go out like that, they'd smell her a mile away.'

John tried his hardest but he couldn't keep the laughter back. Mick joined him, and then Martha began to see the funny side. Only Jenny managed to keep a straight face. She wasn't going to have a laugh at her best friend's expense.

'Can't she just wash it off, Mrs Porter? The smell would go away then.'

'Where did yer put yours, Jenny?' Martha asked with an amused expression on her face. 'A dab behind the ears, was it?'

Thinking she was helping her friend, Jenny said, 'And a dab on me neck, Mrs Porter. I bet Jan's been a bit heavy with it, that's all.'

'Ah, but my daughter didn't put it on her skin, girl, she put it on her dress. Half a bottle of the bleedin' stuff. She's upstairs now changing her clothes so people won't be fainting all around her. Honest to God, she ponged to high heaven. I had to open the kitchen door to let some fresh air in.'

They all looked up when they heard footsteps on the stairs. And down came Janet, looking so woebegone they all felt sorry for her. 'My mam did the same thing once, curly top,' John said, in an effort

295

to put a smile back on her face. 'Only she couldn't afford an expensive scent so she used Essence of Violets. And yer know me mam, she wouldn't wash it off for anyone. She said she wasn't pouring good money down the plug-hole, and if me dad didn't like it, he could go and sit in Annie Baxter's for a few hours. Well, me dad preferred the smell to sitting in Annie Baxter's.'

'I was stupid,' Janet said, 'and ye're all late now because of me.'

'Who cares?' John asked, while his head was asking him why she always appealed to his soft side. 'We'll be there before the interval.'

'Come on, Jan,' Jenny said, 'yer'll have forgotten all about it once yer get on the dance floor. Yer'll be too busy trying to stop these two from standing all over yer feet.'

'Yeah, come on.' Mick thought the words would choke him, but he managed to get them out. 'I bags the first dance with yer.'

When John said, 'I bags the second,' Janet cheered up considerably and donned her coat. What was the use of worrying about a bottle of scent anyway? She could always get round their Bill to buy her another.

The boys had agreed beforehand to swap partners for every dance. That was the fairest way and would save any arguments. So although it broke his heart, Mick gave way to John when he asked Jenny to dance. And while he was steering Janet around the dance floor, his eyes spent more time watching what John was up to, than they did watching Janet's feet. It was only when the dance was over it struck him that she hadn't done badly at all. 'Yer did well, there, Janet, I'm proud of yer.'

The girl preened. 'Thank you, Mick, and you did well, too.'

Mick looked at her closely to see if she was having him on, but her face was that of an innocent baby. He was an experienced dancer, but she'd managed to reduce him to the status of a beginner. And she'd done it in such a way you couldn't fall out with her.

When the other couple came off the floor, John had his arm across Jenny's shoulder and they were laughing up at each other. This was enough to send Mick's temperature shooting up to boiling point. Just wait, John Hanley, he said to himself, from now on it's no holds barred. Every man for himself and the devil take the hindmost.

After turning the record over and winding up the gramophone, the MC announced a slow waltz. Mick was highly delighted. 'This is you and me, Jenny, and as ye're pretty good at waltzing, we can dance proper.' With a cheeky grin at his friend, he led Jenny on to the dance floor and put his arm around her waist. If this wasn't heaven, it was the nearest he'd ever been to it. 'Just relax, Jenny, and yer'll follow me easy.'

'Ye're not half holding me tight, Mick. I can't see a thing only your chest.'

'If you concentrate on the dancing, I'll give yer a running commentary.' Mick looked down at the top of her blonde head and had to stop himself from planting a kiss on it. He knew she'd clock him one if he did, and besides his mother's words were ringing in his ears. 'Don't yer forget, me darlin', the girl's only fifteen and you're nearly nineteen.' He sighed, wondering how long he was supposed to wait. Hadn't he been wishing his life away for the last ten years?

Jenny pulled herself back and stared up at him. 'I don't think much of yer commentary, Mick Moynihan, yer haven't opened yer mouth yet. There must be something going on, or has everyone gone home?'

Mick grinned and pulled her towards him. 'Well, let's see. John has got hold of Janet's hand and is walking her on to the dance floor. Yes, he's holding her properly and I don't see her complaining. Ay, hang on a minute! He's just kissed her, right in the middle of the floor. Well, that's cheek for yer.'

Jenny jerked herself away and gazed around the dancing couples until she spotted her friend. 'Ye're a lying hound, Mick Moynihan. I've a good mind to tell them.'

'It was wishful thinking, Jenny. Yer know me and John do everything together, and I thought if he'd kissed Janet it was only natural for me to kiss you.'

'You just try it, Mick Moynihan, and yer'll be sorry yer signed.' Jenny went back to staring at his chest so he wouldn't see her eyes dancing with merriment. 'The very idea, indeed.'

'Well, are yer at least prepared to discuss our relationship? That wouldn't do yer no harm, just talking.'

'Our relationship? Well, we're good mates, aren't we?'

'That's what I'm getting at, Jenny.' By this time Mick had given up trying to dance and was walking Jenny around the floor. Still holding her close, though. 'Yer told Auntie Lizzie that yer were looking for a boyfriend, and as I haven't got a girlfriend I thought yer might like to team up with me.'

'Are yer asking me for a date, Mick?'

Mick sighed with relief. After going all around the world, and nearly having a heart attack, Jenny had said the words for him. 'Yes, Jenny, I'm asking yer for a date. Will yer come out with me one night?'

'What about yer mate? I thought you and John went everywhere together.'

'Yer've got eyes in yer head, Jenny, and yer know that me and John both feel the same about yer. We've been rivals for years, even though we're the best of pals. But the time has come, for me at least, to put me claim in before someone else comes along. It's up to John to decide what he wants to do. If he asks yer, and yer would rather have him, then that's the way it is. Me and him will always be pals, no matter what.'

Jenny lapsed into thought. There was no way she would choose between the two boys; it wouldn't be fair. It would ruin their friendship no matter what they thought now. And she didn't want to be the cause of that, even though her heart lay with one of them – and always had. She heard John's familiar laugh and turned her head to see him acting the goat with fancy footwork, and Janet was lapping it up.

'Mick, shall I ask me mam if we can go to the pictures one night as a foursome? I've never had a boyfriend, never even been out with a boy. And I think I should get out and about a bit before I say I'll be someone's girlfriend. Don't yer agree?'

'Yeah, I suppose ye're right.' Mick was disappointed, but at least he'd made a start, put his cards on the table. 'But don't forget, I've got a lot to offer.'

'What have yer got to offer, Mick?'

Mick's dimples appeared. 'Meself, for a kick-off. And I know self-praise is no recommendation, but yer'll not get anyone better. Then there's me mam and dad, they're definitely an asset. Oh, and I almost forgot, there's next door's cat.'

Jenny giggled. 'Mick Moynihan, ye're as daft as a brush.'

'Don't tell yer mam that, or she won't let yer come to the pictures with us.'

'Come on, girl, out with it. What's wrong with yer?' There was concern on Amy's face as she sat across from her friend. 'For the past few days yer've had a face on yer like a wet week. It's a wonder the bleedin' milk isn't curdled.'

Mary sighed. She'd kept her worry bottled up inside her until it was nearly choking her. If she didn't tell someone and get it off her chest, she'd go nuts. And who better to confide in than her best mate? 'Not a word leaves this room, sunshine, okay?'

Amy stiffened a finger and made a cross on her chest. 'Cross my heart and hope to die, if this day I tell a lie.' Hoping to lighten the gloom, she asked, 'Yer haven't got yerself a fancy man, have yer?'

'I'm sorry, Amy, but I haven't got a laugh left in me. I'm drained. I can't eat or sleep, or even think straight.' She came straight to the point. 'Celia's expecting a baby.'

Amy's jaw dropped and she sagged back against the chair. 'Yer what! Christ, girl, yer've got to be joking.'

'I wish I was. I wish to God I was.'

'What's the man thinking of? Has he lost the run of his senses?

Blimey, girl, he must be sixty! And he's got a slut of a wife!' Amy's eyes narrowed. 'Is he sure he's the father? I wouldn't put anything past that one; she's a real trollop if ever there was one.'

'Me dad's not that soft, he'd know if it wasn't his. He's not happy about it, yer can tell, but as he said, what's done is done. He looks terrible and I feel heartily sorry for him. I'm afraid I told him what I thought, and I'm sorry now. He's got enough on his plate without me turning against him.'

'You'd never turn against yer dad, girl, and he knows it. But he couldn't expect yer to welcome news like that, not from a man of his age.'

'Well, he didn't come last night and Wednesday's his usual night to call. I must have really upset him and I'm worried sick.'

'What does Stan have to say about all this?'

'He's not said much because he knows how bad I feel about it. His feelings are that it's done and we can't do anything about it.'

'Do the girls know?'

Mary shook her head. 'I couldn't tell them, I'd be too ashamed. How could I explain that to two young girls? If it was me expecting I'd be too embarrassed to tell them, never mind their grandad. They'll have to know sometime, but me dad said not to say anything to them yet. I think he's dreading the thought of facing them. And I'm such a coward, Amy, I'd rather they never had to know.'

Amy's huge bosom rose and fell as she let out a deep sigh. 'I'm sorry for yer dad, 'cos I think the world of him. But I've got to say, girl, I think he's been a stupid old bugger. Yer'd think, at his age, he'd be past that sort of thing now.'

'Yeah, but don't forget he's got a young wife.' Mary picked nervously at the plush of the chenille tablecloth. 'Whatever I think, I've got to stand by me dad 'cos I love the bones of him. He's been hurt enough, I'll not add to that hurt. So even if it kills me, I'll not upset him any more. But one thing I'm determined on, I'll never visit that house while she's in it, baby or no baby.'

'I dunno, girl, life can be a bugger, can't it? But I know how yer feel about telling the girls because I couldn't tell my kids if I was in your shoes.' Amy stretched her chubby arm across the table and patted her best mate's hand. 'The world keeps on turning, girl, and yer can't stop it. It won't do no good sitting in the house feeling miserable. So come on, get yer coat on and let's get down to the shops. The fresh air will blow the cobwebs away and yer'll feel better. And don't faint when I say the cream slices are on me today.'

Celia was waiting for her as usual. Leaning against the wall, cigarette smouldering between her fingers, she studied Laura's face. 'Ye're a

299

bit late tonight, kid, I was getting worried. I thought there might be trouble at home.'

Laura was in a fighting mood. Last night, when John and Mick had brought her sister home, they'd been full of how much they'd enjoyed themselves. And because of this woman, she wasn't able to bring her boyfriend home. Well, something had to be done about it, she'd had enough. 'I can be late if I want, can't I? And why should there be trouble at home?'

'All right, keep yer hair on, I only asked.' Celia blew the cigarette smoke straight into Laura's face. 'I worry about yer, yer see.'

'Yer must have better things to do than worry about me, Celia. Yer see, I'm quite capable of looking after meself.'

Gary came through the double doors of the dance hall and heard Laura's words. He hesitated just for a second, then walked towards her. 'Come on, babe, don't be standing here nattering when we could be dancing.'

Laura couldn't help her face lighting up when she saw him. 'I'll just stick me coat in the cloakroom, I won't be a tick.'

Putting her cloakroom ticket in her bag, she passed Celia without a glance. One wrong word out of her grandad's wife, and she knew she'd clock her one. So she walked through the doors and into Gary's arms. 'I'll kill her one of these days, Gary, I really will. Who the hell does she think she is?'

Gary put a finger to his lips. 'Yer never know who she's got listening out for her.' He waited for her to put her bag under a chair, then pulled her on to the dance floor. 'Come on, babe, it seems like an eternity since I had me arms around yer.'

'I'm not putting up with it any longer, Gary. I've had a bellyful of this once-a-week lark. Me kid sister can bring her boyfriend home, but not me. So I'm telling yer straight – either yer start taking me out proper, or I'm not coming here any more. And I mean it.'

'Yer might not have to put up with it any longer, babe. I think our Celia has overstepped the mark this time. She's confident she'll get away with it, but I can't see it meself.' His bright blue eyes met her deep brown ones. 'Has there been anything out of the ordinary happened at your house? Any news of anything?'

Laura looked puzzled. 'What's going on? Celia said something about trouble at home, but there's been nothing that I know of.'

'I think you and I are going to have to have a very serious talk tonight.' Gary put his cheek next to hers. 'I want to be yer proper boyfriend. I want to take yer home to meet me mam, and I want to meet your folks. I want to sit on the back row of the pictures with yer, go on the ferry to New Brighton – all the things courting couples do. And I think that between us we can make it happen. All it will take is our sticking together, come what may, and having the guts to

300

tell her to her face to get off our backs. We can turn the tables now, because we've really got something on her.'

'I'll do anything if it means we can see each other as often as we like – but what have we got on her?'

'When Celia and Charlie do their disappearing act, we'll go outside and I'll tell yer what I know. We'll see what yer think, and take it from there.'

They walked a little way from the dance hall so they couldn't be seen or heard, and stood against a wall. Laura shivered. 'I should have got me coat out of the cloakroom, I'm freezing.'

Gary slipped off his navy-blue jacket and draped it across her shoulders. 'That'll keep yer nice and warm.'

Laura snuggled into the jacket and grinned up at him. 'I've never been as close to yer as I am now.' She sniffed up. 'I can even smell yer on it. I think I'll take it home with me so I'll always feel ye're near me.'

'Yer'll be sick of the sight of me pretty soon, if all goes to plan. I'll be knocking on yer door every night.'

'Yer seem very sure of yerself tonight, Gary, and very secretive. What is it that yer've found out about Celia? I hope it's something really bad, so we can tell her to go and jump in the Mersey.'

'She's expecting a baby.'

Laura screwed up her eyes as a dozen thoughts came into her head. And with the thoughts came a picture of her grandad's face. 'Are yer sure?'

'I got it right from the horse's mouth, babe. Celia and Charlie told me themselves. I think I was happier than they were.'

'I don't get it! What's it got to do with Charlie?'

'Well, it's his baby, isn't it? But she was laughing her head off when she said her husband has agreed to let everyone think it's his. She called him all the fools going. But she still never mentioned anything about her husband being yer grandad. Even Charlie hasn't got a clue about that. They're both in for a rude awakening. I can't wait to see their faces when we tell them we'll blow them up if Celia doesn't leave us alone.'

'Maybe I'm thick, Gary, but I don't get it.' Laura's temper was rising. 'D'yer mean yer expect me to let her get away with pulling a stunt like that on me grandad? If yer do, then you're in for a rude awakening, too! I love me grandad, and I'll not go along with her lies just to get me and you off the hook. If I did that I'd be worse than she is – nothing more than a scheming, brazen, lying bitch.'

'What else can we do, babe? If we tell yer grandad, then Celia will get her own back by telling all sorts of lies about us. What we did would be magnified a thousand times to my mam and your family.'

301

Laura dropped her head. She'd got herself into this mess for the sake of one lousy underskirt. But she knew Gary was right. When Celia told her tale, it wouldn't be just about an underskirt; she'd add a lot more on to it. Like her smoking, even though she'd only ever had that one cigarette. And that she'd lied about going to the dance with Cynthia.

'I'll have to have time to think it over, Gary. After all, it's not your grandad she's lied to and cheated, it's mine. He's a lovely, gentle man, and he doesn't deserve what she's doing to him. If yer could meet him, yer'd know what I mean. I couldn't stand back and let him be made a fool of, just so we get what we want. And me mam would hate me if I let someone hurt him without me lifting a finger to help.'

'What shall we do, then, babe? I'll go along with whatever you decide because, as yer said, it's not my family.'

'I'm not thinking straight, Gary, so I don't want to do anything hasty. I mean, where does Charlie fit into this? He's laughing sacks, isn't he? What sort of a man would get a married woman pregnant and then pass the baby off as someone else's? He's a good match for Celia, they're both rotten.' Laura shook her head as though bewildered by it all. 'Will yer give me until next Thursday to think it over? By that time I'll know exactly what I should do for the best.'

'That suits me, babe, as long as we can sort ourselves out. We need to make the most of what we know because we may never get another chance. You're my girl and I want the whole world to know. If yer think we should throw ourselves on the mercy of our families, then I'll go along with that. But please don't let anything keep us apart for much longer, babe, I couldn't stand it.'

Laura stood on tiptoe to kiss him. 'I won't let anyone keep us apart, Gary, I promise. Especially Celia. Somehow I'll pay her back for laughing at my grandad behind his back.'

Chapter Twenty-Four

Laura was looking in the bedroom mirror as she ran a brush through her hair, but her mind was so occupied she didn't even see her reflection. Nor did she feel the stiff bristles of the brush scraping her scalp as she put her strength behind the strokes. She was trying to cover one pain with another but it wasn't working. Last night had been a nightmare and she was no further forward. For hours she'd lain on her back staring up at the ceiling, seeking a solution that would not only help her grandad, but also her and Gary. She knew she was being selfish, and for the first time in her life wasn't proud of herself. She had the solution in her hands but was too cowardly to use it. All she had to do was go downstairs now and tell her mam and dad everything. But she didn't have the courage to do it because suddenly it mattered to her what her mam and dad thought of her. She couldn't bear the prospect of them turning their heads from her in disgust.

She heard footsteps running up the stairs and quickly slipped the brush into a drawer. She hoped Jenny would get what she wanted and go; the last thing Laura needed was to have to listen to her going on about how good life was. She must have been born under a lucky star, her sister, because everything had always gone her way.

Jenny bounced in, her face wearing a big smile and her whole body exuding happiness. 'Are yer going out tonight, Laura?'

'Only down to Cynthia's for an hour.' Laura cringed inside when she heard the bedsprings creak as her sister sat on the side of the bed. Oh Lord, she wants to be matey and this is the wrong time. 'I'm going to have an early night for a change.'

'Me mam's just said I can go to the pictures with John and Mick on Saturday night, and I'm over the moon. Janet's coming as well, of course – I wouldn't go anywhere without me mate.' Jenny bounced gently on the bed. 'I wonder which picture-house we'll go to?'

Laura snapped. The stupid girl was going to ask her to choose between James Cagney and Cary Grant, when she had so much trouble on her mind. She spun round to face her sister. 'I don't know why yer bother with those two stupid nits. It's about time they grew up. They can't even kiss proper.'

The smile slipped from Jenny's face. 'How would you know that?'

303

'How d'yer think I'd know? Down the entry, of course.' Laura grabbed her handbag and made for the door. 'Fumbling and sloppy, both of them.' She didn't stay long enough to see her sister's stricken face. With those few words, spoken without thought or truth, she'd stripped Jenny of her happiness and her belief in the two people she'd have trusted with her life.

'Can we go up to yer bedroom to talk?' Laura whispered anxiously when Cynthia opened the door. 'I've got something terrible to tell yer.'

'Yeah, you go on up, I'll tell me mam.' Cynthia poked her head around the living-room door. 'I'm going to me bedroom with Laura, Mam.' She winked when her father's eyes appeared over the top of the *Echo*. 'Girls' talk, Dad, yer wouldn't be interested.'

When her head disappeared from view, her father looked across the room. 'She seems to have got over whatever was ailing her.'

Fanny lowered her eyes to the sock she was darning. 'Yes, she's a lot better.'

Cynthia bounded up the stairs and closed the bedroom door behind her. 'Well, what's this terrible thing I'm about to hear?'

'Sit down and I'll tell yer.' Laura moved along and patted the eiderdown. 'Don't say anything until I've finished, Cynthia – just listen.'

Laura hesitated, wondering where to start. The incident with the underskirt was the beginning, so her tale began on the night she'd walked out of the factory gates to find Celia waiting for her. She didn't leave anything out, as the words came tumbling from her mouth. The lies she'd told, the way she'd deceived her parents, how she'd met and fallen for Gary, and how Celia had manipulated them both. It was when she came to last night, and what she'd heard about the way her grandad was being made a fool of, that her voice faltered and tears sprang to her eyes. 'I'm at the end of me tether, Cynthia. I just don't know what to do for the best.'

'Of course yer know what yer've got to do, otherwise yer'd take the easy way out and you and Gary would be laughing sacks. But yer know damn well that's not what yer should do, or yer wouldn't be here telling me. Ye're feeling guilty, and ye're hoping I'll tell yer what yer want to hear. But I'm not going to.' Cynthia put a finger under Laura's chin and raised her face. 'I've listened to you, now it's your turn to listen to me. Yer might not like what I'm going to say, but it's the truth. When me and you were at school, we were horrible. We bullied the younger kids, and we cheated and told lies. And we kept on like that even after we'd left school. We did exactly what we wanted to do, and it was to hell with everyone else. We didn't care about hurting our parents, as long as we got our own way. We've

304

been bitches, Laura, and there's no other word for it. I gave my mam a dog's life, treated her like a skivvy. But I've tried to make it up to her in the last few months, and we're getting on fine. It's a bit late in the day for me to find out, but I know now that a mother can be yer best friend.'

'I've noticed that ye're nicer with yer mother, and she looks a lot happier.' Laura wrung her hands. 'What am I going to do, Cyn?'

'Stop telling lies for a kick-off. Yer mam has the right to know about this Charlie, and she'll know best how to handle it.'

'But Celia will tell her everything, and more. And she'll get Gary into trouble.'

'Don't give her the chance – beat her to it. Own up to everything, tell yer mam and dad the lot. And ask Gary to do the same. That way yer'll take the wind out of her sails and she'll be left high and dry.'

'But you don't know what she's like.' Once again Laura was finding that her friend was a much stronger person than she was. 'And what about me grandad? She'd take it out on him and she can be really wicked.'

'Laura Nightingale, I'm surprised at you! Fancy even thinking of letting this person, this Celia, get away with it! If I was in your shoes I'd be up there right now, giving her the bloody good hiding she deserves.' Cynthia felt like shaking some sense into her friend. 'This feller, Charlie, is he married?'

Laura shook her head slowly. 'I don't know. I was that confused last night, I never thought to ask. Why?'

'His baby, his problem. Blow the whole thing sky-high, Laura, and get yer grandad off the hook. Yer can't let him be lumbered with another man's baby, not at his age. And from what I've heard, he's sorry he ever married her in the first place, so yer'd be doing him a favour. If yer don't, and yer go on letting him carry the can while you and Gary waltz off into the sunset, then I'll never speak to yer again, Laura – and I mean it. We've done some lousy things in our lives, but never anything as bad as this. If yer don't do the right thing by yer family, then I wouldn't want yer as a friend.'

No one could have got through to Laura as her childhood friend did. Every word struck a chord. 'I know ye're right, Cyn, I've known all along that's what I should do. I just didn't have the courage. But I have now – you've given it to me. I'll see Gary next Thursday and I'm sure he'll go along with what I say.' Laura sighed. 'I don't know why I have to lie all the time. I even lied to our Jenny, just before I came out. She was telling me she was going to the pictures on Saturday night with Mick and John, and she looked so happy I had to spoil it. So I told her I'd been down the entry with them and they're sloppy kissers.'

'Oh Laura, that was wrong. She's a nice kid, your Jenny, and she's been mates with the two boys all her life. If you've spoiled that friendship, then ye're not worth having for a sister. Yer've got to tell her the truth.'

'I will, Cynthia, I promise. And I'll tell me mam and dad everything next Thursday. I won't go in the dance, I'll get there early and wait outside for Gary. He might come home with me so we can tell me mam and dad together, but if he doesn't, I'll do it on me own.'

Jenny pushed her plate away. 'I couldn't eat that, Mam. I'm sorry after all the trouble yer've gone to, cooking it, but I don't feel well.'

'Yer've probably got a cold coming on,' Laura said, mopping gravy up with a piece of bread. 'Take a Beecham's Powder.'

Mary rounded the table in a flash. Kneeling by her daughter's chair, she felt her head to see if she was running a temperature. 'Have yer got a headache, sunshine, or any pains?'

'I just don't feel well, Mam, me tummy's upset.'

'Yer must be sickening for something,' Stan said. 'I'd go and lie down for an hour if I were you.'

'I think I will.' Jenny pushed her chair back. 'And I think I'll stay in bed, 'cos I feel faint and dead tired.'

'See how yer feel after a couple of hours,' Mary suggested, ' 'cos ye're supposed to be going to the pictures with Janet and the boys.'

'It won't matter if I don't go, the boys will take Janet.' Jenny looked through her sister as though she wasn't there. 'I'll go up to bed.'

'You do that, sunshine, and I'll bring yer a hot drink up.'

Laura put her dirty plate on the draining board. 'I'm just nipping upstairs,' she told her mother. 'I'll help yer with the dishes when I come down.'

Jenny was slipping between the sheets when her sister entered the room. She didn't even turn her head. In fact, Laura was the last person on earth she wanted to see or be near.

'Look, our kid, what I said last night isn't true. So if that's got anything to do with yer not feeling well, I'm sorry. I don't even know why I said it.'

Jenny laid her head on the pillow and pulled the blankets up to her chin. 'Yer wouldn't have thought of saying it, if it wasn't true. And I'll tell yer why yer said it, it was because yer wanted to spoil things for me. Like yer've always spoilt things for me.'

'It was a lie, Jenny.' Laura heard the stairs creak and knew her mother was on her way up. 'Honestly, kid, it was a lie.'

'Yer said it, and yer can't un-say it. So go away and leave me alone.'

Laura was leaving as her mother came through the door with a cup of hot, weak tea. 'I'll make a start on the dishes, Mam, so take yer time.'

Mary put the saucer on top of the chest of drawers before sitting her daughter forward while she plumped the pillows. 'Get the tea down while it's hot, sunshine, and I'll nip to the corner shop for a Beecham's for yer.'

Jenny heard the knock and the sound of Janet's voice. 'Is Jenny ready, Mrs Nightingale?'

'I'm sorry, kids, but Jenny's not well, she's in bed.'

'Ah, isn't she coming with us?'

'What's wrong with her?' John asked. 'It's nothing serious, is it?'

'No, she'll probably be as right as rain tomorrow. But it's not like our Jenny to take to her bed, especially as she'd been looking forward to going out with yer. So she must really be feeling under the weather.'

Mick was looking down in the mouth. 'I don't suppose we could see her for a minute, could we? Just to say hello, like?'

'I don't think so, Mick, she was asleep the last time I looked in on her. Perhaps tomorrow, eh? Anyway, she said to enjoy yerselves and make sure Janet's well looked after.'

'Don't worry, Mrs Nightingale, Janet will make sure she's well looked after.' John chuckled. 'It's me and Mick that Jenny should be worrying about. Anyway, I'll give a knock in the morning, see how she is.'

'Yeah, me too,' Mick said. 'Give her my love and tell her I'll miss her.'

Jenny pulled the bedclothes over her head so she couldn't hear any more. She felt sick all right, but it wasn't a sickness that could be cured by a Beecham's Powder. It was in her heart and mind she felt sick. She'd never feel the same towards John and Mick now. Not when she knew they'd been kissing her sister down an entry. She felt betrayed by them, but knew that was stupid. They were both old enough to have been out with girls and kissed them. She could forgive them that, but not when one of the girls was a fly turn like her sister.

Mary opened the bedroom door and popped her head in. 'They've gone, sunshine, and Janet looks as proud as Punch with her arms through theirs. It's a pity yer couldn't go, yer'd have enjoyed it. The boys were disappointed, especially Mick. He looked as though he'd lost his wage-packet down a grid.'

'He'll get over it.'

'Of course he will. Anyway, if ye're feeling better, yer'll all meet up tomorrow night at yer Auntie Lizzie's.'

When her mother had gone, Jenny lay on her back. She knew she'd have to see the boys again, it couldn't be avoided. But she didn't want to go out with them ever again, and didn't want them to

307

touch her. They'd been part of her life for as long as she could remember – good mates who had looked out for her since she was able to toddle. But the thought of them kissing her sister was more than she could stomach. She wouldn't tell Janet, that wouldn't be fair, but she wouldn't be so friendly with them in future. And losing them from her life was all down to Laura. At that moment Jenny wished she'd never had a sister.

Sighing, Jenny curled up and tried to sleep. But although she could close her eyes and shut out anything she didn't want to see, she couldn't close her mind or her heart. And pictures of a boy with raven-black hair, the deepest of blue eyes and dimples in his cheeks, kept popping up in her head. She could hear him speaking as clearly as if he was standing next to her. 'As I haven't got a girlfriend, I thought yer might like to team up with me.'

And with the words and the pictures came the tears.

Mary opened the door on Monday morning to Lizzie Marshall. 'Well, this is a surprise. It's not often we get honoured with your company. Come on in, Lizzie, me mate's here for her usual cuppa and natter.'

Lizzie didn't look too sure. 'Perhaps I'd be better coming back when yer haven't got any visitors. I don't like to intrude.'

'Visitors, did yer say, Lizzie?' Mary leaned forward and pulled on the old lady's arm. 'Come on in and don't be daft. I haven't got no visitor, but me lodger's here.'

'Ay, I heard that, buggerlugs,' Amy grinned. 'But I ain't no lodger, 'cos lodgers have to pay for what they get. I get mine for nowt.'

'Ye're telling me.' Mary pulled a chair out for her visitor and saw her settled before going on. 'Proper skinflint you are, if there ever was one.'

Amy combined an expression of surprise and hurt. 'How can yer say that, girl? Have yer forgotten those cream slices already?'

'Oh my God, am I going to get that thrown up at me for the rest of me life?' Mary winked at Lizzie. 'She mugs me to a cake once – just the once, mind yer – and never a day goes by that she doesn't remind me of it.'

'Only 'cos ye're getting absent-minded, girl.' Amy shuffled to the edge of her chair, cupped a hand around her mouth and wagged a podgy finger at Lizzie to move nearer. 'She's going a bit senile. Terrible thing to happen to a woman of her age, but there yer go, that's life for yer. So I remind her of me generosity every day, just to keep her mind active.'

'Lizzie, sorry to change the subject, sunshine, but would yer like a cuppa?'

'No, thanks, Mary, I've not long had one. I just came over to see how Jenny was. I didn't think she was herself last night at all. Usually she's always laughing and joking, but last night she was very quiet.'

'Oh yeah, our John mentioned something like that before he went to work this morning,' Amy said. 'In fact, he said every time Mick spoke to her, she nearly bit his head off.'

'That's not like our Jenny, I've never known her be in a temper with anyone. She was quiet this morning before she went out, but that's all. I'll have a good talk to her tonight, make sure she's telling me the truth. I wouldn't like the girl to go to work if she's sick, just because she doesn't want to worry me.'

'I'm going on without yer, Dad,' Mick said as they came out of work. 'I want to catch Jenny on her way home, and I can run faster on me own.'

'Is true love not running smoothly, son?'

'No, it's not, Dad, and I want to find out why. Ask me mam to put me dinner between two plates, will yer?' With that, Mick took to his heels and ran like the wind. He had to know what was wrong with Jenny, because he didn't believe it had anything to do with her not feeling well. And he wanted to be alone when he asked her.

His heart flipped when he saw her walking towards him, shoulders hunched and head down. 'Jenny,' he spoke her name softly so as not to startle her, 'can I have a word with yer, please?'

'Mick, what are you doing here?'

'I want to ask yer what's happened in the last few days to change yer so much? Yer looked at me last night as though I was something the cat had dragged in. I could tell yer didn't want to talk to me, or even be in the same room. And I want to know why, Jenny, 'cos I would never do anything to hurt you.'

'There's nothing wrong, Mick, I just wasn't feeling well. But now ye're here, and we're on our own, I may as well tell yer I've been thinking about what yer said about me being yer girlfriend. I don't think it's a good idea because I'm too young, really, to start courting proper. I haven't been anywhere yet, and never met any other boys.' Jenny saw the hurt on his face and hated herself for putting it there. But she was hurting, too, and it was his fault. She felt like shouting out loud, asking him why he'd kissed her sister. But that would be childish.

'I only asked yer to be me girlfriend, Jenny, I didn't ask yer to marry me. Yer'd have been free to end it any time yer wanted, if yer met another bloke yer liked better.' Looking the picture of dejection, Mick dug his hands in his pockets. 'And where does John fit into your plans?'

'John's never asked me to be his girlfriend, but if he did, I'd tell him the same as I'm telling you. I want to get out and about on me own for a while, do a little growing up.'

'So me and John are not even on yer list of friends? No more going to the dance, or even a game of cards?'

Jenny turned her head away from those deep blue eyes that could make her go weak at the knees. 'Of course we're still friends, we'll always be that. It's just that I don't want to get serious, that's all.'

'All right, Jenny, I've got the message, I'll not bother yer any more.' As he turned away, he said, 'I'll tell John so he won't have to listen to the price yer put on our friendship.'

'I'll be seeing yer around, like at Auntie Lizzie's.'

Mick turned back and looked down at her. 'Yer intend taking our ten years of being mates and tearing it up into little pieces. But yer want to keep some of the pieces that suit yer. Well, it doesn't work like that, Jenny. I have loved you for as long as I can remember. I've never even tried to find anybody else because I've always known you were the one I wanted. But I'll not hang around just in case I bump into yer, like, as yer said, "at Auntie Lizzie's".'

This time when Mick walked away he kept on walking. Slowing down only long enough to say, 'Goodbye, Jenny. I hope yer find what ye're looking for.'

'What's gone wrong in this house, love?' Stan asked Mary. 'We always managed a laugh when we were having our dinner, but lately I can't even raise a titter. I know what your worries are, and I can understand, but what's up with the girls? Our Laura looks as though she's sitting on a time bomb and yer hardly get a word out of Jenny.'

'We'll start with me, shall we?' Mary shrugged her shoulders. 'I'm worried sick about me dad. He didn't come Sunday and this is the second Wednesday he's missed. But I can't bring meself to go to his house 'cos I know once I set eyes on Celia I'd clock her one. I'll give it until Sunday, and if he doesn't come then – well, someone will have to go and see what's wrong.'

'I can take a hint, love – I'll go. If he doesn't turn up Sunday, I'll be there the next night.'

'As for our Laura, I haven't a clue. She comes and goes as she pleases, as she's always done. Never a dickie bird out of her. And I'm not going to ask because I wouldn't believe what she told me anyway.' Mary sighed as she bent to straighten the rug in front of the hearth. 'Our Jenny is a little more complicated. For some unknown reason, she's fallen out with John and Mick. She says she hasn't, she just doesn't want to go out with them like courting couples. Janet's gone to the dance with the boys, but she couldn't persuade Jenny no matter how hard she tried. Molly was over today and she said Mick is devastated. He can't understand why they're the best of mates one day, then out of the blue she told him straight to his face that she wanted to meet other people.'

310

'What about John?'

'Well, apparently our Jenny, who wouldn't say boo to a goose, told Mick she felt the same about John and the message was passed on. Something must have happened to make Jenny the way she is; she thought the world of those boys and would never hurt them for no good reason. But whatever the reason is, she's not saying. Even Lizzie can't get it out of her.'

'I'm surprised about that,' Stan said. 'I always thought she'd end up marrying one of those boys. I'd have bet a pound to a pinch of snuff on it.'

'Oh, I think John's been out of the race for weeks now,' Mary smiled. 'Janet pulled him off the starting line. She set her sights on him from the beginning and yer've got to hand it to her, she's never given up. Amy thinks it's hilarious. She said the lad doesn't know he's been caught yet, but he will when he tries to wriggle out of the fishing net.' She sat back in her chair and rapped her fingers on the wooden arms. 'Before me dad hit me with his troubles, I used to often think how nice it would be if the two boy mates married the two girl mates. I'd be made up to have Mick for me son-in-law.'

Stan chuckled. 'How does Amy feel about having Janet as her daughter-in-law? Mind you, it's Janet we should feel sorry for.'

'Amy seems quite delighted. She said the girl's either a genius or as thick as two short planks. It doesn't matter to her which, because she's a bit of both herself.'

'I'm sorry about Mick, our Jenny couldn't have got a better bloke,' Stan said. 'And we get on well with his family.'

'Yeah, but what we want and what Jenny wants, are two different things. She's a very level-headed girl and she must know what she's doing. You and me, sunshine, will just have to stand by and watch, hoping for the best.'

The card game was over and Fanny Pennington was putting the cards back in the box when Cynthia took hold of Laura's arm. 'Come up to me bedroom, I've got a new lipstick to show yer.'

Laura sat on the bed and was surprised when her friend plonked herself down beside her. 'Where's the new lipstick?'

'That was only an excuse. I've got something to tell yer.'

'I hope it's something nice,' Laura said, pulling a face. 'I'm dreading tomorrow night, I just hope I can go through with it.'

'Of course yer can go through with it, don't be stupid. Just remember how many people yer'd be letting down if yer didn't. Particularly yerself, Laura. For once in yer life do something that counts. Neither of us can look back on the good things we did, because there aren't any. If yer want to make yer family happy, then do this for them. I've changed a lot, kid, since I met Bill. He's been

311

good for me. I told him at the beginning that I'd lost me trust in men, and not to rush me. And I'll always remember what he said to me: "I'll try a little tenderness." Do the same, Laura. Forget the tough girl who lied and cheated, be more caring for those who love yer, and remember – a little tenderness will go a long way.'

Laura took a deep breath and squared her shoulders. 'I will, Cynthia, even if it kills me, I'll do it. And now, what's this news of yours?'

Cynthia hugged herself. 'Bill's asked me to get engaged on me seventeenth birthday.'

Laura's mouth opened wide. 'Go 'way! Ooh, isn't that marvellous!'

'I don't know whether I'm on me head or me heels, I'm that excited. I haven't told me mam and dad yet, I'll wait until Bill's with me and we can do it together. And when we've told my parents, we'll go round and tell his. I think they'll be pleased because we all get on so well together.'

'I'm going to start being the new me right away,' Laura decided. 'No more lies, no more cheating. So I'll be honest and say that when yer said yer were getting engaged, I was as jealous as hell. But it's made me more determined to sort meself out, so me and Gary can get engaged. Then he can take me to meet his mam, who he loves the bones of, and he can meet my family.' Laura closed her eyes. 'I just hope I don't make a hash of the whole lot.'

'Ay, look at me, kid. You are not going to make a hash of it, or I personally will kill yer. All yer have to do is tell yer mam and let her take over. But tell her everything, don't leave a thing out for Celia to latch on to.' Cynthia gave her a hug. 'Come down on Friday and let me know how yer got on. If it's possible, bring Gary with yer. I can't wait to see this blond's answer to a maiden's prayer.'

Laura stood up. 'I'd better be going. Are yer seeing Bill tomorrow night?'

Cynthia's smile was her answer. 'He's the best thing that ever happened to me.'

Chapter Twenty-Five

Gary was startled when he saw Laura walking towards him, his first thought being that she was in trouble. He ran to meet her and took both of her hands in his. 'What's wrong, babe? Has something happened?'

Laura shook her head. 'Not yet.' Her whole body was tingling, as it always did when he touched her. She loved him so much, she'd go through hell, fire and water for him. 'I came to meet yer 'cos there's something I want yer to do. Something that will get us out of this mess once and for all.'

Gary grinned as he squeezed her hands. 'I'm already out of it, my dearest, darling Laura. I've been and gone and done it: I told me mam everything. So Celia can do what the hell she likes, she can't hurt me now.'

Laura was dumbstruck. She'd imagined having to talk him into going along with her, and had even prepared herself for him refusing. But here he was, with a big smile and a clear conscience. 'What did yer mam say?'

'She called me for all the silly buggers under the sun, said I should have told her right from the start and none of this would have happened. If she ever meets Celia, she'll skin her alive, or so she says.'

'But didn't Celia say she'd go and tell yer old boss, and the place where yer work now? She could still do that.'

'Me mam's sorted it all out. She went to see Mr Brown, he's the owner of the shop, and he was disgusted. Apparently she'd tried it with one of the older workers, but she had the sense to tell her to scram. So she tried me, soft lad, and I fell for it. Anyway, me mam gave Mr Brown five shillings, to help towards what she'd fiddled. He didn't want to take it but me mam made him. Her motto is, out of debt, out of danger. And guess what? He even offered me a job! I wouldn't go back, though, even though he's a smashing feller, because I'm on better wages where I am.'

Laura thought suddenly of Celia, who would be along this way any minute. She pulled on Gary's hands. 'We'd better move. I want yer to come home with me, while I tell me mam and dad. If yer think anything of me, Gary, yer won't let me down.'

'Think anything of yer! Babe, I love yer and adore yer.' His laugh rang out. 'Oh, it feels good to say it at last. I'll be only too happy to come with yer to hold yer hand and give yer support. And to see that worried look disappear from yer eyes.'

As they walked arm in arm, Laura said, 'I'm glad yer've told yer mam, and she was all right about it. I hope my parents are the same.' She glanced up at him and thought how lucky she was to have met him. He wasn't half handsome, and nice with it. 'Your mam must have some guts to do what she did.'

Gary chortled. 'She's not the size of sixpenn'orth of copper, but when she gets her dander up, she can be a real spitfire. When she knew what Celia had done to her lovely son, she went haywire. Mind you, I came in for it. She couldn't believe I'd been stupid enough to let meself be blackmailed without telling her. She knows some choice words, my mam, and I got called every one of them when she was telling me how dumb I'd been. So I'm warning yer what to expect.'

'My Auntie Amy's like that, she's always swearing. She once said that if the King came to her house for tea, she'd still tell him to wipe his bleedin' feet before she'd let him in. And if he pulled a face because his cup had no handle, she'd tell him to bugger off back to his palace.'

'My mam would get on well with your Auntie Amy. The air would be blue if the two of them got together.'

'She'd get on with me mam, as well. Me mam doesn't swear much, but she's full of fun and always laughing.' Laura shuddered. 'I hope she's able to laugh after what I've got to tell her tonight.'

They came to the end of her street. 'Would yer mind waiting outside by the entry, Gary? I think I'd be better doing it on me own; I'd be too embarrassed if you were there. I'll come for yer when it's over, if she hasn't thrown me out before then.'

'Okay, babe. I'll walk up and down in case someone thinks I'm up to no good and thumps me one.'

Laura took a deep breath. 'Here goes.' Before she had time to change her mind, she covered the few yards with purpose in her step. He'd told her he loved her, and she clung to those words.

'I thought yer were going to the dance?' Mary looked up in surprise when her daughter walked in. 'Don't tell me you're not feeling well.'

Laura pulled a chair from the table and sat down next to Jenny, who was reading. 'I want to have a talk to you and me dad. Ye're going to be shocked, but I want yer to hear me out before saying anything.'

Jenny closed her book and stood up. 'I'll go upstairs.'

'No, I want yer to stay.' Laura held on to her arm. 'Please, Jenny?'

Jenny pulled her arm free and looked down at her sister. Harsh

314

words were on her lips but there was something in Laura's eyes that held them back. She put her book on the table and sat down.

'What's all the mystery?' Stan asked. 'Yer sound very melodramatic.'

Laura's tongue flicked over her dry lips. She'd have given anything for a drink, but that would take time and she was eager now to get it over with. 'I haven't been a good daughter, I know that now. I've lied and cheated all me life, and led me mam a merry dance. But lately I've been a bigger liar than even you could imagine. I'm not proud of it, and I only hope yer don't all hate me when I've said what I've got to say.'

Mary and Stan looked at each other with apprehension. The last thing they wanted to hear was that their wayward daughter had got herself into trouble. But they stayed silent and listened to the story unfolding. Several times Mary shook her head and closed her eyes, signs of the disgust she felt at the string of lies her eldest daughter had told. But she never spoke until Laura came to the baby Celia was expecting.

'How d'yer know this?' Mary was red in the face with anger. 'Did the cheeky bitch tell yer herself?'

'No.' Laura felt faint with worry. Her family were going to despise her after this. 'I told yer about the boy I met at the dance, Gary, and the way Celia has been blackmailing him, too. Well, he told me. She doesn't know I know yet. And Gary also told me something else.' The tears she could no longer control, started to roll down her cheeks. 'I know I've been bad, and I'm sorry, 'cos I want yer to love me, not hate me. But I've got to tell yer what Gary found out. The baby isn't me grandad's baby. The father is a bloke called Charlie, and he goes to the dance. I'm pretty sure Celia goes out with him a lot.'

Stan looked at his wife and saw the colour drain from her face. 'Are you all right, love?'

'I can't take it in!' Mary looked dazed. 'How does this Gary know?'

'Celia and Charlie told him. He said they were having a good laugh because she said her husband had agreed to let people think it was his. And she hasn't told them that she's married to me grandad, she said she'd married me uncle, and that's how she knows me.'

Stan asked, 'How long have yer known all this?'

'Only since last week, Dad. I was frightened to say anything right away 'cos Celia's always hinting that she's going to tell yer about me lying. And she'd make up worse tales about me, to get me into trouble with me mam. That's why she started all this, just to get back at me mam, she's so spiteful.'

'And where does this Gary feller fit in to all this?' Mary asked. 'Is he a crony of theirs? He must be pretty thick with them to know all this.'

'Oh no, Mam, he doesn't even like them. I only ever see him every Thursday at the dance, but I really like him. So would you, if yer'd let me bring him in. He's waiting outside for me. He's told his mother what's been going on, and she called him a stupid bugger for letting someone blackmail him. But Gary was only fourteen, Mam, and yer know how wicked Celia is. He was terrified of her 'cos he didn't want his mam to find out. He hasn't got a dad, he died when Gary was very young, so there's only him and his mam.'

'I don't want yer to bring him in,' Mary said. 'Not tonight, anyway. I want to get things straight in me head first. If what ye're saying is true, I'll have to think about what to do about yer grandad.'

'Hang on a minute, love, don't be so hasty.' Stan stroked his chin thoughtfully. 'I'd like to ask the lad a few questions, see whether it is true or whether he's made it all up.'

'He hasn't made it all up, Stan, 'cos we know Celia's pregnant. And if this Charlie is the father, me dad has a right to know.'

'Bring the lad in, Laura,' Stan said. 'Let's see if he can answer some questions.'

'Yer won't take off on him, will yer? It's not his fault I've told yer lies. He's lovely, and I like him better than any boy I've ever met.'

'We'll see about that.' Stan's face was stern. 'Just bring him in.'

Jenny hadn't opened her mouth, even though everything surprised and shocked her. Now she knew why her mother hadn't been herself for over a week now. She'd been worried about Grandad. She looked across and met Mary's eyes. 'Our Laura's done a lot of things to hurt all of us, but I think she's been very brave doing what she's done tonight.'

'I know that, sunshine, and even though she's been very naughty, I admire her speaking up. But we've got to get at the truth now, for everyone's sake.'

All eyes went to the door when Laura came in, hand-in-hand with a tall blond boy who looked nervous at first, until he smiled. 'I've wanted to meet yer for a long time,' he said, 'and I'm sorry it has to be like this.'

Mary studied his face for a few seconds, and knew she was going to like him. His handsome face was as honest and open as could be. 'Sit down, son.'

Jenny moved to another chair, making room for Gary to sit next to Laura. She noticed that their hands stayed gripped, as though they didn't want to be parted.

Stan was more reasonable than he thought he'd be. If he was any judge of character, there wasn't much wrong with this boy. 'We're finding it hard to believe all that Laura's told us, son, so can yer shed some light on it?'

'I don't know where to start, Mr Nightingale, but I suppose

316

Laura's told yer how stupid we've both been for letting Celia get her claws into us?'

'I understand that, and believe it,' Mary said. 'She's as evil as they come. But what's this about the baby she's expecting? I'll be truthful with yer, me dad told us she was expecting, but never gave a hint that the baby might not be his. I've been out of me mind with worry, 'cos he's too old to be starting a family. And I can't stand his wife, I won't have her in the house.'

Stan held up his hand. 'Leave all that for now, love. I would like Gary to answer a few questions for me. Will yer do that, son?'

'If I know the answers, Mr Nightingale, I'll be glad to answer them.'

'Tell me about this bloke called Charlie, and why yer think he's the one got Celia in the family way?'

'I don't think it, I know it! They told me themselves and they thought it was funny! She's been knocking around with Charlie for ages and makes no secret of it. I honestly didn't know that she was married to yer dad, Mrs Nightingale, not until Laura told me a week or so ago.'

'And is Charlie a married man?' Stan asked. 'Or don't yer know?'

'No, he's definitely not married, he lives with his mam. I'm certain of this 'cos he only lives a few streets away from me. He doesn't half fancy his chances, does Charlie, he's a real ladies' man.'

'Is he now?' Stan stroked his chin. 'I wonder if he fancies being a family man?'

'What are yer thinking of, Stan?' Mary asked. 'I don't want me dad getting into a fight with a younger man, it would kill him.'

'Yer dad doesn't need to know anything, love, if we play our cards right.' Stan looked at the young couple still holding hands. 'Are yer willing to help me put Celia and this Charlie in their place? And help Grandad to be happy again – give him his life back?'

'Oh yes, Dad, I'd do anything to help me grandad,' Laura said. 'And I know Gary will too, after what she's done to us.'

Gary grinned. 'It would give me great pleasure to see them squirm. And the thought of Charlie pushing a pram down Walton Road – well, it's a sight I'd like to see.'

There was hope springing in Mary's heart. She'd often said to Stan that if Laura met a nice boy he might be the makings of her. Well, from what she could see, the boy sitting opposite to her was a nice boy, and he'd certainly changed her daughter.

'Jenny, will yer put the kettle on for us, sunshine?' Mary smiled at the daughter who had never caused her a moment's anxiety. Please God she'd now have two daughters to be proud of. 'We'll have a cuppa while yer dad tells us what he's got in his mind.'

Laura followed her sister out to the kitchen. 'Seeing as I'm getting

317

all me sins off me chest, kid, I can't leave you out because I've made you suffer more than anybody. I've been a lousy sister to yer, and I am so sorry. Yer see, I've always been jealous of yer.'

Jenny raised her brows. 'Jealous of me! Why?'

'I know it sounds daft, but it's the truth, and I feel so guilty. I was jealous of yer blonde hair because yer looked like me mam, and I didn't. Jealous because yer were always laughing and happy, and everybody loved yer. Jealous because yer were good at school and I was a dunce. Yer were too good, and I walked all over yer. I can't tell yer how sorry I am and I want yer to forgive me. Give me a chance and I'll prove I want to be a real sister to yer. To share things, like sisters should do. I want yer to believe I mean all that from the bottom of my heart. I also want yer to believe me when I tell yer again, I was lying about John and Mick. I have never been down an entry with either of them, or kissed them. They wouldn't have touched me with a barge-pole. Please believe that, and then I'll have a clear conscience.'

Jenny didn't answer for a while, then a slow smile spread across her face. 'You make the tea, big sister, I'm going on a message.'

Molly opened the door and her eyes widened in surprise. 'Yes, me darlin'?'

'If Mick's in, Mrs Moynihan, can I have a word with him?' Jenny knew he was in, she'd seen him through the window. Although she would never admit it, she'd been keeping tabs on him since Monday night. He hadn't been out any night, and she was glad he was as miserable as she was. 'If he's not, it doesn't matter, I'll come back tomorrow.'

Molly felt herself being pulled backwards. 'It's all right, Mam, I'll see what Jenny wants. You go in.' He waited until his mother had closed the living-room door. 'What can I do for yer, Jenny?'

'Would yer like to be me boyfriend, Mick?'

There was no smile on Mick's face. There hadn't been for three days and four nights. 'If this is yer idea of a joke, Jenny, I don't think it's funny.'

'It isn't a joke, Mick. I've never been more serious in me life.'

Mick's heart wanted to beat faster with hope, but he wouldn't let it. 'Yer were dead serious on Monday, Jenny, when yer told me, in no uncertain terms, that yer wanted to get out and about on yer own. So I decided I'd do the same thing.'

'But yer haven't been out, have yer?' Jenny wasn't going to be put off. 'I know yer've been in every night 'cos I've watched yer through the window.'

'You haven't been out, either.'

'How d'yer know?'

318

'Because I've seen yer through your window.' Mick realised how childish it sounded and almost laughed out loud. But he didn't. Jenny had hurt him so much, he wasn't about to let her hurt him more. 'Anyway, what have yer come over for?'

'To ask if I can be yer girlfriend. I know yer haven't found another one, 'cos yer haven't been anywhere to meet one.'

'Yer've changed yer tune, haven't yer? What about all those things yer said to me about meeting other boys?'

Jenny thought if Laura could admit to lying, so could she. 'It was all lies, Mick, I didn't mean a word of it. I've wanted to be your girlfriend for as long as I can remember. I don't want no one else. But I'll not crawl to yer, Mick Moynihan, so either yer close the door in me face or yer get yer coat and come out with me. Which is it to be?'

'Yer do know that if I'm yer boyfriend, I'm entitled to kiss yer?'

'I can't wait, Mick. In fact, if yer come down off that step we can have our first kiss in the street and give the neighbours something to talk about.'

'Don't tempt me, Jenny.'

'I'm not tempting, Mick, I'm offering.'

When Mick stepped on to the pavement, he expected Jenny to back up, but she didn't. 'Yer mean it, don't yer?'

'Of course I mean it! Now, when a girl gets her first kiss, it's a big day in her life. One she can look back on with happiness. So will yer put a smile on yer face, just for me?'

It was a brief kiss, but lasted long enough for Mick to see stars and Jenny's knees to buckle. 'This is for keeps, isn't it, Jenny?' His voice was husky.

'For ever and ever, Mick.'

'Hang on, I'll get me coat and we'll go down to Auntie Lizzie's. John and Janet are there and I want them to be the first to know.'

Molly was standing inside the living-room door with his coat in her hand. May God forgive her, but hadn't she been listening to every word that was said? 'Romance back on track, is it, me darlin'?'

His dimples deep holes in his smiling face, he kissed his mother's cheek. 'On track and it's full steam ahead, Mam.'

Seamus chortled. 'Sure, now, isn't it meself yer take after? It's a one-woman man yer are, right enough.'

'We're only going to Auntie Lizzie's, Mam, so I won't be late.'

'Will John not be thinking he's had his nose pushed out of joint? Yer know he's always had a soft spot for Jenny.'

'That's why I want to be the first one to tell him. But somehow I don't think he'll be that upset. Janet seems to have found favour with him. Anyway, I'll see yer later. Ta-ra.'

* * *

Lizzie Marshall's face lit up when she saw Jenny. 'Oh, it's good to see yer, love, I was beginning to think yer'd fallen out with me.'

Jenny kissed her and lightly pinched her cheek. 'I fell out with everyone, Auntie Lizzie – I was a real misery guts. Even me mam couldn't get a smile out of me.' She would never tell anyone how Laura had lied to her. 'I can only put it down to feeling under the weather.'

'Well, let's hope it doesn't happen often,' John said, 'otherwise none of us will have heads left. Yer'll have bitten them all off.'

'Ay, don't you talk to my friend like that.' Janet wagged a finger at him. 'She can't help it if she's not well.'

John grinned at her. 'If yer don't put that finger away, I'll bite it.'

'You do that and see what'll happen. Either I get me mam to come after yer with the rolling pin, or yer kiss me finger better.'

'I'll give both options my consideration and let yer know.' John turned his eyes to Jenny. 'How come you and Mick have both turned up?'

'I called for him. I wanted to say I was sorry for being nasty the last time I saw him. I'm glad to say he accepted my apology.'

'I've asked her to be me girlfriend, John.' Mick put his arm across Jenny's shoulders. 'I finally plucked up the courage.'

It was difficult to read anything from John's face. 'I gather, seeing as ye're both grinning like Cheshire cats, that Jenny's answer was the one yer wanted to hear?'

Mick nodded. 'We've come to see if yer approve, or whether yer want to throw down the gauntlet and challenge me to a duel, at dawn, in the North Park.'

John searched Jenny's face, and a feeling came over him that he couldn't put a name to. He'd loved her for so long he couldn't imagine stopping loving her. But he now knew that though he would always love her, it would be the love of a brother for a special sister. He turned to Mick, and grinned. 'What d'yer mean, the North Park? That's flipping miles away! What's wrong with Walton Park?'

Relief flooded Mick's body. He wasn't going to lose his best mate after all. 'Well, it's like this, yer see, pal. Knowing what a lazy begger yer are, I knew yer wouldn't travel all that way just to kill me.'

'So after years of rivalry, it's you who's won the fair maiden's hand? Well, I don't think ye're good enough for her, she deserves better.' John put his arms around Jenny and held her close. 'I'm cut to the quick, I really am. Me poor heart is bleeding.'

'I'll bet it is,' Jenny laughed, hugging him back. 'But we'll always be mates, won't we, John? Nothing will change that.'

'We'll always be that, Jenny, and I'll always be there for yer.' His arms dropped to his side. 'At least, I will when me bleeding heart is mended.'

'Ah, yer poor thing.' Janet sidled up to him, and in her childish voice, asked, 'Shall I kiss it better for yer?'

'Not as long as yer mam's got a rolling pin and you talk like a parrot. I like the shape of me head as it is, thank you.'

Janet patted his head as she would a child, then moved close to her friend. 'So is it all settled, Jenny? Mick is officially yer boyfriend?'

'Yeah, I think so.'

'Yer think so! Hasn't he asked yer yet?'

'No, I asked him, Janet.'

'Ooh, er!' Janet pursed her lips. 'You asked him, eh?'

John bent his elbow and gave Mick such a hard dig in the ribs, he caught his breath. 'Just watch this, Mick. Can yer hear her head ticking over? Let's see what gem she comes up with this time. Honest to God, she comes out with some corkers.'

While this was going on, Lizzie was drinking it all in. She needed to go down the yard but she didn't want to miss a single word. Mind you, she might have to if they didn't hurry up. At her age, she'd die of humiliation if she disgraced herself.

Janet wanted a bit more information before she decided. 'What did yer say to him, Jenny? Did yer come right out with it, or did yer go all round the world?'

Jenny giggled. 'There wasn't much point in going around the world, Jan, so I just said, "Will yer be me boyfriend?" '

Janet tapped her lips with a finger. Then, her mind made up, she walked over to John, stood in front of him and looked him straight in the eyes. 'Will yer be me boyfriend, John Hanley?'

'Ooh, I'd have to think about that, Janet. After all, it's not only you I'd be taking on, but yer mother and her rolling pin.'

'Me mam doesn't hit members of the family, she only hits people who do things she doesn't like. And she wouldn't like it if you turned me down, so there. It would be in yer own interest to say I can be yer girlfriend.'

'Oh dear.' John couldn't look at her because he knew he'd burst out laughing. 'Are yer listening to this, Auntie Lizzie? I've got a choice between a duel to the death with Mick, or Mrs Porter's rolling pin. And I'm not a strong lad, as yer know, so for either one I'd have to get a stuntman to stand in for me.'

'Ye're not palming me off with any stuntman, John Hanley. If yer won't be me boyfriend, I'll have to pinch Mick off Jenny.'

'I can't let yer do that, curly top, 'cos they're me two best mates. It looks as though yer've got me over a barrel and I'll have to give in to yer.'

Lizzie could no longer resist the call of nature. She struggled to her feet, and on her way to the door, she said, 'I'll be gone a couple of minutes, that's plenty of time to seal yer relationship with a kiss.

But for heaven's sake don't tell yer mam I suggested that, Janet. I've never been partial to rolling pins.'

As she hastened down the yard, Lizzie could hear the laughter, and she knew that John and Mick would be doubled up, while the girls waited for their kiss.

'Yer are sure this is Charlie's address, aren't yer, Gary?' Stan asked as he made notes on a notepad. 'And that his mother's name is Hettie?'

'That's definitely his address, and he calls his mam by her first name. I've heard it hundreds of times. Their surname is Owens.'

'What do yer intend doing with all this information, now yer've got it?' Mary asked. 'I'm not going to call on the woman, if that's what yer've got in mind.'

'We're all in this, love, so I don't expect any one person to do what needs to be done. We mustn't forget that Charlie's mother is not to blame for what he does. It could come as a terrible shock to her.'

'She's quite a nice lady, actually,' Gary said, 'keeps her house like a little palace. And she dotes on Charlie, waits on him hand and foot. But unless she's blind, she must know what he's like for the ladies. Everyone else does, he's got quite a reputation.'

'I'd go with yer to see her, Mam,' Laura said, 'if yer wanted.'

Stan brushed the offer aside. 'This will take some working out, so yer grandad doesn't know anything about it until it's over.' He glanced at Mary. 'Yer did say that none of the women in the street liked Celia, didn't yer?'

Mary nodded. 'They can't stand the sight of her. Especially the near neighbours, who were me mam's friends. I know they wouldn't need asking twice if we wanted them to help. But what they could do, I don't know.'

'I do,' said her husband, 'but we need to work from two sides. Someone, who they won't know from Adam, has to go and see Charlie's mother with the news that she's to become a grandmother. And at the same time – and this is the tricky part – we need to get Celia out of that house for good. That's where I think yer mam's old neighbours would come in – they could drive her out.' He saw the look on Mary's face and reached for her hand. 'Strong measures are needed, love, to keep her away from yer dad. Otherwise she'll be pestering him for money and we don't want that. It has to be a clean break. And if she knows the neighbours are gunning for her, and that they mean business, she'll think twice about setting foot in the street again.'

There was a look of concern on Laura's face. 'Dad, she'll know something's up with me and Gary not being at the dance. Whatever ye're thinking of doing, it'll have to be soon.'

Mary conjured up her father's face to give her the strength she needed. 'We'll do it tomorrow and get it over with. Laura, you take a day off work and come with me. If she sees us together, she'll know her little game hasn't worked.'

Stan raised his brows. 'Who's going to see to Charlie and his mother?'

'Just leave it to me, Stan. I'll get Amy and Molly over first thing and I'll enlist their help. They're me best mates, and I know they'll get stuck in and help because they think the world of me dad. If we're going to do it, let's do it properly, with our own army.' Mary jerked her head and rolled her eyes. 'I'll never hear the last of it off Amy, 'cos she didn't believe it was me dad's baby from the start.'

All eyes turned to the door when Jenny walked in with Mick. And Mary was quick to note that for the second time that night, one of her daughters had come in holding the hand of a boy.

Jenny was all smiles. 'We've made it up, Mam, and Mick's come to ask if he can start taking me out. And me dad, of course, he'll have to ask me dad. I'm going to be his girlfriend and I'm very happy about that.'

For the first time that night, there was laughter in the room. But the tears that rolled down Mary's face weren't all from laughter. They were emotional and sentimental. 'Oh sunshine, that's the second surprise we've had tonight.' She smiled across at Gary. 'And both pleasant surprises.'

Mick's grin couldn't be wider. 'Is it all right then, Mr and Mrs Nightingale, if I come courting yer daughter? I know I'm older than her, but that doesn't matter, because I'm young for me age and Jenny's old for hers. And yer know I'll always look after her and she'll not come to any harm from me.'

'I know that, sunshine, and I couldn't be happier.' Mary turned to her husband. 'They've got my permission, have they got yours?'

'If I don't give it, I won't get invited to any parties over there. And the Moynihans give the best parties in Liverpool. So, permission granted.' Stan suddenly remembered his manners. 'Oh, this is Gary, a friend of Laura's. I'm afraid I don't know yer second name, son.'

'It's Stevens, Mr Nightingale.' Gary stood up to shake Mick's hand. 'It's nice to meet yer, Mick, and I think yer've got a very pretty girlfriend.'

The two boys liked each other on sight. 'Ay, keep yer eyes off her, Gary, I've only just got her – she's brand new. If I ever get tired of her, I'll give yer a shout.'

'You won't ever get tired of me, I won't let yer.' Jenny leaned against him as she grinned at her mother. 'And guess what, Mam? Janet's going to be John's girlfriend. She's absolutely over the moon. Mind you, I'm not quite sure that John knows it yet.'

'Oh, he knows it all right,' Mick said. 'It started to dawn on him a few weeks back. He wouldn't have it though, when I told him.'

Mary's heart felt lighter than it had done in days. 'So the four mates have become two two's eh? I'm delighted for yer.' Her attention was caught by Laura pulling on Gary's arm. And she saw her daughter mouth the words, 'Go on!'

Gary cleared his throat. 'I'm the new boy in the camp and I'm embarrassed and blushing like mad. But have I your permission, Mr and Mrs Nightingale, to call for Laura tomorrow night? And the next night, and every other night after that?'

Mary saw the way her daughter was looking up at this handsome blond boy, and knew he was the one for her. She also knew he'd keep her on the straight and narrow. 'As long as yer promise to look after Laura, like Mick did over Jenny. Yer see, me and Stan, we love both our daughters dearly.'

Chapter Twenty-Six

'Don't get yerself involved in any fighting, d'yer hear?' Stan looked up at his wife as he pulled his cap lower on his forehead. 'Any sign of trouble and you get out of there quick.'

'Don't worry, love, I won't be on me own. Anyway, last night was such a lovely night I'm convinced everything is going to go fine for us from now on. I'm made up over Mick, I really am, he's a smashing lad. And although it was the first time I'd clapped eyes on Gary, I can feel it in me bones that he's going to be good for Laura.' Mary unfolded her arms and shooed him away. 'If yer don't hurry, yer'll be late clocking in.'

'Will yer be here when I get home?'

'I don't know, love, we'll have to take things as they come. I'm hoping for big things, all in one day, and perhaps I'm hoping for too much. If all me dreaming and scheming comes true, I'll be the happiest woman in Liverpool and I'll greet yer with a smile on me face. But anyway, if I'm a bit late, Jenny will do yer beans on toast or something – it won't kill yer to do without a cooked dinner for one day.' Once again she shooed him away. 'Get going, love, 'cos I can't afford to stand gossiping, I've got a busy day ahead of me.'

Mary closed the door and paused in the hallway for a while when she heard her daughters talking. It was a sound seldom heard and was like music to her ears. It was with hope in her heart she entered the room. 'Laura, will you see to the beds while I tidy up in here? I don't want it looking like a muck-midden when Amy and Molly come. As soon as I think Seamus and Ben have gone to work I'm going to give them a knock.'

Amy opened the door rubbing the sleep out of her eyes. 'Christ, girl, fancy calling on anyone at this ungodly hour! The bleedin' streets haven't been aired off yet.'

'It's an emergency, sunshine – I need yer help.'

The hour was early, but not too early for Amy's brain to look for humour in any situation. 'Ay, girl, ye're not going into labour, are yer?'

Mary tutted. What would you do with her? 'Me dad's in trouble and I want yer in our house in half an hour – fully awake.'

Amy's face showed concern. 'Serious, is it, girl?'

Mary nodded. 'Very.'

'Right, half an hour it is.'

When Molly opened her door, she agreed without question. Except to ask, 'D'yer need me to bring anything, me darlin'?'

'Only yerself, Molly, thanks.' Mary hurried across the cobbles to make sure the house was tidy. She didn't worry about Amy because her best mate didn't give a continental what her place looked like. But Molly was a different kettle of fish. As soon as her husband and Mick left for work, she got stuck in and the whole house was spick and span by nine o'clock. That's unless it was the day for changing bedclothes, then she finished a little later.

'Laura, yer've got five minutes to get yerself washed, then I can get to the sink.' Mary caught her daughter's arm as she passed. 'There's no need to come out with the whole story. Yer just went to a dance and Celia happened to be there. Yer met Gary, fell for him and started going to the dance every week. From that point, we tell the truth. Okay, sunshine?'

Laura felt choked. Her mam and dad had been great, and she knew it was more than she deserved. She gave Mary a big hug. 'Thanks, Mam, for everything.'

Jenny popped the last piece of toast in her mouth and stood up to take her plate out. 'I was saying to Laura, Mam, that she's got a good-looking boyfriend. And he seems to be nice inside as well as out.' Her body still feeling the effects of the excitement of last night, and her heart singing with happiness, she laughed. 'Mind yer, he's not as handsome as my Mick – no one is.' Then she added, 'Except for me grandad – he's the most handsome man in the whole wide world.'

After Jenny had left for work, mother and daughter rushed around like mad to get everything done before Amy and Molly arrived. And Laura had just finished the last job of wiping the hearth over when the knock came.

'This emergency had better be good, girl.' Amy waddled in, followed closely by Molly. 'Every bleedin' bone in me body is complaining about the way it's been rushed this morning. Me face doesn't even know it's been washed yet.' Her brow rose when Laura walked in from the kitchen. 'What are you doing at home this time of the day? Did yer sleep in?'

'No, she didn't, I kept her off work.' Mary pulled the chairs from under the table. 'Thanks for coming over this time of the morning, both of yer. Sit yerselves down and when yer've heard what I've got to say, I'm hoping yer'll help me out. It's about me dad.'

'I'll make meself scarce, Mam,' Laura said, knowing she'd be embarrassed to listen to them talking about someone having a baby, especially her grandad. 'I'll go upstairs and dust the bedrooms, shall I?'

'You do that, sunshine, there's a good girl.' Mary understood and was relieved because she didn't think it was a fit subject for young girls. 'It'll save me having to do them tomorrow.' She waited until her daughter was out of the way, then with her head bent and a finger running along the plush of the chenille tablecloth, she began to speak.

Amy opened her mouth several times, her face red with anger and disgust, but Mary silenced her with a shake of her head. However, keeping silent didn't sit well with the big woman and she could be heard muttering under her breath, 'The bleedin' bitch, she deserves to be skinned alive.'

Molly, who didn't know anything about a baby, listened with mounting horror. And when Mary had finished, the Irishwoman made the sign of the cross and said, 'In the name of God, what sort of a person is she?'

'A very wicked woman, Molly.'

Amy had so much to say she spluttered. 'What did I tell yer, girl? Didn't I say it might not be yer dad's baby? It was the first thing I thought of when yer told me. But yer wouldn't have it, would yer?'

'Me dad didn't give a hint that it wasn't his, so why would I think different? He probably thought it was the easiest way out. But that bitch has ruined his life. He didn't look his age until she got her claws into him, now he's old and haggard. He looks so unhappy, as if he's got the troubles of the world on his shoulders.'

'So he doesn't know what yer've found out?' Amy asked. And when Mary shook her head, her neighbour tutted. 'What are yer going to do about it? If I was in your shoes, and it was my dad, I'd break her bleedin' neck for her.'

'Stan thinks we should get her out of me dad's house without him knowing anything about it until it's all over. So I've got a plan in me head, which might work, but I'd need the help of me friends. That's why I asked yer over.'

Amy lifted her ample bosom and laid it on the table so she could lean forward. 'If yer want someone to kick her out, I'll be more than willing to do the job. It's what yer dad should have done ages ago, when he first found out what she was really like.'

'Me dad hasn't got the strength to argue, never mind throw her out. But I'll do that, with the help of me mam's old neighbours. That's why I kept Laura off, for some moral support. What I'm short of, is someone who'll go and see Charlie's mother and tell her she's going to be a grandmother. Her son's got this girl in the family way, her parents are throwing her out and she's nowhere to go. Under no circumstances is me dad's name to be mentioned, or our real names.'

'I'll do that,' Amy said, with a look of relish. 'I'm good at that sort of thing. What did yer say her name was, Hettie Owens? Well, I'm sure me and Hettie will get on like a house on fire. I'll have her feeling heartily sorry for the girl and the unborn baby what her son is the father of. What I won't tell her, is that the girl in question is the devil in disguise.'

'Yer'd have to be diplomatic, Amy. She wouldn't have to know who yer are in case it gets back to me dad. He'd never show his face around here again if he thought everyone knew his business.'

Molly read the misgiving on Mary's face and was quick to reassure her. 'Don't you worry, me darlin', I'll go with Amy and we'll be discretion itself.'

Amy's eyes flew sideways. 'What did yer say we'll be, Molly?'

'Discreet, me darlin'. We'll be careful what we say.'

'Oh aye, we'll be that. I'm good at being careful, I am.'

Mary wrote the address down and they discussed how the two women should go about it. Then she told them of her plans to get her mam's old friends to rally round and help her put the frighteners on Celia. 'I know things don't always go to plan, but I hope these do. I said so many prayers last night, God must surely have heard them.'

'When we've done our bit, d'yer want us to go up to yer dad's?' Amy asked. 'To let yer know how we got on?'

'Call in to Monica Platt's first, see how the land lies. Celia isn't going to take this without putting up a fight, I can tell yer.'

'Yer'll have Laura with yer, so it's two against one.' Amy showed her serious side. 'Just keep thinking of yer dad and what she's done to him. And what she's done to the home yer mam was so proud of. That should give yer enough courage to belt merry hell out of her.'

Molly pushed her chair back. 'Let's go and get dressed properly, Amy, and make a start. We need to get there early before the woman goes to the shops.'

Mary waved them off, then called Laura. 'Ten minutes, sunshine, then we're on our way.'

Amy put on her brightest smile when the door opened. 'Hello, are you Hettie Owens?'

The woman smiled back. She was quite tall, ramrod straight, with steel-grey hair plaited into a bun at the nape of her neck. 'That's me, queen, can I help yer?'

'We'd like a word with yer, if yer don't mind. It's about your Charlie.'

The door was opened wider and the woman stepped back. 'Come in.'

The hallway and living room were spotlessly clean. Furniture highly polished, grate rubbed until you could see your face in it, and the brass companion set gleaming. 'Yer've got a nice house, Mrs

Owens,' Molly said, trying to hide her Irish accent which would be a dead giveaway. 'It's a credit to yer.'

'Thank yer, queen. And the name's Hettie, that's what everybody calls me.' Hettie gestured towards the couch. 'Sit down and take the weight off yer feet.' She sat in a rocking chair at the side of the fireplace. 'Did yer want to leave a message for Charlie?'

'Well, no, not really.' Amy pulled a face. 'I don't know whether this will be good news for yer, or bad. But your Charlie's been a naughty boy, and he's put a girl in the family way. Well, she's not a girl really, she's in her thirties. But her family are up in arms about it and they're going to throw her out. She'll be on the streets today, with nowhere to go. Being a mother meself, I didn't think yer'd want that to happen, not when your Charlie has admitted to everyone that he's the father.'

The rocking chair stopped and Hettie looked shocked to the core. 'I don't know nothing about this, Charlie hasn't said a word. Does he know this woman's being thrown out?'

'That I couldn't tell yer, Hettie. It's just that I know the family and they're very religious. They're mortified with the shame their daughter's brought on the house. So I just thought yer should know, seeing as the baby will be your grandchild. If it was me, I'd take the girl in, rather than see her roaming the streets looking for somewhere to lay her head. I'd feel it was my Christian duty.'

'What's this girl's name?' Hettie asked, some colour returning to her cheeks. 'And where does she live?'

'Her name's Celia, but that's all I'm going to tell yer. After all, it's got nothing to do with me, except I couldn't live with meself if I hadn't tried to do something. I'm not so worried about the girl, it's the baby I'm thinking of. And I can tell just by looking at yer, Hettie, that yer've got a kind heart. So ask Charlie when he comes in, he'll tell yer all yer want to know.' It took three attempts before Amy could push herself up off the low couch. 'I know yer'll see yer son does the right thing and I'm glad me and – er – and Margaret came. My name's Olive, by the way.'

Hettie looked shell-shocked as she followed them down the hall. 'How can I get in touch with yer, if I need to?'

'I've done what I thought I had to, Hettie. I don't want to get involved any more. Have a word with yer son 'cos, after all, it *is* his baby.'

Amy linked her arm through Molly's and the two women set off down the street, leaving Charlie's mother with very unChristian feelings towards her son. But as the day wore on, and the shock wore off, she began to think it might be nice to be a grandmother. A baby would certainly put a halt to her son's gallivanting. It was about time he settled down.

Halfway down the street, Amy asked in a muffled voice, 'How d'yer think it went, Molly? Did I do all right?'

Molly squeezed her arm. 'I'm proud of yer, me darlin', so I am. Yer were that convincing I got carried away and almost offered to take the girl in meself, so I did. It's an actress yer should have been, Amy.'

'And did yer notice, girl, I did it all without using one swearword? That's a record for me. If I told my Ben, he wouldn't believe me.'

'Yer could hardly swear when yer were doing yer Christian duty, Amy. Sure, wouldn't that have been very unChristian of yer? And wouldn't yer have had the Good Lord frowning?'

'D'yer think it worked, though? Or have I given the performance of me life for nothing? I should have had an audience – I was wasted there.' Then came her mischievous chuckle. 'I know, I'll go over it again tonight for my Ben. He can take the part of Hettie, 'cos she didn't have much to say for herself, did she?'

'Sure, the poor woman didn't have much chance, not when you were in full flow. She was flabbergasted, and that's putting it mild. I'll bet a pound to a penny she's sitting in that rocking chair wondering whether she imagined it all.'

'I hope not, Molly, I hope it sunk in. Otherwise Mary will have me guts for garters.'

'Oh, it sunk in, right enough. Charlie might be in for an ear-bashing when he comes home, but I doubt if she'd turn Celia away. It was the use of the words "religious" and "Christian" that did it. Did yerself not notice the statue of Our Lady on the sideboard? Sure, the woman's a Catholic and she'll not be tempting the wrath of God.'

'I wonder how Mary's getting on?' Feeling as though her mission had been accomplished and successful, Amy's thoughts went to her best friend. 'We got the easy bit – she'll have a fight on her hands. Celia is one tough cookie; she won't leave like a lamb, all meek and mild.'

'Then let's get to her side as quick as we can.' Molly tugged on her arm. 'We're in luck – there's a tram coming.'

'It's a fine how-d'yer-do, isn't it?' Monica Platt had thought nothing that Celia did would surprise her any more, but this latest news had knocked the stuffing out of her. 'All the neighbours thought yer dad was mad at the time for marrying a woman half his age, but if it had worked out, we'd have been glad for him. But the queer one didn't even try, she wrapped him around her little finger from day one. And he's too much the gentleman, he let her get away with it. But this latest trick goes beyond the pale. He wants his head testing if he doesn't throw her out, bag and baggage.'

'I don't want to give him the option – I don't think he could stand up to it. So I want to do it for him, and I was hoping you, and some of me mam's other old mates, would help me.'

'I will, queen, I wouldn't hesitate. And I know three or four others who would rub their hands in glee if they were asked.'

'The thing is, I want to do it today, before she can get her hands on him. I've seen marks on his face that couldn't have got there by accident, and I'll swear it was her that put them there. Yer see, if she went for him, he wouldn't fight back because he thinks any man who lifts his hand to a woman is a bully and a coward.'

Monica looked at her with sympathy and understanding. 'Yer don't need to tell me anything about yer dad, Mary – I've known him since before you were born. And as for Celia, yes, she would have put the marks on his face. These walls are very thin and we've heard her carrying on. She shouts and yells at the top of her voice, and her language, for a woman, is terrible. Sure enough, the next day we'd see Joe with scratches on his cheeks, or bruises.'

Laura hadn't said much, but now she ground her words out. 'If I get my hands on her, I'll give her a good hiding for doing that to my grandad.'

Mary patted her hand. 'Let's be content if we can get her out of me dad's house and out of his life.' She appealed to the woman who'd been her mam's best friend. 'How about it, Monica, will yer help?'

'With the greatest of pleasure.' The older woman smiled. 'Besides, I've got nothing on today, so it'll fill in me time and I'll consider it time well spent.'

Mary explained what she had in mind, and also what Amy and Molly were doing right this minute. And while she was speaking, Monica was nodding her head in agreement. 'Good planning, queen, yer'd make a good army captain. Now if you'll put the kettle on and see to a pot of tea for yerselves, I'll go and make a few calls.'

It was half an hour before Monica came back, but she didn't come back alone. With her were four neighbours whom Mary had known all her life. Maggie Smith, Nellie Mitchell, Lizzie Thompson and Ada Bullen. Tears came to her eyes when they stood in a line facing her across the table. They spoke as one. 'Hello, queen.'

Remembering the laughs her mother had had with these women who, when times were bad, would help each other out with half a loaf, a shovel of coal or a cup of sugar, Mary had to speak through the lump in her throat. 'If me mam's looking down on yer now, she'll be smiling and saying "thank you".'

'Ay, girl, we're doing it for yer dad,' Maggie Smith said, folding her black knitted shawl across her chest. 'But we'll be doing ourselves a favour at the same time.'

'Ye're not kidding, we'll be glad to see the back of her.' Nellie Mitchell turned her head to make sure her neighbours were nodding in agreement. 'Have yer seen the state of her bleedin' house?'

'Bloody disgrace it is,' Lizzie Thompson said. 'Spoils the whole street.'

'Aye, and that's what we see when we look out of our window,' Ada Bullen complained, playing with the long hairs that grew from a mole on her chin. 'It'll be good riddance to bad rubbish.'

'*If* we can pull it off. Still, we can but try.' Mary sighed. 'Has Monica told yer what's happened, and what I'm trying to do?'

'Yeah, girl, we know about the baby and what yer friends are doing.' Maggie Smith took it upon herself to be the spokeswoman. 'I hate to say this, but the woman yer dad married is no more than a whore. Am I right, Monica?'

'I'm afraid so. I don't want to pile the agony on, Mary, but the more yer know, the more determined yer'll be. Many a night me and Phil have heard her in the entry with a bloke. And we could tell from the noises that they weren't just having a friendly conversation.'

'Right, that does it.' Mary stood up so quickly the chair would have toppled over if Laura hadn't caught it in time. 'Me temper's on the boil now, I'm just in the mood for her.'

'She'll still be in bed queen.'

'She was in bed last time I came, but I got her up. If you ladies will give me fifteen minutes after I get in, then will yer stand in a group outside her window?' Mary waited for their nods, before tapping her daughter on the shoulder. 'Come on, sunshine, let's go.'

Celia heard the banging on the door and pulled the bedclothes up to her chin. 'Whoever it is can sod off, I'm not getting up for no one.' The banging became louder but she still ignored it. 'Bleedin' cheek knocking like that, I've a good mind to go down and belt them one.'

But the sound of breaking glass had her slipping her legs out of bed and struggling into a scruffy dressing gown. 'Just wait, whoever yer are. Yer'll be sorry yer signed by the time I've finished with yer.'

Celia was prepared for a slanging match, but she was not prepared for the two people who confronted her when she opened the door. Her surprise showed briefly, then an evil smile crossed a face that still bore the traces of yesterday's make-up. 'Well, if it isn't the stuck-up bitch herself, and her lying daughter.' Her laugh was scornful. 'I don't know which window yer broke, but it doesn't worry me 'cos yer old feller will pay for it. Now, yer can just bugger off to where yer came from, 'cos this time ye're not getting in.'

Laura moved before her mother. She was in the hall before Celia

332

had time to stop her. 'Come in, Mam, it's me grandad's house, not hers.'

'Oh, you'll be sorry, yer little bitch. Wait until I tell yer dear mother what you've been up to.'

Mary squeezed between them and went straight to the living room. She shut her eyes at the sight that met her, but she couldn't stop the smell of dirt from invading her nostrils. And her beloved father had to live in this pigsty. She shook her head; not any more he didn't, not after today.

Celia crossed to the mantelpiece and picked up a packet of cigarettes. She lit one and took a few puffs before brazenly staring at her husband's daughter and granddaughter. 'I don't know why ye're here, but seeing as yer are, yer may as well listen to a few home truths about this daughter of yours. Perhaps yer won't be so high-and-mighty when I've finished.' She moved to stand in front of Laura and pushed her sneering face close. 'I wonder where I should start?'

Laura put her hand in the middle of Celia's chest and pushed with all her might, sending the woman reeling backwards. 'Don't come near me, yer smell dirty.'

Mary stood in front of her daughter when, mad with rage, Celia went to grab her. 'Take yer filthy hands off her. And I know about the underskirt, the lies, the smoking and Gary. So that leaves yer with little to say to me. But I have a lot to say to *you*. We'll start off with the baby ye're carrying, and its father, Charlie.' She heard Celia gasp and smiled. 'Oh, there's much we know about you. Down the back entry with every Tom, Dick and Harry, like a woman of the streets. Well, yer heydays are over, at least from this house. It's up to Charlie to look after yer now, ye're his responsibility. So I want you out of here now. And I mean within the next half-hour.'

Celia's lip curled. 'Some hope you've got, yer stupid bitch. I'm not going anywhere so yer can forget it and bugger off.'

'Ye're leaving, Celia, if I have to kick yer out.'

'Just you try it, yer bleedin' cow! Wait until Joe hears about this.'

Laura lunged forward. 'Don't yer call my mother names.' She smacked Celia across the face. 'Ye're not fit to be in the same room as her.'

Mary pulled her daughter back. 'She's not worth it, sunshine, just leave her. She's got half an hour to pack her things and get out. Then we can clean this place up before yer grandad gets home.'

'Are yer deaf or something?' Celia asked. 'I'm not going anywhere, and you can't make me.'

Mary's eyes went to the window. 'The neighbours can make you.'

'Neighbours! They're not going to chase me, why should they?'

'Because they don't like yer. And they can chase yer, don't worry. They'll be glad to see the back of yer.' Mary jerked her thumb. 'Look

333

out of the window, Celia – can yer see them? They know all about yer baby, and Charlie, and what ye're trying to do to me dad.'

Celia saw five women, all with their arms folded across the handles of stiff brushes. And she no longer felt sure of her ground. 'They can't throw me out, it's my home.'

'Shall we invite them in and yer can ask them? But I'd take my word for it if I were you, 'cos they don't think very kindly of yer at the moment and I wouldn't vouch for yer safety. If I don't go out there in the next five minutes and tell them yer've agreed to leave, then heaven help yer. And if ye're wondering why they're doing it, it's because they know ye're an out-and-out rotter, not fit to lick me dad's shoes.'

'I'd better go and tell them what's happening, Mam,' Laura said. 'Otherwise they might break the door down.'

'Yes, okay, sunshine. Tell them to give me another five minutes.'

As soon as Laura was out of the room, Mary turned on Celia. 'If yer know what's good for yer, yer'll leave without fuss. And yer won't show yer face in this street again.'

'How the hell can I leave? I've got nowhere to go.'

'Oh yes, yer have! Yer can make a home with the father of yer baby. In fact, Hettie Owens will probably be expecting yer any time.'

The colour drained from Celia's face. 'You cow. You bleedin', stuck-up, toffee-nosed cow. One of these days I'll meet yer when ye're on yer own and I'll scratch yer bleedin' eyes out.'

'I'll give yer two bits of advice before yer go upstairs to pack yer things. Don't even think of retaliating 'cos yer'd come off worse, I promise. And secondly, keep away from my father. Don't be waiting for him outside work to wheedle money off him, because I'll find out and yer'll live to regret it. From this day, you and the baby are Charlie's responsibility. He's had his fun, now let him pay for it.'

Laura came running in. 'Mam, the neighbours said they're coming over.'

'Go and tell them to wait, Celia's just going upstairs to pack her things.'

Mary and Laura got home five minutes before Stan was due. Jenny was already there and had set the table. 'I didn't know what yer had in for tea, Mam, otherwise I'd have got it ready.'

'That's all right, sunshine, we'll have to make do with egg and chips. Yer can start peeling the spuds if yer will, to give me time to get me breath back.'

'Tell me how yer got on first, I'm dying to know. I've been a bundle of nerves all day, I couldn't settle to work.'

'Can yer wait until yer dad gets in? He'll be here any minute. If I start telling you, it would mean me starting all over again with him.

334

And it's a long story, sunshine, I can't tell it in five minutes.'

Stan popped his head around the door. 'I'm here now, and I'll have a heart attack if I have to wait much longer to hear how it went.'

Mary looked surprised. 'I didn't hear yer coming in!'

'One of yer had left the door open.' Stan slung his cap on the couch and sat down. 'Ye're all in one piece, so yer didn't have a fight on yer hands, thank God. Now tell us, is Celia still at yer dad's house?'

'I don't want to tell it in dribs and drabs, so wouldn't yer like yer dinner first? Not that ye're getting anything to write home about, I'm afraid, just egg and chips. But if it's any consolation, Ben and Seamus are having the same, 'cos Amy and Molly have only just got home.'

'Me dinner can wait, I want to know what happened.'

'Okay, let's all sit around the table and I'll start from half seven this morning, when I knocked on Amy's door.'

It took well over half an hour, and in that time Stan smoked three cigarettes. He wasn't normally a heavy smoker, but his nerves were on edge. He did raise a smile when Amy's and Molly's part in the operation was told. But although he had many question flying around in his head, he never spoke. And Jenny felt as though she was sitting in the pictures watching a sad but exciting film.

Mary was coming to the end of the saga. 'So the last I saw of Celia, she was walking down the street carrying a suitcase with all her belongings in. And behind her marched five women clutching stiff sweeping brushes. Amy and Molly had arrived by then, and they helped me clean me dad's house. We sent Laura to the shops for everything we needed because there was no Aunt Sally, no dusters or floorcloths. In fact, there was nothing – she must never have done any housework. Anyway, I left me mates to it and went down to me dad's works when I knew he'd be on his dinner break. That was the hardest part, because I didn't know how he'd take it. But he seemed relieved, although ashamed that we'd done what he couldn't bring himself to do. And he did no more than ask his boss for the rest of the day off, saying there was a problem at home. On our way back, I did some shopping and made a big pan of scouse for him.'

'I can't take it all in, yer've done so much in one day.' Stan gazed at his wife with love and admiration. 'I take me hat off to yer.'

'I didn't do it on me own, love. I had all my friends to help, and also me mam's. I could never have done it without them.'

'And all without a fight! I thought she'd be like a raving banshee!'

'Ah, well, I was saving that until the last.' Mary gazed across the table at her eldest daughter. 'There wasn't a fight, but there was a hand raised. Celia called me a not very nice name and Laura gave her a really hard slap across the face.'

Jenny looked at her sister in awe. Then she put an arm across her shoulders and squeezed. 'I'm glad yer did that, sis. I'm proud of yer.'

'And me, too, love,' Stan said. 'Thanks for sticking up for yer mam.'

Mary was dog-tired, but it was a pleasant tiredness. 'Me dad's coming here straight from work tomorrow dinnertime, and he's staying for dinner and tea. And talking of food, I'd better get cracking on feeding yer, 'cos Amy and Molly are coming over later to go over it all again.'

She stretched her arms above her head. 'I'll sleep without rocking tonight, with no worries on me mind. Oh, peace, perfect peace.'

Chapter Twenty-Seven

They were just finishing their meal when Laura saw a figure pass the window. She was off her chair like a shot. 'I'll open the door – it's Gary.'

'It looks like he's the one for her,' Stan said, smiling at his wife. 'He seems to have done wonders for her.'

'He'll do for me, he's a nice boy,' Mary said. 'And we've got him to thank for what we've achieved today.'

Gary was laughing as he was pulled into the room. 'Nice to see yer again, Mr and Mrs Nightingale – and you, Jenny. I've only heard a few garbled words, but it sounded as though yer've had a good day.'

'A brilliant day, son, thanks to you. But I'll leave Laura to tell yer the part we played, and Amy and Molly will be here soon to tell yer theirs. I must warn yer though, that me best mate, Amy, has a wicked sense of humour and a vocabulary that includes quite a few words yer won't find in no dictionary. So I hope ye're not easily offended.'

'Laura's told me about her Auntie Amy, and I can't wait to meet her. She sounds like a barrel of fun.'

Stan grinned. 'She's the funniest thing on two legs, son, and as sound as a pound.' He'd only just finished speaking when there was a knock on the window that had the pane of glass quivering in its frame. 'Yer didn't have to wait long, this is her.'

'Oh Lord, look at the state of the place.' Mary tucked a stray lock of hair behind her ear. 'Dirty dishes still on the table and me without the energy to move.'

'I'll clear the table, Mam.' Jenny was already collecting the plates. 'Laura can open the front door.'

Amy waddled in, followed by Molly. 'Is your Laura stuck to that feller? Silly buggers, they shouldn't mess around with glue, their hands are stuck together now. We had to flamingwell squeeze past them.'

'This is me boyfriend, Auntie Amy,' Laura looked so proud as she said it, 'and his name's Gary. I told him all about yer and he said he was dying to meet yer.'

Amy stretched to her full height, which was up to Gary's chest. 'Me reputation has gone before me, has it? Anyway, lad, it's nice to meet yer.' Amy pumped his hand before saying, 'This is me partner in crime, Molly Moynihan.'

Molly held out her hand. 'It's a pleasure, so it is. Mary has told us about yer.'

'Will yer all sit down,' Mary said, 'yer make the place look untidy.' She noticed Laura was still gripping Gary's hand. 'If ye're not going to let go, you two had better sit on the couch.'

Amy gave Stan a dig in the arm before plonking herself on one of the wooden chairs. 'Eh, Stan, have yer heard I've added another string to me bow? I'm in the acting lark now, and if I do say so meself, Ethel Barrymore's got nothing on me.' She leaned forward to seek confirmation from Molly, and being top heavy, nearly overbalanced. Everyone held their breath as she steadied herself, and laughed when she muttered, 'God strewth, I nearly went arse over elbow.' She covered them all with her cheeky grin. 'Anyway, Molly, me darlin', am I right about me acting, or am I right?'

'Yer were so convincing, me darlin', didn't meself get carried along? I felt so sorry for the pregnant girl who was being thrown out by her family, I only just stopped meself in time from saying I had a spare room she could have. And didn't poor Hettie Owens look as though she'd been struck by lightning?'

'Amy has that effect on people, Molly,' Mary said. 'I often feel I've been struck by a thunderbolt.'

'It's what yer need, girl.' Amy's chins did a quickstep as she nodded her head. 'Ye're that bleedin' slow on the uptake, sometimes I feel like sticking a firework up a certain part of yer – er – yer atemy.'

'The word is anatomy, Amy,' Mary told her, biting on the inside of her cheek to keep a smile at bay, 'and I'd prefer yer not to mention my unmentionables in mixed company, if yer don't mind.'

The chair seat was hidden under Amy's rather large bottom, but it creaked its protest when she shook with laughter. 'Ay, girl, if I had to go through life without mentioning the unmentionables, I'd never open me bleedin' gob! And, anyway, God gave us everything we've got, and He wouldn't have done if we couldn't mention them.' There was more than a hint of mischief in the look she gave Mary. 'Or make good use of them. I can't speak for you lot, but me and Ben make good use of what the Lord gave us.'

Mary capitulated and chuckled when she said, 'This is only the second time Gary's been in this house, and the poor lad must be wondering what sort of family and friends Laura's got. I only hope he knows that ye're just a one-off, there's no more like you.'

Gary was in a state of bliss. Holding the hand of the girl he was head over heels in love with, and being made welcome in a home full of warmth and friendliness – well, his cup of happiness was overflowing. 'I'm not easily offended, Mrs Nightingale, and I'm really

338

enjoying meself. I just wish me mam was here, she'd be in her apple-cart.'

'You bring her to me, son,' Amy said, 'I'll teach her a thing or two.'

Gary burst out laughing. 'Yer don't know me mam – there's not much she doesn't know. In fact, she could probably teach you a thing or two.'

Amy studied him for a while before turning to Mary. 'Ay, girl, he's all right. Your Laura has her Auntie Amy's permission to court him.'

Laura finally let go of Gary's hand and jumped up. She gave Amy a big hug and said, 'I'm glad ye're me auntie.' Then she turned to her mother. 'Me and Gary will wash the dishes, Mam, and I can tell him what we did today. Then I want to take him to meet Cynthia.'

'Is it all right if I go and get changed, Mam?' Jenny asked. 'I'm going down to Auntie Lizzie's with Mick.'

'Yes, to both of yer. But remember, Grandad's business is his own and that's the way it stays. It is not a subject for discussion.' She gazed at her two daughters who seemed to have changed overnight from young girls to young ladies. 'Anyway, I'm sure yer've got more important things to talk about.'

Cynthia weighed Gary up as they shook hands. He was certainly everything that Laura had said he was. 'Well, we meet at last. I was beginning to think yer were a figment of me mate's imagination.'

'No, I am real, I can assure yer. And I hope we'll be seeing a lot of each other from now on. Laura tells me yer've been friends since yer started school.'

'Yeah, a real pair of horrors we were. Anyway, come and meet me mam and dad. I'm expecting Bill any minute – perhaps we can go for a walk and get to know each other?'

'Ooh, yeah, I'd like that,' Laura said. 'I want us all to be friends. Is that all right with you, Gary?'

'Anything you want, babe, suits me. As long as you're happy, I'm happy.'

Cynthia's parents made him welcome and were soon engaged in an easygoing conversation. Fanny Pennington was finding a peace in her home she had not experienced since her daughter was old enough to know she could get her own way if she played up to her father. But those bad days were behind them now, never to return. Her husband treated her with affection and respect, and her daughter with a love that grew stronger every day.

When Bill arrived, Gary noticed he greeted Cynthia with a kiss, and he promised himself he'd do the same next time he called for Laura. After all, he was nearly nineteen; he wasn't a kid.

'D'yer feel like a walk, Bill?' Cynthia asked, after introductions were made. 'Just for an hour or so.'

'Yeah, that's fine.'

'I'll go up and get me coat, then. Come up with me, Laura – I've got something I want to show yer.'

Cynthia closed the bedroom door behind her and leaned back against it. 'Well, did yer do it, kid?'

Laura nodded. 'Celia's out of me dad's house now, and although we're not sure, we think she may have gone to Charlie's. Gary will find out 'cos he knows people who know Charlie and his mam. I haven't got time to tell yer now 'cos it would take too long. I'll come down tomorrow afternoon and we can have a good chinwag. But it would never have happened if you hadn't told me straight what a bitch I've been.'

'We've both been, kid, not just you. Anyway, I'm happy for yer mam and yer grandad. And I've got to say, I think Gary's smashing. We've both done well – better, I suppose, than we deserve. I for one know how lucky I am, with Bill.'

'Me too! I love the bones of Gary, and me mam, dad and Jenny. They've been really brilliant with me. I'm going to make it up to them, I've promised meself that.'

'Going out with Gary will help yer. When yer love someone, it doesn't half change yer. I was as hard as nails before Bill came along, now I'm as sentimental as anyone can get.'

Laura smiled. 'I know, don't tell me: "Try a little tenderness".'

'That's it, kiddo! Keep singing the song.' Cynthia opened the wardrobe and took out her best coat. 'Wouldn't it be smashing if we both got engaged on the same day?'

'It would be more than smashing, it would be heaven.'

'Janet's late,' Jenny said as they sat in Lizzie's. 'Didn't she say she'd meet us here, John?'

John looked at the clock and nodded. 'I think I'll take a walk round there, see what's keeping her. I won't be long.'

'If Mrs Porter opens the door, and she's got a rolling pin in her hand, run like hell.' Mick chortled. 'I've heard she's got a good aim.' As John was opening the front door, his mate yelled, 'Ay, yer didn't kiss Janet good-night last night, did yer? If yer did, then I'd start running now if I were you.'

John set off with a grin on his face. He'd only ever kissed Janet on the cheek – surely that didn't warrant a bash on the head? As he turned into the side street, he told himself it didn't seem the same in Auntie Lizzie's without her.

Martha Porter opened the door. 'Come in, son, she's upstairs putting the finishing touches to herself. She's been that long getting ready, anyone would think she was going to a ball.'

'I heard that, Mam.' Janet came slowly down the stairs. 'I haven't

340

been that long, only an hour.' When she reached the bottom stair, she patted her hair, which was a mass of shining curls. 'Me mam bought me some curling tongs and it took me ages to get the hang of them. I hope I look all right.' She stared at John. 'Well, John Hanley, have I made a mess of meself?'

With her mother looking on, John blushed. 'No, it looks great.'

'Right, then, we'll be off. I won't be late, Mam.'

They reached the top of her street and when she hadn't spoken one word, John asked, 'It's not like you to be so quiet, curly top. What's wrong?'

'I was thinking. In fact, John, I've been doing a lot of thinking these last few days. The last few months, really, but it's only the last few days that are important.'

'That's a lot of thinking for you, Jan, what's on yer mind?'

Janet sighed. 'Can we stand here, on the corner, while I tell yer? I don't want to say anything in front of the others.'

John cupped her elbow and led her to stand against a high wall. 'Don't look so serious, curly top, I don't like to see yer with a frown on yer face. So come on, get whatever it is off yer chest.'

'Well, I know you and Mick both wanted Jenny to be yer girlfriend, I've always known it. And now she's definitely promised to be Mick's, I don't want yer to say yer'll be me boyfriend just because of that. Yer see, I'd be second choice then, and I don't want to be yer second choice, John.'

John closed his eyes and let his head drop back for a second. 'I wouldn't do that to yer, Janet. I wouldn't want to spend me life with someone who was me second choice.' His forehead creased as he sought the right words. 'I've lived next door to Jenny since she was born and she's always been special to me – always will be. And she was twelve and a half when Mick told me he was waiting for her to grow up, then he'd ask her to be his girl. He said he'd loved her since he was six years of age and she was a toddler. I was jealous and told him to get in the queue. And over the years, we've acted out the part of rivals. We've had a lot of fun doing it, 'cos he is me best mate and we like to clown around. I've gone along with it without really giving it any thought.' He reached for Janet's hand. 'Then you came on the scene and it was nice being with yer 'cos yer made me laugh.'

'Yer mean yer thought I was daft.'

'Yes, to be honest, I did! But I know now there's nothing daft about yer. Yer've wormed yer way into my affections, and woven a spell around me heart. I didn't know this was happening until the night of yer birthday party. And even then I wouldn't believe it because me and Mick were still acting as rivals and it had become a habit. The test came the other night when Mick said Jenny had agreed to be his girlfriend. I expected to feel angry, or sad, but I didn't. It was the end of a chapter in me life, but not the end of the story. I love Mick as much as I love Jenny, and nothing will ever change that.'

'Ye're talking a lot, John Hanley, but yer not saying what I want to hear. So will yer get on with it, please?'

John grinned, thinking life would never be dull with her. Placing his hands on her shoulders, he bent to put his face on a level with hers. 'If I'd had any doubts, they disappeared when I was sitting waiting for yer in Auntie Lizzie's. It wasn't the same without yer, and I got this terrible thought that yer might have dumped me. Because if yer won't be me girlfriend I don't know what I'll do – probably join the Foreign Legion.'

'Then for heaven's sake, ask me!'

'Janet, curly top, darling, will yer be me girlfriend?'

'Yes, John Hanley, I will.' There was a twinkle in her eyes. 'If I remember rightly, Jenny got a kiss from Mick.'

John feigned a look of horror. 'Oh no, not without asking yer mam first!'

'I don't tell me mam everything.'

'Yer mean right here on the street?'

Janet pulled his head down, and when their lips met John didn't see the woman who nearly walked into a lamp-post because she was watching them instead of where she was going. And all thoughts of rolling pins fled. He was experiencing a sensation he'd never felt before, and loving it. 'Wow! Even me toes have curled up.'

'Yer can have another one when yer walk me home.'

'Oh no, curly top, not until I've asked yer mam and dad if I can start taking yer out.'

'Yer don't need to do that – I'll tell them.'

'I'll do the job properly, so until then, don't act daft.'

She pulled on his coat-sleeve as they started to walk. 'I'm not daft, John Hanley. I've got you, and I think that's very clever of me.'

'Where the heck have yer been?' Jenny asked as she let them in. 'We were getting very worried about yer.'

Janet's face was one big smile. 'I'm sorry if yer've been worried, Auntie Lizzie, but I've just been proposed to and had me first kiss.'

John doubled up, his laughter louder than anyone's. 'I haven't proposed to yer, curly top!' He spluttered. 'Yer only do that when yer want to get engaged or married.'

But Janet had her own ideas on that. 'Yer can't get engaged or married without courting first, can yer? I mean, yer've got to start somewhere, and you've just proposed that I be yer girlfriend. If yer hadn't done that, we'd never be able to get engaged or married 'cos I'd be a stranger to yer.'

342

Jenny hugged her friend. 'There's logic in there somewhere, Jan, and when I'm in bed tonight I'll try and figure it out.'

Lizzie wiped her eyes. 'Oh dear, you'll never know what joy you children have brought me. In all me eighty odd years I've never laughed as much as I have since I fell off the front step. It was the best thing I ever did.'

Mick said, 'She's got me thinking now. I think I'd better go over it all again 'cos I'd hate it if I could never get engaged or married to yer, Jenny.' He went down on one knee and took her hand. 'Jenny Nightingale, will yer be my girlfriend?'

Jenny's infectious giggle rang out and her pretty face was a joy to behold. 'Yes I will, Mick Moynihan, with the greatest of pleasure.'

Lizzie was saying a little prayer, asking God to leave her on this earth long enough to see these two couples happily married and settled down.

Mick and Jenny stood with their arms around each other's waists and watched their best friends walking down the street. Janet had a habit of moving her head when she spoke, so they knew she was talking fifteen to the dozen. Then they saw John pull her to him as his laughter filled the night air.

'They were made for each other, them two,' Mick said. 'I've been telling him for ages that she was the one for him, but he wouldn't have it.' He gave a quick glance around before planting a kiss on her cheek. 'Just like we were made for each other.'

They were so engrossed in their own little world, high on excitement and emotion, they didn't see the courting couple until they nearly stumbled over them.

'Sorry, pal,' Mick said. 'We weren't looking where we were going.'

Laura and Gary broke apart, but it was with reluctance. 'I'm afraid we weren't looking either,' Gary laughed. 'We were otherwise engaged.'

'Ay, our kid, I'm older than you so I'm pulling rank on yer.' Laura's white teeth flashed when she smiled. 'This is our spot.'

Mick didn't like the sound of that. 'And I suppose yer'll be seeing each other every night, will yer?'

Laura put her arms around Gary's waist and her voice was husky. 'Every night, even Sunday.'

'Then we'll have to come to some arrangement,' Mick said. 'You stay this side of the window, and me and Jenny will take the other. And they'll be reserved places.'

'Suits me fine.' Gary moved Laura the yard needed to make it fair. 'It's best we know where we stand.'

'Right, pal.' Mick pulled Jenny into his arms, then looked across at the other couple. 'And no peeking, right?'

343

* * *

It was Jenny's giggle which alerted Mary. She left her chair and crossed to the window. Moving the draw curtain just a little, she looked out and smiled. Both her daughters were in safe hands, they'd never come to any harm from the boys they had chosen.

'Ay, Stan, come and see this. Things have moved faster this week than I thought. Yer two daughters are standing outside, in their boyfriends' arms being kissed very soundly.'

Stan joined her at the window. 'We shouldn't be doing this, yer know – they'd go mad if they knew.' But wrong or not, he couldn't resist a peep. 'It takes yer back, doesn't it, love? Twenty years ago, we were doing the same thing.' He took her hand from the curtain and let it fall back into place. 'I don't see why they should have all the fun. We're not too old to enjoy a kiss and a cuddle.'

Mary walked into his arms, tilted her head back and waited for the kiss that could still send tingles down her spine. 'This has got to be the happiest day of my life, Stan Nightingale.'

Stay As Sweet As You Are

I dedicate this book to the many readers who have written to say how much they enjoy my books. I appreciate your letters, and hope my characters will find favour with you.

A friendly greeting from Joan

Lucy Mellor is the heroine of this story, and I think you'll love her. But leave room in your heart for the other larger-than-life characters who will have you reaching for your hankies. There is a baddie, and you'll meet her soon enough.

Happy reading!

Chapter One

The flickering flame from the streetlamp cast an eerie glow over the face of the young girl huddled on the step of the two-up two-down terrace house. Her elbows were resting on her drawn-up knees and her two hands cupped her dirty, tear-stained face. Her eyes kept darting up and down the silent street as though anxious for the sight of someone, and occasionally her head would turn to look back through the open front door and into the darkness of the house.

Lucy Mellor let out a long sigh. She was in for a hiding now, no matter what she did. Her mam would say she should have taken herself off to bed while it was still light, instead of staying up until this time. But when she'd gone out at half-past seven, her mam had said she'd only be out for half an hour so Lucy had stayed up waiting for her. Then it had started to get dark and she was afraid to go upstairs with no one in the house. She had thought about striking a match and lighting the gas-light, but her dad had warned her about standing on a chair striking a match. She was small for her eleven years and he said it was too dangerous. And now, with the house in pitch darkness she was too afraid to go inside, never mind climbing the stairs to her bedroom.

She heard a door close nearby and Lucy quickly swivelled her legs around into the hall, hoping whoever it was would pass without seeing her. She was in enough trouble without the neighbours knowing she'd been left alone until this time of night. They wouldn't think twice about having a go at her mam; they were always telling Ruby Mellor that she wasn't fit to be a mother. Then the girl heard the slow slithering footsteps and knew it was old Mrs McBride who lived three doors away. She'd be on her way to the corner pub for her nightly half-pint of stout. That meant it must be nearly ten o'clock because the old woman never went until just on closing-time.

Lucy held her breath, hoping their neighbour would pass without glancing in the doorway, but the old woman had sharp eyesight.

'Is that you, queen? What on earth are yer doing sitting there at this time? Yer should have been in bed hours ago.' There was surprise in Aggie McBride's voice, and her eyes narrowed when she noticed the house was in darkness. 'Are yer all on yer own, queen? Where's that mother of yours got to?'

'She's only gone out for half an hour, Mrs Aggie – I'm waiting for her.' Lucy was used to making excuses for her mother, she was doing it all the time. 'She'll be here any minute now.'

Aggie huffed. This girl had the face of an angel, with thick dark curly hair framing her heart-shaped face, and green eyes as big as saucers. She was a daughter any mother would be proud of, but not Ruby Mellor. She was too fond of herself, out for a good time and to hell with everyone else. All the neighbours had her taped and not one had a good word for her. She treated her daughter like a skivvy, making her do housework, shopping and even sending her scrounging to the neighbours if she ran short of anything. But she'd gone too far tonight, leaving a child in a dark house on her own; she deserved horse-whipping. 'Would yer like me to come in and light the gas for yer, queen? Then yer could get yerself off to bed before she comes in.'

If Lucy had been frightened before, she was now terrified. 'No, I'll be all right, Mrs Aggie, honest. Me mam will be here any minute now, yer'll see.' There was a sob in the girl's throat. 'Yer won't say anything to her, will yer, Mrs Aggie? Please?'

Aggie's temper was rising. How she'd love to give Ruby Mellor a piece of her mind. But if she did, Lucy would be the one to suffer. 'I'll not say a dickie-bird, queen, I promise. Anyway, yer dad will be finishing his two-to-ten shift any minute, so if yer mam knows what's good for her, she'll make sure she's home by then. If he finds you still up, and nothing ready for him to eat, then the sparks will fly.' Wrapping the knitted shawl across her arms, Aggie managed to hide the jug she was taking to the pub for her half-pint of stout. Not that she needed to hide it, everyone in the neighbourhood knew Aggie and her drinking habits. 'I'll be on me way, queen, before Alec puts the towels on and I miss me nightly dose of medicine. And that would be a fate worse than death.' She began to shuffle away. 'I hope ye're not here when I come back, Lucy, 'cos if yer are I'm going to sit with yer and wait for that mother of yours.'

'I won't be, Mrs Aggie,' Lucy said, willing the old lady to move away so she could think of what to do. She had two choices. She could brave the dark and run up to bed, or she could brave her mother's anger. It wasn't often that Lucy rebelled against her life, but right now she was asking herself why *she* should be the one to be afraid. She hadn't done anything wrong. Her mam was in the wrong, she had no right to stay out all this time.

Lucy sighed. She knew she'd get a hiding when her mam came in. Never a day passed without her feeling the force of her mother's hands. And yet she never did anything to deserve it. She never answered back or gave cheek, never even looked sideways. But it didn't take much to send her mother into a temper, and she was always the whipping boy. It wasn't so bad when her dad was in; her mother wouldn't dare hit her in his presence. But he worked three shifts and she didn't see much of him. If he wasn't at work he was in bed. And she'd been well warned what would happen to her if she went running to him telling tales.

Ruby Mellor was gasping for breath as she ran up the street. She'd cut it fine tonight, and she'd be lucky if she got home in time to have Bob's bacon sizzling in the frying pan when he came back from work. She should never have listened to the friends she'd been drinking with when they coaxed her to stay a bit longer. But she'd been flattered by the attention of Wally Brown, who kept paying her compliments and keeping her glass filled. He was a handsome man in his thirties, a bachelor who was fond of the ladies. And Ruby lapped it up, telling herself another five minutes wouldn't do any harm. Well, she now understood that five minutes could make all the difference. If Bob got home before her there'd be hell to pay.

She reached into her coat pocket for the door key and her hand was outstretched when she realised the door was open and Lucy was standing on the step. 'What the bleedin' hell are you doing still up? Get in that house, quick.' Pushing past her daughter she ran into the living room and felt on the mantelpiece for a box of matches. She struck one, held it to the gas mantel and the room flooded with light. Then she spun around. 'What the hell d'yer think ye're playing at, yer little faggot? Why aren't yer in bed?'

Lucy dropped her eyes. 'Yer said yer were only going out for half an hour, and I waited for yer. Then it got dark and I was frightened to be in the house on me own.'

Ruby swung her arm out and her open palm caught Lucy on the side of the face, sending the girl reeling back. 'Frightened, were yer? Well, I'll give yer something to be frightened about, yer little faggot.'

Her hand touching her cheek, Lucy could feel the tears well up in her eyes and their warmth as they rolled down her cheeks. It was so unfair, she just had to speak out. 'It's not my fault, it's you what told lies. Half an hour yer said, and now it's gone ten o'clock.'

'Don't you dare answer me back. And what I do has got nothing to do with you. Ye're big and ugly enough to see yerself

351

to bed, and I'll make yer sorry yer didn't.'

Neither of them had heard the front door open or knew that Bob was standing in the hall listening. It was only when Ruby reached out to give Lucy a hiding that he made his presence known. 'Touch her and yer'll be out in that street on yer backside before yer know what's hit yer.' He put his arm across his daughter's shoulders and bent to kiss her hair. 'Don't cry, pet, you just take yerself off to bed while I have a word with yer mam.'

Lucy shivered. 'I'm cold and thirsty, Dad, could I have a hot drink, please?'

'I'll bring yer one up when yer mam decides a man needs a meal after a day's work. You poppy off and I'll bring yer a cup of tea in a minute.'

After Lucy had fled without a word or a glance, Ruby's face and manner changed as if someone had waved a magic wand. In the place of anger, there was a smile. 'She's making a mountain out of a molehill, the silly thing. I was busy talking in me mate's house and didn't realise the time. But I told Lucy to go to bed before I went out, and she should have done as she was told. Still, there's no harm done.' She made a move towards the kitchen. 'I'll see to yer supper, it won't take five minutes.'

Bob put his cap on the sideboard. 'You stay right where yer are until we get a few things straight.' He didn't speak for a while as he took stock of the woman he'd married fifteen years ago. She'd been nineteen then, and as pretty as a picture. Nice slim figure, mousy-coloured curly hair, laughing hazel eyes and a peaches and cream complexion. The woman he was facing now bore no resemblance to that happy-go-lucky girl. The mousy-coloured hair was bleached to a horrible pale yellow, the hazel eyes were hard and calculating and Ruby's face was caked with make-up. She looked like a brazen, cheap tart, and her actions matched her looks. 'Where have yer been from half-seven until now?'

'I told yer, I was in me mate's and the time just seemed to fly over.'

'Don't you lie to me!' Bob's voice was raised in anger. 'You must take me for a right bloody fool. I can smell the drink on yer from here, and it's not just one glass yer've had – yer've had a bellyful. And while ye're out enjoying yerself, yer leave an eleven-year-old girl on her own in the house. And I'll bet that yer never gave her one thought as yer sat boozing with yer cronies. What sort of a mother are yer? In fact, what sort of a wife are yer?'

Ruby tried to wheedle her way out of it. 'It's the first time it's happened, Bob, so don't get in a temper. I'll see to yer supper now and promise it won't happen again.'

'Ye're not getting away with it that easy, so you just stay right where yer are. I should have put a halt to yer gallop years ago, before yer started going off the rails. I should have done it for Lucy's sake because she deserves a better mother than you. She's a good kid and I'm proud of her. But I can see now that she gets more hidings off you than she does hugs or kisses. And I blame meself for that.' He crossed the room and, putting his hands on his wife's shoulders, he turned her around to face the mirror hanging over the fireplace. 'Take a good look at yerself, Ruby, and see yerself as others see yer. Peroxide blonde, thick cheap make-up, a face as hard as nails and smelling like a brewery.' He dropped his hands and let out a deep sigh. 'You are not the woman I married, but so help me, I'm stuck with yer. And so is our daughter.'

Ruby rounded on him. 'Who the hell d'yer think yer are, talking to me like that? Just because I like to get a bit of enjoyment out of life, instead of being bleedin' miserable, like you. You might be happy with work, bed, the wireless and a pint on a Saturday, but it's not my idea of a good life. I've no intention of being the dutiful wife, who sits knitting or darning every night, so yer can get that out of yer head. Life is short and I intend to get the best out of it while I'm still able.'

He gripped her arm and held it tight. 'Frankly, Ruby, I couldn't care less what yer do. If yer want to drink yerself to death and get a name like a mad dog, then go ahead. But while I am the one working and handing my hard-earned money over to yer, I expect the house to be kept clean and meals on the table on time. I also expect me daughter to be dressed decent and to be treated with kindness and affection. I do not want her to be doing the work which you should be doing, or being ordered around like a skivvy.' His grip tightened. 'And if I ever find yer've raised yer hand to her in anger, then heaven help yer.' He pushed her away as though in disgust. 'Make a pot of tea so I can take a cup up to Lucy before she goes to sleep.'

Ruby glared at him. This was all that little faggot's fault, and by God she'd pay for it tomorrow. There was no fear of Bob finding out, Lucy would be too scared to tell him.

Her husband watched her face and could almost read her mind. 'Don't for one moment think of taking yer spite out on her tomorrow, thinking she'll be too frightened to tell me. 'Cos from now on I'll be taking a very keen interest in me daughter's welfare. Lay a finger on her and I'll know about it.' He waited until his wife was at the kitchen door before adding, 'Oh, yer'll be five bob down in yer money this week. I'm taking Lucy to town on Saturday to buy her something decent to wear. She's the prettiest girl in the street but always looks like an unwanted orphan. But from today there's going to be big changes around here, whether yer like it or

353

not. So yer'd better start getting used to being a housewife and mother again. Yer don't have to worry about being a wife to me, yer stopped being that years ago. And if ye're looking for anyone to lay the blame on for all this, look no further than yerself.'

Aggie McBride was passing the Mellors' house on her way back from the pub, and when she heard raised voices she felt no guilt in standing outside the window and listening. She kept nodding her head when Bob spoke, and muttered, 'It's about time yer came to yer senses, Bob Mellor. That's right, lad, you tell her. Ye're about five years too late, like, but as they say, it's better late than never.'

She ambled on her way, chuckling to herself. She felt happier now she'd heard the queer one get her come-uppance, and when she got home she'd go over every word she heard as she sat in her rocking chair supping her stout.

Ruby was in a foul temper the next morning. Her head was splitting, what with having too much to drink and then the row with Bob. There was malice in her eyes as she dropped the plate of toast in front of her daughter. 'Get that down yer and hurry up or yer'll be late for school.'

Lucy looked down at the burnt bread and knew this was part of her punishment. She picked up a slice and bit into it. Then, in a quiet voice, asked, 'Can't I have some butter on it, please, Mam?'

Ruby mimicked her daughter's voice. ' "Can't I have some butter on it?" ' She closed the living-room door quietly. Bob didn't get up until ten o'clock when he was on the afternoon shift, and for all she knew he could be lying awake listening. So she kept her voice low. 'Yer'll be getting dry toast every morning from now on, seeing as yer dad is docking me money so he can buy yer some fancy clothes.'

Lucy raised her face and stared directly into her mother's eyes. What she saw there caused her to turn away in distress, thinking, she doesn't even like me, never mind love me. 'I never asked me dad to buy me anything, Mam, I wouldn't do that.' She picked up her plate and got to her feet. 'I'll make meself a round of bread and jam because I'll be starving if I don't have anything to eat.'

Ruby watched her daughter go into the kitchen before lighting a cigarette. Inhaling deeply, and with a sneer on her face, she leaned against the door-jamb. 'Yer dad won't always be here, just remember that.'

Instinct told Lucy she would be well advised to get out of the house as quick as possible and away from trouble. She could eat the bread on her way to school. So without a word, she passed her mother, took her coat from the hallstand and let herself out of the

354

front door. She stood for a moment with the bread in her mouth while she slipped her arms into her sleeves, then began to walk up the street.

Aggie McBride was standing on her front step, her shawl around her shoulders. She'd been waiting for Lucy to make sure the child hadn't come to any harm. She was a kindly soul, was Aggie, with steel-grey hair combed back off her face and plaited into a bun at the nape of her neck. She wore false teeth when she was going out, but this morning she'd decided to give her gums a rest.

'Were yer late getting up, queen?' Aggie nodded at the bread. 'No time for a proper breakfast?'

'Just a bit late, Mrs Aggie, but I don't think I'll be late for school.'

'Yer didn't get into trouble last night, did yer? I heard yer mam and dad rowing when I passed on me way back from the pub. I hope she didn't try and lay the blame at your door?'

Lucy shook her head. No matter what her mother did, she would never talk about her to anyone. After all, she was still her mother. 'I went straight to bed and me dad brought me a nice hot cup of tea up.'

'That's good, queen.' Aggie put her hand in the large pocket of her wrap-around pinny and brought out a rosy red apple. 'Here yer are, girl, I kept this specially for you.'

When Lucy's face lit up it was as though the sun had come out. 'Oh, thank you, Mrs Aggie, I'll eat it at playtime.' She rubbed the apple on the sleeve of her coat and held it up to the old lady. 'Look how shiny it is – I can see me face in it.'

Aggie chuckled. 'I bet the apple thinks there's an angel looking at it. Now, run along, queen, or yer'll be getting the cane.'

Lucy took to her heels, shouting over her shoulder, 'Ta-ra, Mrs Aggie.'

Aggie was waving to her when she heard the sound she'd been waiting for. She turned her head to see her next-door-but-one neighbour stepping into the street. Irene Pollard had a part-time cleaning job in the corner pub and she left the house every morning dead on ten minutes to nine. The Pollards lived next door to the Mellors, and Aggie was eager to know if Irene had heard the rumpus.

'Good morning, Aggie! What are yer waiting for – better days?'

'Irene, I had me better days fifty years ago, and, by God, I made the most of them. All I've got left now is to stick me nose into other people's business – which brings me to the reason for standing on me step this time of the morning, getting me bleedin' death of cold.' She gave a toothless smile. 'Did yer hear the carry-on at the Mellors' last night?'

'Couldn't help it, Aggie. They were shouting so loud we could hear every word. Yer know how thin the walls are, yer can't sneeze without the whole street knowing.' Irene Pollard was a bonny woman, with plenty of flesh on her bones. She had auburn hair, brown eyes, a pretty round face and a good sense of humour, and her husband, George, was a riot when he'd had a few drinks on a Saturday. They had two sons, Jack fourteen, and Greg, twelve, and were well liked in the street. If anyone needed a helping hand, it was the Pollards' door they knocked at. 'I don't know what started the row, but Bob certainly had a go at Ruby. She must have gone too far this time because Bob puts up with a lot from her. As George said, she's had it coming for years now, the brazen hussy.'

'I'll tell yer what started it.' Aggie quickly recounted what had happened. 'The poor kid was terrified, all alone that time of night in a house in pitch darkness.'

Irene tutted as she shook her head. 'She doesn't deserve that child. I always wanted a girl but it wasn't to be. How is it that someone like Ruby Mellor has a beautiful girl that she treats like dirt, and me, who was longing for a daughter, can't have one? I love me two boys, yer know that, and having a girl wouldn't have made any difference to the love I have for them. It's just that a girl is a mate to her mother when she grows up, someone to share things with. If Lucy was mine, she'd get as much love off me, and George and the boys, as she gets hidings off her mother. Many's the time the boys have been upset when they've heard her being belted. When they were younger they used to say she was like a fairy, with her being so pretty and dainty.'

Aggie sighed. 'Well, let's hope that Bob sticks to his guns and makes that wife of his toe the line. He must rue the day he ever set eyes on her.'

'Only time will tell, Aggie, only time will tell. But I think in future, when Bob's at work, and I hear any shenanigans from her, I'll poke me nose in.' Irene smiled. 'I'm bigger than her and one swipe from me would knock her into the middle of next week.'

'Give me a knock first, girl, 'cos I wouldn't want to miss that for the world.'

'I'll sell tickets, shall I, Aggie?' Irene started to walk away. 'If I don't get a move on I'll be getting me cards. I'll see yer tonight, sunshine, ta-ra for now.'

By dinnertime, the story had gone the rounds of the street. And when Ruby left the house to go to the shops, she could sense the hostility of the women who were standing at their doors talking to their neighbours. With their eyes boring into her, she tossed her head and sauntered past them, her jaunty step saying she didn't give a damn what they thought. And she didn't either. It was a pity the poor buggers had nothing better to do than stand gossiping. The only time they seemed to enjoy themselves was when two women got into an argument over their kids. Then the whole street would be out watching and shouting encouragement as the two women belted hell out of each other. And, of course, there was always a stir when a football was kicked through a window and none of the boys would own up to being the culprit.

There was a sarcastic smile on Ruby's face as she neared the shops. If the truth were known, there wasn't a woman in the street who wouldn't change places with her, given the chance. They just didn't have the guts. Then she had a thought that took the smile from her face. If she was going to be five shillings down in her housekeeping it would mean she'd be skint all the time. She wouldn't be able to keep up with her friends, splashing out on drinks and handing cigarettes around. She'd be like a poor relation and that idea didn't appeal to her one little bit. The truth was, if she had no money, she'd soon lose her friends.

Ruby hit on an idea as she turned into the butcher's shop. She'd make the money up by cutting down on food, that's what she'd do. If she was clever, no one would be any the wiser. And she'd start right now. 'Just half-a-pound of steak, Stan, and a quarter of kidney.' There, she gloated as the butcher cut the steak into small pieces, a quarter of steak less has saved me a few coppers. If I do that in every shop, every day, I'll soon make up the five bob.

The meat was simmering on the stove when Lucy came running in from school. 'I'm going out to play hopscotch with Rhoda, Mam. I'll only be in the street.'

'Just you hang on a minute, buggerlugs.' Ruby threw her cigarette end in the hearth. 'Yer can get in that kitchen and peel the spuds, never mind playing bleedin' hopscotch.'

Lucy's face fell. 'But it'll be dark soon and we won't be able to play.' There was pleading in her large green eyes. 'Go on, Mam, please?'

'Yer haven't got cloth ears, so out in that kitchen before I belt yer one.'

Lucy was close to tears. 'Just for half an hour, Mam?' When she saw Ruby jump from her chair and make for her, the girl pressed back against the wall and lifted her arm to protect her face. 'Don't hit me, Mam, please.'

Ruby grabbed a handful of the dark hair and pulled. 'Yer get those spuds peeled or I'll break yer bleedin' neck. Now—' Her words were cut short by a loud banging on the open front door. Her face livid, she bawled, 'What the hell d'yer want?'

'Ruby, it's Irene Pollard. Is everything all right? Young Rhoda

357

here's waiting for Lucy to come out to play, and she's been knocking hell out of yer door for the last five minutes but can't get anyone to answer. I just wondered if anything was wrong?'

Ruby bit so hard on the inside of her mouth she could taste blood. Any other neighbour she would have told to sod off, but Irene Pollard was a woman to be reckoned with. And her husband was very pally with Bob, too. 'She's coming now.' Ruby took her daughter's hand and squeezed until it hurt. She pulled her out to the front door. 'I was telling her to wash her face before she went out, it's filthy.'

'Oh, I wouldn't worry about that,' Irene said calmly. 'She'd be dirty again in no time, so what's the point? My two lads are playing ollies in the gutter, and they're both as black as the hobs of hell. To say nothing about the state of their kecks. But they'll be well-scrubbed before they go to bed.'

'Will yer let go of me hand, please, Mam?' Lucy asked. 'Rhoda will be getting called in for her dinner before we've had a game.'

Ruby was almost spitting feathers with temper. And the look she gave her daughter as she joined her friend on the pavement, wasn't lost on Irene. She'd bet a pound to a pinch of snuff that the girl would get a hammering for this. Unless Ruby was warned off. It was worth a try.

Watching the two girls marking the paving stones with a piece of chalk, Irene said casually, 'If yer ever want to go out at night, Ruby, when Bob's at work, yer can always leave Lucy with us, yer know. We'd love to have her.'

You bitch, Ruby thought. I bet yer had yer ears to the wall last night, listening. 'What made yer ask that? Yer've never asked before.'

'It was just a thought. She gets on well with the boys and would probably enjoy playing cards with them.' Irene stretched to her full height and folded her arms under her ample bosom. 'The offer's there, if yer want to take me up on it sometime.'

'No, Lucy usually goes to bed about eight o'clock.' Then begrudgingly, she added, 'But thanks all the same.'

'Well, if yer change yer mind, just knock on the wall.' Irene was determined to get her point across. 'We'd have no trouble hearing yer – these walls are so thin yer can hear *everything* that goes on either side.' She smiled as Lucy hopped from one square to another, her pink tongue peeping out of the side of her mouth. 'She's a beautiful child. I hope yer know how lucky yer are.'

Ruby had no intention of answering that. The nosy bitch had gone far enough. The next thing, she'd be inviting herself in for a cup of tea. 'I'll have to go in, or me stew will be sticking to the bottom of the pan.'

358

There was a half-smile on Irene's chubby face. She'd gone as far as she could; she only hoped the message had got home. She'd keep her ears open tonight, just in case, but she had a feeling Ruby would be keeping her hands to herself, for a while at least.

Irene waited until Rhoda had completed the course before asking, 'Who's winning?'

'We're even, Mrs Pollard.' Both girls were puffing and red in the face. After all, it was hard going hopping from one number to another. If you couldn't keep your balance, and your other foot touched the ground, you were counted out.

Lucy grinned. 'We always end up even, Mrs Pollard. We let each other win, don't we, Rhoda?'

Rhoda's long, stringy hair had been tied back with a piece of ribbon, but with the exertion, most of it had come loose and was hanging down her cheeks. She was the same age as Lucy, but a much bigger girl in every way. Inches taller than her friend, she was very heavily built. She worried about that, but her mam had told her it was puppy fat and she'd lose it as she grew older. A big smile covered her face now. 'Lucy means we cheat, Mrs Pollard.'

Irene chuckled. 'If yer both know ye're doing it, then it's not cheating, sunshine. It means ye're such good friends yer want to share.'

'Me dad's taking me to town on Saturday, Mrs Pollard, to buy me some new clothes.' Lucy's face was aglow. Never before had she had anything so exciting to brag about. 'Aren't I lucky?'

Irene put on a suitably impressed face. 'I'll say yer are! I hope he buys yer a pretty dress to match yer pretty face.' To say she was surprised would be putting it mildly. It sounded as though Bob had changed with a vengeance. 'Will yer call and let us see yer in yer new clothes, sunshine?'

'If me mam will let me.' Some of the shine had gone from Lucy's face. 'I'll ask her, but she might say I'm showing off.'

'Anyone with new clothes wants to show them off, it's only natural. Anyway, seeing as it's yer dad what's mugging yer, it's him yer should ask.'

Lucy thought that over for a few seconds, then smiled. 'Ye're right, Mrs Pollard, I'll ask me dad.'

Rhoda looked down in the mouth. 'I wish me mam would take me with her when she buys my clothes, then I could pick what I like.'

'Your mam buys yer lovely clothes!' Lucy said. 'Yer always look pretty.'

Irene took a deep breath. Next to her friend, Lucy always

359

looked like a tramp, but she never complained. There was no envy or malice in her, she was a good kid through and through. What a pity her mother didn't appreciate it. They say God makes them and matches them, but He had certainly slipped up when He'd matched this angel with a devil like Ruby Mellor.

Chapter Two

Lucy didn't let her excitement show until she was standing on the pavement watching her dad pull the door closed behind him. All morning she'd been on pins in case something happened to spoil the treat she'd been looking forward to. Her mother's face had been like thunder, and although she didn't lift her hand to Lucy, she gave her a dig in the ribs every time she passed. It would have taken very little for her temper to explode, so the girl did as she was told without a word, while willing the hands on the clock to move faster until it was time for her dad to get up at ten o'clock. Even then she didn't feel safe because although her dad seemed at ease chatting to her, not a word was exchanged between him and her mam. Still, it was over now and they were on their way.

Bob took his daughter's hand and smiled down at her. 'I think we'll hop off the tram at Great Homer Street and try the market there, see if there's anything doing. Yer never know, we might just be lucky and pick up a bargain. If not, we won't have lost anything, and we can carry on into town. What d'yer think?'

'I'm that excited, Dad, I don't care where we go.' Lucy began to swing their joined hands. 'I've never been into town before.'

Bob looked surprised. 'Of course yer have!'

'No, I haven't, Dad, honest!'

'I used to take yer through town, when yer were little, to get down to the Pier Head. Don't yer remember going on the ferry boats?'

Lucy's brow creased in concentration. 'I remember little bits, but not much. I must have only been a baby, Dad.'

Bob nodded. 'Yeah, I used to carry yer on me shoulders and yer mam was left to lug the sandwiches and towels and things.' Suddenly he was filled with a great sadness. What had he been thinking of all these years, while his daughter's childhood was passing her by? It would be easy to lay the blame at Ruby's door, but he must bear some of the responsibility. He should have put his foot down at the very beginning, when his wife made the excuse of visiting one of her old workmates and came home smelling of drink. He'd been blind and stupid, and the one to suffer most had been his beloved daughter. All he could do now was try to make it up to her. 'I'll take yer on the ferry to New Brighton next time I've got a Saturday off. Would yer like that?'

'I'd like it, Dad, but ye're buying me new clothes and that's what I'd like most. After all,' she grinned up at him, 'ye're not made of money.'

'Ye're right there, pet, but what I've got I'll have to stretch a long way. Like it was a piece of elastic.'

They didn't have long to wait for a tram, and Lucy made for a window seat. Her eyes were wide as Bob told her the names of the streets and pointed out landmarks. When they reached Everton Valley, he said, 'Next stop's ours, pet.'

The market was absolutely packed. Lucy gripped her father's hand tight, frightened by the mass of heaving bodies. 'We'll never get through there, Dad, we'll get separated and I'll lose yer. I wouldn't know how to get home on me own, and I've no money for a tram.'

Bob put an arm across her shoulders. 'You just hang on to me jacket like grim death, pet, and we'll do what everyone else is doing, push our way through.'

Lucy gradually calmed down as she got used to the pushing and shoving and the noise of the stallholders shouting out their wares. She would have liked to have seen what they were selling, but the crowd standing in front of the stalls was so deep it was impossible to see anything.

'There's a woman selling children's clothes,' Bob said. 'Let's make our way over there.' He elbowed a path through the crowds, pulling Lucy behind him. 'Some of those look nice.' He pointed to a makeshift rail where there was a display of girls' dresses. 'Is there anything there that takes yer fancy?'

'They're all nice, Dad, but it doesn't say how much they are.'

'There's only one way to find out, and that's to ask.' Ignoring the dark looks being cast his way, Bob pushed and manoeuvred until they were in front of the trestle table which was piled high with secondhand children's clothes. 'How much are those dresses, Missus?'

'They're all different prices, lad,' said the stallholder, wearing the uniform long black skirt and black knitted shawl. 'Show me which one and I'll tell yer the price. Dirt cheap, they are – yer won't get anything cheaper if yer travel the length and breadth of Liverpool.'

'Which one, Lucy?' Bob looked down into those wide green eyes which were now shining with excitement. 'What about that one with flowers on, and a lace collar? That would look nice on yer.'

362

But Lucy knew which one she liked the best as soon as she'd set eyes on it. It was in a deep maroon cotton, very plain with a round neck and long sleeves. If she was going to get a new dress, that was the one her heart would choose. She pointed to it. 'That's the one I like, Dad, but it might be too dear.'

Bob crossed his fingers as he asked, 'How much is that one?'

'Two and six, lad, and that's practically giving it away.'

'Would it fit me daughter?'

The stallholder eyed Lucy. 'How old are yer, girl?'

Lucy had never felt so important in her life. Being able to choose her own clothes was something she'd never known before. She took what was thrown at her and was never asked if she liked it. 'I'm eleven, Missus, but I'll be twelve in four weeks' time.'

When the stallholder smiled, she showed a row of yellow teeth, but her smile was wide and friendly. 'Ye're very dainty for yer age, girl, and very pretty, too. That dress will fit yer like a glove, as though it was made for yer. Yer'll have all the lads whistling after yer when yer walk out in it.'

Bob handed the half-a-crown over, and as he waited for the dress to be hooked down, Lucy was looking through the clothes piled on the table. She tugged on her father's sleeve and when he looked down, she beckoned for him to bend so she could whisper in his ear. 'Dad, there's girls' knickers here. Could I have a pair, please?'

'But they're secondhand ones, pet. Yer wouldn't want to wear someone else's cast-offs, would yer? Not knickers, anyway.'

'They'd be clean if I gave them a good wash, wouldn't they?' Lucy was embarrassed and averted her eyes. 'They're better than the two pair I've got. The elastic's gone on them and I have to pin them up.'

Bob closed his eyes. Dear God, what was that wife of his thinking of? He gave her enough money to keep the child well fed and clothed. Had she no love at all for her daughter, no shame that the child was going around with pins in her knickers? And this was only the start. There was plenty more he didn't know about, of that he was sure. 'Pick three decent pair out, pet, and they'll keep yer going until we can get yer new ones.'

The stallholder didn't appear to be listening, but she heard every word. Working the markets gave you an insight into people, taught you how to sort the wheat from the chaff. So when Bob handed over the three pair of knickers, she knocked a penny off the price of each pair. 'That'll be a tanner, lad. And if yer don't mind me saying so, yer've got a little cracker there, so you take good care of her, mind.'

Bob smiled his thanks then guided Lucy through the crowds

and out into the street. 'How would yer like a little treat? What d'yer say about getting a tram down to TJ's and having a cup of tea in the café there?'

Lucy was clutching the paper bag and telling herself this was the best day of her life. She couldn't wait to show Rhoda her new dress. She wouldn't tell her about the knickers though, she'd be too ashamed. 'That would be the gear, Dad, but can yer afford it? Yer've spent a lot of money on me as it is.'

'I've still got a few bob left, pet, so don't be worrying. Come on, let's get down to London Road, me throat's parched.'

The butter ran down Lucy's chin as she bit into the toasted teacake, her eyes wide as she gazed around the tables. Every chair was occupied and the room was buzzing with adults trying to talk above the sound of screaming children. 'All these people, Dad, wouldn't yer wonder where they came from?'

'Liverpool's a big city, pet.' Bob grinned as he passed over a hankie. 'Wipe yer chin before the butter runs on to yer coat.' He groaned as he silently told himself one more stain on the shabby coat wouldn't even be noticed. It was so faded it was difficult to know what its original colour had been, and the sleeves, about three inches too short, were threadbare. 'In a couple of weeks, when I've had time to save up, I'll mug yer to a new coat. Heaven knows, yer could do with one.'

'This one's all right, Dad, I only wear it to go to school.'

Bob shook his head. 'No, it's a complete new rig-out yer need, and that's what yer'll have as soon as I can get the money together. What about yer shoes, are they in good nick?'

Lucy pushed her feet as far back under the chair as she could. 'They're fine, Dad, they'll last me for ages yet.'

'Then why are yer hiding them under the chair? Come on, pet, there's no need to be frightened, let me see.'

Lucy cast her eyes down as she slid her feet forward. 'See, I told yer, Dad, there's still plenty of wear in them. I gave them a good polish before we came out.'

That's her mother talking, Bob told himself as he bent down to remove one of her shoes. They weren't the words of an eleven-year-old girl. And the anger he felt when he examined the shoe was so strong, he could feel his head throbbing. The heel was worn right down on one side, which must have made it agony to walk on, and there was an inch-round hole in the middle of the sole. He turned the shoe over and felt like crying when he saw how his daughter had tried to hide the scuffmarks with shoe polish.

Bob swallowed hard, trying to shift the lump that had formed in his throat. What sort of a father was he, not to have seen all this?

364

'Lucy, why didn't yer tell me yer didn't have a decent pair of shoes? I would have done something if I'd known, but the trouble is, pet, yer never complain. Yer don't have to put up with using pins in yer knickers or wearing shoes that are only fit for the back of the fire. Yer've got to start speaking up for yerself.'

'Me mam said she didn't have any money.' Lucy spoke quietly, afraid of saying too much and then being the recipient of her mother's anger.

Bob sighed. 'I give yer mother enough money to manage on, pet, more than most women in the street get.' He was also careful about what he said. It wouldn't do to criticise his wife to his daughter. 'It's just that she's not very good with money, she spends it on the wrong things. There are lots of women like that, they're just not good managers. So in future, you come to me if yer need anything. And don't be frightened of upsetting yer mam by coming to me, 'cos I'll have a word with her. I'll see to yer clothes, and that'll be one less worry off her mind.'

'Yeah, okay, Dad.' Lucy took her shoe and slipped it on. 'Don't look now, but yer toasted teacake has gone cold.'

'Won't stop me eating it, pet.' Bob folded the teacake and took a bite. 'I noticed the shoe department when we came in. We'll have a gander and see if me money will stretch to a pair of cheap shoes for yer.'

He was counting up in his head how much money he had in his pocket as they entered the shoe department. He had to keep enough for his fares to work, the five Woodbines he bought every day and a couple of bob for drinks tonight. Saturday night was the only time he went out with Ruby. They only went to the corner pub because of leaving Lucy on her own and his wife wouldn't be very happy to forego that pleasure, even for the sake of seeing her daughter in a decent pair of shoes.

Lucy tugged on his sleeve. 'Dad, these plimsoles are only elevenpence ha'penny, they'd do for me.'

'They'd be no good if it rained, yer feet would be sopping wet. Let's look around before we decide.' The price of girls' shoes went from half-a-crown up to the seven and six ankle bands that Lucy was gazing at with eyes and mouth wide open. In black shiny patent leather, with the straps fastening at the front with a button, they were the most beautiful shoes she'd ever seen. Bob saw her face and sighed. She was so pretty, she deserved the clothes to match, but they were out of his reach. 'I'm sorry, pet, me pocket doesn't run to that.'

'Oh, I wouldn't want them, Dad, they're too posh. None of me friends have got them and they'd think I was swanking.' She started to giggle. 'Can yer see me playing hopscotch in them? I wouldn't enjoy meself, I'd be terrified of scratching them.'

Bob picked up a pair of the half-a-crown lace ups. They looked what they were, a pair of cheap shoes. But they were sturdy and she'd get good wear out of them. 'Sit on that stool, pet, and I'll get the assistant to find the right size for yer.'

'Are yer sure yer can afford them, Dad? I can wait a few more weeks, yer know.'

'We'll get them now, while we're here.' Bob had gone well over what he intended spending, and wondered what he could forfeit to make it up. He had to keep his tram fare otherwise he wouldn't be able to get to work, and he wasn't going to give up his Woodbines, they were one of the few pleasures he had in life. So they'd have to give the pub a miss, it wouldn't kill them for one night. And the pleasure on Lucy's face made it worth while.

Ruby sat with a scowl on her face as Lucy brought her new clothes out of the bags. She showed no enthusiasm, passed no compliments. And her silence angered Bob, who tried to make up for her lack of interest. 'I can't wait to see yer in the dress, pet. Nip upstairs and put it on for us.'

Lucy was so excited, even her mother's attitude couldn't dampen her spirits. She felt as though a good fairy had waved a magic wand and she suddenly had a beautiful dress, new shoes and even knickers. And she'd been in a café and had tea and toasted teacakes. She had never known a day like this, and she was too ecstatic to wonder if there would ever be another. 'I'll go and put them on, Dad, and swank.'

When Bob heard her taking the stairs two at a time, he quietly closed the door before facing his wife. 'Would it have killed you to show some pleasure in yer daughter's new clothes? What sort of a mother are yer?' He shook his head. 'I don't know what brought on the change in yer, but ye're certainly not the woman I married. It's like living with a complete stranger – someone I don't even like.'

'Those clothes were bought with my housekeeping money.' Ruby spat the words out. 'So don't expect me to go in a swoon over them.'

Bob felt like wiping the sneer off her painted face, but he would never lift a hand to a woman. So he got his revenge in words. 'Not only yer housekeeping, Ruby, but also yer Saturday-night pleasure. I've no money left for the pub tonight, so yer can settle yerself in to listen to the wireless. It won't worry yer, though, will it? Being the good mother yer are, yer'll be quite happy knowing yer daughter won't have to pin her knickers up again, nor wear a shoe with a ruddy big hole in the sole.'

366

Ruby's eyes were nearly popping out of her head and her nostrils were wide and white. 'Not going to the pub! The one night in the week yer take me out, and yer've gone and spent all yer money on that little faggot?'

'Not on a little faggot, Ruby, on our daughter. And Saturday may be the only night I take yer out, but it certainly isn't the only night you go out. In fact, ye're out more often than ye're in. So I don't think yer have anything to complain about.' He heard footsteps on the landing and spoke quietly, but threateningly. 'You say one word out of place to that child and by God, yer'll be sorry. It won't be five shillings short in yer money, it'll be ten. So think on before yer put yer foot in it.'

Lucy had never had anything to show off before, and she was shy as she stood inside the door. 'How do I look, Dad?'

'Oh pet, yer look as pretty as a picture. The dress looks lovely on yer, fits like it's been made for yer. Go and stand in front of yer mam and see if she likes it.'

Lucy gave him a quick glance before crossing to where her mother sat. 'D'yer like me new dress, Mam?'

The words were so begrudged, Ruby had to force them out. 'Yeah, it's nice.'

Lucy could sense the antagonism in the voice but wouldn't let it prey on her mind. No one was going to spoil today for her. So tossing her hair, she turned back to her father. 'Can I go and show Rhoda? And Mrs Pollard asked me to call and let her see me new dress.'

That was too much for Ruby. 'You keep away from that nosy cow next door. All she's good for is pulling people to pieces. The less she knows about our business, the better.'

Lucy's eyes widened in surprise. How could her mam say that about their neighbour? 'But she's nice, is Mrs Pollard. Everyone likes her 'cos she's always happy and friendly. She never shouts at the kids like some women,' the girl almost stamped her foot at the injustice of her mother's words, 'and she's not a nosy cow, either.'

Ruby was halfway out of her chair when she caught Bob's eye. So the slap she thought her daughter deserved would have to wait for another time. But that time would come. In the meanwhile, she contented herself with saying, 'Don't yer ever dare answer me back like that.'

Bob was thoughtful as he looked down at his clasped hands. He didn't want to set mother and daughter against each other, but Lucy had to learn that when someone said something bad about a person she liked, and she knew it was untrue, she should stick to her guns and say so. 'Lucy wasn't answering yer back, Ruby, she was stating a fact. Irene Pollard is one of the kindest, nicest people ye're ever likely to come across. If you don't like her, that's your misfortune, but don't expect others to agree with yer.'

Lucy thought it would be best if she made herself scarce, then she couldn't cause any more trouble. 'I'm going, Dad, but I won't be long.'

'Yer'll bowl 'em over, pet,' Bob called after her. 'They won't recognise yer.'

Rhoda opened the door and her eyes popped. She turned her head and called, 'Ay, Mam, come and see who's at the door.'

Jessie Fleming came out drying her hands on the corner of her pinny. 'What is it, love, someone on the borrow?' Then she saw Lucy, standing there looking so proud, and her face split into a smile. 'Well, I never! Who is this young girl dressed up to the nines? I don't recall seeing her before.'

Lucy giggled. 'Me dad took me into town and mugged me, Mrs Fleming. D'yer like me dress,' she did a little twirl, 'and me shoes?'

'Yer look a treat, love.' Jessie was thinking it was about time someone took an interest in the girl. 'The dress looks lovely on yer, and the colour suits yer.'

For the first time, since the day they'd started school together, Rhoda had reason to be envious of her friend. 'I bet yer picked it yerself, didn't yer?'

Lucy nodded. 'They were all hanging on a rail, and I liked this one the best.'

'Yer see!' Rhoda flashed her eyes at her mother. 'You won't take me with yer to buy my clothes, so I have to have what *you* like. It's not fair.'

'But yer mam buys yer lovely clothes.' Lucy was feeling sorry she came. Now she'd started a row between her friend and her mother. 'Yer don't know how lucky yer are, 'cos yer gets loads more things than I do.'

Jessie folded her plump arms and leaned back against the door. 'Take no notice of misery guts here, Lucy, she always finds something to moan about. If I bought her a ballgown, she'd complain because I didn't get her a tiara to go with it.'

Lucy grinned. 'She's not always moaning, Mrs Fleming, not to me, anyway. She's me very best friend.'

Rhoda pulled a face at her mother. 'There, yer see, I'm not a misery guts.'

'I know ye're not, sweetheart, ye're all sweetness and light. And for that reason, next time yer need a new dress I'll take yer with me and yer can choose yer own.'

Rhoda flung her arms around her mother's neck and kissed her soundly. 'Ooh, ye're the best mam in the whole world.'

'It'll be a different story if I've left the dinner to burn. I'd better get back in and see to it, otherwise there'll be ructions if I put a burnt offering down to yer dad.' She leaned forward and stroked Lucy's hair. 'Yer look lovely, girl, a real little princess.' She began to chuckle. 'If I ever get down to buying a tiara for our Rhoda, I'll get one for you while I'm at it.'

When her mother disappeared into the house, Rhoda was feeling very kindly towards her friend. 'Yer do look nice, Lucy, the dress really suits yer. And I'm not half glad yer came down to show us, 'cos now me mam's promised to let me choose me own, and she never goes back on a promise. So yer've done me a good turn, kid.'

'Yeah, yer owe me one. So next time we have a game of rounders, yer can let me win. That'll make us even.' Lucy rubbed her arms briskly. There was a cool breeze blowing and the cotton dress wasn't much protection against it. 'I'll have to go, Rhoda, I promised to call in and see Mrs Pollard, and it's nearly teatime. I'll see yer tomorrow, eh?'

'Okay, Lucy. Ta-ra for now.'

Lucy took to her heels and ran the short distance to her neighbour's house. The door was opened by Jack, who at fourteen was the eldest of Irene's two sons. He gaped at Lucy, then bawled, 'Hey, Mam, come and get a load of this.'

Irene came to the door, followed by twelve-year-old Greg. Her face lit up when she saw Lucy. 'Oh, sunshine, ye're a sight for sore eyes. My, but yer do look bonny. Come in and let George see yer.'

Lucy had never been fussed over so much, and she loved every minute of it. 'Wasn't me dad good, letting me choose me own? There were a lot of dresses, but this was me very favourite.'

'Yer've got good taste, queen,' George said, thinking you'd go a long way to find anyone with a face and nature as beautiful as this child. And wasn't it sad that most of the time she was dressed like a backstreet waif. He turned to his sons. 'Don't yer think she looks pretty, boys?'

Blushing to the roots of their hair, the lads looked down at their feet. They both liked Lucy, thought she was a smashing girl. But at their tender age they'd never been called on to pay compliments before. Jack was the first to find his tongue. 'Yeah,' he said, 'she looks great.'

The only thing Greg could think of that might be considered a compliment, was, 'Yeah, she looks the pig's ear – the gear.'

George dropped his head back and roared with laughter. 'The pig's ear, eh? Now that is flattery indeed.'

'Well, what d'yer expect from a twelve year old?' As always,

369

Irene was quick to defend her son. 'And when I was young, to look the pig's ear meant yer looked fantastic. And that is just what Lucy looks – fantastic.' She put her arm across the thin shoulders and squeezed. 'Tell yer dad from me that he's done yer proud.'

Lucy's smile was a joy to behold. 'Thank you. I'm made up, I really am. I don't think I've ever been so happy in me life.'

Irene exchanged glances with her husband before giving Lucy another squeeze. 'Yer mam and dad go to the pub tonight, don't they?'

'Yeah, every Saturday.' Forever mindful of what she said, Lucy added, 'They see me in bed first, though, and they leave the light on in the living room. And they don't stay out late.'

'Why don't yer ask them if yer can come in here tonight, and have a game of cards or Ludo with us? Jack and Greg are allowed to stay up late on Saturday and I'm sure yer parents won't mind. George usually walks home with them from the pub, don't yer, light of my life?'

George averted his gaze. He couldn't stand Ruby Mellor, thought she was as tough as an old boot. He got on fine with Bob, they were good mates, but he couldn't stomach his wife. So he always walked behind them with a bloke from up the street. But now wasn't the time to air his feelings. 'Yeah, we all get thrown out at closing time.'

'Would yer like me to come with yer to see what they say?' Irene asked, seeing the look of doubt on Lucy's face. 'I'm sure it will be all right. After all, yer can't come to any harm with us, can yer? The worst that can happen is yer lose a game and have to fork out a couple of matches.' Her chubby face beamed. 'Mind you, sometimes we go mad and play for old buttons.'

Remembering her mother's set face, and the atmosphere in the room when she'd left the house, Lucy shook her head. 'No, I'll go and ask them. Yer see, me mam likes to know I'm settled in bed before she goes out.'

George put his hands on the wooden arms of his fireside chair and pushed himself up. He was a tall, well-made man with a mop of fine, sandy-coloured hair and a ruddy complexion. And like his wife, he had an ever-ready smile. 'I'll go with her. I want to see Bob, anyway.'

Irene looked surprised. 'Yer'll be seeing him tonight in the pub.'

'I want to ask if he's got a paintbrush I can borrow to whitewash the kitchen, and I don't want the whole street knowing.'

So when Bob opened the door it was to see his daughter holding the hand of their neighbour. He smiled a welcome. 'Come in, George, ye've timed it nicely. There's a fresh pot of tea just brewed.'

370

George pushed Lucy ahead of him. 'I'll come in, Bob, but I won't stay for a cuppa 'cos Irene's got the meal nearly ready.'

Ruby's welcome was a brief nod, and George's was barely noticeable. 'I came on the cadge, Bob, to ask if yer've got a paintbrush to lend. It's to whitewash our kitchen and the brushes I've got are too small. I need a wide one.'

'Yeah, I've got one, and ye're welcome to borrow it. Shall I get it for yer now?'

'No, there's no hurry, I'm not starting it until Monday night. Now I know I can borrow yours, it'll save me coughing up for a new one.' George put a hand on Lucy's shoulder. 'Now another request. Irene wants to know if yer'll let this fashionable little lady come to ours tonight to have a few games with her and the boys? Yer can pick her up on yer way home from the pub.'

'We're not going out tonight, George, we've decided to have a night in.' Bob saw his wife's body stiffen with anger, but ignored it and kept the smile on his face. 'But that's no reason why Lucy can't go and have a few games with the boys. It'll do her good, having youngsters to play with for a change.'

'I'd rather she didn't go,' Ruby said, feeling if she didn't put her foot down now, Bob would take over completely and she'd never have a say in anything. 'I like Lucy to be in bed by eight, that's late enough for a girl of her age.'

'There's no school tomorrow, so she can have a lie-in.' Bob's eyes were like steel as they bored into hers. 'It must be lonely for her, being an only child and no one to play games with. It's about time she began to enjoy her childhood, before it's too late.' He dropped to his haunches in front of his daughter. 'Yer'd like to go, wouldn't yer, pet?'

Her smiling eyes told him the answer before she spoke. 'I would, Dad, if it's all right with you and me mam.'

'Of course it's all right, why wouldn't it be? I mean, next door is hardly the other side of the world, is it?'

Lucy giggled. 'It's fifteen walking steps from our front door to theirs, but if I do long jumps, I can do it in ten.'

George ruffled her hair. 'What about cartwheels, queen? How many of them would it take yer to get from here to there?'

'Ooh, I can't do cartwheels.' Lucy had never even tried. How could yer do cartwheels when yer had a pin in your knickers? 'Anyway, our teacher, Miss Robinson, said it's not ladylike to show all yer underwear off.'

'She has a point, has your Miss Robinson.' George gave her a beaming smile before reaching for the door knob. 'I'd better get going otherwise I'll have me meal thrown at me. Nothing gets Irene's goat more than making a hot dinner and then having to warm it up again. Send Lucy along about seven, we'll have all eaten by then.'

As soon as he'd gone, Ruby turned on her husband. 'I may as well talk to the bleedin' wall, yer don't take a blind bit of notice what I say. That cow next door only wants Lucy there so she can poke and prod into our business. Before the night's over, she'll know how many flamin' blankets we've got on the bed! But you're too thick to see that.'

'When yer talk sense, I might start taking notice of yer. But yer come out with some of the most ridiculous things imaginable, and I'd have to be a fool to agree with yer. It just shows what a warped mind yer've got when yer think Irene Pollard has nothing better to interest her than how many blankets we've got on our bed.' He sensed Lucy moving restlessly from one foot to the other and cursed himself for letting Ruby rub him up the wrong way in front of the girl. There'd be time enough later, when they were alone, for harsh words. 'D'yer want to change into yer old dress, pet, or are yer keeping that one on?'

'I'll get changed, Dad, 'cos I want to keep this one for best.'

'Go on, then, while yer mam gets the tea ready.'

Ruby didn't even wait until her daughter had put her foot on the first stair before saying what was on her mind. And she didn't keep her voice lowered. 'Who the bleedin' hell d'yer think yer are? This is my house too, yer know, I have as much right to have my say as you have. If yer think I'm going to stand here to be bossed around, and walked all over, then yer've got another bleedin' think coming.'

Bob kept a tight rein on his temper. 'That's another thing I won't have in this house, bad language. In future yer'll keep yer filthy tongue until ye're with yer friends. You do not use it in front of Lucy or me. Is that understood?'

'You can just sod off, Mr High and Mighty Mellor. D'yer hear me? Sod off.'

Next door, the Pollards were sitting down to their meal. Irene jerked her head towards the wall. 'Can yer hear them going at it, high ding dong?'

'I can hear Ruby going at it, but I think Bob's taking it all in his stride. He's not messing around this time, he means business. He's put his foot down with a firm hand, all right, it's sticking out a mile. And yer can tell the way they look at each other, there's no love lost there, I'm afraid.' George began to chuckle. 'He might get her to toe the line in some things, but he doesn't stand a snowball's chance in hell of getting her to clean her mouth out. Swearing is second nature to her now, she thinks it's as normal as

372

pulling the chain after yer've been to the lavvy.' He tapped a finger on his chin and looked thoughtful. 'I've got that the wrong way round, haven't I? Yer pull the chain to clean the lavvy, but when Ruby opens that mouth of hers, nothing clean comes out of it.'

'All right, sunshine, that's enough,' Irene tutted. 'We're having a meal and all you can talk about is the lavvy. It's enough to put anyone off their food.'

'It won't put me off me food,' Jack said, spearing a chip and dipping it into the mound of tomato sauce at the side of his plate. 'Nothing puts me off me grub.'

Greg's eyes were serious as he looked across the table. 'Mam, why is Mrs Mellor so cruel to Lucy? She's not a naughty girl, is she?'

'Of course she's not naughty! Lucy is one of the best-mannered kids I know. And I wouldn't say her mother was cruel to her, 'cos we don't really know that, do we?' Irene pointed her fork at him. 'And yer don't discuss things like that with yer mates, d'yer hear?'

'I hear yer. But I'm not half glad Mrs Mellor isn't my mam. I wouldn't like to get shouted at all the time, even when I've done nothing wrong.'

'If she was my mam I'd run away from home.' Jack sounded quite definite. 'I wouldn't stay with her, she's horrible.'

'Oh, aye?' Irene raised her brows. 'And where would yer run to, sunshine?'

Jack's eyes glinted with laughter. 'I'd run to the house next door, where there was a proper mam.'

George saw the funny side and his guffaw was loud. 'It's a pity they don't have humour as a subject in your school, son. At least yer'd be top of the class in something.'

There was love and pride in Irene's eyes as she gazed at her two sons. 'But we're not going to mention Mrs Mellor's name tonight, in front of Lucy, are we?'

Two heads shook vigorously. 'Nah,' Jack said, 'we're not that daft, Mam.'

Chapter Three

'I thought yer said yer'd never played this game before?' Jack placed his fan of cards face down on the table as he looked across at Lucy. 'How come, if yer've never played before, ye're the only one with three cards down?'

'I don't know, do I?' Lucy was dead excited. They'd explained the rules of the game to her before they started, and she couldn't believe her luck when she was sorting the cards she'd been dealt to find she had three fours. She couldn't wait for her turn so she could put them down and beam all over her face. 'I must be lucky.'

'Beginner's luck, sunshine,' Irene said, 'that's what it is.'

Jack turned sharply when he felt his brother move and found Greg bent down, peeking at his cards. 'Ay, you, stop cheating.'

Greg sat up straight, grinning from ear to ear. He wasn't in the least ashamed of being found out. 'He's got a cob on because he's got two fours himself and he'd have to be dead lucky to pick another one up.' He chuckled. 'I hope me mam won't be throwing one down now she knows what he's after.'

Irene shook her head and clucked. 'That's cheating, Greg, and it's not fair. Besides, we're supposed to be teaching Lucy how to play cards, not cheat.'

'Shall we all throw our cards in, Mrs Pollard, and deal another hand?' Lucy asked. 'That would make it fair, wouldn't it?'

'Not on yer life!' Jack said. He did have two fours, but he also had two other pairs. It wasn't a bad hand by any means. 'Take no notice of me brother, he still thinks he's a baby. He's more to be pitied than laughed at.'

'Let's get on with the game,' Irene said, 'otherwise we'll be here until midnight. You leave those three cards down, Lucy, and throw one away.'

Lucy stared at the cards in her hand. Oh, decisions, decisions. She had two kings, two jacks and a six. The six looked out of place, so she threw that on the upturned cards in the centre of the table.

Irene picked a card from the pack, looked at it and snorted

before throwing it down. 'That's not a ha'porth of good to me, I've got a lousy hand.'

Jack shrieked with delight as he snatched up the king his mother had thrown down. 'Ta very much, Mam.' He matched the card with the two in his hand and laid the three down. 'How about that, then? And,' he said with an air of a superior being, 'I can put my two fours on to Lucy's.'

Irene clamped her lips and shook her head. 'Not a very wise move, sunshine. Yer should have kept one back.'

Jack, thinking he'd been very clever, looked puzzled. 'Why?'

'Because yer've got to throw a card in now, which leaves yer with two in yer hands. And yer could sit there all night waiting for somewhere to put them.'

'Well, yer never know.' The lad felt like kicking himself for not hanging on to one of the fours, but he put on a brave face. 'Anything can happen in a game of cards. Come on, Greg, it's your turn.'

His brother picked up a card, checked it against those in his hand before throwing it down in disgust. 'I might as well pack in now, I've got nowt.'

Lucy's green eyes were like saucers as she picked up the card Greg had thrown down. 'Will yer tell me if I'm doing right, Mrs Pollard?' She put three jacks down in front of her and showed the other two cards to Irene. 'I can put these kings on Jack's now, can't I?'

Irene's tummy was rumbling with laughter. 'No, sunshine, yer have to throw one away first. Then yer can put the other one on Jack's run, and yer've won the game.'

As Lucy flipped the card across the table she caught sight of Jack's open mouth, and the look of disbelief on his face. She didn't want to laugh because that would be rude. It wasn't her home, she was only an invited guest. But after another quick glance across the table she had as much chance of keeping the laughter back as she had of stopping the rain which they could hear pelting down outside.

Lucy's laugh started as a tinkle, then gathered momentum until it filled every corner of the room. 'I've won three buttons! Me first game of cards and I won! And because ye're looking at me as though I cheated, Jack Pollard, I want nothing less than a pearl button off you.'

'I'll get it back off yer before the night's over,' Jack threatened. 'Like me mam said, it's just beginner's luck.'

'That's what you think, clever clogs.' Lucy had been shy at first, but now she was really relaxed and happy. There was no tension in her body, no worry in her mind that any minute now she'd get a clip around the ear and not know what she'd done to deserve it. 'I bet I win more games than you.'

'Yer won't if he starts cheating,' Greg said. 'He's very good at cheating, is our Jack. Aren't I right, Mam?'

'It takes one to know one, sunshine, and I'd say that when it comes to cheating, you'd win hands down.'

Lucy had been listening with interest. 'Mrs Pollard, d'yer think yer'd better teach me how to cheat so I'm in with a chance?'

The brothers thought this was hilarious and once again the room rang with laughter. She was good fun, was Lucy Mellor, and they hoped their mam would ask her to come again.

Bob Mellor lowered the newspaper and looked across at his wife. 'Can yer hear them next door? They're having the time of their lives, and I've never heard our Lucy laugh like that for years. It's about time she had someone her own age to play with.'

Ruby's scowl deepened. 'I still think Irene is a miserable cow. She should doll herself up and go to the pub with her husband on a Saturday night, instead of sitting in playing stupid games. Some wife she is, letting him go out on his own all the time.'

'She won't go out and leave the boys on their own. Besides, Irene is not a drinker and doesn't enjoy sitting in a pub all night. George doesn't mind, he understands. It isn't as if they never go out together, they often go to the pictures.'

Ruby's lip curled. 'Aye, with the kids in tow.'

'Which is the way they want it. Those boys are their life, and that's the way it should be. They are a very happy family, and George and Irene have a good marriage.' Bob raised the paper but couldn't concentrate, the words kept running into each other. So he went back to his thoughts. He envied George and Irene and their two children. They were what he would call a perfect family. They laughed together, played together and their love for each other was there for all to see. It wasn't only the wall that separated the two families, it was everything. And his daughter would be experiencing the difference tonight.

Bob rustled the paper as he crossed his legs to make himself more comfortable. He tried to think back to a time when things started to go wrong with his marriage. After much soul-searching he realised things hadn't gone wrong, they were never right! Oh, Ruby had kept the house clean and fed them well. She made sure his clothes were washed and ironed ready for work and his socks were always neatly darned. She'd looked after Lucy properly, too, when she was little, buying her pretty clothes and taking her for walks to the park so she could play on the swings. Bob had been very content in his marriage in those early years, thinking they had everything for a long and happy life. It was only now, looking back, he realised there'd always been something missing: the most important ingredient in any marriage – and that was love and affection. It hadn't worried him at first that Ruby never hugged or kissed him, he thought she was shy. And when she spurned his advances in bed he blamed himself for being over-passionate and selfish.

He shifted restlessly in the chair. Surely to God, in all those years, when she never once kissed or hugged him spontaneously, he should have realised she didn't have any love or affection to give. He must have been blind, or was it simply that he didn't want to rock the boat? Anything for an easy life, that was him. But he should have realised his baby daughter wasn't getting the love she deserved, either. When he wasn't at work, the child was always handed over to him to nurse and play with. He was the one who tucked her up in bed after a kiss and cuddle. The signs were there, but he didn't see them. He thought Ruby lavished her love on the child when he was at work. How could he have been so wrong? Lucy was nearly twelve years of age now, and had never known a mother's love.

'It's a quarter to ten,' Ruby said, through gritted teeth. 'Yer'd better go and get her because they wouldn't think of sending her home.'

Bob threw the paper down and left the room without a word. He had nothing to say to this woman who left her child on her own while she was in a pub drinking with her so-called friends. A woman who gave clouts instead of kisses and used foul language instead of words of praise. A woman who had the gall to scoff at a fine person like Irene Pollard for putting her beloved children before herself.

Jack opened the door wide. 'Come in, Mr Mellor, we're just finishing a game.'

Bob's troubled mind eased when he saw the joy on his daughter's face. She was bouncing up and down on the chair looking more relaxed and happy than he'd ever seen her. 'There's no need to ask if yer've enjoyed yerself, pet, it's written all over yer.'

Lucy held out her hand. 'Look, Dad, I've won six buttons. That means I've won two games.'

'Has she behaved herself, Irene?' Bob asked.

'Behaved herself! She hasn't been a ha'porth of trouble. In fact, we've had more of a laugh tonight than we've ever had. She's got quite a sense of humour, has Lucy, she's had us in stitches. My sons are not very good losers, I'm afraid, but tonight they paid up without any argument. In fact, it was worth losing to see her face.'

378

'Can she come again, Mr Mellor?' Jack asked. 'We haven't half enjoyed ourselves.'

'As long as yer mam doesn't mind. But not when it's school the next day.'

Jack's shoulders went back and his chest came out. 'I won't have to worry about school soon – I leave in four weeks. I'll be getting meself a job, then, and me mam's going to buy me some long trousers.'

'Good for you, son. I can still remember getting me first pair of long trousers, and me first pay packet. And did I think I was somebody that day! Oh boy, me head was so big I couldn't get through the front door. And me mam, God rest her soul, was standing in the hallway with her hand out for me pay packet. She was only joking, like, and we had a good laugh about it. Not that I didn't have to give it to her unopened, mind, 'cos I did. And with me shilling pocket money burning a hole in me pocket, I swaggered down the street like James Cagney. I went to the picture-house and bought meself a fourpenny ticket for the front stalls.'

'Good old days, eh, Bob?' Irene smiled. 'A shilling in yer pocket and not a care in the world. And a bob went a long way in those days, I can remember.'

'It went up to one and six when I got me first rise, and I thought meself a rich man.' Bob sighed inwardly, thinking how carefree life had been when he was a youngster. 'Come on, pet, it's ten o'clock, Mrs Pollard will be wanting to get the boys to bed.'

'Ah, ay!' Greg cried. 'We're in the middle of a hand. Can't we finish it?'

'No,' Irene said firmly. 'Yer dad will be in any minute. Put the cards back in the boxes and put them in the sideboard, ready for next time.'

Lucy didn't want the night to end and was sad as she pushed her chair back under the table. 'Thank you for having me, Mrs Pollard, I've had a smashing time.'

'It's been a pleasure having yer, sunshine, and ye're welcome to come at any time. And don't forget that, either. Any time, night or day, for whatever reason, just give us a knock.'

Bob was working the night shift the following week, and on the Monday night he was hammering an iron rod into shape when the whistle sounded to down tools for their break. He worked in an iron foundry near the Dock Road, where they made everything from small nuts and bolts to huge girders. He'd worked there since he left school and was skilled in all the jobs, so was able to move from a furnace to one of the machines when needed. He got on well with the blokes he worked with, who were easygoing and always willing to help. If one of them was off-colour and not able to keep up the pace, they'd all muck in to keep his job going so he wouldn't have any pay docked from his wages. They all had families to support and every penny counted.

Bob brought the hammer down one more time, then satisfied the rod was perfect he laid it beside the pile he'd been working on, and reached for his carry-out. He could just go a cup of tea, his mouth was parched. He quickened his steps and caught up with Billy Gleeson, who'd been working nearby. 'Me mouth feels like sandpaper.'

'Aye,' said Billy, 'it's the heat from those bleedin' furnaces what does it. The sweat pours off yer, but yer mouth stays as dry as a ruddy bone.'

They walked past the nut and bolt section to the canteen, and as soon as they walked through the door, Billy groaned. 'Blimey, listen to those cackling women. They put me in mind of a flock of turkeys being chased by a farmer with a ruddy hatchet.'

'I heard that, Billy Gleeson, yer cheeky bugger,' one of the women shouted. 'Yer want to listen to yerself some time.'

'Oh, ye're there, are yer, Peg? If yer've nowt else going for yer, girl, yer've got a good pair of lug-holes on yer. I bet if yer shut up long enough to listen, yer'd hear Big Ben chiming.' Billy was smiling as he made his way to the table where the women were sitting. 'Move up and make room for me and Bob.'

'I've a good mind to tell yer to sod off,' Peg Butterworth said as she shuffled her bottom along the wooden bench. 'Turkeys, indeed.'

Bob waited for his mate to sit down, then slid on to the end of the seat. He winked at the woman facing him. 'Billy knows how to flatter a woman, doesn't he, Kate? He's just oozing with charm.'

There were eight women on the shift and their job was sorting and inspecting the thousands of nuts and bolts turned out every day. They were a happy bunch, even if their language would make your hair curl. They could certainly hold their own, too, and gave the men back as good as they got. But Kate Brown was the odd one out. She was always pleasant but kept herself to herself. She was quietly spoken and never a swearword passed her lips. Bob knew she was a widow with a young daughter to keep, and he often thought it must be hard for her trying to hold down a job and bring up a child. But apparently her mother was good and helped out by minding the daughter when Kate was at work.

'That's why all the women run after him,' she said now, her shy smile appearing. 'With his looks and personality, he's a real ladykiller.'

'I'll have to keep me eye on him, then, to see if I can pick up a few tips.' Bob was smiling when he took the lid off his carry-out box, but when he saw the contents his jaw dropped and he couldn't keep the words back. 'Bloody hell!'

Kate followed his eyes and gasped. There were two rounds of bread in the box and they were cut as thick as doorsteps. 'Did yer daughter do yer carry-out?'

Bob tried to control his temper as he shook his head. 'No, the missus did it.' He lifted the top slice of bread and it took all his willpower not to shout out in anger. In the centre of the sandwich was a piece of brawn about two inches square. He couldn't believe his eyes. What the hell did his wife take him for? Did she think he was a bloody fool who wouldn't mind being belittled in front of his workmates? She hadn't even bothered to cut the bread in two, and if he lifted the huge sandwich out of the box as it was, he'd be a laughing stock. Thankfully, apart from Kate, the others were too busy yapping to have noticed.

He put the lid back on the box in disgust. He'd throw it at her when he got home, along with a piece of his mind. He'd rather starve than eat it. 'We had a blazing row over the weekend, and this is my dear wife's way of getting her own back.'

Kate's heart went out to him. 'A bit drastic, isn't it?'

'I think the word that suits her best is spiteful. Still, I'll make sure it doesn't happen again.'

Kate's eyes swept around those sitting at the table and, confident that no one was looking, she slipped two of her sandwiches across the table and put them at the side of his box, out of sight. 'It's not much, but it'll keep the hunger pangs at bay. And I've got a cake yer can have, too, thanks to me mam. She does the baking, and even though I shouldn't boast, she's a dab hand at it. My sandwich cakes always sink in the middle, but not hers. And her fairy cakes melt in yer mouth.'

Kate knew she was talking too much, but it was only to stop any embarrassment Bob might feel. And she sighed with relief when he nodded his thanks and picked up one of the butties. 'They're only meat-paste, I'm afraid, me money doesn't run to boiled ham. But they'll fill a hole.'

'Beggars can't be choosers, Kate, and besides, they're very tasty. I'm beholden to yer on two counts.'

Kate raised her brows questioningly. 'How d'yer make that out?'

'Well, for helping to stop my tummy from rumbling for one thing, and for not laughing yer head off like some would have done. I really appreciate that.'

A faint blush came over Kate's face. 'I've not done anything the others wouldn't have done if they'd known.'

'Oh, they'd have helped, I know that. But they'd have made a song and dance about it.' Bob leaned closer. 'I could have said me wife had played a joke on me, and they'd have laughed their heads off. But I'm not lying about it. It was done for spite, and the missus will be sorry she signed when I get home.'

Kate, her hair hidden beneath the turban all the women had to wear on the shop floor, showed a set of strong white teeth when she smiled. 'Having a row won't solve anything, it seldom does. Wouldn't it be better to just kiss and make up?'

Bob gazed at her for a second before lowering his head. He had no right to burden this woman with his problems, she probably had more than enough of her own. So he met her hazel eyes and smiled. 'Yeah, ye're right. I'll probably throw me carry-out at her, then give her a cuddle. It beats a black eye any day, doesn't it?'

Billy Gleeson, who'd suddenly realised Bob hadn't contributed anything to the general conversation going on around the table, turned to him. 'What beats a black eye, mate?'

Kate surprised herself by stepping in. 'A fairy cake. I was just asking Bob if he'd like one. Me mam baked a batch today and put two in with me carry-out. I couldn't eat both of them so I was trying to palm one off on Bob.'

Holding out his hand, Bob said, 'Which I accept with pleasure.'

Billy pursed his lips and tapped the side of his long, thin nose. 'They say the way to a man's heart is through his tummy, Kate, but don't forget this feller's a married man. In other words he's took, spoken for.'

'Men are the last thing on me mind, Billy.' Kate flicked a crumb from her chin. 'I'd rather have a fairy cake any day.'

'That's put me in me place,' Billy chuckled. 'And you, Bob.'

Peg Butterworth stood up when the whistle sounded. 'Back to the grind, folks.' She leaned over the table and grinned in Billy's face. 'Kate's right. All men are nothing but a load of bleedin' trouble. The only time they're happy is when they're in the pub supping beer, or in bed taking advantage of their poor, longsuffering wives.'

There was a surge towards the door, and Bob just had time to smile at Kate, and say, 'Thanks a million.'

Bob let himself in and closed the front door quietly behind him. He felt like flying up the stairs and having it out with Ruby, but the thought of waking Lucy held him back. He'd keep it bottled up until she'd left for school, then he'd have his say. Usually, when he was on nights, he'd make himself a pot of tea and some toast, then slip into bed as Ruby was getting out to see to Lucy. But today he only made himself a pot of tea. This was one morning he'd have his breakfast cooked for him.

Sitting at the table, smoking a Woodbine and supping his tea, Bob was asking himself where it was going to end. They couldn't carry on like this, at loggerheads with each other all the time. It was no way for a married couple to live, and certainly not the right atmosphere to bring up a child in. Something had to be sorted out, and quickly, because he couldn't stand much more. A row between man and wife was one thing, it happened in every household, but in most cases it could be ended with a bit of coaxing and a kiss. But what was happening here was no ordinary row; it had gone too far to be sorted out with coaxing and a kiss.

He heard a sound from the room above and knew Ruby would be down any minute. He didn't move, just stared at the door. And when it opened and she walked through, yawning and scratching her head, he never uttered a sound, just stared.

'What's the matter with you? Why haven't yer gone to bed?'

Bob closed his eyes to shut out the sight of her matted, dyed blonde hair, the hardness in her eyes and her bloated face still caked with yesterday's make-up. Was this really the girl he'd fallen in love with and married? He opened his eyes and sighed. 'I'm waiting for yer to cook me breakfast.'

'Yer what! You cook yer own breakfast!'

Bob picked up his carry-out box and threw it on the floor at her feet. 'Not after the little trick yer pulled on me last night, I don't.'

'What are yer on about? I didn't pull no trick on yer! I did yer carry-out, didn't I? What more d'yer expect?'

'I'm not going to argue with yer, Ruby, I'm not even going to raise me voice. At least not until Lucy has left for school. Then I intend to raise the roof, and I don't care who hears me. So while I'm waiting, yer can cook me breakfast.'

'I don't know what the bleedin' hell ye're on about, and I don't ruddy well care, anyway.' The washed-out cardigan Ruby was wearing was wrapped across her chest as she bustled out to the kitchen. 'Yer've sat there for an hour, like a stuffed dummy, too bloody lazy to toast two pieces of bread! Yer want yer head testing, you do.'

'No, Ruby, that's where ye're wrong. The day I needed me head testing was the day I married you. But we'll discuss all this later, when Lucy doesn't have to listen to her parents pulling each other to pieces. Right now, though, I'll have me two rounds of toast, lightly done, and a fresh pot of tea.'

Lucy was surprised and pleased to see her father sitting at the table. 'I thought yer'd be in bed by now, Dad. Yer usually are.'

Bob gave her the brightest smile he could muster before biting into a piece of toast. 'I felt like some company with me breakfast this morning, so I waited for yer.'

'That's nice, I'm glad yer did.' Lucy looked down at the plate her mother put in front of her. There was no burnt offering this morning, the bread was toasted to a nice golden brown. She knew her father's presence accounted for this, and she also knew this would be one morning she wouldn't be subjected to her mother's taunts or clouts. 'How did work go, Dad?'

'Same as usual, pet, I can't complain. It's a job, and I'm lucky to have one with so many men out of work.' He looked across at his wife who was sat on a fireside chair with a plate on her lap and her cup of tea close to hand on the fire hob. 'We wouldn't know what had hit us if I wasn't working. We'd really be in Queer Street.'

'I know it's a long way off,' Lucy said, 'but when I leave school my wages will help out, won't they?'

Ruby snorted. 'Blimey, we might all be dead and buried by then.'

'That's right, Ruby, there's nothing like starting the day on a happy note.' There was sarcasm in Bob's voice. 'Always laughing and joking, that's you. The life and soul of the party.'

'Well, I'm not going to die, I'm too young.' Lucy nodded her head to show she meant it. 'I'm going to live until I'm as old as Mrs Aggie.'

'Don't let Aggie hear yer say that, pet, 'cos she's not that old, yer know. I'd say in her early sixties.'

'Oh, I didn't mean I thought Mrs Aggie should die, Dad!' Lucy said. 'I'd be very sad if anything happened to her, she's lovely and she's me friend.'

'She's a nosy old witch,' Ruby snorted. 'All she needs is a broomstick and she could fly away over the houses. And it would be good riddance to her.'

Lucy looked down at her clasped hands for a second, then twisted in her chair. 'Mrs Aggie's not wicked, she's nice and kind.'

'That's enough now.' Bob pointed to the clock. 'Don't yer think yer'd better be making tracks, pet? Yer don't want to be late for school.'

Lucy's heart was beating fast. She'd rather have had a clout off her mam than have her say those things about Mrs Aggie. Why did she hate everyone so much? There wasn't one neighbour she had a kind word for. 'I'll get me coat, Dad.' She pushed her chair back under the table, and knowing her father's presence would prevent her from getting a hiding, she had the courage to face her mother. 'You don't like no one, you don't.'

Bob stood up. 'Come on, get yer coat on and I'll see yer out. One of the reasons I stayed up was to sneak a kiss off yer. I don't get nearly enough.'

This brought a smile to Lucy's face. 'I'll give yer six, that'll be one for every day.'

Bob gave her a playful smack on the bottom. 'I'll put five in me pocket and take one out every morning.'

After waving his daughter off, Bob closed the door with a heavy heart. He was tired after working all night and would have loved nothing better than to get his head down. But things needed sorting out, and they needed doing now. But where to start, when his wife was making it plain she had no intention of meeting him halfway?

Ruby lit a cigarette and drew deeply on it when Bob came into the room. 'Ye're making a rod for yer own back with that girl, she's getting far too cheeky.'

'Let's leave Lucy out of it, shall we? This is just between you and me.'

She raised her eyebrows. 'Aren't yer going to bed?'

'Later.' Bob looked down at the littered table. 'Will yer clear these things away, please?'

'I'll do it when I've finished me cigarette. There's no bleedin' hurry, I've got all day.'

'You might have, but I haven't.' Bob made no move to sit down. 'I want a bit of comfort in me own home, if it's not too much trouble.'

With the cigarette dangling out of the side of her mouth, Ruby began to stack the plates and cups. She did it almost in slow motion, with that hard look on her face and all the while blowing smoke in Bob's direction. Her actions were deliberate, and her way of telling him she wasn't going to knuckle under to him or anyone else.

Bob's temper snapped as the incident in the canteen came back to remind him why he had to put his foot down. He leaned across the table, snatched the cigarette from her lips and flicked it into the grate. 'I have never been nearer to hitting you than I am this minute. Don't try me patience too far, Ruby, or yer'll be sorry. Now get this mess cleared away and we'll sit down and air our differences.'

The table was cleared within minutes and the chenille cloth put back. Then Bob gestured to a chair facing him. 'I'm tired and ready for bed, but I'll not leave this room until we come to an understanding. We can do it in a civilised manner or we can do it the hard way. It's up to you.'

Ruby narrowed her eyes. 'What d'yer mean, an understanding?'

'If we're to live under the same roof, there's got to be give and take. For Lucy's sake, we've got to try and get on together so she

385

has a decent home life. Show each other a bit of respect and politeness. I'll say what I would like, then you can have your turn. I'd like good food on the table when I'm home, and I'd like carry-out that doesn't shame me in front of me workmates. I don't want yer to use bad language in the house and I don't want yer pulling the neighbours to pieces. Especially in front of Lucy.' When Ruby opened her mouth, Bob raised a hand to silence her. 'No, let me have my say first. Yer don't leave our daughter alone in the house while ye're out boozing with yer so-called mates, and I don't want to see her treated like a skivvy. Other women in the street do their own housework and shopping, there's no reason why you can't. God knows, yer've got all day to do it in. And last but not least, I don't want yer raising yer hand to her. She's a good kid, not cheeky or forward. I've only heard her answering yer back twice, and that was called for because yer were saying nasty things about people she likes. She doesn't deserve to be bawled at all the time, a kind word now and again wouldn't go amiss. So I'm asking yer to keep yer voice down and yer hands to yerself.' He met his wife's eyes and could see the blazing anger there. 'I've had my say, now it's your turn.'

Ruby couldn't get her words out quick enough. 'You arrogant bastard! There's got to be give and take, yer say, then reel off all the things I can and cannot do in me own flaming home! I'm a grown woman, not a child!'

Bob said quietly, 'Then act like one.'

'Everything yer've said is what *you* want, not a mention of what *I* might want. If you had your way, I'd be stuck in the house like a bleedin' prisoner. I'm allowed to go to the shops because darling Lucy mustn't do any shopping. She mustn't help with the house-work, either, 'cos she's not a skivvy. No, *I'm* to be the skivvy!'

'I'm only asking yer to do what every other mother does. Keep the home clean and warm, feed and look after yer family, and be pleasant. Is that too much to ask?'

'And be the dutiful little wife? How soft you are!' Anger made Ruby reach for her cigarette packet. And after she'd lit up, she stared him out. 'And what happens if I don't agree to this understanding, as yer call it?'

'Yer'll find out soon enough.' Bob pointed to the cigarette packet she was holding. 'Yer won't be able to afford them, for a kick-off. And there's a lot more yer won't be able to afford. Like the stuff yer bleach yer hair with, and the muck yer thicken on yer face. Yer've had it easy with money up to now, buying yerself everything yer wanted while yer daughter walked around in rags. But all that will change if yer don't agree to mend yer ways.'

Ruby could tell by his eyes and the tone of his voice that he meant every word. She'd be well advised to agree, or pretend to. 'If I agree to everything yer've asked for, what do I get in return? Can I have a night out with me mates now and again, so I get a bit of pleasure out of life?'

'When I'm on early shift, yer can go out every night if yer want, I'm not that interested. But when I'm working, you stay put.'

Ruby was gloating inwardly. As long as she got her housekeeping, and she had a few bob in her pocket, that's all she was interested in. She'd found ways of getting out before when he was at work; she could do it again. Even if it was only an hour, after Lucy was asleep. He'd never find out, she thought craftily, so she'd go along with him. 'What about me money? Do I go back to what I was getting before?'

Bob shook his head. 'Not for a few weeks, until I've got enough saved to buy Lucy a new coat. She certainly could do with one, and I'm hoping to take her to town on her birthday so she can choose one she likes. After that we can go back to normal, but you'll be responsible for buying her clothes and making sure she always looks decent. If it doesn't work out, I'll dock the money again and see to her meself.' He stretched his arms over his head and yawned. 'Have yer anything else to say? If yer have, get it off yer chest now.'

'No, we'll see how it works out. I'll do my bit.'

'Right! I'm off to bed then, 'cos right now I could sleep on a clothes line. If I'm not awake, give me a call about five o'clock.'

Ruby heard him climbing the stairs and pulled a face. What a miserable man she was married to. He had no life in him at all. All he thought about was work, bed, his tummy and his beloved daughter. Not like the men her mates were married to. They liked nothing better than taking their wives to the pub a few nights a week and having a laugh and a sing-song.

She threw the cigarette stub into the hearth, and after telling herself she didn't have much to do and all day to do it in, she decided another smoke wouldn't do no harm. And as she watched a smoke ring drift towards the ceiling, she asked herself what she'd ever seen in Bob Mellor. Oh, he was tall, dark and handsome, all right, but he wasn't exciting. And that's what she wanted, some excitement in her life.

387

Chapter Four

'Hey, Aggie!' Irene Pollard saw her neighbour walking up the street ahead of her and hurried to catch up. 'What's the big rush, sunshine? Have yer got a heavy date?'

'Yer could say that, queen.' Aggie's smile was wide, showing that this wasn't a day for her gums to be on display. 'The postman brought a letter from Titch this morning and his ship's docking some time today.'

Irene linked her arm and squeezed. 'That's what yer call good news, eh?' Tommy McBride was Aggie's son, the only family she had. And she idolised him. 'It's been a long trip this time, hasn't it?'

'Four months. I've been expecting a letter every day, 'cos I knew he was due any time. But he's still caught me on the hop, with a pantry as bare as Mother Hubbard's. So I'm off to the shops to stock up, 'cos yer know what an appetite he's got. He eats me out of house and home when he's here, but it's a pleasure to see the way he tucks into anything yer put before him.' Aggie's chuckle was hearty. 'He used to lick his bleedin' plate clean when he was a youngster, but I had to put a stop to that when he was twenty-one 'cos it didn't look right somehow.'

'Yer can tell he likes his food, Aggie, he's a giant of a man. That's why I can't understand how he got the nickname Titch! There's nothing small about him.'

'The kids called him that when he started school because he was very small and skinny. He didn't start growing until he was about twelve, and so help me, Irene, I thought he'd never stop. But everyone knew him as Titch, and the name stuck. The only time I call him Tommy is when I'm telling him off.'

Irene chortled. 'Yer can't tell a forty-year-old man off, Aggie, that's daft.'

'That's what he gets told off for, queen, being daft. He might be forty, but he's never grown up in the head. He's always playing tricks on me, and if he wasn't so big I'd box his ears for him.' When Aggie laughed, her top set of teeth became loose and she stuck her thumb in her mouth to push them back into place. 'Last time he was home he hid me purse on me. I didn't know he'd hidden it, like, and I searched high and low for the bleedin' thing. I didn't let on to him in case he said I was careless, but after looking everywhere, I was getting frantic. It was only when the club woman knocked he took it out of his pocket and handed it to me, looking all innocent, as though butter wouldn't melt in his mouth. "Is this what ye're looking for, Ma?" he asked. I could have brained him, I didn't think it was a bit funny. But when I came back after paying the club woman, he had one of the wooden chairs in the middle of the room. He held his hand out and said, "Here yer are, Ma, I'll help yer stand on it. I deserve me ears boxing for pulling a stunt like that. I'm a fool to meself, that's what I am. After all, yer could have had a heart attack, and who'd have made me dinner for me then, eh?" '

Irene was shaking with laughter as she pictured the scene. 'There's never a dull moment with your Titch around, is there? But I bet yer wouldn't have him any different, though, because I know yer love the bones of him.'

'Ye're right there, queen. He's been going to sea since he was eighteen, and I don't see that much of him. But I treasure every minute he's with me.' Aggie put a hand on Irene's arm and pulled her to a stop outside a butcher's shop. 'I'm going in here, love, to get some shin beef. When Titch gets home there'll be a pan of scouse simmering on the stove, and four light-as-a-feather dumplings ready to pop in. He always looks forward to his favourite meal on his first day home.'

'I'm made up for yer, Aggie, and I hope he gets a decent leave this time. Tell him to give his friends a knock when he can, we'd love to see him.'

'If I know my son, he'll make sure he's home in plenty of time to eat his meal and go down to the pub. He wouldn't miss either on his first night. Nor would he miss asking George and Bob to go for a welcome home drink with him. So tell George to expect a knock, will yer?'

Irene nodded. 'I'll do that, he'll be tickled pink to see Titch again. And as luck would have it, Bob's on early shift this week, so he can join them.'

'I'll have to go, queen, 'cos I've a fair bit of shopping to do to make me larder look a bit healthier. One egg and one rasher of bacon doesn't look out of place when yer live alone, but yer can't feed a hungry man on it. Besides, I can afford to splash out a bit today because Titch put a pound note in with his letter.'

'So, ye're not only happy, but rich as well?' Irene was pleased for her neighbour. Aggie never complained, but she must get lonely at times. Her husband, Les, had died ten years ago, and although Titch had offered to find a shore job at the time, she wouldn't hear of it. The sea was in his blood, and although he argued otherwise, she knew he wouldn't be happy working in a factory and sent him off to join his ship, so great was the love this mother had for her son. 'I might see yer tonight, then, Aggie, if Titch doesn't bring a bottle of the hard stuff home with him, like he did last time. Yer were too drunk to go down to the pub!'

'Nah, I wasn't, queen.' Aggie's teeth fell down again. The trouble was, her gums felt much better without them and kept pushing them out. So there was a constant war between teeth and gums. But the gums were fighting a losing battle today. No way was Aggie having her son come home to a mother with no teeth in. 'I was a bit tipsy, perhaps, but certainly not so legless I couldn't make it down to the pub. I just felt the men would feel more free to talk if they were on their own.'

Irene laughed. 'I'll believe yer, where thousands wouldn't. Anyway, sunshine, I'll be on me way. Ta-ra for now.'

Aggie heard the key turn in the lock and stood up. Her tummy was doing somersaults with excitement and her heart was crying out with hunger for the sight of her beloved son. Then she heard his familiar voice. 'What's that delicious smell? I must be in the wrong house. We never have no smells like that in our house, 'cos me ma's a lousy cook.'

Aggie rounded the table and held her arms wide. 'Ye're a cheeky bugger. But I'll forgive yer, seeing as it's yer first day home.'

'Ma, it's good to see yer.' Titch put his hands on her waist and lifted her until their faces were on a level. 'Ye're still as pretty as ever. I swear yer look younger every time I come home. Give us a kiss.'

They hugged for a while, then Aggie whispered in his ear, 'I'd better put the dumplings in before the stew burns dry.'

'What! Dumplings as well!' Titch gently set her down. 'Anyone would think yer were glad to see me.'

'And they wouldn't be far wrong, son, I'm over the moon.' Aggie pushed the sleeves of her dress up. 'Let's get this dinner on the go, ye're probably starving.' She turned at the kitchen door. 'Where's yer bag?'

'I dropped it in the hall in me haste to feast me eyes on yer.'

'Well, get yer dirty clothes out and I can put them in the tub to steep overnight.'

Titch leaned against the door jamb. 'There's no need, Ma, yer can do that tomorrow.'

For a brief second, Aggie felt a stab of sadness. He had all the mannerisms of Les, right down to the way he walked, held his head, and even his lopsided grin. He had the same mop of brown hair, too, and blue eyes. But he was taller than his father had been, and broader. And his face was weatherbeaten with being at sea for so long, out in all weathers. She shook her head to dispel the memories. 'Do it now, son, so I'm not rushing to get them washed and ironed at the last minute.'

There was a smile on her son's face as he watched for her reaction to what he had to say. 'Ma, I'm home for two and a half weeks. So yer've got all the time in the world.'

Aggie's mouth gaped. 'If you're having me on, I'll break yer bleedin' neck for yer.'

'Scout's honour, Ma, I'm home for eighteen days. And with being away such a long time, with nothing to spend me wages on, I've got quite a bit saved up. So I'll take yer into town tomorrow and treat yer to whatever takes yer fancy. Yer can have anything yer like, the sky's the limit.'

'I don't want nothing, son, having yer home is treat enough for me.' Then the mother in her came out. 'And don't yer be carrying a load of money around with yer, either. If I know you, yer'll be treating everyone in the bleedin' pub. Throwing yer money around like a man with no flaming hands.'

'I'm not that soft, Ma, it's got to last me until I sail again. And I want to see you're all right when I leave. So I'll just mug me mates, George and Bob, and that's about it, apart from a few pennies for the kids. Does that meet with your approval?'

'I'm not a miser, son, and I'll help anyone out if they're stuck. But yer should be putting some money aside in case yer ever need it. One of these days yer might meet a girl, fall in love and want to settle down. And yer'll need money to do that.'

There was a smile on her son's face as he watched her lift two plates down from the shelf that ran the length of the kitchen wall. 'Ma, it's true what they say about a sailor having a girl in every port, yer know. It's not that I've never had me chances, 'cos to tell the truth I've been spoilt for choice. I've had plenty of flings, because being a red-blooded man I do like the ladies. But I've never met one who I could fall head over heels in love with. One who I would want to spent the rest of me life with. So ye're stuck with me, Ma, because I've not come across one yet that can hold a candle to yer.'

Aggie tutted. 'Go 'way, yer daft ha'porth. Sit yerself down and stop yapping to me, or I'll be burning the backside out of this pan.'

Half an hour later, Titch pushed his empty plate away and rubbed his tummy. 'The captain would have a very happy crew if the ship's cook could make dumplings like you. The ones he makes are so heavy I'm surprised the blinking ship hasn't sunk by now.'

'Ah, well, there's a knack to it, yer see.' Aggie nodded knowingly. 'He probably puts too much suet in them. Tell him I said to just put half the amount in that he usually does, and see how they turn out.'

Titch smiled as he imagined what the scene would be in the galley if he told the cook his mother had advised him to put less suet in his dumplings. The air would be blue with words his mam wouldn't even know the meaning of. 'I'll do that, Ma.' He leaned back against the chair and reached into his pocket for his pipe. 'Any news for me? How are the Pollards and the Mellors?'

'The Pollards are fine. They're a lovely family, the salt of the earth. Young Jack leaves school in two weeks and he's a scream. He was leaning against the wall last night, watching his mates playing marbles, and I asked him why he wasn't playing. "I'm practising, Mrs Aggie," he said. I asked him what he was practising, because all he was doing was leaning against the wall. "I'm practising not playing marbles. Yer see, Mrs Aggie, I'll be going into long kecks when I leave school, and me mam said if she sees me even looking at the gutter while I've got them on, she'll box me ears for me. And as I'm fond of me ears, and don't want them boxed, I'm practising hard at not playing marbles".'

Her son's hearty guffaw filled the room. 'Oh, that's a good one, that is. I can see he takes after his mam. Irene's always had a quick sense of humour. George has too, but he's not as quick off the mark as his wife.'

Aggie sighed. She didn't like gossiping about the neighbours, but if Titch was going to be home for nearly three weeks, he'd notice things for himself. Better he was forewarned so he didn't say anything out of place. 'As for the Mellors, well, what's happening in their house is anyone's guess.' She told him briefly what she knew, and watched him shake his head. 'I feel sorry for Bob, and for Lucy. Their home is not a very happy one, I'm afraid.'

'Trouble's been brewing in that house for a few years now, Ma. Anyone with half an eye could see that. I'm surprised Bob's put up with it for so long. Whenever we go for a pint, which isn't often with me being away, but when we do he never mentions Ruby's name. And as they say, silence speaks louder than words. George is full of Irene and the boys, but Bob only ever talks about Lucy. And that set the alarm bells ringing for me ages ago.' Titch drew on his pipe and there was a look of contentment on his face. He knew he'd be craving for the sea by the time his leave was over, but right now it was bliss to sit with the mother he adored, in the

393

house he was born in. 'I don't know what the solution is there, Ma, only Bob and Ruby can sort that out. And they have to have the will to do it.'

'It's Lucy I feel sorry for,' Aggie said. 'Poor little mite, always has a smile on her face even though her mother gives her a dog's life. Mind you, Irene has brought about a few changes for her. She heard Ruby having a go at the girl one night and knocked to ask was something wrong because of all the shouting and banging. It seems to have done the trick because Irene said it's gone much quieter. And, thanks to George, Lucy goes in their house now to play cards with the boys.'

'Is Lucy still as pretty as ever?'

'As pretty as a picture, son. She'll break a few hearts when she's older.'

'Then I think I'll wait for her to grow up and marry her.'

'I'll knit yer a wife, if yer like. That way, if yer ever got fed up with her nagging, yer could stick her in a sideboard drawer.' Aggie began to clear the dishes. 'I'll get these out of the way, then yer can have the sink to spruce yerself up. I told Irene yer'd be knocking for George, so he'll be expecting yer.' She put the plates on the draining board, then popped her head back in the room. 'Bob's on early shift, so yer'll have yer two mates to jangle to. Yer can tell them all about these girls yer've got in every port, and the goings-on that yer wouldn't dare tell yer old mother about in case she clocked yer one.'

Titch chuckled. 'If I did that, Ma, they'd both pack their bags and sign up on the next ship out of Liverpool!'

'That's as maybe, son. But a life on the ocean wave doesn't appeal to everyone. Heart and hearth are what most men are satisfied with. Especially if they have a family.'

'Yeah, I know, Ma. And in ten years' time I might envy them. But right now I'm happy being foot-loose and fancy free.'

'I'd better get foot-loose and see to the dishes,' Aggie said, disappearing into the kitchen. 'Otherwise yer won't have time for yer usual quota of the liquid brown stuff. We can't have yer sober on yer first night.'

'Ma, I could drink the pub dry and still be able to put the key in the lock. And I'd never be too drunk to miss yer lips for me goodnight kiss. I couldn't sleep without that.'

Aggie smiled as she poured hot water over the dishes. Oh, it was so good to have him home.

'It's great to see yer, Titch.' George's smile was wide when he opened the door. His words were sincere, his handshake firm. 'And yer look the picture of health, as usual.'

'I wouldn't say you were exactly sickly-looking yerself, mate. Irene must be taking good care of yer.'

'And why wouldn't I? He's the only husband I've got.' Irene was waiting for him, her pretty face lit up and her arms opened wide. 'Come and give us a kiss, Titch McBride. And make it a good one, seeing as yer've stayed away a long time.'

They embraced as two friends who had a deep fondness for each other. And his eyes looking over her shoulder, Titch glimpsed the two boys watching with interest. 'Yer don't mind if I kiss yer mam, do yer, fellers?'

'I've got me eye on yer, Mr Titch,' Jack said, his face deadpan. 'Me dad gets one kiss when he comes in. I was watching to make sure you didn't get two. Otherwise me dad would have had to go out and come back in again.'

'Oh, if I'd known that's how yer worked it, I'd have pinched two kisses. Maybe even three! Then yer dad would really have been grateful to me.'

Greg grinned. 'More likely he would have belted yer one. He's very generous, me dad, but not with me mam's kisses.'

'Oh, aye, I think I'm going to have a hard time in a few years. Yer mam will have three big men to make sure no one gets more than one kiss.' Titch winked at Irene as he went to stand behind the boys' chairs. Putting a hand on the back of each of their necks, he turned their faces towards him. 'Anyway, don't I get a welcome-home kiss off you two?'

The boys looked horrified as they tried to pull away. 'Not blooming likely!' Jack cried. 'Only cissie boys get kissed.'

'Gerroff!' Greg twisted his head in an attempt to break free. 'Ye're not getting no kiss off me.'

It was difficult to know who laughed the loudest, Titch or George. 'Yer'll be singing a different tune in a few years,' their dad said, 'when the girls start giving yer the eye.'

Jack gave a superior smile. That time would come for him two years before his brother. 'Ah, well, that's a different kettle of fish. If Mr Titch was a girl, I'd have given her a kiss.'

'Yer mean yer'd have given *him* a kiss,' his brother corrected him.

'I said if he was a girl, soft lad.'

Greg stuck to his guns. 'If he was a girl, he wouldn't be Mr Titch, would he? It means yer'd be kissing a total stranger, and yer can't go round doing things like that. She'd probably slap yer face for yer.'

George was grinning as he walked into the hall for his coat. 'They'll keep that up all night, Titch, so we'd better leave them to it.'

'Does Bob know we'll be giving him a knock?'

'I haven't seen Bob,' Irene said, 'and I don't have much to say to Ruby. If I'd known for sure yer were coming, I'd have made it me business to let him know, but nothing is definite with a sailor, is it? Anyway, I know he'll be that delighted to see yer, he'll have his coat on in five seconds flat.'

George kissed his wife's cheek. 'I won't be late, love.'

'Yer better hadn't be, sunshine, or I'll be waiting in the hall with the poker in me hand.' Irene turned her laughing eyes on Titch. 'If my husband has one over the eight, I'll hold you personally responsible.'

Titch clicked his heels and gave a mock salute. 'Aye, aye, sir.' He put a hand to the side of his mouth and in a loud whisper, said to the boys, 'Blimey, she's worse than our captain.'

The two men walked into the hall with Irene at their heels. Then Titch suddenly turned around. 'I won't be a tick.' He marched back into the living room and grinned at the boys. 'How would yer like to come to first-house pictures with me one night? And we could take Lucy with us.'

'Oh yeah, that would be the gear.' Jack's face was aglow. 'Thanks, Mr Titch.'

'Blinking fantastic!' Greg said, leaning his elbows on the table. Then he narrowed his eyes. 'What night?'

'Unless yer've got heavy dates, we'll make it tomorrow night, eh?' Titch left the room with shrieks of delight ringing in his ears.

Ruby's face was sullen when she opened the door, but it changed miraculously when she saw the two men. 'Well, this is a surprise,' she said, patting her hair into place and hoping her lipstick wasn't smudged. 'Come on in.'

Bob threw the paper down and jumped from his chair. Grabbing Titch's hand he pumped it up and down vigorously. 'Ye're a sight for sore eyes. I didn't even know yer were due home.'

'Me ma didn't know until today, and even then she didn't know what time I'd get home.' Titch's eyes were fastened on the girl sitting at the table, a book opened in front of her. 'Hello, Lucy.'

There was a smile on the heart-shaped face and a twinkle in the green eyes. 'I bet Mrs Aggie's like a cat with two tails. She often talks to me about yer, Mr Titch.'

'Oh, aye? What does she say?'

Lucy's infectious giggle rang out. 'I can't tell yer that, she'd have me life. But she never says nothing bad.'

Titch put on a stern look and folded his arms. 'Now what could she say about me that was bad? I've got a heart as pure as the

396

driven snow and I'm as handsome as a Greek god. Now what more could she want?'

Again Lucy's giggle filled the room. 'Not all gods are handsome, Mr Titch. Have yer seen the state of the God of Thunder? His face is enough to frighten the living daylights out of anyone.'

Ruby was fuming inside. She was being ignored while a chit of a girl was getting all the attention. And she was all dressed up, too, because it was one of her nights out. 'That's enough, Lucy,' she said, pushing her way to stand in front of the fireplace. 'I'm sure Mr McBride came to talk to yer dad, not you.'

'Oh, I don't know,' Titch laughed, 'her dad's not as pretty as her.' He winked before turning to Bob. 'Besides, I've got plenty of time to talk to me mates while we're downing a few pints in the pub.'

Bob glanced at Ruby hoping she would offer to stay in, but one look at her face told him he'd be wasting his time asking. 'I'm afraid I can't go with yer tonight, much as I'd like to. Ruby's promised to go and see a friend of hers and I'll have to stay in with Lucy.'

George raised his bushy eyebrows. 'Can't yer go another night, Ruby?'

If they'd asked her to go to the pub with them, Ruby would have agreed like a shot. But she wasn't prepared to be stuck in the house when she could be out enjoying herself. 'I've promised, and she'll be expecting me.'

The miserable bitch, George thought, before saying, 'Not to worry, there's another way around it. Lucy can go in our house for a couple of hours. It won't hurt her to be late going to bed for one night. Irene and the boys would be delighted to have her.'

Refusing to meet the dark look on her mother's face, Lucy clapped her hands together in glee. 'Oh yes, I'd like that.'

'That's settled then.' George held out his hand. 'Come on, sweetheart, I'll take you to ours while yer dad gets himself ready.'

When Bob was in the kitchen swilling his face, Ruby eyed Titch up and down. God, he wasn't half handsome in a rugged sort of way. Life with him wouldn't be dull, he was a real live wire. 'How long are yer home for?'

Titch shrugged his shoulders. 'Seventeen, eighteen days, it depends when they send for me.'

'If ye're ever stuck for somewhere to go, I'm in every day and yer'd be more than welcome to a cuppa.' Ruby's bold eyes bored into his and she didn't even try to mask the attraction she felt for him. 'As I said, yer'd be more than welcome.'

Titch knew he was getting the 'come on', and was disgusted. If Bob hadn't been in the kitchen, likely to enter the room any second, he would have told her the truth. That he wouldn't touch her with a barge pole. As it was, he said, 'I won't be stuck for somewhere to go. Yer see, I'll be with the only woman in the world for me. That's me ma.'

Bob bustled in, fastening the buttons on his shirt-cuffs. 'I'll just run a comb through me hair, then I'm ready.'

Ruby turned her back on them to stand the fireguard in front of the hearth. 'Don't forget to take a key with yer.'

Bob didn't answer. He was too angry even to look at her. Once again she'd made him look a fool. What would his neighbours think when she wouldn't even forego a night with her so-called friends so he could go for a pint with a mate he hadn't seen for months? The answer to that was easy. They'd think he was crazy.

He jerked his head at Titch and the two men left the room without a word.

'Before we go in, let's get one thing straight. The drinks are on me tonight, so I don't want any argument. Next time, we'll all buy our own, but tonight is my treat.' Titch pushed the door of the saloon open and was greeted by voices from all sides. He was popular with everyone because he was so easygoing and friendly. His weatherbeaten face creased in a huge smile, he punched the air. 'Eighteen days I've got! Eighteen bloody days!' He leaned across the bar and grinned into the manager's face. 'Alec, by the time I go back yer'll be a rich man. I'll be skint, like, but you'll be laughing sacks.'

'Is that a solemn promise, Titch?' Alec kept his face straight. 'Can I give me notice in and look for a cottage in the country to buy for me and Betty?'

There was silence in the bar as men, some still wearing their cloth caps and overalls, listened in anticipation of a good belly laugh. 'Ay, hang about there, Alec,' Titch said, scratching his head and pretending to be deep in thought, 'if I had enough money to spend to make yer rich enough to buy a cottage in the country for you and your Betty, I might as well buy the bloody cottage meself! Mind you, I'd help yer out as much as I could. I'm quite prepared to take your Betty along with me.'

When the laughter had died down, Titch said, 'I'd be good to her, Alec, yer know that. I'm an old softie at heart. And think of the money yer'd save with one less mouth to feed. Yer'd be quids in, able to retire in no time. And then yer could come and lodge with us, in the cottage. I'd let yer have the spare bedroom, what's next to the one me and Betty will be sleeping in.'

The loud laughter and cheers brought Betty down from the

living quarters over the pub. She saw Titch and nodded knowingly. 'I might have known it was the wanderer returned to the fold. It's good to see yer, me darling.'

'And it does me heart good to see you, sweetheart. But before I make the most important decision of me life, can I ask yer something?'

'Fire away, Titch.'

'When you make dumplings, are they as light as a feather?'

'Huh! Some hope! I wouldn't even know how to make the bleedin' things.'

Titch shook his head sadly at the man behind the bar. 'I'm sorry, mate, but the deal's off. What good is a cottage in the country, with roses around the door, cows in the field, buttercups in the meadow and Betty in the kitchen not making dumplings?' He sighed. 'Alec, give us three pints of bitter and I'll sit in the corner with me mates and we can cry in our beer. Yer see, I could tell by George and Bob's faces that they were all set to come to the cottage for their holidays. We've all been dealt a bitter blow, all because your wife can't cook.'

'Ay, yer cheeky bugger, I'll have yer know I'm a good cook.' Betty wagged a stiffened finger while giving her husband a sly kick on his shin. 'Alec will tell yer, he gets food fit for the King himself, don't yer, my heart's delight?'

Alec put the third pint on the counter. 'Anything yer say, dearest heart.' He held his hand out for the ten-bob note Titch was passing over the bar. Through gritted teeth, he growled, 'That bloody brainwave of yours about the cottage just cost me a bruised shinbone.'

Titch chuckled as he picked up the three glasses in his huge hands. 'Look on the bright side, Alec, it's always raining in the country. Yer wouldn't have liked it one little bit.' He spotted an empty corner. 'Come on, lads, let's get supping.'

Bob and George slipped behind the table and sat on the long wooden bench that ran along the wall, while Titch perched himself on a round stool. 'I don't half look forward to me first day home, yer know. Seeing me ma and finding her still as fit as a fiddle, and then meeting me mates for a few bevvies.' He lifted his glass, drank a third of the contents in one go, then wiped his mouth with the back of his hand. 'By, but I enjoyed that. This is the only country where yer can get a decent pint of beer.'

'Where did yer get to on yer travels this time, Titch?' George asked. 'Yer were away long enough to sail around the world.'

'We should have been home a month ago, but we ran into the worst weather I've ever known. There were times I thought I'd never set foot on dry land again. I've sailed through storms before

399

and it's never really bothered me. But this was something else, I can tell yer. For four days and nights the ship was tossed around like a cork. She was built in 1893, the same year I was born, so she's been sailing for forty years. I honestly didn't think she'd stand up to the battering she got, I kept expecting her to break up. And to make things worse, we had a full cargo and the ropes keeping it in place broke, leaving the bloody lot to slide all over the place. We couldn't do a thing about it either, because it would have been suicidal for anyone to venture on deck to get to the hold. They'd have been washed away by waves that were higher than the ship. It was a ruddy nightmare, and one which I wouldn't like to repeat.' Titch saw the rapt expression on his friends' faces and grinned as he picked up his glass. 'Still, I've lived to tell the tale, haven't I?'

Bob shook his head, 'Rather you than me, mate. I feel seasick just thinking about it.'

'Nah, I've never been seasick. Green in the face, maybe, but never sick. Anyway, the old ship was badly damaged, and when we got to India it had to go in dry dock for repairs. That's why I've been away so long, but for God's sake don't tell me ma or she'll worry herself silly every minute I'm away.' Titch finished his pint off and nodded to his two mates to drink up. 'By the way, me ma wouldn't come with me tonight because she thinks I tell yer all about the girls I've got in every port. And the things I get up to that I wouldn't dare tell her about because she'd clock me one.'

George chuckled. 'Yer never say anything, but I bet yer don't go short.'

'I have me moments, George, but I'm choosey. In every port there's young girls and women hanging around outside the docks, hoping to make a few bob. But yer never know what yer could pick up off them. Some of the crew can't wait to get ashore and they'll go with anyone wearing a pair of knickers. But that's too risky for me, I'd rather do without.' Titch picked up the empty glasses. 'I'll get these filled up. I'm hoarse now with all the talking.'

Bob watched him walking to the bar, laughing and chatting to neighbours as he went. 'I can't make up me mind whether I envy him or not.'

George shook his head. 'It wouldn't suit me. I'm more than happy with me life as it is. I've got a job, which is more than can be said for some of the poor buggers around here. And I've got a loving wife and two fine children. I consider meself a rich man.'

And a lucky man, Bob thought. A very lucky man.

'Who's a rich man?' Titch asked, setting the glasses down carefully. 'Has someone come up on the pools?'

'I'd have a job, seeing as I don't do them,' George said. 'No, I was telling Bob I'm very content with me life. There's more ways of being rich than having money.'

'I should bloody well think yer would be content with a wife like Irene! She's got everything it takes to make a man happy, and she's a good mother. I'd even give up the sea if I could find someone like her.' Titch drank deeply, smacked his lips and wagged his head from side to side. 'There's nothing to beat the taste of draught bitter.' He looked across the table as he reached in his pocket for his pipe. 'How about you, Bob? Unless I'm very much mistaken, relations between you and Ruby seemed a bit strained tonight.'

Bob took a deep breath, then blew it out slowly. 'She'd try the patience of a saint, Titch, and that's putting it mild. Look at tonight, for instance. Wouldn't yer think she'd have offered to stay in and mind Lucy? But no, she's too selfish to put herself out. She's only going to see a mate, for God's sake, it's not as though she had something important on.'

Titch puffed until the tobacco caught, then threw the match in an ashtray. His eyes on his pipe, and his voice low, he asked, 'Have yer ever tried putting yer foot down with her?'

Bob was fed up pretending, there was no point in it. Besides, these two were his best mates. If he couldn't talk to them, who could he talk to? 'Apart from giving her the hiding that most husbands would have given her by now, I've tried everything. She's changed so much over the last few years I hardly know her any more. If I said she was as hard as nails, that would be being kind to her. I've tried coaxing, threats, even docking her housekeeping, but none of it has any effect. I just don't know what to do any more. I'm at my wits' end. If it was only meself that suffered I wouldn't mind so much. But it's Lucy I'm concerned about. She's at an age now where she needs a motherly figure, someone she can confide in. She deserves that at least, 'cos she's a lovely kid.'

George had been listening with head bent. He was glad Titch had brought the subject up, it was something he'd wanted to do for ages. It was only because he was afraid of embarrassing Bob that he'd held back. 'I don't like to interfere between man and wife, but for Lucy's sake I will. She does need someone she can talk to. Someone who will explain how yer body changes when yer get in yer teens, and other facts of life. And with the best will in the world, Bob, I can't see Ruby being that someone. I think yer best bet is Irene. She's very fond of the lass, and they're getting to know each other now. She'd be the ideal person to answer questions and confide in. So if I were you I'd have a word with Lucy and encourage her to call into ours more often. Tell her she doesn't have to wait to be invited, like she is when she plays cards with the boys, but any time. Even if it's only a case of popping her head around the door, or staying for ten minutes. That way she'd get to know Irene better, and in time, come to trust her.'

Bob lowered his eyes. Once again Ruby had made him look like a weak fool – a man who couldn't even control the woman he married. Well, he might be weak, but he wasn't going to let his beloved daughter suffer for it. 'I appreciate all yer've said, George, and I'll do me best to see Lucy spends more time in your house. I do worry about her when I'm at work, yer know, she's never out of me thoughts.'

'By the way,' Titch said, 'I'm taking George's boys to first-house pictures tomorrow night and I said I'd ask Lucy to come, too. Is that all right with you?'

Bob's troubled face broke into a smile. 'I'll say it is! She'll be over the moon. And thanks. I might be unlucky in love, but I'm certainly not unlucky with me two mates. Ye're the best, bar none.'

Titch pushed his stool back and reached for the glasses. 'I'll get them in again. The rate we're going, we'll never get drunk tonight. And if I go home sober, me ma will think I'm sick and send for the doctor.'

Chapter Five

'Yer should never go out boozing when ye're on early shift.' Bob sat in the canteen with his elbows on the table and his head in his hand. 'It's nice when it's happening but yer don't half pay for it the next morning.'

'I don't know how yer can afford to go drinking through the week,' Billy Gleeson said, chewing on a sandwich. He was tall and thin, was Billy, with a long thin nose, pale blue eyes, and a mop of ginger hair. He had a sprinkling of freckles on his face right now, but come the summer he'd be covered in them. 'I know I couldn't. Saturday night, and that's me lot. I'm skint the rest of the week. The odd half-pint, maybe, if the wife's got any coppers to spare. But that doesn't happen very often and it's only enough to whet me whistle, certainly not enough to give me a hangover.'

'I wasn't spending me own money, Billy. Well, I mean, yer can't spend what yer haven't got, can yer? No, one of me mates, a neighbour, is a seafarer and he came home yesterday. It's been a ritual for years now, that the day he comes home he takes me and another mate out to celebrate. That's if I'm not on afternoons, of course. The trouble is, he can drink like a fish and thinks everyone's the same.'

'Is this bloke married?' Peg Butterworth asked. 'I could do with meeting a feller with a few bob to his name.'

'Peg, yer've already got a husband,' Billy reminded her, 'and three kids.'

'Yeah, a husband who never has a bean, and three kids what are little buggers.' Peg could call her family fit to burn, which she often did in very colourful language. But let anyone else try and she'd marmalise them. 'Anyway, Billy Gleeson, mind yer own ruddy business, no one asked you to stick yer oak in. There's no harm in me asking Bob a question, even if it does look as though I'm not going to get a bleedin' answer.'

'No, he's not married, Peg,' Bob told her. 'And all the questions I know ye're going to ask, I'll answer in one go. He's tall, built like an ox, and I guess women would say he's very attractive. He's a nice bloke, and very generous.'

'Lead me to him. I've been looking for someone like him all me life.' When Peg smiled, it changed her face from being ordinary, to being easy on the eye. 'Tell him yer've got a mate in work who'd like to meet him.'

'D'yer want Bob to ask if he'd like to meet yer husband, as well?' Billy asked. 'And yer three children?'

'Oh, ye're there again, are yer, nose fever? I'd never get a bit on the side with you around, you old misery guts.' Peg turned to the woman sitting next to her. 'He's a right pain in the arse, isn't he, Elsie? A girl gets the chance of living it up for a change, and he has to go and put the blocks on it.'

Bob felt something brush over his foot, and after checking under the table, he looked across to where Kate was sitting. 'Eat up,' she said, 'it's nearly time to go back to work.'

He pulled a face. 'Me tummy's upset, I've no appetite.'

'Yer can't work on an empty stomach.' Kate had kept a friendly eye on him since the episode of the doorstep sandwich. He and Billy had sat at the women's table every day since, and the two seats on the bench were always left free for them. 'Yer'll feel better if yer get some food down yer.'

Bob smiled and took a sandwich from the box in front of him. 'If you say so.'

'I do say so,' Kate said, returning his smile. 'Anyway, how's yer daughter?'

Interest flared in Bob's eyes. 'She's fine. In fact, I bet at this moment she's got a big smile on her face. The bloke I've just been telling yer about, he's taking her to the pictures tonight, with the two lads from next door. She'll be like a cat on hot bricks all day, full of excitement. And it's her birthday next week, that's something else for her to look forward to.'

'Will she be having a party?'

Bob lowered his eyes. He was too ashamed to tell Kate his daughter had never had a birthday party in her life. 'No. Instead of a party I've promised to take her into town for a new coat. If I've any cash left, I'll treat her to tea in the Kardomah.'

'Oh, that's nice, she'll like that.' Kate looked puzzled. 'Will yer wife be going with yer?'

Bob raised his head and faced her. 'No, my wife will not be coming, Kate.'

'Don't tell me you two haven't made it up yet?'

Bob glanced at the others sat at the table, but they were too busy listening to Elsie Burgess telling them about a woman in her street who was getting her milk for nothing because she was having it off with the milkman. He sighed and turned his gaze back to

404

Kate. 'Me and the wife are having a hard time, I'm afraid. We don't see eye to eye at all.'

'Oh dear, I'm sorry to hear that. It's not still over yer carry-out, is it?'

'No, nothing as trivial as that.' Bob met her eyes. 'It's a long story, Kate, and this isn't the place to tell it. Anyway, yer've probably got enough troubles of yer own without listening to mine.'

'Sometimes it helps to get things off yer chest. And I'm a good listener.'

'Another day, perhaps.'

There was a burst of loud laughter and both turned towards Elsie, who was still holding forth. 'I'm telling yer, it's the truth! Her feller comes out at half-seven, and the milkman goes in at eight. Yer can set yer alarm by them.'

'Come off it,' Peg Butterworth said. 'He probably goes to every house in the bleedin' street! Yer can't tell me he's having it off with everyone, unless he's got the strength of a ruddy lion.'

'Yes, he does go to nearly every house in the street, I'll grant yer that. But he doesn't go inside every house and stay for half an hour, leaving his pony and trap outside. It's a dead give-away, that is. The stupid ców must think we were all born yesterday.'

'D'yer not think,' Billy said, his face straight, 'that ye're all being bad-minded? The poor bloke probably gets a cup of tea off her.'

That got Elsie on her high horse. The arms were folded and the bosom hitched. 'Well, you tell me how come the woman who lives opposite saw the milkman at the bedroom window? He wouldn't be going upstairs for a cup of tea, now, would he, smart arse?'

Peg's eyes were glinting wickedly. There was nothing she liked more than to get Elsie's dander up. 'Perhaps she'd asked him to fix the bedroom curtains or something. Or, she could have had a bad back and asked him to make the bed for her. And being an obliging man, he didn't like to refuse.'

'Oh, he's obliging all right.' Elsie's lips were a thin straight line. Here she was with a bit of juicy gossip, and they didn't believe her. 'And I suppose yer'll say the coalman is obliging as well?'

'What the hell has the coalman got to do with it?' Peg asked. 'Yer can't tell me he comes around at half-eight after the milkman's left?'

'Because she's bleedin' well having it off with him, too!' Elsie was getting to the state where she felt like clocking every one of them. 'Hers is the only house he goes in, and he's there for half an hour. Every Tuesday, like clockwork, he goes in with hands as black as the hobs of hell, and comes out with them snow white.'

'The simple answer to that, Elsie, is that the woman asks him to

405

wash his hands before he makes the bed.' Billy was really enjoying himself, he thought it was hilarious. 'That's what anyone would think if they didn't have a bad mind.'

'What would yer say if I told yer that the milkman doesn't get no money, nor the coalman?' Elsie was red in the face by this time. 'I suppose yer'll say that apart from being very obliging and making her bed for her, the two bleedin' men are also very generous?'

Peg slapped her on the back. 'No, queen, we think it's the woman what's generous. I mean, everyone in your street can't be wrong, can they? But just out of curiosity, what film star does this generous woman look like? She must have plenty going for her, snaffling two men from under yer noses.'

'She's nothing to write home about, that's what we can't understand.' The bell rang to signal it was time to get back to their workbenches, and as she stood up, Elsie got her own back. But she made sure she wasn't standing too close to Peg when she added, 'She looks a lot like you, actually, now as I come to think about it.' Before her mate had time to digest her words, she took to her heels and legged it, with Peg in hot pursuit.

As they walked through the canteen door, Bob said, 'it's amazing what a good laugh can do, isn't it, Kate? I feel a helluva lot better than I did an hour ago.'

Kate grinned. 'I thought Elsie was going to burst a blood vessel when they were pulling her leg. She wanted to be dead serious and they wouldn't let her.'

'We still don't know whether the woman's a harlot or just a pleasant, friendly soul who likes giving out cups of tea.'

'I think that's the trouble. The whole street doesn't know what to make of it either.' Kate veered to the left when they came to the nut and bolt section. 'I'll see yer tomorrow, then, Bob.'

'Yeah, see yer tomorrow, Kate. Take care.'

Lucy sat at the table, her head bent as she chewed on the over-toasted bread. She didn't look at her mother who was sitting in her favourite chair, smoking as usual. It was seldom you saw her without a cigarette these days, she was always puffing away like a chimney. But Lucy wasn't going to do or say anything that would bring on her temper. Today she wanted to go out to school without having to listen to a load of abuse. She was so excited about going to the pictures with Mr Titch and the boys, she wanted nothing to happen that would mar her happiness.

Ruby watched her daughter through a cloud of smoke. She's keeping her nose clean today, she thought. And well she might, with all the attention she was getting. New clothes, bought with money that should have come into the housekeeping purse, going in next door to play cards and be fussed over, even though she knew it was against her mother's wishes that she got matey with that crowd. And now, to top it all, Titch McBride was taking her to the pictures tonight. He'd spurned Ruby's offer of a cup of tea and a friendly chat and was rubbing salt in the wound by taking her daughter out. And all these things had been sanctioned by her dear husband. Well, there was little she could do to pay Bob back, but she could certainly make life unpleasant for his daughter.

Lucy lifted her head when she heard a chair on the opposite side of the table being pulled out, and her heart dropped when she found herself looking into her mother's face. Another five minutes and she'd have been away. Oh, why hadn't she put a move on and been out of the house by now?

'So ye're away gallivanting tonight, eh? Off to the pictures with the great Mr Titch. It's a fine life ye're having these days.'

'He's not only taking me, Jack and Greg are coming, too!' As Lucy picked up her plate, she told herself not to be drawn into an argument. That was what her mother wanted, she could tell by the glint in her eyes. But she couldn't not stick up for someone who was a friend and always good to her. 'I think it's nice of him to take us, so there!' With that, Lucy marched out to the kitchen and put her plate down. The sooner she was out of the house the better. Her mother wouldn't be able to pick on her tonight because her dad would be in.

But Lucy hadn't reckoned on Ruby's burning desire to take her spite out on someone. And the only person available was her daughter. So she waited until the girl was putting her coat on in the hall, with her back to her. Then, silently creeping up behind her, she put her hand up Lucy's dress, and with thumb and forefinger, pinched the flesh at the top of the girl's leg as hard as she could.

Tears welled up in Lucy's eyes. 'Stop it, ye're hurting me!'

'That, you little faggot, is the general idea.' With an evil look in her eyes, Ruby spun the frightened girl around and pressed her face close. 'And that's one place yer won't be showing yer dad, isn't it?'

Lucy made a dash for the front door. When it was open, and freedom at hand, she dared to looked back. The pain, the injustice and the sadness in her heart, gave her the courage to cry out, 'Mothers are supposed to love their children, but you don't love me, you hate me!'

'Are yer putting yer best dress on, pet?'

'Yeah, we can't let the side down, can we?' Although she didn't feel like smiling, Lucy managed one for her dad. He looked so happy for her she didn't want to spoil it. How different it would be if he could see the inside of the top of her leg. There was a big ugly bruise there, and the skin had been broken where her mother's nails had dug in. It hurt like anything when she walked and her two legs rubbed together. And she'd been in pain all day, sitting on a hard bench at school and wishing there was someone she could ask for help without fear of them getting in touch with her dad. 'I'll go and get changed now so I'll be ready in time.'

'It would be nice if yer had a new coat, but it can't be helped. Tell Mr Titch ye're getting one next week for yer birthday, and yer'll be a proper swank then.'

'Now if I told him that, I would be swanking, wouldn't I? The boys would think I was showing off and they'd skit me.' Lucy blew him a kiss before leaving the room to go upstairs. She was on the third stair when she heard her dad speak.

'You could take a brush to her old coat while she's upstairs and try and make it look a bit respectable,' Bob said. 'The lads from next door will be well turned out, Irene will make sure of that. I wouldn't have to ask if yer showed some interest in yer daughter's appearance.'

'She's big enough to brush her own flamin' coat,' Ruby said. 'She'll be wanting a maid next, the way she's getting spoilt.'

Lucy jumped down the stairs and went back into the living room. 'I'll brush me own coat, Dad.'

'Yer mam will do it, it'll only take five minutes.'

'Dad, I'd rather do it meself, honest. I don't want me mam doing it for me.'

Bob looked puzzled at Lucy's tone. 'Are you all right, pet? Yer mam hasn't been shouting at yer, has she?'

'No, it's just that I'd rather do it meself. I've got plenty of time, so I'll have a good go at it when I come down.'

'Oh well, if that's what yer want.' But Bob wasn't completely satisfied, and as soon as Lucy was out of earshot, he glared at his wife. 'Have you been upsetting her? It wouldn't surprise me in the least, it's just the sort of thing yer would do.'

'In the name of God, I only saw the girl for half an hour this morning!' Ruby was so good at telling lies, she didn't even blush. 'You've been home since she got in from school, mollycoddling her, as usual.'

With that, Bob had to be content. But if he could have seen his daughter at that moment he would have gone berserk. The cuts on the top of Lucy's leg were bleeding with the constant rubbing, and she didn't know what to do. Even if she had a bandage it would be no good because the wound was in an awkward place and a bandage wouldn't stay up. She sat on the side of her bed wondering what to do. There was no one she could talk to, so she'd have to think of something herself. How crafty her mother had been, knowing her daughter was far too shy to show anyone what she'd done.

Lucy rested her elbows on her knees and cupped her face in her hands. If the bleeding got worse, it would run down her leg and everyone would see it. And she'd die of shame if that happened. Besides, it would ruin her new dress, and that would be terrible. She racked her brains but couldn't think of anything she could do without help. Then, just when she was about to give up, thinking there was no answer to her plight, she suddenly had a brainwave. She jumped from the bed and crossed to the small chest of drawers. Her old knickers were in there and unless she was much mistaken, the pins would still be in them. Her prayers were answered and she clutched the washed-out knickers to her chest. If she could make a pad out of one of the pairs, she could use the two pins to pin them to the knickers she was wearing and the elastic in the leg would help keep the pad in place. Then came disillusionment when she realised the knickers were far too big to make a pad. But the feeling of hopelessness didn't last long, because she was determined not to be beaten. That would mean her mother had won, and she couldn't let that happen. So she began pulling at the seams of the material and found it ripped easily, being so old and well worn. And five minutes later, with the pad in place and easing the pain, Lucy was smiling as she pulled her best dress over her head.

'Who's a clever girl, then?' she asked herself in a low voice, feeling very proud of her achievement. 'Yer can do anything if yer try hard enough.'

But as she skipped lightly down the stairs, Lucy knew that no matter how hard she tried, she would never forgive her mother for what she had done today.

Bob stood outside the Pollards' house with Irene and George, waiting to wave Titch and his young friends off. 'There's about fifteen pubs between here and the picturehouse,' George reminded him. 'D'yer think yer can resist the temptation?'

'I've got a blindfold in me pocket.' A huge grin covered the weatherbeaten face. Titch wouldn't admit it, but he was as excited as the children. They were doing him a favour, not the other way around. 'When we get to the top of the street I'm going to put it on and the kids can lead me.'

'I'll lead yer, Mr Titch,' Lucy said, her hand held tight in his. 'I won't let yer walk into no lamp-post.'

'And me and Greg will make sure yer don't walk into a pub by accident,' Jack said with his usual deadpan face. 'We'll put a hand over yer nose when we pass one so yer won't be tempted.'

Titch shook his head at Irene and the two fathers. 'Yer had no need to train them, yer know. I got all the instructions off me ma, this afternoon. I'm not allowed to smoke, drink or use bad language. But she gave me permission to breathe, I'm happy to say.' He squeezed Lucy's hand. 'Come on, let's go, or we'll miss the shorts. I hope Laurel and Hardy are on, they're me favourites.'

When they reached the top of the street they all turned around for one last wave. 'They'll worry themselves sick until ye're home again,' Titch said. 'I don't think they trust me, having no family of me own.'

'Even when ye're grown up, do parents still tell yer what to do?' Jack asked, walking on Lucy's other side. 'If they do, there's not much point in growing up, is there?'

'A mother stays a mother all of her life. You might grow up and change, but she never will. She'll always love yer and worry about yer. But yer've got one consolation when ye're grown up, son – yer don't get a clip around the ear if yer don't do what she says.'

'I can't wait to be grown up.' The words were out before Lucy could stop them. 'And my mam doesn't have to worry about me, 'cos I'll be able to look after meself.'

Titch kept his voice casual. 'I'm sure you don't get many clips around the ear off your mam, do yer?'

It was Greg who answered. 'Yeah, she does. Her mam's always clouting her and bawling at her. We can hear it in our house.' He saw the warning glance his brother gave him, but ignored it. 'I'm glad she's not my mam.'

Lucy could feel the colour rise from her neck to cover her face. 'She doesn't hit me no more, me dad told her she hadn't got to.'

'I should jolly well hope she doesn't.' Titch bit on his bottom lip. Out of the mouths of babes comes the truth, he thought. 'If she ever tries to hit yer again, sweetheart, run like blazes out of the house and wait for yer dad to come home.'

'She can always run to ours,' Jack said. 'Me mam would look after her.' He leaned forward and looked past Lucy to catch Titch's eye. 'Me mam always wanted a daughter, yer know. She told us that before each of us was born, everything she knitted was in pink. And of course she couldn't throw it away, so we had to wear the stuff. I've been told I was dressed like a girl until I was two years of age.'

'Ye're not the only one,' Greg told him. 'I was, too! Me mam said she was sure the second baby would be a girl, she didn't think she could be unlucky twice. Me dad used to pull our leg soft about it, didn't he, Jack? He said people used to pop their head around the pram hood and say, "Oh, isn't she lovely, what have yer called her?" '

Titch roared with laughter. 'Your mam wouldn't swap you two for a dozen girls. She loves every hair on yer heads and every bone in yer bodies.'

'Yea, we know that.' Jack stroked his chin thoughtfully. 'Mind you, a dozen girls would be quite a temptation. Six I'd feel safe with, but twelve would have me worried. I believe she'd give the matter careful consideration.'

'Go 'way, soft lad,' Lucy said, not quite used to Jack's dry sense of humour. 'Your mam wouldn't swap you for all the rice in China.' Her brow furrowed. 'Or should it be all the tea in China? I forget.'

'Both commodities are plentiful in China, sweetheart, so either will do.' Titch looked down into a pair of bright green eyes set in a heart-shaped face framed by a mass of dark curly hair. How, he asked himself, could any mother not love this girl? Ruby obviously didn't or she wouldn't hurt her. 'I believe there's two special treats coming up next week, eh? One of yer is having a birthday and the other leaving school. Now which is which?'

Lucy giggled, bringing a smile to all three faces. 'It's me having a birthday, I'll be twelve years of age. I'll change over with Jack if he likes, 'cos I wish it was me leaving school.'

'Fat chance of that!' Jack said, stretching to his full height. 'I've been waiting fourteen years for this.'

'I'm included in these treats, Mr Titch.' Greg gave him a broad wink. 'I've got a brother what's leaving school, going into long kecks, getting himself a job and giving me thruppence a week pocket money.'

'Some hope you've got, soft lad,' Jack said. 'If yer behave yerself I might give yer a penny, and then yer'll have to clean me shoes to get it.'

They reached the cinema entrance and Titch let go of Lucy's hand to delve in his pocket for the ticket money. 'What's it to be? Front stalls, back stalls, the circle or up in the gods?'

'Can we go in the front stalls, please?' Greg asked. 'If we sit at the back, it would be just my luck to sit behind a big fat woman with a hat on.'

'And don't forget the ostrich feather,' Jack said. 'If she's got a hat on, it's bound to have a flipping big ostrich feather sticking up on it.'

'The front stalls it is.' Titch was chuckling to himself as he paid for the tickets. It was a long time since he'd enjoyed himself so much. Then he crossed the foyer to the kiosk where there was a lady selling sweets. 'What would yer like? How

411

about fruit pastilles?' Three eager faces nodded, and Titch gave the order to the assistant. 'Three packets of pastilles and one packet of jelly babies, please.' As he waited for his change, he spied the three children giving each other looks. 'The jelly babies are for me, they're me favourites.'

'Ooh, I like jelly babies,' Lucy said. 'They're my favourites too.'

'And mine!' Greg gave his brother a dig in the ribs. 'And they're yours, as well, so why don't yer open yer mouth?'

'I know,' Jack said, looking sheepish. 'But I thought jelly babies were like marbles. You parted company with them when yer left school.'

'Not on your life! If yer like something, yer don't stop liking it just because ye're getting older.' Titch remembered what his mother had told him, and added, 'Except for playing marbles, of course. I mean, can yer imagine me kneeling in the gutter? I'd look a right nit.' He turned back to the kiosk where the woman was standing with a smile on her face and three packets of jelly babies in her hand. 'I'm sorry to be a nuisance,' he said as they did a swap, 'but they might as well have what they want.'

'Don't worry about it, just enjoy the picture.'

'I'm going next door to wait for Lucy.'

Ruby looked up from the paper she was reading. 'My God, d'yer think the wind might have blown on her?'

Bob walked out without answering. He was weary of all the slanging matches and the arguing. The only way to cope with it, and stay sane, was to ignore it. It didn't seem to worry Ruby, she thrived on it.

Irene opened the door and the welcoming smile on her face had Bob comparing her to the woman he'd just left. He shouldn't compare them, he knew, but the whole atmosphere was so different it was hard not to. This house was in a different world to the one next door.

'I was just going to put the kettle on, so yer've timed it nicely.' She held the door wide. 'The gang should be home any time now.'

'It's to be hoped Titch hasn't taken on more than he can chew.' Bob raised a hand in salute to George. 'Taking three children to the pictures could turn out to be a headache.'

'Don't you kid yerself,' George laughed. 'He'll have a whale of a time with them. He's so good with children, it's a pity he hasn't any of his own.'

They heard the laughter and chattering before the knock came. 'What did I tell yer?' George said, as Irene went to open the door. 'I bet they've had the time of their lives.'

The three children ran in, all trying to get through the door at the same time. Their faces were alive with excitement and eagerness to tell what a marvellous time they'd had. Lucy made straight for her father and sat on his knee. 'I've never enjoyed meself so much, Dad. It's been wonderful.'

He hugged her close. 'I'm glad, pet. In fact, I'm jealous because Titch didn't take me along with yer. I could have put a pair of short kecks on and pretended I was only twelve.'

'Yer'd never have got away with it, Dad. Anyone can see ye're at least fourteen. But yer didn't half miss a treat.'

Titch stood inside the door and viewed the scene with warmth in his heart. Lucy's pretty face was animated as her words poured out. And Irene was standing with an arm around each of the boys' shoulders, listening as they vied with each other to be first to tell all they'd seen and done. There was so much talking going on, George couldn't keep track of it all, so he clapped his hands and called a halt.

'Can we have a bit of hush, please? Now, seeing as yer've had such a good time, don't yer think the least yer can do is show a few manners to the man who made it possible, by asking him to sit down?'

The children were immediately contrite, and three pair of willing hands led Titch to the couch. 'I'm sorry, Mr Titch,' Lucy said, 'but yer gave us such a good time I couldn't wait to tell me dad about it.'

'Yeah,' said Jack. 'If me head hadn't been up in the air I wouldn't have forgot me manners and yer'd have had a cup of tea in yer hand by now. So yer see, Mr Titch, what it boils down to is, ye're a victim of yer own generosity.'

Greg looked at his brother with narrowed eyes. 'Ye're showing off, you are, with yer fancy words. There'll be no living with yer when yer start work. We'll have to get a dictionary out every time yer open yer gob.' He gave Titch a broad smile. 'I'm not as clever as him, so I'll just say it was the gear, and thank you very much.' He started to walk away, then changed his mind. 'I'll pay yer back when I'm older. I'll take yer to the pub on the corner for a pint.'

'I'll hold her to that, son.' Titch laughed heartily. 'I'll be walking with a stick by then, like, but, please God, I'll still be able to lift a pint glass.'

'Aye, look at the time,' Irene said. 'It's nine o'clock and time yer were in bed.'

There were groans from the two boys. 'Ah, ay, Mam, we've got loads to tell yer.'

'Do as yer mam says,' George told them. 'Don't argue with her.'

Irene saw the three young faces drop. 'Yer can tell us everything, from beginning to end, tomorrow night. But right now, I'll let each

413

of yer say what one thing sticks in yer mind the most. Lucy, you can go first.'

'Oh, that's an easy one. Laurel and Hardy were on, and Mr Titch laughed so much he had to hold his tummy. And he had tears rolling down his cheeks.'

George roared. 'Still a kid at heart, eh, Titch?'

'Yer don't have to be a kid to enjoy Laurel and Hardy,' Titch said. 'I think they're the best, bar none.'

'Your turn now, Greg,' Irene said, her eyes on the clock. 'And don't make a meal of it, either.'

'I'll talk fifteen to the dozen, eh, Mam?' Greg moved to the other side of his mother. 'I'm getting out of Lucy's way in case she belts me one. Yer see, the big picture was a sad one. And every time Janet Gaynor cried, Lucy cried. And when she wasn't crying, she had her eyes shut tight. Yet when we came out of the picturehouse, she said it was a lovely film.' He shook his head as though it was a mystery to him. 'How is it, that girls are never happy unless they've got something to cry about.'

'Nobody answer that,' Irene warned. 'Now, Jack, it's your turn.'

'I'm telling tales out of school now,' Jack said, 'but yer could have knocked me over with a feather when Mr Titch bought himself a packet of jelly babies.'

The laughter that piece of information brought was loud and long. And it would have continued if Irene hadn't taken the boys by the scruff of their necks and pointed them to the door. 'Up those stairs, now!'

Jack's eyes slid sideways, 'Mam, if yer strangle me, yer won't only be losing yer lovely son, yer know. Yer'll be losing the wages I'd have been earning if yer hadn't strangled me.'

'And if yer strangle me,' squeaked Greg, 'I'd be losing the pocket money he'd have given me if yer hadn't strangled both of us.'

Her eyes showing her love for them, Irene hugged them close and kissed them. 'If I ever kill yer, it'll be with love. Now, behave yerselves and get up to bed.'

The boys stood in front of Titch and thanked him again. 'If yer were a girl,' Jack said, 'then I would most definitely give yer a kiss.'

'Oh, don't start that again, our kid,' Greg pulled on his arm, 'or we'll have our dad after us.'

As the boys clattered noisily up the stairs, Bob moved Lucy from his knee and stood up. 'Those two boys of yours are real cases,' he said. 'Sharp as a razor, both of them.'

'I know someone who's a match for them, eh, Lucy?' Titch chucked her under the chin. 'She had them fair flummoxed at times, I can tell yer. With her looking so shy, and speaking in such a matter-of-fact voice, they don't know whether she knows she's being funny, or not. But between the three of them, they made tonight very special for me. They were a treat to take out.'

Lucy bent down and kissed his cheek. 'Thank you, Mr Titch.'

'Come on, pet,' Bob took her hand, 'yer'll never get up in the morning.'

'Come back when Lucy's in bed,' George said. 'We can have a good natter.'

'That's a good idea, it'll round the day off for me.' Titch started to push himself up from the couch. 'I'll nip down to the corner and get a few bottles.'

He was thrown back on the couch before he knew what was happening, and Irene was standing over him. 'Oh, no yer don't, Titch McBride. For one night in yer life yer can do without knocking the brown stuff back. Yer can make do with a cup of tea like the rest of us, and one of me home-made scones. So put that in yer pipe and smoke it.'

'What! I wouldn't dream of putting one of yer home-made scones in me pipe and smoking it. Not when it was made by those fair hands of yours.'

George was watching Lucy and could see her eyes becoming heavy. 'Take the lass home, Bob, before she falls asleep on her feet. She's had enough excitement for one day. Titch will still be here when yer get back, Irene will see to that. If he makes one move, she'll sit on him.'

His grin reaching from ear to ear, Titch held his arms wide. 'Oh, yes, please.'

Chapter Six

'What sort of time is this for her to be coming in?' Ruby had been listening to the noise coming through the wall, and with each burst of laughter her temper had grown. 'She'll get used to all this fussing and yer'll never do anything with her – she'll expect it all the time.'

Bob didn't answer, but his eyes spoke volumes. He took Lucy's coat from her and said, 'I'll hang this up, pet, you'd better run down the yard before yer go to bed.'

'Yeah, I think I better had.' Lucy was glad to get away from the room and her mother's spiteful tongue. There were no hugs for me from a loving mother, she thought. Mine couldn't even ask me if I'd had a nice time. Still, she can't take my memories of tonight away from me, that's one thing. I can lie in bed and go over it all again, relishing every second.

Inside the house, Ruby wasn't to be silenced. 'Did yer hear what I said? It's too late for her to be out. She should have been in bed an hour ago.'

'Yer didn't think of that the night yer left her on her own until nearly half-past ten, did yer? But I don't suppose that counts, seeing as you were out enjoying yerself.' Bob shook his head in disgust. 'It's hard to believe that a grown woman could be jealous of her own daughter. You never take her out because, apart from the fact yer can't be bothered, it might cost yer a few pennies, and yer need them to keep up with yer boozing friends. Yet yer don't like it when someone else gives her what you should be giving her. And that's a little love and attention.' He heard Lucy running up the yard and pointed a warning finger. 'One word out of place to her, and by God, yer'll be sorry.'

'I'll go straight up, Dad, I'm dead tired.' Lucy gave her father a kiss and left the room without a glance at the woman who had given birth to her. She didn't act like a mother, Lucy's sore leg reminded her of that, so she wasn't going to treat her like one. But no matter how brave the words were that were running through her mind, in her heart she was hurt and sad. Why didn't her mother love her like Mrs Pollard loved her boys? She wasn't a bad girl, she'd done her best to make her mother love her. If she did, this house would be as happy as next door, and that would be wonderful. And her dad wouldn't have that sad look she sometimes glimpsed in his eyes when he thought she wasn't looking.

Lucy climbed into bed and pulled the clothes up to her chin. She was very tired and it wasn't long before she could feel herself drifting into slumber. And as she did, there was a smile on her face as a picture flashed through her mind of Mr Titch biting the head off a green jelly baby.

Bob stood aside while Billy Gleeson slithered along the bench in the canteen, then he sat on his usual end seat. 'It doesn't seem like twenty-four hours, does it, Kate? I've never known the time to go so fast. It's just flown over.'

'I remember when I was about fifteen, me mam heard me saying I wished I was seventeen and able to go to dances. She gave me a lecture, saying I should make the most of my teenage years, because when I got to twenty-one the years would fly over.' Kate smiled. 'She was right, too, although I didn't believe her at the time. But twenty-two years have gone by since then and I've hardly noticed them passing. It's frightening when yer think about it.'

'Go 'way, ye're still a young woman,' Bob said. 'A mere slip of a girl.'

Billy had had his ear cocked. 'He's flattering yer, Kate, yer want to keep yer eye on him. I knew yer never should have given him that fairy cake.'

'It's not very often anyone flatters me, Billy, so I'm going to make the most of it. Just think what would have happened if I'd given him *two* cakes! Me head would be twice the size. I think when I go home I'll tear me birth certificate up, then when I'm feeling weary I can tell meself I'm only twenty-one. There'll be nothing to prove otherwise.'

'Only that yer'll still feel weary,' Billy said, tapping the side of his long nose. 'Yer body's the one thing yer can't fool. I should know because I feel every day of me thirty years.'

Bob chuckled. 'Yer've lost fifteen years somewhere along the way, Billy.'

'That's only first thing in the morning, mate. I wake up as spritely as a spring chicken, ready to take on the world. But by the time I've bent down to put me shoes on, then try to straighten up again, those fifteen years let me know they're still there.' He cocked an ear. 'Ay out, let's listen to this.'

'Hey, Elsie,' Peg Butterworth spoke through a mouthful of corned beef sandwich. 'Any more news from that house of ill-repute? The one where the woman's having it off with the milkman and the coalman? At least, according to everyone in your street she is.'

Elsie's eyes slewed sideways to see if Peg was making fun of her. But her mate's face was dead straight. 'Not everyone, Peg, there's one silly cow who won't hear of it. Mind you, the tight-fisted bitch is making a few coppers out of it, so she's bound to believe what she wants to believe. It's in her best interest, isn't it?'

Peg put her buttie down and swivelled her bottom round. 'Ye're not going to tell me she stands at the door and charges the men? And then afterwards the two women split the dosh between them? Well, that takes the biscuit, that does. What sort of a street d'yer live in, girl?'

'Don't be so bleedin' stupid, Peg Butterworth, of course she doesn't stand at the door taking money. There'd be a lynch mob out if she did that. Besides, she's a sneaky thing, she doesn't do anything in the open, it's all underhanded.'

'I know I'm a fool for asking,' Peg said, 'but I wouldn't get a wink of sleep if I didn't. How does this sneaky, underhanded woman make money out of the carryings-on of one of her neighbours?' Then Peg banged a closed fist on the table. 'I've got it! The men pay her money to keep her mouth shut. I'm right, aren't I?'

'Are yer hell,' Elsie said. 'Ye're miles out! She doesn't get no money off the men, she gets it from the horse.'

Disbelief showed on all faces for a few seconds, then laughter broke out. 'Elsie, ye're a real case,' Billy chuckled. 'Yer had us going for a minute.'

'I'm not pulling yer legs, it's the truth,' Elsie said, a smug smile on her face. She'd teach them not to make fun of her. 'She makes money out of the horse.'

'I've got it!' Once again Peg banged the table. 'While the milkman's in the house, doing you know what, this sneaky woman gives people rides in the trap and charges them. That's it, isn't it?'

'Ye're not even warm.' Oh, how Elsie was enjoying being the centre of attention. 'I know,' said another workmate, Ada Smithson, 'she lets the kids stroke the horse and charges them a ha'penny.'

'Ye're not even close.' Elsie's face was now wearing a haughty expression. She was going to milk this situation for all it was worth. 'Try again.'

'Not on yer life,' Peg said. 'Ye're taking us for suckers. There's no way she can make money out of the horse.'

'Yes, there is, so there,' Elsie snapped.

Peg was equally determined. 'And I say there isn't.'

'There is, and don't you call me a bleedin' liar, either, or I'll clock yer one.'

'Yer'll have to prove it, 'cos I don't believe yer.'

Those sitting at the table looked as though they were watching a tennis match, as their heads moved from Peg to Elsie. And when it looked as though Elsie wasn't going to deliver the goods, Billy chipped in, 'Go on, Elsie, put us out of our misery. We're all on edge, waiting for yer to solve the mystery. How can she make money out of the horse?'

'Manure.' Elsie was still wearing her haughty face. 'That's what.' Nine voices spoke in unison. '*Manure?*'

Elsie folded her arms and looked down her nose. 'Are yez so ignorant yer don't know what manure is?'

'We know what it is, Elsie, but I don't think we quite understand the connection.' Billy decided to see if a bit of soft soap would work. 'Ye're very good at telling a tale, girl, yer have a way with words. Why don't yer fill the picture in for us? You know, every little detail, so we can see it all in our minds.'

Elsie smiled. That was more like it. Not before time they were beginning to appreciate her. 'Well, this money-grabbing little cow's name is Flo Durning. She's small, as thin as a rake and as miserable as bloody sin. Yer never see her without a mobcap on and a pinny with a big pocket in. She's got beady little eyes, and believe me she doesn't miss a trick. If she's not standing at the door, taking all in, then she's peeping behind her curtains. There's not a thing goes on in our street that she doesn't know about. In fact, she knows about it before it bleedin' happens.' Elsie glanced around the faces. 'Are yer with me so far?'

Peg Butterworth tapped her on the arm. 'Yer did that beautiful, girl. I can see the little squirt as if she was standing in front of me. Now, carry on.'

Elsie beamed. That was praise indeed from her mate. 'Well, now we'll go to the horse. It's a dark brown one, with a patch of white on its face. The milkman, Taffy, he's got it well trained, I'll say that for him. When he says "Wait", then wait it does. And after about ten minutes, out comes droopy drawers, Flo, with a bucket and shovel. And sure enough, the flaming horse obliges and she shovels the manure up as soon as it hits the ground. In the bucket it goes, then the queer one makes a dash for her house with it. Honest to God, can yer imagine what her house smells like? Anyway, down the back entry she scarpers, and sells it to a bloke in the next street what's got an allotment. Tuppence a bucket she charges him, the crafty cow.'

'Well, I'll be blowed.' In repose, Peg's mouth was far too big, it stretched the full width of her face. But when she was animated and smiling, it did wonders for her appearance and drew eyes like a magnet. 'They're an enterprising lot in your street, I must say. Not only do they give the neighbours plenty to talk about, they make a few bob into the bargain.'

'Ay, yer can cut that out for a start,' said Elsie, looking as suitably outraged as she thought the occasion warranted. 'We're not all tarred with the same brush.'

'Only because the milkman wouldn't have the energy to cover the whole street, and the horse will only oblige once a morning.'

'Are you insulting what I think yer are, Peg Butterworth?'

'All I'm saying is, chance is a fine thing. And before yer get on yer high horse and tell me ye're going to knock me block off, just remember I'm bigger than you. You might have the weight, but that can be a disadvantage in a fight. So think on before yer take yer false teeth out and put yer boxing gloves on.'

Elsie's eyes and mouth opened wide. 'Ay, you, ye're asking for it, you are. Yer know bleedin' well I don't wear no false teeth!'

Bob was grinning as he turned to face Kate. 'Are they always like this, at each other's throat?'

Kate nodded. 'All the time. But they've never come to blows yet. In fact, they're the best of mates. If one of them is in trouble, the other is always there to help out.'

'Thank God for that! For one horrible moment I thought either me or Billy would have to be referee and stand between them. I wouldn't fancy that, not with the weight Elsie's carrying. One blow from her and I'd be knocked into the middle of next week.'

'No fear of that, she's as soft as a brush, is Elsie. If yer told her yer neighbour's cat had been run over, she'd cry her eyes out.' Kate gave a quick glance to make sure no one was listening. 'As yer know, Peg can tell a good story. And last time we were on the early shift she went to the pictures. The film was a real weepy by all accounts and she had Elsie in floods of tears, telling her all the sad parts and really piling the agony on. Then when she'd finished, she handed over a piece of cloth for Elsie to dry her eyes on. "Seeing as yer won't need to go and see it now, girl, I think yer should pay me what it would have cost yer. I won't charge yer the tram fare, though, seeing as ye're me mate." That soon put a stop to Elsie's tears. "Yer know what you can do, Peg Butterworth," she said, "yer can just sod off." '

Bob chuckled. 'It sounds something like the picture Lucy went to see last night. By all accounts she cried all the way through it, and then at the end said it was a lovely film. The two boys from next door pulled her leg soft.'

'I was going to ask yer how she got on. Did she enjoy herself?'

'They all had the time of their lives. Especially Titch, the bloke who took them. He said it was a real eye-opener, just listening to them. The boys have inherited their mother's sense of humour and he said the wisecracks out of them had him in stitches. And he surprised me over Lucy. He said she was as quick off the mark as they were and had an answer for them every time.' There was a trace of sadness in Bob's smile. 'Who she inherited that from I don't know, because no one could say I'm the life and soul of the party. And her mother certainly isn't.'

'Oh, come off it, Bob! Listening to you anyone would think yer were a real misery guts. Yer've got as much sense of humour as the next man, so don't be running yerself down.'

If Bob had spoken his thoughts, he would have said his life over the last few years had robbed him of any humour he might have had. Instead, he said, 'Oh, I can laugh at other people's jokes, but I'm no good at telling them meself.'

'You're as bad as me, then. My husband used to laugh when I tried telling jokes, because I always told the end bit first. So I gave it up as a bad job.'

'He must have been very young when he died?' Bob asked the question before giving it any thought. When he saw Kate's hazel eyes cloud over, he cursed himself for being so insensitive. 'I'm sorry, I shouldn't have said that. I've upset yer now.'

'The people who say time is a great healer don't know what they're talking about. It's five years now since Vic died, but it still hurts like hell. There isn't a day goes by that I don't miss him because there's so much to remind me of him. Oh, I've gone past expecting him to walk through the door, and I've got used to his favourite chair being empty. But our daughter, Charlotte, is the spitting image of him and a constant reminder.'

'And then yer've got thoughtless people like yours truly. I really could kick meself, Kate, for being so stupid.'

They hadn't heard the bell, and Bob was startled when Billy clamped a hand on his shoulder. 'It's time to move, mate, but before we do, let us in on the secret. What have yer done that's so stupid yer could kick yerself?'

Once again Kate came to the rescue. 'Don't tell him, Bob, or he'll want one.'

Billy was intrigued. 'Want one what?'

'Ye're a nosy bugger, Billy.' By now, Bob had sorted his head out. 'But since I know yer'll keep at me until I tell yer, it's a fairy cake. I've been promising to bring one in for Kate, and blow me if I don't keep forgetting.'

'A likely tale,' Billy snorted. 'Come on, shift yerself.'

'If I forget again tomorrow, Kate, yer have my permission to kick me.' Bob winked. 'See yer.'

422

'Yeah, see yer, Bob.' Kate picked up her carry-out box and put it under her arm. Then she smiled and called after him, 'I'm not very good at kicking, so I'll get Elsie to do it for me.'

'Come on, Ma, let's go into town and I'll buy yer something.' Titch faced his mother across the table. 'We can go to Blackler's and have a look around – yer like it there.'

'There's nothing I need, son,' Aggie said. 'And there's no use buying something just for the sake of it. That would be a waste of good money.'

'Ma, if I'm going to waste me money, there's no one else in the world I would rather waste it on. I haven't even bought yer a drink yet.'

'Buying me drinks would be money down the bleedin' drain. I'm quite happy with me half-pint of stout every night, suits me down to the ground. It's nice and smooth and puts me in the mood for a good night's sleep.' Aggie had a thought. 'Ay, Irene's going into town to buy some long trousers for Jack – why don't yer go with her? It would save yer hanging around the house twiddling yer thumbs.'

'Oh, aye,' Titch laughed. 'George would love me taking his wife out. And we'd be the talk of every wash-house in the neighbourhood.'

'Not if I was with yer.'

'Yer've just said yer didn't want to go into town!'

'What I said was, I didn't want yer spending money on me just for the sake of it. But I wouldn't mind going around the shops with Irene, in fact I'd be made up. Me and her get on like a house on fire, and she's always good for a laugh.'

'Well, that's settled then.'

Aggie tutted. 'It's not settled, son. Not until we've asked Irene if she minds us going with her. I'm sure she won't mind, but it's manners to ask.'

'You'll have to do the asking, Ma, I wouldn't have the nerve.'

'Oh, my God!' Aggie threw her hands in the air. 'A girl in every port he tells me, but he's shy with a woman's he known for nigh on twenty years.'

Titch grinned. 'I steer clear of married women, Ma, they're not on me list. Yer see, I'm not a good runner.'

Aggie pushed herself up from the chair and studied her reflection in the mirror over the mantelpiece. 'I'll nip up and have a word with her. If it's all right, I'll have to do something to titivate meself up. I can't go out with me son looking like an old hag.'

'Ye're still a fine-looking woman, Ma, and I'd be proud to have yer on me arm even if yer were dressed in a sack. And people would still think yer were me wife, not me mother.'

'Ye're full of flattery, Titch McBride. It's no wonder yer've got a list of girlfriends as long as me arm. But I'm a bit too long in the tooth to fall for such blarney.' Aggie cupped his face and planted a noisy kiss on his lips. 'While I'm out, be a good lad and wash these few dishes for me.'

Irene was drying her hands on a towel when she opened the door. Her face lit up, as it always did when she set eyes on one of her favourite people. 'I've just finished doing the spuds ready for tonight. Save me worrying meself to death while I'm out. Come on in, sunshine, yer don't have to wait to be asked.'

Aggie brushed past and walked into the living room which, as usual, was shining like a new pin. 'I came to see if yer felt like some company on yer shopping trip?'

Irene reached into the kitchen to hang the towel on a nail behind the door. 'I'd be highly honoured to have yer, Aggie. It would be company for me and yer can help me choose Jack's trousers. Then if he doesn't like them, I can put the blame on you.'

'How d'yer fancy Titch's company, as well?'

Irene's eyes widened. 'Your Titch, coming round the shops? I don't believe it, he'd be bored out of his mind.'

'That's for him to find out, girl,' Aggie chuckled. 'He wanted to take me, anyway, to buy me something. Yer know what he's like when he's got money, it burns a hole in his pocket. So I thought it would be nice if we all went together.'

'It's fine by me, Aggie – as I said, I'd be glad of company. But I can't for the life of me see Titch enjoying himself. George only ever came to the shops with me once, and he said blow that for a lark, he'd rather do a hard day's graft.' Her pretty face smiled at a memory almost forgotten. 'He was buying me a dress for me birthday, and the first one the assistant in TJ's brought out, he said, "That's nice, we'll take it." I hated it – it was a dark muddy-brown colour and dead old-fashioned. There was no way I was going to settle for that! And half an hour later, after I'd tried six on, George was nearly spitting feathers. But I was determined. It wasn't often I got new clothes, and I wasn't going to settle for something I didn't like. So I dragged him from TJ's to Blackler's. The third one I tried on there was a smasher, I really loved it. My dear husband was so impatient when the woman was wrapping it, I swore it was the last time I'd take him shopping with me. I didn't have time to tell him that, mind, because once outside the shop he told me straight: "Don't ever ask me again, love, it's a mug's game." '

'Shopping is a mug's game, girl, same as washing and house-work. And women are the mugs what have to bleedin' do it. If it was left to the men the houses would stink and no one would eat. And I've said all along, if it was men what had to have babies, the human race would have died out thousands of years ago. Still, we can call our men fit to burn, but we wouldn't be without them, and that's a fact.'

Irene glanced at the clock and pulled a face. 'We'll have to hurry 'cos I've got to be back for the boys. Go and tell Titch he's very welcome to join us, but on his own head be it. If he starts getting restless and grumbles, I'll put him over me knee and smack his backside good and proper.'

'That's not a threat, girl, it's a bleedin' promise. And I'll not be passing the message on 'cos I know what a devil me son can be at times. Anyway, can yer give me fifteen minutes to doll meself up a bit? Give us a knock and we'll be ready.'

'They're a good strong pair, girl, he'd get plenty of wear out of them,' Aggie said as she fingered the dark grey material. 'A sensible colour, too.'

The assistant at Blackler's hovered behind the counter. 'Are you sure you have the right inside leg measurement, Madam?'

Irene nodded. 'Twenty-nine inside leg, thirty-two waist. He's only fourteen, but he's tall for his age.' She cast a critical eye over the trousers again. 'How much did yer say these were, sunshine?'

'Five and elevenpence, Madam, and they're a good buy. He'll get years of wear out of them.'

'Not if he keeps on growing at the rate he is.' Far from being bored, Titch was enjoying himself. 'He's going to be a six-footer, without a doubt.'

The assistant gave him one of her best smiles. 'He will if he takes after his dad. If you don't mind me saying so, you're well above average height.' She had them down as man and wife, with a mother in tow, and looked surprised when they all burst out laughing. 'Have I said something wrong?'

'Yer've only married me off to me best friend's wife.' Titch was tickled pink. 'Look, yer've got her blushing.'

'Take no notice of him, sunshine,' Irene said, 'I've always got rosy cheeks. It would take more than that to make me blush.' She took three two-bob pieces from her purse. 'Do I pay you?'

'I'll have to call the supervisor over. I'm new here, so I'm not allowed to make receipts out on my own. I'll call her over.'

But Miss Simpson, the supervisor, had been keeping an eagle eye on her new recruit and raised a hand to say she was on her way over. 'Can I help you, Miss Marsh?'

'The lady wishes to purchase these trousers, Miss Simpson, and I need to make out a receipt.'

Vera Simpson was weighing Titch up and down as she walked to stand behind the counter. She liked what she saw, and directed her smile at him. 'I'm sorry to keep you waiting, sir, but Miss Marsh is new and has to be supervised.'

'That's all right, my dear.' Titch could feel his tummy rumbling with laughter. 'My wife and I are not in too much of a hurry.'

Aggie chuckled, Irene turned her head away and the new assistant bit on her bottom lip. As for Miss Simpson, she was telling herself it was just her luck. The only men worth having were already married. Still, she'd keep on trying, otherwise she'd be left on the shelf. And the prospect of being a spinster, living on her own with only a cat for company, was one that didn't appeal to her at all.

The trio waited until they were outside before letting the laughter free. 'Oh dear, oh dear, oh dear!' Aggie wiped her eyes with the back of her hand. 'Yer could have had yerself a click, there, son, if yer hadn't been married.'

'She was too stuck-up for my liking, Ma. I'd have to be on me best behaviour all the time and watch me language. Did yer see the way she looked down her nose at poor Miss Marsh? Blimey, she doesn't half think she's the whole cheese.'

Irene's shoulders were shaking as she dropped the change in her purse. 'Do they send yer to prison in this country for bigamy? I don't think my feller would be too happy, he certainly wouldn't come and see me on visiting day.'

'Well, we've had a good laugh, haven't we?' Titch said. 'And Jack's got a nice pair of kecks, so everyone's happy.'

'He needs another pair for a change, but I couldn't afford two pair in one go. So if yer've got a day free next week, yer can both come with me. It doesn't hurt so much parting with money when ye're enjoying yerself.'

Titch looked at his watch. 'Yer've got bags of time, it's only two o'clock. Let's go to Reece's for a cuppa and a cake. Eh, what say yer?'

Irene shook her head. 'No, I can't afford it, Titch, and I'm not sponging off you. Yer paid me tram fare, and that's enough.'

'In the name of God, Irene, can't yer let a friend mug yer?' Aggie said. 'I could do with a cuppa and a sitdown, me legs are not as young as they used to be.'

Irene tutted. 'Aggie McBride, I've seen yer scarpering up our street like a two year old. Yer can run faster than me, so don't be making that an excuse.'

Titch wagged a finger. 'My ma always taught me never to argue with someone older than meself, it's not good manners. So if she says she's got old legs, then we've got no option but to agree with

426

her.' He put an open hand to the side of his mouth and in a loud whisper, said, 'Even though she climbs our stairs three at a time.'

Irene gave in. 'Okay, if you insist. I'll have a cup of tea, but no cake.'

At the time, Irene meant it. But when Titch ordered a selection of cream cakes, her mouth started to water. 'That's not fair, that. Definitely hitting below the belt. Aggie knows I can't resist cream cakes, that's why I'm so fat.'

'Not fat, Irene, bonny.' Titch handed her the plate. 'The chocolate eclair looks very inviting. And you can have the cream horn, Ma, I know yer've got a weakness for them.'

'Ye're right there, son. What I say is, sod me bleedin' figure.'

'My sentiments exactly.' There was a look of pure bliss on Irene's face when she bit into the eclair and the cream oozed out of the sides. This was a rare treat and she intended to savour it. 'Ye're spoiling me, Titch McBride. My feller won't be able to do a thing with me after this high living.'

Aggie was thoughtful as she nibbled the end of the horn. 'Is it next Friday your Jack leaves school?'

'Yeah. He's already told me he'll wear his short trousers until he goes to bed, then Saturday morning he wants to wear his new ones. So expect a knock on yer door 'cos he'll be doing the rounds, showing off.'

'And it's Lucy's birthday on the Saturday, isn't it?'

Irene licked her fingers before answering. 'Yeah, I'll have to get her a card and a little present of some kind. If me money runs to it, I'd like to get her a nice underskirt. I don't think she's got one, 'cos when she wears her new dress yer can see right through it.'

'You get one, and I'll go half with yer.' Aggie turned to her son who was exchanging smiles with a girl at the next table. 'Ay, you, buggerlugs, behave yerself. There's only two things ever on yer mind . . . beer and women. That's all yer think about.'

Not in the least put out, Titch grinned. 'Ah, be fair now, Ma. Yer know very well that you come before the beer and women.'

'In that case, put yer eyes back in her head and listen to me. Yer said yer wanted to buy me something, and I've just thought of the very thing.'

'Just name it, Ma, your wish is my command.'

'To celebrate Lucy's birthday, and Jack leaving school, I'd like to have a little tea-party for the youngsters. Just Jack and Greg, and Lucy can invite her friend, Rhoda. That's if you'll fork out for the food.'

'Ma, that's the best idea yer've had since I came home.' Titch looked chuffed. 'That wouldn't be money down the drain, would it? But why can't the grown-ups come, as well? I'm not going to be left out, that's for sure, and yer can't leave the others out.'

'Can I butt in?' Irene asked. 'I think yer should have a word with Bob first. I'm sure they won't be having a party for Lucy, and I know she'd be delighted if you had one for her. But yer couldn't invite Bob without Ruby, not if me and George are there.'

'That's no problem – we'll ask Ruby!' Titch looked to his mother. 'That's all right with you, isn't it, Ma?'

'My idea was a children's party, son, but you seem to have taken over. I don't mind, though, the more the merrier. And while I don't like Ruby Mellor, I agree that yer couldn't ask Bob and not her. So you go ahead and make the arrangements, seeing as ye're forking out for it. But I don't want the children to know, I want it to be a surprise. And I'm determined about that, so woe betide anyone who lets the bleedin' cat out of the bag.'

'My lips are sealed,' Irene said.

Titch squeezed his mother's hand. 'My lips are not sealed, Ma, but I'll be very careful what comes out of them. Especially after I've had a few jars.'

'Which is only every bleedin' night.' The tenderness in Aggie's eyes belied her words. 'Yer'll end up with a big red conk and a beer belly, mark my words.'

'Nah, there's no chance of that. And when I pack the sea in, I'll change me ways. It'll be you and me, Ma, down to the pub every night, just before closing-time, for a pint of stout. And I'll carry the jug – save yer hiding it under that shawl of yours.'

'Who's been telling tales out of school?'

'Don't look at me, Aggie,' Irene said. 'I've never said a word.'

'Nobody's been telling tales. It was Alec what mentioned it, and it was a compliment. He said yer might not be his biggest-spending customer, but ye're definitely his most regular.'

'He won't get rich on what I spend, son, but you make up the shortfall when ye're home. He must rub his hands in glee when he knows yer ship's docked.'

'Ye're right there, Ma. He really gave me down the banks for being away so long this time. He said our captain had no consideration for folk like him what are trying to make an honest living.'

Aggie gasped. 'He never did!'

Titch grinned. 'No, Ma, he never did.'

Bob stood outside the confectioner's window and gazed at the cakes on display. He spied what he was looking for and smiled when he saw the sign which said they were three for twopence. He could just about manage that.

The bell behind the door tinkled when he pushed it open, and the sound brought a young assistant through from a back room. Her grin told of a sunny disposition and her voice was friendly. 'What can I get for yer that takes yer fancy?'

'There's a lot of things I fancy, love, but me pocket tells me I can only afford three fairy cakes.'

'Well, that's better than a kick in the teeth.' The girl tugged a white bag from a hook and reached into the window. 'Beats a drippin' buttie, any day.'

'You sound on top of the world,' Bob said. 'Are yer always so cheerful?'

'I try to be. People don't want to be served by someone with a face as long as a fiddle, it only makes them miserable. Mind you, I have a hard time on a Monday. Me face refuses to smile and I can't get a joke past me lips. I've tried giving them a good talking to, but they're not having any. So Monday is misery day.' She folded the top of the bag over and placed it on the glass-topped counter. 'I make up for it on the other days, though, and try to spread a little happiness. I make sure that not one person goes out of this shop without a smile on their face.'

She took Bob's sixpence and opened a drawer for his change. 'There yer go, a thruppenny joey and a penny.' Then, as though she could no longer hold it in, she said, 'I'm very happy today because I've got a date tonight.'

'Ah, yer've got a boyfriend?'

'He's not me boyfriend yet, but I'm hoping he will be after tonight. Yer see, I've had me eye on him for months. I couldn't believe me luck when he asked me for a date 'cos all the girls in our street are after him. He's not half handsome.'

Bob smiled at her openness. 'Keep that smile on yer face, love, and yer'll bowl him over. The other girls won't be in the meg specks.'

'Ooh, I hope ye're right. Next time yer come in, I'll let yer know how I got on.'

Bob waved as he passed the window. She seemed a nice kid and he wished her luck. But it was doubtful she'd ever see him again. That was the first time in his adult life that he'd been in a cakeshop, and it would probably be his last. Now he could repay Kate, there would be no need to.

Chapter Seven

'You go on ahead, Billy, I'll catch yer up,' Bob said. 'I've got to get something out of me coat pocket.' With his carry-out box under his arm, he made haste to the cloakroom. They only got three-quarters of an hour dinner break, so every minute was precious. And he was concerned about the fairy cakes that had been left in the bag in his pocket since he'd bought them the day before. They'd probably be a mass of crumbs by now with his luck. But he couldn't let Ruby see them or there'd have been ructions. He could almost hear her shrill voice shouting that she couldn't afford the luxury of cakes on the money he gave her, but he could find it for his mates all right. He'd never have heard the last of it.

Bob breathed a sigh of relief when he opened the bag and found that the sponge cakes, in their crinkly white paper cases, appeared to be in one piece. Thank goodness for that, he thought, hurrying to the canteen where, even from this distance, he could hear Peg giving forth on the joys of motherhood. 'What a night I had with those blinking kids of mine. They just wouldn't go to sleep even though I promised them a ha'penny each to buy bull's eyes on their way to school. Three times I was up to them, but even a clip round the ear wouldn't shut them up. Mind you, I couldn't hit them hard because I was too tired and didn't have the bleedin' strength to knock them out.'

Elsie, her dimpled elbows leaning on the table, glanced side-ways. 'What did yer do in the end, girl?'

'Threatened to send them to the bleedin' Cottage Homes, that's what. It shut them up all right, but the trouble was I was wide awake by then, and in a right temper, I can tell yer. Not with the kids, but with my feller. Here was me, in and out of bed like a bleedin' yo-yo, and he was away to the world. Sleeping like a baby, he was, without a care in the world. That's until I kicked him out of bed, like.'

Ada Smithson gasped. 'Yer never did, did yer?'

'With both feet, Ada.' Peg nodded slowly. 'And on his way to the floor he banged his head on the tallboy and didn't know what the bloody hell had hit him 'cos he was seeing stars. When he came to, he said, "What the hell did yer do that for, yer stupid cow?" I told him it was for making something and not looking after it. He scrambled to his feet and stood at the side of the bed. "What the hell are yer on about, woman? It's nearly one o'clock in the morning, a fine time to be kicking me out of bed and telling me I've made something and not looked after it." '

'Well, he had a point there, girl,' Elsie said. 'My feller would have marmalised me if I'd done that. Whatever it is he made and doesn't look after, it would have waited for another time, surely? It can't be that important.'

'Ah well, yer see, Elsie, the timing was perfect. As I told him, he'd made the kids, so it was his job to look after them. And in future, he could take a turn in getting out of bed to shut them up.' Peg put her buttie down and pinched the bridge of her nose. 'But d'yer know what? He looked so comical standing there in his long johns and short shirt, with this surprised look on his clock, I couldn't help but laugh.'

'Ooh, ay, he wouldn't like that, I bet.' Ada was small, thin, and downtrodden. Her husband was built like an ox and a bully to boot. She was completely dominated by him; he only had to open his mouth and she jumped. She was afraid to look sideways, never mind laughing at him. 'Was he as mad as hell?'

Peg chuckled. 'He was at first. Called me for everything and his language was choice. But when he climbed into bed, he said, "Well, yer've woke me up now, so I may as well make something else for yer to look after".'

Billy joined in the laughter before saying, 'All in all, Peg, there was a lot going on in your house last night. Yer were busier than Lime Street Station.'

'Yeah, it was all go, Billy. But isn't it surprising how yer can be tired one minute, and full of energy the next? My feller's no oil painting, but he can be very passionate when he's in the mood. And in the dark I can make believe he's me heart throb, Tyrone Power. So, all-in-all, the night had a happy ending and I went to sleep with a smile on me face.'

'Yer must have a bleedin' good imagination,' Elsie snorted, ''cos your feller doesn't look a bit like Tyrone Power. Even if yer met the pair of them together, down an entry on a dark night, yer couldn't make that mistake.'

'I wouldn't want to, smart arse.' Peg's hackles rose. 'I'm quite content with my feller the way he is. At least he's not cross-eyed, like some poor buggers.'

Elsie hitched her bosom until it was nearly touching her chin. 'I hope ye're not insinuating that my feller's cross-eyed?'

'I'm not saying anything, not a dickie-bird. Except,' Peg waved a

432

hand casually, 'if the cap fits, wear it.'

Bob raised his brows at Kate. 'Elsie's husband doesn't squint, does he?'

Kate smiled as she shook her head. 'When will yer learn not to believe a word Peg or Elsie say? They make these things up for something to talk about. I'll bet any money that Peg was in bed sound asleep at half ten last night, and it wasn't the kids that woke her, it was the alarm clock. Elsie goes along with her for a laugh, and yer've got to admit they do brighten things up.'

Billy closed the hinged lid of his carry-out box and moved it so he could rest his elbows on the table. 'The truth is, Peg's husband is nicer-looking than Tyrone Power. He's a good bloke, too, and a ruddy good husband. As for Elsie's feller, he's as quiet as a mouse. The most easygoing man yer'll ever meet. He never gets in a temper or raises his voice. She calls him Tiger, but he's a tiger that never roars.'

'How d'yer know all this, Billy?' Bob asked.

'Well, I don't live far from them, do I? And I meet them in the pub now and again on a Saturday night, when I take my one out for a drink. And yer can take it from me, after a few jars, Peg and Elsie have the pub up. I think the landlord should give them their drinks free, because they're more entertaining than going to the flicks.'

'I'm afraid I can't think of anything to make yer laugh, Billy, but will a fairy cake do instead?' Bob tore the bag open and pushed it across to Kate. 'Ladies first.'

'Ooh, lovely!' Kate picked one with pink icing on the top. 'Yer shouldn't have bothered, but thanks all the same.'

Billy licked his lips. 'I'll have the lemon one.'

Elsie's eyes never missed a trick, and they didn't miss this. 'Ay, Bob Mellor, yer lousy nit! What have they got that we haven't?'

Bob shrugged his shoulders and held out his open palms. 'Sorry, Elsie, but I'm not made of money. If I was I'd have mugged all of yer to cream cakes.'

'Aye, and pigs might fly.' Elsie reached down into her bag and brought out a small parcel wrapped in newspaper. With a jerk of her head, and a quivering of her bosom, she placed it on the table. 'Well, smarty pants, ye're not the only one with a surprise. I've brought one as well.'

Peg was intrigued. 'I love surprises, girl. What is it?'

'Guess.'

'Give us a clue, then. Can yer eat it?'

Elsie's whole body shook with laughter. 'Aye, I suppose yer could. But yer'd have to be bleedin' hungry, though.'

'Oh, I've lost interest now,' Peg said. 'If yer can't eat it, it's not much good to us.' Then her mouth widened. 'I know, yer've brought yer false teeth.'

Now Elsie, who was the proud possessor of healthy white teeth, got on her high horse. 'Ye're too clever for yer own bleedin' good, you are, Mrs Know-it-all. Well, for your information, that,' she pointed to the parcel, 'is me proof.'

Interest flared in Peg's eyes. 'Proof of what?'

'What I've been telling yer about the goings-on in our street. None of yer would believe me, so I've brought yer proof.'

'Yer milkman must be very small if he fits in that,' Billy laughed. 'Mind you, he might have worn himself down to that size.'

'Ho, ho, ho, very funny.' Elsie rolled her eyes upwards. 'None of yer have got an ounce of bleedin' sense in yer heads.'

'Well, it certainly ain't the horse,' Peg said. 'Unless yer've brought a piece of his tail.'

'Near enough.' Elsie's expression was haughty. 'It's a piece of his manure.'

Faces showed their horror as mouths stopped chewing and sandwiches were whipped from the table. 'You filthy cow!' Peg moved as far away from her friend as she could. 'What the hell d'yer think ye're messing at? Yer've put us all off our food now.' She pointed to the offending parcel. 'Get that filth out to the toilet and flush it down the pan.'

Her face as innocent as a baby's, Elsie said, 'Oh, yer can't flush coal down the lavvy, girl, it'll block it up. Yer own common sense should tell yer that.'

Silence reigned as Peg held her head in her hands. 'And to think I bleedin' well fell for it. Me what's known yer all these years, and I fell for a trick like that. I want me head testing.'

Kate grinned across at Bob. 'See what I mean?'

'I certainly do. From now on I'll take everything they say with a pinch of salt.'

Billy was chuckling. 'It was dead funny, though, wasn't it? Mind you, I'm glad I'd eaten that cake. Somehow manure and cake just don't go together.'

Titch was standing at the front door when Bob came down the street. 'Just the man I've been waiting for. Can yer come in for a few minutes, Bob?'

'Yeah, sure,' Bob said, following him into the house. 'I've no heavy date on, me diary is empty.'

Aggie grinned when she saw him. 'Are yer bragging or complaining, Bob?'

'Neither, Aggie. I've got no social life to brag about and complaining doesn't get yer anywhere.'

434

'Well, sit down, son, and make yerself at home. I want to ask yer something, and I hope ye're agreeable. As yer know, young Jack leaves school a week today, and the day after it's Lucy's birthday. I was wondering if yer'd let me have a little party for them? Just the two Pollard boys and Lucy and her friend, Rhoda. I'd be tickled pink to do it, so I hope yer'll agree and make an old lady happy.'

Bob looked at Titch and winked. 'Who's the old lady she's on about?'

'Whenever me ma wants anything, she piles the years on to get sympathy. Yer'd better humour her or she'll bawl her eyes out.'

'I think it's a cracking idea and I know Lucy would be thrilled to bits. But wouldn't yer be putting yerself to a lot of trouble and expense?'

Aggie's eyes were twinkling. 'It wouldn't be any trouble, it would be a pleasure. And my beloved son is footing the bill. He wanted to buy me something, and I said the thing I'd like best would be to see the kids enjoying themselves. Irene knows, but I've asked her not to tell the boys yet. I want it to be a surprise. So, can Lucy come?'

'Of course she can. I think it's very kind of yer and yer have my thanks.'

'Good.' Aggie sat back in her rocking chair and rested her clasped hands on her lap. 'Now Titch has got something to say.'

Bob feigned surprise. 'Let me guess. He's getting married.'

'If the day ever comes when I tell yer I'm getting wed, that's the day yer'll know I've lost me marbles. And I want yer to promise yer'll send for the men in white coats and have me certified insane,' Titch said, crossing his long legs. 'Anyway, back to business. I don't see why the kids should have all the fun. So I've suggested asking Irene and George, and you and Ruby. How does that strike yer?'

'It's fine by me, I'd be delighted to come. But I can't speak for Ruby, I'm afraid.'

'Will you ask her? Or d'yer think it would be better coming from me or me ma? A secondhand invitation isn't very polite, is it? She might be put out if she thought we couldn't be bothered asking her.'

'It's up to you, but yer know what Ruby's like. I'll mention it to her when I go in, then by the time you ask her, she'll have had time to think about it.'

'You do that, son,' Aggie said. 'Then I'll make a point of giving her a knock tomorrow. But don't forget, I don't want Lucy to know.'

'I won't breathe a word.' Bob stood up. 'Yer've been very kind to

435

Lucy over the years, and don't think I haven't noticed or appreciated it.'

'It would be hard not to like or be kind to her, Bob,' Aggie told him. 'She's a little angel, is Lucy, and yer should be proud of her.'

'Oh, I am, Aggie, make no mistake about that. She makes my life worth living.' Bob headed for the door. 'I'll get home now and have a word with Ruby before Lucy gets in from school. Will we see yer in the pub tomorrow night?'

'Not me,' Titch said. 'I'm going into town for a night out with some of me mates off the ship. We usually do a round of the pubs, so I'll probably roll home in the early hours of the morning.'

'Well, enjoy yerself. I'll see yer, Aggie.'

'Ta-ra, Bob, see yer tomorrow.'

As Bob let himself in, he wondered what his wife's reception would be to the invitation. She couldn't stand the neighbours, but that was nothing new. Ruby hadn't a good word to say about anyone. Except her mates, of course. Invisible mates Bob had heard plenty about, but never seen.

'Ye're late today. I had a pot of tea made for yer and it'll be cold by now.' Ruby planned to be pleasant from now on. The week after next she should start getting the extra five bob back in her housekeeping, so it was in her interest to keep her nose clean. 'I'll make yer a fresh brew.'

There was a surprised look on Bob's face as he watched her walk through to the kitchen. She seemed to be in a happy frame of mind today. Usually he didn't even get an acknowledgement, never mind the offer of a fresh pot of tea. Perhaps she'd come round to thinking he was right, and life would be much easier if they could at least be polite with each other. He hoped so, for everyone's sake.

Ruby came through from the kitchen with two cups and saucers. As she set them on the table, she said, 'It won't be long, I'll just let it mash for a few minutes.'

'There's no hurry.' Bob flopped into his chair and stretched his legs. He was never going to get her in a better mood, so perhaps now was a good time to say what he had to. 'I've been talking to Titch and Aggie, and they've invited us up there next Saturday.' He saw her face change and went on quickly before she had time to say anything: 'Aggie's having a little celebration tea-party for Jack's leaving school, and as it's Lucy's birthday, she asked if we'd let her go. And her friend, Rhoda. I said yes, of course, because I know Lucy would be over the moon.'

Ruby huffed. 'I'm not going to no kids' tea-party, so yer can forget it.'

'We haven't been invited to the tea-party.' Bob was determined not to lose his patience. 'Titch wants us to go along later, with Irene and George.'

'Oh, I might have known the queer one would be in on it. It wouldn't be a bleedin' show without Punch.'

Bob's sigh was deep. 'Ruby, you are my wife and we've been invited as a married couple. Can we not, for once, act like one? I'm asking you to come for my sake, and for Lucy's. Remember, it's our daughter's birthday. Let's not spoil it for her.'

'Oh no, we mustn't do anything to spoil Lucy's day. It doesn't matter about what *I* want as long as she's happy. Well, I'll not set foot over the door of any of them to please her or anyone else. I don't want to go, and I'm not going. That's all there is to it.'

'Then we'll have the birthday party here and invite our friends and neighbours. If you don't want to go to them, I'll bring them to you.' Bob knew there was no possibility of this, but he wanted to shake his wife into some sort of action.

Ruby looked at him as though he'd gone mad. 'Some hope you've got. If yer think I'm going to run around after that lot, yer've got another think coming.' Then that hard-boiled look came to her face. 'And where d'yer think the money's coming from for yer grand idea?'

'I wouldn't be able to get Lucy's coat for her birthday, she'd have to wait a few more weeks.' Bob saw the flash of anger in her eyes and knew his words had hit the mark. 'She wouldn't be upset – she'd rather have a party.'

You sly bugger, Ruby was thinking. That's my five bob a week you're talking about. My extra ciggie and beer money. But she wasn't going to give in so easily, she'd give him a run for his money. 'Anyway, they wouldn't miss me if I didn't go because they don't really want me. If they did they'd have asked me themselves, instead of making you the messenger boy. You go on yer own and they won't even know I'm not there.'

'Not true! Aggie's coming down tomorrow to ask yer. Oh, and don't forget, Lucy's not to be told.'

Ruby was blazing inside. If she made a big deal out of it and refused point blank to go, she'd be cutting off her nose to spite her face. It would take Bob at least six weeks to save up the money for Lucy's coat, and that meant being the poor relation amongst her friends for all that time. Having one drink to their two, and waiting for them to offer her a cigarette because she didn't have enough to go round. So even though she couldn't stand the thought of spending a couple of hours in the company of the Pollards and the McBrides, the alternative was even worse. There was five bob a week at stake here, and for that money she'd sup with the devil himself if need be. But she had one more try to turn things in her favour. 'Why can't we all go to the pub? It would be a damn sight more lively than sitting in the McBrides' twiddling our fingers.'

'Because Irene won't go to the pub and Aggie wouldn't dream of leaving her out. Besides, they've been good enough to ask us and it would be an insult to refuse. So it's up to you. We accept their invitation or we ask them here.' Bob could read her like a book and knew he was on safe ground. Otherwise he'd never have mentioned it because he wouldn't let Lucy down for the world. She'd been looking forward so much to getting a new coat. 'I could tell them you would like to have your daughter's party in her own house, and they are welcome to come.'

'Oh, I'll go with yer, then, because I'm not having them here, that's a dead cert. But I'm going under duress, and if there's any snide remarks or dirty looks, I'll be out of that house like a shot. I won't stay around to be insulted.'

'Ruby, yer ask for everything yer get. If you're not pleasant with people, yer can't expect them to fawn over yer. Give a smile and yer'll get one back. Crack a joke and yer'll get one back. Give a sneer or a dirty look, and that's what yer'll get back. Life is what yer make it, but your trouble is, yer can't be bothered. If there's nothing in it for you, then yer don't want to know.'

'I've said I'll go, so there's no need for a lecture. And I'd better see to that tea, it'll be stiff by now. I'll add more boiling water to it 'cos I can't afford to throw another pot away.'

Bob cocked an ear. 'Here's Lucy. Remember, not a word.'

There was a half-smile on Ruby's face as she struck a match under the kettle. The silly bugger thinks he's got one over on me, and I'm going to be the dutiful little wife. If that makes him happy, then let him get on with it. When next Saturday comes I might just be feeling sick with a bad headache or an upset tummy. And if that doesn't work – well, what the hell. A couple of hours of misery won't kill me. I'll just think of the weeks ahead when I'm in the money and can doll meself up and go out and really enjoy meself.

She could hear Bob talking to Lucy, and her smile turned into a full one as an idea came into her head. This is where I put on me act as the dutiful wife and mother, she thought, and I can't wait to see their faces. Popping her head around the kitchen door, and her smile still intact, she said, 'There's a pot of tea made, Lucy, would yer like a cup?'

Lucy's surprised expression turned to one of suspicion. She never ever got a smile off her mother, and the offer of a cup of tea was unheard of. There had to be a catch in it somewhere. 'I'll have one if me dad's having one,' she said cautiously.

'Of course he's having one, I made it for him.'

438

'I was just saying she looks pale today,' Bob said. 'She's got no colour in her cheeks and her eyes look dull.'

Ruby threw a brief glance at her daughter. 'She looks all right to me.'

'I am all right, Dad, honest! I don't know why me face is pale, 'cos I feel the same as I always do.'

But Bob wasn't convinced. He'd got a hug and a smile off his daughter when she came in, but he'd noticed the smile didn't reach her eyes. 'I think yer might be sickening for something, so to be on the safe side yer can take a Beecham's Powder before yer go to bed.'

'Ah, ay, Dad! I promised Rhoda I'd play out with her until dinner was ready. Just for half an hour, please?'

When those large green eyes looked so appealing, he didn't have the heart to refuse. 'Okay, after yer've had a cup of tea. But remember, it's a Beecham's before yer go to bed.'

Lucy looked to make sure her mother was in the kitchen before throwing her arms around his neck. 'I love you, Dad.'

'And I love you, pet, more than yer'll ever know.'

Lucy stretched her arms wide. 'As much as this?'

'Oh, much more than that.' Bob smiled. 'Run around the world twice, and that's how much I love yer.'

A sparkle appeared briefly in Lucy's eyes. 'If I ran around the world twice, Dad, there'd be nothing left of me for yer to love.'

Ruby carried two cups of tea through and set them on the table. 'Come and sit here and drink it, it's too hot to hold in yer hands.'

Lucy blew on the piping hot tea, wishing she dared ask for more milk to cool it down. 'I can't drink any more, Dad, I've had enough. Can I go out now?'

'Yeah, okay, we'll give yer a shout when dinner's ready.'

She was near the front door when Lucy heard her mother's voice. 'I've told yer, ye're making a rod for yer own back, spoiling her like that.'

And she heard her dad answer, 'It's my back, Ruby, not yours.'

Lucy sighed as she jumped down the step, right into the path of Jack and Greg.

'Hey, watch where ye're going, yer nearly sent us flying,' Jack said, securing the football under his arm. 'Where are yer going in such a hurry?'

'I'm not in a hurry, I just jumped off the step, that's all. I can't see around corners, clever clogs.' Lucy nodded to the ball. 'I see ye're off for a game of footie.'

'He's making the most of it,' Greg said, chuckling. 'Me mam said that this time next week, footie will be a thing of the past. And marbles and kick-the-can. It'll be long kecks, hair combed and

439

flattened down with sugar and water, a tie when he's going out, and mind yer manners if yer please.'

Lucy grinned. 'It'll be worth it when he's got money jingling in his pocket.'

'Yeah, too true.' Jack gave his brother a dig. 'And before yer start making cracks when I put me long kecks on, just remember yer penny pocket money is at stake.'

'Blimey, what I've got to do to get this penny is nobody's business. I've got to polish his shoes and run any messages he wants. I haven't got to laugh when he's got his long kecks on in case he thinks I'm laughing at him, which means on top of everything else I've got to lose me sense of humour, as well.' Greg appealed to Lucy. 'Be fair, now, don't yer think all that is worth more than a miserly penny?'

'Oh, I'm not taking sides, Greg, that wouldn't be right. But when Jack sees how well yer polish his shoes, I'm sure he'll think it's worth tuppence.' Lucy wanted to be on her way, there was something she had to do. 'I'll have to go, or Rhoda will think I'm not coming. Enjoy yer game of footie, but don't break any windows.'

She waited until the boys reached the end of the street, then went to stand in front of their house. She was nervous, and biting her fingernails. But Mrs Pollard had told her to knock if she ever needed help, and right now Lucy was desperate to talk to someone. And she'd never get another chance like this. The boys were out and Mr Pollard wouldn't be home from work until six o'clock. Plucking up courage, she knocked on the door.

'Hello, sunshine.' Irene's smile was welcoming to the frightened girl. 'Come in.'

Lucy stood by the table in the living room, wondering how to start. 'Yer said I could come to yer if I needed anything, Mrs Pollard, so yer don't mind, do yer?'

'Of course not, sunshine, sit down.' Irene's heart went out to the girl who had a look of fear in her eyes. Her voice gentle, she coaxed, 'Come on, out with it. Whatever it is will remain a secret between the two of us, I promise.'

'I've got a sore at the top of me leg and it's getting worse. I don't want to tell me mam, and I can't show it to me dad because of where it is. So I wondered if yer'd look at it for me and tell me what to do to make it better.'

'Is that all! Come on, don't be shy, show it to me.'

When Lucy lifted her dress and took away the dirty pad, Irene gasped. There were large bruise marks which had now faded to a pale blue and yellow, but there were two slits in the skin which were oozing a yellow pus. And in the pus were bits of navy-blue fleece from the piece of knickers. 'In the name of God, sunshine, how did yer do that?'

Lucy dropped her head. 'One of the girls in school did it in the playground.'

'Good God! Did yer tell the teacher? Yer should have done and she'd have cleaned it up for yer and put a dressing on.'

'I didn't want to get the girl into trouble.'

Irene closed her eyes and tried to calm her rising temper. Lucy was telling lies, and she wasn't very good at it. 'Come into the kitchen and I'll bathe it in warm water. I've got some antiseptic ointment we can put on, and I've got lint and plasters. We'll have yer cleaned up and comfortable in no time.' Gently, Irene cleaned the wound and dressed it. 'Ye're lucky, sunshine, it was about to turn septic. Yer should have told me before, instead of going round with a dirty old piece of cloth on it. And how have yer managed to walk? Yer must have been in agony.'

Not used to tenderness and sympathy, Lucy was near to tears. 'It has been sore. But I couldn't come to yer before because yer were never on yer own.'

Irene used two strips of plaster to keep the lint in place. 'There yer go, all done and dusted. I'll have a look at it tomorrow and put a clean dressing on. In a few days yer'll be as right as rain, please God. Now come and sit down.' She led the girl to the couch and sat down beside her. Taking her hand, she said softly, 'I promised this would be our little secret, and I meant it. But we've got to be honest with each other. And I'm afraid yer haven't told me the truth, have yer, sunshine?'

Lucy hung her head in shame. Shame for having lied to this warm, kind-hearted woman, and ashamed to have to admit that her own mother would deliberately hurt her. 'No, I told yer a lie, and I'm very sorry.'

'It's not a sin to tell a lie to protect someone, Lucy, and that's what ye're doing, isn't it? But yer don't have to tell me who did it if you don't want to.'

The tears came then, and rolled down Lucy's face to fall on Irene's hand. 'Me mam did it, but she didn't mean to hurt me, she was acting daft. She does love me, yer know.'

Irene took her in her arms and held her tight. 'I'm sure she does, sunshine. She couldn't help but love yer.' She rocked her like a baby. No mother who loved her child could be so cruel to her, it wasn't natural. But they were the words Lucy wanted to hear. 'She wasn't to know she'd hurt yer that much. She'd never forgive herself if she knew.'

'Ooh, yer won't tell her, will yer?' Two large frightened eyes begged. 'Yer won't tell anyone, will yer, 'cos yer promised.'

'I won't tell a living soul, cross my heart and hope to die.' Irene held her away so they could face each other. 'Anytime ye're worried about anything, even if it's only a little worry, yer can come to me knowing it won't go no further. And if ever I need a shoulder to cry on, or I'm feeling down in the dumps, I'll come to you, eh?'

'You're never down in the dumps, Mrs Pollard, ye're always happy and laughing.'

'Everybody has times when they're down, sunshine, and I'm no different. Sometimes I feel dead miserable without even knowing why. I don't tell George or the boys because men don't understand how temperamental a woman can be when she's having an off day. So I'd be glad to have someone to talk to and get all me moans off me chest. It's surprising how much it helps.' Lucy's tears had stopped now and Irene kept on talking in a matter-of-fact way. 'If yer could see me on a Monday morning standing in front of the pile of dirty clothes I've got to wash, yer'd soon find out I'm not always happy and laughing. Monday is one day I could do without.'

'Yer could talk to me, Mrs Pollard, but I couldn't help yer 'cos I'm only young. I would if I could, though.'

'There's lots of ways yer could help. For instance, if I change me hairstyle and ask the boys or George if they like it, they always say they do without even looking at it. Now if I asked you, it would be different. You could tell me which style suited me best.'

Lucy's eyes brightened with interest. 'Ooh, I could do that! That would be easy, 'cos I could comb yer hair in different ways and see which suited yer best.'

Irene's heart lifted. 'Right, that's settled then. I'll be your confidante and you can be mine.'

'What does that word mean, Mrs Pollard?'

'A confidante is someone yer tell yer secrets to. And that's what we're going to be from now on. But right now, I think yer'd better get down to Rhoda's before she decides to call for yer. We don't want yer dad having the police out looking for yer, do we?'

Lucy, a much happier girl now, grinned and jumped to her feet. 'We're going to have a game of skipping, to see who can do the most cross-overs. And it's Rhoda's turn to cheat. So before we start, she's the winner.'

Irene followed her to the door. 'She's a good friend, isn't she?'

'Yeah, she's the best.' Lucy turned before stepping into the street. 'Thanks for doing me leg for me, Mrs Pollard, it feels a lot better now. I've been really worried about it.'

'Call in tomorrow and I'll get rid of the boys for five minutes while I change the dressing. It's thanks to them I had all the stuff

442

to dress it with. They're always coming in with cuts and scrapes.' Irene waved a hand. 'Poppy off now and enjoy yer game of skipping.'

'Ta-ra, Mrs Pollard.' Now her worries were over, Lucy ran up the street with wings on her heels. She felt so relieved and happy, she didn't mind that it was her friend's turn to cheat.

Chapter Eight

'Ah, ay, Rhoda, I know it's your turn to win, but ye're not half cheating.' Lucy was leaning against the wall outside her friend's house, her arms folded and a look of impatience on her face. 'Ye're not even doing proper cross-overs! Little Milly Simpson could do what ye're doing and she's only five.'

'I am doing proper cross-overs, so there!' Rhoda was red in the face with jumping up and down. 'This is the way you do them, so if I'm wrong, then you are as well.'

'I do not do them like that!' Lucy dropped her arms and stood to attention. Cheating proper was one thing, but this was double cheating. 'All ye're doing is crossing yer wrists and ye're supposed to cross yer arms.'

'Here, you have a go.' Rhoda was happy to pass the piece of clothes line over. She had more weight to heave up and down and she was out of breath. It was all right for Lucy, she was a real skinny links and never got puffed. And as for her mother telling her it was only puppy fat she was carrying and she'd soon lose it – well, she was getting fed up hearing about it and it never happening. 'Let's see how you do it, clever clogs.'

Lucy took in her friend's red face and the beads of sweat on her forehead, and was immediately contrite. 'Let's not do any more cross-overs, yer've won anyway. So how about tying one end to the lamp-post and take turns swinging the rope?'

Rhoda looked relieved. 'Yeah, that's more like it.'

Lucy was tying the rope when a boy came up behind her. 'If yer want any help, Lucy, just sing out.'

'Hello, Steve.' Lucy gave him a bright smile. 'I've done it now, so I don't need no help. But thanks for asking.'

Rhoda's face was set. She glared at the boy who was so poorly dressed he looked like a tramp. His pullover was full of holes, his short trousers torn and frayed, and both his shoes and socks looked as though they were going to fall to pieces any minute. 'Even if we did need help, Steve Fletcher, we wouldn't want it off you, 'cos ye're all dirty.'

'Rhoda!' Lucy looked horrified. 'That wasn't a nice thing to say.'

Her friend was unrepentant. 'Well, he is dirty, just look at him. And he's got scabs on his legs, as well.'

The boy's face flushed a bright red. He was thirteen, and tall and well-built for his age. And anyone bothering to ignore the clothes and look at the lad himself, would see he had the makings of a fine-looking young man. His untidy hair was fair, his eyes a bright blue and he had a cleft in his chin. He stared at Rhoda and half opened his mouth as though he was going to answer her. Then he shook his head and began to walk away. 'I'll see yer, Lucy.'

'Yeah, okay, Steve, I'll see yer.' Lucy waited until he was out of earshot before turning to her friend. 'I'm surprised at you, Rhoda Fleming. That was really mean and cruel of yer.'

'It's true, what I said. Everyone in the street knows the Fletcher house is filthy. He's probably got fleas as well, and I don't want to catch them off him.'

'He can't help being poor! He's got no dad and his mam's too sick to go out to work. They barely have enough money coming in to pay the rent, never mind clothes and food. His mam's a lovely woman, and he thinks the world of her. He goes around asking people if they want any jobs doing so he can earn a few coppers. He helps the coalman after school, lugging heavy bags of coal, and he chops firewood for the corner shop. I admire him for that, and I think he's a nice boy.' Lucy was sick at heart for the way her friend had belittled someone who, through no fault of their own, wasn't as well off as they were. 'I'm surprised at yer, Rhoda, I really am. I just wish I hadn't been here when yer said it, 'cos I'm ashamed for yer.'

'Yer've no need to be ashamed for me, Lucy Mellor, nobody asked yer to. Steve is dirty and I said so. And if he ever comes near me, I'll tell him again.'

Lucy sighed as she untied the knot in the rope. This was the first time she and Rhoda had ever argued, but she wasn't going to let it pass. Her friend was wrong to make a fool of Steve the way she did. He was a friendly boy, always had a smile when he saw you. He didn't deserve to be insulted and he must be feeling terrible now. 'Here's the rope, Rhoda, I don't feel like playing any more.'

'I don't know why ye're getting a cob on over him for.' Rhoda snatched the rope from her friend's hand. 'He's not worth it.'

'That's what you think, I think different. Yer don't judge people by what they've got, but what they're like inside.' Lucy was so upset she could feel the tears welling up behind her eyes. 'I'm going in now.'

Rhoda was feeling sorry inside, she didn't want to fall out with

Lucy. But she wasn't going to give in. 'Suit yerself.'

As Lucy crossed the cobbled road, tears blurred her sight. She was wiping them away when she walked headlong into Titch, who was standing outside his front door.

'Hey, young lady, watch where ye're going.' He looked closer. 'Have yer got something in yer eye?'

Lucy shook her head, and in a muffled voice, said, 'No, I'm all right.'

'Are they tears I can see in yer eyes?'

So full up she couldn't speak, Lucy nodded and made to walk past him. But Titch barred her way. 'I don't think I've seen yer cry before, Lucy, so something bad must have happened to upset yer. Come inside and tell me all about it.' He cupped her elbow and propelled her into the house. 'Things don't seem so bad when yer talk them over with someone.'

Aggie was sitting in her rocking chair and at first sight of Lucy, her face lit up. Then she saw the red eyes. 'What is it, queen? Has someone hit yer?'

'No, I'm all right, Mrs Aggie, honest.' But Lucy's trembling voice said otherwise.

Titch pulled a chair from the table. 'Sit down, love, and tell me and me ma what's happened to make yer unhappy.'

Lucy sat down and wiped a hand across her eyes. 'It's nothing, really, I've got meself all upset over nothing.'

'Tell us what the nothing is, queen,' Aggie coaxed, 'and we'll tell yer whether ye're making a mountain out of a molehill.'

'Yer'll think I'm a big baby when I tell yer, but it didn't half upset me at the time.' Lucy sniffed up. 'Yer know Steve Fletcher from the top of the street?'

Aggie looked puzzled. 'Of course we know Steve! He hasn't done anything to upset yer, has he? I'll be surprised if he has 'cos he's a lovely boy, wouldn't hurt a fly.'

'Me and Rhoda were playing skipping, and I was tying the rope to the lamp-post when Steve came up and asked if I needed any help. And for no reason at all, Rhoda told him we didn't need his help because he was dirty and had scabs on his legs.' Lucy closed her eyes as she relived those few awful seconds. 'I didn't know where to put meself, Mrs Aggie, I felt so sorry for him. It was a horrible thing for Rhoda to say and he must have felt terrible.'

Aggie leaned forward in her chair. 'It was a terrible thing for her to say, and she needs her bottom smacking for it. If she was my daughter, I'd drag her by the hand and make her apologise to Steve. Him and his mam have a hard time, and everyone in the street feels sorry for them. And God knows the lad does all he can to bring a few coppers into the house.'

447

'I told Rhoda all that, Mrs Aggie! But she said she didn't care. He was dirty, their house was filthy, and everyone in the street said so. And if he comes near her again, she'll still tell him he's dirty.' Lucy swallowed the lump in her throat. 'We had a row about it and I gave her the skipping rope back and said I didn't want to play no more. And that's the first row we've ever had in all the years she's been me friend.'

'It'll blow over, queen, don't fret. She's probably feeling worse than you do, 'cos after all it was her what caused the row. But I'm glad yer told her off because she was very naughty to say what she did, she had no right. She must have upset the poor lad something terrible.'

'I won't sleep tonight for thinking about him,' Lucy said. 'I hope he doesn't tell his mam because it would upset her, and with her being sick, she shouldn't be disturbed.'

Titch, who had been listening intently, now said, 'When his dad was alive, things were different in that house. They were the most loving family yer could meet. He was a fine man, was Jim Fletcher. A good husband and a good father. It was a tragedy that he died so young, and losing him nearly killed Olive, his wife. She's been ailing ever since. And hearing all this has put me to shame. I used to call there often when Jim was alive, but it's years since I knocked on their door. Some friend I've turned out to be.'

'It's never too late to put a wrong right, son. I'm sure Olive would love to see yer. And it would do the boy good, 'cos they don't seem to get many visitors.'

'Oh, yes, Mr Titch, please call and see them,' Lucy said eagerly. 'Steve hasn't got many friends because he's always busy doing jobs for people. He'll do anything to earn some money, turn his hand to anything. He'd be made up to have a man to talk to.'

'I'll go tomorrow, I promise.'

'Never put off till tomorrow what yer can do today,' Aggie told him. 'Ye're only sitting on yer backside twiddling yer thumbs, so make the effort now. The lad must be at home if Lucy's just seen him, and if yer leave it until tomorrow he might be out.'

'He will be out tomorrow, Mr Titch. He helps the milkman on a Saturday morning, then takes orders out for the corner shop.' Lucy held out her palms as though pleading. 'If yer go now, it will help him feel better after what Rhoda said. Cheer him up a bit.'

Titch lifted his own hands in surrender. 'Okay, okay! I'm not going to argue with two women because I know I wouldn't stand an earthly. So I'll go out of the door with you, Lucy, and yer can watch me walk up to the Fletchers' house. Then yer can sleep contented in yer bed tonight.'

It was on impulse that Lucy threw her arms around his neck and planted a kiss on his cheek. 'Oh, thank you, Mr Titch, it's no wonder Mrs Aggie loves the bones of yer. But yer won't let on about Rhoda, will yer? Otherwise he'll think that's the only reason yer called to see them.'

Titch grinned, and with a stiffened finger made a cross on his chest. 'Cross my heart and hope to die, sweetheart. Yer can count on me, I'll be the soul of discretion.'

Across the street, Mrs Fleming was eyeing her daughter. 'What's up with you, coming in before ye're shouted? And why have yer got a face on yer like a wet week?'

'I've had a row with Lucy, that's what, and we've fallen out.' Rhoda was feeling angry with herself. Deep down she knew she was at fault; she should never have said that to Steve. She didn't even know why she had done so, except that it was always Lucy he spoke to, never her. Not that she was jealous. I mean, why would she be jealous of *him*?

'It's not like you two to row. What have yer fallen out over?'

'It was over that Steve Fletcher. He was hanging around and I told him we didn't want him because he was dirty and he's got scabs on his legs. Lucy didn't like what I said, and when he'd gone yer should have heard the way she took off on me! Called me for everything, she did. Then she gave me the rope back and said she wasn't playing out no more.'

Jessie Fleming folded her arms and hitched up her ample bosom. 'Are you telling me that yer told Steve to his face that he was dirty?' She didn't wait for an answer because guilt was written all over her daughter's face. 'You little flamer! Just wait till yer dad gets in and hears that. He'll tan your backside so hard yer won't be able to sit for a week.'

'I don't know what all the fuss is about,' Rhoda said defiantly. 'He is dirty and their house is filthy. Everybody knows it and I was only speaking the truth.'

'Oh, aye, and who is everybody, pray? Yer've never heard me speak ill of the Fletchers because I've had no cause to. They're down on their luck, there's no two ways about that, but we were in the same boat ourselves a couple of years back, when yer dad was out of work. You won't remember because yer were too young, but we were living from hand to mouth then, just like the Fletchers are now. Only it's worse for them because they've no man in the house. So don't you go looking down yer nose at anyone, Lady Muck, 'cos that person could very easily have been you.'

'Mrs Bentley thinks they're dirty,' Rhoda said, feeling sorrier with every second the clock ticked away. 'She won't let her Andrew even talk to Steve, never mind play with him. And she said they've got fleas and bugs.'

'That stuck-up cow! Listen to me, young lady, that Sheila Bentley thinks we're all dirt beneath her feet. She reckons she's a cut above the rest of us, but it's all show. Her husband is only a labourer, like yer dad, but to hear her talk yer'd think he was a bleedin' director or something. She gives the impression they're rolling in money, but yer should stand behind her in the shops and yer'd soon realise very little money goes on food. Outward appearances are more important to her than putting food in their bellies. Her husband's not a bad man, but he's under her thumb and jumps when she tells him to. And as for Andrew – well, he's a proper little snob. Any other kid around here would be called Andy, but that's too common for him. He has to have his full title.'

Rhoda hung her head. 'I'm sorry I said what I did, Mam. Me and my big mouth have got me into trouble. I've lost me best friend, and now me dad will start on me when he comes in from work.'

Jessie tilted her head. 'Are yer truly sorry, or just saying it to get out of being given a hiding off yer dad?'

'I was sorry as soon as I'd said it. I could have bitten me tongue out.' The girl looked the picture of misery. 'And when Lucy took off on me, I felt really ashamed.'

'She's got a head on her shoulders, that girl. She's kind and wouldn't intentionally hurt anyone for the world. It's a pity ye're not more like her.' Jessie saw her daughter's face crumble and held out her arms. 'Come here, yer daft nit. What am I going to do with yer, eh?' She patted Rhoda's back as sobs shook her body. 'Come on now, be a big girl. I won't tell yer dad if yer promise me two things. One, that yer'll say sorry to Lucy and make up with her. And two, that when yer see Steve yer'll give him a nice, big, friendly smile.' She held her daughter away and looked into her red-rimmed eyes. 'Is that a deal?'

Rhoda wasn't so sure about the whole deal. 'I'll see Lucy 'cos I don't want to fall out with her for ever. We've always said we'll be friends all our lives. But I don't think Steve will want to have anything to do with me after what I said.'

'You're the one who started all the trouble, so it's up to you to sort it out. And don't forget, ye're twelve years of age now, and it's time to grow up. Steve's had to grow up quick, he had it thrust upon him. The day his dad died, he became the man of the house. And God only knows, he's done his level best to be just that.'

With every word her mother spoke, Rhoda became more ashamed. Her voice choked, she said, 'I'll do what yer said, Mam. I'll see Lucy and Steve, and I'll tell them both how sorry I am.

And in future, when I hear that Andrew Bentley calling Steve names, I'll clock him one.'

Jessie smiled and gave her a hug. 'That's my girl. But I wouldn't go as far as clocking him one, I don't think yer dad would like that. Just call him Andy – that should get his goat.'

Steve opened the door and gaped when he saw who was standing there. He vaguely remembered, when he was a toddler, this man used to come to their house when he was home on leave. But that was all he could remember, and it was years ago. He knew who he was, though, 'cos everybody in the street knew Titch, he was such a colourful character. 'Did yer want something, Mr McBride?'

'I want to offer an apology to yer mam for not coming to see her for so long. If it's possible, Steve, I'd like to have a word with her.'

Steve hesitated. He knew his mam didn't like visitors because of the state of the house. 'I'll have to ask her. She's not been well and she's lying down on the couch.'

'I understand that, son, but a visit from an old friend might just cheer her up. Don't you agree? She used to be full of spirit, your mam, so she'll probably tear a strip off me for staying away so long.'

Steve was torn. He knew if he asked his mother, she'd tell him to make an excuse to this man and send him away. But she never went over the door to meet people to talk to. She said he was all the company she needed, but he worried about her. She was too young to shut herself away from the outside world, and he was too young to know how to change things. If he let this chance slip, he might never get another. 'Step inside, Mr McBride, and I'll give her a shout.'

Titch stepped into the hall and waited for Steve to close the door. Then the boy called out, 'Yer've got a visitor, Mam.'

'Oh, don't let anyone in, son, I'm not fit to be seen.'

Titch took over. 'Then cover yerself up, Olive Fletcher, 'cos I'm coming in whether ye're respectable or not.'

'Oh, my God!' Olive covered her mouth with a hand as she pulled a knitted shawl across her chest. Her eyes darted around the room, seeing it as she knew Titch would and wishing the floor would open and swallow her up. 'What possessed you to come after all this time? As yer can see, we're not exactly ready for visitors.'

'I haven't come as a visitor, Olive, I've come as an old friend. I'm expecting yer to throw the book at me, so go ahead. Whatever names yer call me, I deserve for not keeping in touch with yer to see how yer were getting on.'

Olive waved a hand around the room. 'Yer can see how I've

451

fared, I don't need to tell yer. I've come as low as it's possible to come. And I've brought me son down with me.'

Titch pulled a rickety chair from the table. 'I never used to wait to be asked to sit down, and I'm not waiting now. Yer might think I've got a bloody cheek to land meself on yer after all these years, and yer'd be right. But we used to be good friends, Olive, and that should stand for something. I'm away a lot, as yer know, but I've watched Steve grow up, and he's a credit to yer.'

Olive's face softened as she looked to where Steve was leaning on a sideboard that was minus a drawer and had a door hanging loosely on its broken hinges. 'My son is one in a million. I don't think I'd have survived without him.'

'Yer've had it hard, have yer?' Titch asked softly, afraid of overstepping the mark and being told it was none of his business.

'It's been a nightmare, a living nightmare. I managed to cope for a couple of years after Jim died, by pawning things. But I never had the money to redeem them, so you can see for yerself how we've ended up. Ornaments, pictures, everything we had went to the pawnshop. And I've never been able to replace them. The furniture, bedding and curtains, they're all on their last legs and there's not a snowball's chance in hell of me being able to renew them.'

'I leave school in nine months,' Steve said, 'and my wages will help.'

Olive smiled at him, and all the love she felt for her son showed in that smile. 'Yeah, we'll be in clover, then, love. And yer never know, I might start to feel better and I'll be able to look for a little job.'

'Have yer been poorly for long?' Titch asked. 'When I used to come, yer were always the picture of health.'

'I've never been the same since Jim died. I just don't seem to have the energy or the willpower. And I've got to say that we don't get the right food to keep us strong and healthy. We can only afford the cheapest of everything.'

Titch was thoughtful. She's not really sick, he thought, she's still grieving for Jim. And until she accepts that, she'll spend her life on that couch. And that's not fair to her son. It was clear that she needed an incentive to bring her to life again. 'That's like asking which comes first, Olive, the chicken or the egg. Yer can't get a job until yer build yerself up, and yer can't build yerself up until yer get a job! Couldn't yer get an hour here and there, doing light work?'

'Me mam can't go to work,' Steve said, quickly defending his mother. 'She's not strong enough to take a job on.'

'It was only a thought, son. I had it in mind that if she got out a

452

bit and mixed with people, she might start to feel better.' Titch smiled at the boy who was left to carry a burden of work and worry that was too great for his young shoulders. He sent a message with his eyes, hoping Steve would understand he wasn't trying to run their lives for them, he was only trying to help. 'Your mam used to be a real goer when she was younger. She could dance the feet off anyone. And she was so pretty she could charm the ruddy birds off the trees. The fellers at the Grafton used to queue up to dance with her.'

Steve seemed to grow in stature and his face filled with pride. 'Me mam's still pretty. I bet she's the prettiest woman in the street.'

This gave Titch the opening he was waiting for. 'She's pretty all right, but there's someone else who would be joining her on the stage if there was a beauty contest. I wouldn't know which one to choose.'

Olive was now getting embarrassed. 'Hey, knock it off, you two. Any man who fell for me charms now would have to have very bad eyesight.'

Titch leaned forward, elbows on knees and fingers laced. 'The other woman I'm talking about is Irene Pollard. D'yer remember her?'

'Of course I remember Irene! I haven't spoken to her for years because I never go over the door. But I see her passing the window on her way to the shops.' Olive's voice was stronger now and there was interest in her eyes. 'A smashing woman, she is. One of the best yer'll find.' A faraway look came over her face as memories flooded back. 'God, when I think of the laughs we used to have. Her and George, and me and Jim, used to go out together until the children came along. They were good times, and I remember it was always Irene who was the one who made people laugh.'

'She hasn't changed,' Titch said, fully aware that Steve was drinking in every word. 'She's put weight on, but it suits her and she's still as pretty as ever.'

Olive looked down at her flat chest and skinny arms. 'Tell her I'll have some of her fat – I could do with it, God knows.'

'Why don't yer tell her yerself? Good grief, if she passes yer door, why can't yer just invite her in?'

'Invite her in to this?' Olive flung an arm wide. 'No thanks, Titch. Leave me with what little pride I've got left.'

Titch raised an eyebrow. 'I thought yer said yer knew Irene well?'

'I do! Well, at least I did. We were the best of pals for years.'

'Olive, if yer think Irene would worry about the state of yer house, then yer really don't know her at all. At least not the Irene

I know. She wouldn't care if yer lived in a pigsty.'

'She mightn't, but I would, Titch. I don't want anyone to see what I've come down to.' Olive hung her head. 'Irene did knock here a couple of times, but I pretended I wasn't in. That was years ago, mind.'

'I didn't know that, Mam!' Steve's voice was high with surprise. 'Why did yer never mention it to me?'

Olive sighed. 'Because I didn't want yer to know that yer mother was such a coward she hid behind the door when one of her friends knocked. I wasn't very proud of meself, I can tell yer.'

'Would yer still hide behind the door if she knocked?' Titch asked.

'I couldn't face her, Titch, I'd be too ashamed. It's not only the state of the house, it's me as well. Just look at me! I haven't got a decent stitch to put on me back. And me son, who I love more than words could ever say, has to walk around like a tramp. He gets his clothes from a secondhand stall at the market, and they're worn out when he gets them.'

'I don't mind that, Mam! I don't care what people think, I've told yer. If I had a wish, it wouldn't be for new clothes or a nice house, it would be that you get better.'

Titch sensed the emotion in the air and changed the subject. 'Talking about Irene, did yer know she has a little job?'

'Go 'way!' This was news to Olive. 'No, I didn't know that.'

'Yeah, she does two hours a morning at the corner pub. It's a cleaning job and she's made up with it. Apart from bringing in a few extra bob, she said it gets her out of the house.'

'Well, I never! I didn't think she'd need to go out to work with George's wages coming in every week. That is a surprise.'

'She's got two growing lads to feed and clothe, so the money comes in useful.' There was a reason behind Titch's words. 'Mind you, her eldest, Jack, leaves school next Friday so she may decide to pack the job in then.'

Olive narrowed her eyes in thought. Many of the things Titch said had hit home. But Irene taking a job to give her boys a better life had struck home the hardest. 'Is it a heavy job she's got?'

'That I couldn't tell yer. All I know is that she cleans at the pub. Why?'

'D'yer think I could do it?'

Steve was about to say it would be too hard for her, but thought better of it. Mr McBride had got his mother talking more than she had done for years and he seemed to know what he was doing. So the boy leaned his elbows on the sideboard again and listened.

'I don't know about that, Olive.' Titch was overjoyed and thanked God that Lucy had spurred him into this visit. 'Besides, she hasn't said yet that she's leaving. I could ask her for yer, if yer like.'

'She'll think I've got a bloody cheek after not opening the door to her. I'm certain she knew I was in, and hiding.'

'I wouldn't know, she never mentioned it to me. But when I see her I'll ask and let yer know.' Titch turned his attention to Steve. 'I believe you do odd jobs, son?'

'Yeah, when I get the chance.'

'Have yer ever painted anything? I don't mean a picture, or a house. I'm thinking of whitewashing a wall.'

'Yeah, I've done a couple of walls, and an outhouse. It's easy work, that.'

'Me ma wants her yard wall doing, and she asked a bloke how much he'd charge. He said it would be four bob, including the whitewash. If yer feel like having a go, the money would be better in your pocket than his.'

'I'll say it would!' Steve was beaming. Four bob would keep him and his mam in food for nearly a week. 'When does Mrs Aggie want it doing?'

'Hadn't yer better look at the job first, see what ye're letting yerself in for?' Titch dropped his head back and roared with laughter. 'Me ma's terrible fussy to work for. Spill a drop of paint on her yard and she'll have yer guts for garters.'

It was so long since the house had heard the voice and laughter of a man, Olive and her son savoured the sound before allowing their faces to break into a smile. 'Will yer ma stand over me with a broom in her hand?' Steve asked. 'Or will it be the poker?'

'That all depends, son, on the mood she's in. If her corns are giving her gyp, she'll likely as not have both broom and poker. And every twinge she gets, she'll lash out at yer. But ye're lucky, 'cos her eyesight's not what it used to be and I guarantee she'll miss yer more often than she hits yer.'

'I'm good at ducking and running, Mr McBride, so unless Mrs Aggie's nifty on her feet I should be safe.' Steve was thinking that for four bob he'd work for a maniac, never mind Mrs Aggie, who was liked by everyone. 'But what about the bloke she's asked? Won't he be expecting to get the job?'

Titch was safe in saying what he was going to say because there was no such bloke. And he'd have a lot of explaining to do to his ma, as well. 'No, there was nothing definite arranged so he won't know the difference. Anyway, come up and see the yard for yerself. I've got another week at home, so if yer decide yer want to do the job, I can get the whitewash for yer on Monday. I need to make a call on someone now, so will yer give me fifteen minutes and then follow up?'

The pleasure on Steve's face was a joy to behold, and wasn't lost on his mother. 'Thanks, Titch, yer've made him a happy lad. And d'yer know why he's happy? Because he'll have a few bob to give me. He won't keep a ha'penny for himself no matter what I say. There's not many mothers can say that about their sons.'

Titch chuckled. 'Me ma would argue with yer on that, Olive. She's always saying that I'm a gift from God.'

'Your ma always doted on yer. Spoilt yer soft, she did.'

'Well, yer just admit, I'm a very lovable bloke. Yer don't get many like me in a pound.' Titch got to his feet. 'I'll see Irene tonight and have a word with her. I think the pub job might be too much for you, but we'll see. I'll give yer a knock tomorrow and let yer know. And I want to see yer off that couch, Olive, even if yer've got to wear a curtain to hide yer modesty. I've got a kink in me flippin' neck looking down at yer.'

There was a trace of colour in Olive's thin face now, as she said, 'Still the same old Titch. Yer haven't changed a bit, have yer?'

'Now who would want to change perfection, Olive?' Titch grinned as he picked up one of her hands and held it in his. All he could feel was skin and bones, and this saddened him. But not for the world would he let this once proud woman see how her appearance had affected him. 'I'm glad I came, it's been great seeing yer. There's no friends like old friends, eh?'

Olive's eyes were shining with unshed tears. 'I'm glad yer came, Titch, yer've bucked me up. And I'm glad yer were cheeky enough to barge in after being told I didn't want to see no one.' She gave his hand a squeeze. 'Yer didn't give me time to hide behind the door.'

'Now I'm up to yer little tricks, I'll come the back way in future.' He laid her hand down on her lap. 'I'd better skedaddle, but I'll see yer tomorrow. And you, Steve, I'll see in fifteen minutes.'

The boy followed him to the front door. 'Thanks, Mr McBride. Not just for the job, which I'm grateful for, but for cheering me mam up. She looks better than she has for ages.'

'Don't thank me, Steve, because I feel like a heel for not coming to see her before now. But we'll talk about yer mam, later, eh? Right now I've got to be on me way. Ta-ra for now.'

Chapter Nine

Titch covered the ground quickly. He could do with more than fifteen minutes to talk his mother round. She'd lay a duck egg when she knew what he'd done. Still, it was all in a good cause so he'd just have to try and out-talk her. A grin covered his face as he told himself it would take some doing to out-talk his mother. She said herself she'd been born with the gift of the gab. To which she'd added, with a smile, that she'd passed the gift on to him.

He let himself in and, as he was taking the key out of the lock, he called, 'it's only me, Ma! Yer don't need to put yer false teeth in or take yer knickers off the fireguard.'

'Well, I know it's not the bleedin' coalman, yer silly bugger.' Aggie was sitting watching the door when he came in. 'Well, how did yer get on? Was Olive pleased to see yer, or did she die of shock?'

'I'll tell yer that in a minute, Ma, but tell me this first. Didn't yer once say that yer'd like the backyard wall whitewashing?'

'Yer what? I've never said I wanted no backyard wall white-washing!'

'Yes yer did, Ma, I distinctly remember. Some time last year it was.'

'Ye're imagining things, son, 'cos it's never entered me head. I don't want me wall whitewashed, and as it's my wall, I should know.'

'Yer only THINK yer don't want it doing, Ma. But deep down yer one ambition in life is to see yer wall whitewashed.'

'D'yer know, son, I often wonder about you. An hour ago yer went out of here to go and visit Olive, who yer haven't seen for years. But yer come back, not with news of her, but with some notion about the state of me backyard! Am I missing something, or have yer lost the run of yer senses?'

'There's nowt wrong with me mind, Mam, yer can rest assured. I just thought it would be nice to look out of the window and see it all nice and white. Those brown bricks are enough to give anyone the willies.'

'Okay, son, spit it out. What have yer been up to?'

Titch grinned. 'I'll tell yer, Ma, if yer promise me yer'll stay in that chair and not reach for the poker.'

Aggie was having trouble keeping a smile off her face. 'Okay, I'll hear yer out. But I'm not making no promises about the bleedin' poker until I know what yer've let me in for. I can't be up to you, I don't know what ye're going to do next.'

Titch glanced at the clock. Time was running out and he'd better make it snappy. So with the words tumbling from his mouth, he told the whole story in as few words as possible. But they were enough to have Aggie hanging on to every one of them. When he'd finished, he asked, 'Shall I pass yer the poker, Ma?'

Aggie looked shocked and was shaking her head. 'Is it as bad as that, son?'

'It's worse. There's not a pick on Olive, she's as thin as a rake. If she doesn't get off that couch soon, and get some decent food down her, she'll just fade away. Some fresh air would do her good, too. And the house is bare, not a bit like the bright home it used to be. It's my belief that Olive has got herself in a rut and hasn't got the energy or the inclination to pull herself out of it. But it's not fair on the boy, he worries himself to death about her. Something needs to be done there, and quick.'

Aggie's sigh was deep. 'Are yer going to see Irene? If anyone can do anything, it's her. And I'll do me bit, too. That's if Olive will let us help, of course. I wouldn't want to stick me nose in where it wasn't wanted.'

'I'll go and see Irene when we've had our tea. But Steve will be here any minute, so it's make-yer-mind-up time, Ma. D'yer want yer yard wall whitewashed or not?'

'It's like yer said, son, I didn't think I did, but yer've shown me the error of me ways. As long as you're forking out, 'cos I couldn't afford it.'

There was a loud ran-tan on the knocker and Titch jumped to his feet. 'This will be Steve. Don't mention anything I've told yer, Ma, just let's play it by ear.'

'I'm not thick, Titch McBride,' Aggie said as he left the room. 'You go and teach yer grandmother how to milk ducks.'

There was a smile on Titch's face when he opened the door. 'Come in, lad, me ma's waiting to see yer.' In a loud whisper, he added, 'Just humour her. She's getting on in years so yer have to make excuses for her.'

'Ay, I heard that, buggerlugs,' Aggie said. 'I may be getting on, but I can still run bleedin' circles around you.' The smile she bestowed on Steve was warm and friendly. 'It's nice to see yer, lad. Take a pew and make yerself at home.'

'Is it true yer want yer yard walls whitewashing, Mrs Aggie?' Steve couldn't bear the suspense any longer. The last fifteen

458

minutes had seemed like an eternity. Getting this job meant so much to him and he was afraid of having his hopes dashed. 'Mr McBride said that yer did.'

'Don't be so formal, lad,' Aggie said with a smile. 'All the youngsters call him Mr Titch, so why don't yer do the same? Sounds more friendly, like.' She sat back, set her rocking chair in motion and tried to keep her eyes on the lad's face, not on the rags that were almost falling off his back. 'I've always wanted me yard doing, but never seemed to get down to it.' She gave a broad wink. 'That's because I'm getting on in years, yer see, lad.'

'I'll do it good for yer, Mrs Aggie. I won't spill no paint or anything, and I'll clean up after meself.' The flicker that Steve had felt the minute he stepped in the room and saw Aggie's smile had grown into a warm glow coursing through his whole body. These two people weren't put off by his appearance – in fact, they seemed not to have noticed. I bet they wouldn't treat me any different if I was dressed like a toff, he thought. And this made him daring enough to say, 'So yer won't need to stand over me with the broom and poker when yer corns are giving yer gyp, will yer?'

Aggie forgot it was wise to alert her false teeth before she laughed, and she just caught them before they parted company from her gums. Beating the chair-arm with a curled fist, she shook with laughter. 'I can see me son's been telling yer tales, eh? Well, lad, you and me are going to get along just fine. And don't you worry none about me corns, they only bother me every blue moon.'

Steve's face was eager. 'When can I start?'

'As soon as yer like, lad. But don't you come knocking on the door at six o'clock in the morning 'cos then I might take the broom to yer.'

'Would nine o'clock be all right?'

'Ay, hang on a minute.' Titch knew these two were going to get along like a house on fire and was delighted. 'We haven't got the blinkin' whitewash yet.'

'The shops open at nine, son,' Aggie told him, knowing it would spoil his lie-in. But the lad was really eager to start. The poor bugger was probably thinking about the money. He could do with spending it on himself, but from what Titch had said, he would turn every penny over to his mam. 'Yer could be waiting outside when they open up.'

'I would go for yer, Mr Titch, save yer getting up early, but I don't have any money.'

'We'll go together,' Titch said. 'I'll do without me lie-in for once.' He explained that they had a brush and a tin for mixing the

459

whitewash in. 'So give me a knock before nine and we'll have yer hard at work by half-past.'

Now everything was arranged, Steve thought he should leave. He was rising from the chair when Aggie said, 'I believe yer mam's not too well, lad?'

'No, she's been sick for a long time. But she seemed better when I left the house and I think it was Mr Titch calling that bucked her up.'

'Yeah, he's good at bucking people up, is my son. He's good at a lot of things, like springing surprises on yer when ye're least expecting them. And he's a bugger for playing tricks that no one thinks are funny but himself.' Aggie could see the lad was far more relaxed than he had been and she was pleased. So she told him the tale about Titch hiding her purse on her. 'He watched me searching high and low and didn't say a dickie-bird. The club woman was banging hell out of the door and I was nearly having a heart attack. Then the bold laddo passes it over as cool as yer like. He thought it was hilarious and couldn't understand why I was hitting him over the head with the poker.'

Steve roared with laughter. 'Ooh, I'd love to have seen it.'

'Yer wouldn't have liked it,' Titch told him, his face deadpan. 'There was blood everywhere. I had to be carted to hospital and they put a hundred stitches in me head. The doctor said I was lucky to be alive.'

Aggie's whole body was shaking. 'That's why he's not quite with us in the head. So while ye're keeping an eye on me, lad, to make sure I haven't got a weapon in me hand, keep the other one on the queer feller here. Yer never can tell when he's going to have a funny turn.'

Not to be outdone, Titch said, 'She's right, yer know. Our captain was sick once, and he asked me to steer the ship. We only ended up in China when we were supposed to be going to India. And d'yer know what? The miserable so-and-so has never let me steer the ship since. The trouble is, he's got no sense of humour.'

'Wait until I tell me mam all these things,' Steve said. 'She won't half have a good laugh.'

'Yeah, you tell her, lad.' Aggie was wiping her eyes on the corner of her pinny. 'And while ye're at it, ask her if I can call one day to have a natter with her.'

The smile dropped from Steve's face. 'Me mam doesn't like visitors, Mrs Aggie, 'cos our house is like a dump and she doesn't like anyone to see it.'

'Listen to me, lad, and tell yer mam what I said. People see what they want to see, and in my case I want to see an old friend. If she was living in the workhouse, I'd still like to visit her. Tell her she should know better than to think her old mates are snobs. We've all hit rock bottom some time in our lives, but we've managed to claw our way up. And you and yer mam will, too, lad, take my word for it.'

'We'll be a bit better off when I leave school.' Steve felt some of the weight being lifted from his shoulders. It was good to have someone to talk to. 'I know I won't earn much, but I'll still help out at the corner shop, and do any odd jobs I can to bring in a few coppers. I'm not frightened of work, Mrs Aggie.'

'I know ye're not, sweetheart,' Aggie gave him a smile, 'even when there's an old biddy standing behind yer with a poker in her hand.'

'I can't wait.' Steve was eager to be away, to tell his mam the good news. And to brighten her up with the tales he'd heard. 'I'll see yer in the morning, then.'

Aggie eyed him up and down. 'Ye're a big lad for yer age, aren't yer? I'd say yer were only a few inches shorter than Titch.'

Steve drew himself up to his full height. 'Me mam said me dad was very tall and I take after him.'

'Yeah, yer dad was tall all right, and good-looking. If yer take after him yer won't go far wrong.' Titch made a move towards the door. 'I'll see yer at nine in the morning, Steve. And tell yer mam I'll be calling, but not that early.'

When he came back after seeing the lad out, Aggie was in the kitchen. 'I'm putting the spuds on, then I'm going upstairs to sort yer clothes out.'

Titch leaned against the door jamb. 'What d'yer mean, sort me clothes out? Everything in the drawers and wardrobe are all neat and tidy.'

'There's clothes there yer haven't had on yer back for years, and probably never will. Rather than let the moths get at them, they may as well go where they'll do some good. And that's on the back of the boy who's just walked out of this house. The poor bugger, me heart went out to him.'

'Be careful Ma, 'cos yer could embarrass him. And Olive might not take too kindly to it, either. If she thinks ye're doing it out of pity, she could shut the door on us for good. And I wouldn't want that.'

'Me neither, son.' Aggie put the pan of potatoes on the stove and struck a match under them. Then talking to herself, she asked, 'Now have I salted them or not? Better put a bit more in, just in case.' The salt in the water, the lid on the pan, she turned to Titch. 'So ye're going to have to be very diplomatic, aren't yer, son?'

'What d'yer mean?'

461

'When yer ask Olive if she would mind yer giving Steve some of yer clothes. If yer use the right words, I'm sure she won't take umbrage.' Aggie bit on her bottom lip to keep a smile back. 'And if anyone knows the right bleedin' words, it's you. Look what yer've achieved today! The last thing on me mind was having me yard wall whitewashed, but tomorrow morning there'll be a lad out there whistling his head off as he slaps the stuff on in good style. All because I couldn't resist yer smooth tongue and yer charm.'

Titch chuckled as he held his arms wide. 'Come here and give us a kiss.' He held her close and whispered in her ear, 'I love the bones of yer, Ma, and it's not me smooth tongue or me charm talking, either.'

'Away with yer,' Aggie said, loving every minute of it. 'Keep yer eye on the spuds, and lower the light when they come to the boil. Then come up and make sure I'm not giving something away that yer want to keep.'

Titch looked at the lone pan on the stove. 'What are we having with them?'

'I was going to say fresh air, but we haven't got time for jokes. We're having bacon, sausage and egg. And I'm going to mash the potatoes with butter. How does that sound?'

'Music to my ears, Ma, music to my ears.'

'I knew she was in when I knocked,' Irene said, 'but I couldn't understand why she didn't want to see me. After the third or fourth attempt, I gave up.'

'Yer'd understand if yer saw the state of her house.' Titch looked from Irene to George. 'And yer wouldn't know Olive, she's like a bag of bones. Anyway, I'll fill yer in on what's gone on today. It all started with Lucy falling out with her mate.' He went on from there, right through to his mother and his clothes. 'She's got them all stacked up nicely, even to socks. And she said she'll ask Steve tomorrow what size shoes he takes.'

'I feel terrible now,' Irene said. 'I should have made more of an effort.'

'You weren't to know, love.' George reached for his wife's hand. 'I should have given some thought to how Olive and the son were managing. I owed it to Jim to do that. But the years go by and the longer yer leave it, the harder it is to make it up. I've seen how badly dressed the boy's been, and I could kick meself now for not getting off me backside to offer some sort of help. For old times' sake, if nothing else. Jim would have expected that of me because we were good mates.'

'I haven't thought of packing me job in,' Irene said. 'I want to stay on a while to renew some of me furniture and bedding. But if

462

I thought Olive wanted the job, I would pack in. Although, if she's as weak as yer say she is, she'd never manage it. It's hard graft, cleaning the pub in two hours. Yer've got to get on yer hands and knees and scrub hell out of the floor. Then there's all the woodwork and tables to polish.'

'I wouldn't expect yer to pack yer job in, Irene,' Titch said. 'I only mentioned it to try and liven Olive up. I think it worked, too, because in her heart she knows it's not fair on Steve to have to carry all the worry. He's a smashing lad, he really is. I'm just hoping that between us we can do something to get her back on her feet. Give her an interest in life. Are yer game to give it a try?'

'Of course we are!' Irene was blaming herself for not trying hard enough. She often talked to Steve, but never once had she asked about his mother. Not because she wasn't interested, but because she thought that for some reason Olive didn't want to be friends any more. 'D'yer think she'd mind if I came with yer tomorrow, to see her?'

'I think she'd mind, but only for a few minutes. She spoke very highly of you and George and what good times yer had together. And Steve said my calling had bucked her up, she was better than she'd been for a long time. So we can but try, Irene.'

'Well, I'm game. If she throws me out, at least I'll know I've tried. But I'm at the pub from nine until eleven, so it'll have to be after that.'

'That's fine. And leave yer working clothes on, girl, so Olive doesn't get embarrassed.'

'I want to help too, yer know,' George said. 'If there's anything in her house that wants doing, I'm more than willing to get stuck in.'

'Let's see how me and Titch get on first, love. We can't make up for all those years in one day. If we try too hard, we'll put her off. So we'll do things slowly.' They heard the front door being slammed against the hall wall and Irene put a finger over her mouth and said softly, 'Little pigs have big ears.' Then her face lit up when the two boys barged in, elbowing each other out of the way to be first in the room. They looked so happy it brought a lump to her throat. Thank God she'd been able to give her children a good home. 'Here's my two angels back from playing footie. There'll be no more peace now until they're in bed.'

'I'm going for a pint, are yer coming, George?'

George grinned at his wife. 'How's the money situation, love? Will it stretch to a pint?'

'Oh, I think I can spare a few coppers. And just think, in a couple of weeks yer'll be able to borrow off yer son.'

'I'll want interest on it, Dad,' Jack said, his face straight. 'I can't go lending money without getting interest. It'll have to be on a business footing.'

George slipped his arm into his coat-sleeves. 'What interest rate did yer have in mind, son? If it's too high, I'll stick to yer mam.'

'I'll make enquiries and see what the going rate is. I can't be fairer than that.'

Titch ruffled Jack's hair as he passed. 'Yer'll end up a rich man, you will.'

Jack grinned from ear to ear. 'That's the general idea, Mr Titch.'

George's chuckle was deep and hearty. 'If I borrowed money off yer and had to pay yer back with interest, it would mean that in a few weeks yer'd be lending me me own money. So I think I'll stick with yer mam. Otherwise I'd have a rich son, but I'd be a pauper.'

There was a look of fear on Olive's face when she opened the door and found Irene standing beside Titch. 'I told yer I wasn't ready for visitors, Titch.'

'Don't blame him, it wasn't his fault.' Irene mounted the step, her usual smile beaming. 'When he told me he'd seen yer, nothing would keep me away.' She was shocked to the core at the sight of her old friend, but not by a flicker did she let it show as she bent to kiss a pale cheek. 'It's good to see yer. I really thought I'd done something to offend yer and yer'd fallen out with me.'

Olive had no option but to stand aside and let them pass. 'I'd never have any reason to fall out with you, Irene, but when yer see the state of the place yer'll know why I shut meself away from everyone.'

Irene stood at the door of the living room, and it took every ounce of self-control to keep the smile pasted on her face. 'Good God, Olive, anyone would think the place was a pigsty to hear yer talk. Yer've got it spotless.'

'There's not much to keep clean, is there? No ornaments or pictures to dust, no grate to clean out because we never have a fire.' The initial shock had worn off now and Olive pointed to the chairs. 'Now ye're in, why don't yer sit down.'

Irene took one of the wooden chairs, but Titch remained standing. 'Where are you going to sit, Olive?'

For a brief second, they saw a glimpse of the old Olive. With a half-smile, she said, 'It's all right, Titch, I'm not getting on the couch.'

'Thank God for that! I had to get me ma to rub me neck with liniment last night because it had a kink in it. That's with bending down to yer for so long.'

'Me heart bleeds for yer,' Olive said.

'Yeah, mine too,' Irene chuckled. 'Men can be proper babies

sometimes. The least little thing and they're moaning.'

'Thanks for the sympathy, I feel better already.' Titch waited until Olive had seated herself on a wooden chair next to Irene, then he dropped onto the couch. 'Before I forget, Olive, me ma said to ask yer if she could adopt Steve? The two of them have really hit it off. And I've got to say he's a crackin' worker. He'd have the job done today if me ma would stop making him cups of tea every five minutes.'

'Tell yer ma I wouldn't part with him for the world. He's a good son and I'm so proud of him. It grieves me to see him walking around in clothes only fit for the dustbin, because he's really good-looking. But I've made up me mind that somehow or other I'm going to make life better for him. You woke me up, Titch, and I'm determined to start pulling me weight.'

Irene put a hand over Olive's. 'Titch mentioned the job I've got in the pub. I haven't made up me mind whether I'm packing it in yet, but it would be too heavy for you, sunshine. Yer need something a bit lighter, just until ye're feeling a hundred per cent. I'll scout around and see if there's anything going for yer.'

'Thanks, Irene, I would be grateful.'

'You two probably have lots to talk about,' Titch said, 'and I'll only be in the way. But before I go, I've got something to ask yer, Olive, and I don't want yer to fly off the handle about it.' He gave one of his cheeky grins. 'Before I tell me ma something I think she might not like, I always make her promise not to go for the poker. And I'm going to ask you for the same promise.'

'I'll sit on her, if yer like,' Irene said with a laugh. 'Would that help?'

'There's no need, Irene, I won't take off on him. So go ahead, Titch, out with it.'

'Well, it's like this. I've got stacks of clothes I'll never wear. I'm a bugger for hoarding things, and some of them are years old. But they'd do Steve a turn and I'd be made up to see them put to good use. That's if yer wouldn't mind me offering them to him.'

'I wouldn't mind in the least, as long as you're not going to need them. God knows he could do with something decent to wear. Have yer asked him?'

Titch shook his head. 'I wouldn't do that without asking you first in case yer didn't take kindly to the idea.'

'I wouldn't let me pride stand in the way of me son being able to walk around with his head held high. I love him, yer see, and if I could, I'd give him the world. That's not possible right now, so I'm more than willing to accept help from an old friend. And I thank yer from the bottom of my heart, Titch.'

Titch rubbed his hands. 'Thank you for that! Yer can never tell

465

with you women, which way ye're going to turn.'

'Well, I like that!' Irene said. 'We women are an open book compared to you men.'

'And I don't think! It would take a good man to get to the bottom of a woman, believe you me.' Titch pressed his hands on the couch and pushed himself up. 'I'll leave you two to have a good gab, yer've got a lot of years to make up. Me, I'm going to see how the working man is getting on with me ma's yard walls. I'll see meself out, Olive, so stay where yer are.'

'Remember me to yer mother, and say I was asking after her. I often see her passing the window and she still gets around like a two year old.'

Titch turned at the door. 'Olive, a word of warning in yer lily-white ears. Me ma's not going to stay away from here now she's taken a shine to yer son. So be a good girl and keep off that ruddy couch, eh?'

As he walked down the hall he could hear both women laughing, and the sound was like music to his ears.

Titch let himself in and walked through to the living room. He could hear gales of laughter coming from the yard, and when he looked through the window it was to see Steve, paintbrush in mid-air, looking down at his mother. Both of them were in pleats. It would seem that the boy had the same sense of the ridiculous as his mother, he thought, making his way out to the yard. 'Well, you two seem to be enjoying yerselves.'

Aggie had her back to him and his voice startled her. 'Yer silly sod, why didn't yer whistle or something to let me know yer were there? I nearly jumped out of me skin.'

'Ma, yer were that busy gabbing, yer wouldn't have heard me if I'd come in playing "I Belong To Glasgow" on a set of bagpipes.'

'Yer haven't got no bagpipes.'

'There wouldn't have been much point, would there, seeing as yer wouldn't have heard them anyway.'

'Oh, I'd have heard them if yer'd been playing "I Belong To Glasgow". That's one of me specialities, that is. Particularly when I've had a few drinks. Me feet won't keep still when they hear that tune, and I can dance in time to the music, too.'

'I know that, Ma, I've seen yer. And I've seen the way yer show yer bloomers off while ye're doing it.' Titch looked at Steve. 'It's not a pretty sight, lad, for a son to see his mother showing her bloomers off. Particularly when the elastic in one of the legs has snapped.'

Aggie gave him a playful push in the chest. 'Away with yer, yer'll have the lad believing yer. He'll probably go home and learn to whistle "I Belong To Glasgow", just so he can see me bloomers.'

'I can whistle it, Mrs Aggie.' Steve had never heard anyone as funny as these two, nor had he ever laughed so much. He shouldn't be getting paid for this job, he should be paying them. If his mam wasn't so desperate for the money, he'd have done it as a favour. 'D'yer want to hear me?'

'No, lad, I'll sit this one out. Yer see, I haven't got me dance shoes with me.'

Titch put an arm across her shoulders and held her close. 'Shall we stop blabbering and see how the worker's doing?'

'He's doing fine, son, really fine.'

'He certainly is.' Titch nodded his head in appreciation. A grown man couldn't have done better. 'Ye're doing a good job, Steve, it looks really professional.'

Steve blushed with pride. 'Thanks, Mr Titch. But I think it'll need two coats. As yer can see, one coat isn't covering the brown bricks properly. I'll try and get it all done today, then come back tomorrow and give it another coat. We didn't mix all the white-wash, so there'll be enough to finish the job.'

'You're the expert, Steve, so I'll leave it to you.'

'And we'll leave yer alone now to get on with it.' Aggie linked her son's arm and drew him away. 'I'll give yer a shout when I've got a bite to eat ready.' She pushed Titch ahead of her then closed the kitchen door after them, so her words wouldn't carry. 'Did yer ask Olive about the clothes?'

'Yes, Ma. I used me charm, and all the right words, and she said she'd be delighted. It really got to me when she said she wouldn't let her pride stand in the way of her son being able to walk around with his head held high. We don't know how lucky we are, do we?'

'No, son, we don't. And it's because God's been good to us, we should try and help someone who isn't so fortunate.' Aggie hugged herself. 'I can't wait to see his face. I just hope yer clothes fit him, but it's not the end of the world if they don't. It's years since I did any sewing, but I used to be a dab hand with the needle and thread.'

'Ma, I think ye're in yer element with—' Titch broke off as a knock came on the front door. 'I'll see who it is, you start getting something ready to eat.'

He was whistling as he opened the door. 'Irene, I didn't expect yer so soon. I thought you and Olive would have plenty to say to each other.'

'I'll come in for a minute, Titch, but it'll only be for a minute 'cos I've got all me shopping to do and a dinner to get ready.'

Aggie heard the familiar voice and came through. 'Hello, queen.'

'Good morning, Aggie.' Irene leaned sideways to glance in the kitchen. 'Where's Steve?'

'He's in the yard,' the older woman told her with a smile, 'going like the clappers.'

'He won't come in, will he? I don't want him to hear what I've got to say.'

'No, he won't come in.' Titch looked puzzled. 'Why?'

'Olive's a sick woman, Titch. After yer'd gone we were nattering about old times and she seemed fine. But after a while I could see the effort was too much for her and she was getting tired. She did her best to put up a front, God knows, but she just hasn't got the energy or strength. As for her getting a job – well, there's no chance of that. In fact, unless something drastic is done, and soon, I don't think Olive will ever come out of that house alive.'

Aggie gasped, her face white. 'Don't say that, queen.'

'It's true, Aggie. And I feel heartbroken because I blame meself for it. I should never have let her put me off getting into the house years ago. Me own common sense should have told me what was going on, just by looking at Steve. The old Olive would never have let her son walk around the way he does. I feel terrible, racked with guilt.'

'It's not your fault, Irene, we must all shoulder some of the blame,' Titch said. 'But surely it's not too late for all of us to get stuck in and help?'

'There's one drawback to that, Titch, and that's Olive herself. I doubt if she'd accept help, she's too proud. And anyway, to get her back to what she was would take a miracle. She needs plenty of good food down her, and a tonic from the doctor. That part would be easy, if we can talk her round. But we can't do much about her mental state. With the best food and tonics in the world, she's not going to get better while she's living in a house where all the furniture is only fit for a bonfire, and the decoration is enough to send yer round the bend. And on top of all that she hasn't got two ha'pennies to rub together.' Irene sighed, her pretty face showing her sadness. 'I just don't know what the answer is, I feel absolutely helpless.'

'Don't be getting yerself upset, queen,' Aggie said. 'If we put our heads together and all rally round, we'll find a way.'

'Me ma's right, Irene,' Titch said. 'We can't just sit on our backsides and do nowt. I know I'll be away at sea in eight or nine days, and you lot will be left with the worry. But I can muck in with some money.'

'There's plenty we can do, Titch, like me and Aggie making sure she gets wholesome food every day. And George has offered to decorate her house. But it would all come to nothing if we can't

468

find a way to get through to Olive. She has to have the will to live.'

Aggie pinched on her bottom lip, her brow furrowed in concentration. 'I know of a way to get through to her.'

'What's that, Ma?'

'The way to Olive's heart and conscience is through her son. And if it's all the same with you two, I'll go down tomorrow, while Steve's here, and have a good talk to her.'

'It wouldn't do no harm, Ma.'

Irene nodded. 'If she'd listen to anyone, it would be you, Aggie. But tell Steve to warn her that ye're going, otherwise she won't open the door.'

'I've got it all worked out in me head, Irene. I know a good way of making sure she opens the door. And I'll let yer know how I get on.'

'Yeah, don't forget, Aggie, 'cos I'll be on pins.' Irene looked down at her working clothes and grimaced. 'I'll have to go to the shops in these, I haven't got time to change. I've usually done me shopping by now and got the dinner on the go.' She put her arms around Aggie and kissed her cheek. 'Lots of luck tomorrow, sunshine. I hope Olive listens to yer words of wisdom.'

'We'll see, girl, we'll see.'

When Titch came back after seeing Irene out, his mother was busy in the kitchen. 'What have yer got going on in that head of yours, Ma?'

Aggie tapped the side of her nose. 'That's for me to know, son, and you to find out.'

'How can I find out if yer won't tell me? I don't know what's going on in that head of yours.'

'Neither do I, son, so that makes two of us. So we'll both have to wait until tomorrow to find out, won't we? And while yer've got nothing else to do but wait until tomorrow, go and see how Steve's getting on. Tell him it won't be long now before I've got that bite to eat I promised him.'

Chapter Ten

Steve pushed his plate away and licked his lips before sighing with appreciation. Aggie had made him three thick slices of toast and had grilled it with cheese on top. A feast to a boy who was lucky to get a dripping butty. 'I really enjoyed that, Mrs Aggie. It was very tasty, and very welcome.'

'If it wasn't for me son and his queer habits, yer'd have been having a proper dinner,' Aggie told him. 'But he's so used to having his hot dinner at teatime, he doesn't enjoy it in the middle of the day.' Then she added, by way of an explanation, 'That's because he's away at sea more than he's home, yer see.'

'That's right, Ma, put the blame on me,' Titch said. 'Me shoulders are wide enough to take it.'

'And yer legs are strong enough to walk to the kitchen and pour the lad another cup of tea. It's thirsty work, is painting.'

Titch refilled Steve's cup, then sat down to wait for his mother to broach the subject of the clothes. He didn't have long to wait.

'I was cleaning Titch's room out the other day, lad, and he's got more clothes up there than they've got in Blackler's. There's some he'll never wear again, but they're too good to throw out. So I was wondering if yer'd be embarrassed if I asked yer if yer'd like to take a look at them? There's no harm done if they don't fit yer, or yer don't like them. What d'yer think?'

Steve's face was agog. 'Oh yeah, Mrs Aggie, I'd be made up. As yer can see, I'm not well off for clothes.' Then a thought hit him and the brightness in his eyes dimmed. 'But I don't know whether me mam would like me taking clothes off yer. I'd have to ask her first, in case she got upset.'

'I've already asked yer mam, Steve,' Titch said. 'I mentioned it to her when I was up there earlier and she wasn't in the least bit upset. In fact, she seemed highly delighted.'

'That's the gear, that, Mr Titch, thanks very much.' Steve became fidgety. He didn't want to seem forward, or cheeky, not after they'd been so good to him. But the thought of going to school in decent clothes and not having the two school bullies make fun of him, was one he couldn't cast aside. And to be able to walk up this street and feel as good as anyone else, that would be like a dream come true. So he took a deep breath and asked, 'When can I see them?'

Aggie could sense the lad's nerves were as taut as a violin string, and thought, God love the poor beggar. 'Yer can see them now, Steve. Titch will take yer upstairs and yer can try some of them on for size. The trousers might be too long in the leg for yer, but that's easily remedied.' Then she hit her forehead with an open palm. 'I forgot, yer can't wear long trousers for school!'

'Yes, I can. There's a couple of boys in my class who wear them. They were hand-me-downs from their dads 'cos they couldn't afford to buy the short ones the school say we've got to wear. The first boy who came in long trousers was sent home by the headmistress and told not to come back until he was wearing short grey trousers like the rest of the class. But the boy's father dragged him back an hour later and played merry hell with the headmistress. He told her if she wanted his son in short trousers she'd have to buy them herself because he couldn't afford to. And he said if she sent his son home again, he'd keep him at home because he'd learned all he was going to learn. But wouldn't yer think the school would understand that people can't help being poor?' Steve's face took on a look of defiance. 'I'm fourteen in just under six months, but I've got to stay on an extra three months until the end of term. I don't think that's fair, not when me mam needs me working and bringing in a few bob.'

'I've got news for yer, Steve,' Titch said. 'Once ye're fourteen, the school authorities have got to let yer leave as long as yer have a good reason. And being hard-pressed for money is one of the reasons. Yer have to apply, of course, and prove that ye're a deserving case. But that shouldn't cause yer a problem. They'll send someone out to the house to see what yer circumstances are, but that's only a formality.'

Steve looked as though he'd lost a ha'penny and found a ten-bob note. 'One of the lads in our class said he was leaving on his birthday, but I didn't believe him, I thought he was pulling me leg.' He shook his head. 'Wouldn't yer think the teachers would tell yer these things? They know how hard-up some of the families are, they've only got to look at us to see that. I mean, would I walk around like this if I had a choice?'

'Ah well, lad, teachers don't come from poor families,' Aggie said. 'They don't know what it's like to have yer tummy rumbling with hunger and no food to eat. Nor have they ever gone bare-arsed or barefoot, like some poor kids. Not that I'm blaming them for not knowing what it is to be poor, they can't help the families they were born into. But they could be a bit more

472

understanding of those less fortunate. I know they're there to teach yer the catechism, yer five times table, and the date of the Battle of Hastings, but they could show some sympathy while they're doing it.'

Titch was wide-eyed. 'That was a long speech, Ma! Yer had me back in the classroom there, getting me knuckles rapped for not knowing the date of the Battle of Hastings. I had it drummed into me so much, I'll never forget it. And a fat lot of good it's done me because no one has ever asked me.'

Steve was rapping his fingers on the table, a contented look on his face. 'Yer know, I'll remember this day as one of the best in me life. Yer've given me a job so I can give me mam some money, yer've offered me clothes which I badly need, and I've learned I can leave school three months earlier than I thought. And as if that wasn't enough, on top of it all, I've really enjoyed meself.'

'I'm glad about that, lad, 'cos yer deserve a bit of luck.' Aggie leaned across the table and smiled into his face. 'Now yer can make *me* happy by going upstairs and seeing if those clothes are any good to yer. If they're not, I'll let yer look through mine and see if there's anything takes yer fancy. All except me fleecy-lined bloomers, 'cos I'm partial to them and wouldn't part with 'em even for King Tut himself.'

Steve was laughing as he followed Titch out of the room. 'Our teacher must be slipping up, 'cos I've never heard of King Tut.'

'Ye're not missing much, Steve, so don't worry,' Titch said, throwing open his bedroom door. 'Even King Tut's never heard of himself.'

Aggie's heart was singing as she collected the dirty dishes. She'd taken a real liking to the lad and was glad to have been able to put a little happiness into his life. She couldn't always be so generous, not when Titch was away, 'cos she had to live on the allowance he left her each week and the tiny widow's pension she got. But it didn't cost anything to be a friend, and that's what she hoped she could be to Steve.

The few dishes washed, Aggie went to stand at the bottom of the stairs. She couldn't hear the words that were spoken because the bedroom door was closed, but she could tell by the high pitch of Steve's laughter, and her son's deep chuckle, that things were going well in that room. And as she made her way to her rocking chair, she thanked God. He was the one Who made it all possible, and when she was saying her prayers tonight, she'd have a word with Him about Olive. It wouldn't hurt to have a word in the right ear.

There came a clattering of footsteps on the stairs and Aggie leaned forward in anticipation. Titch was the first to enter the room and his beaming smile was a sign of things to come. Waving a hand towards the door and bowing from the waist, he announced, 'Let me introduce you to Mr Steven Fletcher.'

Aggie's jaw dropped. The lad standing before her, grinning like a Cheshire cat, would pass for sixteen in the long navy-blue trousers, and a grey pullover over a white shirt. 'Well, I never would have believed it. Yer look like a real toff! And a handsome one, at that! By heck, lad, when yer mam sees yer all dolled up to the nines she'll be that proud of yer, she'll soon get herself better so she can go out holding on to yer arm.'

'I couldn't believe it meself, Mrs Aggie, when I saw the clothes all neatly piled up. There's everything there, from underclothes, hankies, socks, shirts, pullovers and trousers. I'm going to have to pinch meself in a minute to make sure I'm not dreaming.'

'The trousers are a couple of inches too long for him,' Titch said, 'but everything else fits fine. And he takes a size six and a half in shoes, only half a size smaller than me. So he can have the brown pair I don't wear very much.'

Steve's head was somewhere in the clouds, he just couldn't believe all this was happening to him. 'Tell me I'm not dreaming, Mrs Aggie.'

'Yer'll soon know ye're not dreaming when yer get that paint-brush in yer hand, lad, and I'm standing behind yer with me poker.' Aggie was feeling very emotional and had to force herself to speak as though nothing out of the ordinary was taking place. 'Before yer take those trousers off, let me see how much wants turning up on them. Hang on till I get me box of pins.'

'Leave a big hem on them, Ma,' Titch said, 'because at the rate he's growing they'll need to be let down in a month or so.'

'I know what I'm doing, son, I don't need no help. And I'll sit and sew them tonight, while you're off boozing with yer shipmates. If I can, I'll shorten the grey pair, as well.'

'I can't wait for me mam to see them,' Steve said, his tummy beginning to settle down. 'I know she'll be over the moon.'

'I've been thinking about that,' Aggie said, as she got down on her knees and put the pin box on the floor beside her. 'Yer'd better not let the whole street see yer carrying them, yer know what a nosy lot some of them are. So I thought it would be best if I nip down with them tomorrow while you're busy painting. I'd use the back entries so no one would see me.' She put half-a-dozen pins in her mouth, then lowered her head so she wouldn't see the doubt on Steve's face. 'Tell yer mam to leave the yard door open, there's a good lad.'

Busy pinning the hem up to the required length, Aggie reminded herself of the old saying that sometimes yer have to be cruel to be kind. Well, that's what she was doing, and she hoped Steve and his mam would come to realise that in the near future.

'Ye're a crafty one, you are, Ma,' Titch said, as he watched Steve through the net curtains. 'Yer didn't ask the lad, yer told him.'

'And what d'yer think he'd have said if I'd asked him, eh? He'd have put me off, that's what. And I'm not going to be put off. Come hell or high water, I'm going to see Olive tomorrow. If she throws me out on me backside, then so be it. But at least I would have tried.'

'It wasn't a criticism, Ma, I'm proud to have a mother who's a better actress than Norma Shearer. And better-looking than Jean Harlow.'

'If yer hadn't noticed, son, Jean Harlow has blonde hair. And her waist is about the size of the top of my arm.'

'Ah, well, there's an explanation for that. Yer see, she wears a wig. Her real hair is the same colour as yours. And she's laced tightly into a pair of stays, that's how come she looks so slim in the films.'

Aggie was busy unpicking the hem on the trousers and she stopped for a moment to look up at her son with a smile on her face. 'Oh, yer know the lady well, do yer? A friend of yours, is she?'

'We're like that, Ma.' Titch crossed two fingers. 'As thick as thieves.'

'In that case, why don't yer ask her if she wants her yard whitewashing? Steve could get away with charging her ten bob, 'cos she must be rolling in money. Stands to reason if she can afford wigs and stays. Neither of them come cheap.'

'Alas, Ma, she hasn't got a yard. All the film stars have great big houses and they stand in acres of land.' Titch managed to keep his face straight. 'Mind you, if she had a yard she'd definitely let Steve whitewash it for her, if I asked her.'

'Well, if she hasn't got a yard, where does she keep her lavvy?' That's got you, thought Aggie as the chair rocked with her laughter. 'Caught yer out there, haven't I, clever clogs?'

'D'yer know, I've never thought to ask her. I will next time I see her, though, and I'll let yer know. Interesting point, that, Ma.'

'Write it down so yer won't forget. And underneath it write "a reel of navy-blue cotton". The corner shop will have one, so yer'll be there and back in five minutes if yer don't stop to gossip to the neighbours.'

'I'm on me way, Ma, but one good turn deserves another. I know yer want to get the trousers done, but don't let that make yer late with the dinner. I'm meeting me mates at seven so I'll have to leave here, all spruced up, by half-six.'

'Your wish is my command, oh Great One. I am only on this earth to serve you.' Aggie jerked a thumb towards the door. 'Now get yer bleedin' skates on.' She heard Titch laugh as he opened the front door, and called, 'Don't come back with the wrong message or I'll make yer take it back. That's after I've tanned yer backside for yer.'

When Titch stepped into the street, it was to see Lucy standing with her arms folded listening to Rhoda, whose mouth was going fifteen to the dozen. 'Everything all right, Lucy?'

'Hello, Mr Titch.' Lucy put a hand on her friend's arm. 'Hang on a minute, Rhoda, I want to tell him something.' Lucy skipped over the cobbles. 'Rhoda came to say she was sorry, Mr Titch, and she's going to apologise to Steve when she sees him.'

'That's good. Didn't I tell yer it would all blow over? I'm on me way to the corner shop for me ma, but when I come back I want yer to come in our house for a minute. I've got something to show yer.'

Lucy rolled her big eyes and grinned. 'Ooh, er, it sounds all mysterious.'

'It's nothing to get excited about, sweetheart, just something I think yer'd like to see. By the way, did yer sleep all right last night?'

'Yeah, I slept like a log. I told me dad about what Rhoda had said, and he said not to worry it would sort itself out. So when I went to bed, instead of letting meself worry, I thought of something nice. When I finally dropped off, I was just stepping on the tram with me dad and we were on our way to town to buy a new coat for me birthday.'

'Looking forward to yer birthday, are yer?'

'Oh, yeah! As me dad says, it's not every day a girl gets to be twelve. I'm dead excited, I can't wait.'

'That's the spirit.' Titch grinned, thinking about the surprise birthday party. 'Anyway, I'll see yer when I get back from the shop. Okay?'

'I'll talk to Rhoda till yer come, then I'll go in with yer.'

'What did yer want to tell him?' Rhoda asked, when Lucy came across. 'It took yer long enough.'

'Mrs Aggie asked me to go a message for her, and I was just telling him I'd go and see her when I've finished talking to you.' It's only a white lie, Lucy consoled herself. God won't punish me for that. 'Anyway, I'm glad we're friends again, Rhoda, I didn't want to fall out with yer.' Her green eyes danced mischievously. 'After all, who could I cheat with if I didn't have you? If I cheated with anyone else there'd be more rows than enough.'

Rhoda's smile was one of relief. She'd been so miserable last night, her mam said her face had turned the milk sour. But it was over now; she'd finally plucked up the courage to apologise and Lucy had been smashing about it. 'When I see Steve I'll tell him how sorry I am. That's if I can face him after what I said.'

'Yer'll face him all right, Rhoda, and Steve isn't the type to bear grudges. Then we can all be friends again, like we should be.' Lucy saw the familiar figure walking down on the opposite side of the road, and said, 'Here's Mr Titch, I'll go and see Mrs Aggie while he's got the door open. Shall I call for yer tomorrow and we can go for a walk?'

'Make it about two. After we've had our dinner and before me mam collars me to help her wash the dishes.'

'I'll try.' Lucy stepped off the pavement waving a hand. 'If I'm late it'll be because I'm helping with our dishes.'

Titch waited for her. With a sweep of his arm, and a bow from the waist, he said, 'After you. Ladies first.'

'I'm not a lady,' Lucy giggled, 'I'm only a girl.' She was still giggling when she entered the living room to a warm welcome from Aggie.

'It's good to see yer, queen – and with a smile on yer pretty face. Not like yesterday when yer were so upset.'

'I'm all right now. Rhoda came down to say she was sorry, so we're friends again. And when she sees Steve, she's going to say sorry to him.'

'That's all water under the bridge now,' Titch got in quickly, before his mother could say something that would spoil his surprise. He cupped Lucy's elbow and drew her to the window. Lifting the net curtain, he said, 'That's what I wanted to show yer.'

'Ooh, er!' Lucy blinked to make sure she wasn't seeing things. 'Ay, Steve's making a good job of it, isn't he?'

'He sure is.' Titch left her to gaze while he tapped his mother on the shoulder and pointed to the trousers on her knee. 'Put them away,' he mouthed the words. 'Don't let her see them.'

'Can I go out and say hello to him?' Lucy asked. 'I won't stay long or put him off doing his work.'

'Of course yer can, queen.' Aggie pushed the trousers down to the side of the chair. 'He'll be made up to see yer.'

Steve wasn't made up at first, he was embarrassed. But with Lucy's pretty face wearing a huge grin, and her big green eyes dancing, he soon felt at ease. 'Have yer come to give us a hand? I'll get another brush if yer like.'

'I would if I could. But you're miles taller than me, I couldn't reach that far. I mean, look how long yer arms are to mine.'

'I could always ask Mrs Aggie for a chair for yer to stand on.'

'Oh, yeah, and I don't think!' The picture that came into Lucy's

477

mind brought forth a fit of the giggles. 'I'd spill that much paint, she'd have a chair to match her yard walls.' She gave a closer look to Steve's work and thought he was very clever. There weren't many boys of thirteen who could do the variety of jobs he did. 'Have yer only got that one wall to do now?'

'Yeah, I'll be finished in an hour or so. But it needs another coat to cover it properly so I'm coming back tomorrow.'

Lucy was in two minds whether to tell him about Rhoda, and how sorry she was. But if she did he'd think they'd been talking about him. Anyway, it was up to her friend to tell him herself. 'I better go and let yer get on with it, or Mrs Aggie will be calling me for everything for stopping the work.'

If Steve was asked who his favourite person was, after his mam, he would say Lucy. The girl always had a smile and a word for him, no matter how scruffy he looked. She always looked him in the face when she was talking to him, never at the rags he had on his back. And he would never forget that. 'Perhaps I'll see yer tomorrow?'

'Could be. If not I'll see yer in the street on Monday, after school.' Lucy got as far as the kitchen door and turned. 'Ye're doing a real good job, Steve. It'll look lovely when it's finished. Ta-ra for now.'

Aggie was standing by the kitchen sink peeling potatoes, and there was a delicious smell coming from a pan on the stove. Lucy wrinkled her nose and sniffed up. 'Ooh, that smells lovely, Mrs Aggie. It's started me tummy rumbling.'

'It's mincemeat, queen, with onions in. Titch said he felt like cottage pie, and his word is my command.'

Lucy looked closer. 'Have yer been crying, Mrs Aggie?'

'No, queen, it's the bleedin' onions, they always make me eyes water. Titch has just told me that that's how they make film stars cry in the films. They stick a bleedin' onion under their nose and the tears flow.' Aggie picked an eye out of the potato she was peeling, then threw it in a pan of water before resting her hand on the draining board. 'He's a mine of information, is Titch. If it wasn't for him I'd be as thick as two short planks. Here was me, thinking what a marvellous actress Greta Garbo was because she could cry when there was a sad bit in the picture. While all the time, she'd just had an onion stuck under her bleedin' nose. Yer see, queen, ye're never too old to learn.'

Titch came to lean against the wall. 'What's me ma saying about me now, Lucy?'

'How clever yer are, Mr Titch. That if it wasn't for you being a mine of information, she'd be as thick as two short planks.'

'Don't you believe it, sweetheart. When the day comes that I

478

can outsmart me ma, then I'll put the flags out. She might act daft, but believe you me, she's all there on top.'

'It's just as well I'm one step ahead of yer, son, or yer'd have me out of me mind, the things yer come out with.' Aggie swished the potatoes around in the pan, then emptied the dirty water off and replaced it with clean. 'Now make yerselves scarce, the pair of yer, and let me get this dinner ready in time for me one and only to go out and get plastered with his seafaring mates.'

'I better get home meself,' Lucy said. 'Me dad will wonder where I've got to. I'll see yer, Mrs Aggie, and you, Mr Titch.'

Lucy was humming as she walked through the front door she'd left open when Rhoda had beckoned her through the window. Life felt much happier than it had yesterday. Her and her mate were speaking again, Steve had a little job which would bring him a few bob to give his mam, and she had her birthday to look forward to. This time next week she'd be the proud possessor of a new coat.

'Where did you get to, pet?' Bob asked. 'Yer mam made a pot of tea and I went out looking for yer to see if yer wanted a cup.'

'I was talking to Rhoda, then I went in Mrs Aggie's.' Lucy plonked herself on the arm of his chair. 'Guess what, Dad? Steve Fletcher's painting their backyard wall, and he's making a smashing job of it.'

'Oh aye, whitewashing it, is he?'

'That's the same as paint, isn't it? Yer put it on with a brush, just the same.'

Ruby came through from the kitchen, drying her hands on the corner of her pinny. 'That's one feller I wouldn't have near me house. Apart from being filthy and probably walking alive with fleas, I wouldn't trust him as far as I could throw him. It's to be hoped Mrs McBride keeps her eye on her purse.'

Bob could feel his daughter's body stiffen, and looked up to see her face set. He pulled her down on his knee and put his arms around her comfortingly before saying, 'Ye're bang out of order saying that, Ruby. Steve Fletcher's as nice a lad as yer'll find. Because him and his mam are having a rough time, that doesn't make him a thief.'

'Go 'way, it sticks out a mile. He looks an absolute disgrace, no better than a tramp. And I think he'd nick anything he could get his hands on. He wouldn't get over my door, that's a dead cert, I'd chase him.'

Bob patted Lucy's hand to tell her not to interfere, he'd sort this matter out. 'Has anyone ever said that Steve has pinched something from them? Have yer any proof that he's a thief? Of course yer haven't. D'yer think Joe from the corner shop would let him take orders out if he wasn't honest? Or the milkman he helps? No, that boy's as honest as the day is long, and if I were you I'd be very careful what I said. Yer could find yerself in a load of trouble.'

Ruby threw her head back, a look of contempt on her petulant face. 'Yer can talk till ye're blue in the face, yer won't change what I think. He'll never set foot over my door and that's the end of it.'

'Over your door? What am I, Ruby, a flippin' lodger? No, this is still my house, it's my name on the rent book. So watch what yer say.' Bob pushed Lucy gently from his knee. He wasn't going to get involved in an argument in front of her. But he'd have plenty to say to his wife later. He'd never been as friendly with the Fletchers as Irene and George were, because of working shifts. But he remembered Jim being a fine, honest man, and Olive kind and friendly. Jim would turn in his grave if he'd heard what Ruby had said about his son. And apparently Olive was now a sick woman and couldn't help the dire straits they were in. 'Come on, pet, we'll walk to the shop and see if the *Echo*'s in yet.'

Lucy was glad to get out of the house, she felt as though she was suffocating. Holding on to her dad's hand as they walked up the street, she said, 'I don't care what she says, I like Steve and he's me friend.' Her voice choked, she went on, 'And Mrs Aggie and Mr Titch like him, they think he's a lovely lad, and a good worker. I don't know how me mam can say such terrible things about someone she's never even spoken to.'

Bob tried to appear calm, but he was anything but calm inside. His daughter had come in happy and smiling, and in a few minutes her happiness had disappeared, along with her smile. 'The trouble is, yer mam speaks before she thinks. A bit like your friend, Rhoda. So I wouldn't take much heed to what she says, pet, or get upset about it, it's not worth it. You and I know that Steve's a good lad, as do the McBrides and the Pollards. And that's all that counts in the end, isn't it? He's not without friends.'

When Lucy's answer was a deep sigh, Bob tried to cheer her up. 'Just think, pet, this time next week we'll be back from town and yer'll have yer new coat.'

This went some way towards brightening Lucy up. 'Yeah, I'm looking forward to it. I wonder what colour it'll be?'

Lucy had gone next door for a game of cards with Irene and her sons, and Bob and Ruby were getting ready for their Saturday-night drink at the corner pub. Bob was struggling with the stud at the back of his collar as he looked in the mirror, and he was telling himself that next time he bought a shirt he'd get one of the new-style ones, with the collar attached. He finally succeeded in getting the fiddling stud through the hole and gave a sigh of relief. Most of the men in the pub wouldn't have bothered with a collar and tie, they'd be wearing their silk scarves knotted over their Adam's apple. But Bob didn't go out very much so when he did he liked to make the effort.

When he turned around it was to see Ruby putting more lipstick on a mouth that already looked as though it had been slashed with a knife and was pouring with blood. 'D'yer have to put so much of that muck on? It must be an inch thick. And the bright rouge on yer cheeks makes yer look like a clown.'

Ruby pressed her lips together and looked in the hand-mirror she was holding. She twisted her head from side to side to see the effect from all angles. 'You dress as you want, and leave me to dress as I want.'

'Yer won't give an inch, will yer, Ruby? Yer'll have yer own way and it's to hell with what anybody else thinks. At least I try to be reasonable and meet yer halfway, but I'm fighting a losing battle. If it was only meself I had to think about, I'd throw me hands in the air and say to hell with everything, and let yer get on with it. But yer go out of yer way to upset Lucy, and yer do it deliberately. She can't mention any of her friends, the people she likes, without you having to say something nasty about them. And the sad thing is, I think yer get a kick out of it.'

'Sing us another one, will yer, Bob? It's the same old tune over and over again. You and yer precious Lucy. Because she likes someone, it doesn't mean I've got to. And I'm not bleedin' well going to pretend, just to please her. Yer give in to her too much, she's so soft-hearted she cries at the least thing. It's about time she toughened up.'

'Toughen up? Yer mean like you, Ruby? God forbid that she ends up as hard-boiled as you are. She's kind and caring, and I hope she stays that way. I don't want her to change in any way, I love her just as she is. And I feel sorry for you that yer can't find it in yer heart to love yer own daughter.' Bob's eyes locked with his wife's. 'You don't love her, do yer?'

Ruby turned her head. 'She's all right, but I've never had much time for kids. Not like her next door, she devotes her whole life to her two boys. She doesn't have a life of her own. Well, that wouldn't suit me one little bit. I have a life to live, too, and I intend getting the best I can out of it while the going's good. Lucy can do what she likes with hers when she's grown up.'

'A real mother helps her child to grow up. Is there when she's needed, to give advice or comfort.' Bob stared at his wife long and hard. Then he turned slowly and sat down in his chair. Crossing his legs, he said, 'I have no appetite for a drink tonight. It would be hypocritical of me to sit with you in a pub and pretend there's nothing wrong with our marriage. Not when yer've told me yer

481

have no love for our daughter and don't have one motherly instinct in yer whole body. At the moment I can't even bear to look at yer.'

'You can please yerself what yer do, but I'm not staying in on a Saturday night for you nor no one else.'

'Then go on yer own.'

'I'm not sitting on me own in that dive on the corner. It's as miserable as sin there. And yer can't expect me to sit in and look at your miserable gob all night. The least yer can do is give us a couple of bob so I can go for a drink with me mate.'

Bob leaned sideways and took some money out of his trouser pocket. He picked out a two-bob piece and flipped it towards her with his thumb.

Ruby slipped the coin in her pocket and left the room without a word. But when she'd banged the door behind her, a smile came to her face. She had two bob of her own, money she'd saved by scrimping on food. With four bob she could have a really good night out with people who knew how to enjoy themselves. For once in his life her husband had done her a favour.

Bob was in a sombre mood as he lit a cigarette and inhaled the smoke like a dying man would gasp for breath. His brown eyes were troubled as he contemplated what life held in store for him. He was only thirty-six but felt like an old man. If he lived the three score years and ten which were reckoned to be the average lifespan, it meant he had another thirty-four years to go. Could he endure those years without a woman's loving arms to find comfort in? Without a warm, happy home waiting for him after a day's work? Once Lucy grew up and married, this place would hold nothing for him – only misery.

He could hear the squeals of young laughter coming through the wall from the Pollards', and occasionally George's deep throaty roar could be heard above the others. He was a lucky man, was George, with a loving wife like Irene. It might be the men who brought the money in each week to run the house, but it was the woman who made the house into a home.

The sound of the Pollards' door banging told Bob his neighbour was on his way to the pub. And without even knowing he was going to do it, Bob leapt from his chair and rapped on the window as George came abreast. 'Hang on a minute, wait for me.'

There was surprise on George's face when Bob came out of the house alone. 'On yer own tonight, mate?'

As the men fell into step, Bob said, 'Yeah, but it's a long story. I need a pint first, then I'll bend yer ear back.'

The pub was crowded and noisy. It was pay day, the one night of the week the families could afford a few bob for a night out.

'Grab those two seats, Bob,' George said, nodding his head in the direction of two spare chairs at one of the circular tables. 'I'll get this round in.'

Bob waved and shouted greetings to the regulars he knew, but the din made it impossible for more. And it wasn't the men creating the noise, it was the women. Saturday was the only time they met socially, and there was a week's gossip to be told and savoured. As he watched the faces, Bob thought how much more expressive a woman's face was, compared to a man's. If a bloke was told that So-and-so did this or that, he would probably just raise a brow and promptly forget it. But not so the fairer sex. Their faces went through the whole range of expressions. While their heads were either nodding or shaking, their eyes would be popping out of their head, their lips would purse, their nostrils twitch and arms would be folded to hitch up their bosoms.

'Get that down yer and yer'll soon feel better.' George put Bob's pint down in front of him. 'Alec could do with help, it's murder trying to get served. I'm surprised Betty isn't down to give him a hand.'

'It's filled up early tonight, she probably doesn't know he's got a rush on.'

George picked up his glass, gazed at it with anticipation in his eyes, then took a long swig. 'I needed that,' he said, wiping the froth from his mouth. 'Me throat was parched.'

'That's with all the laughing yer've been doing, I could hear yer through the wall.'

George chuckled. 'Those kids could leave us standing, yer know, Bob. They're so quick off the mark, an answer for everything.' He studied his neighbour's face for a while, then asked, 'You and Ruby fallen out, have yer?'

'We never do anything else, George. Ruby's not easy to live with, I can tell yer. I try to keep the peace, but as I told her tonight, I'm fighting a losing battle. She went too far today though, and I just didn't want to be in her company.' He explained briefly what his wife had said about Steve. 'They were terrible things to say about the lad, and it didn't half upset Lucy. In fact, Ruby goes out of her way to upset her. The girl just has to mention one of her friends and that friend is pulled to pieces. It really worries me.'

'If she'd said that about Steve in front of me, I wouldn't half have given her a piece of my mind. They were wicked things to say and totally without foundation. The lad is no more a thief than you or me.' George would have said more, but Bob was feeling bad enough without him adding to it. 'Anyway, yer've no need to worry about Lucy. She's a sensible girl, got her head screwed on the right way. Of course she gets upset when a friend is called bad names, because she cares for them. And I'm sure yer wouldn't have her any different. She's loyal, too, and no one on God's earth will turn her against someone she's fond of. So stop worrying about her and just be proud that she's yer daughter. I know I would be.' This time, George emptied his glass in one go and set it down. 'As for Ruby, well that's between the two of yer, Bob. I know yer've had problems for a while, even a blind man could see that. And I know it's through no fault of yours. But no one can help yer there, it's something yer've got to sort out for yerself. In the meantime, have yer noticed me glass is empty?'

This brought a smile to Bob's face. 'I don't need a house to fall on me to take a hint.' He picked up the glasses and looked towards the bar. 'I see Betty's down, everyone at the bar's got a full glass in front of him. I'll be back in sixty seconds flat, with two of the same.'

'Tell Betty I said if she's feeling generous, she can put a tot of whisky in mine and I'll love her for ever more.'

Bob laughed. 'Some hope you've got.'

'Hope is what life's all about, mate. If yer lose that, what's left?'

As he watched Betty pulling a pint, Bob told himself George was right. Hope was all he had left and he'd better cling to it.

Chapter Eleven

It was eleven o'clock on the Sunday morning when Aggie carefully negotiated the step down into her yard. Over her arm was her shopping basket, the contents of which were covered over with an old cushion cover. She stopped by Steve, who had arrived an hour before and was busy applying a second coat of whitewash to the walls.

'That's a big basket for you to be carrying, Mrs Aggie.' There was a look of concern on the boy's face. 'It looks heavy, too. Shall I come and give yer a hand with it?'

'No, I'll manage fine. Look, I can carry it in front of me using both hands. I'll go down this entry, cross over at the main road, then go up your entry. There's never many people around on a Sunday morning, so I can't see meself bumping into anyone I know.' She glanced up at the back bedroom window where the curtains were still drawn over. 'Yer'll get a cup of tea when Titch decides to get out of bed. It was all hours when he came in and he's probably got a hangover.'

Steve grinned. 'Had a drop to drink, did he?'

'A drop, did yer say? I bet every pub in Liverpool has been drunk dry. Once he gets out with his mates he forgets to stop. His excuse, and he always has an excuse, will be that each one has to buy a round and his turn didn't come up till last, as per usual. And there was no way he could leave without paying his way, 'cos he'd never hear the end of it.'

'How many mates was he out with?'

'From the state he was in, I'd say about fifteen.' Aggie's face softened into a smile. 'He couldn't get the key in the door and I could hear him fumbling and cursing. Then when he finally got in, he walked into the bottom stair and fell face forwards. I did think of lighting the candle at the side of me bed and going out on the landing with it, so he could see where he was going. Then I thought, To hell with it, he's a big boy now. He got himself in that state, let him get himself out of it.'

'How did he get up the stairs in the end?'

Aggie gave another quick glance at the bedroom window. 'A secret?'

485

'Yeah, a secret. I promise.'

'On his bleedin' hands and knees, the silly bugger. And when I looked in on him this morning, he was lying on top of the bed in the clothes he'd gone out in. But don't yer say I told yer or he'll be embarrassed. And I don't mind, really, 'cos he spends more of his life on the sea than he does on dry land. So the way I look at it, he's entitled to go off the rails once in a while.'

'I agree with yer, Mrs Aggie. I know he's a good son, and I know he thinks the world of yer because he told me.'

'The feeling is mutual, lad. I love the bones of him.' Aggie patted Steve's cheek. 'I'd better get moving 'cos even with a hangover, me dear son will expect his Sunday roast dinner on the table. So I'll see yer later.'

Aggie hurried down the entry, her eyes looking straight ahead. If she did meet someone she'd have to make some sort of excuse. She couldn't say she was going to the corner shop, not when her basket was already full. She was lucky, though. She made it to the Fletchers' yard door without bumping into a soul. But she didn't open the door straight away, she stood for a while to compose herself. It wasn't often she got the collywobbles, but she had them now. What sort of reception was she going to get? 'There's only one way to find out, yer silly cow,' she muttered under her breath, 'and that's get in there.'

Olive had been watching through the back window, and when Aggie walked up the yard it was to find the kitchen door open and Olive waiting for her. 'Hello, Aggie.'

'Hello, girl.' Aggie put the basket down and held out her arms. 'Come and give an old woman a kiss.'

Safe in the warmth and comfort of Aggie's arms, Olive said, 'Titch told me about this old woman yer keep talking about. Is it anyone I know?'

Aggie chuckled. 'I only bring her into play when I'm looking for sympathy. Otherwise, I'm like a spring chicken.'

Olive bent and picked up the basket. 'Come on through, but be warned, it's no palace.'

'Oh, I thought it was, that's why I put me false teeth in.' Aggie gazed around the bare room and nodded. 'Ye're right, girl, it's no palace. But then, who the bleedin' hell wants to live in a palace? With all those servants around, yer'd never be able to soak yer feet in a bucket of nice warm water or have the tin bath out in front of the fire.'

Olive's smile turned into a full laugh. 'Oh Aggie, yer haven't changed a bit.'

'Only got older, girl, and perhaps a little wiser. But you've changed. Look at yer, there's not a pick on yer.'

'Life hasn't been kind to me, Aggie. It made me older, but not wiser.'

'Aye, well, ye're back in the fold now, one of us again. And I'm not having anyone in my gang who's as thin as a lath.' Aggie told herself she'd gone far enough for now. One step at a time was the right way in this situation. 'Anyway, I've brought the clothes for Steve. There's another pair of trousers to come, I didn't have time to turn them up last night.'

'That's all I could get out of him last night, he was full of it. He described everything in detail, the trousers, shirts, pullovers, socks, and even a pair of shoes.'

'Have a look at them for yerself, girl. They're not new, mind, but they're in good nick. Steve should get plenty of wear out of them.'

Olive put the basket on the couch and sat down beside it. When she took the cover off and saw everything all neatly ironed and folded, she shook her head as though she didn't believe what she was seeing. 'No wonder he was excited. These clothes look as though they've just been bought.'

'Some of them are years old,' Aggie said. 'Titch isn't home very often, as yer know, so he didn't get to wear them all that much and it seemed a shame to leave them lying there when they could be put to good use. And I don't know anybody better to get them to than your son. He's a fine lad, Olive, and I bet ye're proud of him.'

'I have a son in a million, Aggie, and I'm more than proud of him. Nobody will ever know the life that lad's had since his dad died.' She put her hand on top of the clothes. 'He deserves to wear clothes like this, and I'll never be able to thank yer enough. One day, please God, I'll be able to pay yer back in some way.'

'Yer've nothing to pay me back for – that clobber belongs to Titch.' Aggie gave her cheeky grin. 'Still, seeing as he's away all the time, yer can pay me back by letting me be a friend to Steve. I've really taken to the lad, and I'd be over the moon if he called in now and again for a natter. Yer see, it gets lonely when Titch is away.'

'Yer've no worries on that score, Aggie, because I think ye're stuck with Steve whether yer like it or not. He thinks you and Titch are the funniest things on two legs. I must have heard every word yer've spoken in his presence. The tricks Titch plays on yer, and the jokes and wisecracks that fly between yer. I was a bit jealous that I wasn't a fly on yer wall and could have heard it all first hand. Olive stood up and placed the folded clothes carefully on the broken-down sideboard. Then she put the basket on the floor and sat on the couch with her legs curled under her. 'I'm glad he's making friends, Aggie, he needs them. It's not healthy for a young lad to have no other company than a sick mother.'

Aggie was beginning to see what Irene had seen. Olive could only keep up the pretence of normality for so long, then she flagged. 'What sickness have yer got, Olive? What does the doctor say it is?'

'Oh, I haven't seen no doctor, we can't afford it. Anyway, he'd only tell me what I already know. Years of money worries have worn me down and the lack of good food hasn't helped. And living in this hovel would break anyone's spirit. I just haven't the strength or the will to do anything about it.'

Aggie's sympathy was mixed with impatience. 'Olive, years ago, before yer got in this mess, all yer had to do was walk down the road and knock on my door, the Pollards' or the Mellors'. We could have helped yer out. I would have minded Steve for yer while yer got yerself a job – yer should have thought of that. But all that's by the wayside now. It's the future yer should be looking to.'

'Get off me backside, yer mean, Aggie? I can't, I haven't got the strength. An hour after I get out of bed, I'm lying on this couch, drained.'

Aggie closed her eyes and sighed as she tried to think of the right words. 'Olive, would yer listen to the thoughts of an old woman?'

Olive smiled. 'Yer told me before yer were only an old woman when yer were after sympathy. So what's on yer mind?'

'There's a few things on me mind, but the main two are you and Steve. At his age he deserves some pleasure and happiness. But he can't have either because he's always worrying about you. So for his sake, if not yer own, yer should make a valiant effort to change things. Also on me mind, are the friends who want to help yer. None of them are well-off, so they can't wave a magic wand and change yer life overnight. But they can help in little ways and they'd get a kick out of doing it. And before yer tell me ye're too proud to accept our help, I'll ask yer to think of that lovely son of yours.'

Olive's eyes were guarded. 'What sort of help are yer talking about? I'll accept the clothes and be more than grateful. But I'd never accept money.'

Aggie huffed. 'Yer'd not be getting offered money, girl! What the bleedin' hell d'yer think I am? A ruddy moneylender?'

In spite of herself, Olive laughed. And memories of the old days came flooding back. Life had been good then, with so many friends and lots of good times. And she remembered in particular how Irene and Aggie had always made her laugh. You could never be downhearted when they were around, they wouldn't let you. 'I'll accept anything within reason, Aggie, except money or blows.'

Aggie rolled her eyes to the ceiling. 'At last, a glimmer of light at the end of the tunnel. I've never suffered with nerves in me life, girl, but right now yer've got me a bleedin' nervous wreck. Anyway, see what yer think of me first offer of help. And keep yer gob shut until I've had me say.' She laced her fingers across her tummy and licked her lips before starting. 'I'm making a roast dinner when I get home, and 'cos Steve's there, I was going to make enough for him. That's if Titch ever gets out of bed, like, 'cos he came in at two this morning, blind drunk. If he doesn't get up, that's his look-out. Me and Steve will share his dinner between us.' A lock of hair fell down to cover her eyes and she brushed it aside, only for it to fall again. 'Blasted nuisance. I've gone off the bleedin' track now. The way I'm going on, no one will be getting anything to eat. So I'll just rush things along, Olive, and ask would yer like some of me roast dinner? And I'll have yer know I'm noted far and wide for me crispy roast potatoes. A proper treat, they are.'

Olive asked, tongue in cheek, 'Oh, how far and wide are they known, Aggie?'

'From me front door to me back door, girl.'

'In that case, I can't refuse, can I? Not when they come with a recommendation like that. So, yes, please, Aggie. And thank you.'

Aggie jerked her head backwards. 'Blimey, anyone would think I was offering yer a dose of arsenic! If it wasn't for me false teeth falling out I'd shout for joy.'

'Aggie, you do me more good than any dinner.'

'That's as maybe, girl, but ye're still getting a dinner.' Aggie got to her feet and reached for the basket. 'I'll take this and Steve can bring it back with enough to eat for both of yer. Seeing as it's a celebration, like, I'll let him have an hour off so he can eat with yer. And I'll tell him to watch yer like a hawk, and report back to me if yer don't eat every scrap.'

'I'll do me best, I promise. And it's been lovely to see yer again, Aggie, I'm really glad yer came.' Olive lowered her eyes. 'I've been stupid, haven't I? Like yer said, I should have knocked on yer door years ago, before all the things I held dear went to the pawnshop.'

'It's no good fretting about what might have been, queen, 'cos yer can't turn the clock back. But that clock is still ticking away, taking yer into the future. And yer can do something about that. For you and Steve.'

'How was me mam?' Steve asked before Aggie had time to get through the entry door. 'Was she all right with yer?'

Aggie tilted her head. 'Yer don't see any black eyes, do yer? She was fine, lad, and as happy to see me as I was her. But she'll tell yer all about it when ye're having yer dinner. Me meat should be done by now, so I'll get the carrots and turnips on the go, and the potatoes. It'll be about an hour, then I'll fill two plates and yer can take them home and eat with yer mam, eh? How does that sound?'

Steve was already thinking of Aggie as his guardian angel, now he could almost see a halo hovering over her head. 'I don't know what to say, Mrs Aggie, except ye're a little love and a really good woman. I know me mam's going to get better now, with you and Mrs Pollard helping her. Oh, and I mustn't forget Mr Titch, he's been brilliant.'

Aggie's face did contortions. 'Has that son of mine seen light of day yet?'

Steve tried to keep a straight face but wasn't successful. 'Yeah, he came down about half an hour ago and made me a cup of tea.' He gave a throaty chuckle. 'I think he was putting it on for my benefit, but he was staggering all over the place. I would have believed he was still drunk except he didn't spill a drop of tea.'

'Never take my son at face value, lad, or yer'll come a cropper. He's the best bleedin' actor I've ever seen. The number of times I've fallen for his tricks, I must want me brains testing. I get me own back now and again, like, but I've got a sneaking suspicion it's because he lets me.' She winked broadly before making her way up the yard. 'I bet he's got a good yarn to tell me about last night, and I bet there won't be a word of truth in it. Still, I wouldn't have him any different.' She stepped into the kitchen then popped her head back out. 'Give me an hour, lad, that's all.'

Titch heard her open the kitchen door and quickly folded the *News of the World* and threw it on the couch. Then he slid forward in his chair, his legs spread out and his head in his hands. He peeped through his fingers, and it was with great difficulty he kept his face straight when his mother appeared in the doorway, shaking her head and tutting. Oh, how he loved to pull her leg, particularly as he knew she enjoyed it as much as him.

'In the name of God, will yer look at the state of him?' Aggie could see the quick rise and fall of his stomach, telling her he was laughing inside. 'If yer picked him up in the dark yer'd bloody soon drop him as soon as it was daylight.'

His voice halfway between a moan and a groan, Titch said, 'Me head is splitting and I feel sick. I won't be able to eat no dinner Ma, I'd only bring it all back.'

'That's all right, son, not to worry. It'll save me doing any extra.' She deliberately turned around slowly and made her way to the sink. Her hand went to the tap, but before she turned it on, she said, 'Olive can have your dinner.' The running water covered any reply her son might have made, but as she knew it would, her remark brought him to the door.

'Yer did it then, Ma?' Looking as sober as a judge, Titch came

490

to lean against the sink. 'Yer got in to see Olive?'

'Did yer ever have any doubts that I wouldn't?' Aggie looked down her nose as her eyebrows were raised in a haughty expression. 'Yer haven't got much faith in yer old mother, have yer?'

'I've got so much faith in yer, Ma, I've already parboiled enough potatoes for four people. And if yer eyesight wasn't failing because of yer age, like, yer'd see there's a pan of carrots and turnips boiling away happily on the stove.'

Mother and son gazed at each other, and the love that flowed between them needed no words. Aggie felt like throwing her arms around him, but knew that when she got sentimental it brought on the tears. And the last thing she wanted was for him to see her crying. He'd be legging it back to his ship before his leave was over if she bawled every time she looked at him. 'Ye're too quick for yer own good, you are. One of these days yer'll meet yerself coming back.' She placed a stiffened finger on her chin and put on a thoughtful expression. 'Mind you, if yer did meet yerself coming back, yer could ask yerself if yer'd had a good time. And if yer hadn't, then yer needn't bother going.'

Titch chuckled. 'Ay, Ma, I had quite a few pints last night. I'd need a clear head to sort that one out. But it sounds good, so it's one up to you today. That's until I'm sober, then I'll see if I can beat it. Anyway, how did yer get on with Olive?'

'Just hang on until I get me meat out of the oven, then I can put the potatoes in while the fat's hot.' Aggie took a towel from the kitchen door and was about to open the oven when her son took the towel from her.

'Stand back, Ma, let me do it.' He bent down and took out the roasting tin, sniffing up as he did so. 'That smells delicious. I see we're doing ourselves proud today with a leg of lamb.'

'That's because you're home, son. If I was on me own it would be a mutton chop.' Aggie pointed to the stack of plates on the shelf. 'Pass one down for us, there's a good lad.' While Titch held the plate, she speared the leg of lamb with a fork and transferred it over. 'Done to a turn, that is. Just the way I like it. A slice of that with a spot of mint sauce and I'll think I'm in heaven. Now you go and sit down while I set everything in motion. Then I'll make us a cuppa and tell yer how I got on.'

Ten minutes later they were sat facing each other either side of the hearth. Titch with his big cup, which Aggie always said was big enough to have a bath in, and her with a dainty china one. In her opinion, tea tasted better out of a china cup. And it was the one luxury she wouldn't do without. She only ever possessed one, and if it got broken she'd hot-foot it down to TJ's to root through their basket of seconds until she found one which was perfect except for a flaw in the pattern. 'I'm glad I've seen Olive for meself. Now I can understand what Irene was saying. It'll take more than a few hot dinners to get her back on her feet again. She made me very welcome, and was fine at first, but it didn't last long. She admitted that after she'd been out of bed an hour, she was whacked.' Aggie shook her head sadly. 'It's no wonder she's lost all her spirit – it would bring anyone down. To think of all those lovely ornaments and pictures she had, all gone to the pawnshop. And she wouldn't get much off them, yer know what pawnbrokers are like. They know the poor buggers wouldn't be there unless they were desperate, and they give yer next to bleedin' nothing for things. They probably paid Olive out in coppers for all those possessions that held her memories. And what gets me mad is, the sods know there's not much chance of people redeeming the things they put in, so yer'd think they'd give a fair price.'

'It's business, Ma. Yer can't afford to have a heart when ye're in business.'

'Aye, well, bad cess to them, I say. If I was them I wouldn't be able to rest me head on me pillow at night. I know they've got to make a living, but they don't have to fleece people who are on their uppers.'

Titch's eyes were looking over his mother's shoulder to the back window. He could see Steve busy at work and veered the conversation back to the lad's mother. 'Any ideas over Olive, Ma? I was talking to Steve when I took him his tea out, and he seems very confident you and Irene are going to work miracles with her. He's got in his head she'll soon be up and about.'

'I'm not making any promises, son, 'cos that wouldn't be fair. If Olive can be helped at all, then there's a few of us will be there for her. But I'm no doctor – I don't know whether she's let herself go down so much there's no turning back.' Aggie stopped the rocking motion of the chair and stood up. 'I'm nipping to Irene's after dinner, and we'll see what the two of us can come up with between us. But right now me potatoes must be browning nicely and I don't want them too crisp.' She bent to smile into her son's face. 'After all, me reputation is at stake here. I've been blowing me trumpet to Olive about me roasties being the best she'll ever taste, so I'd never hear the last of it if she ends up with a plate of burnt offerings.'

'It would be the price of yer, though, Ma, for bragging. Ye're always telling me yer can't stand bigheaded people who never stop bragging.'

'Yeah, but I didn't mean meself, son, I meant everybody else. I'm not daft enough to call meself bigheaded when I know I'm not. Shame on yer, son, for thinking that of yer poor old mother. I'm hurt to the quick, I really am.' With that, Aggie flounced out to the kitchen before allowing a smile to crease her face.

Steve placed the basket carefully on the table. 'I've carried it straight all the way, Mam, and Mrs Aggie packed some newspapers down the side, so I don't think any of the gravy will have spilled out.' His pleasure and excitement was such, Olive felt she could stretch her hand out and touch it. 'I've had this wonderful smell wafting up me nose all the way home and me mouth is watering.'

Olive slipped her legs over the side of the couch. She didn't have any appetite, never did these days because usually there was nothing to eat. And after a while your tummy got accustomed to not eating and didn't send out the hunger pangs. But for her son's sake she would eat the meal Aggie had sent down, even if she had to struggle. 'You get the knives and forks, son, and I'll take the plates from the basket.'

'I'll do it, Mam, you stay where yer are.'

'This is one day I'm sitting at the table to eat, Steve. If I don't do the thing proper, Aggie will have me guts for garters. And I don't want it to get cold, not after her going to all the trouble. So hurry up, sweetheart.'

When Steve came back from the kitchen it was in time to see his mother taking the covering plates off. And they stood together and gazed down at the slices of lamb, mounds of carrots and turnips, and the crispy potatoes. 'That looks and smells really good,' Olive said. 'I just hope I can do it justice.'

'Yer will, Mam, once yer get started. Even if yer don't eat it all, do yer best.' He gave a start as he remembered something and pushed a hand into his pocket. 'I almost forgot! Mrs Aggie gave me this little bottle with mint sauce in. She said to tell yer the bottle had been well washed and that she wasn't trying to poison yer.'

Olive pulled out a chair. 'Come on, son, let's get stuck in.' As she sat down she gave a half-smile. 'It's a wonder the table doesn't collapse with shock. It's the first time in years there's been a proper dinner on it.'

'Things are going to get better, though, Mam, I know they are.'

'I'm sure they are, love, I'm sure they are.'

Watching anxiously as his mother picked at her food, Steve asked, 'Yer will let them help yer, won't yer, Mam? Yer won't send them away?'

'Of course I won't send them away, that would be unkind and ungrateful. And I'll let them help us until we get on our feet.

That's as long as I know they're not going without themselves, just to give to us.'

Steve suddenly burst out laughing. 'What yer've just said reminded me of Mrs Aggie, and I know what her answer would be if she heard yer saying that. Mr Titch asked her for something yesterday, and what she said didn't half tickle me.' He pushed his chair back and jumped to his feet. 'Pretend I'm her and I'll show yer how she said what she did.' Steve's hands folded over his tummy and his head tiltted. ' "I haven't got none, son. And if I haven't got none, I can't give yer none. I mean, it stands to sense doesn't it? If I held me hand out, palm upwards, and there was nothing on it, then I couldn't give yer nothing off it, could I?" ' He was delighted when he heard his mother chuckle. He took his seat and picked up his knife and fork. 'Honest, Mam, they're both a treat to listen to.'

'What did Titch say to that?'

Steve was laughing so much it took a while to compose himself. 'Mr Titch said, "If I had nothing, Ma, I'd still give yer half of it." Then Mrs Aggie said, "That's bleedin' generous of yer, I must say. But if it's all the same to you, son, I'll wait until yer've got something and then I'll have half of it." '

Olive was shaking with laughter. 'They haven't changed a bit – they could always make a joke out of nothing.' She looked down at her plate. 'I know yer've been told to watch me like a hawk and report back, so we'll stop talking for a while and eat this delicious dinner.'

'That's right, Mam, get it down yer. It'll do yer the world of good.'

Aggie took the plates out of the basket and asked, 'Did yer wash these, lad, or lick them clean?'

'Both, Mrs Aggie. I licked and me mam washed. She ate every bit as well, and she told me not to forget to tell yer that. It was lovely and we didn't half enjoy it.'

'It does me heart good to hear that, lad, it really does. There's enough lamb over for tomorrow, so give us a knock when yer've finished yer little job at the corner shop and see what I've got ready for yer. I might go down and see yer mam during the day, but although Titch will have his Sunday roast at midday, he flatly refuses through the week. So you'll have to come up for it.'

'It suits me, Mrs Aggie, I like coming here.' Steve was hopping from one foot to the other, unable to contain his excitement. 'I'll be wearing me long trousers tomorrow, and one of the shirts and pullovers. Yer won't know me when yer see me.'

'In that case, yer'd better introduce yerself in case I mistake yer

494

for the landlord.' Aggie smiled and patted his cheek. 'You get on with what yer've got to do, lad, 'cos I'm going up to the Pollards' for a natter. Titch is having forty winks, so if he wakes up, tell him where I've gone. He's like a fish out of water on a Sunday, with the pubs being shut.'

'Think of the money he's saving, Mrs Aggie.'

'He doesn't see it like that. As he says, money is round to go round. And God knows he tries to spread as much of it around as he can. He can't get rid of it quick enough.' Aggie peeped through the side of the living-room door. 'He's well away, so I'll go out the back to save banging the front door. I'll be back before yer've finished, to pay yer.'

Steve hung his head. 'I wish I could say I don't want nothing for doing it, 'cos yer've been so good to me. But we need the money, Mrs Aggie.'

'Ay, lad, yer've done a job and yer want paying for it, same as any man would. So don't be going all soft-hearted, yer can't afford it. And I'm on me way now, before the queer feller wakes up. I'll see yer later.'

Irene was at the sink washing the dinner dishes when Aggie walked up the yard. 'Yer pick yer time, don't yer, sunshine? Ten minutes earlier and yer could have helped me with the dishes. I think yer've got second sight.'

'I'll dry them for yer, save yer moaning.' Aggie reached for the tea towel. 'I sent a roast dinner down to Olive, and she ate the lot.'

'Go 'way!' Irene rested her dripping hands on the sink. 'Ay, that's a good sign, isn't it? Apart from getting some goodness down her, it means she's willing to let us help.'

'I think there's a few ways we can help that won't cost anything and will brighten the place up. God knows, it needs something doing to it, it's like a bleedin' morgue. A couple of days stuck in there and I'd be ga-ga.'

Irene grinned at her neighbour's way of putting things. 'The boys are out so we can sit and talk in peace when we've finished these. George has already read the paper from front to back so he'll be glad of someone to talk to.'

'Oh, he won't be talking to me, girl, it'll be the other way round. He's going to sit and listen to what I've got to say first, then he can put his twopennyworth in.'

They heard the rustling of paper, then George's voice boomed. 'I heard that, Aggie McBride. Don't yer be coming here throwing yer weight around. On the Sabbath, too!'

Aggie put the last plate on the shelf before hanging up the towel. 'Ye're going to listen to me whether yer like it or not, George

Pollard. I'm pulling rank here, being the oldest, like, and the one with the most sense.'

Irene finished drying her hands and pushed Aggie through the living-room door. 'If you two are going to argue, at least do it in the same room.'

'Argue? Me, argue!' Aggie looked hurt to the quick. 'Me, what's as quiet as a mouse and as timid as a rabbit? Well, that's a new one on me.'

Irene pulled a chair out and motioned for her neighbour to sit down. 'Would yer like to take yer wings off first, sunshine, so they won't stick in yer back?'

'I left them at home, queen, 'cos I didn't want yer to feel inferior.' Aggie chuckled before sitting down and becoming businesslike. 'Olive said she'll accept any help except money. Now there's a few little jobs that want doing that will only need a couple of nails. One is the sideboard cupboard that's hanging on one hinge. The other hinge is still on, but the screws are missing. It wouldn't take a man two minutes to fix that. And the drawer that's missing, I noticed it standing up under the stairs, with the handle beside it. That would be another two-minute job.' She looked at George. 'Those two things alone would improve the appearance of the room. Yer can't expect Steve to know what to do, he's only a lad. And when he's not at school he spends most of his time trying to earn a few coppers. So are yer still prepared to help, George?'

'Of course I am. And I know someone else who'd pitch in, and that's Bob from next door. Yer'd be doing him a favour by asking, 'cos sometimes I think he'd like to get out of the house for a while.' George pushed himself out of the chair. 'Just hang on, Aggie, and I'll give him a knock. More hands make light work, and he knows Olive and Steve.'

Bob was indeed glad to get away from the house. Lucy was out with Rhoda and the place was like a graveyard with never a word passing between him and his wife. He'd been in bed last night when Ruby came in after midnight, reeking of drink. The pubs closed at ten o'clock so she must have gone back to someone's house. He'd been so disgusted he intended to have it out with her this morning, but changed his mind in the light of day. What was the use, it wouldn't achieve anything.

Aggie gave him a smile of welcome. 'How's the world treating yer, Bob?'

'So-so, Aggie, I can't complain.' Bob had only been in the room a matter of seconds but already he felt a different man. What a change it was to see smiling faces and know those smiles were genuine. 'And yerself and Titch? Are yer both okay?'

'I'm fine, but I can't speak for me son. He was out on a bender

496

last night and I've left him sleeping it off on the couch. He never tells me anything about where he goes, and I don't ask. But I've no doubt you and George will hear all about it.' Aggie laced her fingers and rested them on her knee. 'We're having a conflab about Olive, and George said you wouldn't want to be left out.' She quickly brought him up to date on the situation. 'So, d'yer want to join our gang, Bob?' Before he could answer, she held up her hand. 'There's something yer should know before yer decide. I'm the gaffer, and I'm a hard taskmaster. If yer step out of line, yer get punished. Yer'll have to write out a hundred lines saying, "Aggie is the boss". So speak now or forever hold yer peace.'

'Yer can be my boss any day, Aggie.'

'Right, let's get down to business then.'

Chapter Twelve

'Will you stop running in and out every minute?' Ruby grabbed hold of Lucy's wrist and held it in a vice-like grip. 'Ye're getting on me nerves and yer'll know it if I lose me temper.'

'I only want to know the time.' Lucy didn't meet her mother's eyes. It was her birthday but it had never been mentioned. There'd been a card for her this morning with both her parents' names on, but the girl knew it was her dad who bought the card and wrote the greeting. He'd left it propped up on the mantelpiece before he went to bed after finishing his night shift. Lucy had thanked her mother because her name was on it, but all she got in reply was a grunt. 'Me dad said he'd get up about one o'clock to take me into town and I thought I'd get meself ready about twelve. I want to look clean and tidy for him.'

'Listen to me, yer selfish little faggot. The world doesn't stop because it's your birthday, even though yer seem to think it should.' Ruby was giving vent to a temper that had been building up all morning. Every time she thought of the money that was going to be spent on her daughter today, she could scream. 'I don't want to see yer in here again until yer dad's up, d'yer hear?' Her grip tightened and Lucy winced with the pain. 'I said, did yer hear me?'

'I heard yer, Mam. Will yer let go of me hand now, please, 'cos ye're hurting me.'

'It's nothing to what I'd like to do to yer. Ye're nothing but a spoilt little brat.' Ruby gave one last squeeze before releasing her grip. 'Now, get out of me sight.'

Lucy stood by the front door, squared her shoulders and put a smile on her face before running to join Rhoda. 'Me dad's not up yet, so we can have another game.'

Rhoda was bursting with excitement. She'd been invited over to the McBrides' to a tea-party, but had been sworn to secrecy. She hadn't got to say a word to Lucy or the Pollard boys. And she was finding it very hard to keep the secret. 'What time are yer going into town?'

'About half-one to two o'clock. Whenever me dad's ready.

Don't forget he's been on night shift, so he needs some sleep.'

'But yer'll have to be back for four o'clock.' Rhoda nearly bit her tongue off. She shouldn't have said that, she nearly gave the game away. 'What I mean is, yer'll be back about four, won't yer? I don't want to have to wait until tomorrow to see yer new coat.'

'Oh, don't worry about that.' Lucy managed to put her hurt and sadness aside. 'I'll be swanking up and down the street in it, yer won't be able to miss me.'

'Ye're lucky, you are. I wanted a coat for me birthday but me mam said the two I've got will last me a while, 'cos there's not a break in them.'

'She's right, too! Yer've got a lovely mam, Rhoda, and it's not often she says no to yer. Yer've got more clothes than any other girl in the street.'

Something caught Rhoda's eye. 'Yer dad's outside your door, Lucy, and he's waving like mad.'

Lucy's face lit up. 'He got up early! I've got a lovely dad, Rhoda, I'm very lucky.' She gave her friend a grin before turning to cross the cobbled street. 'I'll see yer later. Ta-ra.'

Bob swept her up in his arms. 'How's my birthday girl?'

'I'm very happy, Dad.' Lucy grinned down into his face, thinking how lost she'd be without him and his love. 'Ye're up early.'

'Yeah, well, by the time we get ready it'll be one o'clock. And we don't want to be rushed into buying a coat, do we?' He set her down and they walked into the house arm-in-arm. 'We have to be sure yer get one yer really like.'

'We will, Dad, I know we will.' Lucy put a hand over her heart. 'I've got a feeling in here that I'm going to see a coat and fall head over heels in love with it.'

'I hope so, pet. Anyway, yer mam's made a pot of tea, we'll have a drink and then get ourselves ready.'

'I'll use the sink first to get washed, Dad, so yer won't have to wait. Then I'll have me drink before I get changed into me best dress.'

The tea had cooled down by the time Lucy had washed, and she was able to drink it quickly. She didn't want to be alone in her mother's company because she knew there'd be sarcastic comments passed, and she didn't want anything to mar her birthday. It should be a day of happiness and she was determined it would be. To prove her intention, she hummed as she changed into her maroon dress and combed her dark curly hair until it shone.

'Yer look as pretty as a picture, pet,' Bob said, bending his arm for her to link. 'Let's go and search the town for a coat that looks as good as you do.'

500

Ruby didn't even come out of the kitchen to see them off. She didn't trust herself to keep her thoughts to herself. And a few wrong words now could jeopardise the increase in her housekeeping she was relying on to start next week.

When they were passing the Pollards' house, Lucy said, 'I thought Mrs Pollard would have come out to wish me a happy birthday. She said last night she hadn't forgotten it and she'd see me today.'

'The day's not over yet, pet, so give her time. Yer know she works for a couple of hours in the mornings, then she's got the shopping and dinner to get ready.' Bob thought of the surprise in store for his daughter and it gladdened his heart. It wasn't often anything nice came her way.

'Yeah, ye're right, Dad.' Lucy mentally scolded herself for being selfish. Mrs Pollard had been really good to her. Every other day she'd changed the dressing on leg, and last night when she was taking the pad off, she'd said it was better now and didn't need covering any more. 'I'll give her a knock and show her me new coat. And Mrs Aggie and Mr Titch.'

'Then we'd better make sure yer get a posh one, eh?'

Lucy giggled. 'It doesn't have to be posh, Dad, just nice.'

The assistant in Blackler's couldn't have been more helpful if Bob had said price was no object. But he hadn't. He told her the truth, that four pounds was the limit.

The assistant held out her hand. 'Come with me, Miss, and we'll look along the rails and see if anything takes your eye. Your father can sit down while he's waiting.'

The first and second rails held nothing that Lucy liked. It was while the assistant was taking one from the third rail, that a colour caught her eye. 'Could I have a look at that one, please?'

The coat, in deep cherry red, was brought out for her inspection. It had a pointed collar, slanted pockets, revers that could be turned up to fasten at the neck for warmth, and there were five cherry-red buttons fastened down the middle. 'I like that one, I think it's lovely.'

The assistant looked at the price tag. 'I'm afraid this one is four shillings more than your father said he could go up to. Shall I go and ask him?'

'No, don't do that, please. I'm very lucky to be getting a coat and I shouldn't be greedy. Shall I try that navy blue one on? That looks nice.'

When Lucy came out of the fitting room wearing the navy-blue coat, Bob tried to be enthusiastic but he didn't think it suited her. It was serviceable all right, and wouldn't show the dirt, but it was dull and made Lucy look dull. 'Are yer sure that's the one yer want, pet?'

'Yes, I like it, Dad.'

But the assistant thought the same as Bob. The coat was too dowdy for such a pretty girl. So forgetting the rule that the customer was always right, she made a try. 'There was another coat your daughter really liked, but unfortunately it was four guineas.'

'I like this one just as much, Dad,' Lucy cried, not wanting her father to feel she was getting second-best. 'Honest, I do!'

Bob knew his daughter too well to believe her. He had intended treating her to tea and cakes at Reece's, and then a trip on the ferry. If they did without the cakes and the ferry, he could just about manage the extra four shillings. 'Let me see yer in the other coat, pet.'

The assistant was away like a shot, tugging Lucy after her. And the girl who came out of the fitting room was a different girl altogether. The colour suited her down to the ground, bringing out the rosy blush of her cheeks and highlighting her shining hair. And her stance and bright green eyes told how much she enjoyed the fit and feel of the coat.

'That's the one, pet,' Bob said, swallowing the lump in his throat. 'That's the one yer knew yer were going to fall head over heels in love with. It's a beauty, like yerself.'

The assistant breathed a sigh of relief. She wouldn't have slept tonight if the girl hadn't got the coat she wanted. And it really looked as though it had been made for her. 'Is she having this one, sir?'

Bob nodded, waving Lucy's objections aside. 'I'd like you to wrap her old one up and let her keep that one on. It's her birthday, yer see.'

'And it's a lovely birthday present. But I'll have to take it off her to take to the counter. Once it's paid for, and you have a receipt, she can change into it.'

'Here yer are, pet.' Bob took hold of Lucy's hand and counted out four pound notes and a ten-shilling note. 'Ye're a big girl now, you go with the lady and pay. And don't forget I want me change.'

Lucy felt as though she was floating on a cloud. 'I know, Dad, yer want six shillings change.' She bent and whispered in his ear, 'This will open a few eyes, eh, Dad? I'll be the talk of the street.'

Bob grinned. 'And the washhouse, no doubt. In fact, I'll be disappointed if ye're not the talk of the whole flippin' neighbourhood.'

When Lucy came back to where he was sitting, dressed in her finery and carrying a bag with her old coat in, Bob thought he had never seen her look so pretty or happy. 'I'm very proud of yer, pet, and the luckiest man alive to be yer father.'

'It's me what's the lucky one.' Lucy linked his arm, then dropped it to wave a thank you to the assistant who was watching them leave with a huge smile on her face. 'She was awful nice, Dad.'

'Yes, she was. Very kind and helpful.'

When they stepped from Blackler's into Elliot Street, Bob pulled her to a halt. 'Now comes the bad news, pet. I intended to take yer for tea and cakes, then a trip on the ferry, as a treat. But I can't afford that now or I won't have the tram fare home. So how about a walk down to the Pier Head, just to watch the ferries coming and going? It's very interesting, lots of hustle and bustle, and it'll pass an hour away.' He'd had strict instructions to stay out until four o'clock. Then on the dot of the hour, he was to knock on Aggie's door. 'It'll blow the cobwebs away, too, 'cos it's always nice and fresh by the river.'

'I'd like that, Dad. I'll be able to swank in me new coat.'

'Come on, then, let's go. Give me that bag to carry, it's too heavy for you.'

When they stepped off the tram, Bob glanced in the pawnshop window at the big round clock on the wall. Five minutes to four – he couldn't have timed it better. Walking at a steady gait, they'd be knocking at Aggie's dead on the hour.

'Shall we call at the McBrides' and let them see yer birthday present?'

'Oh, yeah! Mrs Aggie won't half get a surprise when she sees me. She won't be expecting me to be wearing the most beautiful coat in the whole world.'

But it was Titch who opened the door. And being Titch, he was able to hide his surprise and keep a straight face. 'Hello, young lady. I think yer've come to the wrong address, 'cos I've never seen yer in this street before. Have yer lost yer way, dear?'

This brought forth peals of laughter from Lucy. 'Don't be daft, Mr Titch. I know I look different in me new posh coat, but not that different.'

Titch slapped an open palm on his forehead. 'Well, blow me down, if it isn't little Lucy Mellor! And in the poshest coat I've ever seen. Yer'd better come in and let me ma see yer. She'll have to put her glasses on to make sure she's not seeing things.' He stepped back and bowed her in, winking broadly at Bob as he followed.

'It's only me, Mrs Aggie,' Lucy called as she walked to the living room. 'I've come to show off me new coat.' She stopped on the threshold, her eyes and mouth wide. The room seemed to be full of people. Apart from Mrs Aggie, there was Mr and Mrs Pollard with Jack and Greg, Rhoda and Steve. And as she wondered why they were all there, it flashed through her mind that Steve looked more posh than she did.

Titch pushed his way past her and raised his two hands as though he was conducting an orchestra. 'Right, everyone in tune, now.' And suddenly the rafters were ringing with voices wishing Lucy a happy birthday. She was dumbstruck at first, until her father put his arm around her waist and hugged her as he sang his head off. Then joy and excitement replaced the shock and her face beamed with sheer delight and pleasure. What a wonderful day it was turning out to be!

When the singing finished, Lucy found herself being kissed and hugged while birthday cards were pressed into her hand. And she got a parcel off Mrs Pollard, who said it was a present from her and Mrs Aggie, one off Rhoda, and another from Steve. The lad looked so embarrassed as he explained it wasn't much, but the thought was there.

Lucy grinned at him. 'Yer've stolen me thunder, you have, Steve Fletcher. Yer look posher than I do in yer long trousers.'

Aggie saw the lad blushing to the roots of his hair and was quick to stand beside him. No one, except her and Titch, knew where the clothes had come from. 'He's been working hard and saving hard, queen. And doesn't he look the young gentleman?'

'He certainly does.' Lucy eyed him up and down. 'He looks very smart.'

Rhoda pushed her way to her friend's side. 'I told Steve he looked nice, Lucy.' She had her eyes on her friend's coat and was green with envy. She might have two coats, but neither of them was a patch on Lucy's.

Lucy was bewildered. She gazed around the smiling faces and was lightheaded with happiness. All her best friends were here. But how did it come about? 'Mrs Aggie, how come they're all in your house?'

'It's all Titch's doing, queen, not mine. Not only is it your birthday, but for Jack, here, it's a big day in his life. He's no longer a schoolboy, but a young gentleman setting out in life. So my son decided we couldn't let the day go by without a celebration. So a small tea-party is his present to both of yer.'

Lucy ran to put her arms around Titch. 'Oh, thank you, Mr Titch. Ye're not a little love, ye're a big one.'

'It's my pleasure, sweetheart. And might I say how elegant yer look in yer new coat? It really is a knock-out.'

There were shouts of approval and praise, causing Lucy to blush

504

with shyness. 'I feel daft, now. A real show-off.'

'Seeing as we're sharing this day,' Jack said, feigning disgust at the fuss over Lucy, 'what about me? I'm standing here in me new long kecks, and not a peep out of yer.'

'How was I to know, soft lad, when ye're hiding behind the table? Come and stand next to me and we can both look posh and swank together.' When he was beside her, her eyes travelled the length of him. 'Jack Pollard, you are a very, very handsome lad.'

'Yeah, I know. I was told that before I left the house.'

'Oh, aye,' Irene said, her eyebrows raised. 'Who told yer that?'

'The mirror in your bedroom wardrobe.' Jack stuck his two hands in his pockets, feeling very grown up. 'I was standing in front of it, weighing meself up in me long kecks, and the mirror spoke to me. It said, "Jack Pollard, ye're a very, very handsome lad." And as yer know, Mam, mirrors don't lie.'

George chuckled before saying, 'Self-praise is no recommendation, son.'

'But I told him he was handsome, Mr Pollard,' Lucy said. 'And that's not self-praise.'

'So yer did, sweetheart, so yer did. And seeing as he's me son, I can't contradict yer, can I?' Me dear wife would give me the rounds of the kitchen if I did.'

Aggie squared her shoulders and became businesslike. 'I'm going to throw you out now, George, and you, Bob, so I can start setting the table. And as Lucy is the only one who doesn't know what's going on, I'll tell her. The tea-party is only for the youngsters. Then at seven o'clock they're all being packed off to the Pollards' to play cards, so the grown ups can have a knees-up, jars out, booze-up.'

Bob put a finger under Lucy's chin and raised her face. 'Enjoy yerself, pet, and I'll see yer at seven o'clock.'

'Is me mam coming to the party with yer?'

'As far as I know, she is.'

Lucy laid her cards and presents on the couch. 'Will yer take me coat home with yer, Dad? And will yer put it on a hanger so it doesn't get creased?'

Bob took the coat from her and jerked his head at George. 'Come on, mate, before Aggie throws us out.' He was halfway down the hall, with George behind him, when Steve caught up with them.

'Mr Mellor, I want to thank yer for doing those jobs for me mam. I really am grateful.'

'Think nothing of it, Steve, it was only half an hour's work. I was glad to be able to help, and as I'm on the early shift next week, I'll nip up one day and fix that loose shelf in the kitchen for her.

They're only little jobs, but every little helps, as they say.'

George waited until he and Bob were on the pavement so their voices wouldn't carry. 'There's a lot we could do for yer mam, but we don't want to rush things. Ye're a sensible lad, and I know yer'll understand that if we try to do too much, yer mam won't like it and we'll be back to square one. So we'll take things slow and easy.'

'I do understand, Mr Pollard. But she seems to be brighter now that people are calling to see her. And she eats the dinner that the ladies take down to her every day. Yer've all been so kind, I really don't know how to thank yer. Mr Mellor says the jobs he did were nothing, but they've made a difference to the house.' Steve grinned. 'The sideboard looks like a sideboard now, not a heap of scrap. And I'm not banging me leg against the broken door like I used to. Anyway, I just wanted to say thanks.'

'We're here any time yer want us,' Bob said. 'Just remember that.'

'Can I open me presents now, Mrs Aggie?' Lucy shouted through to the kitchen where there was a lot of activity going on. 'And me cards?'

'Of course yer can, queen.' Aggie put the last jelly cream on a plate and rubbed her hands down the side of her pinny. ''Cos I'm a nosy bugger, we'll take a five-minute break to see what yer've got.'

Lucy's face was a joy to behold as she read out the verses in each card and the name of the sender. 'Six birthday cards, aren't I lucky?' Each card was put back in its envelope so she could take them home and treasure them. Then she opened the present from Aggie and Irene and let out a squeal of delight at the sight of the pale pink underskirt. 'Oh, it's lovely, thank you so much.' She'd never owned an underskirt before, not since she was a toddler, anyway. 'I'll take really good care of it and only wear it for best.'

Rhoda's present was a perfumed tablet of Lux soap and a cream-coloured flannel. Lucy closed her eyes as she held the soap to her nose. 'Thank you, Rhoda, I'll smell lovely when I get washed with this.'

Steve was dreading her opening his present. It was a tuppenny slab of Cadbury's chocolate, all he could afford. It seemed so cheap compared to the other two presents. But to Lucy it meant just as much. 'Ooh, me favourite chocolate! Thank you very much, Steve. And don't be put out if I don't offer to share it 'cos I'm going to be real tight with it. One square every night in bed and it'll last me nearly all week.'

The knots in Steve's tummy began to relax. He'd been expecting to see a look of disappointment of Lucy's face, but she'd welcomed his cheap gift with the same enthusiasm as the others. And he vowed that next year he'd buy her an extra nice present. He'd be working then, and money wouldn't be as tight. With a bit of luck his mam might be well enough to take on a light job and they'd be quids in.

Lucy's eyes grew wider as Aggie and Irene carried plate after plate through. There were sausage rolls, boiled ham and corned beef sandwiches, colourful jelly creams, iced fairy cakes, crackers with cheese on top and a sponge sandwich cake on a glass stand with a fancy doily underneath. 'Doesn't everything look lovely?'

'It sure does,' Jack said, rubbing his tummy. 'Can yer hear it rumbling? And me mouth's watering that much I'm dribbling.'

Steve was feeling the same symptoms. He couldn't remember seeing a table so heavily laden with such fare. 'Mrs Aggie doesn't do things by half.'

Greg was sitting facing the back window and he suddenly burst out laughing. 'Neither does Mr Titch. He's just coming up the yard lugging a crate of ale. If there isn't high jinks here tonight, I'll eat my hat.'

His brother shook his head. 'Greg, yer haven't got a hat.'

'I know that, soft lad. Yer don't think I'd be daft enough to say I'd eat it if I had one, do yer? I'd have to be barmy.'

Rhoda thought it was about time she got a word in. They'd think she didn't have a tongue in her head. 'I've always said yer were barmy, Greg Pollard.'

'Well, you should know, Rhoda Fleming, seeing as ye're barmy yerself. They say it takes one to know one.'

Aggie came through from the kitchen, minus her pinny. 'Right, kids, take yer seats at the table and get stuck in. The barmy ones on this side, Lucy and Jack on the other, and me and Steve at either end. So help yerselves to whatever takes yer fancy. Titch will be bringing yer some lemonade in, unless yer'd prefer tea.'

The vote for lemonade was unanimous. After all, they could get tea any time. And when Titch carried a tray of glasses through, he brought coloured paper hats with him. 'Get them on yer heads and let's do the thing in style.'

'Isn't Mrs Pollard coming in to join us?' Lucy asked.

'No, queen, she's slipped home the back way. She's going to put her feet up for an hour because she's been on the go all day. But she'll be back later to give me a hand with the washing-up.'

'I'll wash up for yer, Mrs Aggie,' Steve said, putting the brown paper hat on his head. 'There's no need for Mrs Pollard to come back. She may as well have a rest and be ready for the party tonight.'

'I'll help with the dishes,' Lucy said. 'It won't take long.'

507

Rhoda thought it would look bad if she didn't offer. 'I'll help, too.'

Jack gave his brother a dig in the ribs. 'Go on, say something.'

Greg grinned. 'What would yer like me to say?'

'That yer'll give a hand to clear up.'

The grin was replaced by a bulldog expression. 'Why don't you offer to give a hand? I don't see anyone holding yer back.'

'I've got me long kecks on, haven't I? And if I get a mark on them me mam will have a duck egg. That's after she's kicked me into the middle of next week.'

Greg considered this piece of information. 'I've a good mind to drop this jelly cream on yer lap. It would be worth it to see me mam lay a duck egg. And the thought of you being kicked into the middle of next week is very tempting.'

'I'll tell yer what,' Jack said, a twinkle in his eye. 'You help Mrs Aggie and I'll leave yer these long kecks in me will. And I'll even leave yer the braces to keep them up. Now I can't be fairer than that, and ye're not likely to get a better offer.'

Greg looked at Aggie while jerking his head at his brother. 'How long d'yer think he's good for, Mrs Aggie?'

'Ooh, let's see now.' She rubbed her chin thoughtfully. 'I'd say, at a guess, he's got at least sixty, seventy years.'

'I'm not hanging around that long for a pair of kecks that will have been eaten by the moths.' Greg patted Jack on his shoulder. 'Sorry, pal but the only way ye're getting out of helping with the dishes is by breaking a leg. I could arrange that for yer if ye're desperate.'

Lucy's giggling attracted their attention. 'You two don't half look daft with yer paper hats hanging down over yer eyes. And while ye're arguing the toss, we're eating all the goodies.'

Jack glared at his brother. 'See what yer've done? Why d'yer have to talk so much?' He reached out and took a jelly cream in one hand and a fairy cake in the other. 'Honest, ye're like a flippin' parrot what's been living with that Mrs Gibson for a few years.'

This brought forth howls of laughter. Mrs Gibson lived at the very top of the street. She was a thin wiry woman who waved her arms about when she was speaking and her mouth was in constant motion. She lived on her own and because she had no one in the house to talk to, she made up for it by standing at her front door and gossiping to everyone who passed. And once she had you in her clutches she hung on tight. No one knew where she got her information from, but everything that happened in the surrounding streets was known by Mrs Gibson. And she was always willing to pass it on to anyone who would stand and listen to her. The trouble was, she went all around the world to tell you something

508

and people didn't always have the time.

Aggie wiped the laughter tears away. 'We shouldn't be mocking the poor soul, she's harmless enough. Just a lonely old woman, that's all.'

'Yes, she's all right, really,' said Steve, who only lived a few doors from Mrs Gibson. 'She's always got a smile for yer.' Then he couldn't keep the grin back. 'Mrs Aggie, I'm not making fun of her, honest. But have yer ever noticed that people stop just before they get to her house, take a deep breath and then make a run for it?'

Titch, who'd been leaning his elbows on the sideboard, straightened up. 'I've done that meself, son, I've got to admit. She's a nice woman, but by God can she talk! I was coming home on leave one day, with me rucksack over me shoulder, when she stopped me. And I couldn't get a word in edgeways. D'yer know, me leave was up before I could shut her up? I had to turn right around and go back to the ship without even seeing me ma.'

Oh, how Jack was enjoying this. He thrived on laughter. 'Were they only giving yer a few hours' leave, that trip, Mr Titch?'

Titch shook his head solemnly. 'No, son, I had ten days' leave due to me.'

Rhoda gaped. She wasn't used to the McBride and Pollard humour and had taken Titch seriously. 'That's terrible, that is. Yer should have told her. I know I would have done.' She couldn't make out why this brought forth more laughter. But so she wouldn't look daft, she laughed along with them. What she had succeeded in doing though, was to convince Greg that she was indeed barmy.

By seven o'clock every dish had been washed and the place tidied. All done by the youngsters, who made Aggie sit with her feet up. They'd had the time of their lives and it was their way of saying thank you to her and Titch. And the day wasn't over for them, they'd enjoy themselves playing games in the Pollards'. But Steve was worried about leaving his mother for so long.

'Mrs Aggie, I'll have to nip home and see how me mam is. I wouldn't enjoy meself if I didn't know she was all right.'

'I'm on me way down there right now, lad, so yer've no need to worry. I'm taking her a plate of sandwiches and cakes, seeing as she couldn't come to the party. But if I think there's the least thing wrong, I'll let yer know. Yer have me promise on that.'

Chapter Thirteen

'I can't stay long, girl, 'cos as yer know, our Titch has invited a few friends in for a drink.' Aggie placed the plate on the table and was heartened to see Olive's eyes showing appreciation. 'The kids have had a whale of a time, really enjoyed themselves. And of course, seeing them happy made me happy. Some youngsters are hard-faced and pushy, but not the Pollard boys, or Lucy or Steve. The world won't go far wrong if everyone grows up like them.'

'Thanks for inviting Steve, Aggie, I really do appreciate it. He went out of here with his head held high, his chest sticking out a mile and a real swagger to his walk. All courtesy of the McBride family.'

'He's worrying about leaving yer for so long, but yer don't mind, do yer, Olive? Let him get as much enjoyment out of life as he can, eh?'

'Tell him not to worry, I'm fine. As soon as yer've gone, I'll be tucking into those sausage rolls, sandwiches and jelly creams. God, it's years since I had a jelly cream, and I used to make loads of them.'

'I'll be on me way then, queen, to welcome the guests.' Aggie got to the door before putting into play the plan she'd concocted in her head. Tutting loudly, she turned. 'I've got a head like a sieve. I was going without giving yer this.' She pulled a folded piece of beige linen from her pocket and opened it up. It was a sideboard runner, and it had small coloured flowers embroidered on it. 'I came across this yesterday, when I was cleaning me cupboard out. It's that long since I've seen it, I'd forgotten I had it. I've got no use for it, and it would be a shame to throw it in the bin. Would yer be insulted if I asked if yer wanted it for yer sideboard?'

'Are you sure yer don't want it?' Olive looked suspicious. 'It looks too good to throw in the bin.'

'That's what I thought, girl.' As quick as a flash the runner was on the sideboard and Aggie was standing back admiring it. 'There yer are, it looks a treat.'

Olive thought the runner looked lovely, but she wasn't convinced. 'I've got a feeling ye're telling me fibs, Aggie McBride.'

'What would I gain from telling lies, girl? Not a bleedin' thing. I've got loads of stuff at home that'll never see daylight. Our Titch used to bring me all sorts home after every trip, until in the end I had to put a stop to it 'cos I had nowhere to put the things. A lot of stuff was stored in me loft and I haven't seen I for years. There's vases, ornaments and pictures, everything yer could mention.' Here goes, thought Aggie. In for a penny, in for a pound. 'I'll get Titch on the ladder tomorrow and ask him to hand some of the stuff down. Yer may think it's rubbish, and I wouldn't be offended if yer said so. But yer may as well have a root through it and see if there's anything yer like, instead of it rotting up there. This place could do with a few things to brighten it up, God knows. So how about it? D'yer want to have a dekko, or are yer going to go all stubborn and get yer knickers in a twist?'

'I'm not a stubborn person, Aggie, and I never get me knickers in a twist because they're that old they wouldn't stand the strain.' Olive smiled. 'How can I refuse such kindness?'

'That's settled then. I'll see yer tomorrow, please God. And now I'd better be on me way, queen. Ta-ra.'

Aggie was nearing her house when she saw Bob closing his front door. And even at this distance she could see Ruby wasn't in a very happy mood. If she spoils my son's night, I'll marmalise her, the miserable bleeding cow, Aggie thought, but for Bob's sake she raised a smile. 'I hope yer singing voice is in tune, Bob.' She inserted the key in the lock and looked over her shoulder. 'And you, Ruby – we'll expect a song from you as well.'

'Some hope you've got.' Ruby managed to inject a sneer into her voice. 'I've no intention of making a fool of meself.'

Bob looked sideways and shook his head. With her hair dyed a horrible yellowy blonde, and thick bright make-up plastered on her face, his wife didn't need anyone else to make a fool of her, she did that herself.

As Aggie stood aside to let them enter the house before her, she groaned inwardly. Ye gods and little fishes, this was a fine start to a party. If Ruby kept that face on her all night, Titch wouldn't think twice about telling her. And that would put the cat among the pigeons. Still, one way or another, the evening promised to be a lively one.

Irene and George greeted Ruby warmly, but all they got in reply was a curt nod. Titch was the only one favoured with a smile. 'What's yer poison, Ruby?' He pointed to the array of bottles on

512

the sideboard. 'I've got beer if yer want it, or there's port, whisky or gin.'

'I'll have gin, please, Titch.' Ruby sat in a chair on the opposite side of the room to her husband. A move not lost on the rest of the company. And each one asked themselves why this woman always had to belittle Bob. She didn't know she was born with a husband like him, he was far too nice a person for her.

Irene broke the silence. 'Do yer like Lucy's new coat, Ruby?'

'Yeah.' Ruby smiled up at Titch and took the glass from him. Then, sensing all eyes on her, she added, 'It's very nice.'

George stared down into his glass of bitter. Why should they all put themselves out to be nice to a woman who couldn't be bothered to be pleasant in return? 'Nice, did yer say, Ruby? I thought it was more than nice. I thought it was a real beauty, like the girl herself.'

Titch glanced at his mother as she rocked in her chair, a glass of stout in her hand. He could read her mind and knew that right now she would willingly wring someone's neck. He wasn't surprised at Ruby's behaviour, he hadn't expected anything else. She was an unhappy woman who thought she deserved more out of life than she was getting. A loving husband and daughter weren't enough for her, she didn't want the ties that bound her down.

His elbow leaning on the sideboard, and a grin on his face, Titch said, 'George is right about Lucy being a real beauty, Ruby. A few years from now there'll be broken hearts lying all over the place.'

'So they say.' Ruby lifted the glass to her lips and downed the gin as though it was water. 'Can I have the same again, Titch?'

'Ay, yer'd better watch it, Ruby, this is strong stuff.' Titch had given her a generous measure to begin with, and she'd drunk it in about ten minutes. At this rate she'd be flat out in no time. 'I don't want to see yer rolling home.'

Ruby's lips curled. 'Don't worry, Titch, I can hold me drink. Yer'll never see me rolling home, no matter how many I have.'

Her bragging inflamed Bob. Self, self, self, that's all she ever thought about. 'You get drunk and yer can crawl home on yer hands and knees,' he interjected. 'I won't be carrying yer.'

Ruby lit a cigarette before taking her refilled glass. Then she inhaled deeply and blew the smoke in her husband's direction. 'Yer'd be the last one I'd want to carry me home.'

The rocking chair was brought to a halt and Aggie sat forward. 'That's enough of that. Any families differences yer can air at home, not here. This is supposed to be a friendly gathering, so let's keep it that way. And I don't want to hear no more talk of drunken women, 'cos there's no worse sight than to see a woman the worse for drink.'

George had had enough. At this rate they'd be coming to blows. 'When are yer due back at yer ship, Titch?'

'I'll go down to the docks on Tuesday, see how things are. We'll likely be sailing on Wednesday or Thursday. But it'll be a short trip this time, probably only two or three weeks.'

'Will yer be glad to get yer sea legs back again?' Irene asked, glad the conversation had been steered to safer ground. 'Have yer missed it?'

'I won't be sorry to get back, but I can honestly say I haven't missed it this time. There seems to have been a lot going on to keep me occupied. And of course I've enjoyed me ma's company and good food.'

'I suppose yer've been helping that Olive Fletcher, like soft lad here.' Ruby drained her glass. 'I don't know why yer bother, the house will be filthy again in no time.'

Titch had no intention of going down that road. And he could see his mother's set face and knew she was ready to explode. 'Drink up, fellers, there's a crateful to get through.'

'I'll have a whisky this time, mate,' George said, 'if it's all the same to you.'

'And me.' Bob was on tenterhooks, afraid of what his wife would come out with next. She didn't care who she insulted or offended. Never again would he inflict her on his friends.

'Fill mine up while ye're at it, Titch.' Oblivious to the tension in the room, Ruby held her glass out. 'It's a nice drop of gin, that.'

'Yer'll have to wait until I see to the men. And me ma and Irene.' Titch's even temper was beginning to fray. 'You're last in the queue.'

Ruby put her glass down at the side of her chair and lit another cigarette. 'Like I was saying about the Fletchers, ye're all wasting yer time.'

Irene got to her feet to take her drink off Titch, then she looked down into her neighbour's face. 'Listen, Ruby, we're all friends of the Fletchers in this room, so we'd be grateful if yer would just keep yer mouth shut. Yer don't know the first thing about them, so ye're in no position to discuss their private affairs. So do yerself, and all of us, a favour by keeping yer trap buttoned up tight.'

Ruby was about to let fly with a tirade of abuse, when Titch intervened. 'A gin again, is it, Ruby?'

By a quarter to nine you could cut the atmosphere with a knife. Ruby never stopped talking, and it was always to pull people down. She'd had too much to drink, her eyes were glazed and her words slurred. Bob was so ashamed he couldn't take any more.

'I'll go and get Lucy – it's time she was in bed.' He handed his glass to Titch, his eyes telling of his torment. 'Come on, Ruby, time to go home.'

'I'm all right here, you go for her.'

'I'm not asking yer, I'm telling yer.' Bob snatched the cigarette from her mouth and threw it in the grate. Then he grasped the top of her arms and jerked her to her feet. 'Get yer bag and let's go.'

Ruby struggled as a stream of obscenities left her lips. But too much drink had made her unsteady on her feet and she was no match for her husband. 'I'll be back when I've seen Lucy to bed, Titch,' Bob said, 'if that's all right with you?'

Aggie got her words out before her son had a chance. 'Of course it is. Ye're always welcome in this house, Bob, yer know that.'

'Thanks.' Bob literally dragged Ruby into the hall. 'Needless to say, my wife will not be with me.'

Titch went to the door to make sure Bob could manage the woman who was struggling to get free, even though she would have fallen without her husband's hands holding her up. And her language was the language of the gutter.

'Well, did you ever!' Aggie said when her son came back into the room. 'Fancy having to live with the likes of that! I don't know how Bob puts up with it, he must be a saint.'

'He deserves a medal,' Irene said, her heart filled with sympathy for the man who had been humiliated in front of them all. 'He's a smashing bloke, far too good for her. What she needs is a man who'll give her a go-along now and again when she steps out of line.'

'I'll tell yer what,' Titch said, 'if I wasn't off marriage before, I certainly am now.'

'Ay, all women are not like Ruby, yer know.' George reached for his wife's hand. 'Take Irene here, she's a perfect wife and mother. Bob just picked the wrong one.'

'Yer can't say that, George.' Aggie pushed her feet down on the floor to set her chair in motion. 'If yer think back to the early years of their marriage, Ruby was a different person. She was friendly and easy to get along with.'

'She wasn't bad looking, either.' Titch crossed the room and held his hand out for George's empty glass. 'But I believe she let us see what she wanted us to see. People don't change that much, and the Ruby we saw tonight was the real Ruby.' He poured a generous measure of whisky and handed it over. 'If we cast our minds back, we can practically put a date on the time she decided life was too dull and she let her true self come to the fore.'

'Titch is right,' Irene said, thinking back. 'It was just after Lucy started school that she started to bleach her hair. Then gradually the make-up became thicker, as though she'd put it on with a trowel, and her nails were painted a bright red. I know Bob's had rows with her over it, yer can hear them through the wall. But she takes no notice of him. She's only interested in herself and couldn't care less for him or Lucy.'

'She doesn't still hit the girl, does she?' Aggie asked. ''Cos if I thought she'd laid a hand on her I wouldn't be responsible for me actions.'

Irene dropped her eyes for a brief second. Bob had suffered enough, she wasn't going to add to his suffering. 'Not as far as I know, Aggie.'

'Let's forget about Ruby for now, eh?' Titch said. 'She managed to spoil a couple of hours for us, but don't let her spoil the whole night. Yer've all got full glasses, so drink up and be merry. And for God's sake, will someone tell a joke to put a smile on our faces?'

'I know,' Aggie chuckled, 'tell them about the parrot and Mrs Gibson.'

'Oh, aye, that was dead funny, that was.' Titch related the whole story and it brought not only smiles, but roars of laughter. 'The funniest part, the one that tickled me most, was that Lucy's friend believed me when I said Mrs Gibson had kept me talking all through me ten days' leave. She said, all serious like, "That's terrible, that is. Yer should have told her. I know I would have done." And the poor girl had no idea why everyone went in a pleat.'

They were still wiping their eyes when Bob came through the door Titch had left ajar for him. He was smiling, but they could see the strain on his face and in his eyes. 'I'm glad you lot can still laugh. I thought me wife had blighted the night for yer. I can't tell yer how sorry I am, but it's me own fault. I should have known better than to bring her.'

'Did yer manage to get her home all right?' Titch asked. 'I would have given yer a hand but thought I'd better not interfere.'

'I had to half carry her up the stairs, and she was a dead weight. Then I took her coat off and lifted her onto the bed. I left her there and went for Lucy. And when she was settled in bed, I looked in on the wife. She was just as I'd left her, out like a light and snoring her head off.'

'She certainly likes her drink,' George said. 'She must have gone through half a bottle of gin in that short time.'

'Perhaps it's my fault,' Titch said. 'I should have refused to give her so much.'

'Don't blame yerself,' Bob told him. 'Ruby sober is no nicer than Ruby drunk. She's got a chip on her shoulder as big as a ruddy tree, and nothing yer do or say will please her. I should

516

know, I've tried everything under the sun but it doesn't have the slightest effect.'

'Forget about it for now,' Irene said, 'and sit down and relax. Get a glass in yer hand and drown yer sorrows.'

Titch raised his brows. 'How about a good stiff whisky, pal?'

'Just the job, mate.' Bob sat down and stretched his legs. He was physically and mentally exhausted. 'Then yer can tell me what yer were laughing about when I came in. I could do with cheering up.'

'Before that, Bob, will yer tell us how the kids got on in Irene's?' Aggie leaned forward in expectation. 'Did Lucy enjoy herself?'

The mention of his daughter's name brought a genuine smile to Bob's face. 'Enjoy herself! She was full of it – they all were. I couldn't get a word in edgeways with them all talking at once, saying they'd had the time of their lives. I felt like an ogre breaking the party up. Lucy said it was the best birthday she'd ever had, and young Jack said he'd never forget the day he wore his first pair of long kecks.' Bob held the glass to his lips and closed his eyes as the liquid warmed and soothed him. 'I'll tell yer what – that Steve's a good 'un. He said he'd stay and help the lads clear up so their mother didn't have to come back to dirty dishes and crumbs all over the floor. Yer'd not get many boys his age being so thoughtful.'

Aggie sat back feeling contented. As long as the children enjoyed themselves, that was the main thing. At least Ruby hadn't been able to spoil their party. 'They're all good kids. I don't know Lucy's friend, Rhoda, as well as I know the others, but she seems a nice enough girl.'

Titch chuckled. 'She's an exceptional girl is Rhoda, with a very unusual sense of humour. Which brings me to what we were laughing at when yer came in, Bob.' Leaning back against the sideboard with a glass in his hand and a twinkle in his eye, he started with Jack telling his brother he talked like a parrot that had lived with Mrs Gibson for years. And he ended with Rhoda's serious reaction to a story that had been made up for a laugh.

If Titch had told the tale once again in the hope of cheering his neighbour up, then he'd been very successful. For Bob, with a warm glow inside him, and feeling relaxed, roared with laughter as he pictured the scene in his mind. 'I wish I'd been here to see it. I bet our Lucy saw the funny side.' He shook his head. 'Rhoda didn't really believe Mrs Gibson kept yer talking for ten days, did she? No, she couldn't have. She was having yer on.'

'If I never move from this spot, she fell for it, hook, line and sinker.' Titch looked to his mother for confirmation. 'Isn't that the truth, Ma?'

Aggie chuckled. 'It is, son. And I bet she'll lie in bed tonight wondering how yer could stand on yer feet for ten days without going to the lavvy.'

'She either believed it, or is a ruddy good actress,' Irene said. 'But either way she's done us a favour. Especially you, Bob. Yer look heaps better than yer did half an hour ago.'

'That's the whisky, sweetheart,' George said. 'It's amazing what a drop of the hard stuff will do.'

'No, George, it's not the whisky,' Bob said. 'It's being with me friends. I was all wound up before, me nerves shattered. But now I feel nice and relaxed. In fact, I feel so full of goodwill to all men, I wouldn't mind if Mrs Gibson walked through that door right now and talked the head off me all through the night.'

George let out a loud guffaw. 'I told yer it was amazing what a drop of the hard stuff will do. But even I didn't think it was powerful enough for anyone to brave Mrs Gibson's company for a whole night. Give him another one, Titch.'

'All in good time, mate,' Titch said. 'The last thing I want is for him to get legless and me have to carry him up the stairs and throw him down next to Ruby.'

Mellowed by the drink and good company, Bob chuckled. 'Yer need have no fears on that score, 'cos I'm kipping down on the couch. I'm at ease with meself now, as happy as a pig in you-know-what. And I'm not about to let the sight and sound of me drunken wife spoil things for me. Time enough tomorrow for rows and recriminations.'

'Take the advice of an old woman, Bob,' Aggie said, 'and forget about it. It's over and done with now and yer can't change things. What's the good of getting all het-up when nothing will come of it? 'Cos I'll tell yer now, lad, no matter how hard yer shout, yer'll never change Ruby.'

'Aggie's right, Bob, yer'd get yerself all worked up for nothing,' Irene said. 'Put it out of yer head and pretend it never happened.'

Bob was thoughtful as he swirled the whisky around in his glass. And when he looked up, he nodded. 'The ladies are right, as usual. I won't forget about it, I can't. But kicking up a stink won't get me anywhere, so to all intents and purposes, it never happened.'

'It's very sensible of yer to take me ma's advice when she becomes an old woman,' Titch said, trying to control his laughter. 'I took her advice, that's why I never married. She told me there wasn't a girl in the world good enough for her son, so I never bothered looking.'

Aggie gaped. 'That is a bleedin' lie, Titch McBride. I never said no such thing.'

'Yes, yer did. I was about twenty-two at the time.'

'Yer must have been hearing things, 'cos if I never move from this chair I never said no such thing.'

Titch slapped a hand on his forehead. 'Well, blow me down! Here I am, forty years of age and unmarried. All because I've gone through life thinking there wasn't a girl good enough for me. And now I find out I must have dreamt yer said it.'

Irene looked at the smiling faces and thought, this was more like it. Mother and son were just getting into their stride and there was a lot of laughter on the way. It was a bit late for it, thanks to Ruby, but better late than never. The disastrous start to the evening had been pushed to the back of their minds and merriment was taking its place. Which was as it should be when friends got together.

Aggie stood on the small landing and watched her son heaving the wooden ladder up the stairs. 'I dunno,' Titch grumbled, 'fancy getting me up at this ungodly hour on a Sunday morning.'

'Ah, yer poor thing. The bleedin' streets were aired off hours ago.'

Titch stood the ladder against the wall. 'Where d'yer want me to put it? And I don't want a rude answer, 'cos it wouldn't fit, anyway.'

Aggie chuckled. 'Ye're wide enough awake to give me yer old buck.' She nodded her head towards the front bedroom. 'By me wardrobe.'

Titch opened the ladder in front of the large wardrobe. 'Now what?'

'I want yer to get up there and pass some of the parcels down to me. I want to see what's in them.'

'Ah, ay, Ma! Did yer get me out of bed just so yer could do some spring-cleaning?'

'No, I didn't, so stop yer moaning. I think there's some things up there that would brighten Olive's house up. They're not doing me any good sitting up there, so she may as well have the use of them. So get cracking, son, 'cos I've got a dinner to get ready.'

Titch climbed on to the third rung. 'Is there anything in particular ye're looking for?'

'I don't know until I see it, do I? Just give me the first thing yer put yer hand on.' Aggie reached up to take the small, newspaper-wrapped parcel. While her son looked on, she opened it up to find a pretty, blue glass vase. 'That's nice, she'll like that. Another one now, son.'

The next parcel revealed a statue of a Japanese lady in a bright kimono with a fan hiding the bottom half of her face. Then came another statue. This time it was an old man with a walking stick, bent over with the weight of the pack on his back. The fourth parcel contained a framed picture, and Aggie studied it with a smile on her face. It was a pretty scene, with children playing in a field of buttercups and daisies. 'That's enough for now, son, otherwise Olive will send yer packing with them.'

Titch nearly fell off the ladder. 'Send *me* packing! I'm not taking them up to her, yer can do it yerself.'

Aggie looked all innocent. 'I'd be happy to do that, son, if you'll see to the dinner. I'll put the meat in the oven for yer, so all yer'd have to do is peel the carrots and turnip, and the spuds. Then when the meat's nearly done, yer can put the potatoes around it to roast. Oh, and yer'd have to make the gravy, as well.'

'Ye're a crafty so-and-so, Ma. Why can't yer put the meat in the oven now? Then yer'd have time to go to Olive's and be back in time to see to the rest of the meal.'

'That sounds all very well, son, but yer see, I can't knock a nail in the wall. If you go, yer can take a hammer and a nail with yer and put the picture up for her.'

Titch shook his head. 'Yer've got it all figured out, haven't yer, Ma? When did yer plan this little manoeuvre?'

'In bed last night. Yer can blame Ruby for it if yer must blame someone. I couldn't sleep thinking about the brazen hussy, so to take me mind off her, I got thinking of Olive. And I came up with this idea. Mind you, it never entered me head that you'd be so bleedin' contrary.'

'I'm not being contrary, Ma, it's just that yer don't tell a person what's on yer mind. And when they refuse, yer blackmail them. Yer know darn well I'd rather go to Olive's for half an hour than eat a dinner I'd made meself.' Titch put his arms around the ladder and lifted it from the floor. 'Are yer sure that's all, before I lug this thing downstairs?'

'Yes, light of my life, that's all. Except I've just remembered I told Olive all this stuff was in the loft, so don't you go making a liar out of me.'

The ladder was lowered to the floor as Titch shook with laughter. 'But yer are a liar, Ma!'

'Yes, I know that. And you know it, too. But yer've no need to let the whole bleedin' street know.' Aggie spread her hands out. 'It's not meself I'm thinking of, it's you. How would yer like to be walking down the street and hear a woman saying to her neighbour, "His mother's not half a liar. Yer can't believe a word what comes out of her mouth." '

'Ma, I'll do a deal with yer. I'll tell lies for yer, if you make a rice pudding for after our dinner. How does that sound?'

'Yer drive a hard bargain, son. But, yeah, it's a deal.'

Titch was on the landing preparing to lift the ladder down the top stair. Then over the rustling of the paper as the parcels were rewrapped, he heard his mother talking to herself. 'If he had eyes in his bleedin' head he'd have seen the rice in steep on the draining board. Still, he wanted a deal and he got one.'

'I heard that, Ma.'

'Oh, did yer now! Well, now yer know it's true what they say about listeners never hearing good about themselves. It's coming to something when an old woman can't have a decent conversation with herself without some nosy bugger butting in.'

'Well, this nosy bugger is on his way downstairs now to make a cup of tea for an old woman. She doesn't deserve it, like, 'cos she tells lies and all sorts of things. But I'll be lenient and make allowances for her age.'

'Sod off, Titch McBride.'

Steve opened the door and his face stretched in a smile. 'Hello, Mr Titch, it's nice to see yer. Come on in.'

'Is yer mam respectable?'

'Keep yer voice down, Titch McBride,' Olive called. 'Yer'll have the neighbours thinking there's times when I'm not respectable.'

'Only the bad-minded ones, Olive, only the bad-minded ones.'

Steve put a hand on his arm. 'I want to thank yer for yesterday, Mr Titch, we all had a smashing time. And me new clothes went down a treat.'

'Think nothing of it, lad, it was my pleasure.'

Olive eyed the bag with suspicion. 'What's Aggie sent yer down with now?'

'Don't you start on me, Olive, 'cos me ma's had me up since the crack of dawn. The last Sunday of me leave and she drags me out of bed at ten o'clock.'

'And that's the crack of dawn, is it?'

'It is when yer've had a few drinks the night before.' Titch put the bag on the table. 'Me ma said yer know about these. They're things she's had for years and has no use for.'

'Don't tell me she's had yer in the loft this morning?'

'I haven't been in the loft, Olive.' Titch thought half a lie wasn't so bad. 'I just stood on the ladder and pulled out the first things that came to hand.'

'Can I have a look, Mam?' Steve's hand was already on the bag. 'We're not half getting a lot of surprises these days. Everyone's been very kind.'

'We shouldn't really take them.' But Olive's words were half-hearted. She was dying to see what Aggie had sent. 'I feel as though I'm scrounging.'

'Scrounging! Olive, me ma's got enough stuff at home to open a

521

shop. Yer'd be doing her a favour by taking them off her hands.'

'I'll believe yer, Titch, because I want to.' Olive smiled into the weatherbeaten face. 'I feel like a little girl when she finds out Father Christmas has been.'

That was good enough for Steve, and his hand went into the bag. And as he and his mam showed their pleasure as each piece of paper was opened, Titch stood by and watched in silence. How little it took to make these two happy.

'There's a hammer in the bottom of the bag, Mr Titch.' Steve looked puzzled. 'Fancy carrying that around with yer, 'cos it's heavy.'

'I've got a nail in me pocket to go with it, lad. And strict instructions from me ma that I wasn't to go home until that picture was on yer wall. She said if I didn't do it, she'd come down and have a go herself. I didn't fancy letting her do that because I think she'd knock yer wall down in the process.'

Olive stood with a finger in her mouth, looking first at the sideboard and then the mantelpiece. 'I think the vase in the middle of the sideboard, and an ornament each end. What do you think, Titch?'

'Move them around until yer get them where yer think they look best. And while ye're doing that, I'll put the picture up. Which wall would yer like it on?'

There was no hesitation. 'On that wall, so everyone can see it when they walk in.'

Steve watched the pleasure on his mother's face and thought of how much they owed to the McBrides. Yesterday he'd felt equal to the other children because he was dressed as well as any of them. And he'd never forget the two people who'd made that possible.

Olive stood behind the table and looked across at the sideboard. Only a couple of weeks ago it had been falling to pieces, only fit for the scrapheap. Now, with the lovely runner, the ornaments and vase, it looked a treat. And the picture hanging over it was just the right finishing touch. The trouble was, the wallpaper didn't do them justice. Dark with age, and torn in so many places, it took the shine off the nice things. She didn't say anything, though, because it might sound as if she was dropping hints. 'Thank yer mam for me and tell her I'm thrilled to bits.' She pointed to a chair. 'Yer can sit down, yer know, we don't charge. Not even for the spring that'll stick in yer bottom and leave a mark.'

When Titch sat down he felt the truth of her words and grinned. 'No one will see it. I've been changing me own nappies for nearly forty years now.'

Steve was in his element having a man to talk to. 'How did yer party go, Mr Titch? I bet it wasn't as good as ours.'

'Well, the first couple of hours were interesting, and quite lively at times. But they were nothing to write home about. It was nearly ten o'clock when it really got going, after we were all well-oiled.' He lifted a finger and corrected himself. 'I should say when the men were well-oiled. Irene and me ma don't need drink to make a party go, and they had us in stitches.'

'How was Ruby?' Olive asked. 'Did she enjoy herself?'

'Least said, soonest mended, Olive.'

'Oh.' She had gathered from snippets of conversation with Aggie and Irene that Bob's wife wasn't very popular. Whenever she mentioned her name they changed the subject. So she now followed their example. 'When do yer sail, Titch?'

'I'm reporting on Tuesday, so we'll probably sail the day after. I was told it would only be a short trip, but yer can't rely on them. I didn't expect to be away four months on the last one. But when I get home, I'll be taking the Pollard boys and Lucy to the flicks one night. And yer'd be very welcome to join us, Steve, if yer want to.'

Steve was agog. If someone had given him a pound note he couldn't have looked any happier. 'Ooh, yeah! That would be the gear, Mr Titch, thanks very much.'

'Just look at the face on him,' Olive said, feeling so pleased for her son. 'That's all I'll be able to get out of him now, so yer'd better not be away for four months, Titch McBride, or he'll drive me round the bend.'

'I was going to suggest that yer come with us. That's if ye're feeling better, like. It would do yer good to get out.'

'Oh, please, Mam,' Steve said. 'That would be brilliant.'

Olive was flabbergasted. Her hand to her throat, she croaked, 'I couldn't go with yer, Titch, I haven't been over the door for nearly two years. Anyway, what would the neighbours say? They'd have a field day!'

'Don't be acting daft, Olive, I'll have four kids with me. And if it makes yer feel better, I'll get me ma to come along.' Titch leaned forward and rested his elbows on his knees. 'Anyway, what the hell's it got to do with the neighbours? They don't pay yer rent for yer, or put bread on yer table, so why care what they say? I took Irene into town the other week, while her husband was at work, but there's been no gossip about us having an affair.' He grinned. 'Mind you, if George wasn't such a big feller, I might have tried me luck.'

'Let me think about it, Titch.' Olive didn't need to think about it, she'd already decided she wouldn't go. 'It's such a long time since I've been out, just the thought frightens me.'

'It's coming up summer, Olive. Hot, sunny days. Yer can't spend them in the house, it wouldn't be healthy.' Titch looked at his watch. 'I'd better get back, me ma will have the dinner ready. But will yer promise to give it some thought?'

'I will, I promise. Now don't forget to thank Aggie for me. And if I don't see yer before yer set sail, have a good trip and take care of yerself.'

'So Olive was pleased with the things, was she?' Aggie sat facing her son across the table as they tucked into a roast dinner. She'd already asked Titch half a dozen times since he came home. 'And the picture looked nice on the wall, did it?'

'Ma, the picture was a joy to behold. And Olive was so delighted she jumped up and down for joy.'

'There's no need for sarcasm, Titch. And as it's Sunday, keep a civil tongue in yer head if yer don't mind. Yer never hear me being sarcastic, or swearing, on the Sabbath.' She wiped a trickle of gravy from her chin before adding, 'Well, only in extreme circumstances, of which this will be one if yer give me any more lip.'

'A paragon of virtue, yer are, Ma, and no mistake.' Titch bit on the inside of his mouth to stop himself from smiling as he told her, 'By the way, I've asked Olive for a date.'

Aggie nearly choked on a piece of crispy roast potato. Swallowing hard, she gasped, 'What did yer say?'

'I've asked Olive to come to the pictures with me one night on me next leave.'

Aggie searched his face for a while then burst out laughing. 'Pull the other one, it's got bells on.' She laid down her knife and fork and sat back in the wooden chair. 'Oh, that was a good try, son, but yer didn't really think I'd fall for it, did yer?'

'If yer don't believe me, ask her yerself. Yer'll be seeing her tomorrow 'cos it's your turn to make them a dinner. Just ask her, casual like, and see what she says.'

'Will I heckerslike! The woman would think I've gone off me rocker. She'd die of embarrassment.'

His face still straight, Titch said, 'Well, she was alive and kicking when I left. She wasn't the least embarrassed when I asked her.'

'Titch, the joke's gone far enough.'

'Yeah, ye're right, Ma. What happened was, I told Steve I'd be taking the kids to the pictures one night next time I'm home, and I asked if he'd like to come with us. He was absolutely over the moon. Then it struck me that it might be one way of getting Olive out of that house, and I asked if she'd like to come with us. She said she'd think about it, but I know she won't come. Which is a pity, 'cos she needs fresh air. She needs to get out, even if it's only to the shops. Wouldn't you or Irene have a go at asking her?'

'We've already tried, with no luck. It was thoughtful of yer to ask her, and I'm proud of yer. But I think the reason she won't go out is because she's no clothes to go out in. It's never been mentioned, like, but I'll bet a pound to a pinch of snuff that the two washed-out dresses I've seen her in are all she possesses. And they're nearly falling off her back – she wouldn't want to be seen out in them.' Aggie picked up her knife and fork. 'This dinner will be stiff if we leave it any longer, so get stuck in.' She cut a potato in half and speared it with her fork. 'It's early days, yet, son, just give it time. Me and Irene will keep working on her, and George and Bob will do as much as she'll allow them to do. Only God can do more than that.'

Chapter Fourteen

Titch walked up the street with a swagger. With his seaman's bag slung over his shoulder, his navy-blue peaked cap at a rakish angle and a twinkle in his eye, he was feeling in high spirits. He'd been away for two months and was looking forward to seeing his mother. He had the key ready in his hand and was smiling as he imagined the delight he'd see on her face. And he knew his heart would lurch, as it always did, at the love that was plain to see in eyes moist with tears of emotion. He was about to insert the key in the lock when he heard a piercing whistle and turned his head to see Steve Fletcher running towards him, a hand waving in the air.

'Mr Titch, I've got a job!' Steve was breathless with excitement. 'I started two weeks ago. I've been dying for yer to come home so I could tell yer.'

'Good for you, lad.' Titch was highly delighted for the boy. 'Come inside and tell me all about it.'

'Nah, I won't come in. Mrs Aggie's been so looking forward to yer coming home, she won't want me in the way.'

'Yer know me ma better than that, Steve. She's always glad to see yer.'

'I'll wait here for five minutes, so yer can give her the kiss and cuddle she said she always gets. I don't want to spoil yer home-coming.'

'Okay, I'll leave the door open and give yer a shout when the coast is clear.'

Aggie was in the kitchen when she heard the key in the lock. Her heartbeat quickened as she dried her hands on the corner of her pinny. She entered the living room at the same time as Titch came in from the hall. Her arms wide, she walked towards him. 'It's a sight for sore eyes yer are, sweetheart. Welcome home.'

He held her close and they rocked from side to side. 'It's good to be home, Ma. And I'm happy to say yer've got me company for at least ten days.'

'Oh, that's good. The last couple of leaves ye've had were a waste of time. Yer barely had time to unpack before yer were off again.'

'Listen, Ma, Steve's outside. Is it all right if he comes in? I told him it would be, but he wasn't having any. He said he didn't want to spoil yer kiss and cuddle.'

Aggie grinned. 'I told him yer were due about this time – he must have been watching out for yer. I'm not going to say anything, he'll want to tell yer the news himself.'

And Steve couldn't get his news out quick enough. The words tumbling from his mouth, he brought Titch up-to-date. 'Yer know Jack got a job at Dunlop's when he left school – well, he got an application form for me from the office. Mrs Pollard helped me fill it in, then she asked Mr Whittle from the corner shop if he'd give me a reference. He gave me a good one, too, and so did the headmistress at school. They must have done the trick because I got an interview and was told to start on the Monday.'

'I'm really pleased for yer, lad.' Titch eyed him up and down. 'Yer haven't half shot up in the last few months. Either that or I'm shrinking.'

'It's me what's growing, Mr Titch.' There wasn't an inch of Steve's face that wasn't smiling. 'Me mam had to let the hem down on the trousers.'

'I bet she's proud of yer, is she?'

'Not half! I had to work a week in hand, but I got me first wage-packet on Friday. I couldn't get home quick enough to see her face when I handed it over.'

'And he wouldn't take a penny back.' Aggie knew the lad wouldn't say it, so she did. 'He walks to work every day, there and back, to save the tram fare.'

Titch looked surprised. 'That's some walk, that is. How long does it take yer?'

'I can do it in half an hour. And I don't mind. If I went on the tram, there and back, six days a week, it would be two bob out of the seven and six I earn. Then there's me carry-out. Me mam has to buy that as well.'

This lad is a bloody hero, Titch thought. For years he'd been deprived of even the basic needs in life. Things other kids took for granted. But it hadn't made him bitter or resentful. He was healthy in mind and body, kind and caring, and appreciative of the good things that came his way. A son to be proud of. 'How is yer mam?'

'I think she's a lot better, Mr Titch. Don't you think so, Mrs Aggie?'

'It certainly seems that way. She's been out to the shops a couple of times and that's a good sign.' Aggie chuckled. 'Me and Irene pulled a fast one on her. Steve knows about it so I'm not telling tales out of school. We'd been taking turns getting her

528

messages in, like bread and something for the lad's carry-out. But we decided that as long as we did that, Olive would never go out. So one day we told her we wouldn't be able to see her the next day until late, 'cos we were going to visit Irene's family. We both felt a bit mean about it, but it had the desired effect. If she didn't go to the shops, there'd be no bread for carry-out. And she wouldn't see her son go without, 'cos as we all know, she loves the bones of him.'

Titch clicked his tongue on the roof of his mouth. 'The older yer get, Ma, the worse yer get. Is it you leading Irene astray, or the other way around?'

'Six of one and half-a-dozen of the other, son. Me and Irene think alike, always have done. And that little trick paid dividends. Since that first day, Olive's been to the shops a few times. Once with me, once with Irene and once on her own. So things are definitely looking up.'

'I'll go and leave yer in peace now,' Steve said. 'I can smell Mrs Aggie's got a nice dinner ready for yer.' He hesitated for a second. 'How long are yer home for, Mr Titch?'

'Ten long, beautiful days, lad. Ten days of being spoiled rotten by me ma. And that dinner yer can smell is only the start.'

'I know what it is, but I'm not going to tell yer. Me and me mam had the same, thanks to Mrs Aggie.' There was fondness in the look he gave the woman who was like family to him. 'She's a smashing cook.'

'She's everything a mother should be, and more.' When Steve moved towards the door, Titch followed. 'I'll have a look down the paper tonight and see what's on at the pictures this week. Then we'll let the gang decide if they want to see a cowboys and Indians, a thriller or a comedy.'

'That's smashing. I don't care what we go to see.' Steve turned on the top step. 'Are yer going to ask me mam if she'll come?'

Titch pursed his lips. 'I don't think so, lad. She hasn't wanted to come the other times I've asked her, and I don't want to put her in an embarrassing situation.'

'She might do, this time. She's been out now, she hadn't before.'

'We'll see how the land lies, eh? Tell her I'll nip up and see her tomorrow. Tonight is my night for a drink with me mates. If I'm not mistaken, Bob's on night shift, so we might get a couple of pints in before he goes to work.'

'Okay, Mr Titch, I'll tell me mam.' Steve lowered his head to gaze down at his shoes. 'I don't know how we'd have managed if you hadn't come down to our house that day. I used to worry meself sick about me mam, but I didn't have no one to turn to. I could see she was really ill, but she wouldn't let me get the doctor 'cos we had no money. I knew we weren't getting enough to eat, that the house was a tip and I was walking around like a tramp. None of that worried me, I didn't care what people said about me. But I did care what was happening to me mam, and I used to have nightmares that she was going to die and I couldn't do a thing to stop it.'

Titch put a hand on his shoulder. 'Listen to me, lad, all the neighbours in this street have nothing but praise for yer. Yer've come through that bad patch with flying colours. Put it behind yer and look towards the future. Ye're a working man now, with yer whole life ahead of yer.'

'Without you, Mr Titch, I wouldn't have had a pair of trousers to wear for the interview for a job. Without Mrs Aggie and Mrs Pollard, me mam wouldn't have been getting a decent dinner every day. She doesn't spend all her time lying on the couch now because she's got good friends that visit and have given her an interest in life.' His blue eyes told of a wisdom beyond his years. 'We've come through the worst of it, as yer say, but I'll never forget we didn't do it alone.'

'Ay, it's a good job me ma isn't here listening to yer, she'd be crying buckets. Life has made yer grow up quick, Steve, but yer've got the guts and courage to make a good life for yerself, and yer mam. And all yer friends are behind yer and dead proud of yer.' Titch punched him good-naturedly in the chest. 'Now will yer go on home before yer have me bawling me eyes out. Me ma thinks the world of yer, but if she thought yer'd made her lovely son cry, she'd be chasing yer down the street with the poker in her hand.'

He stood for a while watching the lad walk down the street, his back straight, his stride long. A young man with a purpose who deserved to get on in life. 'Olive might not have been able to give that lad any luxuries, Ma,' Titch said when he went back in the living room to find his mother setting the table, 'but she's given him something more important. She's taught him honesty and a respect for people. I think she's done a damn good job on him.'

'There's no doubt about that, son. There's not a better-mannered lad in this street.' Aggie bent over the table, straightening the knives and forks and making sure the condiment set was close to where her son would be sitting. 'Did I hear yer telling him yer'd be taking the kids to the pictures during the week?'

Titch chuckled as he pulled a chair out from under the table and sat down. 'My God, yer've got good hearing, Ma – yer don't miss a thing. Yes, I did say I'd be taking them to the flicks. They look forward to it, and so do I.'

'And are yer going to ask Olive?'

'There's not much point, is there? She'd only refuse.'

530

'Then I'll ask her. I'll say I want to go with yer but I don't fancy being the only female.' Aggie bustled out to the kitchen. 'Come and stand by the door so I can talk to yer while I'm putting the dinner out. Once yer go out to the pub, that's the last I'll see of yer until tomorrow.'

Titch leaned against the door jamb, his arms folded and his legs crossed at the ankles. 'Okay, Mam, let's have all the news. I've got a couple of months to catch up on.'

'We'll stick with Olive. She has improved a lot, although once she steps out of that house she gets very nervous. But that'll pass in time. Irene had some dresses that won't go near her now she's put weight on, and she told Olive she was welcome to them if she could alter them to fit. It turns out she's very handy with a needle and thread and she made a good job of them. That's why I suggested yer asked her to come to the pictures. Now she's got some decent clothes she might be glad of a night out.'

'She'd be more than welcome, Ma. I'd be made up to see her getting out and about. But I'd feel happier if you asked her.' Titch waited for his mother's agreement, then asked, 'What about the Pollards? Everyone well, I hope?'

'They're fine. Irene's still doing her morning job, she's saving up for some new furniture. They're pretty comfortable now with three lots of wages coming in, even though young Jack thinks it's his few bob that keeps the house going. He takes after his mam, always with a smile on his face and a joke on his lips. They're a very happy family, the Pollards.'

'Shall I ask how the Mellors are, or would it put me off me dinner?'

'It's hard to say. Sometimes Bob looks as though he's got the troubles of the world on his shoulders, but he never mentions his wife's name. They don't go over the door together, so things haven't improved. But to give Bob his due, he keeps his worries to himself. I very seldom see Ruby. If we meet in the street we just walk past each other. I've no time for her and I'll not pretend otherwise.' Aggie drained the potatoes and put a knob of butter in the pan before plunging the masher up and down. 'Lucy is a little treasure. Every time I see her I want to give her a big hug to make up for the ones she doesn't get off her mother. She is always happy and cheerful, but I think deep down she's a sad child. She spends a lot of time in the Pollards', especially when Bob's at work. I think she confides in Irene, but I wouldn't like to say for sure. Irene's not one to break a confidence.'

Titch moved away from the wall and stretched his arms over his head. 'In other words, Ma, things are just the same as they were when I went away?'

'Not quite, son, not quite. I've got another wrinkle in me forehead, three more white hairs in me head and a hole in the heel of me stocking that yer could put yer fist through.' Aggie pointed the masher at him. 'I'm not complaining, mind. I wouldn't have mentioned them if yer hadn't asked.'

'Ma, yer've got steel-grey hair and there's not a white hair to be seen. Nor have yer got a wrinkle in yer face. What's more, I'll bet a pound to a pinch of snuff there's no hole in the heel of yer stocking. In all, I'd say ye're a remarkable woman for yer age. And now, while ye're dishing the dinner out, I'm going to give George and Bob a knock to ask them to be ready for half-seven. I'll be back in two ticks.' Titch was passing the sideboard when he heard his mother talking to herself.

'I'll have a little bet on the side meself. I bet that when the world comes to an end, my son will be sitting in a pub somewhere with a bleedin' pint glass in his hand.'

Titch crept up behind her. 'Ma, can yer think of a better way to go?'

Lucy was in the Pollards' when Titch called for George that evening. As soon as he walked through the door she flew to him and put her arms around his waist. 'I'm glad to see yer, Mr Titch.'

'And I'm glad to see you, sweetheart.' He stroked her hair, thinking here was a child starved of affection. Oh, Bob was affectionate with her, he idolised her. But she wasn't getting any from the one person, who above all, should be showering it on her. 'Are we all set for the pictures one night, gang?'

'Oh, yes please, Mr Titch.' Greg's face was one big smile. 'I'm looking forward to it.'

Jack stood up, and with his two hands in his pockets, sauntered across the room. 'I thought yer were never going to ask.'

'Ay, you,' Lucy said, 'where's yer manners?'

'I keep them in me back pocket so no one can pinch them. I got a lot of smacks learning those manners, so I'm not taking any chances on them getting nicked.'

'That's enough now, all of yer,' Irene said. 'I'm still waiting for me kiss.'

'Don't mind me, I'm only yer husband!' George said with mock indignation. 'It's getting to be too much of a habit, this kissing lark.'

'Take no notice of him, Titch.' Irene winked. 'Pretend he's not here.'

Titch wagged his head from side to side. 'Ooh, I don't know about that, he's bigger than I am.' He eyed the youngsters. 'I'll take a chance though, 'cos it's worth it. But hold the door open in case I have to make a quick getaway.'

Irene held her cheek up and Titch's mouth was two inches away when George banged his fist on the wooden arm of his chair. 'That's enough now. Don't be making a meal out of it.'

Titch was laughing so much he only managed a peck on the cheek. 'See what yer've done, mate? Two flaming months I've waited for that.'

George's hearty chuckle filled the room. 'Tomorrow's another day, mate, and I might be feeling more generous.' He pushed himself out of the chair and shook his trouser legs until the crease was straight. 'We'd better be off, Bob will have to leave just after nine.'

'Yeah, okay. I'll see yer all tomorrow.' Titch held his hand out to Lucy. 'Are yer coming home with us?'

The girl seemed to shrink from him. 'No, I'm staying here to have a game of cards.'

'I'll take her home when it's bedtime,' Irene said. 'We'll have a couple of hands, first.'

'Lucy always wins, yer know, Mr Titch,' Jack said. 'As sure as eggs is eggs, she'll end up with another eight buttons tonight. That's because me mam taught her how to cheat.'

'You big fibber! It's you what cheats, not me.'

'Come on, Titch, or we'll be here all night.' George led the way out of the house. 'Those boys of mine would talk yer into an asylum.'

Bob answered their knock and stepped into the street, banging the door behind him. 'Yer'll have to excuse the clobber but I'm a working man. I wish I could get a day job, but there's none going in our place and there's too many men out of work to look elsewhere.'

They fell into step for the short walk to the corner pub. George had a few bob in his pocket through the week these days, so he said he'd get the first round in. While he went to the bar, Titch and Bob found seats in a corner.

'How's the world treating yer, Bob? Okay?'

'It's ticking over, Titch.' Bob was on edge, hoping they wouldn't mention his wife. He didn't want to talk about Ruby. He could lie, and say they were getting on fine, but the words would stick in his throat. 'Nothing exciting, like, but it's ticking over.'

'That's all we can expect, I suppose. There's always someone worse off than yerself, but then there's always someone better off.'

George was laughing as he put the three pint glasses down. 'There's an argument going on over the bar and it's a scream to listen to them. Yer know the old man from the top of the street – Bert? Well, he's trying to get a half-pint of stout on tick. And

Alec's telling him he can't have it because he hasn't paid for the one he got on tick last week. Bert asked, "Which one was that? I don't remember getting half a pint on tick." Alec was very patient with him at first, explaining it was Friday night and he had it written on his slate. And if Bert couldn't pay him for one, he certainly wouldn't be able to pay for two. And d'yer know what the old man said? "If that's yer attitude, I'll have to take me custom elsewhere." '

Titch saw the funny side and turned in his seat to see the old man's head going as he argued the toss. Lifting his arm, Titch snapped his fingers to attract the manager's attention. Then he pointed to the old man's back and mouthed, 'Give him one. I'll pay for it.'

Alec shrugged his shoulders and reached up for a glass. 'There's one born every minute, so they say.' He filled the glass, put it in front of old Bert and nodded to where the three men were sitting. 'Yer can thank the bloke in the navy reefer.'

Bert turned with the glass in his hand and a smile that showed he didn't have a tooth in his head. 'Ye're a gent. Ta very much.'

'Ye're welcome, mate, enjoy it.' Titch swivelled back in his seat. 'Poor old bugger. We could end up like him one day. None of us knows what's in store for us.'

'My two lads say they'll look after me when I'm old and grey,' George said with a smile. 'They won't see me without a few coppers for me beer money.'

Bob nodded. 'Lucy must have heard them saying it because she said the same thing last week. I wondered what had put the idea into her head.'

'It doesn't say much for me, does it?' Titch said. 'I'll have to hope the manager who's here when I'm old is an easier touch than Alec.'

'The solution's in yer own hands, mate,' George told him. 'Get yerself a wife and family before it's too late.'

Bob drained his glass. He wasn't so much on edge now and told Titch, 'I'd give that very careful thought if I were you. Weigh up all the pros and cons.'

'Oh, don't worry, mate. To me it sounds like a choice between the devil and the deep blue sea, and I don't fancy either.' Titch scraped his chair back and reached for the empty glasses. 'Looking at old Bert though makes yer think, doesn't it? He mustn't have had any children.'

'What! Are yer joking?' George laughed. 'He only had six! Four boys and two girls. They're all married with children of their own, but I know they slip him a few coppers when they can, 'cos I've seen them. But he likes his stout, does Bert, and this isn't the only

534

pub he frequents. He does the rounds and I'll bet he never goes home without a drink, even though he seldom has a penny to bless himself with. Ask the manager of the George – he'll tell yer all about the tricks Bert gets up to.'

'In other words, I've been had?'

'Well and truly, mate. Well and truly.'

Titch gave an exaggerated sigh. 'There's nothing down for me, is there? No wife, no kids and no ruddy brains.'

Ruby paced the floor after Bob had left, feeling really hard done by. What a bloody miserable life she was expected to lead. If he had his way, she'd be stuck in this house every night looking at four walls and she'd had enough. It had been like that for months now, and she was fed-up to the teeth with it. Every third week, when Bob was on the early shift, she had three nights out with her mates, but it wasn't good enough. She'd go stark staring mad if she thought this was how her life was going to be until she was too old to want some fun.

Not once did it enter Ruby's head that her life was of her own making. If she was friendly with the neighbours she'd have had plenty to do to pass the time away. Like the Pollards, where Lucy was now, playing cards. She could be in there if she'd put herself out to be friendly. But that wasn't what Ruby called having a good time. She wanted to be with her mates, sitting in a pub having a few drinks and being fawned over by Wally Brown. Now there was a man who appreciated her and made her feel like someone special.

She looked at the clock to see it was nearly eight o'clock. She'd give a knock on the wall in half an hour, a signal for Lucy to come home. And when the girl was in bed and fast asleep she'd take a chance and slip out for an hour. Bob would never know, and anyway she didn't give a monkey's whether he did or not. He couldn't expect her to live like a ruddy hermit.

With her mind made up, Ruby sat down and reached for her purse. Counting the money into her lap, she smiled. She had plenty to buy a round for everyone. Bob had never given her the extra five shillings housekeeping back, he'd reduced it to three. But with what she saved on food, it was enough for her nights out. She scooped the money up and put it back in her purse before running up the stairs to get changed. After that, she got the mirror out and began to apply thick layers of make-up.

'There's yer mam knocking for yer, sunshine.' Irene saw the look that always came to Lucy's face when it was time to go home. It was a look of disappointment mixed with fear. But she couldn't ignore the knock, otherwise Ruby would come banging on the door creating merry hell. 'It must be yer bedtime.'

Lucy put her cards down and pushed her chair back. Although she would never say it, she hated leaving this warm, happy house to go back to her home where there was never any laughter or smiles when her dad wasn't there. She hadn't done anything wrong, she always made sure she kept on the right side of her mother. But she knew something would be picked on as an excuse for a telling-off.

'We'll see yer tomorrow night, Lucy,' Jack said, hoping to bring a smile to the pretty face. 'It's a pity yer only won three buttons tonight, but yer luck might change tomorrow.'

'Yeah,' Greg grinned. 'And when yer've got enough to open a button shop, I'll be yer very first customer. Every time me mam washes a shirt, she manages to lose one of the pearl buttons. I don't know how she does it, but she definitely has the knack because all me shirts are missing a couple of buttons.'

'You cheeky beggar!' Irene put her arm across Lucy's shoulders. 'Take no notice of him, sunshine, he's pulling yer leg.'

'I know he is.' Lucy put out her tongue at the grinning face. 'Your mam looks after yer, she always has yer well turned out.'

'I'll come to the door with yer, sunshine, and make sure yer get in all right.'

The Mellors' front door was open and Lucy waved before stepping inside to be confronted by her mother. She was startled and took a step back, expecting a hand to lash out at her. But to her surprise and suspicion, there was a smile on the heavily made-up face. It wasn't a proper smile, but one that Lucy called a put-on one.

'I've made a hot drink for yer,' Ruby said, closing the front door and following her daughter into the living room. 'It'll warm yer up before yer go to bed.'

This was so out of character it put Lucy on her guard. 'I'll take it up with me and have it in bed.'

'Yeah, okay, if that's what yer want. But I'd like yer to do me a favour.'

Lucy took in the best dress, the made-up face and the sickly-sweet smell of cheap scent. Her mother was up to something. 'What d'yer want?'

'I've got a message for me mate Josie, and I want to slip round to her house for a few minutes. I won't be out long, just there and back. But yer know what yer dad's like, he'd do his nut if he knew. So it would be daft to tell him and start a row, wouldn't it? Just for the sake of half an hour at the most. So I want yer to be a good girl and not mention it to him. I'll give yer a ha'penny in the morning to buy some sweets on yer way to school.'

She's trying to buy my silence, Lucy told herself. But she needn't bother because for my dad's sake I wouldn't tell him. I know he'd get upset and there'd be a big row. And I wouldn't want that. 'I don't want any money for sweets, and I won't tell me dad unless he asks me.'

Ruby breathed a sigh of relief. Bob wouldn't ask, he had no reason to. He was stupid enough to think he had her under his thumb. 'I'll stay until ye're fast asleep, and I'll leave the light on for yer.'

Lucy didn't answer. She went down the yard to the lavvy, came back and washed her hands before pouring herself a cup of tea. She carried it through the living room and up the stairs without so much as a glance at her mother. And not a word was spoken.

When Alec called time, he motioned to Titch and George to stay put. He often did this, and would sit with the two mates and have a pint in the peace and quiet of an empty pub. He said it gave him time to wind down before clearing glasses and ash-trays. They just talked about things in general and had a good laugh. What the pub manager heard standing behind the bar counter was nobody's business and the three men would be in stitches. Until he called time on them, too.

Alec slid the heavy bolts back and opened the door. He peeped out to make sure the coast was clear, then stepped back to let the two men out. 'See yer tomorrow, eh, Titch?'

'More than likely, Alec. Goodnight.'

George was still smiling at something Alec had said which tickled his fancy. 'Yer wouldn't believe the stories he hears behind the bar, would yer? He should write a book about it.'

'Yeah, but as yer say, George, no one would believe it was the truth.' Titch suddenly took hold of his mate's arm and drew him into the darkness of the pub door. 'Not a word,' he said softly. Seconds went by before he let go of his grip. 'Yer can turn around now. Ruby Mellor's just gone past on the other side.'

George turned and watched the figure covering the ground quickly. 'What the hell's she doing out this time of night?'

'She certainly hasn't been on an errand of mercy, George, that's for sure. I'd say she's been up to no good.'

'She must have left Lucy on her own in the house. Bob will go mad when he knows.'

'He won't hear it from me, George. He's got enough worry on his plate without us adding to it. I think this is something we should keep between the two of us. I won't tell me ma, and I don't think yer should tell Irene. It's none of our business and it's not

537

our place to interfere. That doesn't mean I condone it, far from it. I'd really like to give that woman a piece of my mind. But I don't think Bob would thank me for it.'

'No, ye're right, he wouldn't.' George had seen Ruby disappear into the house and knew it was now safe for them to walk up the street. 'I won't breathe a word to Irene because I know she wouldn't keep it to herself. She thinks the world of Lucy, and would go mad if she thought the girl was in danger. And she could be, yer know, Titch. All it would take is a piece of coal falling out of the fire on to the rug. Or even the gas mantle flaking, as they sometimes do, and a burning piece falling on to the tablecloth. Yer do hear of these things happening.'

They were outside the Pollards' house now, and Titch said, 'We'll talk about it tomorrow, George. Me ma will wonder where I've got to. She might even think I've met the only girl in the world that's good enough for me, and run off with her.'

George chuckled. 'Aye, and pigs might fly.' He inserted the key in the lock. 'See yer tomorrow, mate. Goodnight.'

'Goodnight, George.' Titch waited until his neighbour was in the hall before saying, 'Oh, will yer give Irene a kiss for me? The one I would have got earlier if you hadn't been so flaming miserable.'

Kate Brown looked across the canteen table at Bob. 'Did yer have a pint before yer came into work?'

'Yeah, I had two as a matter of fact. How did yer know?'

'I tell fortunes. And looking at the tea leaves floating on the top of yer tea, I can see yer sitting in a pub with a pint glass in yer hand.'

Silence descended on the table and all eyes were on Bob as he said, 'Ye're pulling me leg, aren't yer?'

Kate shook her head, feeling she was pretty safe in what she was saying. She'd come to know a lot about Bob in the last six months and knew he only ever went for a pint before work when his friend was home from sea. 'I can see yer as plain as day. Ye're sitting with a man who has some sort of peaked cap on his head and he's wearing a navy-blue jacket.'

Peg Butterworth stopped munching and her eyes were wide with excitement. 'Is she right, Bob?'

Bob looked mystified. 'Yeah, she is. Me mate, Titch, is home on leave.'

'Well, I'll be a monkey's uncle.' Down went Peg's butty and she lifted up her cup. 'Yer can read my cup, Kate, when I've drank me tea.'

'And mine.' Elsie Burgess wasn't going to be left out. 'Ooh, I don't half love fortune-tellers. I went to one in Queen's Drive last year and yer should have heard some of the things she told me. She didn't half buck me up.'

Ada Smithson shook her head knowingly. 'I wouldn't have me fortune told, it's bad luck.'

Billy Gleeson had been listening with a smirk on his face. He could have told Bob what Kate did because he'd come to know his habits as she had. But he wasn't going to spoil the fun. 'You women would fall for the bloody cat. Thick as two short planks, the lot of yer.'

'Billy, ye're like a wet week,' Peg said, in between trying to drink tea that was too hot. 'If Aladdin had been as miserable as you, he'd have told the genie to sod off.'

Kate, after winking at Bob and mouthing that it had been guesswork, now looked on in amusement. She didn't know the first thing about telling fortunes but was game for a laugh. 'Don't blame me if I tell yer something yer don't like.'

Billy chuckled. 'Kate, be warned. If you tell Elsie something she doesn't like, she'll crack yer one.' He looked over to where the big woman sat. 'By the way, Elsie, this woman yer went to see on Queen's Drive, did the things she told yer come true?'

'Well, er, no they didn't. But she cheered me up for a week, so it was worth the tanner I'd paid.' The table began to bounce up and down as her mountainous tummy shook with laughter. 'Wait till yer hear this, Billy, it's a belter. She told me, all mysterious like, that she could see money around me: "I can't tell you exactly, but I think you're going to come into money. That's the message I'm getting through the cards." She spoke dead posh, as though she had a plum in her mouth. And she was right about seeing money. Yer see, ten days later I lost me purse with five bob in it.'

Peg nearly choked on her tea. 'Yer never told me that, Elsie Burgess.'

'Well, I don't tell yer everything, Peg. I mean, I don't say to yer that we've got three blankets on our bed. Or that the tap in the kitchen is leaking. And I wouldn't dream of telling yer that my feller kisses me every night and tells me how beautiful I am.'

'No, but ye're quick enough to tell me when ye're skint. Or like the time we were walking to work and yer said the elastic had snapped in yer knickers. I didn't know where to put meself when I looked down and there they were around yer ankles.' Memory of the scene had Peg rocking in her chair. 'I must have looked a right nit, standing there holding yer hand while yer stepped out of them.'

Everyone around the table went in a pleat, even Elsie. 'Yeah, it was funny that. It wasn't at the time, like, 'cos there were a lot of people about. But I had a good laugh afterwards and told my feller how funny it had been.'

'Elsie, the only thing I've ever seen that was funnier, was a Laurel and Hardy film. The only difference is, they get paid for making fools of themselves and you don't.' Peg leaned across her friend and handed her cup to Kate. 'Try and come up with something nice for me, girl. I need cheering up.'

'It'll have to be short if Elsie wants her reading as well. We haven't got that much time before the bell goes.' Kate pretended to concentrate, while her mind was trying to remember anything Peg had said that she could use. Then she had a brainwave. 'I'm probably miles out, but have yer bought anything recently, or are yer thinking of buying a dress or coat?'

'Well, I never!' Peg gaped. 'Yeah, I'm thinking of buying meself a new dress. Remember, Elsie, I told yer last week?'

Elsie was wide-eyed. 'Yeah, yer did, queen.'

Kate was glad her workmates had loud voices and she'd heard every word of their conversation. She turned the cup around and pretended to study the tea-leaves in the bottom. 'I think I see the colour blue.'

Well, that had Peg and Elsie banging on the table. 'That's the very colour I had in mind, girl! Isn't that right, Elsie?'

'It is, queen, I can vouch for that.' Elsie was by now convinced they had a fortune-teller in their midst and she wasn't going to be left out. 'Do mine, now, queen, before the bell goes.'

Kate was stumped. She couldn't think of anything she'd overheard. So she decided to go for a bit of fun. She turned the cup round and round, a puzzled expression on her face. 'I can't make this out. When yer were little, Elsie, were yer ever a May Queen?'

Elsie preened at the very thought, but had to admit it wasn't true. 'No, queen.'

'I don't know what it is, but it looks like a throne. And you're sitting on it, surrounded by light.' Kate had a funny ending in her head for this piece of fortune-telling, but it wasn't needed as Elsie had a funnier one.

Her chubby cheeks all screwed up and covering her eyes, Elsie shook her head as she tried to find a connection to what had been said to her. Then suddenly she blurted out, 'Bloody hell!' and every head in the canteen was turned towards her. 'Ay, queen, ye're not far out on that one. The throne yer see me sitting on is me lavvy. And the light around me comes from my feller having whitewashed the walls last week.'

When the laughter had died down, Peg said, 'Yer didn't tell me your feller had whitewashed the lavvy for yer.'

'Well, as I said before, queen, I can't remember to tell yer everything.'

Bob smiled across at Kate. 'You're not half coming out of yer shell lately. Yer used to be as quiet as a mouse.'

There was shyness in Kate's smile. 'Yer can blame yerself for that. I used to be as quiet as a mouse until you started sitting at our table. Yer must be having a bad influence on me, Bob Mellor.'

'I hope that's not true. I hold yer in very high esteem, Kate Brown.'

She lowered her eyes as a faint blush covered her cheeks. 'Then I'll have to try and live up to it, won't I?'

Chapter Fifteen

'It's a shame your Titch never got married,' Olive said, walking between Aggie and Irene, their arms linking hers. 'He loves kids and is so good with them.'

'Yeah, I know. I keep telling meself it's not too late, 'cos I'd like to see him settled down with a family. But he's either too bleedin' choosey or no one will have him.'

'Your son would have no trouble finding a dozen girls who'd be more than willing to marry him,' Irene said. 'He's a fine-looking man and if he was that way inclined he could have his pick.'

After much persuasion they'd finally talked Olive into coming to the pictures. She was worried because she didn't have a decent coat to wear, so Aggie had lent her a black knitted shawl to wear over a thick cardigan. It was a cold winter's night and there was a stiff breeze blowing, but cushioned between her friends, Olive was sheltered from the worst of it. 'He's got a lot of patience with kids. Just look at him now, they're all over him and he's lapping it up. Our Steve idolises him, I know that much.'

Titch was walking ahead with the youngsters, one hand holding Lucy's while the three boys walked on his other side. Their laughter was carried on the wind, bringing smiles to the faces of the three women. 'That's our Jack,' Irene said. 'I don't think he's stopped talking since we left the house.'

'Oh, I don't know,' Aggie said. 'They're all doing their fair share, even Lucy. She's not behind the door when it comes to getting her twopennyworth in.'

Olive saw Lucy look up at Titch with a smile on her face. She couldn't hear what the girl said, but loud laughter followed her words. 'I see what yer mean, Aggie. She's a beautiful-looking girl, I bet her parents are proud of her.'

There was no immediate reply to that, then Irene said, 'I'll tell yer what, Olive. You scratch my back and I'll scratch yours. If you say my two are handsome lads, I'll say the same about your Steve. Then we'll all be happy.'

'Oh, no we won't,' Aggie tutted. 'Yer seem to forget that I have a son, too. Now let's hear it for Titch. Is he handsome, or is he not?'

'Very, very handsome,' was Olive's verdict.

While Irene thought he was, 'Film-star handsome.'

'That's better. He may be forty, but he's still my little boy.' They grinned at each other before quickening their steps to catch up with Titch and company outside the picturehouse. The children had all opted for a comedy, *The Gay Divorcée*, starring Fred Astaire and Ginger Rogers. And it was hilarious. Jack got so carried away with mirth he kept banging his fist on the back of the seat in front of him, until the woman turned around and told him if he didn't knock it off she'd knock his block off. Lucy was captivated by the dancing, Steve was captivated by the changing expressions on her face, and Greg was too busy enjoying himself to worry about anyone else.

On the walk home, it was unanimously agreed that a good time had been had by all and the evening had been a great success. For Olive it had been more than that. It had been a much-needed tonic.

It was when they turned into their street that Titch noticed a change in Lucy. The smile had gone from her face and she seemed tense. 'Are yer all coming back to ours for a cup of tea?' he asked.

'No thanks, Titch,' Olive said. 'I'll go straight home if yer don't mind.'

'Me too.' Irene gathered her sons to her. 'It's nearly time for Greg to go to bed. But thanks for a lovely night, I thoroughly enjoyed meself.'

There was a chorus of thanks from the children. It was Steve, a gentleman at fourteen years of age, who held out his hand. 'Thanks, Mr Titch, it's been smashing.'

Titch shook his hand warmly. 'Ye're welcome, lad. We'll do it again, soon.' He put his arm across Lucy's shoulder. 'Are you coming in for a cuppa, sweetheart?'

'Oh no, Mr Titch. Me dad won't have left for work yet, so I'll be in time for me goodnight kiss. I wouldn't want to miss that.'

'Then I'll walk down with yer and have a short natter with yer dad.'

The group went their separate ways, leaving Titch with his mother and Lucy. 'Are yer coming with us, Ma?'

Aggie shook her head. 'No, I'll go in and put the kettle on. You see Lucy home.'

Bob had been watching out and the door was quickly opened. 'Good time, pet?'

'Oh Dad, the picture was lovely. It was very funny, but I liked the dancing the best.'

'Come in, Titch.' Bob threw the door wide open. 'I don't have to leave for half an hour, so there's time for a cup of tea.'

544

'I'll come in, but I won't stay for a drink, thanks. Me ma's gone in to put the kettle on.'

Ruby managed a smile. 'Was it a good picture?'

Titch looked to Lucy, expecting her to reply. When she didn't, he said, 'Yeah, it was great. Everyone enjoyed themselves.'

'I don't know how yer've got the patience to take a gang of kids out. Yer wouldn't catch me doing it, they'd drive me potty. It certainly wouldn't be my idea of a good night out.'

Titch saw the look of disgust on Bob's face. And he saw Lucy standing with her head bowed, a stranger in her own home. Leaning an elbow on the sideboard and injecting a note of interest in his voice, he asked, 'Oh, and what's your idea of a good night out, Ruby?'

'A couple of drinks in pleasant company. Friends yer can have a laugh and a joke with.'

'Yer won't get many of those nights with Bob being on shift-work, will yer? I mean, when he's on afternoons and nights, yer won't manage to get out, will yer?'

There was something in the tone of his voice and the look in his eyes that caused Ruby to feel uncomfortable. He seemed to be goading her, as though he knew something. Could she have been seen on the two nights she'd been out? She'd been very careful, using the back entry when she went out. But she'd come home the front way because she didn't fancy the dark entry late at night. She hadn't given a thought to anyone seeing her because the street had been deserted on both nights. No, she told herself, he doesn't know anything, it's just my imagination. So she brazened it out. 'No, the only social life I get is when he's on mornings, worse luck.'

'Count yer blessings, Ruby, 'cos that's more than most women get.' Titch pushed himself up and stretched his well-built frame. 'I'd better be going or me ma will tell me off if the tea gets cold.' He gave Lucy a hug. 'I'll see yer, sweetheart.'

'Yeah, okay, Mr Titch, and thanks again.'

'I'll see yer out, then I'll have to put a move on meself.' Bob followed his neighbour to the door, 'I appreciate yer taking Lucy out, she doesn't half enjoy herself. I'm sorry to say me daughter doesn't get many treats in life.'

'She's got a lot of friends, Bob, that think the world of her. And she's got the best father anyone could ask for.' Titch began to laugh and pointed a finger. 'Just look at me ma, standing on the step shaking a fist at me. Anyone would think I was fourteen instead of forty. She used to do that when I was a slip of a lad and wouldn't come in when she called me. I'd better skedaddle or I'll be getting a clip around the ear. Don't work too hard, Bob.'

Bob stepped down to wave to Aggie. 'Goodnight and God bless, Aggie. Sleep well. And you, Titch. I'll see yer.'

The night before Titch was due to sail, he went to say goodbye to Olive and Steve. He also went with a plan in mind.

'How long are yer away this time, Titch?' Olive asked. 'A couple of months?'

'Could be longer this time, Olive. That's why, if you don't mind, I'd like to ask Steve to do a job for me.'

'Of course I will, Mr Titch.' Steve would willingly run to the ends of the earth for this man. 'Just name it and I'll do it.'

'Only on certain conditions, Steve. I want to pay yer for it. Not much, mind yer, but I don't want yer to do it for nothing.'

'Steve wouldn't take money off you, Titch!' Olive protested. 'After all you've done for him, he wouldn't dream of it.'

'Me mam's right.' Steve was highly indignant. 'I wouldn't take no money off yer.'

'But it's a big job I'm asking yer to do, Steve. Yer see, I'm worried about me ma, now the winter has set in. I don't like the thought of her having to lug coal up the yard in freezing weather. I have visions of her slipping on the snow or ice or laying in the yard with no one knowing she's there. So I was going to ask if yer'd slip up there each night and fill her coal scuttle for her and make sure she's all right. I'd have an easy mind when I'm away if I knew she was being cared for.'

'I'd do that with pleasure,' Steve said, looking happy at just the thought. 'Yer don't have to pay me no money to look after Mrs Aggie.'

'I'll keep me eye on her, too,' Olive said. 'I won't go up at night, but I'll call in each day.'

This was what Titch had been hoping for. It was a good way of getting Olive out of the house. 'That's taken a load off me mind. But if I'm away for two or three months, it's a lot to ask of yer. So if yer won't take money off me, will yer let me do something for yer?'

Olive tilted her head and narrowed her eyes. 'Oh, aye, what are yer up to now? I don't trust you, Titch McBride.'

Titch winked at Steve. 'Will yer sit on yer mam for me, so she can't scratch me eyes out or wallop me one?'

Steve left the wooden chair to sit next to his mother on the couch. He put his two arms around her and held her tight. 'Safely anchored, Mr Titch.'

'What I've asked you two to do is a very big favour. Now I'd like yer to let me give a little back in return. It's not much, but it would please me to do it.'

546

'I don't like the sound of this,' Olive said. 'Spit it out and get it over with.'

'Promise yer won't hit me, fall out with me or throw me out?'

'In the name of God, what's the man up to now?' Olive managed to keep her face straight while asking herself how could anyone fall out with Titch when he had that huge smile on his face and mischief dancing in his eyes. 'Come on, out with it.'

'Well, now I know me ma's going to be well looked after, I'd like to think you two were happy and comfortable. So let me buy the wallpaper to brighten this room up.'

'You what!' Olive's voice was shrill. 'Not on yer blinking life.'

'Excuse me, Mrs Fletcher, but I haven't finished yet. There's more to come.' Titch wagged an admonishing finger. 'So be a good girl and listen before disagreeing with me. I knew I'd have trouble getting Steve to take money off me, so I went ahead and bought wallpaper for this room. I didn't pay full price for it because I've got a mate what's got a mate with a wallpaper shop. So I'm not being as generous as yer think. It only cost me a few bob. And George and Bob have said they'd be delighted to do the work.' Titch grinned before letting out a deep sigh. 'Now I'll ask Steve to keep tight hold of yer until yer've had time to think it over. But to help yer come to the right decision, close yer eyes and imagine how nice and cheerful this room would look for Christmas. And remember, I wasn't too proud to accept your help, so to keep things square, the least yer can do is accept mine.'

When Olive stayed stony-faced, her eyes fixed on the far wall, Titch wagged his head at Steve before asking, 'Is yer mam still breathing, lad?'

'I think so, Mr Titch, I can see her nostrils going in and out.'

'That's good. It means she hasn't gone and died on us.' He leaned forward and looked into the solemn face. 'I'm glad about that, 'cos I'd have been left with eight rolls of wallpaper and a lot of explaining to do.'

Without moving a muscle, Olive asked, 'What colour's the paper?'

His face as straight as hers, Titch said, 'Pea-green.'

'I'm not having no pea-green wallpaper on my walls, Titch McBride – yer can take it right back and change it.'

'How about a pale beige with little sprigs of pink flowers on?'

'That sounds more like it.' Olive faced him with a beaming smile. 'How soon can the workmen start?'

'Bob's on mornings, so he could do a bit in the afternoons. Then on Saturday him and George could go like the clappers and get a fair bit done. But you and Steve could help by stripping the old paper off and rubbing the paintwork down.' With a cheeky grin on his face, Titch reached into his pocket and brought out a scraper and two sheets of sandpaper. 'I've come prepared for any contingency. These for if yer said yes, and running shoes in case yer came after me with the poker.'

'It wouldn't have made a scrap of difference what I said, and you know it. I could have argued until I was blue in the face, yer'd still have got yer own way in the end.'

'Excuse me, Mr Titch,' Steve said. 'Can I let go of me mam now?'

'Just make sure she's not frothing at the mouth first. It's a bad sign that, frothing at the mouth.'

'I'll froth you at the mouth, yer cheeky beggar.' But Olive was feeling very light-hearted inside. It would be lovely to see this room nice and bright. 'I should tell yer off for being underhanded and arranging all this behind me back. But I'm not going to because I'm really delighted. I'm indebted to yer, Titch.'

'Ay, remember there's a price to pay for this. I'm relying on both of yer to look after me ma for me.' Titch wondered what his mother would say if she knew she'd been used as a weapon in his plans. She'd probably stand on a chair and box his ears for him. 'It means a lot to me, knowing she's being looked after.'

'I'll keep an eye on her, Mr Titch, I promise yer that. Me and Mrs Aggie get along fine together, we're good mates.'

'It does me heart good to hear that, lad. I know she thinks the world of you.' Titch stood up and put the scraper and sandpaper on the table. 'I'll take me leave of yer now 'cos I'm going for a pint with me two drinking buddies. It's me last night so I've got to make the most of it.'

'Well, look after yerself, Titch,' Olive said. 'Next time yer come we'll be all posh and yer won't get in unless yer wipe yer feet.'

Titch chuckled. 'I'm a clever bugger, Olive, but even I can't walk on walls.'

Olive raised her brows. 'Oh, no? According to Aggie yer can walk on the ceiling when yer've had one over the eight.'

'I wish me ma would stop bragging about me achievements, it's embarrassing. But if she ever tells yer I can walk on water, take it with a pinch of salt.' Titch glanced at the clock before holding his hand out to Steve. 'Look after yer mam, lad, take good care of her. And, of course, yer mate, Mrs Aggie.'

Steve felt ten feet tall. 'Yer can rely on me, Mr Titch. But I wish yer weren't going away, I'll miss yer.'

'We all will,' Olive said. 'Even if it's only for yer cheek.'

Titch bent and kissed the top of her head. 'Yer've come on a treat, Olive. Keep it up at this rate and I won't recognise yer when I come home.'

Mother and son felt sad when they heard the door close behind him. Tommy 'Titch' McBride had come into their lives like a ray of sunshine, and picked them up when they were down. They had much to thank him for.

'Me mate sails today,' Bob said, flicking a crumb from his lips. 'We had a cracking night out with him last night. Mind you, me and George can't keep up with his drinking. If Titch had had his way, neither of us would have been fit for work today.'

'When are we going to meet this mate of yours?' Peg Butterworth wanted to know. 'Tall, tanned and handsome, he sounds right up my street.'

Elsie Burgess, her plump elbows leaning on the table, looked sideways. 'Any man in trousers is right up your street, queen.'

'Ay, watch it, you!' Peg looked put out. 'Be careful what yer say about my good name, unless yer fancy wearing a black eye.'

'It's true! Everyone knows ye're man mad.' Elsie's elbow slipped off the table and her sandwich ended up in her eye. But, undeterred, she carried on: 'It's not so long ago that yer asked me about the milkman what was having it off with a woman in our street.'

'But the poor man wasn't having it off with the woman in your street, was he?' Billy Gleeson said. 'It was your bad minds. If he'd known what yer were saying about him, he could have had yer all up for defamation of character.'

Elsie's mouth gaped. 'What was that yer said, Billy?'

'He could have had yer all up for defamation of character.'

'Yeah, I heard that, but could yer say it in English, please?'

Peg gave her friend a dig. 'Don't show yer ignorance, girl. That *was* English.'

'Well, I didn't never learn nothing like that in my school. Some of it, yeah, but not that defation. I didn't never hear that word before.'

'The word is defamation, Elsie.' Billy was highly amused. 'It means he could have sued yer for every penny yer've got.'

Up and down went the table with Elsie's tummy. 'Blimey, if he can get his tongue around a big word like that, he'd deserve to take every penny I've got. But he'd have to do it on a Saturday, 'cos I've never got two ha'pennies to rub together the rest of the week.' Her face straightened. 'Anyway, clever clogs, Billy Gleeson, yer'd better be careful what yer say or I'll have you up for that deffy thing. We didn't do no wrong, it was a genuine mistake. How were we to know our neighbour was a friend of his missus? And that he stopped for a cuppa and a butty every morning? It was an easy mistake to make.'

Peg sat sideways in her chair and weighed her friend up. 'And what about the coalman? Was his missus a friend, too?'

'How the hell do I know!' Elsie was getting all het up. 'Yer'll be asking me next if the bleedin' horse was a cousin of hers.'

'Keep yer hair on, girl.' A glint came in Peg's eyes. 'Yer can't afford to lose any hairs 'cos yer haven't got many to start with.'

'Are you looking for a fight? If yer are, I'll give yer one,' Elsie said. 'I've got as many hairs on my head as you have, if not more.'

Peg pursed her lips. 'I'll bet yer any money yer haven't.'

'And I bet yer any money I have.'

'Okay,' Peg said. 'Put yer money where yer mouth is. How many hairs have yer got on yer head?'

Oh, she's not catching me out there, thought Elsie. She thinks she's clever, but she's picked on the wrong one. 'You tell me how many you've got first, then I'll tell yer.'

Peg's expression was superior to say the least. 'At the last count it was two million, three hundred thousand and twenty-five.'

Elsie managed to look astounded. 'Well, would yer believe it?' She gazed around the table. 'That's exactly the same number I've got.' She turned to her friend, and before Peg realised what she was up to, Elsie reached over and pulled out a few hairs that were sticking out from under her turban. 'Now yer've got three less than me.'

'That does it.' Peg banged her fist on the table. 'Prove it.'

Elsie looked blank. 'What d'yer mean?'

'Start pulling them out and count them. And we'll all sit here and witness that yer play fair. When yer've got to two million, three hundred thousand and twenty-five, if yer've still got a hair left on yer head, then you win.'

'Yer can sod off, you can! Yer must think I've just come over! It was you what started all this, so it's up to you to prove what ye're saying. Start counting, queen.'

'I haven't got time, girl, 'cos the bell will be going in ten minutes. So we'll call it quits, eh?'

'Yeah,' Elsie smiled, 'we're both winners.'

Peg delved into the pocket of her overall and brought out a threepenny joey, which she handed over. 'Here's yer winnings, girl.'

'Thanks, queen.' Elsie stared down at the small chunky coin nestling in her chubby hand. Smiling, she picked it up and held it out to Peg. 'And here's yours, queen. It was a good, clean, fair fight and we both deserved to win.'

Bob winked across at Kate. 'D'yer know, it's a pleasure to come to work. Apart from when I'm out with me mates, this is the only time I get a few laughs and some decent conversation. Plus the added bonus of having a pretty woman sitting opposite to me.'

Billy swivelled in his seat. 'Ay, I heard that.'

'Yer were meant to.' Bob chuckled. 'I don't see why all the gossip should come from the women, so I thought I'd add a bit of spice to liven things up.'

'That's a good idea, mate. Just listen to this.' Billy leaned across the table and gestured for everyone to follow suit. Then in a loud whisper, he said, 'Don't any of yer repeat this, but Kate and Bob are having a clandestine affair.'

'Oh, the gear!' Peg said. 'That's something we can really get our teeth into.'

'I don't agree with it.' Little Ada Smithson's thin lips became a narrow line in her pale face. 'It's a sin, that is.'

'What did yer say Kate and Bob were having, Billy?' Elsie asked, not bothering to keep her voice down. 'I didn't hear yer properly.'

'A clandestine affair, Elsie.'

'What school did you go to, Billy Gleeson? It certainly wasn't the same one as me 'cos we don't speak the same language.' Elsie leaned her elbows on the table and looked along to where Kate was sitting. 'You speak English, queen, so you tell me. What are you and Bob having?'

It was with great difficulty that Kate kept her face straight. 'We're having an affair, Elsie.'

'Go 'way!' Elsie mulled the information over for a few seconds, then asked, 'What exactly d'yer mean, queen?'

'Me and Bob are having what you thought yer milkman and neighbour were having. Only they weren't and we are.'

The bell sounded then and chairs were scraped back. 'Why didn't yer tell us that earlier, Billy Gleeson?' Peg asked. 'Now we've got to wait until tomorrow for the next instalment.'

Bob stood at the end of the table and waited for Kate to pick up her belongings. 'I dropped yer in it there, I hope yer don't mind. I just thought it would be a laugh.'

'So yer think having an affair with me would be a laugh, do yer, Bob Mellor? Well, thanks for the compliment.'

Bob blushed to the roots of his hair. 'I didn't mean it like that, Kate. Any man having an affair with you would be a lucky man indeed.'

'Don't take it to heart, Bob, I was only pulling yer leg. And it was a laugh. But we'll never hear the end of it, so be prepared. Peg and Elsie will have a field day with this.'

'I'll sort it out with them tomorrow, then they won't embarrass yer. I should have had more sense, a man of my age.'

'Will yer stop worrying? Peg and Elsie are not soft, they'll know

551

it was only a joke. They'll have a few laughs at our expense then it'll die a natural death. You mark my words.'

Kate turned off when they reached her section. 'I'll see yer tomorrow, Bob.' Then in a loud voice she called after him, 'I'll meet yer at eight, outside the Forum.'

He smiled and waved back. 'Don't be late, like yer were on Monday.'

Peg nudged her mate. 'Yer see, Elsie, I told yer it wasn't true. They're just having us on. The trouble with you is, yer'd fall for the bleedin' cat.'

'Which cat, queen? I haven't got no cat.'

Peg rolled her eyes. 'Why did I pick a friend what's got nothing between her ears only fresh air?'

When Bob came home from work on the Thursday he went straight into the kitchen to swill his hands and face. 'I'm going up to the Fletchers' after I've had a cup of tea. I want to get the room prepared for Saturday, so me and George can start hanging the paper.'

Ruby was by the stove, pouring boiling water into the tea pot. 'You men are bloody fools falling for a hard luck story. Talk about act soft and I'll buy yer a coalyard, isn't in it. Olive Fletcher is too lazy to do anything for herself, so she flutters her eyelashes, pretends she's sick, and has the lot of yer running around after her.'

Bob didn't answer as he dried his face on the towel. He refused to be drawn into an argument with someone who wouldn't get off her backside to help anyone. His wife didn't know anything about the Fletchers and the hard time they'd had. Even if she did, they'd get no sympathy from her. She didn't have a compassionate bone in her body.

'It would do yer more good to decorate yer own house,' Ruby said. 'Never mind wasting yer time up there.'

Bob hung the towel back on the nail behind the door. It wasn't twelve months since he'd papered the living room, but it wouldn't do any good reminding her. She'd set her mind against the Fletchers, and every other family in the street for that matter, and no amount of persuasion would alter that. 'I won't bother with a drink, I'll have one when I get up there. I'll be back at half-five for me dinner.'

'But I've made this pot of tea now!' Ruby followed him into the living room, intent on giving him a piece of her mind. But her mouth closed on the words when she saw him looking down at the *True Confessions* magazine she'd bought that morning. She bought one every week but never cracked on because he'd have a go at her

552

for wasting money when Lucy needed clothes. She usually hid it behind the cushion on her chair but she'd slipped up today.

'I'm sure yer'll manage to get through a pot of tea while ye're reading this tripe.' Bob saw the price on the top of the magazine and was filled with hopelessness and despair. 'The cost of that would have bought Lucy a pair of socks.'

Ruby stared him out. 'I didn't buy it, smart arse. Me mate called round and lent it to me.'

'Telling lies is the only thing ye're good at, Ruby. Oh, and calling everybody fit to burn. I suppose I should feel sorry for yer really, but I can't. Yer see, where ye're concerned, I no longer have any feelings whatsoever. You killed them long ago.' With that, Bob turned on his heels and left the room. He told himself to put it out of his mind; getting upset wouldn't do him any good. So when he was knocking on Aggie's door, there was a smile on his face.

'I've come for the paper and paint, Aggie. I know there's a lot to be done before we can make a start, but seeing as me hands are empty I thought I'd carry it up and get it over with.'

'Come in, lad.' Aggie closed the door behind him. 'Yer can take the paint 'cos they're big tins and too heavy for me to carry. But yer can't take the paper or border 'cos it wants trimming. Me and Irene are going to make a start on it tonight, so it'll be ready when yer need it. Oh, and your Lucy's going to help. We're meeting at Irene's at half-six, when she's got the dinner out of the way.'

'A hive of activity, eh, Aggie? I'm glad to have something to do to occupy me mind.'

Aggie studied his face. He was still smiling, but it was an empty smile. And she detected a sadness in his eyes. 'Glad of a chance to get out of the house, are yer, Bob?'

Bob's nod came with a sigh. 'Yes, Aggie, ye're right. It's a terrible thing to say, but when Lucy's not there, there's nothing in that house for me. I must be the only feller in Liverpool that's glad to go to work. But as they say, I've made me bed and I must lie on it.'

'Yer shouldn't have to spend a lifetime in misery, lad, no one deserves that. Perhaps when Lucy's grown up yer can do something about it. There is such a thing as divorce, yer know.'

'I've thought of everything, Aggie, believe me. But a divorce is complicated and nasty. Ruby wouldn't consent to it anyway and she'd cause merry hell. I wouldn't want to put Lucy through that. But in a few years – well, who knows.'

'Yeah, ye're right, lad. God works in mysterious ways and none of us knows what's going to happen in the future. But I've got a

553

feeling in me bones that there'll come a time when you and Lucy are happy and contented.'

'I hope so, Aggie. Now can yer show me where the paint is and I'll be on me way to Olive's and get some work done. George is hoping I'll have the room ready for papering by Saturday.'

'They're on the floor in the kitchen. Yer'll have to get them yerself, I can't lift them.'

Bob put the tins down and stared at the bare walls. 'I wasn't expecting this, Olive. Steve must have worked like mad to get this stripped.'

'Ay, Bob Mellor, I helped, yer know. Steve did the top, I did the bottom. The paper was hanging off anyway, so it was easy.'

'Right, I'll start rubbing the paintwork down, then. But is there any chance of a cuppa? I work better after I've had a drink and a ciggie.'

'I'll put the kettle on, but I've only got conny-onny. Is that all right?'

'I was brought up on conny-onny, Olive, it suits me fine.'

Bob started on the door leading to the hall. He was on his knees when Olive came through carrying two cups of piping hot tea. 'Come and get it. I've no saucers, I'm afraid.'

Bob pulled a chair out and sat facing her. 'Olive, I was brought up in a house with no saucers.' They were both laughing when there was a knock on the door.

Olive's hand went to her throat. 'I wonder who this can be?'

'It won't be a bogeyman – they only come when it's dark.' Bob laughed and stood up. 'I'll answer it.'

Olive sat with her ear cocked. She heard a man's laughter and her heart lurched. It sounded like Titch, but it couldn't be. He'd be on the high seas by now. 'Who is it, Bob?'

'I was wrong, it *is* a bogeyman. I'll let him in though, 'cos he looks harmless enough.'

Olive's eyes were on the door when Titch walked in. 'In the name of heaven, am I seeing things or is it a ghost?'

'The ship developed engine trouble and we had to turn back. It's in for repairs now, and they could take a few days. So ye're honoured with my company again.' Titch eyed the two cups. 'What are yer doing, Olive Fletcher, entertaining a strange man the minute me back's turned? A married man at that.'

'He's only been here about five minutes.'

'I know how long he's been here, 'cos I went home first and me ma told me. Anyway, where's my cup of tea?'

Bob chuckled. 'Only conny-onny, Titch, and no saucer.'

'Just the way I like it. And you can pour it out, Bob, while I fill

Olive's heart with happiness by telling her I'll probably be home long enough to see this room decorated.'

'Yer'll be getting stuck in, mate, like the rest of us,' Bob told him. 'With everyone working flat out, it should be finished on Saturday.'

Titch grinned. 'In time for the pub opening, I hope.'

Chapter Sixteen

Bob and Titch worked like Trojans, and by half-past five all the paintwork had been rubbed down. 'That's a good job done,' Titch said. 'But with the best will in the world I don't see how we can get the room finished on Saturday.'

'It can be done.' Bob was more optimistic. 'If Olive will wash the paintwork down while we nip home for our dinner, we can start putting the undercoat on when we come back. I'll bring a brush and the two of us can get cracking. We should get it finished tonight, then the gloss can go on tomorrow.'

Olive looked uneasy. 'I don't want to stop Titch going for his pint.'

'Yeah, that's an important point,' Titch said, pursing his lips as his head wagged from side to side. 'A whole day without a pint doesn't bear thinking about.'

'Yer could keep telling yerself it's Sunday,' Bob said. 'And all the pubs are shut.'

'I've got a better idea. Every time I get a pang, I'll look at Olive and remind meself that even a pint of bitter with a frothy head on isn't as pretty as she is.'

'Will yer go home for yer dinner and stop embarrassing me.' Olive could feel herself blushing. 'Our Steve will be in soon and he'll want something to eat before he gives me a hand washing the paintwork.'

'Aren't some people ungrateful, Bob?' Titch slipped his arms into his reefer jacket. 'I sabotaged the engine for this woman, and that's the thanks I get.'

Olive pointed to the door. 'Will yer go now, the pair of yer?'

Bob chuckled as he grabbed Titch's arm and pulled him into the hall. 'We'll be back in an hour, Olive.'

As soon as she heard the door close after them, Olive bustled out to the kitchen where the mince and onions were simmering gently and the potatoes were ready for mashing. She turned the gas off but left the pan lids on to keep the food warm. An hour wasn't very long to eat a dinner, wash the dishes and then start cleaning the paintwork. But she was determined to do as much as she could. God knows, everybody was doing all they could to help her, the least she could do was pull her weight.

The sound of the key in the door had her reaching for two plates. 'Hurry up, son, we'll be having visitors soon.'

Steve gave her a hug and a kiss. 'Who's coming?'

'Mr Mellor and Mr Titch.'

'Mr Titch!' The lad's voice was high with surprise. 'Is Mr Titch home?'

Olive nodded as she spooned potato on to the plates. 'The ship developed engine trouble and had to turn back. He reckons he'll be home for a few days. Him and Bob have been here all afternoon, rubbing down. They asked if we'd make everywhere clean so they can start on the undercoating tonight.'

Steve took a plate from her and sniffed up. 'It smells good, Mam.'

'Yeah, thanks to Mrs Aggie. She brought the mince down early on and I only had to heat it up. But we'll have to wolf it down, son, 'cos they'll be here before we know it.'

The men were a quarter of an hour late, for which Olive was thankful. The extra minutes gave her time to wash up after their dinner and then really get stuck into the woodwork. She started one side of the room, her son the other.

Steve sneaked a look at his mother as she stretched up to reach the top of the door. Just a few short months ago, she wouldn't have had the energy to do that. Even washing the dishes would have tired her out. So she really must be getting better. His spirits lifted, he went back to washing the windowframe with renewed vigour.

When the knock came, Olive said, 'This'll be them. Open the door, love.' She stood with the wet cloth in her hand and listened as her son welcomed his hero. But she was proud to hear Bob get as warm a welcome. She waited for the two men to enter, then said, with mock severity, 'You are late.'

'It's his fault,' Bob said, nodding at Titch. 'I called for him on time.'

'And I'd have been ready if it hadn't been for me ma. We had fish for tea, and didn't I go and swallow a bone this size.' He held his hands about two foot apart. 'I'm not kidding, I nearly choked to death.'

Steve, never happier than when he was in this man's company, chuckled. 'And the bone was really that big, Mr Titch? It must have been some fish.'

'I told me ma it must have been a whale, but she would have it that it was a piece of cod. And this'll tell yer how serious it was. When I was choking to death, instead of hitting me on the back to dislodge the thing, me ma was searching the sideboard drawer for the insurance policy.'

'Titch McBride, yer can't half tell some whoppers,' Olive said, shaking with laughter. 'And yer have to drag poor Aggie into it.'

' "Poor Aggie", did yer say? If that bone had finished me off, it would have been "rich Aggie". Mind you, she did say she was pleased when I coughed the thing up. And I know she meant it 'cos there were tears in her eyes.'

'I thought yer were having mince and onions for yer dinner.'

'Yeah, we did. But I had to have some excuse for being late and I couldn't very well say I'd choked on a bit of mincemeat. I mean, yer wouldn't have believed that, would yer?'

'No, not really,' Olive said, her face deadpan. 'The two-foot bone was far more believable.'

'We came to work, mate,' Bob reminded him. 'Or had yer forgot?'

And work they did. Stopping only once for a cuppa and a smoke. And by half-past ten, all the woodwork had been under-coated. Titch was as pleased as Punch. 'Not bad going, eh, mate?'

Bob nodded, satisfied they'd achieved their goal. 'Ruddy good going, mate.'

'It's brilliant,' Steve said. 'Yer've done wonders.'

'The room looks brighter already.' Olive was tired, but it was a nice tiredness. 'I didn't realise how horrible that brown paintwork was.'

'Wait until the room's finished, love, yer won't know yerself.' Titch was glad he'd be here to see her face. 'We'll make tracks now 'cos Bob's on early shift. But I'll make a start on the gloss paint in the morning and should have it in hand by the time he gets home from work. Would nine o'clock be too early for yer?'

Olive tutted. 'Titch, no woman looks her best at that time of the morning – at least, I don't. So could yer make it ten? I'll have tidied up by then.'

'Vanity, thy name is woman.'

'Okay, Titch, come at nine and take me as yer find me. But don't say I didn't warn yer, 'cos I'll look like death warmed up.'

Bob yawned. 'I'm off, folks, or I'll never get up in the morning. Goodnight and God bless, everyone. Sleep well.'

'Thanks for everything, Bob. I'll never be able to repay yer for what yer've done. And you, Titch, yer've been brilliant. Now go home and get yer beauty sleep. I'll see yer tomorrow.'

'I'll see them out, Mam, and bolt the door.' Steve was afraid his mother might be overdoing it. 'You get yerself off to bed.'

When the two men stepped into the street, Titch said, 'That's right, lad, you take good care of yer mam.'

559

'I'll always take care of her, Mr Titch, because she's a good mam and I love her very much.'

Aggie was with her son when Olive opened the door next morning. 'I know it's early for visitors, queen, but I thought I'd bring yer up to date on what's happening.' Her basket in the crook of her arm, she marched through to the living room. 'Me and Irene trimmed all the rolls of paper yesterday and we're starting the border when she gets home from work. Oh, and young Lucy's been a great help. She made as good a job at trimming as any grown up could have done.'

'Ma, where's yer manners? Good morning, Olive,' Titch said with a wink.

Aggie snapped her fingers. 'Yer know, I knew I'd forgotten something. I left me manners on the table, and if yer don't behave yerself I'll send yer down to get them.'

Olive grinned. 'Titch, yer might know yer'll never get one over on yer ma. She's got an answer for everything.'

'I'll catch her one of these days, when she's not looking.' Titch folded his coat and laid it on the couch. 'I'll get the ladder out of the yard and make a start.'

'Yer said yer had to report to yer ship,' Aggie said. 'What time are yer going?'

'I'll go about one. I should have a fair bit done here by then. And I'll be back for when Bob arrives.' Titch shook his head, a look of doubt on his face. 'I still can't see us getting this room finished tomorrow.'

Aggie tutted. 'Oh ye of little faith. Would yer like to have a bet on it?'

'Not with you, Ma, 'cos I've tried that before. I never win.'

'I wouldn't take yer money off yer, son, 'cos it would be like taking sweets from a baby. Yer've never seen George Pollard working, have yer? He's that fast, yer eyes can't keep up with him. And I'll be cutting the paper to size, 'cos this room's exactly the same as ours. So if you or Bob do the pasting, all George has to do is put it up. And as I've said, the man is like greased lightning.'

'I'll take your word for it, Ma. Now, if yer don't mind, I'm going to get the ladder. And once I make a start, I don't want no interruptions.'

'I'll be going anyway, I'm off to do some shopping. But before yer put the silence board up, can I just say one thing? I'll be down at half-twelve with some sandwiches for you and Olive. I can't have me one and only son working on an empty tummy.'

When Aggie had gone, Olive felt uncomfortable being alone in the house with Titch. He was busy working away, and she didn't

560

know where to put herself. 'I'm going upstairs to give the bedrooms a clearout, Titch. If yer want anything, just holler.'

It was eleven o'clock when he shouted up the stairs. 'Ay, Olive! I know I said I didn't want any interruptions, but a cup of tea wouldn't go amiss. Everybody has a break this time in the mornings. Even ruddy slaves! Get yerself down here, woman!'

As Olive walked down the stairs, she was thinking how strange it was to have a man in the house. Strange, but somehow comforting. 'There's still only conny-onny, Titch.'

Titch, back on the ladder and painting the picture rail, said, 'If it's wet and warm, it'll do me fine. Yer should try the tea we get on the ship, it's so thick yer can stand yer spoon up in it. And yer won't hear one complaint from the crew because the cook's six foot six. And that's in his stocking feet.'

When they were facing each other across the table, Titch admired his handiwork. 'Not bad going in two hours, is it?'

'Yer've done well, Titch. I won't know meself when it's finished.'

'Well, at least you and Steve can sit in comfort. Ye're a lot better than yer were a few months ago, aren't yer? Yer've put a bit of flesh on yer bones and yer face has filled out.'

'I feel a lot better. I'm hoping to look for a part-time job soon. A few extra bob coming in would make a lot of difference. Me and Steve could both do with some clothes, and we need new bedding.' Olive grinned. 'Actually I could do with throwing every stick and stitch out, and starting from scratch. But we will get there, given time.'

'Of course yer will.' Titch looked at her over the rim of his cup. 'Yer don't have to hide yerself away upstairs, yer know. I won't eat yer.'

'I'm not hiding meself away! I just don't want to distract yer by walking in and out and generally getting on yer nerves.' Olive put her cup down. 'I'm not used to having a man in the house, yer see, Titch. I'm out of the habit of having someone to talk to.'

'Yer'll feel different when yer start getting out and about a bit. Ye're still a young woman, Olive, and a pretty one. The chances are yer might just meet a man and fall for him. Then yer'd never be lonely again.'

Olive shook her head. 'No, I'll never marry again, Titch. I had a good man in Jim, and nobody could ever come up to him.'

'I wouldn't be so quick to dismiss the idea, Olive, 'cos there might be a man out there yer could take to. Yer wouldn't love him as yer did Jim, but love comes in many different ways. So while I'm not saying yer should go out and look for him, I think yer should keep an open mind.'

'You're a fine one to talk, Titch McBride. Forty years of age and still unmarried. And yer can't tell me yer've never met a girl yer liked.'

'I've met dozens that I liked, but not one of them set my heart on fire.' Titch drained his cup and smiled across at her. 'And I believe that's what happens when yer meet the one that's meant for yer. I've been told that when yer lips meet, bells start ringing in yer head and yer see stars. Well, so far there's been no bells, stars or heart set on fire. But being an optimist, Olive, I'll keep on trying.' Titch stood up and leaned his two curled fists on the table. 'Mind you, falling in love doesn't sound very exciting, does it? Who in their right mind would want to see stars, have ruddy bells ringing in their ears and be dashing around for a bucket of water to put out the fire in their heart?'

'Go on with yer, Titch. Don't yer ever take anything serious?'

'I take this painting lark very serious, Olive. I've got an hour before me ma comes with some eats for us, so for that hour I'm going to go like the clappers. 'Cos after that I've got to get down to the ship to see what's happening. So I'll thank yer not to keep me talking like this, it puts me off me work.'

Peg Butterworth had barely planted her bottom down before asking, in a loud voice, 'How are the lovebirds today? Enjoying life to the full, are yer?'

Elsie gave her a dig in the ribs. 'Ay, you! You said they weren't having no affair.'

Peg gave a sigh. 'Yer don't get it, do yer, girl?'

'What is it I don't get, queen?'

'Yer see what I mean? Yer don't even know what it is yer don't get.'

'I will if yer tell me, queen.'

'I'll draw yer a bleedin' picture if yer like.' Then Peg shook her head. 'No, yer still wouldn't get it. Ye're as thick as two short planks, Elsie Burgess, yer haven't got the brains yer were born with.'

'Ay you! Of course I've got the brains I was born with.'

'Yeah, and they haven't developed since the day yer were born. Now will yer shut yer gob and listen?' Peg's expression became all sweetness and light as she looked along the table. 'Are you two still all lovey-dovey?'

Kate gave Bob a sly kick before answering. 'No, Peg, I'm sorry to say we're not. Yer see, our consciences were pricked when Ada said yesterday that it was a sin to have an affair. And because me and Bob don't want to commit no sin, we've decided to end what we had going.'

Peg leaned across the table until her nose was within an inch of

Ada Smithson's. 'Ye're a miserable little sod. Why don't yer mind yer own business? That tale would have given us enough gossip to last a couple of weeks.'

'Ay, queen, what are yer shouting at Ada for?' Elsie put on a bewildered expression. 'It wasn't Ada what had an affair. Mind you, no one would blame her if she did. Not with the bleedin' husband she's got.'

Ada Smithson, the size of sixpennyworth of copper, sprang to her feet and shook a clenched fist in Elsie's face. 'You leave my husband out of this. He'd make six of yours.'

Elsie didn't flinch. 'Ye're right there, Ada. He's six times more bad-tempered, six times more tight with money and six times more handy with his fists. I won't argue with yer on that, queen, 'cos yer've got him bang to rights.'

Kate smiled across at Bob. 'I told yer it would blow over.'

Bob glanced at Billy to see if he was listening. But his mate was too interested in what was taking place at the other end of the table. 'I'm sorry, in a way. It would be very nice to have an affair with yer, Kate. Even if it was only a make-believe one.'

Peg didn't know what to do for the best. She could hear Kate and Bob talking and was eager to know what they were saying. But she had two women near who were spoiling for a fight, and she didn't want to miss that. So she jerked a thumb at Billy. 'You see what the lovebirds are up to, while I keep me eye on these two.'

'Nah, there's nothing doing down here. Besides, if those two come to blows I want to be ready to separate them before Elsie makes mincemeat of Ada.'

Kate winked across the table. 'In our dreams, eh, Bob?'

'Yeah, Kate, in our dreams.'

Six o'clock on Saturday came, and Olive didn't know whether she was on her head or her heels. She'd never known the house be so crowded or noisy. George was on the ladder hanging lengths of wallpaper and singing at the top of his voice. No one knew what he was singing because he was off-key, but he seemed to be enjoying his work. For such a big man he was very agile on the ladder, and its rocking from side to side didn't seem to bother him. But young Steve's heart was in his mouth a few times, so he took it upon himself to stand and hang on to the rickety ladder like grim death. Titch and Bob were kept busy pasting so that when one strip was up there was no delay in waiting for another. To say that George was quick and efficient would be the understatement of the year.

And the women weren't going to be left out, either. Irene had come up armed with cups, tea, sugar and milk, and she was busy in the kitchen brewing up every half-hour or so. Aggie's excuse was that she'd just nipped in to see how things were going. But really she'd come to supervise. 'George, sweetheart, there's a bubble in the paper, just above yer head.'

'I've seen it, Aggie.' When George turned, Steve's hands tightened on the ladder. 'If it weren't for yer age, Aggie, and the fact that I love the bones of yer, I'd tell yer to go and teach yer grandmother how to milk ducks.'

'And I'd do it, George, except for two things. Me grandma's been dead for fifty years and I haven't never seen no ducks in Kirkdale. I haven't seen no ducks anywhere, come to think of it. Wouldn't know one if I tripped over it.' Aggie lifted a finger. 'I'm sorry, George, but I tell a lie. I've seen them lying on slabs in the butchers' stalls in St John's Market. The poor buggers are dead, though, so it would be no good trying to milk them. They haven't even got no bleedin' feathers, never mind milk.'

'Ma, will yer let the man get on with his work?' Titch said. 'There's only three more pieces to put up, then the border, and the room's finished. Don't forget I've got to be back at the ship for ten at latest – we're sailing on the morning tide. And I dearly want to see the job finished.'

'If I had something to stand on, I could start putting the border up on this back wall,' Bob said. 'I wish we had another ladder.'

Irene came through from the kitchen. 'We've got a small stepladder. Would that be any use, George?'

'Yeah, that should do the trick. Bob's tall enough to reach on that. It's not as though he'd have the lengths of paper to fiddle with.'

'I'll nip down and get it.' Irene was nearly out of the front door when she called, 'The kettle's almost boiled, will yer see to it, Olive?'

Half-past seven the ladder was out in the yard, Steve was brushing the floor and Titch was helping Bob move the sideboard back into place.

'I never thought yer'd do it,' Olive said. 'Yer've worked wonders, all of yer.'

George had to bend his head to look her in the eyes. 'It's not finished yet, lass. If yer look up, yer'll see the ceiling laughing at the rest of the room. We wanted to get as much done as possible to please Titch, but I'll be back tomorrow to do the ceiling and frieze. And don't worry, I won't splash over yer new walls, I'm a clean worker.'

Titch came to stand next to her. 'George will finish the job off for yer, don't worry. But from what's been done so far, I think it's going to look a treat. Are yer happy with it?'

'Happy is one word I'd use, Titch. Along with thankful and grateful. I'm not very good at expressing meself, but I want yer all to know that me and Steve appreciate everything yer've done for

564

us. And when I find meself a little job, and we're in the money, we'll throw a big party as a thank you to yer.'

'Are yer really going to look for a job, sunshine?' Irene asked.

Olive nodded. 'Not a full-time one, I couldn't manage that yet. Just a couple of hours a day to earn a few bob for things we need for the house.'

'Then hang on for a few weeks. I'll be packing my job in soon, so I could put in a word for yer with Alec. I've been paying off some new furniture and I reckon I've got another four payments to make. How would that suit yer, sunshine?'

Olive's face glowed. 'That would be marvellous, it's so close to home. But Alec might not think I'm suitable for the job.'

Titch grinned at George and Bob before saying, 'Oh, yer'll have no trouble with Alec. He'll be only too happy to give yer the job.' He didn't say that he would be having words with the pub landlord that night. 'And talking about the pub has made me realise me mates must be as thirsty as I am. So we'll get off now, 'cos I haven't got much time.'

'Ye're not going drinking on an empty tummy, me lad,' Aggie said. 'I've made a stack of sandwiches, enough for you, George and Bob. So come on, before yer tell me yer haven't got time to eat.'

'I'll have to go, as well,' Irene said. 'The boys will be starving.'

'You take care of yerself, Olive.' Titch kissed her cheek, causing her to blush and his mother to raise her eyebrows. 'I'll see yer next time I'm home.' He stretched his hand out to Steve. 'I don't need to tell yer to look after yer mam, 'cos I know yer will.'

'I will, Mr Titch.' Steve looked at each face to show his words were for everyone in the room. 'Like me mam said, we both appreciate what yer've all done for us. Ye're good people, and true friends.'

Olive and Steve stood at the door and waved their neighbours off. Then they went back to admire the white paintwork and bright wallpaper with little sprigs of pink flowers on.

'While you're putting the kettle on, Aggie, I'll slip home and take me overalls off,' Bob said. 'And I'll have to tell Ruby I'm going for a pint. She won't be too happy because Saturday is her night for going out with her mates.'

'Lucy can come to us if Ruby wants to go out,' Irene said. 'After all, yer won't be late home and it's Sunday tomorrow so no school for Lucy.'

'Thanks, Irene, I'll send her in. She'll be made up.'

When Bob got home it was to find Ruby with a face like thunder. 'Where the bleedin' hell d'yer think yer've been? It's turned eight o'clock and I've been walking the floor like a bloody fool.'

Lucy was sat at the table, as quiet as a mouse. She could see her mother getting more angry by the minute and had been careful not to speak or move in case the anger was directed at her. She had been expecting a full-blown row when her dad came in, so was surprised when he ignored his wife, and said, 'I'm going for a pint, would yer like to go next door for a game of cards, pet?'

Lucy scrambled off the chair. 'Oh yeah, I'd like that, Dad.'

'Go on, then. I won't be late because Titch has to leave at half-nine.'

Lucy was near the front door when she heard her mother, and she stood to listen. If she thought her dad was going to be upset, she'd go back in the room to him.

'I asked yer where yer've been until now. Yer know I like to be out by half-seven.'

'I don't ask you where ye're going, or who these mysterious friends of yours are, so I don't see why I should tell yer where I've been. Just go about yer business, Ruby, and leave me to mine.'

Lucy could tell by her father's tone that he wasn't prepared to argue, so she skipped the few steps to the house where she knew she'd be welcome and would never hear a voice raised in anger.

Ruby watched her husband step out of his overalls before walking past her as though she wasn't there. His lack of emotion angered her even more and her fists curled in readiness to rain blows on his back. But a little voice in her head told her she would be unwise to start anything that would jeopardise her night out. Anyway, why bother? In half an hour she'd be with her mates having a good laugh.

The pub was packed and Ruby's eyes were everywhere, searching for her friends. Then she saw Wally Brown waving his hand in the air. 'Over here,' he shouted above the din. 'We saved a seat for yer.'

Ruby pushed her way through the crowd, flattered that he must have been watching out for her. She was surprised he wasn't married because he was a good catch – tall and slim, with fine sandy hair and deep blue eyes. He had plenty of clothes, too, and was always well dressed. She knew he was a flirt because he was always chatting the women up. But he'd told her it was only a bit of fun and they meant nothing to him.

'I'm a bit late 'cos I just missed a tram.' Ruby smiled at Jessie Armitage and her husband Harry. She'd gone to school with Jessie but had lost touch until they'd bumped into each other two years ago. It was a lucky encounter for Ruby, because the women had arranged to meet one night in the pub and through that came her escape from the boredom of married life. And it brought her into contact with friends of the Armitages, Mabel and Jim Bowler, and of course, Wally Brown.

'We thought yer weren't coming,' Jessie said. 'Didn't we, Harry?'

Harry merely nodded. He wasn't keen on Ruby and didn't know why his wife bothered with her. He knew she was married and couldn't understand why she came out drinking without her husband. She looked like a fly turn with her dyed hair and painted face, and he felt sorry for the bloke she was married to. And the way she wallowed in the compliments Wally plied on her was pathetic. He was like that with all the women, but none of them took him seriously because it was so obvious he was a womaniser. All except the silly cow standing there waiting for a space to be found for her to sit down. And ten to one when she sat down it would be next to Wally. Then the flattery would start and Ruby would simper as her eyelashes fluttered, her bright red lips pursing and her giggle that of a teenager.

Harry picked up his glass and gulped down several large swallows of his bitter beer. They'd been enjoying themselves until this stupid woman came on the scene. Just looking at her was enough to put anyone off their drink.

'Can yer slide along a bit, Mabel, and make room for Ruby?' Wally asked. 'Just about six inches will do, she's only got a small bottom.'

Mabel gave her husband a dig. 'Shove up, Jim.'

Wally waited until she was seated, then bent down to smile into her face. 'What would the lady like to drink? Name it and it's yours.'

'I'll have a port, please, Wally. And the next round's on me.'

'There's no need for that, Ruby,' Jessie said, 'we've got a kitty going. We've put two bob each in.'

'If yer want to buy yer own drinks, yer can do,' Harry said gruffly. 'If not, throw two bob in that ashtray with our money.'

'I'll do whatever you're doing.' Ruby took her purse from her handbag. 'We're all pals together.' She tossed a silver coin into the glass ashtray then took a packet of twenty Capstan from her bag. 'Anyone like a cigarette?'

Both men shook their heads, but Jessie and Mabel leaned forward. 'Ooh, I'll have one,' Jessie said. 'It'll be a change from Woodies.'

'Yeah, not half.' Mabel drew deeply as Ruby held a match to the cigarette. 'I can only afford five Woodies a day.'

'Yer should consider yerself lucky yer can afford any,' Jim said. 'With only my wages coming in, and two children to keep, I think yer do very well with yer five Woodies a day and at least two nights out.'

'Ye're dead right there, Jim,' Harry said. 'These two don't know they're born.' He gazed at Ruby's face for a few seconds before saying, 'Your husband must have a good job, yer never seem to be short.'

'Who never seems to be short?' Wally set the glass of port down. 'What am I missing?'

'You wouldn't understand, mate, being footloose and fancy free. The only one you've got to worry about is yerself.'

'My husband does shiftwork, so he probably earns a bit more,' Ruby said. 'And we've only got one child, that makes a difference.'

'I'm not complaining, love.' Jessie was on the plump side, with a round face, rosy cheeks and a happy disposition. She now linked her husband's arm and squeezed. 'I'm more than happy with what I've got, Harry. I wouldn't swap you for a big clock.'

'And I wouldn't swap you, Jim Bowler,' Mabel said. 'I know when I'm well-off.'

'Oh lord, listen to the lovebirds.' Wally winked at Ruby as though they were two of a kind and shared a secret. 'Make yer sick, wouldn't it?'

Conversation was general after that, until a bloke standing by the bar started to sing 'The Rose of Tralee'. This was what the crowd had been waiting for, and soon the rafters were ringing with the popular songs of the day. And the loudest voice belonged to Harry who, with his head thrown back, sang with gusto. And a fine voice he had, too. Requests were shouted from every corner of the room and there wasn't one song he didn't know. With his arm across Jessie's shoulder, he had everyone singing and swaying. Mabel and Jim couldn't sing for toffee, so they let themselves go by clapping their hands and stamping their feet.

When Harry stopped for a breather and a swig of beer, he noticed Wally bending down to whisper in Ruby's ear, while his hand rested on her knee. To hell with them, they're both as bad as one another, he thought, wiping the back of his hand across his mouth. They make a fine pair, neither of them are any bloody good. With that he put his glass down, cleared his throat and to everyone's delight, began to sing 'Wait Till the Sun Shines, Nellie'.

There were howls of disapproval when time was called, but the manager didn't fancy a visit from the police, so he was strict. 'Towels have been on for fifteen minutes now, plenty of time to finish yer drinks. Out yer get, before I lose me licence.' He held the door open while disgruntled customers filed out, then when the last one was through, he shot the bolts. Turning to the barman who was collecting the empty glasses, he said, 'There must be an easier way of making a living than this, Brian. I just wish I knew what it was.'

Standing on the pavement, Ruby said, 'I've had a smashing night, thanks very much. I'll see yer next week some time.'

'Yeah, okay, kid.' Jessie linked her husband's arm. He'd been looking at her with passion in his eyes for the last hour, and she knew he was eager to get home. 'We'll see yer.'

'Be careful going home, now,' Mabel said. 'Yer never know who's lurking about these dark nights.'

'I'll walk Ruby to the tram stop.' Wally cupped her elbow. 'I'll make sure she gets on the tram safely.'

'Come on, let's go.' Harry's mind was on bed and his wife's voluptuous body. 'Are yer coming, Jim?'

'Yeah.' Jim's mind was running along the same lines. Only Mabel wasn't voluptuous. She had slim legs, a neat bottom and a small waist. But she was well-endowed where it mattered. As he had once said to Harry, it was like nestling his head down on a feather pillow. 'I'm ready for me bed.'

As goodbyes were exchanged, Ruby and Wally began to walk in the opposite direction. 'I'll be all right, yer know. There's no need to walk with me.'

'I'm coming because I want to, not because I need to. We never get any time on our own, we're always in company.'

Ruby's heart quickened. 'There's not much we can do about that.'

'Of course there is, if we really wanted some time on our own. I know ye're married, Ruby, but I get the feeling you and yer husband are not exactly crazy about each other.'

'No, we're not. He's a good bloke, but dull and uninteresting. He's quite content to sit in every night, but I'm not. I want to get some fun out of life.'

'Then meet me one night and we'll go for a drink, just the two of us.'

'Oh, I couldn't do that. We might be seen, and then all hell would break loose.'

'But the idea appeals to yer, doesn't it?' Wally had decided that this was the night he'd make his move. He'd played her along until now, and felt sure she was ready to respond to his advances. 'Tell the truth.'

'Yeah, it would put a bit of excitement back in me life. But I wouldn't want to get caught.'

'Meet me one night next week and I'll take yer to a little club where no one will know yer. We can have a drink, just like friends. That wouldn't harm anyone.'

Ruby did some quick thinking. Was she prepared to take such a risk? The thought that Wally might walk away from her if she refused, was enough reason to say, 'Bob's on afternoon shift next week, he's home about half-ten. The most I could manage is an hour.'

'That's enough time for a drink and to get to know each other a bit better.' Wally was gloating inside. She was just the ticket for him. A married woman who wouldn't tie him down. He'd lived alone since his mother had died and left him a comfortably furnished house, and it suited him fine. He wasn't the marrying kind, he'd rather love them and leave them. 'How about eight o'clock on Wednesday, outside the Rotunda?'

'As long as it's only for an hour. I've got to be home by half-nine.'

'Yer have my word on it.' And Wally meant it. He had no intention of scaring her off by rushing things. He'd take it nice and easy until he had her eating out of his hand. 'Is that a date, then?'

Ruby thought of Lucy. She shouldn't have any problem there, 'cos the girl wouldn't tell tales for fear of hurting her father. 'Yeah, it's a date.'

Wally lifted her hand to his lips and kissed it, sending a thrill running down her spine as he knew it would. Here was a woman ripe for excitement, and he'd see that she got it. But all in good time. 'I'll look forward to Wednesday.'

Chapter Seventeen

Aggie came bustling through from the kitchen with a tea pot in one hand and a cup and saucer in the other. 'I told Irene I'd give her a knock when yer got home, so she can have a cup of tea with us and hear yer news first-hand.'

Titch had been away for four months, much longer than he'd expected, and his eyes had been following his mother's every move. He worried about her when he was away so long and was relieved to find her looking well and in high spirits. 'It's your news I want to hear, Ma. I'm sure yer wouldn't be interested in anything I've got to say, 'cos nothing much happens when ye're on board. The only thing of note that happened during the trip was that the skipper had a gumboil and was like a raving lunatic for a week. I did offer to punch him and burst the thing, but he didn't appreciate the offer.'

'A hot poultice is the best thing for that. It brings the boil to a head and draws the pus out.' Aggie put a cosy over the tea pot before making for the door. 'I'll give Irene a knock. She comes in every afternoon for a natter, 'cos with not working now she has plenty of time on her hands.'

Titch sat back and his eyes swept the room. Everywhere was spotless, as usual. Even the leaves on the aspidistra plant standing on a table in front of the window looked as though they'd been polished. His mother had always been houseproud and she hadn't let age change the habits of a lifetime.

'Well, here is the sailor, home from the sea.' Irene breezed in like a breath of fresh air. Her face was beaming and her arms open wide. 'Come and give us a kiss, sunshine. And seeing as my feller's not here, yer can take as long as yer like.'

'Oh, no he can't,' Aggie said, laughing. 'We'll have no hanky-panky in this house.'

Titch hugged Irene and pecked her cheek. 'One of these days we'll meet down a dark entry and I'll finally get to give yer a proper kiss.'

'In the meantime, will the pair of yer sit down while I pour the tea out?' Aggie said. 'Any longer and it won't be fit to drink.'

When Irene sat down facing him, Titch asked, 'Did Olive get the job when you packed it in?'

'Yeah, she's been there three months now.' Irene's brows drew together. 'Apparently someone told Alec that if he didn't give her the job he'd lose three good customers. Now I wonder who that could have been?'

'Don't be looking at me, I've been away for four months. I can only think it must have been your George, or Bob.'

Irene shook her head. 'No, Alec said good customers, and yer could hardly say George or Bob were good customers. The pub would shut down if it was relying on their couple of pints a week.' Again she shook her head. 'No, I think Olive has got a secret admirer.'

'Secret admirer or not, Alec isn't the type to do someone a favour. If she wasn't up to the job she'd be out on her ear.'

Aggie sipped her tea as she took it all in. It was funny that the first person her son should ask about was Olive. Was there an attraction there, or was he just asking out of interest for a friend? Well, he said he had three week's leave, that was plenty of time to find out how the land lay.

'She's doing fine. I went with her for the first week to show her the ins and outs,' Irene told him. 'There's so many jobs to do, I couldn't see her thrown in at the deep end. But she's taken to it like a duck to water and likes it. And the few extra bob a week certainly mean a lot to her. Her and Steve are not living in the lap of luxury, but there's a definite improvement in their standard of living. And it's brought her out of her shell. Yer'll notice a big difference to the last time yer saw her.'

'And young Steve has been a godsend to me.' Aggie nodded to emphasise her words. 'Every night without fail he comes up to get me coal in and see I'm all right for paper and firewood for the next morning. I was glad of him when we had snow six inches deep, I can tell yer. And he's never without a smile on his face. He's a cracking lad, one in a million. And Olive calls in every morning on her way home from work and has a cuppa with me.'

'So yer've not been short of company, Ma?'

'What! Sometimes this house has been busier than Lime Street Station. But that's the way I like it, son. Better that than sitting on me own looking at four bleedin' walls and talking to meself. Not that I don't enjoy a conversation with meself, 'cos as yer are well aware I can hold a very intelligent conversation with meself. The only thing is, it's very difficult to tell yerself to sod off and mean it.'

Titch put a hand over hers. 'I'll do anything for yer, Ma, yer know that. But telling yer to sod off is the exception.'

'I should think so!' Aggie huffed. 'That would be very disrespectful and would call for me to stand on a chair and box yer ears for yer.'

'Knock it off, you two,' Irene laughed. 'Anyway, Titch, aren't yer going to ask how I am?'

'How are you, Irene?'

'I'm fine, thank you. George is fine, Jack's fine and Greg's fine. Me new sideboard is beautiful and me new couch a dream. I was going to tell yer about me lovely new bedding, but I think Aggie would think it was disrespectful to mention the word "bed" and I wouldn't want to end up getting *my* ears boxed.'

Titch sat back in his chair feeling very contented. It was good to be home. 'So yer got everything yer were saving up for?'

'Yes, Mr McBride, I'm very happy to say I did. When yer call for George tonight yer'll think yer eyes are deceiving yer. Of course yer won't be allowed to sit on me couch, or lean yer elbows on me sideboard. If I let you get away with it, the boys would complain about me making them sit on the floor. So while yer can look, sunshine, yer cannot touch. Those are the rules of the house now.'

Titch thought it was hilarious. 'I'll stand on the step and wait for George to come out. From the sound of things, yer'd lay a duck egg if me coat happened to brush against yer sideboard. I bet George is having a dog's life.'

'Don't you believe it! He's as happy as Larry in his old fireside chair. He wouldn't part with that thing for all the money in the world. And my chair has been taken over by Jack. He says he's a working man now, and his wages entitle him to the same comfort as his dad.' Irene's laughter ricocheted off the walls. 'He's asked me to buy him a whip for his birthday, so he can crack it when I don't move fast enough for him.'

'Ye're well blessed with yer family, Irene. Good husband and good kids.'

'She certainly is,' Aggie said. 'But then she's a damn good mother.' Under her breath, she muttered, 'Not like some I could mention.'

'Does Lucy still come in for a game of cards?' Titch asked. 'And if she does, does she still win all the time?'

If there was a slight hesitation before Irene answered, it went unnoticed. 'Yeah, she still comes in, and much to Jack's disgust, she's still very lucky.' Then she quickly took the conversation away from Lucy. 'Yer won't be seeing Bob tonight, by the way, 'cos he's on afternoon shift. So it's just you and George. And please don't let my husband have too much to drink, he's the very devil to get up in the mornings.'

573

'Okay, we'll just have a couple of jars and save the serious drinking until Saturday, when Bob's with us.'

Lucy sat at the table and watched her mother combing her hair in front of the oval-shaped mirror over the mantelpiece. She knew if she said anything it would bring forth a load of abuse, but the burden of guilt she was carrying around with her was getting too heavy to bear. 'Ye're not going out again, are yer, Mam?'

Ruby swung around. 'And what if I am?'

'Me dad would go mad if he knew yer went out so often when he's at work. The first time yer went out and left me, yer said it was only for that one night. But that was months ago and now ye're going out more than ever. It's not fair on me dad.'

'The only way yer dad would know is if you told him.' Ruby forced herself to remain calm. 'And it would be daft to cause a row when I'm only going round to me mate's. I'm not doing anything wrong.'

'Then why don't yer tell me dad? He wouldn't mind if ye're only going to yer mate's, and I could go in next door instead of being in the house on me own.'

Ruby gritted her teeth. 'If you want to cause a big row, then tell yer dad if yer want. But I can't understand what all the fuss is about. I'm always in when he gets home from work and there's always something ready for him to eat. And as for you being on yer own in the house, well, at thirteen years of age yer should be old enough to put yerself to bed.'

'I'm not thirteen until next month. And yer know I've always been frightened on me own in the house. Why can't I go next door and play cards with them?'

'Because I say so, that's why. I don't want the whole bleedin' street knowing me business.' Ruby's temper was reaching boiling point. Her hand was itching to lash out at Lucy. But she couldn't take a chance on her daughter getting upset and running next door. If Irene Pollard found out what was happening, she could say goodbye to her nights out and to Wally Brown. 'Look, I've promised me mate I'd go tonight, and I don't want to let her down. But I won't go out again this week, honest. And as yer dad's on nights next week, I won't be able to get out at all, then.'

Lucy lowered her head, not knowing which way to turn. How could her mother look her straight in the face and tell barefaced lies? Lucy knew she went out when her dad was on nights because she'd heard her. Ten minutes after the front door closed on her dad, she'd hear the kitchen being closed and locked, footsteps down the yard, then the latch on the entry door being dropped. And it wasn't only one night, it was at least two in each week. The

574

knowledge Lucy carried around with her was making her ill. She didn't know where her mother went or what she got up to, but she did know it was wrong for a married woman to behave in such a way. She also knew her mother was using her to deceive her father and that was the worst part because he didn't deserve it and she loved him so much. Many times she'd been on the point of telling him, but was afraid of the consequences. What if it were the straw that broke the camel's back and he walked out of the house for good? That didn't bear thinking about because she couldn't live without her father's love.

'Well, don't just sit there,' Ruby said, her hands on her hips. 'Are yer going to take yerself off to bed, or not?'

'Only if yer promise it will be the last night yer ever go out without me dad knowing. It's not fair to expect me to go along with your lies and I won't do it.'

'But yer haven't told any lies, have yer?'

'Not telling the truth is just as bad as lying.'

Ruby looked at the clock. Wally would be arriving at the club on the dock road any minute now, and he didn't like to be kept waiting. She'd promise anything rather than have him upset. 'I've told yer this will be the last night, and I mean it.'

Lucy kept her head down; she couldn't bear to look her mother in the face. 'I'll see meself to bed.'

Ruby's sigh was one of relief and anger. Fancy having to kowtow to a chit of a girl. If it weren't for the fact she had a sneaking feeling Lucy confided a lot in that cow next door, and Irene Pollard and Bob were as thick as thieves, she'd give her a good hiding and kick her up the stairs.

Ruby gave one last pat to her hair before leaving the room without a word or a glance at her daughter, who was still seated at the table. Her head was bowed and tears were trickling down her cheeks.

Wally Brown didn't look very pleased when Ruby hastened down to where he was sitting. 'Where the hell have yer been? I felt like a right mug sat here on me own.'

'I'm sorry, but me daughter kept me back. Yer know I wouldn't be late if I could help it. But she wouldn't go to bed and we had words.'

Wally wasn't at all happy with the way the affair was progressing. They still met on a Saturday night in the pub and sat with the Armitages and the Bowlers, but they were careful not to let their friends know they were meeting twice a week on the quiet. This seedy little club, frequented by sailors and women of ill-repute, was their meeting place. Wally hadn't expected to wait so long for

575

what he was after from Ruby, but the furthest he'd got in four months was passionate kisses and fumbling down a dark entry. 'I don't know why yer won't let me come to your house. Once yer daughter was in bed she wouldn't know any different. I could come and go the back way so no one would see me, and I'd leave well before yer husband was due in from work. At least we'd have an hour to ourselves. I'm browned off coming to this dive, it gives me the willies.'

'Ooh, I don't know about that. Me neighbours are nosy buggers, and they wouldn't think twice about telling Bob. Besides, if Lucy heard us talking she'd be down like a shot and that would really put the cat amongst the pigeons.'

'I don't want to come to talk, Ruby – we've done enough of that in the last four months.' Wally resorted to flattery. 'I'm not made of stone, yer know. I can't be satisfied with the odd kiss, not the way I feel about yer. When we're together, I can hardly keep me hands off yer. I want to make love to yer and it's driving me crazy.' He ran a hand over her thigh. 'Yer said yer wanted some excitement in yer life and I can give yer that, and more. But I'm beginning to think yer don't feel the same about me.'

Ruby covered his hand. 'I do feel the same about you, Wally, yer know that. Otherwise I wouldn't be here tonight.'

'Then find a place where we can be alone, even if it's only for an hour. And let me make love to you like yer've never been made love to before.'

The nagging doubt in Ruby's mind fled when she felt her whole body thrill to his words. He'd practically said he loved her. She couldn't lose him now, she'd never find anyone else to please her the way he did. She'd be back to her boring life, with her boring husband and boring daughter. 'I'll do me best, Wally, I promise. Perhaps we can take a chance next week when Bob's on nights. If yer came about ten, Lucy should be fast asleep.'

Although he was gloating inside, Wally managed one of his smarmy smiles. It wouldn't have fooled any of the tough prostitutes sitting near them with sailors of every nationality, but it fooled Ruby. 'Yer won't be sorry, love, I promise. I'll please and satisfy yer so much yer'll be floating on air. And I'll show yer how to make me happy.'

'I'll write the day down, and me address, on a piece of paper and slip it to yer on Saturday in the pub. The entry door's got the number painted on it in white, so yer can't miss it. And I'll be watching and waiting for yer.'

Bob leaned across the canteen table. 'How old is your daughter, Kate?'

576

'Just a couple of weeks older than yours. Why?'

'I was just wondering. Has she changed at all? I mean, has she gone quieter, more withdrawn, like?'

'Not so I've noticed. She doesn't act daft like she used to, but yer can expect that when they're growing older. In twelve months, Iris will be leaving school, same as your Lucy. They won't be our little girls any more, they'll be working young ladies.' Kate could see this wasn't what Bob wanted to hear. He was obviously worried about his daughter. 'What is it? Is Lucy not well?'

'Oh, she's not sick or anything like that. It's just that she doesn't laugh as easily and is much quieter than she ever was.'

'Well, haven't yer asked her? That would be the best thing to do.'

Bob blushed. 'I wondered if it was her age. You know, a girl's body changes when she gets in her teens. And I couldn't ask her that because she'd get embarrassed.'

'I know things are not good at home, Bob, but surely it's her mother's place to tell her the facts of life. It shouldn't be left to you.'

'I know that, Kate, but yer see, my wife isn't a normal mother. She has no time for Lucy and I doubt if she's even noticed the change in her. All Ruby thinks about is her make-up, dyeing her hair, her ciggies and her nights out in the pub with her mates. She doesn't give a toss for me, I'm just the man who hands his money over every week. There are times when I feel like packing me bags and finding lodgings somewhere. But I'd have a job finding a place that would take me and Lucy. And I'd never leave her there, she's my whole life. I love her more than anyone else on this earth.'

'I wish I could help yer, Bob, but there's not much I can do. Lucy doesn't know me, and she wouldn't take kindly to a stranger asking her questions.'

'No, I realise that. I'll have a word with Irene, next door. Lucy thinks the world of her, so she'd be the best one to have a chat with her.' There came a loud burst of laughter from their workmates, and Kate and Bob leaned forward to see what was going on.

Peg Butterworth had her chin cupped in her two hands as she glared at Elsie Burgess. 'Say that again, girl, but start at the very beginning.'

'All right, queen, I'll start from the night before last, when I put me washing in the dolly tub to steep overnight. Well, it was all me sheets and pillowcases, so I put some bleach in the water to bring them up nice and white. But when I took the clothes out of the tub yesterday morning, I found I'd accidentally put my feller's blue shirt in the wash. At least, it *was* my feller's blue shirt, but now it's his patchy grey one. I was beside meself, queen, 'cos he loved that bleedin' shirt more than he loves me. While I was getting the dinner ready for our Edna to put on, I was trying to think of what I could do to make amends. I'd peeled the potatoes and carrots and turnip, and I was just salting them when I had this brainwave.'

'You with a brainwave?' Peg said, tongue in cheek. 'That's a novelty.'

'Who's telling the tale, queen, you or me?'

'I'm sorry, girl.' Peg lifted her hands in surrender. 'My lips are sealed from now on.'

Happy she now had the undivided attention of all her mates, Elsie went on: 'I thought of a way to sweeten him up, so he wouldn't pulverise me when I showed him his shirt. I set a tray with a nice lace cloth on, filled me best glass sugar bowl, got out me china milk jug what hasn't seen daylight since Adam was a lad, and put them on the tray with his favourite cup. It looked a treat, dead posh and fit for the King. And I left a note for our Edna to make her dad a nice cup of tea before she put the dinner out.'

'Did it do the trick?' Billy Gleeson asked. 'Did it sweeten him up?'

'Well, it would have done if I hadn't gone and got meself all mixed up. What with all the worry and one thing and another, I'd filled the sugar bowl with salt and put sugar in the potatoes and carrots and turnip. And my feller takes three sugars in his tea, so yer can imagine he wasn't best pleased when he gulped half the cup down in one go before making a dash for the sink and spewing it up. Our Edna said he was drinking cup after cup of water until she put his dinner down to him. She said that was when all hell broke loose. Yer see, my feller doesn't only like a lot of sugar in his tea, he likes plenty of salt in his spuds and vegetables. And I'd gone and got them all mixed up, hadn't I?'

The howls of laughter were so loud, Elsie knew there was no point in going on because she wouldn't be heard. So she folded her arms across her tummy and waited for the noise to subside. Then she said, 'Well, anyone can make a mistake, can't they?'

Peg was pressing her hands to her cheeks which were stiff with laughing. But she couldn't resist a leg-pull. 'Anyone can make a mistake, girl, but very few could make as many in one go as you. It's beyond my comprehension how anyone can be so feckless.'

Elsie's eyes narrowed. 'Is she insulting me, Billy Gleeson?'

'Yeah.' Billy's eyes were red-rimmed with wiping away the tears of laughter. 'She said she can't understand why ye're so daft.'

'Yer mean that's all those big words meant?' Elsie looked down her nose at Peg. 'Ye're wasting yer time here, queen, yer should be standing behind the counter at Cooper's. That's the posh shop where all the rich people go, and they talk so far back yer can't hardly hear them. I think yer'd go down well there, queen, as long as yer remembered yer can't tell them to bugger off, like yer do me.'

Billy was getting impatient. 'Elsie, will yer get back and finish the tale off? What did your feller have to say?'

'Oh yeah, yer'll like this bit, Billy. I didn't, but you will. Yer see when I got home last night, I didn't know what I'd done, did I? So when Tiger put this dinner in front of me I thought he was being all lovey-dovey. "I've saved this for yer, petal," he said. "I hope yer enjoy it as much as me and the kids did." ' Elsie rolled her eyes and hitched her bosom. 'I thought my ship had come in, didn't I? So when I picked up me knife and fork, I was planning in me mind what to do, seeing as he seemed in a good mood. I'd finish me dinner, then sit on his knee, give him a big kiss and stroke his hair. Then I'd break the news about his shirt.'

Little Ada Smithson's eyes and mouth were twitching. 'I know what's coming next. Yer couldn't eat the bleedin' dinner 'cos yer'd ruined it.'

Elsie rested her soulful eyes on each of them for a second. Then in a dramatic voice that would have done credit to Bette Davis, she said, 'If I never move from this chair, I sat there and stuffed mouthful after mouthful in me gob. I could feel my feller's eyes on me and I tried to look as though I was enjoying it. But halfway through I had to give up. I looked at him and asked if this was his idea of a joke. Then of course, I got the lot thrown at me. I can't tell yer what he said because the air was blue. So suffice to say my dear husband was not in the least amused.' She looked at Peg with a haughty expression. 'Yer see, queen, ye're not the only one what knows big words. So if yer ever do get a job in Cooper's, yer can always put in a good word for yer best mate. And don't forget to tell them I'm house-trained.'

'I wish yer'd finish what yer started, Elsie.' Billy hated missing out on anything. 'What did your feller say about his shirt?'

'Ooh, he doesn't know, yet. The mood he was in I wasn't about to confess to another sin. Not ruddy likely, I wasn't.'

'That's daft, that is,' Peg said. 'Yer should have told him and got it over with. Come Saturday, when we're going to the pub, he'll be wanting to wear that blue shirt.'

'I'll have had time to think of something before then. In fact, queen, I was going to ask yer to lend me half-a-crown so I can buy him a new one. I'll pay yer back next week.'

'Blimey! If that's not cheek, I don't know what is. Yer ruin yer husband's best shirt, yer don't know the difference between salt

579

and sugar, and yet it's Muggins here what's going to be out of pocket.'

'Don't shout at me, queen. What with all the carry-on, I've got a splitting headache. And I didn't get much sleep last night because my feller had to get up to go to the lavvy every half hour after drinking so much water.'

'I'll lend yer the half-crown, Elsie,' Billy said. 'The laugh we've had was worth that.'

'Yer will not!' Peg was highly indignant. 'You've got a cheek, Billy Gleeson. She's my mate, and if anyone's going to lend her half-a-crown, it'll be me. So there!'

Aggie glanced at the clock when a knock came on the door. 'This'll be Olive on her way home from work.'

'I'll go.' Titch was halfway out of his chair when his mother waved him back.

'Stay where yer are, sweetheart, I'll go.' She gave a cheeky grin. 'Me legs are younger than yours.' Aggie swayed along the hall with a smile on her face. Unless she was very much mistaken, her son's interest in Olive was more than friendship. He might not know it himself yet, but she could see the signs were there. He'd been clockwatching for the last hour without even realising he was doing it. 'Come in, queen, the kettle's on the boil.'

Titch sprang to his feet and grasped the hand Olive had extended. 'Hello, Olive, it's good to see yer.' He bent to kiss her cheek. 'And it's good to be home.'

'It's good to see you, Titch.' Olive cursed the colour she could feel rising from her neck to cover her face. Fancy a grown woman like her blushing because an old friend kissed her. In front of his mother, too. 'Aggie's been running around like a two-year-old since she knew yer were coming home. And Steve can't wait to see yer.'

Titch pulled a chair out for her. 'I'd have come down last night but yer know I always go for a pint with me mates. Or I should say mate, because there was only me and George.'

'I'll see to the tea while you two catch up,' Aggie said, humming as she went through to the kitchen. After pouring the boiling water into the tea pot, she leaned back against the sink. She knew she shouldn't let her imagination run away with her, but if a romance blossomed between her son and Olive, she'd be the happiest woman alive.

'Ma, have yer gone to China for that tea?'

Aggie shook herself out of her dreaming. She'd been miles away and had forgotten what she was doing in the kitchen. 'Keep yer hair on, son, I'm not a ruddy whippet.'

Olive pushed her chair back. 'I'll give yer a hand, Aggie.'

'I'll do it,' Titch told her. 'You stay where yer are, yer've been working hard.'

Well, well, thought Aggie as her heart began to sing. Things are definitely looking up.

'How's the job going, Olive?' Titch had already quizzed Alec last night, but he wasn't going to say so. 'D'yer like it?'

'It's great. Alec and Betty are very friendly and we have a good laugh. I found it hard going at first, but I'm used to it now.'

'I can see the likeness between you and Steve, now yer face has filled out. Same fair hair and bright blue eyes. He's got your mannerisms, too.'

'But he's got a dimple in his chin like Jim had, and he's got the same square jaw.' Olive turned to Aggie and winked. 'If your son tells me I've put a lot of weight on, I'll clock him one.'

Aggie grinned. 'I'll hold him while yer do it.'

'I wasn't going to say that at all,' Titch said. 'You women have a happy knack of jumping the gun. What I was going to say is that ye're just right now, Olive. Nice and slim but with a bit of flesh in the right places.'

'He's getting personal now, Aggie, and making me blush. I'm going before he tells me me hair needs setting and me eyebrows plucking.' Olive stood up and pushed the chair back into place. 'Next time I see yer, Titch McBride, it'll be me asking all the questions. Like what did yer get up to while yer were away? And have yer added any more conquests to yer long list of girlfriends?'

'Yer can ask me on the way down to your house, 'cos I'm coming with yer. Don't forget I haven't seen yer living room since it was finished.'

'Oh no, you are not! I don't have time to do me housework before I go out in the mornings and the place is a tip. I wouldn't dream of letting yer see it, I'd die of humiliation.'

'Olive, I'll only be looking at the walls! I'm not going to run me fingers over the dust on yer sideboard, or look under yer bed.'

'I know ye're not, 'cos ye're not getting the chance.'

Aggie put a hand over her mouth to hide a smile. That's right, queen, she thought, make him toe the line. Give him a run for his money and he'll come to his senses quicker.

Titch wasn't the least bit put out. 'What time is visiting time then, Mrs Fletcher?'

'Half past six, when Steve's had his meal.' Olive's face broke into a smile. 'He'll be made up to see yer, Titch. And so am I.'

Steve eyed his mother as he stood beside her at the sink. 'Yer hair looks nice, Mam, and the lipstick suits yer.' He dried the plate she passed over and reached up to put it on the shelf. 'In fact, yer look very pretty.'

'I had a spare half-hour so I put a few dinky curlers in.' Olive moved away from the sink and waved a hand down the figure-hugging, soft wool blue dress she was wearing. 'Does this look as though I bought it secondhand from Paddy's Market?'

'No! It looks smashing on yer, Mam, it really suits yer.'

'Yer won't tell anyone where it came from, will yer?'

'Of course I won't, I'm not that thick.' Steve put the last plate on the shelf and hung the tea towel behind the door. 'Did Mr Titch say yer looked well?'

Olive grinned as she dried her hands. 'Yeah, he said I've come on a treat. I must have looked ruddy awful before, 'cos everyone I meet tells me how well I look.'

Steve cocked an ear. 'There's the knocker, Mam. Shall I go?'

'Yes, please, son.' Olive scolded herself for being nervous. After all, Titch was an old friend and there was no reason for her tummy to be doing somersaults.

Titch came in with an exaggerated sailor's roll. 'I gave me ticket in to the man at the door. He didn't give me half back, so I mustn't be getting a cup of tea in the interval.'

'Go on, yer daft nit. I'll have yer know that not only are yer getting a cup of tea, but there's fresh milk to put in it.'

Steve was hopping from one foot to the other. 'What d'yer think of the room, Mr Titch?'

'It looks grand.' Titch tore his eyes away from Olive. 'Yer wouldn't think it was the same room, it's made such a difference.'

'Yeah.' The cleft in Steve's chin deepened with his smile. 'For the first week I kept thinking I'd come into the wrong house.'

'It's not only the room that's changed,' Titch said. 'Look at yer mam! She looks like a film star.'

'You start that, Titch McBride, and I'll send yer packing.' Olive didn't possess a full-length mirror, so while she knew the dress was a good fit, she had no idea it showed off every curve of her body. Or that the colour accentuated the blue of her eyes. 'Sit down and behave yerself.'

'I'll swap yer a list of my conquests for a cup of tea.'

'That should be interesting,' Olive said. 'I'll put the kettle on.'

'What conquests are they, Mr Titch?'

'Yer mam thinks I've got a girl in every port, and she wants to know how many new ones I got this trip.'

'Oh.' Steve looked puzzled. 'Yer haven't, have yer?'

Titch shook his head. 'No, but I don't want to disillusion her.'

'If we go to the pictures while ye're home, Mr Titch, I can pay for meself this time.'

Olive hurried through from the kitchen. 'Steve, don't be so forward.'

'He's all right love, don't be getting at him. As a matter of fact, I was going to suggest we all go on Saturday night. That's yerself, me ma, Irene and all the kids. It would have to be first house because of Lucy and Greg, but I thought the grown-ups could go for a drink afterwards. Just to the corner pub, like. We could meet up with George and Bob.'

Steve's face was a joy to behold. 'That would be the gear, Mr Titch.'

'Excuse me,' Olive said. 'But have yer forgotten I work in the pub?'

'What difference does that make? Yer don't work there at night. And if you came, I'm sure we could persuade Irene and me ma to come. The children would be all right in the Pollards' for an hour or so. Jack and Steve are old enough to see the others don't come to any harm.'

'Go on, Mam,' Steve urged. 'Yer never go out for a drink.'

Her son's face looked so eager, Olive didn't have the heart to refuse outright. Anyway, she was probably reading more into this than there really was. Irene always got a peck on the cheek off Titch when he came home, and he called her love. It was just his way of being friendly, that's all. 'See what Aggie and Irene say first. If they go, I'll come too.'

Chapter Eighteen

Rhoda had her arm across Lucy's shoulder as they turned the corner of the street. 'Are yer playing out after?'

'I don't know yet. I'm not playing skipping or hopscotch, though, 'cos we're too big for that now.'

'Well, come over to ours and have a game of Ludo, if yer like. But it'll have to be after we've had our tea and me mam's cleared away.'

'We'll see, eh?' Although Lucy didn't feel in the mood for games, the prospect of staying in the house all evening with her mother was even less appealing. 'I'll call for yer after tea and see what we want to do.' They stopped opposite Rhoda's house and Lucy watched her friend skipping over the cobblestones. 'See yer later.'

Irene Pollard stepped from her doorway and into Lucy's path. 'I've been watching for yer, sunshine, I want to have a word with yer. But yer better go home first to see if yer mam wants yer for anything. I'll leave the door ajar, so just walk in.'

'Yeah, okay, Mrs Pollard.' A smile came to Lucy's face. 'Did Mr Titch get home?'

Irene nodded. 'He came yesterday, but he didn't call to yours with yer dad being at work. He asked about yer, though, and he's looking forward to seeing yer.'

'I can't wait to see him. I love Mr Titch, he always makes me laugh.'

'He has that effect on everyone, sunshine. Like his mother, he can turn any situation into a joke. He wouldn't let yer be miserable, even if yer wanted to.' Irene thought the word 'miserable' summed up Lucy's life. They never heard laughter coming through the wall of the Mellors', only Ruby's bawling and screeching. And this pretty girl standing in front of her deserved better than that. She deserved to be loved and cherished. 'I'll tell yer what, sunshine, I'll come up to Aggie's with yer when we've had our talk. Then yer can see yer heart-throb. How does that sound to yer?'

'Oh, yes, please! But I'd better go and see if me mam wants me first.'

'I'll leave the door open for yer.'

Irene was seated in the chair, her hands in her lap when she heard the front door crashing back against the hall wall. 'I'm home, Mam!'

'I gathered that, sunshine. I hope the front door's still on its hinges?'

Greg grinned. 'The door's fine, Mam. There's a big hole in the wall, like, but as I say, the door's fine.'

'Listen, son, I want yer to go on a message for me. And I want yer to take at least half an hour over it.'

'Where's the shop yer want me to go to, Mam? In Scotland?'

'I haven't got time to explain, son, except to say I need a quiet word with Lucy. And I want you out of the way. So I'll give yer a penny for some sweets and yer can go and play with yer mates and annoy the neighbours.'

Greg held out his hand. 'Sounds like a fair exchange to me, Mam.'

There was a timid knock at the door. 'It's me, Mrs Pollard.'

'Come in, sunshine. Greg's just going on a message for me.'

'Hi, Greg!'

'Lucy, the button millionaire.' Greg patted her cheek. 'I'm going to marry you when I grow up, just so I can get me buttons back.'

'Chance is a fine thing, Greg Pollard. When I get married it'll be to someone handsome and rich.'

'Yer need look no further, 'cos he's standing in front of yer. At the moment I'm only handsome, but one day I'll be rich as well.'

Irene tutted. 'Will yer get going, son, I've got a lot to do before yer dad gets in.'

When her son's footsteps had died away, Irene moved to the couch and patted the seat next to her. 'Come and sit down, love, I want to have one of our little discussions.'

'What about, Mrs Pollard?'

'It's about you, Lucy. Yer look so miserable and sad lately that I'm worried about yer. And anything that is said in this room will go no further, yer know that.'

Lucy looked down at her hands and laced her fingers. 'I'm all right, Mrs Pollard. I feel a bit fed up sometimes, but it's nothing, really.'

'I'm sorry, Lucy, but I don't believe yer.' Irene put a finger under the girl's chin and lifted her face. 'I thought you and me were friends, and yer trusted me.'

'Oh, we are, Mrs Pollard, ye're me very best friend. And I trust yer more than anyone, except me dad.'

'Then tell me what's worrying yer. And don't say ye're not worried because I know full well that yer are – and have been for

586

months now. I give yer me solemn promise I will not say or do anything about it, but I need to know to set me mind at rest. And don't forget, sunshine, a trouble shared is a trouble halved. Yer'll feel a lot better if yer get it off yer chest.'

'It's me mam,' Lucy said in a quiet voice. 'She's been going out at night when me dad's at work. And I've been real worried because I feel I'm doing wrong by not telling me dad. I know I should have told him in the beginning, but she said I'd only cause trouble and I was frightened.'

Irene's temper was rising but she kept her voice calm. 'And is she still doing it?'

'I pulled her up about it on Tuesday night when I saw her dolling herself up. I said if she didn't stop I would tell on her. She promised she wouldn't do it again, but I don't believe her. I know I shouldn't say things like that about me mother, but I'd be lying if I said otherwise. She's a married woman and she shouldn't be going out drinking when me dad thinks she's at home minding me. That's cheating, and she's making me into a cheat as well.' Lucy's voice became stronger with emotion. 'Me dad's a good husband to her but she hasn't got a kind word for him. And that makes me sad because he's a lovely man and I idolise him.'

'Yer dad *is* a lovely man, one of the best. And I know yer dote on each other. As for yer mother – well, we'll just wait and see if she keeps her promise, eh?' Irene had no intention of setting the girl against her mother, that wouldn't be fair. So her thoughts on Ruby stayed in her head. 'Perhaps one day yer mam will come to her senses and realise what a good husband and daughter she's got. So forget about it, sunshine, and see how things go.'

'D'yer really think she will change, Mrs Pollard?'

If Irene were to be honest, she'd have said there wasn't a snowball's chance in hell of Ruby Mellor ever changing. But she hadn't the heart to extinguish the light of hope she could see in the girl's eyes. 'Only time will tell, Lucy. But if yer'll take my advice yer'll put it out of yer mind for now. There's no point in making yerself ill over it, that wouldn't solve anything. And yer've got yer dad to think about. If he sees you're unhappy, it's going to make him unhappy as well. I'm sure yer don't want that, do yer?'

'I would never do anything to make me dad unhappy, never.'

'Then let's see a smile back on yer pretty face and the laughter back in yer voice. Then everyone that loves yer will be happy.' Irene held out her arms and Lucy moved into the shelter of them as though it was the most natural thing in the world.

'Yer really are me very best friend.' She looked up into Irene's face. 'And I do feel better now I've told yer what's been worrying me.'

'I said yer would, didn't I? So in future, don't keep things bottled up inside yer.' Irene held the girl away from her. 'Now, let's go and see your Mr Titch. I won't be able to stay long because I'll have to put the dinner on soon.'

Titch saw them passing the window and had the door open before the knock had even sounded. His face creased in a smile as he held his arms wide. 'My little sweetheart.'

Lucy seemed to fly through the air. 'I don't half love it when ye're home, Mr Titch.' Her arms around his waist, she grinned up at him. 'And I'm not so little any more. See, I'm up to yer shoulder now.'

'That's 'cos I'm bending down, soft girl.' He stretched to his full height. 'Another couple of inches, then yer'll be up to me shoulder.'

Aggie's voice called out, 'Will yer come in so I can hear what ye're saying? I'm sitting here like a bleedin' stuffed dummy, straining me ears.'

Titch pushed Lucy towards the living room and waited for Irene to follow before closing the door. 'Yer haven't missed anything, Ma.'

'That's for me to decide.' Aggie moved to the side of her rocking chair to make room for Lucy to sit beside her. 'If I don't hear what's said, I won't know whether I've missed anything, will I?'

'I'll tell yer what Mr Titch said, Mrs Aggie.' The rocking chair wasn't made for two people and when Lucy turned she could feel her bottom slipping off the seat. So she held on to Aggie's arm for safety. 'He said he was going to take me back to the ship with him and hide me in one of the lifeboats until the ship was hundreds of miles out at sea. He'd bring me food every day, of course, and make sure I was warm enough. Then when we were that far out the skipper couldn't turn back, Mr Titch would pretend he'd found a stowaway.'

'Well, I never!' Aggie's eyes were wide. 'He told yer all that in a couple of minutes? He's a fast talker, is my son.'

'Yer've got to be fast these days, Ma,' Titch said. 'All the prettiest girls get snapped up in no time. If I don't watch out I'll be left on the shelf.'

'And what did yer tell him, queen?'

Lucy giggled. 'I told him I would give it serious consideration.'

'Well, now yer've had time for this serious consideration, queen, thank him for his kind offer, but say that unfortunately yer'll have to decline. If he wants to know why, tell him yer have too many friends here who wouldn't be without yer.'

Lucy played her part well. With a hand over her heart, she said, 'But he'll be broken-hearted, Mrs Aggie.'

'He'll get over it, queen. I mean, he can always give Irene a kiss if he's feeling lonely. That's as long as George doesn't catch him at it.'

'Ay, hang about, Aggie!' Irene said. 'If any of the neighbours heard yer say that, they'd think there was something going on between me and Titch.'

Titch chuckled. 'I should be so lucky.'

'Sod the neighbours, Irene, they shouldn't be so bleedin' bad-minded.' Aggie thought it was time to throw another name into the pot. 'Anyway, ye're not the only one me son has taken to kissing. Olive's on his list now, as well.'

'Go 'way!' This wasn't news to Irene, but she pretended it was. 'Well, you fickle thing, Titch McBride. Here's me thinking I was yer one and only.'

'And I thought yer were waiting for me to grow up.' Lucy put a sob in her voice. 'Ye're a flirt, Mr Titch.'

'Oh dear, I'm in the doghouse now.' Titch sat down and held his head in his hands. 'I can see I'm better to conduct me love-life in another country. The girl in Rotterdam, now she's a nice quiet little thing – I wouldn't get any trouble from her. Or there's Anna, a beautiful Chinese girl. And I mustn't forget my French girlfriend, Giselle. Now there's a beauty if ever there was one.'

'Don't yer be bringing no foreign girls to this house, me lad. I'm too old to be learning to speak Chinese or bleedin' French.'

'Yer'd have no trouble with the Dutch girl, though, Ma, 'cos yer speak double Dutch all the time. Yer'd get on like a house on fire with Bertha.'

'Listen to me, buggerlugs, there's enough English girls around for yer to choose from.' Aggie was really enjoying herself. And part of her enjoyment came from seeing a genuine smile on Lucy's face. 'If yer can't find one of yer own kind to marry, then all I can say is ye're too bleedin' hard to please and yer deserve to stay a bachelor for the rest of yer life.'

'See what yer've started, Lucy?' Irene asked, her face straight. 'If yer'd told Titch right away that yer didn't want to be a stowaway, none of this would have happened.'

'It's been funny, though, hasn't it, Mrs Pollard? Especially the part about Mr Titch and his girlfriends.'

'Yes, it has, sunshine. But I'd better get home and put the dinner on. My feller won't see the funny side if his meal's not ready for him. He says he's got no sense of humour when his tummy's empty.' Irene waved goodbye. 'I'll see you folks later.'

Lucy slipped from the chair. 'I'd better go as well.'

'Hang on for a few minutes, sweetheart, while I tell yer what we've got planned for Saturday night. Then yer'll have something to look forward to.'

Aggie patted the chair. 'Sit down again, queen.'

Lucy was wide-eyed as Titch's plan unfolded. 'We're all going to the pictures, first house. That's me ma, Irene and the two boys, Olive and Steve and yerself. And after the pictures, the grown ups are going to the corner pub for a drink, while you youngsters can amuse yerselves playing cards in the Pollards' house. I saw yer dad this morning before he went to work to make sure it was all right with him.'

'It sounds wonderful, Mr Titch, I really will look forward to it.' There was mischief in Lucy's eyes. 'Can I just say that no matter how beautiful yer Dutch and Chinese girlfriends are, they can't have yer. I mean, how could yer take us to the pictures if yer were living in China? Yer couldn't travel on the twenty-two tram, 'cos it doesn't go any further than the Pier Head terminus.'

'D'yer know, sweetheart, I hadn't thought of that. Oh well, I'll have to say goodbye to Anna, Bertha and Giselle. They were nice while they lasted, but they'll have to go.'

'D'yer see how fickle he is, Lucy? Now he won't marry anyone who doesn't live on the twenty-two tram route. That narrows the field down to about ten thousand.'

When Lucy had left, Titch kept looking at his mother. Then he finally plucked up the courage to ask, 'Why did yer mention me kissing Olive, Ma?'

'Did I do wrong, son?' Aggie looked the picture of innocence. 'I wasn't to know yer wanted to keep it a secret.'

'It's not a secret, Ma, I just wondered why yer mentioned it.'

'Well, I said yer kiss Irene, so what's the difference? After all, they're both just good friends so there's no harm in yer kissing them. Is there?'

'No harm at all. As yer say, they're both just good friends.'

'Now I've got a question for you, son. Who the hell are these girls yer mentioned? This Anna, Bertha and Giselle? I always thought a giselle was an animal.'

'A gazelle is an animal, Ma. And the three girls I mentioned don't exist. I picked their names out of thin air. So does that answer yer question?'

'I'll mull that over in me head, son, while I'm seeing to something to eat. I'll come back to yer if I find yer answer unsatisfactory.'

'You do that, Ma,' Titch laughed. 'While ye're at it, I'll think up another three answers to be on the safe side. Then yer can pick which one yer find acceptable.'

★ ★ ★

Titch walked ahead with the youngsters while the three women walked behind. He had hold of Lucy's hand as she walked between him and Steve – an arrangement that didn't suit Jack one little bit. 'What are yer walking on the outside for, Steve? Yer should be with me and Greg. All boys together, like.'

'I like walking beside Lucy, she's prettier than you and Greg.' Steve glanced along the line, a smile on his lips. 'Yer don't mind, do yer?'

'I do, as a matter of fact.' Jack was wearing a new shirt and trousers, and he strolled along feeling all grown up and a real toff. 'Ye're not the only one to appreciate a pretty face, yer know. I mean, even I can see the difference between Lucy and our Greg.'

'Thanks a bunch, our kid.' Greg looked really put out. 'If I'm stuck with your ugly mug, it's only fair you should be stuck with mine.'

Jack took his hands from his pockets so he could spread them out for effect. 'Yer see, he admits himself that he's no oil painting. So come on, swap over.'

'Not on yer life. That's like expecting someone to swap a bull's-eye for a slab of Cadbury's. I'm quite happy here, thank you very much.'

Ho, ho, thought Titch, there's rivalry for the fair maiden's hand. Friendly rivalry at the moment, but would it be so in a couple of years' time? 'I hope ye're not going to come to blows over this. We're supposed to be out to enjoy ourselves.'

'I've got the perfect answer,' Greg said. 'And none of yer can say it's not fair. Let Steve carry on walking with Lucy now, then our Jack can walk beside her on the way home. And as I'm the one who sorted yer problem out, I get to sit next to her in the pictures.'

'You can go and take a running jump,' was Jack's answer to his brother's solution. 'And preferably into the River Mersey.'

'Yeah,' Steve agreed, 'and without a lifebelt.'

'That's charming, that is.' Greg put on a pained expression. 'Our kid knows I've got me best kecks on, and he saw me polishing me shoes until I could see me face in them, yet he wants me to go for a swim and get them all wet. That's brotherly love for yer. So I've decided that if him and Steve want to fight dirty, I'm more than a match for them. When we get to the Astoria, it's every man for himself.'

'Don't mind me,' Lucy said, 'I'm only here to make the numbers up. I can think for meself, yer know. And I'm sitting next to Mr Titch and Mrs Aggie. So there!'

Walking between Irene and Olive, her arms linking theirs, Aggie chuckled. 'Thirteen next week and she's got three suitors. Not bad going, eh?'

'Our Steve thinks the world of Lucy,' Olive said. 'When we were down on our luck, he used to say she was the only one who had time for him.'

'I think our Jack's got his eyes on her, too. But the one to watch is our Greg. He might be an outsider at the moment, but very often it's the outsider that wins the race.'

'They're young yet. They've got years ahead of them before they even think of courting.' Aggie saw the group outside the picture-house, and as she quickened her step she noticed the young girl clinging to Titch's hand. 'I hope when Lucy starts going out with blokes she doesn't pick a wrong 'un, like her dad.'

'I'll go along with yer on that, Aggie,' Irene said. 'I vote we form a committee and vet every feller that looks sideways at her.'

Titch waited for them to catch up before marching in and buying the tickets. He passed the sweet counter because his mother had eight bags of sweets in the large handbag she carried. Mr Whittle from the corner shop had made them up for her with a mixture from the wide selection of jars that lined a shelf in a shop that sold everything from food, to gas mantles, firewood and small bags of coal.

The first-house performance hadn't started and the lights were still on when Titch passed the tickets to the usherette. But the performance in the aisle was well in hand. Jack had given Steve the nod, and they frogmarched Lucy down the aisle to a row where there were enough empty seats for them all. And when Titch turned around with the torn tickets in his hand, it was to see Lucy sat between the two boys, giggling her head off. So he now had to manoeuvre himself into the position he wanted. 'Greg, you go in and sit next to Jack. Ma, you go next.' Then, horror of horrors, Olive followed Aggie and then Irene pushed herself past him. He was left standing at the end of the row with his plans lying in shreds at his feet. 'Blow that for a lark,' he muttered. 'The kids have got more nous than I have.'

Aggie noticed his predicament and chuckled softly. 'What are yer standing there for, son? The lights will be going down in a minute and yer might find yerself sitting next to a strange woman. It does happen, yer know, there's some queer folk around.'

It was the opening Titch needed. 'In that case I'm not sitting at the end. Irene, let me get between you and Olive, before some strange woman tries to take advantage of me.'

So it ended up with everybody being pleased with the seating arrangement, except Greg. He was plotting his revenge when the lights went down, but he put his thoughts to one side for the time being while laughing loudly at the antics of Charlie Chase. The big picture was *Annie Oakley*, a Western with Barbara Stanwyck. And while the boy watched open-mouthed as guns blared and there were dead bodies everywhere, he forgot the girl called Lucy Mellor who was being plied with sweets from both sides, even though she had a bag of her own on her lap.

Aggie was nearly cross-eyed as she tried to watch the film without missing anything that went on beside her. Not that there was anything going on. Olive was sitting as stiff as a board with her hands clasped on her knee, while Titch sat with his arms folded staring at the screen as though he'd never seen such an exciting film. He's too bleeding slow to catch cold, Aggie thought. I bet he's late for his own ruddy funeral.

Meanwhile, Titch was quite content with the way things were going. Last time he was on leave, four months ago, Olive had said she would never marry again because there'd never be anyone to come up to Jim. It hadn't bothered Titch at the time because although he knew he was attracted to her, he thought it was friendly affection and didn't amount to anything more serious. But the whole time he was away, she was never far from his mind. And when the ship was homeward bound, he found himself counting the days until they sailed into Liverpool. He'd always welcomed the sight of the Liver Birds, but never as much as he had this trip.

'She's a good actress, isn't she?'

Titch blinked rapidly as he turned to Olive. 'What did yer say, love?'

'I said she's a good actress, isn't she?'

'She is that. One of the best.'

Aggie hadn't missed a word. 'She can act all right, but I don't like her eyes. They're too close together for my liking and she's always got them screwed up.'

Olive and Titch looked at each other and laughed. 'Ye're there, are yer, Ma?'

'Of course I'm here, yer daft nit. Didn't yer see me coming in with yer?'

Irene leaned across Titch to say softly, 'For the money she's getting, Aggie, I'd screw me eyes up too, if that's what they wanted.'

Greg flopped back heavily in his seat. 'I wish yer'd all shut up, I can't hear what they're saying. I've a good mind to go and ask for me money back.'

'It wasn't your money,' Jack hissed. It was Mr Titch what paid.'

A man sitting behind Greg tapped him on the shoulder. 'Do us all a favour. Go and get yer money back and toddle off home. Then perhaps the rest of us can enjoy the film.'

Lucy's giggle brought a loud tut-tut from the man's wife. 'I think some people only come to the pictures to stop others enjoying themselves. For two pins I'd call the manager and have them put out.'

Greg slid down in his seat and there wasn't a peep from him until the lights went up.

Ruby left the house at seven o'clock, while Bob was upstairs getting changed. She'd decided to leave early so she could meet Wally on his way to the pub. It was too dangerous to slip him a piece of paper while they were sitting with Jessie and the gang. Especially when she knew full well Jessie's husband didn't like her and was only looking for an excuse to tell her to get lost. He'd made it quite clear he didn't approve of married women being in pubs without their husbands and she didn't want to upset the apple-cart.

Ruby didn't know where Wally lived, but she knew the direction he came from. So she walked past the pub, crossed a few side streets, then took shelter in a shop doorway. There was no fear of bumping into the Armitages or the Bowlers because they got to the pub very early to get decent seats.

Wally's expression changed three times in as many seconds when Ruby stepped out of the shop doorway into his path. Shock registered first, then annoyance, followed by slyness. 'What on earth are you doing here?' he asked.

'I thought it would be safer this way. We can't make proper arrangements for next week with the others looking on.'

Wally's mind was working overtime. 'I don't live far from here – just two streets away, actually. Would yer like to come and see my house, seeing as we're so near?'

'The others might think it's queer if we're both late.'

'We won't be late. Ten minutes is all it'll take to show yer where I live. Then you can go to the pub and I'll follow five minutes later. They won't think anything of it.'

'What about yer neighbours?'

'They don't bother me and I don't bother them. Besides, they don't know you, so why get all het up about it?'

'It's your good name I'm thinking of.'

Wally grinned. 'What makes yer think I've got a good name? Come on, we're only wasting time standing here.'

Ruby kept her eyes lowered until she was standing in the hallway of the small two-up two-down house. 'I felt as though I was running the gauntlet.'

Wally didn't tell her the neighbours were so used to him bringing women home they wouldn't give it a second thought. Cupping her elbow he ushered her through to the living room. 'Just a quick look around then we'll go.'

594

Ruby's face showed her surprise. The room was spotless and very comfortably furnished. 'You don't clean this place yerself, do yer?'

'No, I have a woman comes once a week and cleans it right through. And seeing as there's only me, and I'm a tidy person, the place doesn't get untidy or dirty.'

'Yer've got a nice home, it's a credit to yer.'

Wally led her through to the well-fitted kitchen where, once again, everything was clean and in its right place. 'Now a quick look upstairs and then yer can make yer way to the pub.'

The two bedrooms each held a double bed, covered with expensive eiderdowns. And the wardrobes and dressing tables were of good quality. 'I think yer've got a very nice home, Wally,' Ruby said as she made her way down the stairs. 'Ye're better off than most people.'

She didn't go back into the living room, but went towards the front door. 'I'll be on me way and see yer later.'

Wally put his hand on the door to stop her from opening it. 'Yer haven't told me what's happening next week.'

'D'yer know, I'd forget me head if it was loose.' Ruby brought a piece of paper out of her pocket. 'Here, yer can read it for yerself.'

Wally's eyes scanned the note. *Monday, around ten, number painted on yard door.* He folded the paper and handed it back to her. 'I've got a better idea, and we wouldn't be on pins in case yer daughter woke up and caught us. You come here instead of me coming to you. We could enjoy ourselves without worrying about being heard or seen.' He saw the indecision on Ruby's face and coaxed, 'Come on, love, yer must admit it would be a hundred times better. I don't want to have our first taste of intimacy ruined by worrying about whether yer daughter's going to walk in on us. I'm not one of these blokes who's satisfied with a quickie down an entry. I want to take me time and show yer what it's like to be really loved.'

He loves me, Ruby thought. He really loves me. I can't let him down now. If I start raising objections he'll think I'm childish and get fed up with me. 'Okay, I'll come on Monday night. If I can get here before ten I will, depending upon Lucy and if I don't have to wait for a tram.'

'Yer won't be sorry, I promise yer.' Wally opened the door for her. 'I'll follow in five minutes.' He went back into the living room and lit a cigarette. God, but she was gullible. She believed every word he said. Still, he had a feeling she'd be very good at what he wanted her for. If she wasn't, it would just be a one-night stand and goodbye Ruby.

Chapter Nineteen

'Mrs Pollard, would yer mind if Rhoda came over for a game of cards?' Lucy asked. 'It would save me being the only girl and I know she'd love it.'

'I wouldn't mind in the least, sunshine, as long as her mother will let her stay out until ten o'clock. D'yer think it would be better if I asked Mrs Fleming?'

'Ooh, yes please, if yer would.'

'Right, I'll be back in two shakes of a lamb's tail. I told the others I'd follow them on, so I'll have to be sharpish.'

When his mother had gone, Greg said, 'I don't know why yer want that Rhoda here, she's as soft as a brush.'

'She is not!' Lucy was quick to defend her friend. 'She's always near the top of the class so she can't be that soft.'

'Which is more than can be said for you, our kid.' Jack was at the sideboard drawer getting the packs of cards out, and he turned to wink at Lucy before adding, 'I think yer were third from the bottom, weren't yer?'

Greg was speechless for all of two seconds. 'I was third from the top, and you know it. If you'd ever got so far up yer'd have been dizzy 'cos yer don't like heights.'

'Who doesn't like heights?' Irene came through the door with a very happy-looking Rhoda in tow. 'I hope you two are not fighting.'

'Me fight with our Jack? I wouldn't do that, Mam! He's me ever-loving brother and no one fights with their ever-loving brother.'

'Well, see it stays like that. I'm relying on the two working men to see there's no shenanigans.' Irene gave a quick glance in the mirror before bustling out. 'Enjoy yerselves but don't go mad.'

'Yer don't need to worry, Mrs Pollard,' Steve called after her. 'Me and Jack will make sure nothing gets broke.'

'Does that include noses?' Greg contorted his face to look vicious. 'Because if anyone cheats tonight, that's what they'll get.'

'Take no notice of him, Rhoda,' Lucy said. 'Come and sit down.'

'Yeah, make yerself at home, Rhoda.' Jack believed that when his dad wasn't at home, he was the man of the house. So what he said went. 'Ignore the face on our kid, he couldn't burst a hole in a paper bag, let alone someone's nose.'

'I'll sit next to you, Lucy.' Rhoda plonked herself down on the chair coveted by the three boys. With a shy look on her face, she said, 'Hello, Steve.'

He gave her a bright smile. 'Welcome to the gang, Rhoda.'

'We'll have to play with two packs tonight, seeing as there's five of us.' Jack placed two packs of cards on the table. 'I'll shuffle, then Steve can cut.'

'I've never played with two packs before,' Lucy said. 'Is it just the same?'

'Exactly the same, but yer stand more chance of getting the cards yer want 'cos there'll be two of everything.' Jack shuffled the cards and pushed the pack over to Steve. 'You cut and Lucy can deal.'

Greg was eyeing Rhoda. 'Have yer ever played cards before?'

'Of course I have.' When Rhoda nodded, her long mousy hair bounced on her shoulders. 'Me and me mam often have a game of Snap.'

Greg's grin was one of pure delight. Oh boy, they were going to have some fun tonight. His anticipation of seeing her beaten in every game made him magnanimous. 'I'll tell yer how to play.' So while Lucy dealt, Greg outlined the rules. 'It's easy-peasy when yer know how.'

'We're not playing for buttons tonight,' Jack told them in his capacity of man of the house. 'I'll buy the winner of the first game a tuppenny slab of Cadbury's.'

Rhoda was still sorting her hand out when it was her turn to go. 'Ooh, er, can yer help me, Lucy? I've got three twos, but they're not the same suit.'

'Of course they're not the same suit, soft girl.' Greg nearly swallowed his Adam's apple. Then he consoled himself by think-ing it was beginner's luck. 'There's only one of everything in a pack of cards, so how could yer get three out of two packs?'

'Leave her alone, you!' Lucy said. 'Go on, Rhoda, yer can put them down.'

The first hand went to Rhoda, the second hand went to Rhoda and she ended up winning the game comfortably. 'Aren't I lucky? And Cadbury's is me favourite chocolate.'

'She's cheated.' Greg looked disgusted. 'I don't know how, but she's cheated.'

'I have not!' Rhoda looked indignant. 'I'm going to tell me mam on you.'

'There's nothing worse than a bad loser, Greg,' Steve said. 'Yer should act like a gentleman in defeat.'

'Yeah, she won it fair and square,' Jack said. 'So behave yerself.'

'How could she win fair and square?' Greg wasn't going to give in without a fight. 'She said she only ever plays Snap with her mam.'

Lucy was laughing inside as she listened and waited for the truth to emerge. Greg was about to get his eye wiped.

Rhoda's face was set and her hazel eyes sending out sparks as she leaned across the table and glared at Greg. 'Yeah, I do play Snap with me mam every night. That's until me dad has finished reading the *Echo*. Then we all play Rummy, or Whist.'

Jack, Steve and Lucy were convulsed with laughter. The expression on Greg's face was a picture no artist could paint. His voice came out as a high squeak. 'Whist! Yer mean yer can play Whist?'

Rhoda tossed her head. 'Yeah, of course I can. And I can play Patience, as well.'

'Then she should be disqualified.' Greg glanced towards his brother. His look was fierce, but anyone who knew him well would have seen the laughter lurking beneath the surface. 'She was playing under false pretences. A professional among amateurs.'

'Ye're only jealous, Greg Pollard,' Lucy said. 'Why don't yer be a good sport?'

Jack nodded. 'Yeah, take it like a man.'

Steve came up with, 'Give in gracefully and admit yer were wrong.'

'Go on, give in.' Rhoda gave Greg a beaming smile. 'If yer give in I'll share me slab of Cadbury's with yer.'

Greg pretended to perk up. 'Well, that puts a different light on things. Did yer say yer'd share yer slab of chocolate with me?'

Rhoda nodded. 'Yeah, and I always keep me promises. When I've eaten the chocolate I'll give yer the silver paper.'

'Now that's what I call having a heart of gold.' Greg wasn't half enjoying himself. Rhoda wasn't so daft after all. 'And for being so generous, if yer win the next game I'll give yer the silver paper back.'

'Ye're not soft, are yer? Yer haven't got the paper yet.'

'You haven't got the chocolate yet. And if I know my brother, yer never will have. Yer see, he's one that never keeps a promise.'

'You watch where ye're flicking yer ash, Titch McBride,' Olive said, wagging a finger. 'I'm the one who has to clean this floor.'

'I'll ask Alec for a brush before we go if yer like.' Titch was sitting opposite, between George and Bob. It was a position he'd chosen deliberately, having decided that he stood much more chance with Olive if he let things take their course. She seemed to be happy in his company and was always glad to see him. That was good enough to be going on with and he'd work on what he had. 'Why pick on me, anyway? Why don't yer have a go at these two. They're dropping ash all over the place.'

'Then they can hold the shovel while you brush up.' Olive had been apprehensive about coming to the pub, but Alec and Betty had greeted her like an old friend and she was soon at ease and soaking up the atmosphere. 'That's if the three of yer aren't legless by the time the night's over.'

'I've never seen George legless,' Irene said. 'I don't know whether I'd see the funny side or hit him on the head with the poker.'

'Oh, I think yer'd see the funny side, queen.' Aggie took a swig of her milk stout. 'As long as it wasn't yer rent money he got drunk on, then I doubt yer'd be laughing.'

George stubbed his cigarette out before leaning his elbows on his knees and smiling across at his wife. 'You've never seen me legless, but I've seen you.'

'I beg your pardon?' Irene looked flabbergasted. 'I have never been drunk in me life, and you know it.'

'Oh, I've seen yer blind drunk, love. And I should know because it cost me enough to get yer that way.' George let out his hearty chuckle. 'It was the night I asked yer to marry me and I was making sure I got the right answer.'

Irene's bonny face lit up as she and her husband exchanged that special look that said they were as much in love now as the night he proposed. 'D'yer know, I've often wondered what I was thinking about, marrying you. But ye're telling me now I wasn't capable of thought.' She leaned towards him. 'I wasn't drunk that night, love, but the girl sitting next to me was. She must have thought it was her birthday, 'cos every time you went to the bar I passed me drink over to her. So yer see, sunshine, I was as sober as a judge and knew perfectly well what I was saying. And never for one minute have I regretted it.'

'You two are lucky,' Bob said. 'I think I must have been drunk the night I proposed and I have lived to regret it.'

There was a trace of sadness in Aggie's smile. 'I've told yer, Bob, there's happiness in store for you and Lucy. Don't ask me how I know, I just do. Yer'll not spend the rest of yer life as yer are now.'

'I think me ma's right,' Titch said. 'Something will blow up one of these days and yer'll say enough is enough. And yer'll be free to start a new life. There's plenty of good women around who'd make yer a good wife, and be a good mother to Lucy.'

'I know that, I've already met one.'

Silence descended as the news was digested. Then Irene found her voice and asked, 'Yer mean yer've already met a woman yer'd like to spend the rest of yer life with?'

'It's a bit premature of me to say it, but yes, I could quite easily spend the rest of me life with her. That's if she'd have me, of course. We sit on the same table in the works canteen, with about eight other people. That's the only time I see her. Her name's Kate, she's a widow with a girl the same age as Lucy. And yer'd go a long way to meet a nicer person.' Bob wasn't usually a talker, but tonight he just wanted to bring his feelings out into the open. 'I think she likes me, but never by word or deed have either of us shown our feelings.'

'Yer just talk to her in the canteen?' Titch asked. 'Is that as far as it goes?'

Bob nodded. 'That about sums it up. But she's kind and caring, everything that Ruby's not. There is a spark between us, I can tell, but that's the way it'll stay as far as she's concerned. And I wouldn't expect, or want her to be any different. I'm just telling yer because ye're me friends and I wanted yer to know. I don't have to pretend to you that I have a happy marriage, and everything in the garden's rosy, 'cos yer know different. If I was on me own I'd walk away tomorrow and breathe a sigh of relief. But Lucy's too young to have her life turned upside down, so I'll have to stick it out until she's old enough to understand.'

'Lucy's not soft,' Titch said. 'She probably understands a lot more than yer give her credit for.'

'Oh, she understands all right. In fact, I believe my daughter knows more about the underhanded antics of my wife than I do. But nevertheless I think the shock of the family splitting up would be too much for her. So I'll leave things as they are for a while, at least until she leaves school.'

'This woman at work,' Aggie said, 'what's her name?'

'Her name's Kate Brown, and yer'd get on with her like a house on fire, Aggie. She's very shy until she gets to know yer, then surprises yer with her quick sense of humour.'

'Never mind all that.' Titch was eager to learn more. 'What's she like to look at? Is she pretty and has she got a figure like a film star? If she has, then she sounds as though she'd be right up my street and yer can introduce me to her.'

'Oh dear, oh dear, oh dear,' Aggie tutted. 'There's that son of mine at it again. It's coming to something when he can't get a girl of his own and has to resort to asking his mate to fix him up with a blind date.'

Bob laughed. 'I wouldn't need to introduce him – Kate knows

more about him than he knows himself. In fact, if she walked in here now, she'd greet yer all by name because she's heard so much about yer.'

'That's scuppered my chances then, before I've even met her,' Titch said. 'I suppose yer've told her I've got a girl in every port?'

'No, I told her yer were a bachelor at the moment. But I said that one of these days yer'd meet a woman and yer'd fall for her like a ton of bricks.'

Olive sat back on the bench and laced her fingers over her tummy. 'It'll take a good woman to catch Titch McBride.'

Titch met her eyes for the first time that night. 'It's a good woman I'm after, Olive. D'yer know of one?'

She blushed and lowered her eyes. 'I'll keep a look-out for yer and let yer know.'

George had been sitting very quietly supping his beer and taking it all in. They say life is full of surprises, he thought, and Bob had certainly dropped one on them tonight. Not that they should be surprised, because God knows, the man had put up with more than anyone should have to put up with. He was a nice bloke and deserved some happiness in his life. So good luck to him.

There'd been another surprise for George in the last hour. One that had sneaked up on him unexpectedly. He might be wrong of course, but if the relationship between Olive and Titch wasn't developing into something more than friendship then he was a monkey's uncle. They hadn't said a word to confirm his belief, but that in itself was what made it more obvious. It was as if they were deliberately being cool with each other. Oh well, George thought, perhaps they don't know it themselves yet. But if I had anyone to bet with, I'd have a little flutter on them getting together in the near future.

'Tell us more about this Kate Brown,' Aggie said. 'Don't forget, she's got to pass our inspection to see if we think she's good enough for yer.'

Bob knew it was all wishful thinking on his part, but he wanted to talk about Kate and surely there was no harm in that. 'Let's see. She's got a round, pretty face, mousy-coloured hair, hazel eyes and strong white teeth. She doesn't wear make-up, at least not in work and that's the only place I see her. Since her husband died she hasn't had an easy life. She works to support herself and her daughter, and her mam helps her out by minding the girl and doing odd jobs for her. If I was asked who she reminded me of, I'd say Irene. I've always thought of Irene as the perfect wife and mother. She's pretty, always got a smile on her face, keeps her home like a palace, is sensible with money, always willing to help anyone out, and is wonderful with the boys. And I bet George is the most contented husband on this earth.'

Irene put her hands to her cheeks. 'Ay, Bob, yer've got me blushing. Anyone would think I was a saint, and I'm far from it.'

'You are to me, love,' George said. 'Ye're everything that Bob said yer are, and more. If he's found a treasure like you, he'd be a fool to let her slip through his fingers.'

Aggie was wishing they had rocking chairs in pubs. Words seemed to come easier to her when she was rocking back and forth. 'Bob, in all the years I've known yer, I've never heard yer talk so much. This woman must be having quite an effect on yer.'

'Aggie, I've never had anyone to talk about before. And I haven't really got the right to be discussing Kate like this when I've only ever seen her in the canteen, with a yard of table separating us. For all I know she might think I'm a dead loss.'

'Yer don't really think that, do yer, Bob?' Irene asked.

'No, I don't. I honestly believe that if I wasn't married, me and Kate would have got together ages ago.'

'Ay, I'm beginning to feel left out with all this talk of love and marriage,' Titch complained. 'Yer'd better find me a good woman soon, Olive. If yer haven't found one by the time I come back off me next trip, yer'll have to marry me yerself.'

'Yer cheeky thing! Did yer hear that, Aggie?' Olive turned to see Aggie grinning all over her face. 'He just wants to get married so he won't feel left out, so anyone will do. He must think I want me bumps feeling.'

'Why, is that what happens?' Titch looked the picture of innocence as he faced George. 'When yer get married, mate, do yer get yer bumps felt?'

'Don't yer dare answer that, George Pollard,' Irene said. 'Unless yer want a bump on yer head the size of a football after I've clouted yer with the poker.'

George chuckled. 'Surely yer wouldn't begrudge Titch feeling a bump on me head? I mean, it wouldn't be neighbourly to refuse.'

'Ho, ho, very funny.' Irene pointed to the table. 'Have yer not noticed me glass has been empty for the last half-hour?'

'I'm sorry, my love.' George stood up and collected the ladies' glasses. 'It was Bob's fault, he took me mind off things with his startling revelation. And now Titch, of all people, is on the look-out for a good woman. If they both get their wish, we'll have to put an order in with Alec for a bigger table. We'll not get many more glasses on this fiddling little thing.' He began to walk away, thought of something and came back. 'D'yer realise it'll take a full week's wages to buy one round of drinks?'

Titch chuckled. 'I never thought of that. It does put a different

603

complexion on things. Unless the women find themselves a job to pay their way. Or they could take in washing.'

'Yer can sod off, Titch McBride,' Irene said. 'My working days are over.'

'And I'll have a job finding yer a good woman, Titch,' Olive said. 'It's no good me singing yer praises and then saying yer'd stipulated that the woman ye're looking for has to go out to work. I think ye're doomed to stay a bachelor.'

'And yer can count me out, 'cos my dreams are too good to come true.' Bob spread out his hands. 'So we won't be needing a bigger table after all, George.'

Bob lay in bed staring at the ceiling. Ruby wasn't home yet so he was free to let his thoughts wander. And he was going over what he'd said in the pub. Perhaps he should never have mentioned Kate because now his friends would be asking about her and he'd have nothing to tell. They wouldn't ask out of curiosity, or because they were nosy, but because they really cared about him and Lucy. He'd be a very lonely man indeed without his good neighbours. It was his loneliness that had brought about his outpourings tonight. He was always the listener, as his friends talked about their wives, husbands and families. But apart from his beloved Lucy, he had no one to talk about. He couldn't talk about his wife because there was nothing good he could say about her. She lived her own life and didn't give a damn about him. Like tonight – she'd gone out without even telling him. Where she got to, God only knows, and he'd reached the state where he didn't even care. So just for once, when Irene and George were telling of their love for each other, he had felt the need to have someone in his life that he could talk about.

Stretching his arms high, Bob laced his fingers and put his hands behind his head. This was one of the times he craved the love of a woman. Someone whom he could hold, who would cuddle up in bed beside him and tell him she loved him. Surely that wasn't too much for a man of thirty-eight to ask for? And he knew without any doubt that the woman he wanted was Kate Brown. But it would take a miracle to bring them together, and miracles were few and far between.

Bob heard the key in the front door and glanced at the alarm clock on the tallboy. The illuminated hands told him it was a quarter to twelve. Where the hell had his wife been until this time of night? He gave a deep sigh and was about to turn on his side when he heard a clatter on the stairs, followed by a loud thud. Then the bedroom door was pushed open to bang against the wardrobe and Ruby walked into the end of the bed. Cursing under her breath, she felt her way round to the side she slept on and, so drunk she couldn't stand, she fell on the bed. The smell of alcohol filled the room and Bob felt sick. He'd been in the company of three women tonight, and two drinks each was all they'd had. Sherry for Irene and Olive, and milk stout for Aggie. Yet his wife, this drunken woman who wasn't even capable of undressing herself, must have had ten times that amount to get in this state. And where had the money come from to pay for it?

The smell was overpowering, and filled with disgust, Bob moved as far away from Ruby as the bed would allow. There was no movement from her now, and he assumed she was too drunk to undress herself properly and had fallen asleep on top of the bedclothes. But minutes later he could feel the mattress on the bed being pushed down and knew Ruby was trying to sit up. At this rate he wasn't going to get a wink of sleep tonight. He could feel his temper rising, but knew it was no use trying to talk sense into her, she was far too drunk. It would end up in a blazing row and Lucy would be disturbed. The best thing he could do was sleep on the couch.

Bob pushed the bedclothes back and was about to slip his legs over the side of the bed when he heard a match being struck. He turned his head to see Ruby trying to light a cigarette. Her eyes wouldn't focus and the hand holding the match was waving all over the place. 'Oh no, you don't.' He quickly rounded the bed, and seeing the matchbox lying on the eiderdown he picked it up before taking the flickering match from between her fingers. 'I don't mind yer setting yerself on fire, but yer'll not set the house on fire.'

Her words slurred, Ruby said, 'Give them here.' She hiccupped several times and the stench caused Bob to step backwards. But he didn't move fast enough, and as she made a grab for him her nails raked the back of his hand. 'Ye're a bleedin' miserable swine, that's what yer are. Call yerself a man, do yer? Ye're not a man, ye're a bleedin' little sissy.'

Bob didn't answer. He knew if he didn't get out of the room quick he wouldn't be responsible for his actions. So, keeping the box of matches in his hand so she couldn't cause any damage, he walked out and crept down the stairs, hoping Lucy had slept through the last fifteen minutes.

But Lucy had been wakened by the noise her mother made coming up the stairs and had heard every sound and word. Tears welled up in her eyes and she felt like running down the stairs after her dad. She wanted to put her arms around him and tell him how much she loved him. But it would upset him to know she'd heard what had gone on. So she pulled the sheet over her head and

605

curled up like a baby. All her life she'd tried to win her mother's love. She'd done everything to try and find favour with her. But right now, her heart filled with sadness for the father she adored, the girl knew she would never again crave the love of a woman who said such wicked things to hurt him. He had never wronged her, but she thought nothing of cheating on him.

Lucy sniffed up and used the sheet to dry her eyes. You were supposed to honour your mother, but how could you honour someone who couldn't speak without using bad language? Who came in drunk at this time of night, and who told terrible lies? No, she couldn't honour the woman whom she could hear muttering drunkenly in the next room. She wasn't a real mother. Not like Mrs Pollard and Mrs Aggie, who loved their children. And Steve's mam, who loved him to bits.

Downstairs, Bob put a match to the gas mantle and the room flooded with light. He blinked for a few seconds until his eyes became accustomed to the brightness, then gazed down at his hand. There was blood running from three deep scratches and dripping on to the floor. Shaking his head, partly in anger and partly in sadness, he went to hold his hand under the tap in the kitchen. He'd need to find something to use as a bandage to stem the bleeding for tonight. Then tomorrow he'd see if the corner shop had any large plasters to cover the back of his hand completely. If they couldn't be seen he could always say he'd injured himself while doing a job in the house. He'd rather tell a lie than admit to the truth.

Bob opened the cupboard that was set in the recess at the side of the hearth and took out a pillowslip. After folding it, he wrapped it around his hand several times. The cuts were stinging like mad, but he knew there'd be no ointment in the house so there was no point in looking. Ruby didn't believe in spending money on the likes of that. 'No,' he muttered softly as he brought his coat in from the hall, 'but she can find money for booze.'

After placing two cushions at the end of the couch, Bob put the light out and lay down. He shivered as he pulled his coat around him and the cold lining came into contact with his bare skin. Taking a deep breath, he spoke softly to the empty room. 'What sort of a life is this? I can't stand much more of it and one of these days I'll just snap. Then Ruby won't know what's hit her.' He moved his position to try and find comfort, but the couch wasn't made to accommodate his long frame and his feet were hanging over the side. 'I won't say anything to her tomorrow, I'd only be wasting me breath. But one thing I can do is cut her money again. It won't change her attitude but it will stop her from coming home blind drunk.' His eyes closed tight, he said, 'May God forgive me, but I wish she would go out one day and never come back. And if I'm wicked for saying so, then it's her who's made me wicked.'

Kate was already seated in the canteen when Bob sat down. And right away she noticed the plasters on his hand. 'What have you been doing with yerself?'

Billy Gleeson answered her. 'I bet he's hit his hand with a hammer, the silly bugger. I've told him to lay off the whisky.'

'Ye're wrong, as per usual,' Bob said. He'd had time to think clearly and he knew the scratch-marks would be there for weeks, long after the plasters came off. 'Not wrong about me being a silly bugger, 'cos I'm that all right. And I'm paying the price for it. A flaming shelf in the kitchen fell down yesterday, and soft lad here,' Bob poked a finger in his chest, 'stood it up against the wall with the nails sticking out. Well, yer can guess the rest. I raised me arm and scratched meself to blazes on the nails.'

'Ay, ye're not the only wounded soldier,' Billy said. 'Look at the black eye on Elsie. It's a real beauty.'

'I heard that, Billy Gleeson.' Elsie glared at him. 'Yer don't miss much, do yer?'

'Don't miss much!' Billy grinned. 'Blimey, anyone would have to be blind to miss that. Who the hell did that to yer?'

'I walked into a door, if yer must know.' Elsie definitely didn't think it was funny. 'Not that it's any of your business.'

Peg Butterworth was struggling to keep her face straight. 'Which door was it, girl? The lavvy door?'

It was difficult for Elsie to put on a haughty expression because her eye was almost lost in the swelling of the angry black and blue bruise. But to her eternal credit she did her best to look down her nose at her friend. 'I've already told yer what happened, so d'yer mind if we forget about it?'

'The only way I can forget about it, girl, is if I stop looking at yer altogether.'

Elsie bit into a sandwich. 'Then don't look at me. Nobody's forcing yer to.'

'But I want to look at yer. Ye're me best mate, aren't yer?' Peg put an arm across the wide shoulders. 'I always thought yer liked a bit of fun and a joke.'

'I do like a joke, queen, yer know that.'

'Then why don't yer loosen up and see the funny side of what happened?'

'The funny side!' Elsie's voice was shrill as she pointed to the offending eye. 'Yer expect me to see the funny side of this?'

'No, girl, 'cos that's not a bit funny.' Peg's tummy was shaking.

'But how yer got it is bloody hilarious. The funniest thing I've heard in years.'

'Yer can sod off, Peg Butterworth. And if yer say one word, I'll never speak to yer again as long as I live.'

'Oh, I wouldn't say anything, girl, 'cos nobody can tell a story like you. But yer have to admit that being on night shift is miserable, and a good laugh would cheer us all up.' Peg gave the shoulders a squeeze. 'And I don't know anyone who can make us laugh like you do.'

'Ooh, I don't know, queen.' Elsie was beginning to weaken. 'I'd feel daft.'

Bob had spent the day in a house where the atmosphere was so tense you could almost touch it. A good laugh right now would be a tonic to him. 'Elsie, never a day has gone by that yer haven't livened up our dinner break. Yer really cheer us up, and not once have we ever thought of yer as being daft. In fact, you are anything but daft.'

The buttons nearly popped off Elsie's overall as her chest expanded with pride. That was praise indeed, and she'd have to remember every word so she could tell her feller.

Peg could tell they were nearly there, so she added a little more pressure. 'Go on, girl, tell them what really happened. And I bet by the time ye're halfway through it, yer'll be laughing yer bleedin' head off.'

'Okay, queen. And before yer say it, I will start at the very beginning.' Elsie shuffled her bottom on the chair and hitched up her bosom. 'It was on Saturday teatime and I was in the kitchen getting our eats ready. Tiger had gone to find the bookie who owed him a couple of bob from the day before, and the kids were playing in the street. Then suddenly I heard this screaming and our Rosie came dashing in, crying her eyes out and holding her nose. When I asked her what had happened, she said Joan had punched her in the face.' Elsie stopped for a second, then said, 'By the way, Rosie is me next to youngest – she's seven. Anyway, I did no more than dash out into the street. I found Joan Craven playing with a mate outside her house and I was that mad, I grabbed hold of her arm and started shaking her. I told her if she ever hit me daughter again I'd give her a good hiding. The next minute her mam, Annie Craven, came flying out of the house screaming, "Take yer bleedin' hands off my daughter before I brain yer". I was going to say I wouldn't let go until the girl had said she was sorry, but before I got the words out, this fist came flying through the air and nearly knocked me over. Yer think I'm big, but yer want to see Annie Craven. She's as big as a ruddy six-roomed house. Anyway, the pair of us were going at it hammer and tongs,

608

and we had an audience by this time. Half the flaming street was out and the neighbours were egging us on. "Go 'ed there, Annie!" they were shouting, and: "Get stuck into her, Elsie." The next thing I know, our Rosie's pulling at me skirt and screaming, "What are yer fighting for, Mam?" '

Elsie couldn't say any more for laughing. She covered her face with her two hands and her whole body shook with laughter. 'Yer were right, queen,' she spluttered, 'it is bleedin' funny.'

'Ah, ay, Elsie, come on.' Billy was sitting on the edge of his seat in anticipation. 'What happened next?'

Elsie wiped her chubby hands across her eyes, savouring the words that were to come from her mouth. 'Well, in between trading punches, I told our Rosie I was trying to get Joan to apologise for hitting her. And Rosie started jumping up and down like a jack-in-the-box. "It wasn't this Joan what hit me, Mam, it was Joan Smedley." '

In the midst of all the laughter, Bob felt like giving Elsie a big kiss. This time last night, lying on the hard couch, his mind in turmoil, he thought he would never laugh again. 'Elsie, you are one good sport.'

'I thought I was a good boxer, too, until I came up against Annie Craven. She can't half pack a punch, believe me. The tops of me arms are black and blue.'

Ada Smithson's thin lips were working overtime. 'It serves yer bloody well right for jumping to the wrong conclusion.'

Elsie leaned across the table. 'I might not be a match for Annie Craven, but a little one like you I could make mincemeat out of. So just watch it.'

'Yer must have landed a few punches, though, Elsie,' Billy said. 'I mean, ye're capable of handling yerself.'

'Oh, I landed more than a few, Billy. But the crafty cow made sure she kept her bleedin' face out of the way. Still, she took it in good part and we shook hands to make up. And the neighbours didn't half enjoy it – they fell about laughing. I met a woman this morning who said she laughed that much she wet her knickers.'

'What did yer husband have to say about it?' Kate asked. 'Did he think it was funny?'

'Did he hell's like! He ranted and raved until me head was splitting. "Fighting in the street like a fishwife! Only women as common as muck do that." ' Elsie's round face beamed. 'But I got round him in bed with some sweet-talking and a few other things, and he went to sleep with a smile on his face. And another good thing came out of it. If the kids in the street break every bone in our Rosie's body, she'll never come crying to me again.'

Bob smiled across at Kate. 'I could do with Elsie in our house. I bet there's never a dull moment when she's around.'

'She is a case, there's no doubt about that.' Kate leaned her elbows on the table. 'I didn't have you down as someone careless enough to cut yerself on nails that yer knew darn well were sticking out of the wood. It doesn't sound like you, somehow.'

Bob made sure Billy was still listening to the women talking before replying: 'It's my story and I'm sticking to it, Kate. Except to you. I'm not going to lie to you. My wife came home on Saturday night at a quarter to twelve, rotten drunk. She could barely walk or stand up. I'd been out for a drink meself, with the neighbours, but we got home just after ten, when the pubs close, and I was in bed when Ruby came in. We don't even speak to each other now, so I turned on me side and was going to leave her to get on with it. But I heard her striking a match to light a ciggie, and the condition she was in, I was afraid of her setting the house on fire. So I took the matches from her for safety. She made a grab for them and scratched the back of me hand in the process. They're quite deep scratches, too, 'cos she has her nails very long and painted a bright red.' Bob gave a hollow laugh. 'It's a good thing for me that she was too drunk to stand or she'd have made for me face.'

Kate pursed her lips and blew out her breath. 'That's terrible, Bob. I don't know what to say, except I really am sorry.'

'Can yer imagine what this lot would say if I told the truth? I'd be a laughing stock.'

Kate nodded. 'Stick to yer story. They'll believe yer 'cos they've no reason not to. It's just that I've come to know yer so well over the months, I can tell when yer've got something on yer mind.'

Bob puffed on his cigarette and made a smoke ring. He watched it rise towards the ceiling as his heart urged him to say what was on his mind. 'Kate, I want to ask yer something. Yer don't have to answer if yer don't want to, but whether yer do or not, I'm asking yer not to fall out with me over it.'

'What is it, Bob?'

'If I was a single man, and I asked yer to come out with me one night, for a drink or to the flicks, would yer come?'

'If yer were single, Bob, yes, I would go out with yer.'

'Thanks, Kate, yer've made me a very happy man. I'm not in a position at the moment to take yer up on it, but who knows what the future holds?'

Chapter Twenty

'Last day of yer leave, eh, son?' Aggie rapped her fingers on the wooden arm of her rocking chair. 'Are yer sorry it's over, or will yer be glad to get back to the sea?'

Titch shrugged his shoulders. 'All good things come to an end, Ma, whether we like it or not.'

'That doesn't answer me question, son. Will yer be glad to get back or not?'

Titch looked uncomfortable. 'Yeah, I suppose so. Although I've got to say I've enjoyed being home. We've had some good laughs, haven't we?'

'We certainly have. Particularly on Lucy's birthday when we all went to the flicks. I don't think I ever seen anyone as happy as she was that night. She was beside herself with excitement. I think she looks on yer as a second father when Bob's on shiftwork. She won't half miss yer when yer've gone.'

'I'll miss her, too, she's a lovely kid. I'll miss you most of all, though, Ma, but that goes without saying. And the rest of the gang, they're real good mates.'

Oh God, Aggie thought. It's like trying to get blood out of a stone. But she had to bring it up now, 'cos he'd be gone tomorrow. 'Isn't there someone in particular that yer'll miss more than anyone else?'

'Yeah, I've just told yer. I'll miss you the most.'

'Well, seeing as I'm yer mother, I'd expect that.' Aggie raised her eyes to the ceiling and asked the Good Lord to give her patience. 'But what about Olive?'

While Titch's face turned the colour of beetroot, he stared at Aggie as though he didn't understand the question. 'What about Olive?'

'Listen, son, I might be old in years, but I'm still sound in mind and body. And there's nowt wrong with me bleedin' eyes or ears, either. Every morning yer've been sat at that table, all spruced up, waiting for Olive to call in on her way home from work. Am I right?'

'Well, yer wouldn't want me to sit here all scruffy, would yer?

Yer'd soon have something to say if I did.'

'Can we stop beating about the bush, son? Have you, or have yer not, taken more than a passing fancy to Olive? And don't start humming and hawing, otherwise yer bleedin' ship will be sailing off without yer.'

Titch dropped his head back and roared with laughter. 'Ma, yer have a very delicate way of phrasing things. No formalities for you, yer believe in getting right down to the point.'

'I'm getting on in years, son, I don't have time to hang around. And I'm not waiting three or four bleedin' months to find out if I'm right, so come on, out with it.'

'I hope this conversation isn't going to be repeated to the lady in question? If it is, then my lips are sealed.'

'I said I was getting on in years, son, I didn't say I was going senile. Ye're all I've got in life, so it's natural I want to share everything with yer. I want to know what's going on in that head of yours and what yer hopes and plans for the future are.'

'There's not much to tell, Ma, I'm afraid. But as I know yer won't be satisfied with that, I'll tell yer where I'm up to. Last year, when we were all trying to get Olive back on the road to recovery, I told her to start getting out and about and meeting people. I said she was young and attractive enough to meet a man who she could come to care for. She told me plainly that she would never marry again because no one would ever take the place of Jim. I can't remember the exact words, but I said something like she shouldn't be so quick to dismiss the idea. Anyway, it was a friendly conversation, and as far as I was concerned, Olive was just a good friend, nothing more.'

Titch smiled at his mother who was leaning forward in her chair, her eyes filled with expectation. 'Are yer with me so far, Ma?'

'Hanging on to every word, son. Ye're taking yer bleedin' time about it, but I'll forgive yer for that as long as the ending is the one I want to hear.'

'That's just it, Ma, I haven't got an ending for yer. But I'll tell yer what my feelings are and yer can figure it out for yerself. As I said, when I went back to sea that time, as far as I was concerned Olive was like Irene, just a friend I was fond of. Then I found meself thinking about her a lot, and when the ship docked in Liverpool I was like a young boy, eager to see her. And I still feel the same way. But I'm afraid of saying anything in case I frighten her off. So I'm just biding me time and waiting for a sign that tells me she feels more for me than friendship.'

Aggie sat back in her chair and for a while her face was serious. Then came a smile and chuckle. 'Here's me thinking yer were too slow to catch a ruddy cold. But ye're right, son, about taking yer time. That's the best way to do it, and it'll come out right in the end. But yer know, sometimes the onlooker sees more of the game than the people taking part. From what I've seen, I'd say that Olive has a definite leaning towards you. And as I'd like yer to go away with hope in yer heart, I'll let yer into a little secret. When Olive comes here every morning for her cuppa she's always got a turban on her head, an old pair of slippers on her feet and there's definitely not a trace of lipstick. Then when you come home it's a different story. The hair's nicely combed, she has a pair of shoes on and her lips are more red than nature intended. So I'd say yer were both dressing up for each other. And that to me, my dearly beloved son, is a very good sign. Ye're both moving forward slowly, and when the time is right, yer'll meet each other halfway.'

'Ye're a sucker for romance, aren't yer, Ma? Ye're wasting yer time, yer should be writing love stories.'

'That's as maybe. But I'm also impatient. So don't be dragging yer heels with Olive.' Aggie rubbed a finger up and down the side of her nose. And trying to sound casual, she asked, 'By the way, are yer seeing her tonight?'

'I'll be going over to say goodbye, yes. Why?'

'Well, always being one who liked to help the course of true love, I'll wangle it so yer have a bit of time on yer own. Just tell Steve I've got a little job for him to do, and that will get him out of yer way for a while.'

'What job's that, then, Ma?'

Aggie shook her head and clicked her tongue. 'It won't be whitewashing the bleedin' yard wall, yer daft nit. But I'll think of something. And if Olive is looking her best, with her hair nice and lipstick on, then take it from me that she's dressed herself up just for you. So don't waste time sitting there twiddling yer ruddy thumbs, make the most of the time yer've got. Drop a few hints and sow a few seeds. That'll give her something to ponder on while ye're away. If ye're too slow, yer might come home to find she's married the flaming coalman.'

Titch smiled. How lucky he was to have this woman for his mother. 'Ma, the coalman's married with half a dozen kids.'

'Which just goes to show he was a damn sight quicker off the mark than you are.'

'Yer've got an answer for everything, Ma, so would yer like to come down to Olive's with me? Yer can tell me what to say and when to say it.'

'Blimey! Would yer like me to hold yer hand and wipe yer nose for yer?'

Titch left his chair and went to kneel in front of Aggie. He held his arms wide and said, 'Give us a hug.'

Locked in each other's arms, Aggie whispered in his ear, 'I only want what's best for yer, son. And I don't know anyone who would make yer a better wife than Olive.' She moved back so she could look into his face. 'And I'd have a daughter and a grandson that I couldn't love any more if they were me own.'

'Don't be counting yer chickens, Ma, 'cos I'd hate to see yer disappointed.'

'I won't be, son, so don't worry.' Aggie had a good feeling about this and her heart was singing. 'Whatever happens I'll still have you.'

'Hello, Mrs Aggie.' Steve was growing more handsome by the day. He was still wearing the clothes Titch had given him and always looked immaculate. He and his mam were still struggling for money, but they took good care of the things they had. 'Mr Titch said yer wanted to see me. He said yer had a job for me.'

'Ah well, that's not strictly true.' Aggie waved him to a chair. 'In fact, sweetheart, it was a downright lie.'

Steve's dimple appeared when he smiled. 'What are yer up to, Mrs Aggie?'

When Aggie sat down and folded her arms, there was mischief glinting in her eyes. 'Whatever it is I'm up to, sweetheart, I want you to be up to it with me. I'd say we'd make good partners, don't yer think?'

'Mrs Aggie, ye're not thinking of robbing a bank, are yer?'

'No, yer need guns for that, son. And I lent mine to Edward G. Robinson for his latest gangster picture. So I can't offer yer anything so exciting.'

'In that case, count me in, partner.'

'I need a promise from yer first, Steve. That this will be our secret and yer won't tell anyone, not even yer mam. In fact, especially not yer mam.'

Steve made a sign on his chest. 'Cross my heart and hope to die.'

Aggie smiled. 'Right then, down to business. I asked yer to come up here so Titch and yer mam could have some time together. Yer see, I've got a sneaking feeling that they like each other.'

'Ye're not the only one, Mrs Aggie, 'cos I think so, too.'

'There yer are, then! I think it and you think it. The only ones that won't admit it are the two silly beggars involved. And that's because they're both afraid of showing their feelings.' Aggie was thinking that as soon as Steve left, her teeth were coming out. How could she think properly when the damn things were getting on her nerves. Vanity was one thing, being miserable was another.

'Tell me, sweetheart, what makes yer think they like each other?'

'Because they're at great pains not to show it. But me mam is a different person when Mr Titch is home. She takes more pride in her appearance for one thing, and she's like a cat on hot bricks when she's expecting him down. And she never used to be shy in his company, but she is now.'

Aggie banged the palm of her hand on the arm of the chair. 'That's exactly how I see things. And we can't both be wrong, can we? So tell me, how would yer feel if they did start courting, serious like?'

'Mrs Aggie, I'd be over the moon. I'd have a permanent smile on me face for the rest of me life knowing me mam was happy.' Steve had a question in his head he had to have answered. 'Does Mr Titch really like me mam?'

'Oh, I think so, son.' Aggie wasn't prepared to say more. 'But we can't force them to do anything just because it's what we'd like. So all we can do is try and help the romance along. And that is why ye're sitting here right now. To help the romance along.'

Unaware that they were the subject of a conversation just down the street, Titch and Olive sat back in the fireside chairs either side of the fireplace. 'How long will yer be away this trip, Titch?'

'I haven't a clue. It depends upon where the cargo's bound for. It could be one month, or it could be four.' Titch thought on about what his mother had said about him being so slow he'd come back and find she'd married the coalman. And while the coalman, with his wife and six kids was no threat, there were plenty of single blokes around. So he took his courage in his hands. 'Why, will yer miss me?'

When Olive nodded, Titch put a hand to his ear. 'I didn't hear what yer said, Olive, I must be getting deaf. Will yer miss me?'

Olive plucked nervously at her skirt. 'Yes, of course I'll miss yer.'

'Will yer miss me like a headache, or miss me 'cos yer like me?'

'Titch McBride, why do yer say these things to make me blush?'

'Well, yer do look pretty when yer blush, but that's not why I asked if yer'd miss me. Ye're not the only one that's shy, yer know. And even though I know me face will turn purple, I'm not going to let it stop me from saying I'll miss you.'

Olive chuckled. 'That'll be the day when you blush, Titch. I hope I'm there to see it.'

'Yer can see it right now 'cos I'm going to ask a favour of yer.'

'If it's about yer mam, yer've no need to ask. Yer know me and Steve will keep an eye out for her. In fact, yer'd have a job stopping me son from going to see his beloved Mrs Aggie. Visiting her is the highlight of his day.'

'I'm glad yer son gets on with my ma, Olive, but will yer stop making things difficult for me? Even me ruddy toes are blushing now. The favour I was going to ask has got nothing to do with me ma, it's for meself. And if I don't get it out now, I never will.' The words came tumbling from Titch's mouth. 'I want to know if yer'll come out with me one night next time I'm home? Just the two of us.'

'Just the two of us?'

'Yeah. You and me, together, like.'

The blush on Titch's face was obvious now, and it chased Olive's nerves away. She began to giggle. 'Yer really are shy, aren't yer?'

'I've never been shy in me life until this minute. And if yer say yer won't come out with me, I'll probably burst out crying.'

'Oh, we can't have that, can we? So I'll have to accept your offer. What was it now? Let's see if I've got it right. Just the two of us. You and me, together, like.'

'Olive Fletcher, I do believe yer've been having me on. Here's me, going through agony, and you've been enjoying me discomfort.'

'Your face was a picture, Titch. But I wasn't having yer on, honest. I felt like a sixteen-year-old girl being asked out on her first date, and you looked like the shy seventeen-year-old boy asking her.'

'I feel seventeen now. I had visions of yer turning me down.'

'Why would I turn yer down? You and me are very good friends, aren't we, Titch?'

'Yes, you and me are very, very good friends, Olive. In fact, I'd go as far as to say you and me are very *close* friends.'

When Steve finally opened the front door he heard them laughing and thought that was a very good sign. They were still in the same chairs they'd been in when he left them, but he detected a difference in their attitude to each other. They were more at ease, more light-hearted. He'd have to tell Mrs Aggie about that tomorrow, she'd be very pleased.

Titch didn't stay long. He'd seen Bob this afternoon with him being on the early shift, but he hadn't said goodbye to the Pollards yet. And he had to be up with the larks in the morning. 'So I'll see you two when I get back – which I hope won't be long.'

Olive got to her feet. 'I'll see you out, Titch.'

Steve's eyebrows shot up in surprise. His mam had never done that before.

He'd have been more surprised if he'd heard Titch asking, 'Do I get a farewell kiss?'

'Of course.' Olive lifted her cheek, but as Titch's face came

616

near, she cupped it in her hands and planted a fleeting kiss on his lips. 'Thank you for giving me me life back, Titch.'

On those softly spoken words, Olive closed the door, leaving Titch looking bewildered. Then a smile lit up his face and he walked away with a spring in his step. He gave a glance up and down the street to make sure there was no one around, then he punched the air with a clenched fist. Nothing had really been said about an understanding between them, but he was certain in his mind that when he came home again there would be a woman waiting to welcome him. Two women, really, because he must never forget his ma.

Titch was going to walk past his house to get to the Pollards', but changed his mind. He had his mother to thank for the progress he'd made tonight, because if Steve had been home he'd never have got the chance to say what he had. So she deserved to share his happiness.

He gave a loud knock on the door and waited for it to open. 'I'm not coming in yet, Ma, I've got to see the Pollards first. But I thought yer'd like to know I've got a date with a certain lady for when I come home.'

'Oh, I am glad, son. I'll sleep happy tonight.' Aggie, minus her false teeth, grinned. 'I owe meself a tanner now.'

'What d'yer mean, yer owe yerself a tanner?'

'I had a feeling tonight was going to be yer lucky night, so I had a little bet with meself.'

'Oh Ma, what am I going to do with yer?'

'Yer can put a move on, that's what. Get yerself settled down, so that when me time comes I can die in peace. I don't want to be standing at the Pearly Gates arguing the toss with St Peter that he had no right to take me until I'd settled all me affairs.'

'Ma, if St Peter knows what's good for him, he won't take yer until ye're too old to argue. And that won't be for another thirty years.'

'Oh well, if I've got that long to wait, I may as well go and make meself a pot of tea and drink to a long life. Then I might take meself off to bed and have an early night. So don't make a noise when yer come in.'

'In that case, I'll come in for a minute now. I want to sort something out with yer and I might not have time in the morning.' Titch ran straight up the stairs to his bedroom and was back down again within seconds with an envelope in his hands. 'Ma, there's thirty pounds in here and I want yer to mind it for me.'

Aggie's jaw dropped. 'Thirty pounds! In the name of God, son, where did yer get that much money from?'

'I'm not the spendthrift yer think I am, Ma, I always keep a bit aside for a rainy day. Not usually this much, but I'm not taking any back to the ship with me. If I haven't got it, I can't spend it. And yer never know, I might be looking for money sometime in the future.'

Aggie took the envelope from him, muttering, 'Think of all the milk stouts I could buy with this. I could be sozzled every day until yer come home again.' Then she smiled up at him. 'This will be safe under me mattress, son, until yer want it. Now go and visit yer mates.'

Titch put his arms around her and kissed her soundly. 'Goodnight and God bless, Ma. I don't half love yer.'

'And I love you, too, son.' Aggie was always emotional the day before her son left to join his ship, but he was so happy tonight she didn't want to spoil things for him. So she did what she always did, she resorted to humour. 'Which is a good job, really, 'cos life wouldn't be worth living if we couldn't stand the bleedin' sight of each other.'

Lucy finished her dinner and carried her plate out to the kitchen. After washing it in the bowl of water in the sink she left it to drip on the draining board. It was April and the nights didn't start getting dark until late, so on the way home from school, she and Rhoda had decided to go for a walk and do some window shopping. They enjoyed pressing their noses against the shop windows and pointing to what they'd buy if they had the money.

'I'm going over to Rhoda's, Mam.' Lucy walked through to the living room where her mother was sitting reading the *Echo* with a cigarette dangling out of the corner of her mouth. 'I won't be late.'

'Yer better hadn't be, yer little faggot. I want yer back in this house by half-seven.' Ruby turned a page of the paper, her eyes screwed up against the smoke swirling upwards from her nostrils. 'And not a minute later.'

'I'm not coming in at half-seven, I'm too big for that now.' Months had passed since the night Ruby had come home drunk, but Lucy had never forgotten or forgiven. Her dad said he'd cut his hand on a nail, but the girl knew better. And she never spoke to her mother unless it was absolutely necessary. 'Yer seem to forget I'm turned thirteen and will be leaving school in seven months.'

'Don't be giving me any of yer bleedin' lip, my girl, or yer'll be sorry. I said half-seven and if yer know what's good for yer, yer'll be in this house by then.'

Lucy was stung by the injustice. Children of eight and nine were allowed to stay out later than that. 'I won't, Mam, 'cos ye're not being fair.'

Ruby threw the paper on the floor and rounded the table to where her daughter stood. 'Yer'll do as I say.' She poked a stiffened finger in Lucy's chest. 'Half-seven in this house, eight o'clock bed. Yer heard what I said, yer haven't got cloth ears.'

Lucy was shaking with fear, but she stood her ground. 'I won't do as yer say, 'cos ye're mean and wicked.'

Ruby grabbed hold of the front of Lucy's gymslip and pulled her forward until their noses were nearly touching. 'Don't have me start on yer, yer little faggot. 'Cos if I do, yer'll be sorry yer signed.'

Lucy never knew where she got the courage from, but she couldn't have stopped the words even if she'd wanted to. 'I know why yer want me in bed early. It's because me dad's on afternoons and yer have to meet yer mates early so ye're back in time to make supper.'

Ruby was dumbstruck. She stared at Lucy for a few long seconds, then dropped the hand holding the gymslip. 'What are yer talking about, yer stupid bitch? I'm not going out! I only go round to me mates when yer father's on an early shift.'

'Mam, why do yer tell so many lies? My bedroom is at the back of the house, remember, and I hear yer closing the kitchen door and the yard door. Yer go out at least twice a week when me dad's on afternoons and nights. Don't deny it, 'cos I don't only hear yer, I've seen yer creeping down the yard when yer think I'm fast asleep. It's been going on for months now, and I have thought of telling me dad but I don't want to add to his worry. He doesn't have a happy life, my dad, and it's all your fault.'

Ruby's mind was in a spin and her temper was raging. But she was crafty enough to know her daughter had her over a barrel and could make life very difficult for her. She was going to Wally's house tonight and he'd go mad if she let him down, so she did something she never thought she would, she crawled. 'Look, I'm sorry if I've upset yer, I didn't mean to. And I do only go to me mates', I swear. I can't be expected to stay in this house day and night, it's not fair. And I'm not doing any harm just sitting in me mates' for a couple of hours having a chinwag and a bottle of stout.'

Lucy turned her head away. She was filled with disgust and didn't believe a word her mother said. But she would never tell her dad, for fear of losing him. 'I'm going out now and I won't come in until I'm ready. You can please yerself what yer do, I'm quite capable of seeing meself to bed.' There was a cardigan hanging over the back of a chair and Lucy picked it up and slipped her arms into the sleeves. She was halfway to the door when she spun round. 'I'm not going to say anything to me dad, but it's not

619

because I'm on your side. Yer see, just because ye're me mam doesn't mean I've got to like yer, 'cos I don't. And me dad will find yer out for himself one of these days.'

When Lucy left the room, little did she know how soon her words were to come true.

'Hello, Mrs Aggie.'

'Hello, queen.' Aggie was standing on her doorstep taking advantage of the nice weather. 'Ye're looking very pleased with yerself. Like the cat what got the cream.'

Lucy giggled. 'I'm happy 'cos I'm going to the pictures with me dad. I've just been over to tell Rhoda I won't be seeing her tonight.'

'That's nice for yer.' Aggie stepped back into the hallway. 'Come in for a minute, queen, and keep an old woman company.'

'Okay, me dinner won't be ready for another fifteen minutes.' Lucy was so full of beans she skipped into the living room. 'I like going out with me dad, just the two of us together.'

'Like a courting couple, eh, queen?'

Lucy tilted her head and fixed her large green eyes on the woman rocking back and forth in her chair. 'Would yer think I was cheeky if I asked yer something, Mrs Aggie?'

'Now how can I answer that if I don't know what it is ye're going to ask me? Go ahead and ask, and then I'll tell yer whether it was cheeky.'

'Is Mr Titch courting Steve's mam?'

The rocking stopped and Aggie sat forward. 'I'll tell yer what, queen. Why don't you and I put all the facts together and see what we come up with, eh?'

'Well, I know he took her to the pictures when he was home on leave last time.'

'Twice he took her. And as yer know he was only home for a week. So what does that tell us, queen? D'yer think it means they're courting?'

'Ooh, I don't know, Mrs Aggie. But he's never done it before, has he? So I suppose it must mean something.'

'Ye're not jealous, are yer, Lucy?'

'Of course not, silly!' Lucy's giggle filled the room. 'I love Mr Titch, but I think he's a bit too old for me. I hope he is courting Mrs Fletcher 'cos I think she's lovely. I did ask Steve, being nosy, like, but he said it's too soon to say.'

'For a lad of fifteen he's very sensible, is Steve. And what a handsome lad he's turning out to be, eh? He'll turn a few heads in another year or so.'

Lucy looked surprised. 'But Steve's always been nice-looking,

620

Mrs Aggie. At least, I think he has. And Jack, next door.' She leaned forward and lowered her voice. 'I'll tell yer who else is nice-looking – that Andrew Bentley from the top of the street. The one whose mother tries to speak posh and thinks she's better than anyone else.'

Aggie chuckled. 'So, yer've got three smashers lined up to choose from when ye're a little bit older. That can't be bad, can it?'

'Ooh, not Andrew Bentley, thank yer very much. He's nice to look at but not nice inside. Every time he sees me he tries to get me to stop and talk to him, but I always say I'm on a message and haven't got the time.'

'He's working now, isn't he?'

'Yeah, he's fifteen, the same age as Steve and Jack.'

'Yer know, queen, yer can't take it out on the lad because his mother's a snob. It wouldn't be fair because he can't help what his mother is.'

This brought a frown to Lucy's face. She'd never thought of it like that before. And she should have done, because she wouldn't like anyone to think that she took after her mother. 'Ye're right, Mrs Aggie, he can't help what his mam is. But he's a bit of a snob himself on the quiet.' She began to giggle. 'Rhoda calls him Andy, and he goes mad.'

'She's very outspoken, your friend. If she thinks it, she says it, and to hell with the consequences.'

'I know, I keep telling her about it. But she says it's better to say what yer think than be polished with someone and then talk about them behind their back.' Lucy glanced at the clock. 'I'll have to go, Mrs Aggie, or I'll get told off.'

'Off yer go, then, queen, and enjoy yerself. Come in tomorrow night and tell me what the picture was all about.'

'Where shall we go, pet? Would yer like to see Claudette Colbert and Robert Young, or Jean Arthur and Ray Milland?'

'Ooh, Robert Young, Dad. He's one of me favourites.'

Ruby pricked up her ears. If these two were going out it meant she could get away early. 'Yer haven't forgotten this is one of me nights out, have yer?'

'I don't see what difference that makes to me taking Lucy to the flicks.' Bob speared the last bit of potato and popped it into his mouth before pushing his plate away. 'We'd better make a move, pet, if we don't want to miss the short comedies.'

Ruby waited until she heard the door close behind them before allowing a smile to appear on her face. The silly bugger thought taking his daughter to the first-house pictures was a big deal. He didn't know what real enjoyment was, but she did. Wally had taught her. And she'd be getting an extra half-hour of it tonight in his bed under the feather eiderdown. He was a real man, was Wally, he knew how to make a woman happy.

Bob glanced in the window of the corner shop as they were passing, and asked, 'Would yer like some sweets, love?'

'Can yer afford it, Dad?'

Bob smiled and ruffled the dark curly hair. He was three shillings a week better off now, since he dropped Ruby's house-keeping money. 'I wouldn't ask yer if I couldn't afford it.' He passed a penny over. 'You get what yer want, I'll wait here for yer.'

Steve was in the shop carrying bags of coal in from the storeroom. He came every night straight from work and at the end of the week Mr Whittle gave him a few bob. His face lit up as it always did when he saw Lucy. 'Hi-ya.'

'I'm going to the pictures with me dad.' Lucy sounded very proud. 'And he's given me a penny for some sweets.' She saw the shopowner waiting to serve her and gave him a broad smile. 'Can I have a ha'porth of mint imperials and a ha'porth of jelly babies, Mr Whittle, please? And can I have them in two separate bags?'

'With a smile like that, how could I refuse?' George Whittle was in his sixties and had owned the corner shop for as long as anyone could remember. Small of stature, he had wispy white hair, kind blue eyes and a deeply lined face. He was very popular in the neighbourhood but he had his favourite customers, and two of them were in the shop now. As he weighed the sweets out, he smiled at the girl he thought had the face of an angel. 'Let me guess. The jelly babies are for yer dad.'

'No, silly! They're for me.' Lucy watched the coloured jelly sweets being tipped on to the scale and said wistfully, 'The red ones are me favourites.'

So it was, as she waved goodbye, Lucy had a bag of white mints for her father and a bag of all-red jelly babies for herself. And as she took her father's hand she thought her happiness was complete.

The picture was a romantic comedy, and Lucy was sighing with pleasure when they came out of the cinema. 'I enjoyed that, Dad. Robert Young's dead handsome, isn't he?'

'I've got to admit, pet, that Claudette Colbert is more my cup of tea.'

When Lucy giggled, Bob put an arm across her shoulders. 'How about getting a pennyworth of chips each to eat on the way home?'

'No, Dad, yer've spent enough. Yer'll leave yerself short of yer ciggie money.'

'I'm not that daft, pet. It's not often I take yer out so I want yer to enjoy yerself. Besides, it's ages since I ate chips from the paper. Me mouth's watering at the thought.'

When they got to the chip-shop, Bob said, 'D'yer think they'd mind if I asked them to wrap them separate? Or would they think I had a cheek?'

'Shall I go in? They know me because I often come for Mrs Aggie.' Lucy held out her hand. 'Yer money or yer life.'

She was still giggling when she came out of the chip-shop with two parcels wrapped in newspaper and letting off steam. 'I asked for plenty of salt and vinegar and he doused them.'

Bob made a hole in the paper and put in a finger and thumb. He pulled out a long chip that was so hot he had to wave it about before popping it into his mouth. With a smile on his face he sighed with bliss. 'Just like I remember. We'll have to do this more often.'

'Next time ye're on mornings, eh, Dad?'

They were eating the last of the chips when they reached home. Lucy took the paper from her father and squeezed it into a ball with hers. 'I'll put these in the bin and then make us a nice cup of tea. We might as well finish the night in style.'

When they were sitting facing each other across the table, talking about the film and things in general, Lucy thought what a wonderful life it would be if it was always like this. No shouting, no sarcastic remarks, no tension. There was nothing in this room tonight except love. Just like the Pollards next door.

It was nine o'clock when Lucy took herself off to bed, and Bob sat down to read the evening paper. He smoked a couple of cigarettes and felt at peace with the world. The silence was soothing and after a while he could feel his eyelids becoming heavy. He looked up at the clock to find it was ten o'clock. Time to hit the hay, he thought, 'cos he had to be up at a quarter to five. So he lowered the gas-light and made his way upstairs. After getting undressed he climbed into bed and was asleep as soon as his head hit the pillow.

Bob thought he'd been asleep for hours when he felt the bed sag. His eyes blinking rapidly, he looked at the alarm clock. A quarter past eleven. He was too drowsy to wonder where his wife got to until this hour, but he was niggled that she had no consideration for him. She knew he had to be up at the crack of dawn.

When Ruby had finished undressing and bent to turn the bedclothes back before getting into bed, the smell of drink wafted over to Bob. He tried to push it from his mind, but he couldn't help asking himself where she got the money from. Then he

623

thought, Oh, what the hell, forget about it. What's the point in going over old ground again?

He grabbed hold of the bedclothes, intending to pull them up to his nose to blot out the stench of drink, at the same time as Ruby climbed into bed. And with the movement of the clothes there came another smell. It was a body odour, but certainly wasn't one he associated with his wife. And after sleeping with her for nearly eighteen years he should know. He couldn't make it out. What the hell was it?

Ruby moved nearer to the middle of the bed and the smell became stronger. And then the truth came to hit him like a blow between the eyes. He caught his breath, and the bile churning in his tummy rose to burn his throat. He knew what the smell was now. It was the smell made by two people whose bodies are joined together in lovemaking. His wife had been with a man. And he knew with a certainty he couldn't understand, that it wasn't the first time. Whether it was one man or ten, made no difference to him now. He would never again share a bed with her. He'd put up with everything she'd thrown at him, but not this.

Bob got out of bed and felt for the clothes he needed for work the next morning. He put them over his arm then dragged the eiderdown off the bed and put a pillow under his arm.

'What the bleedin' hell d'yer think ye're doing?' Ruby asked. 'Yer stupid bugger.'

Bob bent over the bed and kept his voice low. 'You slut. You dirty, cheap slut.' With that he made his way downstairs where he threw everything on the couch before dashing out to the grid in the yard to be violently sick.

Chapter Twenty-One

As soon as Bob sat down in the canteen the next morning, Kate could see there was something amiss. 'You look terrible, Bob. What on earth is wrong?'

For the benefit of Billy, who was listening, Bob said, 'I've got an upset tummy. I must have eaten something that didn't agree with me because I've been up all night vomiting.'

'Yer look like death warmed up, mate,' Billy said, not unsympathetically. 'Yer should have taken the day off and stayed in bed.'

'I would have done if I could have afforded to lose a day's pay. But I'll be all right, me tummy will settle down.'

'What's that I hear?' Peg called. 'Is Bob not well?'

'He's got a tummy upset,' Billy told her. 'Been up all night vomiting.'

'Ooh, er, that's terrible, that is.' Elsie Burgess nodded her to head to emphasise how terrible it was. 'I had it the other week, and d'yer know what?'

Billy decided Elsie's troubles were bound to end up in a laugh, so he turned his back on his workmate. 'Oh, aye, Elsie, do tell.'

This gave Bob his chance. 'Kate, my world's fallen apart and I'm out of me mind. Could yer spare me five minutes when the shift's over? I need to talk to yer.'

'I'll hang around the cloakroom until all the girls have gone, then I'll meet yer outside. You really do look dreadful, Bob.'

'I feel worse than I look, believe me. I never, ever thought it would come to this – I'm at my wits' end.'

'I notice yer've got no carry-out.'

'I couldn't eat anything if yer paid me, Kate. The mere thought of food makes me want to be sick. I'll explain to yer later and yer'll understand the state I'm in.'

'Okay. Ten past two outside.'

They stood in a small side street by an end shop and Kate leaned back against the wall. 'Go on, Bob, get it all off yer chest. I'm a good listener.'

His head down and his voice thick, Bob briefly outlined how his life had been for the last ten years. How it had worsened over the last year to such an extent Ruby lived her own life and had no time for him or Lucy. The way she belittled him in front of his friends, came home the worse for drink and laughed at him when he asked her to try and make a go of it for their daughter's sake.

After a brief pause, Bob went on to the start of last night's events. 'I took Lucy to the pictures last night, and we really enjoyed ourselves. We walked home eating chips out of the paper and I was happier than I've been in a long time.'

'Didn't Ruby go with yer?'

Bob shook his head. 'My wife was out boozing. Who with, God only knows. She wouldn't dream of coming out with me or Lucy, she says we're dull. And I'm a fuddy-duddy who doesn't know how to enjoy himself. Anyway, Lucy went to bed about nine, and I followed an hour later. I was well away when Ruby came in at a quarter past eleven and woke me up getting into bed.' Bob met Kate's eyes, 'I hope I don't embarrass yer with what I'm going to tell yer, but it's the truth and I want yer to know.' It wasn't easy to find the right words and he only managed by keeping his eyes to the ground. When he heard Kate's sharp intake of breath, he looked up to see the colour had drained from her face. 'Not a pretty story, is it?'

'Not a pretty life for you or Lucy, either. I'm very sorry, Bob, I don't know how yer've put up with it all these years.'

'Neither do I, or me friends. But last night was the last straw. I'm getting away from her and I wondered if yer know anybody who takes in lodgers?'

Kate shook her head. 'They're all two-up two-down houses where I live, and you'd need two bedrooms if Lucy's with yer. My mam's got a spare room and she's taken a few lodgers in over the years. But, as I say, it's only the one room, and a small one at that. I will ask around for yer, though, and I'll get me mam to keep an eye open.'

'Thanks, Kate. I bet ye're sorry me and Billy ever came to sit at the same table as yer. I've done nothing but burden yer with me troubles.'

'I don't mind, I really don't. If I could help yer at all I would, 'cos I think ye're a good man, Bob, and I don't like to see yer unhappy. Your wife must be a very stupid woman not to know when she's well off.'

'She might be stupid but she's the one that's going to be left with the house and all the furniture: me and Lucy will end up with nothing. But I've got to get out, I can't live in the same house as her. We haven't lived like a married couple for years, but right now I can't even bear the thought of looking at her face, never mind

626

sharing the same bed. And while I can manage sleeping on the couch for the odd night, I don't fancy doing it for ever. So yer can see how desperate I am. If I had somewhere to go, I'd walk out today, even though it means leaving all me best friends behind.'

'Something will turn up for yer, Bob, I'm sure.'

'Oh, I know it will because I'm going to make it. As soon as I'm out of that house I'm going to make some enquiries about how to go about getting a divorce. I believe it takes a few years but I'm determined not to let her ruin me whole life for me.'

Kate reached out and touched his arm. 'Now, I might be able to help yer there. Yer see, I'm the poor one of the family. Me mam had two daughters, and our Audrey hopped in lucky and married a solicitor. At least he was only training when they got married, but he's a fully fledged solicitor now. They live in a big posh house in Allerton. But he's a nice bloke, Howard, and I'm sure he wouldn't mind giving yer some advice.'

'Ye're an angel, Kate. I feel better already, just talking to yer. If yer wouldn't mind having a word with yer brother-in-law, I'd be grateful.'

'Are yer sure it's what yer really want, Bob? It's a big step to take.'

'It's a step I should have taken years ago. Instead, I put up with being humiliated, degraded, and taunted by a wife who says I'm not a man, but a mouse. And for good measure she adds that she has no feelings for me, or our daughter. I've put up with all that, but I will not put up with a wife who goes with other men. Yer wouldn't expect me to, would yer?'

Kate shook her head. 'No, I wouldn't. I don't think any man would. But I don't want to interfere, you must make up your own mind.'

'I have made it up, Kate, and I'll not change it. So I beg of yer to ask around for some decent lodgings. The sooner I'm away from her the better.'

'I will, I promise. And if I hear of anything I'll give yer the nod in the canteen and we can meet here after work. Now I must go – me mam will wonder where I've got to.'

'Yeah, I'd better scarper, too. I want to call in to see a couple of me friends. They've been good to me and it's only right I tell them what's going on. I'll see yer tomorrow, Kate, and thanks for everything.'

Bob's hand was shaking as he knocked on Aggie's door. It gave him no pleasure to talk about his wife to others, but she'd brought it on herself. And he couldn't just disappear one day without telling his friends the reason.

Aggie beamed when she saw him. 'Have yer had something to eat already?'

Shaking his head, Bob didn't wait to be asked in. He passed her, saying, 'No, I haven't been home yet.'

The wise old eyes noted his pallor and agitation. There was something radically wrong here. 'What's happened, son?'

'I want to talk to yer, Aggie, and Irene. I wonder if yer could give her a knock for us. I don't want to go in, in case Ruby's looking out of the window. The last thing I need now is a slanging match with her.'

'Are things as bad as you look, Bob?'

'Much worse, Aggie.'

'Right, I'll go and get Irene. You sit yerself down.'

Less than five minutes later the two women walked in, worry on both their faces. 'Nothing has happened to Lucy, has it?' This was Irene's first concern.

'No, Lucy's all right. But what I've got to tell yer will affect her as much as meself.'

'I should offer to make a pot of tea,' Aggie said. 'But I can see yer want to get something off yer chest so I'll leave it till later.' She motioned to Irene to sit down while she settled in her rocking chair. 'What is it, Bob?'

'I'm leaving home and taking Lucy with me.'

The enormity of his statement rendered the women speechless. They stared at him, then at each other. Irene was the first to find her voice. 'This is sudden, isn't it? What happened to make yer think of anything so drastic?'

'After years of being taken for a sucker, Irene, I've finally had enough. I did intend waiting for Lucy to leave school, but last night altered all that. Yer see, I found out my wife has been sleeping with another man. I doubt they did much sleeping, but I used the word to spare my embarrassment and your blushes.'

Aggie fell back in her chair, shaken by Bob's words. 'Well, I've always thought the worst of Ruby, but even so I never thought she was that bad.'

Irene too was shaken. 'How did yer find out?'

Choosing words that wouldn't cause offence, Bob related the events of the night before. 'I've been a fool not to have twigged what she was up to before now.'

'Are yer sure ye're not mistaken, son?' Aggie asked.

'Of course he's sure.' Irene couldn't remember ever being as angry as she was now. If Bob moved away they would lose a good friend, and they'd lose Lucy. All because of a woman who wasn't fit to wipe their shoes. 'I'm sorry, Bob, but I've known for ages that Ruby was gadding about when you were on afternoons and nights. Perhaps I should have told yer, but I didn't want to interfere. I've seen her a few times slipping out the back way when Lucy's been in bed asleep.' Irene would never give the girl's secret away. Bob would never find out from her that his daughter knew, and was ill from the worry. 'I didn't know she was seeing a man, though, but I can't say it surprises me.'

Aggie was wishing Titch was home. He would think of some way whereby Bob wouldn't have to leave his home. 'Does Ruby know that yer know?'

'Oh, yes. Before I went down to sleep on the couch, I told her she was a slut. A dirty, cheap slut.'

'And she didn't deny it?'

'She couldn't, Aggie, 'cos it's the truth. Ruby thinks I'm stupid, she's told me often enough, but she knows I'm not that thick.'

'And ye're determined to move out and take Lucy with yer?'

'For the sake of my sanity, I've got to.'

'Does Lucy know?'

'Not yet, Aggie, and I'm not going to tell her until I've found digs for us. I've got a few people looking around for me, so when it's settled I'll tell Lucy. That way she won't be worrying and wondering.'

Irene was feeling sick inside. Bob and Lucy were very dear to her, she didn't want to lose them. 'All these years yer've worked hard to build that home up, Bob, it's not fair that you should be the one to leave. And Lucy won't like being moved away from her friends.'

'Don't think I haven't gone over all this in me mind a hundred times, Irene. I don't want to move away from you and George, and Aggie and Titch. We've been best mates for years and it'll break me heart to leave yer. But there's no alternative. I'm so full of bitterness towards Ruby for what she's done to me and Lucy, I can't bear the thought of being in the same house as her.'

Aggie coughed to clear her throat, because tears weren't far away. 'There is an alternative, Bob. It's your name on the rent book, not Ruby's. So let her move out. She's the one who's wronged you, not the other way round.'

'I haven't got it in me to throw her out, Aggie, and I can't see her leaving of her own free will. There'd be blue murder and I can't take any more, I've had a bellyful.'

But Aggie was still determined to talk him out of it. 'If your name's down as the tenant, it's you who'll be responsible for paying the rent. Ruby won't pay it, that's a bleedin' dead cert, so it's you they'll come after.'

Bob sighed and ran a hand across his brow. 'I'll pay the rent,

Aggie, but I won't give it to Ruby, I'll pass it in to the office. I won't give her money to keep herself though, so she'll have to find a job.'

'I've never heard anything so ridiculous in all me life,' Irene said heatedly. 'Your wife is a bitch and a cheap tart. Any other man would have thrown her out years ago and said good riddance. But you don't throw her out, yer throw yerself and yer daughter out instead! I can see neither sense nor reason in that.'

'Me neither,' Aggie said. 'I wish Titch was here to drum some sense into yer. Why don't yer go home now and tell her to pack her bags and go to the bloke she was with last night? She might just surprise yer and do it.'

'Aye, and pigs might fly.' But Aggie's words set Bob's brain in motion. Everyone would think he was a weak fool for leaving an adulterous wife sitting pretty in a fully furnished house, while he made himself and his daughter homeless. And if he didn't even put up a fight, they'd be right. He didn't think there was much chance of Ruby doing what Aggie said and packing her bags, but to prove to himself that he wasn't the spineless creature she took him for, he had to at least try. He spread out his hands and gave a faint smile. 'However, seeing as pigs have nothing to do with this, Aggie, I might just do as yer say. And because I don't want Lucy involved in any fighting, I'll get home now before she comes in from school.'

'I'll stand at the door and wait for her, Bob,' Aggie said. 'I'll bring her in here and keep her talking for as long as I can.'

'And I'll stay with yer.' Irene was so mad her heart was beating fifteen to the dozen. 'We won't let on, so don't worry. But we'll be on pins wondering how yer got on, so will yer give a knock tonight and let us know?'

Bob pushed himself up out of the chair. 'Of course I will.' He looked from one worried face to the other. And with a catch in his voice, said, 'I can't imagine life without you two.' With that he strode from the room before they saw the moisture of tears in the corner of his eyes.

Rhoda was going to her grandma's straight from school so, being on her own, Lucy used the back entries for quickness. When she opened the yard door, she could hear raised voices coming from the living room. Her heart sinking, she stayed close to the side wall where she couldn't be seen, and stood on the kitchen step. She was in two minds what to do. If her mother was having a go at her dad, she'd go in without hesitation. But if they were discussing something private, it might be better if she went back out again. When she heard her father speaking, though, her feet were rooted to the spot. She didn't intend to eavesdrop, but his words brought fear to her heart and she couldn't move.

Bob and Ruby were facing each other across the table, their faces red and their eyes blazing with anger.

'Who was the bloke yer slept with last night?' Bob asked. 'That's if yer even know his name.'

'Don't be so bleedin' stupid. Ye're away with the mixer, you are, imagining things in that thick head of yours. They'll be putting yer away one of these days.'

'I'm not imagining things, I know for certain that yer slept with a man last night. It's probably not the first time, either, but I can't be sure of that. I can be sure of last night, though.'

Ruby was taken aback. Somebody must have seen her. She was always very careful but Bob was so sure of himself, she must have been seen. She opened her mouth to deny it, then changed her mind. Why bother lying when he couldn't do anything about it, anyway? An evil smile crossed her face. 'Okay, I was with a bloke. So what? If I can't be entertained to my liking here, what's wrong with looking elsewhere for it?'

'I wouldn't lower meself to answer that question. Ye're a bitch, Ruby. A scheming, cruel, heartless bitch. And I want yer to pack yer bags and get out of my house, right now. I don't want to ever set eyes on yer again.'

Ruby's hard laugh rang out. 'Some hope you've got, soft lad. This is my house and no one is going to shift me from it.'

'Wrong! It's my house and I want you out of it. I'm surprised yer want to stay, anyway, seeing how little yer think of Lucy and me. I bet we never entered yer head when yer were being so well entertained last night.'

'Ye're bleedin' right there! Mind you, yer never do enter me head. I wouldn't care if I never saw either of yer again. But this house is a roof over me head and no one will budge me from it. Certainly not you, ye're not man enough.'

Bob was determined to knock that cocky smile off her face and the sarcasm from her voice. 'I've made arrangements to see a solicitor with a view to starting divorce proceedings, so while I'm at it, I'll find out whether you have any legal right, as an adulteress, to remain in my house.'

His words did knock the cocky smile off her face, but not for long. 'Who are yer trying to kid? Yer stupid bleedin' fool, yer don't expect me to fall for that, do yer?'

'Please yerself. But tonight is your turn to sleep on the couch. And I warn yer, I'll not hesitate to throw yer down the stairs if yer make any effort to get in the bedroom.'

★　★　★

Lucy was devastated as she made her way silently out of the yard and walked up the entry to the main road. She wasn't worried about her mother, she wished she would pack her bags and leave. It was her dad she was worried about because she knew her mother was brazen enough to stay put. Nothing would make her move, even though she knew her husband had found out what she was up to.

Lucy sighed as she turned into her street as she normally did each night when she was with Rhoda. What was going to happen to them? Because they couldn't pretend to be a family, not now. She was so deep in thought, she didn't see Aggie standing on her step talking to Mrs Pollard, until she was on top of them.

'Ye're late, sweetheart, where've yer been? We were beginning to think yer'd got lost, weren't we, Irene?'

Irene smiled. 'We nearly had the police force out looking for yer, sunshine. Our Greg got home ages ago.'

'Rhoda was going straight to her grandma's, so we stood talking for a while outside the school gates.' Lucy was wishing her tummy would settle down and her heart stop racing. She just wanted to crawl away somewhere and give way to her sadness with tears. 'Why, did yer want me for anything?'

'Not for anything in particular, sweetheart, we just wanted to see yer pretty face. And we did start to get worried when yer were so late.'

'Aggie's right, sunshine,' Irene said. 'Yer see, when yer love someone, yer can't help but worry about them.'

'And yer do love me, don't yer?' Deprived of love all her life by the one person who should love her more than anyone, Lucy needed reassurance. 'I mean, really love me?'

'Of course we do, don't yer know that?' Irene sensed the girl's unhappiness and was puzzled. Lucy couldn't know what was happening because she hadn't been home yet. 'I'd go as far as to say yer must be the most loved person in this street. What do you say, Aggie?'

'Oh, without a shadow of a doubt. Yer've got yer dad, me and Titch, Irene and all her family and Steve and his mam. That's besides Rhoda and the other neighbours.'

'There yer are, yer see. One thing yer've got plenty of, sunshine, is love.' Irene held out her hand. 'Come on, yer dad will be wondering what's keeping yer. And it's time I thought about what to give my lot for their dinner.'

Lucy took her hand. 'I'll see yer, Mrs Aggie.'

'Yer can count on it, sweetheart. Ta-ra for now.' Aggie watched them walk away with sadness in her heart and tears in her eyes. She dreaded what the future had in store for the girl whose pretty face should never be without a smile. And whose life should never know anything but kindness and affection.

Lucy was reluctant to release the hand that gave her comfort and a feeling of safety. But she had no excuse to cling to it. She was afraid of going home because of what she might find, but knew she couldn't put it off for ever. 'I'll probably see yer later, Mrs Pollard.'

'I hope so, sunshine. And yer know what I've told yer hundreds of times, just knock if yer want a game of cards or fancy a natter. Don't ever forget that.'

'I won't.' Lucy's legs were as heavy as lead as she walked the few steps to her front door. She didn't have a key, so she lifted the knocker hoping her dad would open the door.

'Ye're late, pet.' Bob had never found it so hard to keep a smile on his face. 'I was beginning to worry.'

'I've been talking to Mrs Aggie and Mrs Pollard. Yer know yer don't have to worry about me, Dad, I can look after meself.'

'I know yer can, pet, but it doesn't stop me from worrying. Yer mind plays funny tricks on yer when someone's late, and yer start imagining all sorts of things.' Bob glanced towards the kitchen where Ruby was frying bacon and eggs for their tea. There had been a deathly silence since the flare-up; not one word had been exchanged between them. It wasn't the sort of atmosphere for a young girl to spend any time in. 'Are yer playing out with Rhoda when yer've had yer meal?'

Lucy shook her head. 'She's gone to visit her grandma and won't be back till late. I might go next door for a game of cards to pass the time away.'

'Yer know, I might just come with yer. D'yer think Mrs Pollard would mind?'

'I'll go and ask.' Lucy was out of the room like a shot, and Bob was just as quick making it to the kitchen.

'If yer start acting up in front of Lucy, I won't hesitate to tell her what yer've been up to. And then I'll go and tell all the neighbours. And don't underestimate me this time, Ruby, because I mean every word I say.'

Ruby moved away from the stove and the spurts of fat shooting out from the frying pan before fixing him with her eyes. She didn't say one word, but her look spoke volumes. Bob knew if her thoughts were put into words, they would be to tell him he was a stupid bugger and to sod off. And her dumb insolence brought his blood to the boil. 'Another thing,' he said. 'You don't go over this door tonight. If yer do, yer'll not get back in because I'll bolt up before I go to bed.'

Bob entered the living room as Lucy came in from the hall. 'Mrs

Pollard said to tell yer yer'll be very welcome. But yer've got to take six buttons with yer.'

'Oh, dear. I'll have to empty all the drawers and see what I can find.'

'I'll lend yer them, Dad, 'cos I've got loads. Yer see, I win more than I lose.' Lucy put her arms around his waist and hugged him. 'Yer'll enjoy yerself 'cos we do nothing but laugh.'

Bob could hear Ruby muttering in the kitchen. He couldn't make out what she was saying but knew whatever it was wouldn't be complimentary to him or their daughter.

Ruby was snoring on the couch when Bob crept through the living room the next morning and he closed the kitchen door quietly behind him so as not to wake her. After striking a match under the kettle he cut two slices of bread and put them under the grill to toast. While he was waiting for the kettle to boil, he swilled his hands and face in the sink, donned his working clothes and combed his hair. Then with a cup of tea in one hand and a piece of toast in the other, he leaned back against the wall. What a way to start a working day, standing up in the kitchen eating his breakfast. Still, he'd had the comfort of the bed to himself, even if he didn't get much sleep. With his mind being so active, it must have been one o'clock before he'd managed to drop off.

Draining his cup, Bob put it in the sink before slipping on his jacket. Then he looked around for his carry-out box. He spied it on the small larder-shelf next to the stove and reached for it. As soon as he picked it up he knew it was empty. But not wanting to believe it, he opened the lid. There wasn't even a crumb inside. He closed his eyes and counted to ten, trying to calm himself down, but it was no use, his temper was too high. She was deliberately provoking him, going out of her way to anger him. But how did she expect to get away with it? Surely she must know that one day he'd snap.

With the box in his hand, he went through to the living room and shook Ruby's shoulder. 'Where's me carry-out?'

Her eyes heavy with sleep, she gazed at him as though she didn't know what was going on. Then it all came back to her, the reason for her being on the couch. 'What?'

'I said, where's me carry-out?'

'Oh, I forgot.' Ruby turned on her side, away from him. Not for one moment did she think he'd do any of the things he said he would. Wasn't Wally always telling her how beautiful she was, with a wonderful figure and personality? And how lucky her husband was that she'd married him when she could probably have had her pick from hundreds of men? His constant flattery had filled her head with grand ideas about herself, and had her believing that

634

Bob was indeed a lucky man to have her. And he knew it. That's why he wouldn't carry out his threats. 'Do it yerself, it won't kill yer. Ye're big and ugly enough.'

Bob stood looking down at her curled-up form, his empty carry-out box in his hand. There was something mentally wrong with his wife. There had to be, the way she was acting. No one in their right senses would behave like her and expect to get away with it. He sighed as he quickly made his way back to the kitchen to cut some sandwiches to take to work.

Elsie Burgess glanced across to where Bob was sitting. 'How's the old tummy today, lad? Still got the collywobbles, have yer?'

'No, it seems to have settled down now, thank goodness. I hope so, anyway, because it's not to be recommended.'

'Ye're telling me! I told yer I had it, didn't I? And it was bloody awful. I put it down to some corned beef I got from the corner shop.'

'But the rest of the family didn't have it, did they?' Peg Butterworth said. 'Yer all had the corned beef, so it couldn't have been that what caused it.'

Elsie's look was one of disdain. 'Excuse me, queen, but who was the one what was vomiting every five minutes, you or me? And who, pray, is the one telling the bleedin' story, you or me?'

'Oh, all right, be like that!' Peg huffed. 'Pardon me for breathing.'

'I don't mind yer breathing, queen, as long as yer do it silently and it doesn't interfere with me talking. Nothing puts me off me stroke more than someone butting in.' Convinced there would be no further distractions from her friend, Elsie turned her attention to Bob. 'I was in a right mood when I went back to the shop and told Tom Black it was his corned beef what had made me sick. I said I wanted me money back or the goods replacing. I must have raised me voice a little, yer know how yer do. Anyway, his wife Sheila came through from the back room and stood next to her husband. "That's funny," she said, all sarcastic like. "There was nothing wrong with your feller when he came in for his ciggies. And I've seen all the kids playing out, looking happy and healthy." '

Elsie took a mouthful of tea before picking up the thread of her story. 'I told them it hadn't affected the others, but it had made me really ill and I wanted me money back or the goods replacing. Sheila opened her big mouth, ready for a fight, when Tom put his hand on her shoulder. "Leave it, I'll give her the corned beef. It's not worth arguing over." I was over the moon, thinking I wouldn't have to worry about what to have for our tea. I watched Tom pick up the corned beef and take it to the slicing machine. Then he cut one slice off, put it on a piece of greased paper and brought it to where I was standing. I thought he was showing me how nice and lean it was, and I said it would do fine. The next thing I know, he's wrapped the slice up and was handing it to me. Well, I blew me top, didn't I? I said I'd bought six slices of the meat and I wanted six back. And d'yer know what the smart arse said? "Ah, but there was nothing wrong with five of the slices. And I've only your word that there was anything wrong with the one you had. I'm only giving you this as a goodwill gesture." '

Another mouthful of tea was required before Elsie could continue. 'I was hopping mad and said I had a good mind to wrap it round his bleedin' neck. As cool as a cucumber, he said, "In case yer haven't noticed, Elsie, I take a size eighteen collar. That slice of corner beef would just about cover me Adam's apple." '

When Elsie delved into her box, brought out a sandwich and proceeded to chew at it, Billy Gleeson looked most put out. 'Come on, Elsie, yer didn't leave it at that, did yer?'

'The shop had filled up while this was going on, Billy, and everyone was having a good laugh. So I laughed with them, 'cos by this time I could see the funny side of it. I told Tom he was a gentleman, grabbed me slice of meat and legged it home before he changed his mind. After all, I couldn't prove it was his meat made me sick. I could just as easy have been the fried egg I had for me breakfast. When I cracked it open I thought it ponged a bit, but I ate it just the same. I mean, yer can't waste food just because it doesn't smell as sweet as honey, can yer?'

'Elsie Burgess, yer should be ashamed of yerself.' Peg clicked her tongue on the roof of her mouth. 'Yer've let the whole street think that Tom sold yer meat that was off. I think yer should tell him the truth.'

The table began to bob up and down as Elsie's body shook with laughter. 'Wouldn't make no difference, queen, 'cos I bought the bleedin' egg off him too!'

Bob was wishing he had Elsie's capacity for laughter when he saw Kate trying to catch his attention. She gave a brief nod and he nodded in reply.

'Me mam doesn't know anybody who takes in lodgers, not with two spare bedrooms, anyway. But she said she'll keep her ears open. Sometimes people put cards in shop windows for that sort of thing, so we'll both be looking out. What I wanted to tell yer was that our Audrey and Howard visit me mam every Sunday without fail. So I'll make it me business to go round and have a word with Howard. Unless, of course, yer've had a change of heart?'

'I'm more determined than ever, Kate.' Bob related the blazing row he'd had with his wife. How she had admitted going with a man and wasn't a bit ashamed or repentant. And how she'd laughed in his face when he told her to pack her bags and get out of his house. 'Then when I asked her this morning where me carry-out was, she told me I was big and ugly enough to do it meself.'

'Do yer mind if I tell Howard all this? Just to put him in the picture?'

'He'll have to know, won't he? Otherwise he won't know whether he can help me.'

'Have yer told Lucy, yet, Bob?'

'No, I thought I'd leave it until something turns up.'

'I don't think ye're being fair to her. She has a right to know. Yer can't just take her away from her friends, and the school she goes to, without giving her some advance warning. And yer should ask her how she feels about it. After all, she's not a child any more, and she might not take kindly to being uprooted from everything she's used to. It's her life, too, and I think she should have some say in the matter.'

'I've thought of all that, Kate, but I wouldn't know where to start. Lucy knows Ruby's not a good mother and leads us both a dog's life, I don't need to tell her that. But how to explain the reason and the urgency for me wanting to leave her so suddenly – well, I don't know. How do I explain that her mother's done something so bad I can no longer stand being in the same house as her? Perhaps I'm a coward, Kate, but I just couldn't bring meself to explain that to a thirteen-year-old girl.'

'What about yer friends, Mrs Aggie and Irene? They know Lucy well and could perhaps give yer some advice. But don't just leave things as they are, Bob, because yer might find yer daughter will come to resent yer if yer turn her life upside down and don't even bother telling her why. And I know yer love her too much to want that to happen.'

There was understanding and sympathy in Kate's eyes as she moved away from the wall of the corner shop. 'Do it, Bob, or yer might regret it for the rest of yer life.'

637

Chapter Twenty-Two

'So, there yer have it. Word for word.' Bob pushed his finger along Aggie's green chenille tablecloth, causing the tufts to form a furrow before springing back up again. He'd just finished repeating the conversation he'd had only half an hour earlier with Kate and he looked now to Aggie and Irene for their reaction. 'I think what Kate meant was that I was being selfish for not taking Lucy's feelings into account.'

'If she knew Ruby, she wouldn't think yer were selfish, Bob. I don't know any man who would have been as patient as you've been.' Aggie leaned her elbows on the table. 'But I'll go along with her on everything else she said. Of course yer should tell Lucy, she's got every right to know.'

'I agree.' Irene kept clasping and unclasping her hands with nerves. 'I've thought about nothing else since last night. Yer can't just spring something on the girl like that, it wouldn't be fair.'

Bob sighed. 'I know yer couldn't say anything when we were playing cards last night, Irene, but did yer get a chance to mention it to George?'

'When we were in bed.' Irene nodded. 'We were still talking about it at midnight. He got the shock of his life when I told him, but he's of the opinion that what ye're thinking of doing is crazy. He said if he was in your position he wouldn't be asking Ruby to pack her bags, he'd pack them for her and then throw them in the street. Any woman who was unfaithful to her husband would get short shrift from George.'

'I should bleedin' well think so,' Aggie huffed. 'Anyway, are yer going to tell Lucy?'

'As I told yer, Kate thought I should talk to you and Irene. She knows yer think the world of Lucy, and that she loves and trusts both of yer. So I'm doing as she advised and asking yer to help me do what's right for me daughter.'

'The right thing would be to put her in the picture straight away. I think yer'll find she knows a lot more than yer think,' Irene told him. 'She's quite grown up for her age, and she'll understand what yer've had to put up with. But as for yer taking her away from here, well, I think she'll be devastated. It'll break her heart.'

'I realise that, Irene. But is Lucy grown up enough to understand that her mother has committed the worst sin any woman can commit against her husband? And that is why just being in the same room as Ruby makes me feel physically sick? That is something Lucy would have to be told so she doesn't think I'm disrupting her whole life through spite or childishness. But I don't think I've got the guts to tell her.'

Irene glanced at Aggie, her eyes questioning. It was her neighbour's slight nod that caused her to say, 'Me and Lucy get on well together. We tell each other secrets and share confidences. Nothing of any consequence, like, but she trusts me. And she trusts Aggie. How about if we have a word with her? I could say you'd called in on yer way home from work and told us, and me and Aggie thought we'd get to her first so she wouldn't be embarrassed when you speak to her. We'd be very diplomatic, we wouldn't upset her.'

Bob ran his fingers through his mop of dark hair. That he was a man in torment could be seen in his brown eyes. 'I know yer wouldn't upset her, Irene, or you, Aggie. She loves the bones of both of yer. But d'yer think my letting yer do me dirty work for me, makes me what Ruby said I am – spineless?'

'Don't be stupid, Bob Mellor,' Aggie said with feeling. 'The only trouble with you is ye're too much of a bleedin' gentleman. Any other feller, Ruby would have been out on her backside ages ago. Anyway, with regards to Lucy, I think it would be better coming from me and Irene. Woman to woman, like.'

'And we'll do it today and be done with it,' Irene said. 'When it's all out in the open and we see how Lucy takes it, I might be able to get some sleep tonight.'

'We'll watch for her coming home from school.' Aggie turned to glance at the clock. 'It won't be long now, so I suggest yer take yerself off, Bob, and come back about a quarter to five. That should give us plenty of time.'

It was Aggie who opened the door to Bob. As he stepped into the hall she raised her brows and whispered, 'Ye're in for a shock, lad.'

He didn't have time to question her before Lucy came flying out to put her arms around him. She stood on tiptoe to kiss him. 'I love you, Dad.'

'And I love you, pet.' Bob could see she'd been crying and was filled with guilt. He should never have let things get this far. A firm hand had been needed with Ruby years ago, but he'd opted to put up with her antics for an easy life. 'Let's go in and sit down, me feet are killing me. I've been walking the streets for the last hour.'

Aggie's voice was high with surprise. 'Yer mean yer haven't been home?'

'I can't stand being in the house when Lucy's not there. We'll go home together when we've finished here.'

Irene was sitting hunched up at the table, her hands clasped tightly. 'I've got me dinner on the stove on a low light, so I'm all right for a while. Greg's going to keep an eye on it to make sure it doesn't burn.'

Aggie set her rocking chair in motion. 'We've had a good talk with Lucy, haven't we, sweetheart? And I think she's got something to tell yer.'

'I can see yer've been crying, pet,' Bob said, from his seat on the couch. 'I'm sorry yer've been upset, yer know I'd do anything rather than hurt you.'

Lucy had chosen to sit on one of the wooden chairs next to Irene. 'It's not your fault, Dad, I'd never blame you. It's me mam what's caused all this, she's been horrible to yer.'

'So yer understand why I've got to get away, then? I can't stay with her any longer, pet, you must see that. And if I threw her out, which is what she deserves, she'd cause ructions in the street. And I wouldn't put it past her to come and cause trouble for me at work. You know her well enough to know that we'd never have any peace from her. I don't want that for meself, and I don't want it for you.'

'I understand all that, Dad, and I can see why yer don't want to live with her any more. But it's not only you she's treated badly. She's never been a proper mother to me, always shouting at me and hitting me. I can't ever remember her once, in all me life, saying anything nice to me. I've never told yer all this because I knew yer had enough to put up with. But I've had bruises all over me body where she's hit me, and scratches. And me head's been sore where she's pulled at me hair. She's very sneaky, she never hit me where you would be able to see the bruises. It was always on me body, where no one could see. But Mrs Pollard's seen them, haven't yer, Mrs Pollard?'

Irene looked down at her hands. 'Yes, I've seen them, sunshine. But yer told me in secret and made me promise not to tell yer dad.'

Bob was sitting forward on the edge of the couch, shaking his head in disbelief. 'In the name of God, pet, why didn't yer tell me?'

'Because yer always looked so sad and unhappy. She doesn't hit me now, hasn't done for ages. We had a big row last week and she came at me to give me a belt. That's when I told her I knew she was slipping out the back way at night when she thought I was asleep. She got worried then, and she actually smiled at me. That's never been known before. She didn't get round me though, and I told her so. I said I wouldn't tell you 'cos yer had enough worries, but that one day yer'd find her out for yerself. And yer have, haven't yer, Dad?'

'It seems I'm finding out a lot of things, pet. I must have been going around with me eyes closed not to have realised how bad things were for you. But now yer can see that the sooner we get away from her the better.'

Lucy shook her head. 'No, Dad, I don't see that, or understand. I don't see why it's us that has to move. That house is our home and I think we should stay there.' There was a tremor in her voice, but determination in her heart. She couldn't say she'd overheard her father saying he was seeing about getting a divorce, but if he did then he wouldn't be married to her mam any more and she'd have no right to live in the house. But if they left now, they'd never get it back. 'I don't want us to leave, Dad, please?'

'It's not as easy as that, Lucy. There's grown up things ye're too young to understand.' Bob was wondering what he'd ever done to be punished in this way. Because seeing his beloved daughter like this was indeed a punishment. 'But we'll be all right. I've got the feelers out for some decent digs for us, until I can find us a proper house.'

'Dad, don't take me away from this street and all me friends, please? I wouldn't be happy anywhere else.'

Irene could see the girl was near to tears. And Bob looked like a man who had reached breaking point. 'Look, sunshine, yer've told yer dad how yer feel, so why not give him time to think it over? He's only trying to do what's best for yer.'

'I know that, Mrs Pollard.' Seeing the look of despair on her father's face, Lucy left her chair in such haste it would have toppled over if Irene hadn't caught it in time. Sitting on his knee she laid her head on his chest. 'I don't like to see yer looking so unhappy, Dad, because it makes me unhappy. Let's not talk about it any more now; you take yer time to think things over. Me mam's done bad things to both of us, but she can't part us. No matter what happens we'll always have each other.'

'You and yer dad will never be alone, sweetheart,' Aggie said, trying to swallow the lump in her throat. 'Yer've got lots of good friends and we'll do anything to help yer.'

'I know yer would, Mrs Aggie.' And hoping to bring a smile to her father's face, Lucy asked, 'Can me and me dad come and lodge with yer?'

'Nothing would please me more, sweetheart, if I had the room. I'd be in me bleedin' apple-cart, and that's a fact.' Aggie grinned.

'I can just see Titch's face if he came home and found you sleeping in his bed. He'd think yer were that princess in the storybooks what was asleep for donkey's years and got woke up when a handsome prince kissed her.'

Lucy's giggle brought a smile to each of their faces. 'Yeah, he'd be struck dumb.'

'Ooh, I don't know about that. It would take more than a sleeping princess to rob my son of his powers of speech. He was born with the gift of the gab. The midwife what delivered him said that when she lifted him up by his legs and smacked his bottom, he opened his eyes and said if she did that once more he'd hit her back.'

Now the mood was lighter, Irene pushed herself up from the chair. Greg was very good at watching the stove for her, but he wouldn't think of giving the stew a stir so it wouldn't stick on the bottom of the pan. 'I'm off, folks. Will yer be calling in tomorrow afternoon, Bob?'

'If it's convenient for Aggie. I wouldn't go home anyway, I'd hang around and wait for Lucy to come. To be greeted with a sneer when yer walk in yer own living room after working an eight-hour shift, isn't exactly the best of welcomes.'

'Ye're welcome here, lad,' Aggie said. 'I was going to go to the Adelphi Hotel for afternoon tea, but I'll give it a miss for once.'

'Ooh, ay, Missus,' Irene laughed, 'the state of you and the price of fish! The Adelphi Hotel indeed! That's a new one on me.'

'It's one of my little secrets, queen.' Aggie left her chair and stretched to her full height. 'I'm very well-known in social circles, but it's not something I brag about. I'm not a snob and I wouldn't want my friends to get an inferiority complex.'

'I've already got one, Aggie.' There were the makings of a smile on Bob's face as he pushed Lucy to her feet. 'But you didn't give it to me.'

'Don't let anybody put yer down, lad.' Aggie followed them to the door. 'Ye're as good as anybody and better than most.'

Lucy gave the old woman a kiss before taking her father's hand. 'I won't see yer tonight, Mrs Aggie, 'cos I've promised Rhoda I'd go over there after I've had me tea. But I'll see yer tomorrow. And you, Mrs Pollard.'

'You and yer mate are welcome to come and have a game of cards,' Irene said as they reached her house. 'The boys would enjoy that.'

'Thanks, Mrs Pollard, but I might not to go out at all. I think I'll stay in and keep me dad company.'

'He's welcome to come, too, sunshine.'

'Not tonight, Irene, but thanks all the same.' Bob squeezed

Lucy's hand and smiled down at her. 'I'm going to have an early night in bed and do some serious thinking. Eh, pet?'

'Yes, Dad.' Lucy pulled him towards their door. 'We'll go to bed at the same time.'

After dinner was over and the dishes washed, Ruby picked up her handbag and left the room. Lucy's eyes followed her, and as she heard footsteps mounting the stairs she knew in her heart her mother was getting ready to go out. How has she got the nerve, the girl asked herself, when me dad's told her he knows what she's up to? She doesn't seem to care what he thinks.

Bob lowered the paper he was reading and looked across at his daughter. 'I'm thinking the same as you, pet. She's going out again.'

'Are yer going to tell her she can't, Dad?'

'No, it's no use, love, and anyway, it's too late for that now. At least we'll have the house to ourselves.'

Lucy bit on her bottom lip. Her dad did look very tired, but she had promised her friend. 'Can I ask Rhoda to come over here for half an hour, then? I promised I'd try and do something with her hair. Not that I'm any good at it, but she thinks because mine's curly I can make hers the same. It's only for a laugh, Dad, and we wouldn't get in yer way. I always feel mean not asking her in here, 'cos I'm in her house nearly every day. But she's only been in here once or twice in all the years we've been friends. Me mam wouldn't let her in.'

'Of course she can come over.' Bob's smile turned into a yawn. He was so weary he felt like falling into bed and sleeping for a week. 'But only for an hour, pet, I do want to have an early night.'

When Ruby came into the room, the smell of cheap scent came with her. Her face was caked with powder and rouge, and her lips were scarlet. 'I'm going out.'

'I gathered that,' Bob said, without looking up from his paper, while Lucy pretended to be so intent on pushing the skin back from her cuticles, she didn't hear. But as soon as the front door closed she was off her seat. 'I'll go and get me mate.'

Bob was staring into space when he heard the girls' laughter and he quickly fixed a smile on his face. 'Hello, Rhoda.'

'Hiya, Mr Mellor! How yer doing? And don't say ye're doing everyone because me mam got there before yer.'

'I always was slow on the uptake, love. Anyway, you've changed a lot. Yer used to be a lot bonnier than yer are now.'

There was a look of bliss on Rhoda's face. Bob's words were music to her ears. 'I've lost a lot of me fat, Mr Mellor, like me mam said I would. Mind you,' the girl pursed her lips and her look was comical, 'she was eight years out in the timing. I was six when she said it was puppy fat, and here I am nearly fourteen.'

Bob grinned at the girl who had been Lucy's steadfast friend since they were toddlers. 'Yer look well, Rhoda, very pretty.'

'I'm not as thin as yer daughter yet, but I'm working on it. And I haven't got curly hair like hers, but I'm not working on that, she is.'

'Don't expect miracles,' Lucy told her. 'I'm not a hairdresser.'

'If yer make a mess of it, yer won't be able to blame the tools.' Rhoda placed a bag on the table. 'Me mam's pipe cleaners are in there, together with a brush and comb. So there's no excuse if I don't end up with curls like yours. If I don't, yer'll have me mam to answer to.'

Lucy raised her hands in mock horror. 'Oh no, not yer mam! Let me answer to yer dad instead, please, I beg yer.'

'Shut up and get on with the job.' Rhoda pulled a chair from the table and plonked herself down. 'And I'll be counting the curls when yer've finished. If I haven't got as many as you there'll be skin and hair flying.'

Bob went back to his paper, but not to read. For the next hour he had a real, genuine smile on his face as he listened to his daughter and her friend. They never stopped talking and laughing. When one wasn't rattling off about one thing or another, the other was. And it did Bob's heart good to hear young voices and laughter in the house. This was how life should always have been for Lucy. And Bob was grateful for this short period of normality.

'There yer are, there's thirty pipe cleaners in now.' Lucy put the comb down on the table. 'And if yer hair's straight in the morning I'll eat me hat.'

'Ooh, er, how am I going to sleep with these in? I'll have to sit up all night.'

'Don't be daft! Put a scarf on yer head before yer go to bed and it'll keep the pipe cleaners in place. Anyway, yer've got to put up with some discomfort if yer want to be glamorous.'

'Okay, kid, don't be getting obstreperous.'

Lucy's jaw dropped. 'Don't be getting what?'

'I ain't repeating that! It took me all me time to get it out the once.'

'Well, what does it mean?'

'How the heck do I know? I was in TJ's one day and some kid was screaming his head off. His mam dragged him out of the shop telling him not to be what I've just told yer.'

'I'm going to ask our teacher tomorrow what it means,' Lucy said. 'And if it means something bad I'll clock yer one.'

'What are yer going to ask her?'

'What that word means.'

'What word?'

'The one yer've just used.'

'Can yer say it, then?'

Lucy sent her curls swinging as she shook her head. 'Of course I can't say it. But you can.'

'I'm staying out of it,' Rhoda said, picking up her bag. 'And another thing, I'm staying away from T.J. Hughes' and screaming kids. If I'd know the miserable little blighter was going to cause me this much bother I'd have hit him meself.'

Bob couldn't help laughing aloud. He knew these two had been mates for years, but had no idea how close they were. He was sorry when Rhoda said it was time to go. 'Thank you for a very entertaining hour, Miss Fleming. I sincerely hope yer head is one mass of curls in the morning.'

'Oh, it will be, Mr Mellor. Yer see, Lucy's coming over to ours early in the morning to take the pipe cleaners out and roll me curls for me.'

Lucy gasped. 'I never said I'd do that.'

'No, you didn't say it, I did.' Rhoda pushed her friend into the hallway. 'And don't yer start getting obstreperous with me, Lucy Mellor, or I'll give yer a thick lip.'

Ruby huffed when she walked into the living room at eleven o'clock that night. Why did he have to lower the gas every time she went out? It made the room look miserable, and all for the sake of saving a copper. She pulled the chain at the side of the gas-light to brighten the room, while calling her husband all the tight-fisted buggers she could think of. It was when she was taking her coat off that she saw the blanket and pillow on the couch. 'Oh no,' she said aloud. 'If he thinks I'm sleeping on there again he's got another think coming.'

Wally's lovemaking and flattery had filled her with confidence, and the belief that she was far too good for her husband. And the drink he'd plied her with clouded her judgement. She hung her coat on a hook in the hall, then picked up the blanket and pillow. Without making any effort to be quiet, she climbed the stairs, threw the bedding on the bed and waited for Bob to stir. 'If yer think yer can get away with that, ye're dafter than I thought yer were.'

Bob lay still for several seconds to collect his thoughts. Then, with a deep sigh, he pushed the clothes back. Gathering the blanket and pillow in his arms, he said quietly, 'You will not sleep in my bed.' He started to walk out of the room, intending to throw the clothes down the stairs, but Ruby barred his path. Her two hands pushing him backwards, she yelled at the top of her voice, 'Who the bleedin' hell d'yer think yer are? Yer can't be right in the head if yer think yer can make yer wife sleep on the couch.' All the time she was pushing and beating Bob's chest with her fists. And when he didn't reply, her language became that of the gutter.

Lucy woke with a start and shot up in bed. She heard her mother screaming like a wild woman and was sickened by the swearwords. Then she heard her father speaking in a low voice. 'Will yer move out of my way?' His words sent Ruby into a rage and her screaming intensified.

Lucy scrambled from her bed and flew into the next room. She saw her mother lashing out at her father with both hands and was horrified. 'You leave my dad alone.' She stood behind her mother and began to pummel her back with clenched fists. 'Ye're wicked, you are. Now leave him alone.'

Ruby turned around, pulled her arm back and delivered a stinging slap to the side of Lucy's face. 'Get back to bed, yer little faggot.'

Bob closed his eyes. To think it had come down to this. His daughter trying to protect him from a wife who was clearly not in her right mind. And the neighbours both sides must be able to hear the row. He laid the clothes down on the bed, put his arms around Ruby's waist and lifted her from the floor. 'You either sleep on the couch or walk the streets all night. The choice is yours.'

Lucy stepped away from the thrashing arms and legs as her mother was carried screaming from the room. Holding a hand to her cheek which was smarting from the slap, she watched as her mother clung to the bannister like grim death, screaming like a wild woman as her father tried to carry her downstairs. And, sick at heart, the girl knew that what was happening now had put paid to any thought of her dad staying. It wouldn't be fair to expect him to, either.

'Go back to bed, Lucy,' Bob said. 'I'll handle this.'

'Will yer be all right, Dad?'

'Yes, I'll be all right. You go back to bed, there's a good girl.'

Bob waited for a few seconds, then took an arm from around his wife's waist. He let it fall before bringing it up sharply under her arms and wrenching her away from the bannister. He managed to get her down the stairs and into the living room, where he dropped her on to the couch. She was still shouting and blaspheming as she tried to push herself up, and it was then that Bob saw red. With the sound of Lucy's face being slapped still ringing in his ears, he had come to the end of his tether. 'Shut up, woman, before I make you.'

647

'That'll be the day,' Ruby sneered. 'Yer haven't got the bleedin' guts. Ye're not man enough.'

Bob had always sworn never to raise a hand to a woman, but he had taken enough humiliation from this loud-mouthed, so-called wife of his. He didn't put his weight behind the slap he gave her, but it was hard enough to bring a startled cry from Ruby. 'You bleedin' sod! I'll get yer back for this.'

'That slap was for Lucy. And if yer don't keep that filthy mouth of yours shut, I'll be happy to give yer one from me. And I won't pull me punch next time. So it's up to you. Yer can go upstairs, very quietly, and bring down the blanket and pillow for yerself, or yer can take a chance on me belting yer one before throwing yer out on the street.'

Ruby had sobered up quickly. She had never seen her husband like this, but she could tell by the anger in his voice that he was more than capable of carrying out his threat. However, habit wouldn't let her give in to him. 'I'll be quiet if you sleep on the couch.'

'My terms are not up for discussion, Ruby. Take it or leave it.'

She still wasn't ready to give in. 'And how long is this lark going to go on for – me sleeping on the couch?'

'Oh, not long, Ruby. Not long at all.'

'How d'yer mean, not long? What's going on?'

'I don't have to tell you anything about my private life. You don't tell me anything, never have done. I don't know where yer go or who yer see. I was going to say I don't know what yer get up to, but I know that now.' Bob's sigh came from deep within him. 'I have an eight-hour shift in front of me, I'd like to get some sleep. So go and fetch the bedding if yer don't fancy a night walking the streets.'

Ruby left the room without a word. And when she came down, Bob climbed the stairs hoping to get a few hours' much-needed sleep. Tomorrow was another day. A day in which he had to sort his life out once and for all.

'What in the name of God went on last night?' Irene asked as Bob walked into Aggie's living room the next day. 'The whole street must have heard yer.'

'They wouldn't have heard me, Irene, or Lucy. I was fast asleep when Ruby came home at eleven o'clock. She must have been with her fancy-man and was the worse for drink. I'd left a blanket and pillow on the couch for her because I'd told her I'll never sleep in the same bed as her. If she hadn't gone out, or was home at a reasonable time, I might have slept downstairs meself. But I can't sit up until she decides to roll home, I've got a job to think of.'

'She is one bitch,' Irene said with feeling. 'Shouting her head off, and the language out of her was terrible! What was it all in aid of?'

'She came upstairs with the blanket and pillow and said she was getting into bed whether I liked it or not. Well, I didn't like it. And that started the whole thing off. The noise woke Lucy and she came dashing in to see her mother beating me with her fists. Of course the girl was upset and began to hit her on the back, telling her to leave me alone. The next thing, Ruby turns around and gave Lucy such a belt across the face it must have really hurt. Anyway, it brought me to me senses and I told Lucy to go back to bed while I somehow managed to drag Ruby down the stairs.'

Aggie had been shaking her head and tutting. The more her temper rose, the quicker the chair was rocked. 'Has the woman no shame? A married woman coming home drunk at eleven o'clock at night! And after being told that yer know what she's up to! If yer ask me, she wants horse-whipping.'

'I don't know about horse-whipping, Aggie, and I'm not exactly proud of meself, but I did give her a slap. She just wouldn't shut up when I finally got her downstairs, saying I wasn't a man and I didn't have the guts to do the things I was threatening to do. Like giving her a good hiding and throwing her out into the street. Anyway, I finally lost me rag and slapped her face. I told her that one was for Lucy, but if she didn't shut up I'd give her one for meself and I wouldn't be as gentle.'

'About bleedin' time,' Aggie said. 'Yer should have done it years ago.'

'It must have done the trick, Bob, because all went quiet about half-eleven.' Irene's pretty face was wearing a troubled expression. Last night, through the bedroom wall, she and George had heard a little of what Bob had had to put up with all these years. And it had given her plenty to think about. He was a nice, decent, hardworking bloke who wouldn't do anyone a bad turn. He deserved a good life and she for one wouldn't blame him for walking away from a living hell. 'What happens now?'

'I'm getting out, Irene. Kate and her mam have been looking round for digs for me and Lucy, but haven't come up with anything yet. Her mam's got a spare room, but she couldn't take both of us. I'm just hoping a place turns up quick, or I'll end up doing something I don't want to, and that's doing Ruby an injury.'

'If it helps, I'll have Lucy until something turns up,' Aggie said. 'Then yer could take the room that this Kate's mother's got. It probably wouldn't be for long, so I'm sure Lucy wouldn't mind. I mean, yer could see her nearly every day. There's nothing to stop yer coming home whenever yer've got the time, it's still your house.'

'I couldn't do that to Lucy. Besides, Ruby would give yer a dog's life. You have no idea just how bad she can be. She'd torment the life out of yer.'

'Oh no, she wouldn't, lad! I'm more than a match for that little madam. If she knocked on me door once, she'd never do it again unless she wanted me boot up her backside.'

'Yer wouldn't have to worry on that score, Bob,' Irene said. 'I don't think Ruby would fancy a set-to with me. I'd skin her alive for what she's done to you and Lucy.'

'I couldn't leave Lucy, it would break my heart. She's never had a mother to speak of, and if I walked out on her it would scar her for life.'

'Don't be daft, it would only be for a few weeks. We get on fine together and it would be like a little holiday for her.' Aggie had it all worked out in her head. 'Besides, instead of looking for digs for the two of yer, why don't yer try and get a little house around here? That would mean we wouldn't lose our friends, and neither would you or Lucy.'

'And how would I furnish this house, Aggie? I'll have to pay the rent on the house I've got now, and pay me digs. I won't have much over, and it takes a lot of money to furnish a house.'

'Not if yer take yer furniture with yer. It's you what owns the bleedin' stuff! Just leave the queer one a bed, table and chair. Let her fend for herself.'

'Why don't yer let Lucy decide?' Irene said. 'At least wait until yer ask her thoughts on the matter.'

'Ooh, aye, she'll be home any minute.' Aggie pressed her hands on the wooden arms of her chair and pushed herself up. 'I'd better stand at the door and watch out for her.'

'No need, Aggie,' Bob said. 'Yer can bet yer sweet life she won't go straight home, not after last night. She'll call here first.'

And Bob was proved right ten minutes later when Aggie opened the door to Lucy. 'Come on in, sweetheart, we've been waiting for yer.'

Lucy made straight for her father. 'Are yer all right, Dad? She didn't scratch yer or hurt yer, did she?'

'No, pet, I'm fine.' Bob reached for her two hands and held them in his. 'A bit tired, perhaps, but that's about all.'

'Yer should have seen me mam last night,' Lucy looked over at the two women, 'it was awful. She was screaming and shouting her head off, using bad words. And she was punching me dad with her two fists, saying terrible things to him. She had no right to do that because he never did nothing.' The girl's emotions were running high. Concern for her father was uppermost in her mind, but anger wasn't far behind. 'I want yer to leave, Dad, 'cos I'm afraid she might do something really bad to yer when ye're asleep or something. She's wicked is me mam, and when she's had too much to drink yer never know what she'll do. I want yer to go 'cos I'm frightened for yer.'

'It's not that easy, pet. We have nowhere to go.'

Irene decided to step in. She too was afraid that one day Ruby might go too far. After hearing her last night it was easy to believe she was capable of anything. 'Yer dad knows someone who's got one bedroom, but it wouldn't be enough for both of yer. Aggie has suggested that yer dad takes that room, and you could stay here with her until something comes up where yer can be together.'

There was determination in the shaking of Lucy's head. 'No, I'll stay at home. You take that room, Dad, but I'm not moving. I'm not frightened of me mam, so I'll stay there until yer come back again.'

'Lucy, love, there's no way I'll ever come back to that house once I leave. It'll have to be a clean break.'

In her mind, Lucy didn't agree. She had this feeling that one day her mother would leave, and she and her dad would be back together in their own home. If there was any justice in the world, that's what should happen. But she thought it was wise to keep her thoughts to herself. 'Okay, Dad, we'll do as yer say. If you've got the offer of lodgings, then take it while yer've got the chance. If yer let it go, yer might be ages finding somewhere else. But I'll stay at home until yer've found a place for us to be together.'

'Yer can come here, sweetheart,' Aggie said. 'I'd love to have yer, yer'd be company for me.'

'Thanks, Mrs Aggie, but I'd rather stay put. Yer see, that's my home, and I'm not letting me mam drive me away from it.'

The three adults exchanged surprised glances. Lucy was showing a strength and determination she'd never shown before. And each of them knew that if they talked to her until they were blue in the face, they wouldn't change her mind. Aggie was silently applauding the girl for standing firm. For the old woman still stood by the prediction she'd made – that Bob would one day find true happiness. And she'd never thought his happiness would be anywhere else but in his own little house. 'I'd give it a try, Bob, if that's what the girl wants. After all, me and Irene would always be close at hand.'

Lucy slipped her arm through Bob's and squeezed. 'Yer see, Dad, I wouldn't come to no harm with all me friends around. In fact, Mrs Aggie and Mrs Pollard will be sick of the sight of me before long.'

'That's something that will never happen, sunshine,' Irene said. 'I could take a lot of you without ever getting fed up.' She cast her eyes on Bob, who looked as though he didn't know what to do for the best. 'Give it a go, Bob, and see how it works out. After all, it's not as though yer'll never see each other again.'

'I'll tell yer what. It's Saturday tomorrow, me last morning shift. And you haven't got to go to school, pet, so we could go together to see what this room's like. And to find out what sort of a landlady I'd have. I believe some of them can be real strict. Mind you, if she's anything like her daughter she'll suit me fine.'

'Ooh, yeah, I'd like that, Dad.'

'I'll come home and get changed, 'cos I've got to make a good impression, haven't I? Then we'll pay the lady a visit.'

'Can we come?' Aggie asked. 'Me and Irene would like to meet this Kate.'

'I don't think so, Aggie. Some other time perhaps. If I turned up with you two, the woman would think I couldn't look after meself.'

'Is the lady who's going to be yer landlady called Kate, Dad?'

'No, pet, I don't know the lady's name. Kate is her daughter.'

Chapter Twenty-Three

'I'm not half nervous, Dad, me tummy's turning over.' Lucy was walking along Stanley Road with her father, their joined hands swinging between them. 'And me teeth are chattering like mad.'

'Yer'll be all right, pet. The woman I work with, Kate, said she'd try and be there with her daughter. She's the same age as you, so yer'll have someone to talk to.' Bob stopped at the end of a side street and checked the name sign on the wall. 'Primrose Street, this is it. Now we need to look for number twenty-three.'

Lucy pulled on his hand. 'Dad, I think that woman's waving to us.'

A smile crossed Bob's face when he saw Kate standing on the pavement outside a house about eight doors away. 'That's the woman I work with, pet, the one I was telling yer about.'

'Ooh, er, me nerves have gone mad.'

'After the first two minutes yer'll be wondering what yer were worried about.' Bob put his arm across her shoulders and coaxed her along. 'Kate, this is me daughter, Lucy.'

'Oh, I've heard a lot about you. Yer dad's always talking about yer.' Kate held out her hand. 'It's nice to meet yer at last.'

Lucy liked her on sight. The smile was so warm and friendly it calmed her nerves, and the chattering of her teeth slowed down. She gripped the outstretched hand. 'I'm very pleased to meet yer, Mrs Kate.'

'Come inside and meet me daughter, Iris. And me mam, who's been polishing the furniture so hard she's nearly worn it away. It didn't need cleaning 'cos she keeps it like a new pin, but she's a real fussy boots. As soon as I told her yer were coming, out came her mobcap and her polish and dusters. Plus loads of elbow grease.'

Bob held his daughter's hand tightly as they stepped into the tiny hall, then into the living room. He was feeling a bit nervous himself, but not for the world would he let Lucy see. In the two seconds it took for the older woman to leave her chair, his eyes had taken stock of the room. It reminded him of Aggie's. Spotlessly clean and tidy, yet homely. A room where a speck of dust would love to settle and make itself comfortable, but wasn't allowed to.

'Bob, this is me mam, Nellie Carson.'

'It's nice to meet yer, Mrs Carson.' Bob smiled at the small, stocky woman whose hair was steel grey and had a natural wave. He could see where Kate got her looks from, they were very alike. 'I hope yer didn't go to any trouble on my behalf.'

'Not at all, lad! I've only been up since the crack of dawn slaving away with me mop and bucket and me dusters.' There was a twinkle in the hazel eyes. 'I hope yer didn't stand on me step on yer way in, 'cos that got the scrubbing of its life at seven this morning.'

Bob rolled his eyes. 'Oh dear, I might have done.'

'Don't take any notice of her, Bob, she's pulling yer leg,' Kate said, giving her mother a fond look. 'Anyway, Mam, this is his daughter, Lucy.'

'Hello, queen. My, ye're a pretty little thing, aren't yer? And there's another pretty girl been waiting to meet yer, but the cat got her tongue all of a sudden and she's hiding in the kitchen.'

'Come on in, Iris,' Kate called. 'Don't be silly.'

'Shall I go out there to her?' Lucy asked. 'She might be shy.' And without waiting for an answer, she walked on through to the kitchen while the three grown-ups, as though by silent agreement, stood and listened.

'Hiya! I'm Lucy. Me dad said you and me are the same age.'

'Yeah, me mam told me. My name's Iris.'

'That's a lovely name, that is. It must be nice to be called after a flower, and live in a street what's got a flower's name, too.'

'Oh, this is me nan's house, I don't live in this street. Me and me mam don't live far away, though, only two minutes' walk.'

'What school do yer go to, Iris?'

Three faces grinned. 'They'll be all right now,' Nellie said. 'We'll leave them for a while to get to know each other, then I'll put the kettle on. In the meantime, Bob, would yer like to see the bedroom?'

'If it's not too much trouble, Mrs Carson.'

'Call me Nellie, lad, everyone else does.'

Lucy appeared at the kitchen door. 'Can I call yer Mrs Nellie, please?'

'Of course yer can, queen. I'd like that.'

'Yer see, yer remind me of one of the neighbours in our street. I call her Mrs Aggie, and she's one of me very best friends.'

'Well, seeing as yer've privileged me by calling me Mrs Nellie, perhaps you and me can become very best friends.'

'Yeah, I'd like that.' Lucy grinned. 'I'll go and talk to Iris while me dad looks at the bedroom.' My father would be well looked after here, she thought. They're nice, kind people and they'd take good care of him until he can come home again. 'I'm sure he'll like it.' With that she disappeared into the kitchen and the two girls could be heard chattering away in good style.

'I'll stay down here,' Kate said, knowing she would feel embarrassed if Bob decided to take the room and asked what the weekly charge was. 'It's not a big room and three in there would be a crowd.'

'Come on, lad.' Nellie jerked her head. 'Yer'll have to be patient 'cos me legs are not as young as yours, and the stairs are narrow and steep.'

She gripped the side bannister with both hands and pulled herself up each stair. When she reached the landing she stood for a moment to get her breath back. 'This is the room, lad.' She threw open one of the two doors and waved Bob inside. 'It's nothing to write home about, but it's any port in a storm, eh?'

There was a small, iron single bed with wooden headboards facing the door. To the side of it was a tallboy, and behind the door a single wardrobe. The furniture was old but so highly polished you could see your face in it. It was easy to see it had been tended over the years with loving care. 'It's just the job, Nellie,' Bob said. 'Just what I wanted.'

'I haven't got enough bedding, I'm afraid, but Kate said she'll help me out.'

'There's no need,' Bob told her. 'I can bring a pair of sheets, a blanket and a pillow with me. And a couple of pillowslips. So we'll manage all right.'

Nellie looked at him through narrowed eyes. 'Kate's told me a bit about yer. She said yer've been having a bad time.'

'That's putting it mildly. My life's been hell for years now, but recently my wife has stepped over the boundary of decency and I can't accept that.'

'I should bleedin' well think not!' Nellie put a hand over her mouth. 'I'm sorry, lad, I don't usually swear. Not in front of visitors, anyway. Our Kate would have been mortified if she'd been here and heard that.'

'Then we won't tell her, eh? Anyway, that's nothing to what I'm used to. My wife can't open her mouth without cursing and blaspheming.' Bob gazed around the room once more. 'Can I ask how much a week it'll be?'

'D'yer want full board? Breakfast, carry-out and dinner?'

'I don't want yer to be put to too much trouble, Nellie, not on my account. If I can have the room, I'll fend for meself for food. I knew yer help Kate a lot, so yer've got yer work cut out as it is, without me adding to it.'

'Don't be daft, lad! What's a couple of rounds of toast in the morning? And if I'm making a pan of stew, one extra won't make no matter.' Nellie cupped her chin in a hand and looked thoughtful. 'How about eight shillings a week, all found? That's yer bed, food and washing.'

Bob shook his head. 'That's not enough. Yer'd be out of pocket.'

'Not on yer life I wouldn't. I'm not daft, lad, I know what I'm doing. I get me dolly tub out every Monday, but it's hardly worth the effort with the few things I've got to wash. So it'll cost me nothing to throw yours in as well. And Kate will tell yer I'm very good in the kitchen. I can make a dinner out of practically nothing. So I'll be making a few bob on yer, lad, and I'll be able to get blind drunk every night.'

Bob chuckled. Kate was always talking about her mother, so he knew more about her than she thought. 'So, yer like a drink, do yer?'

'Aye, I do that, lad, and yer can't beat it. A nice cup of strong tea with two sugars in. Best drink in the world.' Nellie studied him for a brief moment. He was handsome all right, just as Kate said he was. And she knew enough about people to know the man who was standing in her bedroom, who she hoped was going to be her lodger, was decent through and through. 'Well, are my terms acceptable to yer, Mr Mellor?'

'More than acceptable, Mrs Carson. When can I move in?'

'Whenever yer like. Apart from a bit of bedding which yer said yer could bring, the room's ready for yer.'

'Would tomorrow be too soon? I'm off work now until I start afternoon shifts on Monday, so I'd have all day tomorrow to bring me bits and pieces and settle in. That's if it's all right with you?'

'It's fine by me.' Nellie wondered whether to mention what she was thinking or leave well alone. But Bob didn't look the sort to get offended, so she said, 'Yer could kill two birds with one stone, if yer did that. Kate said yer'd like some advice off Howard – well, him and Audrey will be here tomorrow afternoon so yer could have a word with him yerself. They come for tea every Sunday.'

'Wouldn't that look a bit cheeky? First I ask Kate for help, then you, and now this Howard is being dragged into me problems.'

'If he can help yer, he will. He's a lovely bloke, is Howard. Speaks frightfully far back, like, but yer can't blame him for that. It was the way he was brought up.' Nellie made her way to the top of the stairs. 'Let's go down and tell Kate the news. I know she'll be on pins.'

Kate was sitting on the couch with her hands folded on her knees. When her mother told her it was all fixed up for the next day, her mouth turned up at the corners in the gentle smile that

Bob looked forward to seeing every day as he faced her across the canteen table. 'I'm very glad for yer, Bob.'

'And I'm very grateful to you, Kate, and to yer mother. I think I've really hopped in lucky.' Bob glanced towards the kitchen where he could hear the two young girls still nattering away. 'Lucy, will yer come in, please?'

There was some hurried whispering, then Lucy came in leading Kate's daughter. 'This is Iris, Dad, and she's dead shy.'

Bob looked at the girl who was the same height and build as his daughter. He was expecting to see some resemblance to Kate, but there was none. Iris had long blonde hair and deep blue eyes. Then Bob remembered the day they'd been talking about Kate's dead husband, and she'd told him her daughter was the spitting image of her father. 'Hello, Iris, I'm very pleased to meet yer. You and me will be seeing a lot of each other, because I'm coming to live with yer nan.'

Lucy flung her arms around his waist. 'Yer've taken the room, Dad? Ooh, I don't know whether to laugh or cry. I'm glad yer've got somewhere as nice as this to live, but I'm not half going to miss yer. Promise me yer'll come and see me as often as yer can.'

'I will, pet.' Bob stroked her hair. 'Except when I'm on afternoon shift, I'll see yer every day, I promise.'

'Yer can come here as often as yer like to see yer dad, queen,' Nellie said. 'The door will always be open for yer.'

Kate beckoned to her daughter to come and sit beside her on the couch. She put her arm across the girl's shoulders. 'I'm sure Iris would like yer to come, wouldn't yer, sweetheart?'

Iris smiled for the first time. 'I've already given Lucy me address and she's going to come and see me. We leave school on the same day, yer know, Mam. And when we start work we're going to the pictures together.'

Lucy brushed a tear away. It was all right trying to be brave and say she didn't mind her dad leaving home, but she did mind, very much. She wasn't going to say so, though, because that would upset him. 'And me friend Rhoda's coming with us.'

Bob put a finger under his daughter's chin and raised her face. 'Yer mustn't give any addresses to Rhoda, pet. I wouldn't want a certain person to know where I'm living.'

'I understand that, Dad. Rhoda's me best friend and I love the bones of her. But I know she can't keep anything to herself. She opens her mouth and lets it all out, whether yer like it or lump it.'

Bob happened to glance at Iris as the girl smiled. She may have inherited her father's looks, he thought, but that smile is definitely from her mother. 'Rhoda's a smashing girl and a good friend to have, love, but for the time being don't breathe a word to anyone.'

'What time can I expect yer tomorrow, then Bob?' Nellie asked. 'Shall I peel an extra spud and yer can have yer dinner here?'

Bob was dreading the next couple of hours. He had to tell Ruby he was leaving and knew she'd be like a raving lunatic. Especially when he told her she'd have to find a job to keep herself. But if he could get away early in the morning it would mean tonight would be the last time he'd have to listen to her screaming and her bawdy language. 'I would like that very much, Nellie, as long as it's not too much trouble.'

'Kate and Iris will be here for their dinner, so as I've said, lad, all I'll have to do is put another couple of potatoes in the roasting tin.'

Bob could sense Lucy looking up into his face and he asked himself if he could go through with this. Could he leave his beloved daughter with a woman who wasn't in her right mind? Then he asked himself what the alternative was. There wasn't one, not for the time being. But he'd move heaven and earth now to find a place where they could be together. 'Thanks, Nellie, ye're an angel.'

'Oh, these are not wings on me back, lad, they're me shoulders what have rounded with old age. I've got a halo somewhere, though, but I couldn't put me hand on it just this minute. I'll give me drawers a clean-out one day and find it to show yer.'

Lucy's titter turned into a giggle. 'Ye're just like Mrs Aggie. I'm going to tell her all about yer next time I see her.'

'Don't tell her about the halo, Lucy,' Iris said, getting into the spirit of things. 'It's only a piece of tinsel I put on me nan's head last Christmas.'

Nellie wagged her head from side to side. 'Did yer have to go and give the game away, Iris? I think I'd make a good angel.'

'Yer would, Nellie, yer certainly would.' Bob picked up Lucy's hand. 'We'll have to go, pet. I've got some unpleasant business to attend to and the sooner I get it over with, the better.'

Kate, with her daughter and mother, followed them to the door. 'I hope everything goes all right for yer, Bob. We'll see yer tomorrow.'

'Yes, Kate, I'll see yer all tomorrow.'

After they'd walked a few steps, Bob and Lucy turned around to see the trio still watching them. They exchanged waves then carried on walking, Bob's arm over his daughter's shoulder.

'They're really nice people, Dad. Mrs Nellie will take good care of yer.'

'Yes, I know, pet. But I'm not happy leaving you at home. Why don't yer stay with Mrs Aggie until I sort something out?'

'No, Dad, I'm staying at home. Everything will work out fine, you'll see. I'll be all right and it's not going to be for that long.'

Bob sighed as his eyes went heavenwards. Please God, let that be true.

It was when they turned into their street that Bob said, 'Listen, pet, I'm going to knock and ask Mrs Pollard if she'll give yer a bite to eat and let yer stay there until I call for yer. I've got to tell yer mam I'm leaving tomorrow and I'm expecting her to create blue murder. I don't want you to have to go through that, ye're best staying out of it.'

'I'd rather come with yer, Dad. If she takes off on yer I can always help.'

'No! As far as yer mother's concerned, yer know nothing. Yer weren't with me this afternoon, and you haven't a clue where I'm going to live. Otherwise she'll be on yer back all the time and yer'll get no peace. Believe me, pet, it's the only way.'

'Okay, Dad, I'll do as yer say. If she asks, I'll tell her I've been in Rhoda's all afternoon playing cards.'

Irene answered their knock and held the door wide. 'Come in.'

'I won't come right in, Irene, I'll just step in the hall.' Bob pulled the door to behind them so anyone passing couldn't hear what was being said. 'I've been to see that room I told yer about, with Kate's mam. And I've taken it – I'm moving in tomorrow. But I wondered if yer'd do us a favour and have Lucy for an hour or two? I'm going in now to tell Ruby I'm leaving and I don't want anyone there when I do it.'

Irene put a protective arm across Lucy's shoulder. 'Of course she can stay. We're having a late tea so she can have something to eat with us.'

'Thanks, Irene, ye're a pal. I'll bring yer up-to-date with everything when I come back. Ruby's bound to go out, I'm certain of that. Me leaving home isn't going to make a blind bit of difference to her enjoyment. I've got a few things to tell her that she won't like, and I'm expecting verbal and physical abuse, but it won't stop her gallivanting. I'll lay odds she's got a heavy date and she'll be out of the house before eight o'clock.'

'We'll see yer later, then. And don't worry about Lucy, we'll look after her.' Irene reached to open the door. 'Go and get it over with, Bob, and good luck.'

Lucy grabbed his arm. 'Dad, yer know what me mam's like when she gets into one of her tempers – she lets fly with her hands and feet. Don't just stand there and let her get away with it, like yer always do, 'cos she could really hurt yer.'

'Don't worry, pet.' Bob bent to kiss her cheek. 'The days of me

659

just standing there and letting her use me as a punch-bag are over. I'll see yer at eight o'clock and I promise I'll be all in one piece.'

Ruby turned on him as soon as he walked through the door. 'Where the bleedin' hell d'yer think yer've been all afternoon?' And without waiting for an answer, she went on, 'And where's that faggot of a daughter of yours?'

Bob stood by the sideboard, looking a lot calmer than he felt. He weighed his wife up, taking in the best dress, the heavy make-up and the cheap smell. All ready for a night out and annoyed that he'd had the nerve to keep her waiting. 'Lucy is probably with Rhoda, or even next door. Then again, she could be with Mrs Aggie. I really don't know. I do know where I've been though, if you interested.'

Ruby sneered. 'That'll be the day, when I'm interested in anything *you* do.'

'Oh, I think yer might just be interested in this. I've been looking at some lodgings and I've found a place to suit me. I'm moving out of here tomorrow.'

She looked at him as though he'd gone crazy. 'Pull the other one, yer stupid bugger. If yer think yer can put the wind up me by coming out with daft things like that, well, ye're sadly mistaken. And I haven't got time to listen to a load of rubbish, I'm going out. I haven't made yer no dinner, yer can see to it yer bleedin' self.'

'Ye're not setting foot outside this room until I've told yer what I intend doing. Then yer can't say I didn't warn yer. I am moving out of here tomorrow, into digs. Lucy will be staying until I can find suitable accommodation for both of us. I will pay the rent on this house for the time being, seeing as my name is on the rent book. But I'll not be giving you the money, I'll pay it into the office.'

Ruby was beginning to realise he wasn't joking. Still she wasn't worried. It was good riddance as far as she was concerned. 'As long as I get me housekeeping I couldn't give a sod where yer go. Let some other poor bugger put up with yer miserable gob for a change.'

'Ah, but yer won't be getting any housekeeping.' Bob leaned his elbows on the sideboard and told himself he needn't feel pity for this woman who had ruined not only his life, but their daughter's. He'd given her more than enough chances to change, but she chose not to. 'If you want to eat, light the gas or have a fire, then yer must find yerself a job to pay for them because I am certainly not. And of course there's yer ciggie money, the make-up, the magazines and the nights out with yer mates. In future, if yer want them, then yer must work for them. I've kept yer long enough.'

Ruby still didn't believe this of the man who had let her walk all over him since the day they got married. He wouldn't have the nerve to do it. 'If yer are leaving, which I couldn't care less about, yer'll still have to give me housekeeping. A man's got to keep his wife, that's the law.'

'Not an adulterous wife, Ruby. Adultery is against the law and grounds for a divorce. And that is something I'll be setting in motion very soon.'

'What about Lucy, eh? What about yer dearly beloved daughter? Is she supposed to live on bleedin' fresh air?'

'I haven't had time to work that out yet. But yer've had this week's housekeeping which includes the money for her keep. I'll pay for Lucy after that, but it won't be to you. I won't be handing you a penny.'

It was then Ruby went for him. 'You bastard! You bleedin' bastard!' Her hands were outstretched, her palms towards him and her nails on a line with his face. If he hadn't been alert, his face would have been scratched to ribbons.

Bob made a grab for both her wrists and pushed her arms high, while pressing her backwards towards the couch. Her rage was such she fought with superhuman strength and it took Bob all his time to keep her pinned down. All the time she was screaming like a woman possessed. 'I'll get yer for this, yer bleedin' bastard. Yer can't do this to me and expect to get away with it. Yer'll live to regret this, yer swine.' And so it went on and on. 'I'll find yer, no matter how far away yer go. I'll go down to yer works and tell all yer mates about yer, you see if I don't.'

'Don't threaten me, Ruby. You are the last person anyone will believe when I tell them exactly why I'm leaving. Yer'll get no sympathy from my mates, I can assure yer. And if ye're still intending to go out tonight, I suggest yer stop slobbering because yer lipstick is all smudged. I don't think yer'd like yer fancy-man to see yer like this, would yer?'

This incensed Ruby and she lashed out with a foot, catching Bob on his shin. And when he let out a sharp cry of pain, she laughed hysterically. 'Hurt yer, did it?' Again her foot came out, but Bob was prepared and stepped back, managing to keep his grip on her wrists.

'I'm going to give yer one last warning, Ruby, and yer'd do well to listen. If yer don't stop this right now, I'll be down to the rent office on Monday and tell them I'm leaving. And seeing as I'm the tenant, you would be evicted and find yerself without a roof over yer head. If that happens, yer'll have no one to blame but yerself. And the warning stays in place even when I'm gone. If yer give

Lucy a hard time I won't hesitate to have yer put out.'

If looks could kill, Bob would have been dead on the spot. But the expression in her eyes was the only opposition Ruby put up. Whether he would ever carry out his threat, or if his words were just hot air, she wasn't prepared to take a chance. But she remained defiant to the end. 'Let go of me hands, I want to get ready to go out and meet me friends.'

After releasing her hands, Bob pulled a chair from the table and sat down. He was a bundle of nerves. It wasn't in his nature to threaten, but there was no other way of doing it. 'I'll be sleeping on the couch tonight. And if yer come home drunk, full of Dutch courage and bravado, don't bother trying to get in this room because I'll have a chair behind the door so yer can't open it.'

Ruby picked up her bag and left the room without a word. And Bob stayed where he was until, fifteen minutes later, he heard her coming down the stairs then the front door close behind her. Only then did he start putting his plans into action. He rooted out an old battered suitcase from under the stairs, put it on the couch and opened the lid. It was as old as the hills and smelt musty, but there was nothing else, so needs must when the devil drives, he thought. He took a pair of sheets and two pillowslips from the cupboard in the recess and laid them on the bottom of the case before gathering his belongings together. There wasn't much, just his clothes, razor and overalls. And when he'd finished, he looked down with sadness. 'Not much to show after working for twenty-five years,' he said as he closed the lid. 'Me mother would turn in her grave if she saw me now.'

Bob looked around to see if he'd forgotten anything, then took the stairs two at a time to the bedroom. He stripped a blanket off the bed and put a pillow under his arm. All he had to do in the morning was wrap the pillow in the blanket, pick up his case and walk away. The thought gave him no pleasure. It wasn't easy to walk away from a house that had been his home for nearly twenty years. He remembered the day he'd moved in with his new bride, looking forward to a life of happiness. And the day Lucy had been born, in this very room, he thought there was nothing he could wish for that he didn't have. Little did he know then what the future held in store for him. If he had known, would he have acted differently? Would he have been stricter with Ruby? No, he knew he wouldn't. It wasn't in his nature to lay the law down, not to the woman he'd married. And when he finally did wake up to reality, the rot had set in and it was too late. Too late for him, too late for his beloved daughter, and too late for Ruby to change.

Bob sighed deeply as he made his way downstairs. He'd made

the break now and nothing would alter that. Better to have few possessions and be happy, than live a life of misery.

Aggie was firmly settled in Irene's fireside chair when Bob arrived. She noted his pale face and haunted eyes and her heart went out to him. But she was wise enough to know sympathy was the last thing he needed now. 'I know ye're thinking I'm a nosy old cow, Bob, but I didn't want to hear all yer news secondhand. And I'm not nosy, lad, it's because I care what happens to yer; we all do.'

George motioned for Bob to sit on the couch. 'Park yer carcass, mate. Have yer had anything to eat?'

Bob shook his head. 'No, but I'm not hungry. Me tummy's too upset to eat.' Before sitting down, he crossed to where Lucy was sitting at the table, facing Jack and Greg. He bent to kiss her. 'All right, pet?'

'Never mind me, Dad. Are *you* all right?'

'Yes, I'm all right, love.' Bob dropped wearily on to the couch. 'But I wouldn't like to go through that again for all the money in the world.'

'We could hear me mam shouting and I was worried,' Lucy said. 'Did she take off on yer like she always does?'

Irene stepped in before Bob could answer. 'No questions yet until yer dad's had something to eat. I'll do yer a poached egg on toast, Bob, it'll fill a hole. Yer can't go on with an empty tummy, it's not good for yer.'

When Irene bustled out to the kitchen, George asked, 'Are yer coming for a pint later?'

'I could do with one. In fact, I could do with half-a-dozen. As long as it's all right for Lucy to stay here till we get back?'

'Of course it is!' Greg said, with feeling. 'We're going to have a game of cards and it wouldn't be the same without Lucy.'

'And don't forget,' Lucy reminded him, 'yer mam said Rhoda could come over as well.'

'Yeah, well, that's all right. She's not so bad once yer get to know her.'

Jack, in his role of a grown-up working man, looked over at Bob. 'Yer don't have to worry about Lucy, Mr Mellor. We're all going to watch out for her.'

Irene came in carrying a plate and knife and fork. 'Move away from the table, lads, while Mr Mellor tucks into this. The kettle's on the boil so it'll be tea all round in five minutes.'

Bob didn't think he was hungry, but the toast was a lovely golden brown and the egg lightly cooked and runny, just as he liked. The plate was empty in no time. 'By, that was good, Irene. Just what the doctor ordered.'

'Yer needed it, sunshine – a grown man like you can't go without food. Now the tea's ready so we'll all sit quietly and drink it, while Bob tells us as much as he wants to. And before he starts I hope I don't have to remind yer that not one word leaves this room. When Rhoda comes, I don't want to hear a peep out of yer. Have yer got that?'

Greg pulled a comical face. 'Mam, when Rhoda's here no one can get a word in edgeways. She never stops talking. After she's been, me mouth's set from lack of use and I have to exercise it when I go to bed.'

'That's one of Rhoda's good points, sunshine. She's the only one I know who can shut you up.' Irene lifted a finger for silence. 'Now let's hear what Mr Mellor has to say.'

It wasn't a word for word account, because Bob wouldn't use bad language in front of the children. He told them of his terms for Ruby being allowed to stay in the house, and his threats. All the time he was talking, Aggie was nodding her head in agreement. If she'd been in her rocking chair it would have been going like the clappers.

'Good for you,' George said when Bob had finished. 'I still think ye're a fool for not throwing Ruby out, but that's your business. It's always easy to tell someone else what to do when, in their position, yer might do exactly the same yerself.'

'It won't be for long, Mr Pollard,' Lucy said. 'I bet any money me dad will be back home again soon.'

'Don't be banking on that, pet,' Bob said. ''Cos it's not going to happen.'

Aggie tutted. 'Leave the girl be. She could be right for all yer know. Don't forget, God moves in mysterious ways, His wonders to perform.'

'I'll go along with that,' Irene said, giving Bob a look that told him he shouldn't rob his daughter of her dreams.

'Me too!' Jack was gazing at Lucy's pretty face. 'I don't want Lucy ever to move away from next door.'

'Me neither,' Greg said. 'She's like a sister to us.'

Lucy tilted her head and looked at her father. 'Yer see, Dad, there's so many people wishing for it, it's bound to come true.'

'Then I hope you're all right and I'm wrong, pet. Yer see, I don't want to leave all me friends any more than you do.'

George pushed himself from his chair. 'I need something to whet me whistle. Let's go and get that pint, mate. It might be the last one we have together for a while.'

'Don't you believe it.' Bob smiled at his daughter when he saw her face drop at George's words. 'Yer'll be seeing as much of me as yer ever have.'

664

★ ★ ★

Bob woke up at seven the next morning, but didn't stir from the couch. It was far too early to be up and about, particularly as he didn't want to make a noise. He'd said a tearful goodbye to Lucy last night, promising faithfully he'd come as often as he could. It was heart-breaking and he didn't want to put her, or himself through that again. She usually got up on a Sunday between nine and half past, so he wanted to be away by then. Ruby never saw daylight before eleven, not after a night out drinking, so there was no fear of having to face her. He'd heard her come in last night and was waiting for her to try the door, but she'd made her way straight up the stairs.

It was eight o'clock when Bob put his pillow in the middle of the blanket and folded the sides over. He left them on the couch, with the case beside them, while he went into the kitchen to get a good wash down in the sink. Then he made himself a pot of tea and two rounds of bread and jam before donning his best clothes. He'd brushed his suit down and polished his shoes last night, wanting to make a good impression on his new landlady. So now he was all ready to leave. He'd go the back way, so he wouldn't be heard.

Halfway down the entry, Bob stopped. He was filled with despair and hopelessness. There didn't seem to be any light at the end of the tunnel. He was a man who'd worked since the day he left school at fourteen, had never asked for much from life, yet he was sneaking down a back entry like a thief in the night, with all his worldly goods in a battered suitcase and a blanket. He felt like sitting down on the cobbled stones and crying his heart out. But he couldn't afford that luxury, not now. Perhaps in bed tonight.

Nellie opened the door with a smile on her face. 'I've had the kettle on the hob for the last hour, so the tea will be up in no time.'

'Thanks, Nellie.' If she only knew I've walked all the way here to pass the time, she'd go mad. But I didn't like knocking on her door at nine in the morning. 'I could just go a cuppa.'

'Throw yer things on the bed for now, I'll help yer make it up later.'

When they were facing each other across the table, Nellie could clearly see the pain in Bob's eyes. It was naked, there for all to see. 'It's not easy, is it, lad?'

He was afraid to speak because the lump in his throat was growing so big it hurt. He was trying to keep his emotions in check but they didn't want to be bottled up, they wanted to be free. 'No, Nellie, it's not easy.' A lone tear trickled down his cheek and he wiped it away. 'I'm sorry, I can't – I can't . . .' He covered his face with his hands as sobs shook his body. Then he pushed his chair back, and in a voice thick with unshed tears, he said, 'I'd better go upstairs. Yer must wonder what sort of man I am for crying like a baby.'

Nellie rounded the table in a trice. 'Stay where yer are, lad. Yer don't want to be sitting on yer own with yer head filled with all sorts. Talk about it and get it out of yer system. And cry as much as yer want, 'cos I wouldn't think yer were much of a man if yer couldn't cry over what's happened to you and yer daughter. Yer've had yer whole life turned upside down; no one expects yer to walk round with a permanent smile on yer face.'

So Bob talked and cried as he unburdened himself, while Nellie listened. She said very little, only to cluck sympathetically when he said he couldn't get the picture of Lucy out of his mind. She asked no questions, didn't pry. And it was then that a bond was cemented between Bob and his landlady.

Chapter Twenty-Four

Nellie said Kate and her daughter usually arrived between twelve and half-past, and as the clock ticked towards the hour of midday Bob began to get jittery. He'd been for a walk to buy a Sunday paper, hoping the fresh air would take away some of the redness from his eyes. He'd feel so stupid if Kate knew he'd been crying. But he had to admit his tears had eased the throbbing in his head and he was thinking more clearly. He would be eternally grateful to Nellie for her patience and understanding. When he'd knocked on her door he'd been at the lowest point in his life. He felt so useless and helpless. But in a kindly way, she'd told him to snap out of it. Feeling sorry for himself wouldn't get him anywhere, she'd said. He had to start thinking of making a new and happy life for himself and Lucy. And her words had worked wonders. He now felt able to start planning for the future.

When the knock came, Bob quickly folded the paper. 'Shall I go, Nellie?'

'If yer would, lad, 'cos I'm just turning the spuds in the roasting tin.'

Bob opened the door and raised his brows. 'Can I help you?'

'Go on, yer daft nit.' Kate smiled as she let Iris walk ahead of her. 'Been here five minutes and yer've taken over already?'

'If only I was that domineering, Kate, I wouldn't be in the mess I'm in now.'

She smiled up into his face. 'I don't like domineering men.'

'I'm glad about that, Kate,' Bob said as he closed the door and followed her into the living room. 'At least someone doesn't think I'm a spineless idiot.'

Kate crossed to her mother to give her a hug. 'How's the new lodger, Mam? Is he behaving himself?'

'No complaints so far, queen.'

'Me nan's been telling yer some of her funny stories, hasn't she, Mr Mellor?' Iris asked with a grin.

Bob was at a loss. 'Funny stories?'

'I know she has! I can tell yer've been laughing 'cos yer eyes are all red.'

'Now listen to me, sweetheart,' Nellie said, hitching up her bosom before smoothing her pinny. 'I've got funny stories for young girls like yerself, and I've got funny stories for grown ups. And the ones I've been telling Mr Mellor are not for young ears, so don't be pestering him.'

'Okay, Nan.' Iris clamped her lips and narrowed her eyes as she gazed at Bob. 'Your Lucy calls me nan Mrs Nellie. And she said there's a woman in your street she calls Mrs Aggie. Is that right?'

'Yes, that's right, love.'

'Well, can I call you Mr Bob, then?'

Kate wagged a finger. 'Don't be so forward, Iris.'

'She's not being forward, Kate, she's being straight.' Bob smiled at the girl. 'I'd be very happy for yer to call me Mr Bob.'

'D'yer think I could go and see this Mrs Aggie? Lucy said she's very funny.'

'Ask yer mam to take yer one day. Aggie would be delighted.'

'Ooh, will yer, Mam, please?'

Kate looked flustered. 'We'll see, but I'm not making any promises.'

Once again Nellie's bosom was hitched. 'I'll go with them. This Mrs Aggie seems right up my street. Next time yer see her, ask if it's all right. And tell her if she hasn't got enough cups to go round, I'll bring some with me.'

Bob chuckled. 'Aggie's got a son who goes away to sea, and he's always bringing her things back from foreign countries. I bet she's got more cups than the Kardomah.'

Iris was hopping from one foot to the other. 'Lucy told me about Mrs Aggie's son what goes away to sea. She said he's dead funny, like his mam. And his name's Mr Titch.'

Nellie could smell the dinner which, if it wasn't served soon, would be ruined. And she prided herself on her cooking. 'Will yer all sit down, please, ye're making the place look untidy. Except you, Iris, you can set the table.'

'I'll give yer a hand with the dinner, Mam,' Kate said. 'Yer've got an extra one today.'

'I can count, queen.' Nellie jerked her head in disgust. 'I haven't lost me bleedin' marbles yet.' She wrinkled her nose. 'Sorry, queen, it slipped out. On a Sunday, too. And in front of a stranger. Oh dear, oh dear, oh dear, whatever next?' She was chuckling as she made her way to the kitchen. 'I don't need any help, Kate, you keep Bob company. But for crying out loud park yer backside when ye're doing it.'

'What would yer do with her?' Kate smiled as she took a seat on the couch while Bob sat in the fireside chair which Nellie had said was his for as long as he stayed with her. 'Yer never know what she's going to come out with next.'

'That's the beauty of her, isn't it, Kate? Yer know exactly where yer are with her. She'll never go behind yer back to say what she thinks about yer.'

'I know that, Bob, and I love the bones of her. I don't know what I'd have done without her the last few years. She was my rock to cling to when things were so rough I never thought I'd make it.'

In the kitchen, Nellie had a secret smile on her face as she jabbed a fork in a roast potato. Kate had had a hard time since her husband died. She had no friends, no social life. Just bed and work, the same old monotonous routine every week. She idolised her daughter, but she couldn't burden young Iris with her heartache and problems. She needed someone mature to talk to, someone who had known sadness in their own lives. Now Bob had come along and Nellie thought they'd be good for each other.

'Kate said yer were a good cook, Nellie, but I never expected yer to be *so* good. That dinner wouldn't have been out of place at Buckingham Palace.' Bob licked his lips and rubbed his tummy. 'It was delicious.'

Nellie looked as pleased as Punch. 'I'm glad yer enjoyed it, lad. I hope yer've left a bit of room for some rice pudding?'

'I'll not say no, Nellie, even though me trousers are tight now.' It was a long time since Bob had been offered a sweet after his dinner. Ruby bought as little food as possible. She said she couldn't afford it on the money he gave her, but Nellie seemed to manage, even though she must be living on a pittance. 'Don't think yer have to cook special for me, Nellie, 'cos I'm the easiest person in the world to feed. Yer can't afford to be giving me meals like this every day.'

'If I can afford it, lad, then yer'll get a decent meal. If I'm hard-up, yer'll be getting conny-onny butties put in front of yer.'

Kate clicked her tongue on the roof of her mouth. 'Take no notice of her, Bob. Me mam would go mad if she had a man in the house and couldn't feed him properly. We don't go short because we share. When I'm on mornings and nights, and every Sunday, me and Iris have our dinner round here, so I share the cost with me mam. And I've got to say she's a wizard in the kitchen. She can make a dinner out of practically nothing.'

Nellie was lapping up the praise. 'Well, queen, as I've told yer, there's them what can, and there's them what can't.'

'I've learned that the hard way, I'm afraid.' Bob looked across at Kate, but carried on talking to her mother. 'D'yer know what, Nellie? Until yesterday, I didn't know yer daughter had legs. I've only ever seen her from the waist up, across the canteen table.'

Iris began to giggle and it was like a knife turning in Bob's heart. She sounded so like Lucy. What was his daughter doing now? How had Ruby been towards her? He wouldn't be able to see her all week, with working afternoons and her being at school. The earliest would be Saturday morning before he went to work, and it seemed a lifetime away.

Nellie had seen Bob's expression change, and although she wasn't to know the cause of it, she did know his mind was elsewhere. 'Come on, Kate, let's get these dirty dishes out,' she said briskly. 'The rice pudding will be going dry in the oven.'

Kate was on pins. Her sister and her husband were due any minute, and she was worried about how to approach Howard regarding advice for Bob, when Audrey, her mam and Iris were sitting there listening. That was the worst of two-up two-down houses, there was never any privacy. She had been hoping to have a word with her brother-in-law before he met Bob, but things had happened so quickly it hadn't been possible. Catching her mother's eye, Kate nodded towards the kitchen.

'I'll start getting the dishes out, ready for tea,' Nellie said. 'Come and give us a hand, will yer, Kate?'

In the kitchen they went into a huddle. 'Mam, I'm going to the corner of the street to wait for Howard's car. I want to explain about Bob, 'cos yer can't expect the poor man to pour his heart out in front of strangers. It won't be so bad if Howard is put in the picture, and our Audrey knows what's going on. So I'm going to tell a little fib to get out, is that okay?'

'Of course it is, queen. Yer can tell a ruddy big whopper for all I care. You do what yer think best.'

Kate knew she couldn't look someone in the eye and tell a lie without blushing, so she made sure it didn't happen by walking straight through from the kitchen into the hall. 'I've got a horrible feeling I've come out and left the stove on,' she called over her shoulder. 'I'm just nipping home to put me mind at rest.'

'I'll go for yer, Mam,' Iris offered. 'I can run there and back.'

'No, it's all right, love.' Kate was gripping the round handle ready for pulling the door shut. 'I'll be back before yer know I'm gone.' She waved as she passed the window, then pelted it hell for leather to the bottom of the street. Howard always came this way in his little black four-seater car, so she wouldn't miss him. He'd caused quite a stir the first time he came in it, because cars were a rare sight in their street. The neighbours who didn't come out to gape, peeped through their curtains. And the kids would have swarmed all over it if Howard hadn't told them off in his posh voice.

When the car turned the corner Kate stepped into the gutter and waved both hands for it to stop. Howard wound the window down, a look of concern on his rather serious face. 'Is there something wrong, Kate?'

'No, I just want a word with yer before yer go in the house.' Kate opened the back door and scrambled on to the seat. She found her sister twisted round and glaring at her.

'You frightened the life out of me, I thought something terrible had happened to Mother.' Audrey's Liverpool accent had all but disappeared since she'd met Howard. The only time she allowed it to come to the fore was when she was angry and couldn't help herself. But she wasn't a snob. Born and raised in this narrow cobbled street, she never pretended to be anything she wasn't. Two years younger than Kate, she loved her family and was always there to help. So far her marriage was a childless one, but whether that was due to nature, or a deliberate decision taken by her and Howard, she had never said. And her time for childbearing was running out. 'What is it, Kate, that's so important we can't talk in front of Mother?'

'Oh, we can talk in front of me mam 'cos she knows all about it. But I want Howard to help a friend of mine with some advice and he's in the house with me mam and Iris. Would yer mind if I tell yer the whole story, very quickly, so you and Howard don't get it in bits and pieces?'

'Is this person a good friend of yours, Kate?' Howard asked.

Kate nodded. 'He's one hell of a nice feller and he desperately needs advice.'

'Then carry on, Kate.'

Kate told them everything, from the first time Bob had sat facing her in the canteen. And she ended by saying, 'Me mam offered him her spare room and he moved in yesterday.'

Audrey took a deep breath then blew it out. 'Well, that's some story. Are yer sure it's all true, Kate, or is he taking advantage?'

'It's true – I've seen his hand scratched to pieces where his wife had gone for him. He's a quiet man, and he's put up with it for years. Anyway, Audrey, would yer say me mam was a good judge of character?'

Her sister nodded. 'I've never known her to be wrong.'

'And he wants advice on how to go about obtaining a divorce?' Howard tapped his fingers on the steering wheel. 'It's a messy business, divorce, and it can take years.'

'Would yer talk to him about it?' Kate was gripping the back of his seat. 'He's only a working bloke and doesn't know where to turn.'

'I'll be only too happy to help a friend of yours, Kate. But isn't

671

it going to be rather difficult in your mother's house? I would need to ask very personal questions which the man would find hard to answer in front of Iris, Audrey and yourself.'

'I know, but I can't think of any other way.' Kate sighed. 'When yer meet him, and yer've been in his company for a while, yer'll understand why I want to help him.'

Howard was conscious of the fact that this was the first time Kate had ever asked him or Audrey for help. Several times they'd offered to help out financially when they knew she must have been desperate, but each time she'd smiled and said she could manage. It was because of this he was prompted to say, 'Leave it to me, Kate, I'll think of something.'

Bob was nervous at first because he thought solicitors were a cut above the rest, like teachers and doctors. But he soon learned that even if the King came to Nellie's house he would be expected to muck in like everybody else. She didn't stand on ceremony, did Mrs Carson. Howard might be a solicitor, and she thought the world of him, but when he was in her house he was treated the same as everyone else. Even when her tongue slipped and a swearword came out, she merely pulled a comical face and said, 'That came out of its own accord, our Audrey. I had nothing to do with it, so don't be giving me daggers.'

Bob happened to catch Howard's eyes and they exchanged smiles. 'Yer've been blessed with a good mother-in-law, Howard.'

'Yes, I know. And I appreciate it. It was only when I met Nellie that I realised my teacher at school had taught me only half of the English language. It was Nellie who taught me the rest. I can't use it, of course, but I'm indebted to her for widening my horizon.'

'One good turn deserves another then, don't yer think?' Nellie asked. 'Yer can come and help me get the plates ready for the tea while Iris sets the table.'

'Mother!' Audrey looked horrified. 'That's not a job for Howard! Kate and I will help you with the dishes, like we always do.'

But Howard knew there must be a motive behind the very strange, and unusual request. 'Stay where you are, Audrey, this should be interesting. I think your mother wants to widen my horizon still further.' So in his immaculate navy-blue pinstripe suit, pure white shirt with stiff collar and a plain grey tie secured with a gold tie-pin, the man who spent most of his life behind a desk followed his mother-in-law into the tiny kitchen.

'Well, I declare,' Audrey said, then lapsed into her Liverpool accent. 'What's got into me mam? I mean, it's not funny, is it?'

672

'Don't worry, he won't reign long,' Kate told her. 'I'll give him two minutes at the most.'

Bob took the chance to study the sisters. They had the same facial features, but there the resemblance ended. Audrey looked every inch the woman about town. Her clothes were expensive and fashionable and she carried them well. Her stockings were pure silk and her black court shoes boasted a two-inch heel. And her hair was perfectly waved, as though she'd just come from the hairdresser's.

'Oh, get back inside,' Nellie said, pushing Howard into the room. 'Ye're about as much use as our cat.'

'Mother, you haven't got a cat.'

'I know that, queen. But if I did have it would be more use in the kitchen than Howard. At least I could kick it out of me way if it got under me feet.'

It was while they were sitting around the table having their tea that the sisters understood the reason for their mother's behaviour. With an angelic expression on her face, Nellie asked, 'Have yer seen Howard's car, Bob?'

'I've glimpsed it through the window, that's all.'

'Yer'll have to get him to show it to yer after. It's his pride and joy, that car. He'd take it to bed with him at night if he could, wouldn't yer, lad?'

Howard was of medium height and build, his complexion was pale through spending his working life in a stuffy office, and his hair was receding at the temples. But when he smiled he looked almost boyish and showed a set of strong white teeth. 'Before you drop me in deep water, Mother-in-law, may I say the car is my *second* pride and joy. Audrey is my first. And the car has a perfectly good garage to sleep in, where it's safe and warm.'

'It told yer that, did it?'

Iris giggled. 'It would do if it could talk, wouldn't it, Uncle Howard?'

'It can talk, dear. Except you wouldn't understand it because it's more of a splutter. On a very cold morning, when I switch the engine on, it splutters to tell me it would much prefer to stay in the garage than venture out into the cold.'

'Now I've heard everything.' Nellie placed her palms on the table. 'You go and show this amazing talking car to Bob, while me and the girls clear away and wash up.'

The men had only been out of the room for five minutes when Howard came back in. 'I'm taking Bob for a short spin. We won't be long.'

Nellie had a very satisfied smile on her face when she winked at Kate. Everything had worked out a treat.

★ ★ ★

Howard had stopped the car in a quiet spot and for half an hour he'd asked questions and listened carefully to Bob's answers. 'Your wife admitted to adultery, then?'

'Oh yes, she sounded quite proud of herself.'

'Do you know the name of the man she's involved with?'

Bob shook his head. 'I never asked because I knew she wouldn't tell the truth. All I know is she goes out two or three nights a week and usually comes home the worse for drink.'

'It would help if you could find out the man's name in case she denies it. Proof is needed rather than hearsay. I can set the wheels in motion if you'll come down to my office one day and fill in some forms. But I must warn you, it's a very lengthy process.'

Bob flushed with embarrassment. 'Howard, can we leave it for a short while? Yer see, I'm going to be strapped for cash with paying the rent on the house, my daughter's keep and my board and lodgings. I will start saving as much as I can, though, because I need to sort life out for meself and Lucy. I won't be happy until I've got her with me again and Ruby's out of our life for good. So if yer'll give me an idea of what I'll need to start the ball rolling, I'll make an appointment to see you as soon as I've got the cash.'

'You're a friend of Kate's, and I promised I would help you.' Howard smiled. 'She said when I met you I'd know you were a decent man, and she was right. So I'll get the proceedings under way without you coming in to my office. I'll ask Kate to bring you to my home one night and I'll have the forms there ready for you to fill in. That way you will be making the application yourself and my partners need not be involved. There may be a legal charge in the future, but we'll cross that hurdle when we come to it. At least you will have set the ball rolling.'

Bob hung his head. 'I don't know what to say. I seem to be asking so much and giving nothing in return. Kate has been a good friend to me, always ready to listen. Nellie has taken me, a complete stranger, into her home and is treating me like one of the family. And now you are offering to help a man yer have never seen in yer life before.'

Howard could see Bob was choked with emotion and hastened to say, 'Bob, Kate needed someone she could confide in, and from what I hear she found that someone in you. And she really wants to help you. As for Nellie, she's told me she's over the moon having you to keep her company. Her actual words were, and I quote, "He's the nicest and most handsome bleedin' lodger I've ever had. The neighbours will be green with envy." '

Bob raised his head and smiled. 'I can just see her saying that.'

'So, because these ladies are very dear to me, I want to make them happy by doing what I can for you. I'll get Kate to bring you

674

to my home one night, when it's convenient for you, and we'll start writing a new chapter to your life.'

Four weeks later, Aggie was sitting in her rocking chair when she heard the key turn in the lock. She jumped to her feet and was standing by the table when Titch came into the room. 'Did yer call to Olive's first?'

Titch dropped his seaman's bag on the floor. 'Now, Ma, I might be living in hope that Olive will become me intended, but until we're married it'll always be you I come to first.'

Aggie didn't know where to start. 'Yer'll never believe what's been happening while yer've been away.'

'Ma, don't I even get me welcome-home kiss?'

'Oh, I'm sorry, son, I'm all hot and bothered.' She put her arms around him and kissed his cheek. 'Bob's left home.'

'What!' Titch held her away from him. 'What did yer say?'

'I said Bob's left home. Four weeks ago it was. He found out Ruby had been sleeping with some bloke and he packed his bags and left. He's down here nearly every day, though, except when he's on afternoons. And Lucy goes to visit him. He's got good digs with the mother of that Kate he told us about. And he's started divorce proceedings as well.'

'Whoa, there, Ma, I can't keep up with yer. Sit down and start at the very beginning.'

'I'll make yer a cup of tea first. I can't have yer coming home without even a drink ready for yer. The dinner's in the oven, it'll be an hour yet.'

Titch leaned forward and rested his elbows on his legs, a cup and saucer in his hands. 'I can't believe it. Yer mean Ruby actually admitted she'd been sleeping with a bloke?'

Aggie nodded. 'As bold as brass. And to see her walking up the street with her nose in the air – well, it's enough to make yer sick. She's had to take a part-time job in some laundry 'cos, although Bob pays the rent, he won't give her any money.'

'And what about Lucy in all this? Doesn't Ruby take it out on her?'

'Lucy has most of her meals in Irene's. Bob pays her a few shillings a week. And Ruby daren't look sideways at Lucy because Bob threatened to stop paying the rent and she'd be turfed out. Besides, the girl isn't the least bit frightened of her mother now. She's turned out to be very strong-willed. She's got it into her head that her dad will come home again one day, so she's making sure the house is kept right for when he does.'

'Bob won't come back – he'd never be able to lift his head up if he did.'

'No, he won't come back if Ruby's there, Lucy knows that. She's of the opinion that her mother will up sticks and leave. And before yer say anything, I think the girl's right. I don't know why I think that, it's just a gut feeling I've got. I pray to God every night that we're both right. The whole sorry mess is taking its toll on Bob. He's lost weight and his face is haggard. He's pining for his daughter, which is only natural.'

'Fancy me being away and missing all this.' Titch shook his head slowly. 'I'm sorry for Bob, he's as nice a feller as yer'll ever meet. And yer say he's already put in for a divorce?'

Aggie nodded. 'Someone related to Kate is a solicitor and he's helped him with all the rigmarole. He wanted to know if Bob knew the name of the bloke Ruby's been sleeping with, but no one knows that.'

'It shouldn't be too hard to find out. Someone could follow her one night. If it's down on the divorce papers that she's been unfaithful to Bob, he could be asked to prove it.'

Aggie sighed as she got to her feet. 'What a bleedin' awful life. I'll be really upset if Bob and Lucy go to live miles away, I wouldn't half miss them.' She sniffed up. 'I'll get the dinner moving 'cos I suppose ye're dying to see Olive.'

'Yer could say that, Ma, seeing as she's me intended. And I'd like to see young Lucy before the day's out.'

'She calls in here every afternoon after school, before she goes to Irene's, so ye're bound to see her. Anyway, if she knows ye're home yer won't need to go looking for her, she'll find you.'

Olive opened the door and held her arms wide. 'Where've yer been all this time? I saw yer passing the window hours ago and I've been sitting on the edge of the chair waiting for yer.'

Titch held her tight, his kisses warm and eager. 'Oh, this feels so good, sweetheart. I've really missed yer this trip. I only intended to call at me ma's for five minutes, but she had so much news for me I couldn't get away.'

Olive took his hand and led him through to the living room. 'Yer've heard all about Bob's troubles, then?'

'Yeah, I only wish I'd been here.' Titch sat close to her on the couch and slipped an arm across her shoulders. 'Not that I could have done anything to prevent what happened, but at least I could have lent him an ear.'

'From what I've heard, Kate and her mother are marvellous with him. Lucy is quite taken with them. She said Mrs Nellie, that's what she calls Kate's mother, is just like yer ma. Always ready to put the kettle on and forever telling jokes.'

'I'm concerned for Lucy. I wouldn't have thought it safe to leave

676

her in the house with Ruby. The woman's as mad as a hatter – she's capable of anything.'

'Don't worry about Lucy, she's being watched over night and day. She has her dinner with Irene and stays to play cards until it's her bedtime. Steve goes there after he's visited yer ma, and when it's time for her to go home, he takes her and waits until she's at the top of the stairs before closing the door. Then the Pollard boys take over. They sleep in the back room and it's only a thin wall separating them from Lucy's. Jack's told her to give a knock at the least sign of trouble and they'll be with her in seconds.' Olive chuckled. 'Greg said he'd come waving a rolling pin. Luckily, Bob gave Irene a spare key just in case, so they'd have no trouble getting in.'

'To think a woman would cause so much heartache to her husband and family.' Titch sounded disgusted. 'And me ma said she walks round as bold as brass.'

'Oh, yeah! She goes out nearly every night, and she doesn't bother using the back entry now. She walks up the street as though she owns it. Dolled up to the nines and enough make-up on to sink a ship.'

'She'll get what's coming to her one of these days, mark my words. And I hope that day comes sooner rather than later.' Titch removed his arm to take her hands in his. 'Anyway, my love, tell me about how much yer've missed me.'

'What? And give yer a big head! Not likely.' Olive nestled closer and kissed his cheek. 'I've missed yer more than yer'll ever know, love.'

Titch blew little puffs of breath into her ear. 'Have yer made up yer mind when ye're going to marry me, then?'

The reply came quickly. 'In six months' time. That's how long it'll take to save up enough to get the house as I want it, and to buy the clothes to get married in.'

'I've told yer over and over again yer don't have to worry about money, love! I've got enough for everything yer need.'

'And I've told yer over and over that after we get married, yer can keep me. Until then I'll hang on to me pride and independence.'

Titch knew it would serve no purpose to argue. They'd been over this ground dozens of times. 'Have it your own way, love. Six months it is.'

The knock on the door brought a look of surprise to Olive's face. 'I wonder who this can be? Steve's not due in till after half-five.'

'Only one way to find out.' Titch got to his feet. 'I'll go and chase whoever it is away. How dare they interrupt us when I've just got home? Have they no tact?'

When Olive heard him say, 'Hello, sweetheart,' she knew who would be coming through the door clinging to Titch's hand.

'Mrs Aggie said if I didn't get an answer the first time, I wasn't to knock again 'cos yer'd be kissing and cuddling.' Lucy's face was one big smile. 'And she said I wasn't to stay long 'cos yer had to make up for lost time.'

'Oh, did she now?' Titch put his hand around her waist and lifted her from the floor. Smiling up into her face, he asked, 'And how's my girl, then?'

'I'm all right, Mr Titch, but I don't half miss me dad. Mrs Aggie told yer what happened, didn't she?'

'Yes, she did, sweetheart, and I'm very sorry. But don't be too unhappy – look on the bright side and tell yerself it won't be for long.'

'We keep telling her that,' Olive said. 'And I know something that will make her very happy. But ye're to keep it to yerself, Lucy, until Titch tells Mrs Aggie himself.'

Lucy's face was agog. 'Cross my heart, Mrs Fletcher, I won't say a dickie-bird.'

Olive glanced at Titch. 'Do you want to tell her, or shall I?'

'I'm sure you'll do it much better than I would, love.'

'Ye're getting married.' Lucy could barely contain herself as she clapped her hands. 'Oh, I bet that's what it is.'

'Yes, we are getting married, but not for another six months.' Olive wanted to give this young girl something to look forward to. 'What I wanted to tell yer, or rather to ask yer, is would yer like to be me bridesmaid?'

Titch felt like hugging Olive for being so caring and thoughtful, but Lucy beat him to it. She threw herself at Steve's mother, tears of happiness rolling down her cheeks. 'Oh yes, yes, yes! And thank you, thank you, thank you! Wait until I tell me dad, he'll be over the moon. I've never been to a wedding, never mind being a bridesmaid.'

'I'll tell yer what, sweetheart,' Titch said. 'I'll ask me intended if she'll come with me now to tell me ma. Then yer won't have to keep it to yerself. Yer can tell the whole world if yer like.'

'I wouldn't tell the whole world, Mr Titch. Just everyone in the street and all the girls in me class at school. I'll be that proud there'll be no keeping up with me.'

Titch was feeling excited himself now that arrangements were finally being made. He reached for Olive's hand. 'Let's go and make me ma as happy as Lucy is. I can't wait to see her face.'

Lucy walked between them, her arms linking theirs. 'How long are yer home for, Mr Titch?'

678

'Only a week, sweetheart.'

Olive brought them to a halt. 'A week! Ye're only on leave for a week?'

'That's the bad news, love. The good news is that I'll only be away a month on the next trip, then it's two weeks' leave.'

Lucy's mind went back to the wedding. 'Six months isn't long, it'll soon pass. And I'll be a working girl by then.'

'It's half-past nine, sunshine, time for you and Rhoda to be going to bed.'

'I won't be able to sleep, I'm that excited.' Lucy began to gather the cards together. 'Your mam is lovely, Steve, for asking me to be her bridesmaid.'

'I've never been a bridesmaid,' Rhoda said. 'D'yer think if I asked her nicely she'd consider having two?'

'No chance.' Steve grinned. 'It's only going to be a quiet wedding.'

'I'd fit in, 'cos I'm only a quiet girl.'

'Just listen to her!' Greg said. 'She gabs more than anyone I know. I bet a pound to a pinch of snuff that she talks in her sleep.'

'She wouldn't be the only one, would she?' Jack winked at Rhoda who was giving his brother daggers. 'You talk in yer sleep every night.'

Irene banged her fist on the table. 'That's it for tonight. Come on, girls, take yerselves off home to bed.'

Jack scraped his chair back. 'I'll see Rhoda to her door while you see to Lucy, Steve.'

George looked up from his paper. 'Remember, no goodnight kisses until the girls have left school.'

'You're awful, Mr Pollard,' Lucy said, giggling. 'But ye're awful in a nice way.' She pecked his cheek before flinging her arms around Irene. 'I'll see yer tomorrow.'

'Goodnight, sunshine. And yer'll make a lovely bridesmaid.'

When Lucy opened her front door, she said to Steve, 'If me mam's not in I won't go straight upstairs, 'cos I want to wash me hands and face.'

'I'll wait here until yer make sure.'

Lucy was back within seconds. 'She's gone out. I'll be all right now, Steve, thanks very much. I'll see yer tomorrow.'

'Okay, but don't forget to knock next door if she comes in and tries anything.'

'I won't. Goodnight, Steve.' Lucy closed the door and made her way through the living room to the kitchen. She had a headache with excitement and a swill in cold water might help shift it. She didn't waste any time because she didn't know when her mother

679

would be in and she didn't fancy coming face to face with Ruby. After what she'd done to her dad, the less she saw of her the better.

Lucy was halfway across the living room when she happened to glance at the fireplace. She stood with her chin in her hand, wondering why she thought it didn't look right. Then it struck her. The carved wooden candlesticks were missing from the mantelpiece. She frowned as she tried to think where they could be. They'd been there this morning before she went to school. Then she spied the bag at the side of her mother's chair. It was a big bag, one her mother took to work with her overall in.

Without thinking, Lucy did something she'd never done before; she lifted the bag on to the chair and moved the newspaper that was spread over the top. And there lay the candlesticks that she knew meant a lot to her dad because they'd belonged to his mother. What on earth were they doing in the bag? Where was her mother taking them? She had no right to move them, they weren't hers. There was only one way to find out, Lucy told herself, feeling very angry, and that was to ask.

Ruby came home at half-ten to find her daughter sat at the table with the candlesticks in front of her. 'What the hell are you doing up at this time, yer little flamer?'

'Waiting to ask yer where yer were taking these.'

'I'm taking them to the pawnshop, yer hard-faced faggot. Now get up them stairs to bed and mind yer own business.'

'It *is* my business. They are not yours to pawn, they belong to me dad.' Lucy got to her feet and picked up the candlesticks. 'I'm taking them upstairs with me so yer can't get yer greedy hands on them.'

'If yer bleedin' father gave me enough to live on, I wouldn't have to pawn anything.'

Lucy wrinkled her nose. 'Yer smell of drink. It's funny how yer can always find the money for that. But if yer take anything out of this house that you haven't paid for, I'll tell me dad on yer.'

There was rage on Ruby's face, but she was crafty enough to know how far she could go. 'One of these days I'll give yer the hiding of yer bleedin' life, yer snotty-nosed little faggot. It's something I should have done years ago.'

'There's lots of things yer should have done years ago, but yer didn't and it's too late now. I used to pray that yer'd love me like a mother should, but I don't bother any more. That's because I've realised yer don't know what the word love means. I suppose I should pity yer, really, but I can't even bring meself to do that.' Lucy turned on her heels and left the room.

Chapter Twenty-Five

Lucy jumped down from the step of Rhoda's house then spun around to gaze up at her friend with a face that was full of excitement and joy. It had been a very hectic but happy day for both of them. It was their last day at school and they'd been allowed time off to go for an interview at Vernons Football Pools. To their delight they'd both been taken on and were to start work on Monday morning at the football pools office in Linacre Lane.

'I can't get over it, can you?' Lucy asked, hugging herself. 'I bet my dad will be as glad as your mam was that we're going to be working together.'

'Is yer dad coming down tonight?'

'Yeah, he said he'd come to see how I got on. He'll be dead pleased for me.'

'No sign of him finding a place for both of yer?' Rhoda pulled a face. 'I don't know why I keep asking yer that, because I hope he never does. Especially now when we can travel to work together.'

'He hasn't found a place he can afford. With needing two bedrooms, the people he's been to see are asking a lot of money.' Lucy looked down at the ground and kicked the step with the toe of her shoe. 'I don't tell me dad because he gets upset about it, but I don't want to leave here. I thought me mam would have moved out by now, but there's no sign of it. She seems quite happy because she's got the house, no one to answer to, and can come and go as she pleases.'

Rhoda always said what was in her mind, and she grinned now at what she was thinking. 'With a bit of luck she'll fall and break a leg and end up in hospital. And with a lot of luck she'll manage to break both legs. Then she'd be in hospital for ages and ages.'

Lucy tutted. 'Ye're terrible, you are, Rhoda Fleming.'

'No, kid, I'm just honest. And yer know what they say about honesty being the best policy.'

'That's not always the case,' Lucy said. 'Anyway, I'm going to tell Mrs Aggie the news before I go to the Pollards' for me tea. Me dad won't be here until about eight o'clock, so I'm going home after tea to sort me clothes out. I'll be wearing me skirt and blouse to start work in, so I want to make sure they're cleaned and pressed over the weekend.'

'Don't forget yer'll need long stockings.' Rhoda was nodding her head. 'If yer turn up in short socks I'll pretend I'm not with yer.'

'Okay, okay! I'll ask me dad for the money tonight. And I'm going now 'cos I can't wait to see Mrs Aggie's face when I tell her I've got a job. She'll be over the moon for me.'

Rhoda watched her friend running across the cobbled street and shouted after her, 'Er, yer wouldn't forget to tell her I've got a job too, would yer? I don't see why you should be allowed to hog all the limelight.'

Lucy turned after knocking on Aggie's door. 'Keep yer hair on, I won't forget.'

Rhoda wanted to make sure all her neighbours knew her good news, so at the top of her voice, she shouted, 'Talking about hair, Lucy, don't forget I want yer to do mine for when we start work on Monday.'

Lucy was grinning when Aggie opened the door. 'What am I going to do with that mate of mine, Mrs Aggie? She'll get me hanged one of these days.'

'I heard what she said, sweetheart. The interview went well, then, did it?'

'The interview was the most terrifying thing I've ever gone through in me life, Mrs Aggie. We had to go to the main office for it. You know, the one in Aintree, near the Old Roan? There were about ten girls there beside me and Rhoda, and they all looked as frightened as I felt. Our names were called out one at a time, and by the time my turn came, me legs were shaking so much I thought I'd never be able to stand on them. I had to follow this woman to an office, and there was a small, oldish woman seated behind a desk. I was told her name was Miss Jones. She didn't half look strict, and I never thought I'd get taken on 'cos I was stammering and stuttering. She asked me all about meself after she'd read the reference I'd got off the headmistress, and she wrote everything down in this big book. Not a smile crossed her face the whole time, and I nearly fell off the chair when she said I could start on Monday in the Linacre Lane branch.'

'I'm made up for yer, sweetheart. And Rhoda got taken on too, I gather?'

Lucy nodded. 'Yeah, we'll be able to travel to work together every day. I'm glad she'll be with me, I won't feel so shy.'

'Wait until yer dad knows, sweetheart, he'll be so proud of yer.'

'Yeah, it's a bit of good news for him for a change. And I'm not bigheaded, Mrs Aggie, but I've got to say I'm dead proud of meself. I'll be a working girl earning a wage. I won't get any money the first week, like, 'cos it's a week in hand, but I will the week after. And that'll make things a bit easier for me dad.'

'Are yer going to tell yer mam?'

'Not likely! She'll want to take me wages off me. She's bound to find out – I mean, I can't go out every morning, come home at night, and her not know what's going on. But she won't hear it from me, nor will she get a penny of me money. I'll hand it all over to me dad and he can give me whatever pocket money he can afford.' Lucy hunched her shoulders and pulled a face. 'I've got to cadge off him tonight when he comes. Rhoda said if I turn up on Monday in short socks, she'll disown me.'

Aggie chuckled. 'She would say that. Sounds as hard as nails sometimes, but her heart's in the right place. I bet if you knock on her door on Monday morning in short socks, by the time yer get to Vernons yer'll both be wearing one stocking and one short sock each.'

Lucy could see it in her mind's eye and she giggled. 'I wouldn't put anything past my mate, she's got the nerve for anything.' The giggle got louder until it filled the room. 'D'yer know what the daft nit told me? That Miss Jones was as nice as pie with her and gave her a cup of tea and a biscuit. Having seen Miss Jones, I can see the funny side, 'cos the woman never cracked her face.'

'At least she gave yer the job, sweetheart. Better that than someone who smiled sweetly at yer and said she was sorry but yer weren't suitable.'

'Ye're right, Mrs Aggie.' Lucy couldn't sit still, she was so highly strung. 'I've got a lot to look forward to, haven't I? Starting me first job and earning money, then in a couple of months I'm to be a bridesmaid. I'm a very lucky girl.'

'No more than yer deserve, sweetheart. Yer can start making up for lost time now.'

'If only me dad could come back home, then I wouldn't ask for anything else in the whole world. I still miss him terrible, Mrs Aggie. I know I see him often, but it's not the same as him living in the house. We're not like a family any more.'

'Let's hope yer dad has a run of good luck, like you have. Yer know what they say about things happening in threes.' Aggie began to rock slowly, thinking that with the number of prayers she'd said, something good should have come along for Bob by now. Either God hadn't heard her prayers or He had a lot on His plate. Even so, He should give everyone a fair hearing. 'Have yer told Irene yet?'

'No, I'm going there when I leave here. Mr Pollard and Jack will be in from work then, so I can tell them all at once and get it over with. Otherwise I'll be telling it in dribs and drabs and it'll take all night. And I want to go home before me dad comes so I can look through me clothes and get them ready for Monday.'

Bob always met his daughter in either Aggie's or Irene's. He'd only been back home the once since he left, and that was to pick up a couple of things he'd forgotten to take with him.

'Are yer all right for clothes, sweetheart?' Aggie asked. She would have loved to have bought the girl something as a leaving-school present, but was afraid of upsetting Bob.

'I've got a skirt and blouse, and one dress that'll be suitable. They'll see me through until I can save up for another blouse to change into.' Lucy looked at the clock and scrambled to her feet. 'I'd better go – Mr Pollard and Jack will be home any minute.'

Aggie walked her to the door. 'I'll see yer later, with yer dad. Ta-ra, sweetheart.'

Mealtimes were always noisy at the Pollards', but tonight everyone was talking at once and it was chaotic. It had been the last day at school for Greg, too, and they couldn't get a word in edgeways with him. What he was going to do, and what he wasn't going to do was nobody's business. He had an interview at the woodworks on Monday, and to hear him talk he had no intention of starting on the bottom rung of the ladder, it was a supervisor's job he was after.

Irene put a hand over her ears. 'Will yer all shut up for a minute, me head's splitting with the din ye're making.'

'There's only one person making a din, Mam,' Jack said, jerking his head towards his brother. 'It's talk a bit, here. He's never closed his mouth once since me and me dad came in. He's making more noise than a steam train chugging into Lime Street Station.'

Greg was so happy at never having to go to school again, nothing would have upset him. No more getting the cane for staring out of the window when he should have been doing his sums, or for answering the teacher back. He wouldn't know he was born without the threat of that blinking cane hanging over him. 'I can remember the day you left school, our Jack, and the day yer wore yer first pair of long kecks. Yer really thought yer were somebody, you did.'

'You'll be in long kecks on Monday, son,' George said. 'So yer can expect to have as much fun poked at yer as Jack did. And I hope ye're man enough to take it in the same spirit he did.'

Greg took that as a compliment. 'I will, Dad. Yer can laugh at me as much as yer like, and I'll laugh with yer.'

'Well, now that's settled to everyone's satisfaction,' Irene said, 'can we hear a bit more about how Lucy's day went?'

So Lucy had the floor to herself without any interruptions. She was very good at imitating people and had them in stitches over Miss Jones. The serious, straight face, the cool voice and the dismissive wave of her hand as she told Lucy, "You may go now." Then came Rhoda's joke about the cosy chat she'd had with the woman who'd interviewed them, and the tea and biscuits she'd been served.

'That's not fair, that,' Greg said, his face unsmiling as he pretended to believe what Lucy had said. 'She shouldn't have given Rhoda tea and not you. Mind you, that Rhoda would talk her way into anything. She was probably given the tea to shut her up.'

'I wish yer wouldn't keep pulling my friend to pieces,' Lucy said. 'She's never done you no harm, so I don't know why yer dislike her.'

'I don't dislike her.' Greg speared the last piece of sausage on his plate and popped it into his mouth. He banged the end of his fork on the table until he'd chewed the sausage sufficiently to be able to speak. 'She's just like the other girls, I suppose. Yer all talk too much and yer love bossing people around. That comes with playing with dolls when yer were kids. Dolls can't answer back, yer see, so girls grow up thinking no one should answer them back.'

'Well, fancy that now!' Irene pinched on her bottom lip. 'I wouldn't have thought of that meself, but I'll put it to the test.' She leaned towards her son and held his eyes. 'Clear the table, Greg, and take the dishes out to the kitchen.'

'Ah, ay, Mam! What's wrong with Lucy or our Jack?'

'This may come as a surprise to yer, sunshine, but I was a little girl once. And I used to play with dolls. So according to your theory, I don't expect to be answered back.'

Lucy giggled. 'Nice one, Mrs Pollard.'

'Yeah, yer've got him stumped there, Mam,' Jack said. 'Look at his face, yer've taken the wind out of his sails.'

'Yer dropped yerself right in it, son,' George said. 'Now take a bit of advice from one who learned the hard way. Never, ever, try and get the better of a woman 'cos yer don't stand a snowball's chance in hell. If she says a thing is black, then agree with her. It could be sky-blue pink with a finny-haddy border, but if she says black, then black it is. That's if yer want an easy life, like. Otherwise she'll come at yer with both guns blazing and yer won't know what hit yer.'

'Ah, yer poor thing, me heart bleeds for yer.' Irene wiped away an imaginary tear. 'Sure there's not a sorrier sight than a hen-pecked husband.'

Greg had recovered his voice by this time, and his sense of fun.

'Lucy, when you and me get married, yer won't henpeck me, will yer?'

'I won't be henpecking yer, Greg Pollard, 'cos I won't be marrying yer. Any girl what marries you would want her head testing.'

'Too true they would.' Jack nodded. 'He only left school today and he wants to put the banns up to get wed!'

'I don't intend to hang around like you,' Greg said. 'Ye're turned sixteen and haven't even got a girlfriend yet.'

'That's what you think.' Jack tapped the side of his nose. 'I don't tell you everything.'

'I don't blame yer for not telling him anything,' Irene said, 'but I'd expect yer to tell yer mother. Come on, who is she?'

'I'm not telling yer, Mam. All I will say is that she's very pretty and yer'll like her.'

'He's pulling yer leg, Mrs Pollard,' Lucy said, collecting the plates. She didn't want to hear any more. If Jack had a girlfriend then soon everything would change, and she didn't want it to. 'I'll take these out and wash them. Then I want to nip home to get me blouse and skirt. I need to make sure they're all right for Monday.'

'Leave those, I'll do them,' Irene told her. 'You go and get yer skirt and blouse and bring them back here.'

Lucy didn't need telling twice. 'I'll take the key and let meself in. I won't be a matter of minutes 'cos I don't want me mam asking me questions. That's if she's in, of course.'

Lucy stepped into the hall, and as she was taking the key from the lock she thought she heard voices coming from the living room. This was unusual because her mother never had visitors. So instead of going straight upstairs as she'd intended, the girl opened the door of the living room, and became rooted to the spot. There was a strange man sitting in the chair by the fire, and he seemed quite at home with a cigarette in his hand and his long legs crossed.

'Who are you? That's my dad's chair ye're sitting in.'

Ruby had jumped to her feet in surprise. Lucy never came back from the Pollards' until it was time for bed. 'Well, yer dad's not here now, is he? And don't you be so bleedin' impudent, yer little madam.'

'Watch your language, Ruby,' Wally Brown said, before turning his eyes back to Lucy. 'My name's Wally Brown, my dear, and I gather you are Lucy.'

'I don't care what yer name is, yer have no right to be sitting in me dad's chair.' Lucy had taken an instant dislike to him. He was too smarmy for her liking. As Mrs Aggie would say, he was too

686

sweet to be wholesome. And seeing him sitting in her dad's chair was making her feel sick and angry. 'What are yer doing here, anyway?'

'Mind yer own business,' Ruby said, trying to remember not to swear because Wally didn't like it. 'And mind yer manners.'

'She has every right to ask what a strange man is doing in her home,' Wally said, thinking he'd never seen such a beautiful young girl in his life. With those huge green eyes set in a heart-shaped face, topped by the mass of thick, dark glossy curls, she really was a stunner. 'I came to see your mother on some business, that's all. I'll be leaving very shortly.'

Ruby was beside herself with rage. She'd been so sure that she and Wally would have the house to themselves for a couple of hours, now this little faggot had gone and spoilt all her plans. She'd belt her one if it wasn't for Wally. He wouldn't like it and she wouldn't do anything to upset him. He treated her like a slave and she lapped it up. She was obsessed with him.

'I'll say goodbye to yer now then,' Lucy said with as much dignity as she could muster. ''Cos yer'll be gone when I come downstairs in about fifteen minutes.'

'Take no notice of her,' Ruby said, when her daughter's footsteps had died down. 'She can't do anything about it. I'm entitled to have visitors – it is my home.'

'Let's take things slowly, Ruby. You flying off the handle isn't going to help. Of course the girl would get a fright finding a strange man in the house, it's only natural. So I won't come again for a few weeks; we'll use my place as usual. The next time Lucy sees me it won't be such a surprise, and eventually she'll get used to me.'

'Whatever you say, love,' Ruby said meekly. 'Shall I come home with yer now?'

Wally shook his head. He enjoyed the power he had over her. She catered to his every whim and he loved to be the one pulling the strings. 'No, leave it until tomorrow night.' To keep her sweet, he said softly, 'I promise we'll have twice as much fun to make up for tonight.'

When Lucy came downstairs it was to see her mother leafing through a magazine. There was no sign of Wally Brown.

'I'm very proud of yer, pet.' Bob was sitting on the couch, holding his daughter close. 'Mind you, the thought of having a daughter working makes me feel a lot older.'

'Ye're not old.' Lucy smiled into his eyes. 'Ye're just the right age for a dad.'

'Ye're not the only one what's proud of her,' Aggie said,

comfortable in the chair she'd claimed off Irene as soon as she'd walked in. 'We're all proud of her.'

'She's had quite an exciting day all round,' Irene said, her bonny face creased in a smile. 'Got her first job, and her first marriage proposal.'

George's deep chuckle ricocheted off the four walls. 'Don't jump out of yer seat, Bob, she turned it down.'

'She won't be getting offered it again, Mr Mellor,' Greg said. 'She didn't only turn me down, she insulted me into the bargain.'

'Try again in about four years, Greg,' Bob told him. 'I'm not parting with her until I have to. And then it'll be under protest.'

Lucy was smiling while this was going on, but her mind was active in another direction. Would she be doing right in telling them about Wally Brown? Or would it cause trouble? Her father was looking so happy she really didn't want to spoil it. But she knew he'd been asked if he knew the name of the man her mother was going with, and told that it would help. So surely it would be wrong not to tell him.

'Dad, would it upset yer if I talked about me mam?'

'Of course it wouldn't, pet. Why, what's she been doing to yer?'

'Well, didn't yer want to know the name of the man she was seeing?'

The room was so silent you could have heard a pin drop. 'What made yer suddenly ask that, Lucy?'

''Cos I know it.'

Five people leaned forward as their eyes widened in surprise. This was definitely not something they expected, and they waited with bated breath.

'How d'yer know it, pet?' Bob asked.

Lucy took a deep breath, hoping she was doing the right thing. 'He was in our house before, and when I asked him who he was he said his name was Wally Brown.' When her father took his arm from around her shoulders and went to stand up, she held him back. 'He's not there now, Dad. He'd gone by the time I came downstairs.'

'Well I never!' Aggie said. 'The bleedin' cheek of him!'

'The cheek of her, yer mean.' Irene ground the words out. 'She must have invited him in. My God, but she's got some nerve.'

'Tell us exactly what happened, love,' Bob asked her quietly. 'I want to know everything he said and what he looked like.'

'He was dressed all right, but he's not nearly as nice-looking as you are, Dad.' Lucy then began at the beginning and repeated everything that had been said. 'And as I told yer, he'd gone when I came downstairs.'

Aggie was rubbing her hands with glee. 'Did yer really tell him he had no right to be there, sweetheart?'

Lucy nodded. 'Well, he didn't, did he, Mrs Aggie? It's me dad's house and me mam can't be asking strange men into it.'

'I'm proud of yer, sunshine,' Irene said. 'I would have loved to have seen your mother's face when you walked in.'

'She would have belted me one if she'd got the chance, I could tell by her face. But she's frightened of upsetting this Wally Brown. He told her to watch her language and she never said a wrong word after that. He's the boss and what he says goes. But he's not nice, Dad. He's one of these smooth-talking fellers, all sweet and honey on the outside. But I wouldn't trust him as far as I could throw him.'

'Then don't have anything to do with him, pet. If he comes again, get out of the house as fast as yer can.' Bob was worried. There were some evil men in the world and he didn't want one of them near his daughter. And this bloke was no saint, he'd been going out with a married woman for God knows how long. 'I'll take yer home later, in case yer mam's got anything to say. But don't worry, I won't start a row. I'm too disgusted to look her in the face, never mind talk to her.'

'Steve usually comes down to take me home, Dad. He'll be here soon.'

'I'll take yer, just for tonight, pet. Then I'll sleep easy in me bed.'

'How come you and Kate come to work together these days, Bob?' Elsie pushed the turban out of her eyes. 'Yer live miles away from each other.'

'We used to, but we don't now.' Bob and Kate had been expecting this and were prepared. 'I've moved in with her family.'

'Go 'way!' Elsie's sandwich was put back in the box. 'Did yer hear that, Peg?'

'I'm all ears, girl. Go on, you're the nosy one, find out what's going on.'

'Oh I will, queen.' Elsie's bosom was hitched and her nose scratched. 'D'yer mean, like, that yer've moved in?'

'That's what I said, Elsie. I'm part of Kate's family now.' Bob didn't care any more that people knew about his marriage break-up. That's why he and Kate had decided to walk to work together instead of splitting up when they got near the factory. It was bound to come out sometime, they couldn't keep it a secret for ever. 'And very comfortable I am, too.'

Never one to mince words, Elsie asked, 'Yer mean ye're living over the brush?'

'What does that mean, Elsie?'

689

Billy Gleeson didn't know whether this was a legpull or not. It was something he would expect of Elsie, but Bob wasn't one for telling jokes. And he couldn't read anything from Kate's face; she was half-smiling and didn't seem to be uncomfortable with the way the conversation was going. But, nah, she wasn't the type to live tally with a feller. So he waited for Elsie's answer.

Elsie and Peg had their heads together, whispering. 'He doesn't know what living over the brush means, queen, so how else can I put it?'

'Yer'll think of something. Go on, girl, ye're doing fine.'

Elsie racked her brains but couldn't think of any other way to put it. 'Are the pair of yer living in sin?'

'Good heavens, no!' Bob was quite enjoying the exchange. 'How can yer think such a thing? I'm surprised at yer being so bad-minded, Elsie.'

'It was you what said yer'd moved in with Kate's family.' Elsie was getting flustered. 'So don't you be saying I'm bad-minded.'

Peg tapped her on the arm. 'Move over, girl, and let an expert have a go.' She looked across at Bob. 'Are yer living at Kate's, then, Bob?'

'No, Peg, I'm living with her mother. She was kind enough to offer me lodgings when I left home.'

Elsie nearly fell off the chair. 'Ooh, er! Yer've walked out on yer wife, have yer?'

Billy scratched his head. If this was a joke, it was a bloody long one.

'Yes, I walked out on me wife when I discovered she was having an affair with another bloke. I've put up with a lot from her, but that was the last straw.'

'I hope yer gave her a good hiding before yer left, Bob,' Peg said. 'I can't stand women who cheat on their husbands.'

'Yer wouldn't say that if yer got the chance to have a bit on the side with Robert Young, would yer, queen? I remember yer telling me once that if yer were in bed with Robert Young yer wouldn't be lying there counting the cracks in the ceiling.'

Peg chuckled. 'I was just thinking the same thing, girl. Bob's as handsome as Robert Young any day. And he's more available.'

When Elsie jerked her head in one direction, her chins went the other way. 'I've always said yer were man mad, queen, and yer'll get yerself into trouble one of these days.'

Kate spoke for the first time. 'She won't be getting into trouble over Bob, Elsie, 'cos he's spoken for. I saw him first.' Because she was laughing, nobody took her seriously. Quiet Kate, who'd run a mile if a man looked sideways at her.

'Yer wife wants her bumps feeling,' Peg said. 'There's not many

690

fellers as good-looking or as nice as you. But perhaps he's loaded and it's his money she's after.'

'I couldn't tell yer, Peg. He could be a tramp or a millionaire for all I know. He does exist, me wife admitted to sleeping with him, but that's all I know. Oh, and his name's Wally Brown.'

Elsie's elbow slipped and her chin came crashing down on the table, but she was too excited to feel any pain. Pushing herself up and straightening her turban, she squeaked, 'Did yer say his name's Wally Brown?'

Peg put a hand on her arm to silence her. 'What's yer wife like to look at, Bob? Is she fair, dark, redheaded, blonde or what?'

'Nature intended her to be dark, but she's a bottle blonde.'

'Her name wouldn't happen to be Ruby, would it?'

Bob looked puzzled. 'Yeah. How did yer know that?'

'Me and Elsie go out every Saturday night with our fellers. We don't go to the same pub every week 'cos we like a change. But our local is Wally Brown's local, and he's there every Saturday with a blonde called Ruby. Unless it's a million to one coincidence, his Ruby and your Ruby are one and the same person. And I'll tell yer what, Bob, ye're well out of that marriage. Wally Brown's never married, but he didn't need to – he gets all the fun he wants and none of the worry. He's been with more women than you've had hot dinners.'

Bob nodded. 'So yer've seen them together?'

Peg turned to her mate. 'Am I telling the truth, girl?'

'Yes, queen. Thick as thieves they are. Can't keep their hands off each other. And from what I've heard, he doesn't need no cracks in his ceiling.'

'I don't suppose yer happen to know where he lives, do yer? Yer see, I've put in for a divorce on the grounds of my wife's adultery, and his name will be down on the application as co-respondent. It would help if I had his address.'

'I'll have it for yer tomorrow, Bob, without fail. I'm not quite sure of the number of his house and it's no good guessing. I even know his flippin' neighbour! I see her at the shops a couple of times a week and we always have a good natter. She'd tell yer some tales about the queer feller and the women he's had at the house since his mother died.' Peg turned to her mate with some impatience. 'What the hell are yer digging me for? I'll be black and blue tomorrow.'

'What is Wally going down on the application as, queen?'

'Yer mean yer've cracked six of me ribs to ask me that! If yer hadn't sagged off school so often, yer wouldn't need to keep asking me questions. The word is co-respondent.'

'What does that mean, queen?'

691

Peg sighed. 'It means he's the one what's been having it off with Bob's wife.'

'Why can't they just say that, instead of using big words what no one can understand? I'll have forgotten that by the time I get home.'

Bob smiled across at Kate. They'd been apprehensive about telling their workmates, but it was out in the open now and he felt relieved. And some good had come from it. Tomorrow he'd have the address for Howard.

Lucy and Rhoda were linking arms and laughing as they turned into their street. They'd been working for two months now and loved it. They didn't sit near each other at work, so they always had plenty to talk about on the way home. 'That Vera must get a lot of pocket money to spend on herself,' Rhoda said. 'She reeks of Evening in Paris and has a different coloured nail varnish on every day. Yesterday it was pink, today it was bright red. And she always wears lipstick to match.'

'She's older than us, so she's bound to earn more.' Lucy squeezed her friend's arm. 'Our day will come, kiddo, have patience.'

They came to a halt when Andrew Bentley stepped from his house and barred their path. 'Hello, Lucy. How's the job going?'

'Fine, thank you, Andrew.' The girls moved sideways to walk around him but he moved with them. 'Can we get past, please?'

'I was going to ask if yer'd come to first-house pictures with me one night?'

Lucy shook her head. 'I always go out with Rhoda, but thanks for asking.'

'Surely yer can go without her one night? You're not joined together at the hip or anything.'

'I said no, Andrew, and I meant it. I don't want to go to the pictures with yer.' Lucy tugged on Rhoda's arm and they stepped into the gutter. They'd only gone a few steps when the boy's voice brought them to an abrupt halt.

'I don't know where you get your airs and graces from. You've got nothing to be stuck up about. Your father's left home and your mother is no better than a common prostitute.'

Lucy closed her eyes and froze. But Rhoda moved like a bullet from a gun. She jumped back on the pavement and laid into Andrew with her fists. 'Don't yer dare talk to my mate like that, you stuck-up, snotty-nosed little pig.'

Steve had turned the corner of the street a minute after the girls and he'd seen Andrew stop them. They seemed to be chatting and he thought nothing of it, until he heard Rhoda shouting as she attacked the boy with both fists flying. Then Steve took to his heels and covered the ground between them in no time. Andrew was bent down and had his arms across his face for protection against the blows that were raining down on him.

'Stop it, Rhoda.' Steve put his arms around her waist and pulled her away. 'What's all this in aid of?'

Andrew straightened up and growled, 'She's mad! Crazy! If she wasn't a girl I'd knock the stuffing out of her.'

'Yer haven't got the guts,' Rhoda said, struggling to get free. Her face red with anger, she twisted her head around. 'Let me go! I'll kill him for what he said to Lucy. No one talks to my friend like that and gets away with it.'

Steve then noticed that Lucy was standing with her back to them, as still as a statue. 'What did yer say to Lucy, Andrew?'

'Nothing! Take no notice of her, she's crazy.' Andrew didn't fancy getting on the wrong side of Steve, he was a big bloke. 'She's can't take a joke, that's her trouble.'

'Shall I tell yer his idea of a joke, Steve?' Rhoda said, nearly in tears. 'Because Lucy said she didn't want to go to the pictures with him, he asked her where she got her airs and graces from. She had nothing to be stuck up about because her dad had left home and her mother was a common prostitute.'

Steve stared so hard at Andrew that the boy lowered his head. 'I'll see you later, and what yer said to Lucy yer can repeat to me.'

'You come near me and I'll tell my mother.'

'You won't need to. I intend to have yer mother present when yer repeat what yer said to Lucy. Your mam might be a snob, Andrew, but she's not wicked.' Steve carried Rhoda to where Lucy stood and lowered her to the ground. 'Come on, girls, he's not worth bothering about.' Then he noticed Lucy's silent tears. 'Come on, love, don't let him see he's got to yer.' He gave Rhoda a nod and they placed themselves either side of the girl who was trying hard to stem the tears. And they walked her to Irene's, where they knew there would be two loving arms waiting to hold her.

'I think he should be pulled up over it,' Irene said. 'And his mother should be told. Otherwise, who's to stop him from shouting his mouth off to everyone?'

'I'll have a word with his mother, if yer like, love,' George said. 'The boy needs a ticking off, no doubt about it. They weren't the sort of things yer'd expect to hear from the lips of one so young.'

'I told Andrew I would be calling to see his mam.' Steve was sat on the floor next to the chair Aggie was sitting on. When Lucy hadn't knocked as usual on her way home from work, the old lady had come down to see if there was anything wrong. And she was hopping mad when she heard what had transpired.

'I'd like to take him over me knee and smack his backside so hard he wouldn't be able to sit down for a week.' Aggie looked at Lucy's red, tear-stained face and thought the boy deserved to be hurt as much as he'd hurt her young friend. Still, she didn't agree with what she'd heard. 'But, much as I'd like to give him a hiding, I think it would be far better to just let the matter drop. The whole street would know about it in no time, and yer'd only be filling their mouths. Someone would be bound to mention it to Bob, thinking he'd know, and he'd be very hurt and upset.'

'Mrs Aggie's right. I wouldn't want me dad to know.' Lucy sniffed up. 'Anyway, I should have given him a go-along meself, instead of standing there crying like a baby. I shouldn't have left it to Rhoda to stick up for me. The trouble is, I've been too soft. All me life I've been too soft. But not any more. I'm going to start sticking up for meself – be hard instead of soft. Then the likes of Andrew Bentley, and me mam, won't be able to hurt me.'

Jack and Greg had listened in silence, each thinking that if they ever met Andrew in an entry, he'd come out with two black eyes for the unhappiness he'd brought to the girl who was like a sister to them.

'Oh, don't say that, sunshine!' Irene said. 'We all love yer and don't want yer to change. We wouldn't want the kind, sweet Lucy we know to become hard and bitter.'

'No, we wouldn't.' Jack dared to speak out. 'You just stay as sweet as yer are, Lucy Mellor, or me and our Greg won't play cards with yer no more.'

'There yer have it, sweetheart,' Aggie said. 'Yer've been out-voted.'

'Yer can't change now, love,' George said. 'Not even yer hair-style.'

'Lucy will never change,' Steve said. 'It isn't in her nature.'

Looking around at the faces who were so dear to her, Lucy asked herself why she should let a little twerp like Andrew Bentley upset her. She had more than he would ever have.

Steve knocked on the Flemings' door on his way home. And when Jessie answered, he looked shy. 'I'm sorry to knock so late, Mrs Fleming. I hope yer don't mind?'

'Not at all, lad, it's only just turned ten.'

'D'yer think I could have a word with Rhoda? That's if she's in.'

'Oh, she's in all right. And calmed down a bit. She was in a right state when she got home, crying and calling that lad from the top of the street fit to burn. Mind you, he was way out of order, saying what he did.'

'Your daughter sorted him out, Mrs Fleming. I think he'll have a few bruises to show for it tomorrow.'

'D'yer want to come in, lad?'

'No, I won't if yer don't mind. Yer see, me mam's on her own.'

'Okay, I'll get her for yer.'

Rhoda looked surprised but pleased. 'If I'd known yer were coming I'd have combed me hair and put some lipstick on. Just my luck to be caught on the hop.'

'I just want to say I think yer were great for sticking up for Lucy the way yer did. Ye're a good friend to her, Rhoda, and I'm glad yer were there when she needed yer.'

'I'll always be there when she needs me, Steve. We've been mates for twelve years now, and we'll carry on being mates all our lives. I know I'm outspoken, even rude at times, but not where Lucy's concerned. I love her to bits.'

'You proved that tonight. She'll tell yer tomorrow how proud she was of yer. And I was proud of yer, too. Anyway, I just wanted to thank yer. I'll be on me way now 'cos me mam will be wondering where I've got to.'

As he turned away, Rhoda stepped down on the pavement and caught his arm. 'I've been wanting to bring this up for years now, but never had the nerve. Remember the time I said I didn't want yer to help me and Lucy because yer were dirty? Well, that wasn't the case at all. I was jealous because it was her yer offered to help and not me. Childish, wasn't it? I've had many a nightmare over it, I can tell yer. But I've got it off me chest now and can face yer with a clear conscience.' She turned and walked back into the house. 'Goodnight, Steve.'

'Goodnight, Rhoda, and thanks again.'

Chapter Twenty-Six

Aggie came in from the yard with a shovelful of coal and was about to carry it through to the living room when she sensed a movement in the hall. 'Oh, my God, someone's broken in.' She put the shovel down on the tiled floor and quickly glanced around for something to use as a weapon. Her eyes lit on the flat iron on the stove and she made a grab for it. 'No one's going to rob from this house if I've got anything to do with it. I'll kill the bugger.'

With the iron held high, she marched into the living room to face Titch coming through the door leading from the hall. 'In the name of God, son, yer frightened the life out of me. I thought yer were a burglar.' She sighed with relief as she placed the iron on the table before giving him a hug and kiss. 'Why didn't yet let me know yer were coming home?'

''Cos I didn't know meself until half an hour before I left the ship. We're only in port for two days, just long enough to unload and load up again. I asked the skipper if I could have the two days off to make all the arrangements for the wedding and he told me to scarper but be back before the ship sails.' Titch pulled a chair out and sat down. 'The banns have to be called for three weeks, so there wouldn't be time if it's left until I come home again.' His grin was that of a young boy. 'This wedding lark isn't as easy as yer think, is it, Ma?'

'It'll all work out, sweetheart, so don't be worrying. It's not going to be a big wedding, not with Olive having been married before, so once yer've seen the priest about having the banns called, there's nothing else for you to do except get yerself a new suit.'

'There's the flowers to think of, and we'll have to have some sort of reception afterwards. I'm not getting hitched without having a bit of a do for me friends.'

'Me and Olive will sort everything out while you're sailing the high seas. When yer get home everything will be organised. Women are much better at this than men. We can have things done while the bleedin' men are still scratching their heads and thinking about it.'

'I've just called into Olive's, and when I said we were going to see the priest tomorrow I could see her nerves go. But when she realised her son would be walking her down the aisle, she was soon happy and smiling. And Steve looked so proud, his face was a joy to behold.'

'Ah, God bless them,' Aggie said, trying not to let him see she was filling up. 'I'm going to have to take half a dozen hankies to this wedding of yours.'

'I've got a problem over me best man, though, Ma. Me two mates are Bob and George. How to ask one without hurting the other?'

Aggie frowned as she pinched on her bottom lip. Then her face lit up. 'I've got it! Yer could put it to them that yer've been agonising over it, not wanting to upset either of them. But with Lucy being a bridesmaid, yer thought it only fair the Pollards should be represented, and you'd be honoured if George would be yer best man. Bob certainly won't get upset 'cos he's so delighted over Lucy. It'll be a big day in the girl's life.

'Sounds good to me, Ma. That way I don't upset anyone.'

'If yer want to go away with an easy mind, son, why don't yer get it sorted out right away? Bob's in the Pollards' now, so go and get it over and done with.'

'I'll do that, Ma.' Titch left his seat to cup her face in his two hands. 'Yer could make all the arrangements for this wedding standing on yer head, couldn't yer, Agnes McBride?'

'I'll certainly see it all goes off without a hitch, son.' Aggie smiled, and her eyes were full of the love she felt for him. 'It'll be the third happiest day of me life. The first was when I married your dad, the man I adored heart, body and soul. The second was the day you were born. I loved yer from the minute yer were put into my arms, and I've loved yer ever since. Now my life is going to be enriched with a new daughter-in-law and a grandson. There's nothing more I could ask for.'

'Hey, Ma! Yer'd better bring an extra six hankies to the wedding, I think I'm going to need them. I can see me standing at the altar blubbering like a baby.'

'You do, and I'll have yer life! Yer wedding day is one yer'll look back on in later years with fond memories. And one of those memories won't be of you standing there blowing yer nose all through the ceremony.'

'I'd be the talk of the washhouse, would I, Ma?'

'What! The washhouse, the poorhouse and every bleedin' alehouse from here to the Pier Head. Yer'd never be able to show yer face in the street again. And me – well, I'd be that ashamed I'd have to move house.'

Titch chuckled. He'd been a nervous wreck for weeks, thinking

698

of all the things he had to do in a few days. But now he'd calmed down, thanks to his mother. Nothing would go wrong on his wedding day, she'd make sure of that. 'I'd better go and see Bob and the Pollards. That'll be one worry off me mind.'

'Yer'd better put a move on then, son, because Bob sometimes goes for a pint with George.'

Titch was whistling a sea shanty when Irene answered his loud rat-tat on the door. 'Well, I'll be blowed! Aggie never mentioned yer were coming home.'

'She didn't know.' A couple passing on the opposite side of the street turned when Titch let out a roar of laughter. 'She thought there was a burglar in the house and nearly crowned me with the flat iron.'

'Come on in and tell us what we owe this pleasure to.' In the hall, Irene lifted her cheek and said in a loud voice, 'Kiss me out here, so my feller doesn't go all jealous and get a cob on. Yer know what he's like.'

'As long as it's a secret and me intended doesn't find out.'

'I won't tell Olive if you don't tell George.'

'Get in here, woman!' George yelled. 'If there's any kissing to be done, I want to see it's all above board.'

Lucy flung herself at Titch as soon as he entered the room. 'This is a nice surprise, it's lovely to see yer.' She moved back to grin up at him. 'It won't be long now, will it, Mr Titch?'

'No, sweetheart, only about seven weeks.' He smiled a greeting at the eager faces who were waiting for his news. 'The ship's only in port for two days, it's a quick turnaround, and the skipper said I could have the time off to start making arrangements for the wedding. So me and Olive are going to see the priest tomorrow about having the banns read.'

'Ooh, it's all happening now, isn't it?' Irene beamed. 'Is it still at St Anthony's on Scotland Road?'

Titch nodded. 'That's what Olive wants. And Steve is going to give her away.'

'That's just how it should be,' George said. 'I bet the lad's over the moon.'

'I'd say that was the understatement of the year, George. I think he's got seven weeks of sleepless nights in front of him.' Titch told himself to make a start and get it over with. 'I was thinking about me best man, and with you and Bob both being me mates, I didn't know what to do. But I figured that if Lucy was to be bridesmaid, it would be fair to ask George to do me the honour of being me best man.'

'Of course it would!' Bob said. 'And a fine handsome best man he'll be too.'

Titch put a hand to his mouth and gave a slight cough. 'He hasn't said he would be, yet, Bob. But I can see he's thinking about it.'

George was a big man, but right now he looked twice his size. And the smile on his face was so bright it would have lit up a dark room. 'Yer didn't think for a second I'd refuse, did yer? I'll be highly delighted, and honoured. It's not often I get the chance to show off in me best bib and tucker.'

'Will I be getting a new shirt?' Greg asked, looking pleadingly at his mother.

Irene tutted. 'Yer'd get anyone hanged, you would! Yer haven't been invited to the wedding and it's manners to wait until ye're asked.'

'Ye're all invited, every one of yer,' Titch said. 'As though I'd get married without all of me friends around me.'

Jack was beginning to feel a stir of excitement. He'd never been to a wedding. 'Does that include me, Mr Titch?'

'Most definitely!' Then Titch remembered what Steve had told him about the Andrew Bentley incident, and how Rhoda had rushed to her friend's defence. 'And Lucy can ask her mate if she'd like to come.'

'Oh, I've no need to ask her, Mr Titch, she's always going on about how lucky I am. I'll go over after and ask her.'

'I'm very happy for yer, Titch,' Bob said. 'Yer couldn't have chosen a better women for yer wife than Olive. She's a lovely lady.'

'I know how lucky I am, Bob.' Bearing in mind Bob's unhappy circumstances, Titch left it at that. 'Anyway, I'm off now. Me and Olive have got a lot of planning to do. We've got a busy day ahead of us tomorrow, then it's back to the ship for me the morning after. I'll let yer know the date and time before I go back, though, because of yer jobs.'

'We'll all fit in with your arrangements, mate,' George said. 'If necessary we'll take the day off. What do you say, Bob?'

'I'd have no problem with that. I can't remember the last time I took a day off, so the boss could hardly complain.'

'What about me and our Greg, Mam?' Jack asked. 'Would we be able to stay off?'

'We've got seven weeks, yet.' Irene kept her face straight. 'That's plenty of time to think of what illness yer can have that'll keep yer off work for a day. Perhaps you can have the measles and Greg the chickenpox.'

'Ah, ay, Mam!' Greg looked disgusted. 'Only little kids have the chickenpox!'

'So they do.' Irene was laughing inside at the expression on his face. 'It'll have to be something a grown up gets, then. I know, you

700

can have a sore throat and Jack can have an upset tummy.'

'Neither of those are as bad as a broken neck,' Titch said. 'And that's what I'll be getting off Olive if I don't put in an appearance pronto.'

'I'll see yer out, mate.' George pushed himself out of the chair. 'Then me and Bob are going for a pint.'

Titch winked at Irene before asking, 'Ay, George, when we're married, d'yer think Olive will let me off the leash now and again to go for a pint with yer?'

'If yer train her properly from the very start.' George nudged his friend towards the door. 'Like I did, with my missus.'

The cushion Irene threw fell well short of the mark. 'Never mind, I'll get him later,' she told Bob. 'He's not getting away with that.'

'Me mam said she'd buy me a new dress.' Rhoda didn't have her mind on the game and she'd already thrown the four of diamonds away before she realised she'd played right into Greg's hands. She watched him snaffle up the card with the look of a victor on his face and shrugged her shoulders. 'If you win this game, Greg Pollard, it won't be because ye're clever, but because I let yer.'

'Because yer talk too much, yer mean?' Greg laid three fours down with great aplomb. 'You and yer flippin' new dress, it's all yer can think about.'

'Oh, aye?' Irene raised her brows. 'So ye're not really interested in the new shirt and tie ye're after? Yer were full of it before.'

'Of course I want a new shirt and tie, but I'm not talking about it all the time.' Greg wasn't going to give them the satisfaction of knowing that in his mind he could see himself dressed to the nines in his navy-blue trousers, a new white shirt and a pale blue tie. 'It's nearly ten o'clock and we're still on the second game. All because the girls won't give their mouths a rest.'

'I'd rather talk about the clothes we're wearing for the wedding,' Lucy said. 'I mean, I've got to look nice, being a bridesmaid.'

'And I'm an invited guest,' Rhoda said, with more than a little pride in her voice. 'So I've got to look nice, as well.'

'I'm sure yer'll both look lovely.' Irene too had been wondering what colour dress to buy for herself. Something in blue, perhaps, or a deep lilac? 'And I'll make sure my two don't let the side down. They'll look like film stars.'

Greg grinned. 'Yeah! I'll be George Raft. He's always dressed to kill.'

'He's a gangster, yer daft nit,' Jack said. 'He doesn't only dress to kill, he carries a flippin' gun around with him.'

701

'What about you, Steve?' Lucy asked. 'Ye're very quiet, and you've got to look nicer than anyone 'cos yer'll be walking down the aisle with yer mam.' She giggled. 'I don't mean yer've got to look nicer than the bride, though. I bet yer mam will look lovely.'

'I won't let me mam down, don't worry.' Steve's grin hid the excitement he felt inside. Titch had brought a suit home for him and he was thrilled to bits. It was in a dark navy and fitted him to perfection. He was as tall as Titch, but not as stocky, so it was easy for his future step-dad to get the fit right. He said the words over again in his mind, relishing them. 'My step-dad.' Never had he known such happiness. 'Yer'll see me in all me finery on the day.'

'I bet yer'll look dead handsome,' Rhoda said, glaring knowingly at Greg. 'More like Randolph Scott than George Raft.'

'Who shall I be?' Jack scratched his head. 'Who's more handsome than those two?'

Lucy didn't hesitate. 'Robert Young. He's me favourite.'

Irene heard the key in the lock. 'Here's the men. Get the cards back in the packs and take the cups and saucers out. It's time yer were going home, Rhoda, or yer mam will start to worry.'

'Okay, Mrs Pollard, and thanks for having me.'

Bob came in rubbing his hands. 'Have yer won a fortune, pet?'

George chuckled. 'She's in the wrong house for that.'

'We've hardly played cards, Dad, we've been talking about clothes for the wedding. At least me and Rhoda have, the boys couldn't care less.'

'Well, let's get yer home now. Nellie waits up for me and I don't want to be too late.' Bob noticed Rhoda making her way to the door. 'Hang on, love, I'll see yer home once Lucy is safe in the house.'

'That's all right, Mr Mellor,' Steve said. 'I've got to pass her house on me way home. I'll hang on until she's inside.'

Lucy tossed and turned in bed, her mind too active for sleep. She was telling herself to put everything out of her head and count sheep, when she heard the front door open. Her mother was home. Then she heard a man speaking in hushed tones and she shot up in bed. It was Wally Brown, she could recognise the smooth, silky voice even though he was whispering. What was he doing here this time of night? It was nearly eleven o'clock. Then the voice faded and Lucy fell back against the headboard. They must be in the living room, but why would her mother bring him here so late at night? She had no right to, and her dad would go mad if he knew.

It was impossible to sleep now, with that man in the house. So Lucy drew her knees up to her chin and pulled the bedclothes

702

around her. She'd stay awake until he'd gone. And she'd have something to say to her mother in the morning. The alarm clock on the chest of drawers ticked away, the only sound in the house. Until Lucy heard whispering at the bottom of the stairs. Alert now, she could make out her mother's voice. 'Don't go up, she'll scream the house down if she sees yer.'

'I'm only going up to see if she's asleep.' Wally's low voice carried up the stairs to the now terrified girl. 'She won't even know I'm there.'

Lucy knocked on the bedroom wall. And when she heard the footsteps reach the landing, she knocked again, harder.

Greg shook his brother's shoulder. 'Jack, Lucy's just knocked.'

Jack was wiping the sleep from his eyes when the knocking was repeated. The two boys scrambled out of bed and rushed down the stairs. 'Mam, Lucy's been knocking. There must be something up for her to do that.'

Irene and George were enjoying a cup of tea before going to bed, and they both looked startled at the sight of the boys. 'What did yer say, sunshine?' Irene asked.

'Lucy's been knocking.' Jack was impatient at their slowness to understand. 'There must be something wrong. Twice she's knocked.'

By the time he'd finished speaking, Irene had taken the key for next door from the glass dish on the sideboard and George was on his way out of the front door. The boys followed quickly on their heels.

Ruby was standing at the foot of the stairs when her front door was opened, and she looked bewildered when she was pushed aside by George, who took the stairs three at a time.

'What the hell d'yer think ye're doing?' Ruby was very worried now. 'Get out of my house.'

Irene passed her without a word. And she reached the bedroom just as her husband grabbed the man who was standing at the side of Lucy's bed. 'You dirty swine,' George roared. 'I'll flay yer alive for this.'

'Who the hell are you?' Wally blustered, knowing he didn't stand an earthly with the size of this bloke. He could only try and talk himself out of it. 'I only came up to see if Lucy was all right.' He saw Ruby hovering near the doorway. 'Tell this maniac to take his hands off me, will yer?'

Ruby came into the room, but made sure she kept out of Irene's reach. 'He's a friend of mine and you have no right to be in here.'

George, still holding Wally by the throat, asked, 'Oh, so yer allow men to come into yer daughter's room, do yer?'

703

Ruby lowered her head, lost for words. So it was up to Wally to bluff his way out of it. 'It's all a misunderstanding. Let's go downstairs and I'll explain.'

Irene looked at Lucy, who was backed against the headboard, her eyes wide with fright. 'Lucy, did you want this man to come into your bedroom?'

'No! I don't like him, he's horrid!'

'Then this is a police matter,' Irene said. 'You,' she gave Ruby a push which sent her flying against the wall, 'are not fit to be a mother. You allow a dirty old man to come into your daughter's bedroom, and the police wouldn't take kindly to either of yer. Yer'd both be locked up. I'll make sure neither of yer are allowed near Lucy again.'

'Oh, come on!' The thought of involving the police scared the life out of Wally. 'I didn't mean no harm. Yer've taken it the wrong way. Leave go of me and let me go home.'

'Ye're not moving from this spot until the police come.' George tightened his grip. 'But before I send me son to the police station, just tell me why yer came into this room?'

'I told yer! Just to make sure she was in bed and asleep!'

'Rubbish!' Irene said. A plan had formed in her mind and she prayed to God she could pull it off. 'There's only one way yer can crawl out of this, without us calling the police. And that's if yer walk away from here now, and take Ruby with yer. Not just for tonight, but for good. If either of yer show yer face around here again, I'll make sure yer go to jail. That's if the neighbours don't lynch yer first. It's up to you, so make up yer mind.'

'Yer can't do that to me,' Ruby cried. 'This is my home.'

'Wrong,' said George. 'It's Bob's house, he only lets yer live in it. We already know this evil bastard has his own house, and when yer visit him yer behave like a married couple, so I suggest yer go and live with him.'

Wally couldn't think any further than getting away from the huge hands around his throat. 'Go on, Ruby, put yer coat on and let's get out of here.'

'Not so fast!' Irene said. 'Ruby won't be allowed back for any of her belongings, so she'll be a while packing. George will sit with you downstairs and I'll stay here until she's got everything together. This is the last time either of yer set foot in this house. That's if yer've got any sense.'

The boys moved into the front bedroom out of the way of their father, who was literally carrying a struggling Wally down the stairs. No way was he going to be allowed to scarper without taking Ruby with him.

'Come in here and sit with Lucy, boys,' Irene called. 'So I can

704

keep me eye on what's going on.'

'Mrs Pollard.' Lucy grabbed her arm to stop her from moving away. 'Does this mean me mam won't ever be coming back?'

Irene sat on the side of the bed and held her close. 'That all depends, sunshine. I've taken a lot on meself by telling her to leave because, after all, I'm only a neighbour and shouldn't really be interfering. If this situation hadn't come up, Ruby would have been within her rights to tell me to mind me own business. But that man was wicked to come into yer bedroom, and yer mam was as bad for not stopping him. I wouldn't trust her after that, and there was no way I was going to let her stay in this house tonight with you. Your dad will be very upset and angry when he knows, and I know he'll agree with me and George about throwing them out. But it depends upon how you feel, sunshine. She is your mother, after all. So think about it carefully, and be sure in yer mind. Would yer be very unhappy if yer thought yer were never going to set eyes on her again?'

Lucy plucked nervously at the bedclothes. 'I'll probably spend the rest of me life being unhappy because me mother never ever loved me, Mrs Pollard. And I'll always wonder why. But she's hurt me so much, and me dad, and I know she'll never change. Yer can't make someone love yer if they don't want to. So I'd rather she left so me dad can come back home again.'

'Are yer sure, sunshine?'

Lucy nodded as she wiped the tears away with the back of her hand. 'I'm sure, honest I am. I want me dad back 'cos I love him and he loves me. We'll be happy together, just the two of us. Me mam spoiled things for us, always skitting, telling lies and cheating. And there was never any comfort or laughter in the house.'

Irene put a finger under the girl's chin and lifted her face. 'In that case, I think yer dad's in for a very pleasant surprise tomorrow. We'll talk about it later, when yer mam and her friend have left. And there's nothing for yer to worry about because I'm certain neither of them will have the nerve to show their faces in this street again, not after me and George have given them a good talking to. And I'll be sleeping with yer tonight in case ye're a bit nervous. We'll cuddle up and keep each other company.' She beckoned to her sons who were hovering near the door. 'Yer can come and sit with Lucy for a while, now. I know ye're missing yer beauty sleep, but it'll soon be all over.'

'We don't mind that,' Jack said. 'As long as Lucy's all right.'

'I'm fine, now.' Lucy pulled the sheet up to her chin. 'I've got to admit I was terrified when I heard that man walking up the stairs, though. I knew he was coming 'cos I heard him and me mam talking in the hall. She told him not to come, but when he took no notice of her she didn't even try and stop him. And she should have stopped him. Even if she doesn't love me, she should have stopped him. But it's over now, and I do feel a bit better knowing me dad will soon be back home.'

'Yeah, in a couple of days when you and yer dad are settled down, yer'll be fine,' Jack said. 'And we can come in your house for a game of cards, for a change.'

'And don't forget we've got the wedding to look forward to.' Greg wanted to see the smile back on Lucy's face. 'Yer'll have yer dad here to make sure ye're the prettiest bridesmaid this street has ever seen. And he'll be so proud of yer.'

Before the smile came to Lucy's face, she allowed time to finish what she was thinking. That one day, when she was a bit older, she'd go and see her mother. Just to ask why she couldn't find it in her heart to love her husband and her daughter.

Ruby struggled to keep up with Wally while carrying three big, heavy bags. He was walking with his hands in his pockets, his anger showing in every step he took. Not once did he offer to help by taking one or two of the bags from her. 'What a bloody performance,' he growled. 'For two pins, that big feller would have marched us off to the police station and we'd have been in big trouble.' Not for a second would he allow himself to admit to being in the wrong. He'd only gone up to Lucy's room to take a peek at her. To stroke her long hair, or her pretty face, perhaps. He only wanted to touch her, not hurt her.

'I did tell yer not to go upstairs.' Ruby daren't raise her voice or say that everything that had happened was his own fault. 'I told yer what she's like.'

'Oh, shut up, woman!' Wally needed a scapegoat, someone to vent his anger on. Gone now were the words of flattery as he looked sideways at her. 'If ye're coming to live with me, there's going to be some big changes. D'yer understand?'

'Yes, Wally.'

'For a kick-off, yer get yerself a full-time job to pay yer way. I'll get rid of the cleaner and you can do the housework – that'll save me a few bob.' Wally was beginning to think he might be on to a good thing here. More money coming into the house and his own personal servant who would cater to his every whim. And she'd put up with it because she was crazy about him. He'd be waited on hand and foot, and she'd be there for the taking, any time he felt like it. 'And another thing – that blonde hair looks ridiculous, let it grow out.'

'But it'll look terrible while it's growing out! It'll take ages!'

'Ask the hairdresser if she can dye it back to its original colour.

I don't care what yer do, but get rid of the blonde, it makes yer look like a tart.'

'All right, Wally, I'll have a word with the hairdresser. And I can go full-time where I work, they've asked me to a few times. Anything you say is all right with me, yer know that. I only want to make yer happy.'

I speak and she jumps, Wally thought. I'd never get another woman as obliging as her. He held out a hand. 'Give us one of those bags to carry, they must be heavy.'

Nellie Carson opened her door to find herself facing a woman of about her own age, with her hair combed back into a bun, a black shawl draped around her shoulders and wearing a big grin. 'I know who you are,' she said instantly. 'Ye're Mrs Aggie.'

'And you are Mrs Nellie.'

Both women laughed and Nellie held the door wide open. 'Come in, ye're very welcome. I've been dying to meet yer 'cos I've heard so much about yer.'

'All good, I hope.' Aggie's eyes were taking in the spotlessly clean and comfortable living room. Here was a woman after her own heart.

'Well, from what Bob and Lucy have told me, yer've got the heart of a saint and are the funniest woman on two legs.'

'Only when I'm standing on me two legs, queen? I thought I was just as bleedin' funny standing on me head.'

Nellie chuckled. 'If yer wear fleecy bloomers like I do, then ye're probably a damn sight more funny standing on yer head.' She waved Aggie to a chair. 'Sit yerself down and I'll put the kettle on.' Her hand on the kitchen door, she turned. 'Did Bob know yer were coming?'

Aggie shook her head. 'There was bleedin' murder at Bob's house last night, that's why I'm here. But you put the kettle on first, then while we're waiting for it to boil I'll tell yer what went on.' She followed Nellie into the kitchen and when the gas plopped under the kettle, she leaned back against the sink. 'I wasn't there to see all this, more's the pity. But Irene repeated it word for word, so I'll give it to you as she gave it to me.'

Her arms folded across her tummy, Aggie soon got into her stride. And before long there were gasps of horror and tuts of disgust coming from Nellie. 'I'd have strangled the buggers with me bare hands.'

'Yeah, me too, Nellie. They want stringing up. But you haven't met Irene yet, or her husband, George. They're a match for anyone, believe me. And they think the world of Lucy. I believe they did right not sending for the police because it would have

707

only filled neighbours' mouths. As it is, George and Irene put the fear of god into this Wally feller, so he'll never show his face again. And Irene, God love her, had the sense to send Ruby packing with him. Lucy was very upset, she was as white as a sheet going to work this morning. It must have given her an awful fright having this man come into her bedroom. But she'll soon get over it when her dad's back home. They dote on each other.'

'Yeah, Aggie, I know. Bob will be over the moon at being able to go back to his house, but he'll be blazing about how it came about. I've got to know him really well, and I know he'll blame himself for leaving Lucy there. Still, once they're settled down they'll soon put all the trouble and heartbreak behind them.' Nellie poured boiling water into the brown teapot. 'Now we'll sit and have a nice cuppa. Are yer waiting for Bob to come home, to tell him?'

'No, I'll leave that pleasure to you. I left Irene cleaning the house so it's nice for him to come home to, and I'm buying a bit of shopping for their larder on me way back. But I will have that cuppa with yer, Nellie, 'cos me throat's parched. And yer can tell Bob we're all looking forward to seeing him later on today.'

'Would yer think it was cheeky if I came with him?' Nellie asked. 'I've heard so much about all of yer, I feel as though I know yer.'

'We'd love yer to come.' Aggie knew if Titch could hear what she was about to say, he'd shake his head and tell her not to be so nosy. 'Why don't yer bring Kate along with yer? I'd like to see if she's all Bob said she is.'

Nellie finished pouring the tea and set the pot down. There was a twinkle in her eyes when she asked. 'Yer wouldn't be matchmaking by any chance, would yer, Mrs Aggie?'

'I certainly am, Mrs Nellie. I most certainly am.'

'Good! That makes two of us! I can see you and me are going to get along like a house on fire. We're both as devious as each other.' She handed a cup to Aggie. 'I've grown very fond of Bob, and I want to keep him in the family. I know he's a married man, but me son-in-law, Howard, said there'll be no problem with a divorce. And after what happened last night, and Ruby going to live with another man – well, that should make it easier.'

Nellie sipped her tea, then rested the cup and saucer on her lap. 'The trouble is, Aggie, both our Kate and Bob are so shy, they'll never make a move. I think you and me are going to have to give them a nudge in the right direction.'

'You have my full support, Nellie. Even if I say it meself, I'm pretty good at giving nudges. So let's drink to our partnership.' Aggie had the cup to her lips when she said, 'D'yer know, I haven't

708

used a swearword since I came in?'

'Oh yes, yer have. Yer halo slipped when yer were telling me how bleedin' funny yer are standing on yer head.'

Both women laughed so much the tea spilled over on to their skirts. But they didn't care. It wasn't every day you found a friend and ally.

'Ay, I wish yer'd slow down a bit,' Rhoda said, red in the face and puffing. 'I know ye're dying to see yer dad, but there's no need to kill me in the process.'

Lucy's face was aglow. She'd told her friend what Mrs Pollard had said they would tell all the neighbours – that Ruby had left home and gone to live with another man. Nobody knew the man or where he lived. There'd be gossip for a few days then it would be forgotten. 'I can't wait to see me dad, Rhoda, so I'm going to run on. You can take yer time, then.'

'Will I see yer tonight?'

'Not tonight, Rhoda, 'cos me and me dad will have loads to talk about. I'll call for yer as usual in the morning. Ta-ra.' With a wave of her hand, Lucy took to her heels and didn't slacken her pace until she came to her front door. With her heart beating like mad, and her tummy churning with excitement, she delved in her pocket for the key. Holding it in the palm of her hand, she gazed at it for a while. Then, with a grin on her face, she put it back in her pocket and lifted the knocker.

When Bob opened the door he had to swallow hard to keep the tears back. Never, even in his dreams, did he think he'd be back in this house and opening the door to his daughter. He stepped down to the pavement and picked Lucy up to spin her around. 'I feel drunk, pet,' he said, laughing up into her face. 'Drunk with happiness.'

'I don't half love yer, Dad.' Lucy's arms were tight around his neck. 'More than anything in the whole world.'

'And I love you, pet.' Bob set her down. 'Let's go in and see what a nice surprise I've got for the working girl.'

'Have yer made me a dinner, Dad? Is that the surprise?'

Bob tapped his nose. 'Wait and see.' With a secret smile on his face, he pushed her ahead of him and closed the door. Then, filled with emotion, he watched as his daughter stood on the threshold of the living room, her eyes and mouth wide open.

There wasn't a sound in the room that was full of people with happy, smiling faces. Mrs Aggie and Mrs Nellie were sitting in the fireside chairs either side of the hearth, Titch and Olive were seated at the table opposite Irene and George, and Mrs Kate occupied a corner of the couch. And standing in the kitchen doorway, still in their working clothes, were Jack and Greg Pollard, with Steve.

Lucy took her hand from her mouth. 'I don't know what to say. I think I'm going to cry.'

'Don't you dare cry, sunshine,' Irene said, not far from tears herself. 'We've all come to welcome yer dad back to where he belongs.'

Titch scraped his chair back and held out his arms. 'Come here, sweetheart.' And holding her close, he said, 'How can I tell yer the plans me and Olive have made for the wedding if ye're crying yer eyes out?'

Lucy sniffed up. 'I won't cry, I promise. Tell me what the plans are, I'm dying to know.'

'Hadn't yer better say hello to yer visitors first?'

'Never mind saying hello, I'm so happy to see them I could kiss them all to death.' Her eyes swept the room, taking in Mrs Nellie and Kate. 'Me old friends and me new ones.'

'Yer can kiss them as much as yer like when I've told yer what the arrangements are.'

Lucy grinned up at him. 'I'm all ears, Mr Titch.'

'Well, before I begin, can I ask Bob to sit down on the couch with Kate? She's all on her lonesome, there. Anyone would think she had an infectious disease.'

When Bob did as he was told with alacrity, Kate smiled that gentle smile that had already made her a favourite with Bob's neighbours. They'd taken to her right away.

Titch chuckled. 'That's better. I don't like having me thunder stolen by someone else sharing the stage.' He pulled on one of Lucy's curls. 'Now to the big day. Me and Olive are tying the knot five weeks on Friday. We couldn't get a Saturday because the priest said they're booked solid for three months ahead. It's at two o'clock and I want to see yer there with a big smile on that pretty face of yours.'

'I'll have a smile on me face every day, now me dad's home. But I'll have an extra special one on the day you and Mrs Fletcher get married.' Lucy's infectious giggle filled the room. 'I'll cry me eyes out all morning and get it over with. Then I'll put a cold flannel over me face to take the red blotches away. How about that, then?'

Titch gave her a hug. 'Me and Olive will have to go now, we've got a lot of sorting out to do. I've to be away by six in the morning.'

'If there's anything I can do while ye're away, just shout out,' Bob said, feeling he was at last the master in his own house. 'And remember, everyone is welcome here now. My front door is always open to yer.'

Jack piped up, 'Does that mean we can come here and pl.
cards, Mr Mellor?'

Bob thought his heart would burst. He owed so much to these
people he'd never be able to pay them back. When he got home it
was to find Irene had cleaned right through the house and it was
warm and welcoming. Aggie had stocked their larder and made a
steak and kidney pie which was now in the oven on a low light and
smelling delicious. 'Of course yer can! At last I can repay the
hospitality yer've always shown me and Lucy.'

George chuckled. 'I think yer might have reason to regret saying
that, mate. My two will never be away.' He rapped his fingers on
the table and for a few seconds considered whether anyone would
be upset if he said what was on his mind. Having decided, he
turned to Aggie, who had been unusually quiet. 'Ay, Aggie,
haven't yer always said the day would come when Bob would be
back home?'

Looking very superior, Aggie nodded. 'I did predict it, George,
yes. Yer all thought I was crazy, but I've been proved right.'

Olive smiled across at the woman who would soon be her
mother-in-law. 'Aggie, in all the years I've known yer, yer've never
been wrong.'

'I've been thinking about that,' Bob said, from his seat next to
Kate. 'I'll sit up and take notice next time yer make a prediction.'

'I'll make another prediction for yer lad, so take notice. The
happiness yer feel right now is nothing to the happiness that's
going to come your way.'

Nellie leaned forward in her chair. 'I agree with yer, Aggie. I
have the same feeling.'

Titch roared with laughter. 'Nellie, don't get too carried away
by what me ma says, she'll get yer into trouble.' Then he glanced
at his mother, and the face he held so dear caused him to shake his
head. 'I didn't mean that, Nellie. Yer won't go far wrong with me
ma, she only does what's right. The best mother a son could have,
she is, and I love and adore her.'

Olive punched his arm. 'Ay, it's me ye're marrying, Titch
McBride.'

Irene followed suit, giving George a hefty punch. 'How come
yer never say nice things like that to me? Yer've no romance in yer,
George Pollard.'

Bob turned to smile at Kate. Neither would say it, but both were
wondering whether the time would ever come when they'd be
close enough to act daft with each other.

Aggie and Nellie didn't miss the wordless exchange. They
smiled across at each other and winked, as if to say Bob and Kate
might be slow, but they were on the right tram lines.

711

Bob had his arm across Lucy's shoulder as they were seeing Titch and Olive off. 'Only a few weeks before the big day, eh, mate?'

'Yeah, it'll fly over.' Titch tucked Olive's arm in his. There was a twinkle in his eye when he said, 'Kate is everything yer said she was, Bob. If ye're daft enough to let her get away, yer want yer head testing.'

Lucy's wide green eyes rolled from her father to Titch. What did he mean about Mrs Kate? Then, before she had time to put her foot in it, the penny dropped. She felt a thrill of excitement travel down her spine and a smile played around the corners of her mouth. Oh, that would be the best thing ever! 'I'll go back to our visitors, Dad, while you talk to Mr Titch and Mrs Fletcher.' After a quick hug and kiss, she made her way back inside.

'Where's Iris, Mrs Kate?'

'She'll be at home now, love. I left her a note explaining I was coming here, and wouldn't be late. She could see to her own dinner, it only needed warming up.'

'Well yer come down again one night soon, and bring Iris with yer? She could have a game of cards with us young ones and you can keep me dad company.'

'Yes,' Kate smiled. 'I'm sure Iris would love that.'

Aggie and Nellie looked at each other. 'Another partner, d'yer think, Nellie?'

Nellie grinned. 'Most definitely, Aggie. One on the spot, too!'

'Me and George are going now, sunshine, so you and yer dad can have yer meal in peace,' Irene said. 'Will yer see to the boys, they're talking about a game of cards tomorrow.'

Lucy went into the kitchen. 'Yer can't come tomorrow night because I've promised to do Rhoda's hair. But yer can come the next night.'

'Rhoda won't mind us seeing her with curlers in,' Steve said. 'I bet if yer ask her in the morning she'll tell yer she couldn't care less.'

Jack nodded. 'Tell her we promise not to laugh at her.'

'I'm not promising anything of the sort,' Greg said. 'If she looks funny, I'll laugh.'

Lucy giggled when Jack went for his brother's throat. What a wonderful day this was.

Chapter Twenty-Seven

'So, yer mate's getting hitched tomorrow, eh, Bob?' Peg Butterworth's elbows were resting on the table as she held an enormous sandwich between her two hands. 'Yer should have introduced me to this Titch feller, he sounds right up my street. He wouldn't be getting married if he'd seen me, I'd have put him off anyone else.'

'How's that, queen?' Elsie asked. 'D'yer mean that because ye're a woman, yer'd have put him off all women? Oh, I don't think so, queen. I mean, ye're no oil painting but ye're not exactly ugly.'

'You cheeky sod!' Peg huffed with indignation. 'Have yer looked in the mirror lately? If yer had yer'd know what ugly means. It would be staring yer in the face.'

'Oh, I don't ever look in no mirror, queen. Me sense of humour wouldn't run to that. I can't understand why you do, it must be very disheartening for yer.' Elsie narrowed her eyes to look at her friend. 'Is that why ye're a bit miserable some days? Down in the mouth, like?'

'Elsie Burgess, what would yer say if I parted yer from yer two front teeth?'

'I wouldn't say nothing, queen, 'cos I'd be too busy knocking the stuffing out of yer. I'm very proud of me teeth, I am. My feller says they're me best feature.'

'They're yer only feature, girl.' Peg was gloating inside. She'd been dying to use this big word on Elsie, but there'd never been the right occasion to fit it into a sentence. 'Apart from them, there's nothing. Ye're just nondescript.'

Elsie's jaws stopped chewing and her eyes slid sideways. Putting on a posh voice, she asked, 'Would yer kindly explain the meaning of that word?'

'It means ye're very ordinary.' Little Ada Smithson's thin face was twitching. 'It means yer wouldn't be noticed in a crowd.'

Elsie pondered for a while, then slowly put her sandwich down. Lifting her bosom to rest on the table, she glared at the little woman. 'Is that so, now? Well, listen to me, smart arse, and take heed. Me and me mate are having a private fight, and we don't like anyone poking their noses in. So just mind yer own bleedin'

ess.' She turned to Peg. 'It's coming to something when yer
t have a fight in peace, isn't it, queen?'

'Yeah, I don't know what the world's coming to, girl. Years ago,
olk would go out and pick their own fight, they wouldn't muscle
in on someone else's.' Peg winked at Ada to let her see this was all
in fun. She felt sorry for the little woman 'cos, God knows, she
didn't have much of a life with that bully she had for a husband. 'It
makes yer think, though, girl, doesn't it?'

'What makes yer think, queen?'

'Well, us fighting so much. Perhaps that's why we're both ugly. I
mean, you with yer cauliflower ear and me with me broken nose,
that's bound to detract from our attractions.'

'I haven't got no cauliflower ear, queen! But if yer don't stop
using those big words, so I don't know whether I'm coming or
going, I'll break yer bleedin' nose for yer with pleasure.'

Bob was shaking with laughter. He laughed easily these days. In
work, having a pint with George and when the neighbours or
Lucy's friends called. His house was a real home now, not a place
where he and his daughter knew nothing but misery. They were
happy and contented, and as free as birds. And he felt no guilt
over Ruby, because Peg and Elsie made it their business to find
out how she was. From all accounts she'd settled in well with
Wally Brown and Bob was pleased about that. For all the heartache she'd caused him, he bore her no ill-will.

'Ay, Bob?' Peg interrupted his thoughts. 'Is Titch having a party
tomorrow night? I'm only asking because me and Elsie would
come along and entertain.'

'Sorry, Peg, but it's only a quiet wedding. Just a few friends for a
drink, that's all.'

Peg jerked her head. 'Just our luck. But when you get married,
Bob, me and me mate will expect an invitation.'

Elsie slapped an open hand on her chest. 'Ooh, er! Is Bob
getting married, queen?'

'Well, he's bound to, isn't he? I mean, it stands to sense, a man
as good-looking as him won't be on the shelf for long.'

'You and Elsie will be top of the list if I ever get married.' Bob
was grinning like a Cheshire cat. 'Mind you, yer'll have to wait a
long time.'

Billy Gleeson, nursing a toothache, had his chin cradled in his
hand. 'Are yer taking a full day off tomorrow, mate?'

Bob nodded. 'Yeah, me and Kate.'

Peg turned to face Elsie, and without a tape measure anyone
would be hard put to say whose mouth was opened the widest.
'Yer mean Kate's going to the wedding?' Peg croaked. 'How come
she can go and we can't?'

714

Kate spoke for the first time. 'I've been kindly invited by bride. And I've got to say I'm really looking forward to it.'

'And yer never said a dickie-bird!' Peg pursed her lips. 'Ye're dark horse, Kate Brown.'

The bell rang to signal the end of their break, and tops were put back on carry-out boxes and chairs scraped back. 'Enjoy yerselves tomorrow, both of yer,' Peg said. 'And don't forget to have a drink for me.'

'Yeah, have a really nice time.' Elsie smiled as she linked her friend's arm and they made their way out of the canteen.

'We'll have to buy a new dress for the wedding, girl,' Peg said.

'What wedding, queen?'

'Bob's, of course!'

'Bob's not getting married, is he, queen?'

Peg squeezed her arm. 'My money's on him marrying Kate as soon as his divorce comes through.'

'Ooh, er! Ye're right, queen, we will have to buy a new dress.'

Lucy was up bright and early on the Friday morning, and the first thing she did was draw the curtains. The sky was clear blue and the sun was doing its best to shine. 'Oh, it's going to be a beautiful day.' She was hugging herself when she heard a noise from the living room and knew her dad was already up and about. The cardigan she'd worn the night before was lying on the bed and she slipped it on before tripping lightly down the stairs.

'Good morning, Dad. It's going to be a beautiful day for the wedding.'

'It looks like it, pet.' Bob plumped the cushions on the couch and picked up last night's *Echo* ready to take to the bin. 'Have yer got yer day planned out?'

Lucy stood with her hands on her hips. 'What are yer doing, Dad? I'll tidy up in here, I've got loads of time. Rhoda's coming over at eleven so I can curl her hair with the curling tongs, then I'm going next door at twelve so Mrs Pollard can dress me up like a dog's dinner. I've got plenty of time to tidy this place.'

'I'm only doing it to occupy meself, pet.' Bob grinned and spread his hands. 'Anyone would think it was me getting married, not Titch. I'm a bundle of nerves and God knows what me tummy's up to, it's fluttering like mad.'

'Today will be good practice for yer, Dad, for when you get married.'

'Yer mean *if* I ever get married, pet! Nothing is certain in this life.'

'Oh, that is, Dad. If yer don't believe me, ask Mrs Aggie or Mrs Nellie. We all think yer'll get married and we can't all be wrong.'

b lowered his head and pretended to straighten the chenille
ecloth. 'And have the three of yer decided who I'm going to
d?'

There was no hesitation. 'Mrs Kate, of course.'

'Lucy, me and Kate have never discussed the future. She
probably doesn't think of me in that way.'

'Yer'll never know if yer don't ask her! Don't tell me ye're not
taken with Mrs Kate, 'cos I wouldn't believe yer.'

Bob pulled out a chair and sat down. 'Of course I'm taken with
her, she's everything any man could wish for. But I'm still a
married man, pet, and likely to be for another year or so. I'm not
in any position to ask Kate to marry me.'

'Yer could ask her to wait for yer and see what she says. Then at
least she'd know how yer felt about her and could decide for
herself. But she does like yer, Dad, anyone can see that. And
there's nothing to stop yer taking her out and courting her. There's
no law against that.'

Bob couldn't keep the smile back. 'Who was it told yer that?'

Lucy giggled. 'Me two partners, Mrs Aggie and Mrs Nellie.
And Mrs Nellie's son-in-law who's helping yer with the divorce.
He said that me mam is the guilty party and there's nothing to
stop you courting. Yer can't get married, though, not until the
divorce is through.'

'I didn't realise my life was of such interest to people.'

'They want what's best for yer, Dad. They all love yer and want
yer to be happy.' Her head tilted to one side, and her hands on her
hips, Lucy said, 'Mrs Kate's only waiting for yer to say something,
so don't keep her waiting.'

'This is all supposing Kate would have me, but would you be
happy if I married her?'

'Oh yes, Dad! She's kind and caring and I couldn't ask for
anyone better for a step-mother. And Iris said she'd be made up to
have you for a dad and me for a sister.'

Bob puckered his lips and let out a whistle. 'So, Iris is in this
too!'

Lucy dropped her head back and her laughter filled the room.
'Dad, you and Mrs Kate are the only ones *not* in it! So yer'd better
pull yer socks up unless yer want to be the only one not at yer own
wedding.' She wrapped her arms around his neck and kissed him.
'I'm going to get washed now, but you sit and think about it. If yer
don't put a move on, Mrs Aggie and Mrs Nellie will get fed up
waiting and propose for yer.'

Irene stepped back for a better look at Lucy. 'Yer look beautiful,
sunshine, a real treat. What do you say, George?'

716

'Yer look good enough to eat, love.' George wasn't a person for showing his feelings but he had to fight hard to keep them hidden when he looked at the young girl from next door. She made a beautiful picture in her pale blue dress which fitted her to perfection. And Irene had made her a bandeau for her hair with pale blue flowers sewn on. But it was the smiling face that would capture anyone's heart. And for the umpteenth time, George asked himself how any mother could walk away and leave her. 'In fact, love,' he told her, 'I think yer'll steal the show today.'

Lucy shook her head. 'No, I won't, Mr Pollard. Mrs Fletcher will do that.'

'Well, I think yer look lovely, Lucy,' Jack said. 'Like a film star.'

'Yeah, I think I will marry yer after all, Lucy.' Greg was leaning against the sideboard. 'Yer are pretty, and on top of that yer've got stacks of buttons.'

Jack glared at him. 'She'd have to be hard up to marry *you*.'

'It's only me buttons he's after, Jack,' Lucy said. 'I'll give him half of what I've got and that should shut him up.'

'The only thing that will shut my youngest son up, is a gobstopper.' Irene looked down at herself. 'I'd better get a move on, I'm the only one not ready. And don't forget, Lucy, you won't be leaving with me and the boys. You are going in the wedding car with Olive and Steve.'

Lucy rolled her eyes. 'Aren't I going to be the posh one!'

'Is there any chance of a cuppa, Ma?' Titch stood at the kitchen door moving from one foot to the other. 'Me mouth's not half dry.'

'Listen, son, will yer go and sit down. Me and Nellie are up to our eyes in it and we can't work with you under our feet.'

'I've tried that, Ma, and it won't work. I can't sit 'cos me nerves are shattered.' Titch held his hands out and started shaking them. 'See, I'm a wreck.'

Aggie grinned as she smoothed the front of her wrap-around pinny. 'Don't try and soft soap me, son, 'cos it won't work. I bet if I held a pint of bitter out to yer, yer hands would soon stop shaking in case yer spilled a drop.' Then she took pity on him. After all, it was his wedding day and he was bound to be nervous. She wouldn't let herself dwell on the thought that this was the last day this house would be his home. If she did, she'd end up bawling her eyes out and the sandwiches would never get done. 'Go and sit down and I'll put the kettle on. Me and Nellie could do with a drink, we're gasping.'

'That's the spirit, queen, it's no good flogging ourselves to death.' Nellie had been there since nine o'clock and had baked enough fairy cakes to stock one of Sayer's shops. She'd also made jellies in little white pleated paper cases and these were standing a tray in the yard to set. When they were ready she would finish them off with a blob of cream on top.

'I don't know what I'd have done without yer, Nellie,' Aggie said, filling the kettle. 'I'd have had to buy the cakes from a shop, I couldn't have managed all this if I'd been on me own.'

'Olive did offer to help yer, Ma,' Titch said. 'And Irene.'

'What! Olive making sarnies on her wedding day! Not bleedin' likely, son. She needs the time to make herself look nice for yer. And Irene's got her two boys to see to, and George. Not to mention helping Lucy. Besides, this kitchen is only big enough for two. Me and Nellie fit in fine, don't we, queen?'

'I like being busy and I've enjoyed meself.' Nellie's hands moved like clockwork as she buttered slices of bread and piled them high ready for the fillings to go on. 'Another half-hour should see the end of it. Then you and me can start to titivate ourselves up. Me best dress and shoes are in the bag I've left in the hall. And I've even borrowed one of our Kate's lipsticks.'

'Go 'way!' Aggie poured the water into the teapot. 'Yer haven't, have yer?'

'I certainly have! It's not often I go to a wedding so I thought I'd go the whole hog. It's a pale lipstick, mind yer, not a bright red colour.'

'I think I'll have a bash at that meself, Nellie. Can I borrow some?'

'Of course yer can, queen! We'll both look like mutton dressed as lamb, but I couldn't give a sod, so there!'

'What time is Kate coming?'

'She's going straight to the church with Iris. She said yer'd have enough to do without an extra two.'

Titch had been listening to the conversation with a smile on his face. He was glad his mother had found a friend her own age. And they got along so well, there was no doubt that it would be a firm and lasting friendship. He walked to the kitchen and leaned against the door. 'Ma, just out of curiosity, how can yer borrow lipstick? Once it's on yer lips yer can't give it back, can yer?'

'Only if yer kiss them, clever clogs. So I'll make it me business to kiss Kate first, then she'll get the bulk of it back. And if that answer satisfies yer, will yer pour this tea out and then go and get yerself ready?'

'Anything yer say, Ma. Anything yer say.'

Steve paced the floor as he waited for his mother to come down. She was cutting it fine for time because the car was due in ten minutes. Then he heard the creaking of the stairs and his eyes were on the door when Olive walked through. She looked so lovely his heart burst with pride. Her pale beige dress had a pleated cross-over top, long tapering sleeves and a full flared skirt. And perched on the top of her head was a pill-box hat in the same colour, with a veil that came down to her eyes. 'Oh Mam, yer look beautiful. Mr Titch will be knocked out when he sees yer.'

'And you look very handsome, love. I'm really proud of yer.'

Steve pointed to two posies on the sideboard. 'Is the biggest one for you, Mam?'

Olive nodded and picked up her posy. It was made up of small white and blue flowers with sprigs of fern, and there were strands of ribbons in the same colours hanging from it. 'We'll give Lucy hers in the car. She'll be delighted with it.'

'We just made it in time, the car's pulled up now.'

The street was deserted and Olive breathed a sigh of relief. But Steve was puzzled. He thought some of the neighbours would be out to see his mam off. It only took the car a minute to get to the Mellors' and Lucy had been watching for it. She had the door open before the chauffeur had time to knock.

'Doesn't she look lovely, Mam?'

'Lucy always looks lovely, Steve. And she's got a lovely nature to go with it.'

The chauffeur opened the passenger door and Lucy, careful of her dress, climbed in. Her smile was as wide as her face. 'Yer look a picture, Mrs Fletcher. Very beautiful.'

'So do you, sweetheart. I'm well blessed with me handsome son and a pretty bridesmaid.' Olive passed the posy over and Lucy's eyes nearly popped out of her head. 'Is this for me? Oh, it's absolutely gorgeous.' She was still staring at it when the car pulled up outside the church.

Steve had rehearsed his role over and over again, and he carried it out to the letter. He tucked his mother's arm in his and covered her hand. Then he looked back and asked, 'All right, Lucy?' When she answered with a wide grin, he straightened his shoulders and led his mother into the church. He only faltered when he saw the church was packed. They were only expecting their close friends to be there, but it seemed every neighbour in the street had turned out to see his mother and Mr Titch get married. And it filled his heart with joy.

When the guests arrived back at Aggie's house, they found Olive and Titch waiting for them. Titch had his arm around Olive's waist and they looked as happy as any lovebirds could look. There was much hugging, kissing and shaking of hands as congratulations were given and Olive, no longer nervous, looked radiant.

Aggie stood back and watched with tears in her eyes. She'd

aited a long time for this day and couldn't have been happier about the woman he'd married. But the happiness was tinged with sadness. Well, that's only natural, she told herself. Every mother cries when one of her children leave home. And he'll be living in the same street, for heaven's sake, it wasn't as though he was moving to the other end of the world. So giving herself a pep talk about not crying, she approached the newlyweds.

Olive moved forward to meet her and took her in her arms. 'Is it all right if I still call yer Aggie?'

'Of course it is, Mrs McBride!' This brought laughter from their friends as it was the first time Olive had been addressed by her married name. 'You just look after him, that's all, or yer'll have Mrs McBride Senior to answer to.'

Titch nearly squeezed the breath out of her. 'I've got two lovely women in me life, now, Ma. I must be the luckiest bloke alive.' He set her down and his arm went back around his new wife's waist. 'I'm glad I let her talk me into marrying her. I did say no at first, then she taught me the error of me ways.'

There were loud hoots from all the women present. 'Get a load of him!' Irene said. 'Anyone would think he was God's gift to women!'

'Put yer foot down with him, queen,' Nellie advised. 'Start as yer mean to go on.'

'Don't put it down too hard, Olive, or he might come back home.' Aggie took a sip of sherry from the glass Steve handed to her and tried not to pull a face. She didn't like the stuff, but Titch said she wasn't allowed to toast his marriage with milk stout. 'And he can't come home because his bed will be occupied.'

Titch looked puzzled. 'How's that, Ma?'

'I've asked Steve to sleep here. He can keep me company and it'll give you and Olive some time on yer own to get to know each other.'

Olive blushed to the roots of her hair, but Titch was delighted. 'Ma, yer think of everything.'

'Yes, I do, son. And right now I'm thinking it's time folks found themselves a seat and we can start giving the eats out. I'll leave the men to see to the drinks.'

'I'll help, Mrs Aggie,' Lucy said.

'What – in that dress? Not ruddy likely!'

'I'll help,' Rhoda said, and looked to where Iris was sitting next to her mother on the couch. 'How about it, Iris? It'll give yer a chance to get to know everyone.'

Iris was on her feet like a shot. She wanted to be near the young ones and this was a good chance. 'Yeah, I'd like that.'

'This thing's killing me,' George said, running a finger around the inside of his collar which had been starched and was rubbing his skin. 'I can hardly breathe.'

'Here, let me undo that top button before yer choke yerself.' Irene smiled into his face as she relaxed the pressure on his neck. 'Yer made a really handsome best man, love.'

'I told yer yer were getting a bargain when yer got me, didn't I?' George ran a finger gently down her cheek. 'But I got first prize when I got you.'

When Iris had left her seat, Bob didn't hesitate to slide along to sit next to Kate. 'Are yer all right, Kate?'

'Yes, I'm fine. Everything went off very well, didn't it?'

Bob nodded. In his mind he was telling himself to get on with it and ask her. In the end what he felt in his heart gave him the courage. 'Kate, would yer come out with me one night?' He put a hand on her arm before she could answer. 'No, let me get it all out while I've got the nerve. Can I court yer with a view to marriage when I'm a free man?'

The slow, gentle smile made his heart flip. 'It's taken yer long enough, Bob Mellor. If yer hadn't asked me by the end of the night, I'd made up me mind to ask you.'

Bob closed his eyes and took a deep breath. Her words were music to his ears. 'We'll talk about it tomorrow, eh? All I'll say now is that I'm a very happy man.'

When everyone had a full plate in their hand and a glass either on the arm of a chair or on the floor, the six youngsters congregated in the kitchen. 'Yer don't half look nice, Lucy,' Rhoda said. 'Very pretty.'

'So do you, that new dress really suits yer. And Iris looks lovely, as well.' Lucy's infectious giggle rang out. 'Make the most of it, 'cos tomorrow we'll be back in our scruff.'

Jack was munching a sandwich, his face thoughtful. Then he took the plunge. 'Lucy, will yer come to the pictures with me one night?'

'Oh yeah, I'd love to!' Lucy had made her mind up a long time ago that Jack was the boy for her. She thought he was very handsome, but that wasn't the reason. He was kind and caring, and on the bad days, when she'd suffered from her mother's hand, he always had the power to put a smile back on her face. 'I'd better go and ask me Dad, though, eh?'

Jack looked as though he'd lost sixpence and found a pound. Reaching for her hand, he said, 'I'll come with yer.'

'Hang on a minute,' Steve said. 'We agreed to do this together.'

Jack huffed. 'Well, go on, ask her.'

Steve's face was red as beetroot. 'Rhoda, will yer come out with me one night?'

'I certainly will, Steve Fletcher, I'd be delighted.'

Jack didn't wait to hear any more before leading Lucy through to the living room. And without bothering to lower his voice, he asked, 'Mr Mellor, is it all right for Lucy to come to the pictures with me one night?'

There were smiles all around, and the widest was Irene's. Was the wish she'd harboured all these years going to come true?

'If that's what Lucy wants,' Bob said, 'then I've no objection.'

Nellie pulled her chair nearer to Aggie. 'That lad's got more gumption than Bob.'

'Don't speak too soon, queen, 'cos Bob and your Kate are looking very pleased with themselves.'

Steve strode from the kitchen to the door leading to the hall. 'I'm going out for a minute, Jack, I won't be long.'

'Where are yer going?'

'To ask Mrs Fleming about taking Rhoda out.'

'Yer've no need to ask me mam.' Rhoda appeared with her face aglow. 'I've already asked her.'

Amid roars of laughter, Steve asked, 'How could yer have asked her? I've only just mentioned it!'

'Well, it's like this, yer see, Steve. I think it's best to be prepared for any eventuality. So I hinted to me mam that yer might ask me, and would it be all right with her. And of course she said it would be okay because ye're a fine, upstanding man.'

'Oh, I'm enjoying this.' Aggie wiped a laughter tear away. 'It's better than going to the bleedin' pictures any day.'

'Listen, queen,' Nellie said. 'If a house comes empty round here, give us the wire, will yer? You've got some lovely neighbours.'

'The secret of keeping yerself feeling young, Nellie, is to mix with youngsters. This lot have taken years off me.'

'I wondered why yer only looked about twenty,' Nellie chuckled. 'I thought yer were on some special miracle pills.'

'Ay out,' Aggie said when Greg and Iris came through from the kitchen. 'All we need now is for these two to say they're putting the banns up.'

Iris was looking very shy, but not Greg. He looked his brother straight in the eye and said, 'Me and Iris would like to go to the pictures, but they won't let me in at the door. Even though I'm working, they say I'm too young. So will you take us in?'

'Will I heckerslike! I'm not having you tagging along on me first date.'

'Don't be so miserable, Jack,' Irene said. 'Once yer got in, yer wouldn't have to sit near each other.'

'Oh, all right.' Jack relented. 'But yer'll owe me a favour.'

Bob coughed before saying, 'Can I get a word in, please? Would you all let me know what night ye're going out, and which picturehouse ye're going to? Just so me and Kate can go to a different one.' He waited until his words had sunk in and all the faces around him were lit up with pleasure. Then he said, 'To Aggie, Nellie and Lucy, who, for those who don't know, are the members of the committee, I'd just like to say their work is finished. I've asked Kate to be me intended and she's agreed.'

'Yer forgot to say I was very happy to agree,' Kate said. 'And very honoured.'

Titch jumped to his feet. 'That's the best news I've had in a long time. Except for Olive saying she'd marry me, of course. So I think we should get all the glasses filled up for a toast.'

'Me and Jack will do that, mate,' George said, lumbering to his feet. 'Seeing at it's your wedding day.'

When everyone was holding a full glass, Titch held out his hand to Olive. 'Come and join me, sweetheart.'

'I'm no good with words, Titch. You're much better at it than me.'

'Mrs McBride Junior,' Aggie said, 'are yer saying my son talks too much?'

'Okay, Aggie, I give in.' Olive joined her husband, who put his arm around her waist and held her tight. 'The first toast from me and my wife, is to all of you. To thank you for all the help yer've given us, and the presents we have yet to open. But most of all to thank you for being such good friends. We think we are well blessed.' The couple raised their glasses before sipping the wine. 'Now I'd like yer all to toast the best mother a man could have. This is for you, Ma.'

'Don't start me off crying, son, for God's sake.'

'Okay, Ma, we'll move on to the next one. To Bob and Kate. And I don't think there's a person in this room who isn't happy for them. Two nice people, with two lovely children, they'll make a perfect family when the time comes. And it's what they deserve.'

Not a word passed between them, but Lucy and Iris moved together. Lucy to sit on Kate's knee, and Iris on Bob's.

Aggie pulled on Jack's jacket. 'Ay, lad, run and get the bucket out of the yard, will yer? The way things are going I'll be shedding enough tears to fill the bleedin' thing.'

'Don't cry, Mrs Aggie,' Lucy said. 'Today I've been a bridesmaid, I've learned I'm going to have a new mam and sister, and I've got meself a boyfriend. This is the happiest day of me life.'